THE COLLECTED

PHILIP K.
DICK VOLUME
THREE

THE COLLECTED STORIES OF
PHILIP K. DICK

VOLUME THREE

First published in Great Britain in 2023 by Gollancz
an imprint of The Orion Publishing Group Ltd
Carmelite House, 50 Victoria Embankment
London EC4Y 0DZ

An Hachette UK Company

1 3 5 7 9 10 8 6 4 2

A CIP catalogue record for this book is
available from the British Library.

ISBN (Mass Market Paperback) 978 1 39961 127 5
ISBN (eBook) 978 1 39961 128 2

Printed in Great Britain by Clays Ltd, Elcograf, S.p.A.

MIX
Paper from
responsible sources
FSC® C104740

www.gollancz.co.uk

CONTENTS

THE COLLECTED STORIES OF PHILIP K. DICK VOLUME THREE

THE CRAWLERS

He built, and the more he built the more he enjoyed building. Hot sunlight filtered down; summer breezes stirred around him as he toiled joyfully. When he ran out of material he paused awhile and rested. His edifice wasn't large; it was more a practice model than the real thing. One part of his brain told him that, and another part thrilled with excitement and pride. It was at least large enough to enter. He crawled down the entrance tunnel and curled up inside in a contented heap.

Through a rent in the roof a few bits of dirt rained down. He oozed binder fluid and reinforced the weak place. In his edifice the air was clean and cool, almost dust-free. He crawled over the inner walls one last time, leaving a quick-drying coat of binder over everything. What else was needed? He was beginning to feel drowsy; in a moment he'd be asleep.

He thought about it, and then he extended a part of himself up through the still-open entrance. That part watched and listened warily, as the rest of him dozed off in a grateful slumber. He was peaceful and content, conscious that from a distance all that was visible was a light mound of dark clay. No one would notice it: no one would guess what lay beneath.

And if they did notice, he had methods of taking care of them.

The farmer halted his ancient Ford truck with a grinding shriek of brakes. He cursed and backed up a few yards. 'There's one. Hop down and take a look at it. Watch the cars—they go pretty fast along here.'

Ernest Gretry pushed the cabin door open and stepped down gingerly onto the hot mid-morning pavement. The air smelled of sun and drying grass. Insects buzzed around him as he advanced cautiously up the highway, hands in his trouser pockets, lean body bent forward. He stopped and peered down.

The thing was well mashed. Wheel marks crossed it in four places and its internal organs had ruptured and burst through. The whole thing was snail-like, a gummy elongated tube with sense organs at one end and a confusing mass of protoplasmic extensions at the other.

What got him most was the face. For a time he couldn't look directly at it: he had to contemplate the road, the hills, the big cedar trees, anything else. There was something in the little dead eyes, a glint that was rapidly fading. They weren't the lusterless eyes of a fish, stupid and vacant. The life he had seen haunted him, and he had got only a brief glimpse, as the truck bore down on it and crushed it flat.

'They crawl across here every once in a while,' the farmer said quietly. 'Sometimes they get as far as town. The first one I saw was heading down the middle of Grant Street, about fifty yards an hour. They go pretty slow. Some of the teenage kids like to run them down. Personally I avoid them, if I see them.'

Gretry kicked aimlessly at the thing. He wondered vaguely how many more there were in the bushes and hills. He could see farmhouses set back from the road, white gleaming squares in the hot Tennessee sun. Horses and sleeping cattle. Dirty chickens scratching. A sleepy, peaceful countryside, basking in the late-summer sun.

'Where's the radiation lab from here?' he asked.

The farmer indicated. 'Over there, on the other side of those hills. You want to collect the remains? They have one down at the Standard Oil Station in a big tank. Dead, of course. They filled the tank with kerosene to try to preserve it. That one's in pretty good shape, compared to this. Joe Jackson cracked its head with a two-by-four. He found it crawling across his property one night.'

Gretry got shakily back into the truck. His stomach turned over and he had to take some long deep breaths. 'I didn't realize there were so many. When they sent me out from Washington they just said a few had been seen.'

'There's been quite a lot.' The farmer started up the truck and carefully skirted the remains on the pavement. 'We're trying to get used to them, but we can't. It's not nice stuff. A lot of people are moving away. You can feel it in the air, a sort of heaviness. We've got this problem and we have to meet it.' He increased speed, leathery hands tight around the wheel. 'It seems like there's more of *them* born all the time, and almost no normal children.'

Back in town, Gretry called Freeman long distance from the booth in the shabby hotel lobby. 'We'll have to do something. They're all around here. I'm going out at three to see a colony of them. The fellow who runs the taxi stand knows where they are. He says there must be eleven or twelve of them together.'

'How do the people around there feel?'

'How the hell do you expect? They think it's God's Judgment. Maybe they're right.'

'We should have made them move earlier. We should have cleaned out the whole area for miles around. Then we wouldn't have this problem.' Freeman paused. 'What do you suggest?'

'That island we took over for the H-bomb tests.'

'It's a damn big island. There was a whole group of natives we moved off and resettled.' Freeman choked. 'Good God, are there *that* many of them?'

'The staunch citizens exaggerate, of course. But I get the impression there must be at least a hundred.'

Freeman was silent a long time. 'I didn't realize,' he said finally. 'I'll have to put it through channels, of course. We were going to make further tests on that island. But I see your point.'

'I'd like it,' Gretry said. 'This is a bad business. We can't have things like this. People can't live with this sort of thing. You ought to drop out here and take a look. It's something to remember.'

'I'll—see what I can do. I'll talk to Gordon. Give me a ring tomorrow.'

Gretry hung up and wandered out of the drab, dirty lobby onto the blazing sidewalk. Dingy stores and parked cars. A few old men hunched over on steps and sagging cane-bottom chairs. He lit a cigarette and shakily examined his watch. It was almost three. He moved slowly toward the taxi stand.

The town was dead. Nothing stirred. Only the motionless old men in their chairs and the out-of-town cars zipping along the highway. Dust and silence lay over everything. Age, like a gray spider web, covered all the houses and stores. No laughter. No sounds of any kind.

No children playing games.

A dirty blue taxicab pulled up silently beside him. 'Okay, mister,' the driver said, a rat-faced man in his thirties, toothpick hanging between his crooked teeth. He kicked the bent door open. 'Here we go.'

'How far is it?' Gretry asked, as he climbed in.

'Just outside town.' The cab picked up speed and hurtled noisily along, bouncing and bucking. 'You from the FBI?'

'No.'

'I thought from your suit and hat you was.' The driver eyed him curiously. 'How'd you hear about the crawlers?'

'From the radiation lab.'

'Yeah, it's that hot stuff they got there.' The driver turned off the highway and onto a dirt side-road. 'It's up here on the Higgins farm. The crazy damn things picked the bottom of old lady Higgins' place to build their houses.'

'*Houses?*'

'They've got some sort of city, down under the ground. You'll see it—the entrances, at least. They work together, building and fussing.' He twisted the cab off the dirt road, between two huge cedars, over a bumpy field, and finally brought it to rest at the edge of a rocky gully. 'This is it.'

It was the first time Gretry had seen one alive.

He got out of the cab awkwardly, his legs numb and unresponding. The things were moving slowly between the woods and the entrance tunnels in the center of the clearing. They were bringing building material, clay and weeds. Smearing it with some kind of ooze and plastering it in rough forms which were carefully carried beneath the ground. The crawlers were two or three feet long; some were older than others, darker and heavier. All of them moved with agonizing slowness, a silent flowing motion across the sun-baked ground. They were soft, shell-less, and looked harmless.

Again, he was fascinated and hypnotized by their faces. The weird parody of human faces. Wizened little baby features, tiny shoebutton eyes, slit of a mouth, twisted ears, and a few wisps of damp hair. What should have been arms were elongated pseudopods that grew and receded like soft dough. The crawlers seemed incredibly flexible; they extended themselves, then snapped their bodies back, as their feelers made contact with obstructions. They paid no attention to the two men; they didn't even seem to be aware of them.

'How dangerous are they?' Gretry asked finally.

'Well, they have some sort of stinger. They stung a dog, I know. Stung him pretty hard. He swelled up and his tongue turned black. He had fits and got hard. He died.' The driver added half-apologetically, 'He was nosing around. Interrupting their building. They work all the time. Keep busy.'

'Is this most of them?'

'I guess so. They sort of congregate here. I see them crawling this way.' The driver gestured. 'See, they're born in different places. One or two at each farmhouse, near the radiation lab.'

'Which way is Mrs Higgins' farmhouse?' Gretry asked.

'Up there. See it through the trees? You want to—'

'I'll be right back,' Gretry said, and started abruptly off. 'Wait here.'

The old woman was watering the dark red geraniums that grew around her front porch, when Gretry approached. She looked up quickly, her ancient wrinkled face shrewd and suspicious, the sprinkling can poised like a blunt instrument.

'Afternoon,' Gretry said. He tipped his hat and showed her his credentials. 'I'm investigating the—crawlers. At the edge of your land.'

'Why?' Her voice was empty, bleak, cold. Like her withered face and body.

'We're trying to find a solution.' Gretry felt awkward and uncertain. 'It's been suggested we transport them away from here, out to an island in the Gulf of Mexico. They shouldn't be here. It's too hard on people. It isn't right,' he finished lamely.

'No. It isn't right.'

'And we've already begun moving everybody away from the radiation lab. I guess we should have done that a long time ago.'

The old woman's eyes flashed. 'You people and your machines. See what you've done!' She jabbed a bony finger at him excitedly. 'Now you have to fix it. You have to do something.'

'We're taking them away to an island as soon as possible. But there's one problem. We have to be sure about the parents. They have complete custody of them. We can't just–' He broke off futilely. 'How do they feel? Would they let us cart up their–children, and haul them away?'

Mrs Higgins turned and headed into the house. Uncertainly, Gretry followed her through the dim, dusty interior rooms. Musty chambers full of oil lamps and faded pictures, ancient sofas and tables. She led him through a great kitchen of immense cast iron pots and pans down a flight of wooden stairs to a painted white door. She knocked sharply.

Flurry and movement on the other side. The sound of people whispering and moving things hurriedly.

'Open the door,' Mrs Higgins commanded. After an agonized pause the door opened slowly. Mrs Higgins pushed it wide and motioned Gretry to follow her.

In the room stood a young man and woman. They backed away as Gretry came in. The woman hugged a long pasteboard carton which the man had suddenly passed to her.

'Who are you?' the man demanded. He abruptly grabbed the carton back; his wife's small hands were trembling under the shifting weight.

Gretry was seeing the parents of one of them. The young woman, brown-haired, not more than nineteen. Slender and small in a cheap green dress, a full-breasted girl with dark frightened eyes. The man was bigger and stronger, a handsome dark youth with massive arms and competent hands gripping the pasteboard carton tight.

Gretry couldn't stop looking at the carton. Holes had been punched in the top; the carton moved slightly in the man's arms, and there was a faint shudder that rocked it back and forth.

'This man,' Mrs Higgins said to the husband, 'has come to take it away.'

The couple accepted the information in silence. The husband made no move except to get a better grip on the box.

'He's going to take all of them to an island,' Mrs Higgins said. 'It's all arranged. Nobody'll harm them. They'll be safe and they can do what they want. Build and crawl around where nobody has to look at them.'

The young woman nodded blankly.

'Give it to him,' Mrs Higgins ordered impatiently. 'Give him the box and let's get it over with once and for all.'

After a moment the husband carried the box over to a table and put it down. 'You know anything about them?' he demanded. 'You know what they eat?'

'We–' Gretry began helplessly.

'They eat leaves. Nothing but leaves and grass. We've been bringing in the smallest leaves we could find.'

'It's only a month old,' the young woman said huskily. 'It already wants to go down with the others, but we keep it here. We don't want it to go down there. Not yet. Later, maybe, we thought. We didn't know what to do. We weren't sure.' Her large dark eyes flashed briefly in mute appeal, then faded out again. 'It's a hard thing to know.'

The husband untied the heavy brown twine and took the lid from the carton. 'Here. You can see it.'

It was the smallest Gretry had seen. Pale and soft, less than a foot long. It had crawled in a corner of the box and was curled up in a messy web of chewed leaves and some kind of wax. A translucent covering spun clumsily around it, behind which it lay asleep. It paid no attention to them; they were out of its scope. Gretry felt a strange helpless horror rise up in him. He moved away, and the young man replaced the lid.

'We knew what it was,' he said hoarsely. 'Right away, as soon as it was born. Up the road, there was one we saw. One of the first. Bob Douglas made us come over and look at it. It was his and Julie's. That was before they started coming down and collecting together by the gully.'

'Tell him what happened,' Mrs Higgins said.

'Douglas mashed its head with a rock. Then he poured gasoline on it and burned it up. Last week he and Julie packed and left.'

'Have many of them been destroyed?' Gretry managed to ask.

'A few. A lot of men, they see something like that and they go sort of wild. You can't blame them.' The man's dark eyes darted hopelessly. 'I guess I almost did the same thing.'

'Maybe we should have,' his wife murmured. 'Maybe I should have let you.'

Gretry picked up the pasteboard carton and moved toward the door. 'We'll get this done as quickly as we can. The trucks are on the way. It should be over in a day.'

'Thank God for that,' Mrs Higgins exclaimed in a clipped, emotionless voice. She held the door open, and Gretry carried the carton through the dim, musty house, down the sagging front steps and out into the blazing mid-afternoon sun.

Mrs Higgins stopped at the red geraniums and picked up her sprinkling can. 'When you take them, take them all. Don't leave any behind. Understand?'

'Yes,' Gretry muttered.

'Keep some of your men and trucks here. Keep checking. Don't let any stay where we have to look at them.'

'When we get the people near the radiation lab moved away there shouldn't be any more of—'

He broke off. Mrs Higgins had turned her back and was watering the geraniums. Bees buzzed around her. The flowers swayed dully with the hot wind. The old woman passed on around the side of the house, still watering and stooping over. In a few moments she was gone and Gretry was alone with his carton.

Embarrassed and ashamed, he carried the carton slowly down the hill and across the field to the ravine. The taxi driver was standing by his cab, smoking a cigarette and waiting patiently for him. The colony of crawlers was working steadily on its city. There were streets and passages. On some of the entrance-mounds he noticed intricate scratches that might have been words. Some of the crawlers were grouped together, setting up involved things he couldn't make out.

'Let's go,' he said wearily to the driver.

The driver grinned and yanked the back door. 'I left the meter running,' he said, his ratty face bright with craft. 'You guys all have a swindle sheet—you don't care.'

He built, and the more he built the more he enjoyed building. By now the city was over eighty miles deep and five miles in diameter. The whole island had been converted into a single vast city that honeycombed and interlaced farther each day. Eventually it would reach the land beyond the ocean; then the work would begin in earnest.

To his right, a thousand methodically moving companions toiled silently on the structural support that was to reinforce the main breeding chamber. As soon as it was in place everyone would feel better; the mothers were just now beginning to bring forth their young.

That was what worried him. It took some of the joy out of building. He had seen one of the first born—before it was quickly hidden and the thing hushed up. A brief glimpse of a bulbous head, foreshortened body, incredibly rigid extensions. It shrieked and wailed and turned red in the face. Gurgled and plucked aimlessly and kicked its *feet*.

In horror, somebody had finally mashed the throwback with a rock. And hoped there wouldn't be any more.

SALES PITCH

Commute ships roared on all sides, as Ed Morris made his way wearily home to Earth at the end of a long hard day at the office. The Ganymede–Terra lanes were choked with exhausted, grim-faced businessmen; Jupiter was in opposition to Earth and the trip was a good two hours. Every few million miles the great flow slowed to a grinding, agonized halt; signal-lights flashed as streams from Mars and Saturn fed into the main traffic-arteries.

'Lord,' Morris muttered. 'How tired can you *get*?' He locked the autopilot and momentarily turned from the control board to light a much-needed cigarette. His hands shook. His head swam. It was past six; Sally would be fuming; dinner would be spoiled. The same old thing. Nerve-wracking driving, honking horns and irate drivers zooming past his little ship, furious gesturing, shouting, cursing ...

And the ads. That was what really did it. He could have stood everything else—but the ads, the whole long way from Ganymede to Earth. And on Earth, the swarms of salesrobots; it was too much. And they were everywhere.

He slowed to avoid a fifty-ship smashup. Repair-ships were scurrying around trying to get the debris out of the lane. His audio-speaker wailed as police rockets hurried up. Expertly, Morris raised his ship, cut between two slow-moving commercial transports, zipped momentarily into the unused left lane, and then sped on, the wreck left behind. Horns honked furiously at him; he ignored them.

'Trans-Solar Products greets you!' an immense voice boomed in his ear. Morris groaned and hunched down in his seat. He was getting near Terra; the barrage was increasing. 'Is your tension-index pushed over the safety-margin by the ordinary frustrations of the day? Then you need an Id-Persona Unit. So small it can be worn behind the ear, close to the frontal lobe—'

Thank God, he was past it. The ad dimmed and receded behind, as his fast-moving ship hurtled forward. But another was right ahead.

'Drivers! Thousands of unnecessary deaths each year from inter-planet driving. Hypno-Motor Control from an expert source-point insures your safety. Surrender your body and save your life!' The voice roared louder. 'Industrial experts say—'

Both audio ads, the easiest to ignore. But now a visual ad was forming; he winced, closed his eyes, but it did no good.

'Men!' an unctuous voice thundered on all sides of him. 'Banish internally-caused obnoxious odors *forever*. Removal by modern painless methods of the gastrointestinal tract and substitution system will relieve you of the most acute cause of social rejection.' The visual image locked; a vast nude girl, blonde hair disarranged, blue eyes half shut, lips parted, head tilted back in sleep-drugged ecstasy. The features ballooned as the lips approached his own. Abruptly the orgiastic expression on the girl's face vanished. Disgust and revulsion swept across, and then the image faded out.

'Does this happen to you?' the voice boomed. 'During erotic sex-play do you offend your love-partner by the presence of gastric processes which—'

The voice died, and he was past. His mind his own again, Morris kicked savagely at the throttle and sent the little ship leaping. The pressure, applied directly to the audio-visual regions of his brain, had faded below spark point. He groaned and shook his head to clear it. All around him the vague half-defined echoes of ads glittered and gibbered, like ghosts of distant video-stations. Ads waited on all sides; he steered a careful course, dexterity born of animal desperation, but not all could be avoided. Despair seized him. The outline of a new visual-audio ad was already coming into being.

'You, mister wage-earner!' it shouted into the eyes and ears, noses and throats, of a thousand weary commuters. 'Tired of the same old job? Wonder Circuits Inc. has perfected a marvelous long-range thoughtwave scanner. Know what others are thinking and saying. Get the edge on fellow employees. Learn facts, figures about your employer's personal existence. Banish uncertainty!'

Morris' despair swept up wildly. He threw the throttle on full blast; the little ship bucked and rolled as it climbed from the traffic lane into the dead zone beyond. A shrieking roar, as his fender whipped through the protective wall—and then the ad faded behind him.

He slowed down, trembling with misery and fatigue. Earth lay ahead. He'd be home, soon. Maybe he could get a good night's sleep. He shakily dropped the nose of the ship and prepared to hook onto the tractor beam of the Chicago commute field.

'The best metabolism adjuster on the market,' the salesrobot shrilled. 'Guaranteed to maintain a perfect endocrine-balance, or your money refunded in full.'

Morris pushed wearily past the salesrobot, up the sidewalk toward the residential-block that contained his living-unit. The robot followed a few steps, then forgot him and hurried after another grim-faced commuter.

'All the news while it's news,' a metallic voice dinned at him. 'Have a retinal vidscreen installed in your least-used eye. Keep in touch with the world; don't wait for out-of-date hourly summaries.'

'*Get out of the way*,' Morris muttered. The robot stepped aside for him and he crossed the street with a pack of hunched-over men and women.

Robot-salesmen were everywhere, gesturing, pleading, shrilling. One started after him and he quickened his pace. It scurried along, chanting its pitch and trying to attract his attention, all the way up the hill to his living-unit. It didn't give up until he stooped over, snatched up a rock, and hurled it futilely. He scrambled in the house and slammed the doorlock after him. The robot hesitated, then turned and raced after a woman with an armload of packages toiling up the hill. She tried vainly to elude it, without success.

'Darling!' Sally cried. She hurried from the kitchen, drying her hands on her plastic shorts, bright-eyed and excited. 'Oh, you poor thing! You look so tired!'

Morris peeled off his hat and coat and kissed his wife briefly on her bare shoulder. 'What's for dinner?'

Sally gave his hat and coat to the closet. 'We're having Uranian wild pheasant; your favorite dish.'

Morris' mouth watered, and a tiny surge of energy crawled back into his exhausted body. 'No kidding? What the hell's the occasion?'

His wife's brown eyes moistened with compassion. 'Darling, it's your birthday; you're thirty-seven years old today. Had you forgotten?'

'Yeah.' Morris grinned a little. 'I sure had.' He wandered into the kitchen. The table was set; coffee was steaming in the cups and there was butter and white bread, mashed potatoes and green peas. 'My golly. A real occasion.'

Sally punched the stove controls and the container of smoking pheasant was slid onto the table and neatly sliced open. 'Go wash your hands and we're ready to eat. Hurry—before it gets cold.'

Morris presented his hands to the wash slot and then sat down gratefully at the table. Sally served the tender, fragrant pheasant, and the two of them began eating.

'Sally,' Morris said, when his plate was empty and he was leaning back and sipping slowly at his coffee. 'I can't go on like this. Something's got to be done.'

'You mean the drive? I wish you could get a position on Mars like Bob Young. Maybe if you talked to the Employment Commission and explained to them how all the strain—'

'It's not just the drive. *They're right out front.* Everywhere. Waiting for me. All day and night.'

'Who are, dear?'

'Robots selling things. As soon as I set down the ship. Robots and visual-audio ads. They dig right into a man's brain. They follow people around until they die.'

'I know.' Sally patted his hand sympathetically. 'When I go shopping they follow me in clusters. All talking at once. It's really a panic—you can't understand half what they're saying.'

'We've got to break out.'

'Break out?' Sally faltered. 'What do you mean?'

'We've got to get away from them. They're destroying us.'

Morris fumbled in his pocket and carefully got out a tiny fragment of metal-foil. He unrolled it with painstaking care and smoothed it out on the table. 'Look at this. It was circulated in the office, among the men; it got to me and I kept it.'

'What does it mean?' Sally's brow wrinkled as she made out the words. 'Dear, I don't think you got all of it. There must be more than this.'

'A new world,' Morris said softly. 'Where they haven't got to, yet. It's a long way off, out beyond the solar system. Out in the stars.'

'Proxima?'

'Twenty planets. Half of them habitable. Only a few thousand people out there. Families, workmen, scientists, some industrial survey teams. Land free for the asking.'

'But it's so—' Sally made a face. 'Dear, isn't it sort of underdeveloped? They say it's like living back in the twentieth century. Flush toilets, bathtubs, gasoline-driven cars—'

'That's right.' Morris rolled up the bit of crumpled metal, his face grim and dead-serious. 'It's a hundred years behind times. None of this.' He indicated the stove and the furnishings in the living room. 'We'll have to do without. We'll have to get used to a simpler life. The way our ancestors lived.' He tried to smile but his face wouldn't cooperate. 'You think you'd like it? No ads, no salesrobots, traffic moving at sixty miles an hour instead of sixty million. We could raise passage on one of the big trans-system liners. I could sell my commute rocket ...'

There was a hesitant, doubtful silence.

'Ed,' Sally began. 'I think we should think it over more. What about your job? What would you do out there?'

'I'd find something.'

'But *what*? Haven't you got that part figured out?' A shrill tinge of annoyance crept into her voice. 'It seems to me we should consider that part just a little more before we throw away everything and just—take off.'

'If we don't go,' Morris said slowly, trying to keep his voice steady, 'they'll get us. There isn't much time left. I don't know how much longer I can hold them off.'

'Really, Ed! You make it sound so melodramatic. If you feel that bad why don't you take some time off and have a complete inhibition check? I was watching a vidprogram and I saw them going over a man whose psychosomatic system was much worse than yours. A much older man.'

She leaped to her feet. 'Let's go out tonight and celebrate. Okay?' Her slim fingers fumbled at the zipper of her shorts. 'I'll put on my new plastirobe, the one I've never had nerve enough to wear.'

Her eyes sparkled with excitement as she hurried into the bedroom. 'You know the one I mean? When you're up close it's translucent but as you get farther off it becomes more and more sheer until—'

'I know the one,' Morris said wearily. 'I've seen them advertised on my way home from work.' He got slowly to his feet and wandered into the living room. At the door of the bedroom he halted. 'Sally—'

'Yes?'

Morris opened his mouth to speak. He was going to ask her again, talk to her about the metal-foil fragment he had carefully wadded up and carried home. He was going to talk to her about the frontier. About Proxima Centauri. Going away and never coming back. But he never had a chance.

The doorchimes sounded.

'Somebody's at the door!' Sally cried excitedly. 'Hurry up and see who it is!'

In the evening darkness the robot was a silent, unmoving figure. A cold wind blew around it and into the house. Morris shivered and moved back from the door. 'What do you want?' he demanded. A strange fear licked at him. 'What is it?'

The robot was larger than any he had seen. Tall and broad, with heavy metallic grippers and elongated eye-lenses. Its upper trunk was a square tank instead of the usual cone. It rested on four treads, not the customary two. It towered over Morris, almost seven feet high. Massive and solid.

'Good evening,' it said calmly. Its voice was whipped around by the night wind; it mixed with the dismal noises of evening, the echoes of traffic and the clang of distant street signals. A few vague shapes hurried through the gloom. The world was black and hostile.

'Evening,' Morris responded automatically. He found himself trembling. 'What are you selling?'

'I would like to show you a fasrad,' the robot said.

Morris' mind was numb; it refused to respond. What was a *fasrad*? There was something dreamlike and nightmarish going on. He struggled to get his mind and body together. 'A what?' he croaked.

'A fasrad.' The robot made no effort to explain. It regarded him without emotion, as if it was not its responsibility to explain anything. 'It will take only a moment.'

'I—' Morris began. He moved back, out of the wind. And the robot, without change of expression, glided past him and into the house.

'Thank you,' it said. It halted in the middle of the living room. 'Would you call your wife, please? I would like to show her the fasrad, also.'

'Sally,' Morris muttered helplessly. 'Come here.'

Sally swept breathlessly into the living room, her breasts quivering with excitement. 'What is it? Oh!' She saw the robot and halted uncertainly. 'Ed, did you order something? Are we buying something?'

'Good evening,' the robot said to her. 'I am going to show you the fasrad. Please be seated. On the couch, if you will. Both together.'

Sally sat down expectantly, her cheeks flushed, eyes bright with wonder and bewilderment. Numbly, Ed seated himself beside her. 'Look,' he muttered thickly. 'What the hell is a fasrad? *What's going on?* I don't want to buy anything!'

'What is your name?' the robot asked him.

'Morris.' He almost choked. 'Ed Morris.'

The robot turned to Sally. 'Mrs Morris.' It bowed slightly. 'I'm glad to meet you, Mr and Mrs Morris. You are the first persons in your neighborhood to see the fasrad. This is the initial demonstration in this area.' Its cold eyes swept the room. 'Mr Morris, you are employed, I assume. Where are you employed?'

'He works on Ganymede,' Sally said dutifully, like a little girl in school. 'For the Terran Metals Development Co.'

The robot digested this information. 'A fasrad will be of value to you.' It eyed Sally. 'What do you do?'

'I'm a tape transcriber at Histo-Research.'

'A fasrad will be of no value in your professional work, but it will be helpful here in the home.' It picked up a table in its powerful steel grippers. 'For example, sometimes an attractive piece of furniture is damaged by a clumsy guest.' The robot smashed the table to bits; fragments of wood and plastic rained down. 'A fasrad is needed.'

Morris leaped helplessly to his feet. He was powerless to halt events; a numbing weight hung over him, as the robot tossed the fragments of table away and selected a heavy floor lamp.

'Oh dear,' Sally gasped. 'That's my best lamp.'

'When a fasrad is possessed, there is nothing to fear.' The robot seized the lamp and twisted it grotesquely. It ripped the shade, smashed the bulbs, then threw away the remnants. 'A situation of this kind can occur from some violent explosion, such as an H-Bomb.'

'For God's sake,' Morris muttered. 'We—'

'An H-Bomb attack may never occur,' the robot continued, 'but in such an event a fasrad is indispensable.' It knelt down and pulled an intricate tube from its waist. Aiming the tube at the floor it atomized a hole five feet in diameter. It stepped back from the yawning pocket. 'I have not extended this tunnel, but you can see a fasrad would save your life in case of attack.'

The word *attack* seemed to set off a new train of reactions in its metal brain.

'Sometimes a thug or hood will attack a person at night,' it continued. Without warning it whirled and drove its fist through the wall. A section of the wall collapsed in a heap of powder and debris. 'That takes care of the thug.' The robot straightened out and peered around the room. 'Often you are too tired in the evening to manipulate the buttons on the stove.' It strode into the kitchen and began punching the stove controls; immense quantities of food spilled in all directions.

'Stop!' Sally cried. 'Get away from my stove!'

'You may be too weary to run water for your bath.' The robot tripped the controls of the tub and water poured down. 'Or you may wish to go right to bed.' It yanked the bed from its concealment and threw it flat. Sally retreated in fright as the robot advanced toward her. 'Sometimes after a hard day at work you are too tired to remove your clothing. In that event—'

'Get out of here!' Morris shouted at it. 'Sally, run and get the cops. The thing's gone crazy. *Hurry.*'

'The fasrad is a necessity in all modern homes,' the robot continued. 'For example, an appliance may break down. The fasrad repairs it instantly.' It seized the automatic humidity control and tore the wiring and replaced it on the wall. 'Sometimes you would prefer not to go to work. The fasrad is permitted by law to occupy your position for a consecutive period not to exceed ten days. If, after that period—'

'Good God,' Morris said, as understanding finally came. 'You're the fasrad.'

'That's right,' the robot agreed. 'Fully Automatic Self-Regulating Android (Domestic). There is also the fasrac (Construction), the fasram (Managerial), the fasras (Soldier), and the fasrab (Bureaucrat). I am designed for home use.'

'You—' Sally gasped. 'You're for sale. You're selling yourself.'

'I am demonstrating myself,' the fasrad, the robot, answered. Its impassive metal eyes were fixed intently on Morris as it continued, 'I am sure, Mr Morris, you would like to own me. I am reasonably priced and fully guaranteed. A full book of instructions is included. I cannot conceive of taking *no* for an answer.'

At half past twelve, Ed Morris still sat at the foot of the bed, one shoe on, the other in his hand. He gazed vacantly ahead. He said nothing.

'For heaven's sake,' Sally complained. 'Finish untying that knot and get into bed; you have to be up at five-thirty.'

Morris fooled aimlessly with the shoelace. After a while he dropped the shoe and tugged at the other one. The house was cold and silent. Outside, the dismal night wind whipped and lashed at the cedars that grew along the side of the building. Sally lay curled up beneath the radiant-lens, a cigarette between her lips, enjoying the warmth and half-dozing.

In the living room stood the fasrad. It hadn't left. It was still there, was waiting for Morris to buy it.

'Come on!' Sally said sharply. 'What's wrong with you? It fixed all the things it broke; it was just demonstrating itself.' She sighed drowsily. 'It certainly gave me a scare. I thought something had gone wrong with it. They certainly had an inspiration, sending it around to sell itself to people.'

Morris said nothing.

Sally rolled over on her stomach and languidly stubbed out her cigarette. 'That's not so much, is it? Ten thousand gold units, and if we get our friends to buy one we get a five per cent commission. All we have to do is show it. It isn't as if we had to *sell* it. It sells itself.' She giggled. 'They always wanted a product that sold itself, didn't they?'

Morris untied the knot in his shoelace. He slid his shoe back on and tied it tight.

'What are you doing?' Sally demanded angrily. 'You come to

bed!' She sat up furiously, as Morris left the room and moved slowly down the hall. 'Where are you going?'

In the living room, Morris switched on the light and sat down facing the fasrad. 'Can you hear me?' he said.

'Certainly,' the fasrad answered. 'I'm never inoperative. Sometimes an emergency occurs at night: a child is sick or an accident takes place. You have no children as yet, but in the event—'

'Shut up,' Morris said, 'I don't want to hear you.'

'You asked me a question. Self-regulating androids are plugged in to a central information exchange. Sometimes a person wishes immediate information; the fasrad is always ready to answer any theoretical or factual inquiry. Anything not metaphysical.'

Morris picked up the book of instructions and thumbed it. The fasrad did thousands of things; it never wore out; it was never at a loss; it couldn't make a mistake. He threw the book away. 'I'm not going to buy you,' he said to it. 'Never. Not in a million years.'

'Oh, yes you are,' the fasrad corrected. 'This is an opportunity you can't afford to miss.' There was calm, metallic confidence in its voice. 'You can't turn me down, Mr Morris. A fasrad is an indispensable necessity in the modern home.'

'Get out of here,' Morris said evenly. 'Get out of my house and don't come back.'

'I'm not your fasrad to order around. Until you've purchased me at the regular list price, I'm responsible only to Self-Regulating Android Inc. Their instructions were to the contrary; I'm to remain with you until you buy me.'

'Suppose I never buy you?' Morris demanded, but in his heart ice formed even as he asked. Already he felt the cold terror of the answer that was coming; there could be no other.

'I'll continue to remain with you,' the fasrad said; 'eventually you'll buy me.' It plucked some withered roses from a vase on the mantel and dropped them into its disposal slot. 'You will see more and more situations in which a fasrad is indispensable. Eventually you'll wonder how you ever existed without one.'

'Is there anything you can't do?'

'Oh, yes; there's a great deal I can't do. But I can do anything *you* can do—and considerably better.'

Morris let out his breath slowly. 'I'd be insane to buy you.'

'You've got to buy me,' the impassive voice answered. The fasrad extended a hollow pipe and began cleaning the carpet. 'I am useful in all situations. Notice how fluffy and free of dust this rug is.' It withdrew the pipe and extended another. Morris coughed and staggered quickly away; clouds of white particles billowed out and filled every part of the room.

'I am spraying for moths,' the fasrad explained.

The white cloud turned to an ugly blue-black. The room faded into ominous darkness; the fasrad was a dim shape moving methodically about in the center. Presently the cloud lifted and the furniture emerged.

'I sprayed for harmful bacteria,' the fasrad said.

It painted the walls of the room and constructed new furniture to go with them. It reinforced the ceiling in the bathroom. It increased the number of heat-vents from the furnace. It put in new electrical wiring. It tore out all the fixtures in the kitchen and assembled more modern ones. It examined Morris' financial accounts and computed his income tax for the following year. It sharpened all the pencils; it caught hold of his wrist and quickly diagnosed his high blood-pressure as psychosomatic.

'You'll feel better after you've turned responsibility over to me,' it explained. It threw out some old soup Sally had been saving. 'Danger of botulism,' it told him. 'Your wife is sexually attractive, but not capable of a high order of intellectualization.'

Morris went to the closet and got his coat.

'Where are you going?' the fasrad asked.

'To the office.'

'At this time of night?'

Morris glanced briefly into the bedroom. Sally was sound asleep under the soothing radiant-lens. Her slim body was rosy pink and healthy, her face free of worry. He closed the front door and hurried down the steps into the darkness. Cold night wind slashed at him as he approached the parking lot. His little commute ship was parked with hundreds of others; a quarter sent the attendant robot obediently after it.

In ten minutes he was on his way to Ganymede.

The fasrad boarded his ship when he stopped at Mars to refuel.

'Apparently you don't understand,' the fasrad said. 'My instructions are to demonstrate myself until you're satisfied. As yet, you're not wholly convinced; further demonstration is necessary.' It passed an intricate web over the controls of the ship until all the dials and meters were in adjustment. 'You should have more frequent servicing.'

It retired to the rear to examine the drive jets. Morris numbly signalled the attendant, and the ship was released from the fuel pumps. He gained speed and the small sandy planet fell behind. Ahead, Jupiter loomed.

'Your jets aren't in good repair,' the fasrad said, emerging from the rear. 'I don't like that knock to the main brake drive. As soon as you land I'll make extensive repair.'

'The Company doesn't mind your doing favors for me?' Morris asked, with bitter sarcasm.

'The Company considers me your fasrad. An invoice will be mailed to you at the end of the month.' The robot whipped out a pen and a pad of forms. 'I'll explain the four easy-payment plans. Ten thousand gold units cash means a three per cent discount. In addition, a number of household items may be traded in—items you won't have further need for. If you wish to divide the purchase in four parts, the first is due at once, and the last in ninety days.'

'I always pay cash,' Morris muttered. He was carefully resetting the route positions on the control board.

'There's no carrying charge for the ninety-day plan. For the six-month plan there's a six per cent annum charge which will amount to approximately—' It broke off. 'We've changed course.'

'That's right.'

'We've left the official traffic lane.' The fasrad stuck its pen and pad away and hurried to the control board. 'What are you doing? There's a two-unit fine for this.'

Morris ignored it. He hung on grimly to the controls and kept his eyes on the viewscreen. The ship was gaining speed rapidly. Warning buoys sounded angrily as he shot past them and into the bleak darkness of space beyond. In a few seconds they had left all traffic behind. They were alone, shooting rapidly away from Jupiter, out into deep space.

The fasrad computed the trajectory. 'We're moving out of the solar system. Toward Centaurus.'

'You guessed it.'

'Hadn't you better call your wife?'

Morris grunted and notched the drive bar farther up. The ship bucked and pitched, then managed to right itself. The jets began to whine ominously. Indicators showed the main turbines were beginning to heat. He ignored them and threw on the emergency fuel supply.

'I'll call Mrs Morris,' the fasrad offered. 'We'll be beyond range in a short while.'

'Don't bother.'

'She'll worry.' The fasrad hurried to the back and examined the jets again. It popped back into the cabin buzzing with alarm. 'Mr Morris, this ship is not equipped for inter-system travel. It's a Class D four-shaft domestic model for home consumption only. It was never made to stand this velocity.'

'To get to Proxima,' Morris answered, 'we need this velocity.'

The fasrad connected its power cables to the control board. 'I can take some of the strain off the wiring system. But unless you rev her back to normal I can't be responsible for the deterioration of the jets.'

'The hell with the jets.'

The fasrad was silent. It was listening intently to the growing whine under them. The whole ship shuddered violently. Bits of paint drifted down. The floor was hot from the grinding shafts.

Morris' foot stayed on the throttle. The ship gained more velocity as Sol fell behind. They were out of the charted area. Sol receded rapidly.

'It's too late to vid your wife,' the fasrad said. 'There are three emergency-rockets in the stern; if you want, I'll fire them off in the hope of attracting a passing military transport.'

'Why?'

'They can take us in tow and return us to the Sol system. There's a six hundred gold unit fine, but under the circumstances it seems to me the best policy.'

Morris turned his back to the fasrad and jammed down the throttle with all his weight. The whine had grown to a violent roar. Instruments smashed and cracked. Fuses blew up and down the board. The lights dimmed, faded, then reluctantly came back.

'Mr Morris,' the fasrad said, 'you must prepare for death. The statistical probabilities of turbine explosion are seventy–thirty. I'll do what I can, but the danger-point has already passed.'

Morris returned to the viewscreen. For a time he gazed hungrily up at the growing dot that was the twin star Centaurus. 'They look all right, don't they? Prox is the important one. Twenty planets.' He examined the wildly fluttering instruments. 'How are the jets holding up? I can't tell from these; most of them are burned out.'

The fasrad hesitated. It started to speak, then changed its mind. 'I'll go back and examine them,' it said. It moved to the rear of the ship and disappeared down the short ramp into the thundering, vibrating engine chamber.

Morris leaned over and put out his cigarette. He waited a moment longer, then reached out and yanked the drives full up, the last possible notch on the board.

The explosion tore the ship in half. Sections of hull hurtled around him. He was lifted weightless and slammed into the control board. Metal and plastic rained down on him. Flashing incandescent points winked, faded, and finally died into silence, and there was nothing but cold ash.

*

The dull *swish-swish* of emergency air-pumps brought conscious-ness back. He was pinned under the wreckage of the control board; one arm was broken and bent under him. He tried to move his legs but there was no sensation below his waist.

The splintered debris that had been his ship was still hurling toward Centaurus. Hull-sealing equipment was feebly trying to patch the gaping holes. Automatic temperature and grav feeds were thumping spasmodically from self-contained batteries. In the viewscreen the vast flaming bulk of the twin suns grew quietly, inexorably.

He was glad. In the silence of the ruined ship he lay buried beneath the debris, gratefully watching the growing bulk. It was a beautiful sight. He had wanted to see it for a long time. There it was, coming closer each moment. In a day or two the ship would plunge into the fiery mass and be consumed. But he could enjoy this interval; there was nothing to disturb his happiness.

He thought about Sally, sound asleep under the radiant-lens. Would Sally have liked Proxima? Probably not. Probably she would have wanted to go back home as soon as possible. This was something he had to enjoy alone. This was for him only. A vast peace descended over him. He could lie here without stirring, and the flaming magnificence would come nearer and nearer . . .

A sound. From the heaps of fused wreckage something was ris-ing. A twisted, dented shape dimly visible in the flickering glare of the viewscreen. Morris managed to turn his head.

The fasrad staggered to a standing position. Most of its trunk was gone, smashed and broken away. It tottered, then pitched for-ward on its face with a grinding crash. Slowly it inched its way toward him, then settled to a dismal halt a few feet off. Gears whirred creakily. Relays popped open and shut. Vague, aimless life animated its devastated hulk.

'Good evening,' its shrill, metallic voice grated.

Morris screamed. He tried to move his body but the ruined beams held him tight. He shrieked and shouted and tried to crawl away from it. He spat and wailed and wept.

'I would like to show you a fasrad,' the metallic voice continued. 'Would you call your wife, please? I would like to show her a fasrad, too.'

'Get away!' Morris screamed. 'Get away from me!'

'Good evening,' the fasrad continued, like a broken tape. 'Good evening. Please be seated. I am happy to meet you. What is your name? Thank you. You are the first persons in your neighborhood to see the fasrad. Where are you employed?'

Its dead eye-lenses gaped at him empty and vacant.

'Please be seated,' it said again. 'This will take only a second. Only a second. This demonstration will take only a—'

SHELL GAME

A sound awoke O'Keefe instantly. He threw back his covers, slid from the cot, grabbed his B-pistol from the wall and, with his foot, smashed the alarm box. High frequency waves tripped emergency bells throughout the camp. As O'Keefe burst from his house, lights already flickered on every side.

'Where?' Fisher demanded shrilly. He appeared beside O'Keefe, still in his pajamas, grubby-faced with sleep.

'Over to the right.' O'Keefe leaped aside for a massive cannon being rolled from its underground storage-chambers. Soldiers were appearing among the night-clad figures. To the right lay the black bog of mists and obese foliage, ferns and pulpy onions, sunk in the half-liquid ooze that made up the surface of Betelgeuse II. Nocturnal phosphorescence danced and flitted over the bog, ghostly yellow lights snapped in the thick darkness.

'I figure,' Horstokowski said, 'they came in close to the road, but not actually on it. There's a shoulder fifty feet on each side, where the bog has piled up. That's why our radar's silent.'

An immense mechanical fusing 'bug' was eating its way into the mud and shifting water of the bog, leaving behind a trail of hard, smoked surface. The vegetation and the rotting roots and dead leaves were sucked up and efficiently cleared away.

'What did you see?' Portbane asked O'Keefe.

'I didn't see anything. I was sound asleep. But I *heard* them.'

'Doing what?'

'They were getting ready to pump nerve gas into my house. I heard them unreeling the hose from portable drums and uncapping the pressure tanks. But, by God, I was out of the house before they could get the joints leak-tight!'

Daniels hurried up. 'You say it's a gas attack?' He fumbled for the gas mask at his belt. 'Don't stand there—get your masks on!'

'They didn't get their equipment going,' Silberman said. 'O'Keefe gave the alarm in time. They retreated back to the bog.'

'You're sure?' Daniels demanded.

'You don't smell anything, do you?'

'No,' Daniels admitted. 'But the odorless type is the most deadly. And you don't know you've been gassed till it's too late.' He put on his gas mask, just to be sure.

A few women appeared by the rows of houses—slim, large-eyed shapes in the flickering glare of the emergency searchlights. Some children crept cautiously after them.

Silberman and Horstokowski moved over in the shadows by the heavy cannon.

'Interesting,' Horstokowski said. 'Third gas attack this month. Plus two tries to wire bomb terminals within the camp site. They're stepping it up.'

'You have it all figured out, don't you?'

'I don't have to wait for the composite to see we're getting it heavier all the time.' Horstokowski peered warily around, then pulled Silberman close. 'Maybe there's a reason why the radar screen didn't react. It's supposed to get everything, even knocker-bats.'

'But if they came in along the shoulder, like you said—'

'I just said that as a plant. *There's somebody waving them in, setting up interference for the radar.*'

'You mean one of us?'

Horstokowski was intently watching Fisher through the moist night gloom. Fisher had moved carefully to the edge of the road, where the hard surface ended and the slimy, scorched bog began. He was squatting down and rooting in the ooze.

'What's he doing?' Horstokowski demanded.

'Picking up something,' Silberman said indifferently. 'Why not? He's supposed to be looking around, isn't he?'

'Watch,' Horstokowski warned. 'When he comes back, he's going to pretend nothing happened.'

Presently, Fisher returned, walking rapidly and rubbing the muck from his hands.

Horstokowski intercepted him. 'What'd you find?'

'Me?' Fisher blinked. 'I didn't find anything.'

'Don't kid me! You were down on your hands and knees, grubbing in the bog.'

'I—thought I saw something metal, that's all.'

A vast inner excitement radiated through Horstokowski. He had been right.

'Come on!' he shouted. 'What'd you find?'

'I thought it was a gas pipe,' Fisher muttered. 'But it was only a root. A big, wet root.'

There was a tense silence.

'Search him,' Portbane ordered.

Two soldiers grabbed Fisher. Silberman and Daniels quickly searched him.

They spilled out his belt pistol, knife, emergency whistle, automatic relay checker, Geiger counter, pulse tab, medical kit and identification papers. There was nothing else.

The soldiers let him go, disappointed, and Fisher sullenly collected his things.

'No, he didn't find anything,' Portbane stated. 'Sorry, Fisher. We have to be careful. We have to watch all the time, as long as they're out there, plotting and conspiring against us.'

Silberman and Horstokowski exchanged glances, then moved quietly away.

'I think I get it,' Silberman said softly.

'Sure,' Horstokowski answered. 'He *hid* something. We'll dig up that section of bog he was poking around in. I think maybe we'll find something interesting.' He hunched his shoulders combatively. 'I knew somebody was working for them, here in the camp. A spy for Terra.'

Silberman started. 'Terra? Is that who's attacking us?'

'Of course that's who.'

There was a puzzled look on Silberman's face.

'Seemed to me we're fighting somebody else.'

Horstokowski was outraged.

'For instance?'

Silberman shook his head. 'I don't know. I didn't think about who so much as what to do about it. I guess I just took it for granted they were aliens.'

'And what do you think those Terran monkey men are?' Horstokowski challenged.

The weekly Pattern Conference brought together the nine leaders of the camp in their reinforced underground conference chamber. Armed guards protected the entrance, which was sealed tight as soon as the last leader had been examined, checked over and finally passed.

Domgraf-Schwach, the conference chairman, sat attentively in his deep chair, one hand on the Pattern composite, the other on the switch that could instantly catapult him from the room and into a special compartment, safe from attack. Portbane was making his routine inspection of the chamber, examining each chair and desk for scanning eyes. Daniels sat with eyes fixed on his Geiger counter. Silberman was completely encased in an elaborate steel and plastic suit, configured with wiring, from which continual whirrings came.

'What in God's name is that suit of armor?' Domgraf-Schwach asked angrily. 'Take it off so we can see you.'

'Nuts to you,' Silberman snapped, his voice muted by his intricate hull. 'I'm wearing this from now on. Last night, somebody tried to jab me with bacteria-impregnated needles.'

Lanoir, who was half-dozing at his place, came alive. 'Bacteria-impregnated needles?' He leaped up and hurried over to Silberman. 'Let me ask you if—'

'*Keep away from me!*' Silberman shouted. 'If you come any closer, I'll electrocute you!'

'The attempt I reported last week,' Lanoir panted excitedly, 'when they tried to poison the water supply with metallic salts. It occurred to me their next method would be bacterial wastes, filterable virus we couldn't detect until actual outbreak of disease.' From his pocket, he yanked a bottle and shook out a handful of white capsules. One after another, he popped the capsules into his mouth.

Every man in the room was protected in some fashion. Each chose whatever apparatus conformed to his individual experience. But the totality of defense-systems was integrated in the general Pattern planning. The only man who didn't seem busy with a device was Tate. He sat pale and tense, but otherwise unoccupied. Domgraf-Schwach made a mental note—Tate's confidence-level was unusually high. It suggested he somehow felt safe from attack.

'No talking,' Domgraf-Schwach said. 'Time to start.'

He had been chosen as chairman by the turn of a wheel. There was no possibility of subversion under such a system. In an isolated, autonomous colony of sixty men and fifty women, such a random method was necessary.

'Daniels will read the week's Pattern composite,' Domgraf-Schwach ordered.

'Why?' Portbane demanded bluntly. 'We were the ones who put it together. We all know what's in it.'

'For the same reason it's always read,' Silberman answered. 'So we'll know it wasn't tampered with.'

'Just the summation!' Horstokowski said loudly. 'I don't want to stay down here in this vault any longer than I have to.'

'Afraid somebody'll fill up the passage?' Daniels jeered. 'There are half a dozen emergency escape exits. You ought to know—you insisted on every one of them.'

'Read the summation,' Lanoir demanded.

Daniels cleared his throat. 'During the last seven days, there were eleven overt attacks in all. The main attack was on our new class-A bridge network, which was sabotaged and wrecked. The struts were weakened and the plastic mix that served as base material was diluted, so that when the very first convoy of trucks passed over it, the whole thing collapsed.'

'We know that,' Portbane said gloomily.

'Loss consisted of six lives and considerable equipment. Troops scoured the area for a whole day, but the saboteurs managed to escape. Shortly after this attack, it was discovered that the water supply was poisoned with metallic salts. The wells were therefore filled and new ones drilled. Now all our water passes through filter and analysis systems.'

'I boil mine,' Lanoir added feelingly.

'It's agreed by everyone that the frequency and severity of attacks have been stepped up.' Daniels indicated the massive wall charts and graphs. 'Without our bomb-proof screen and our constant direction network, we'd be overwhelmed tonight. The real question is—*who are our attackers?*'

'Terrans,' Horstokowski said.

Tate shook his head. 'Terrans, hell! What would monkey men be doing out this far?'

'We're out this far, aren't we?' Lanoir retorted. 'And we were Terrans once.'

'Never!' Fisher shouted. 'Maybe we lived on Terra, but we aren't Terrans. We're a superior mutant race.'

'Then who are they?' Horstokowski insisted.

'They're other survivors from the ship,' Tate said.

'How do you know?' asked Silberman. 'Have you ever seen them?'

'*We salvaged no lifeboats, remember?* They must have blasted off in them.'

'If they were isolated survivors,' O'Keefe objected, 'they wouldn't have the equipment and weapons and machines they're using. They're a trained, integrated force. We haven't been able to defeat them or even *kill* any of them in five years. That certainly shows their strength.'

'We haven't tried to defeat them,' Fisher said. 'We've only tried to defend ourselves.'

A sudden tense silence fell over the nine men.

'You mean the ship,' Horstokowski said.

'It'll be up out of the bog soon,' Tate replied. 'And then we'll have something to show them—something they'll remember.'

'Good God!' Lanoir exclaimed, disgusted. 'The ship's a wreck—the meteor completely smashed it. What happens when we do get it up? We can't operate it unless we can completely rebuild it.'

'If the monkey men could build the thing,' Portbane said, 'we can repair it. We have the tools and machinery.'

'And we've finally located the control cabin,' O'Keefe pointed out. 'I see no reason why we can't raise it.'

There was an abrupt change of expression on Lanoir's face. 'All right, I withdraw my objections. Let's get it up.'

'What's your motive?' Daniels yelled excitedly. 'You're trying to put something over on us!'

'He's planning something,' Fisher furiously agreed. 'Don't listen to him. Leave the damn thing down there!'

'Too late for that,' O'Keefe said. 'It's been rising for weeks.'

'You're in with him!' Daniels screeched. 'Something's being put over on us.'

The ship was a dripping, corroded ruin. Slime poured from it as the magnetic grapples dragged it from the bog and onto the hard surface that the fusing bugs had laid down.

The bugs burned a hard track through the bog, out to the control cabin. While the lift suspended the cabin, heavy reinforced plastic beams were slid under it. Tangled weeds, matted like ancient hair, covered the globular cabin in the midday sun, the first light that had struck it in five years.

'In you go,' Domgraf-Schwach said eagerly.

Portbane and Lanoir advanced over the fused surface to the moored control cabin. Their handlights flashed ominously yellow around the steaming walls and encrusted controls. Livid eels twisted and convulsed in the thick pools underfoot. The cabin was a smashed, twisted ruin. Lanoir, who was first, motioned Portbane impatiently after him.

'*You* look at these controls—you're the engineer.'

Portbane set down his light on a sloping heap of rusted metal and sloshed through the knee-deep rubbish to the demolished control panel. It was a maze of fused, buckled machinery. He squatted down in front of it and began tearing away the pitted guard-plates.

Lanoir pushed open a supply closet and brought down metal-packed audio and video tapes. He eagerly spilled open a can of the video and held a handful of frames to the flickering light. 'Here's the ship's data. Now I'll be able to prove there was nobody but us aboard.'

O'Keefe appeared at the jagged doorway. 'How's it coming?'

Lanoir elbowed past him and out on the support boards. He deposited a load of tape-cans and returned to the drenched cabin. 'Find anything on the controls?' he asked Portbane.

'Strange,' Portbane murmured.

'What's the matter?' Tate demanded. 'Too badly wrecked?'

'There are lots of wires and relays. Plenty of meters and power circuits and switches. But no controls to operate them.'

Lanoir hurried over. 'There must be!'

'For repairs, you have to remove all these plates—practically dismantle the works to even see them. Nobody could sit here and control the ship. There's nothing but a smooth, sealed shell.'

'Maybe this wasn't the control cabin,' Fisher offered.

'This is the steering mechanism—no doubt about that.' Portbane pulled out a heap of charred wiring. 'But all this was self-contained. They're robot controls. Automatic.'

They looked at each other.

'Then we were prisoners,' Tate said, dazed.

'Whose?' Fisher asked baffledly.

'The Terrans!' Lanoir said.

'I don't get it,' Fisher muttered vaguely. 'We planned the whole flight—didn't we? We broke out of Ganymede and got away.'

'Get the tapes going,' Portbane said to Lanoir. 'Let's see what's in them.'

Daniels snapped the vidtape scanner off and raised the light.

'Well,' he said, 'you saw for yourselves this was a hospital ship. It carried no crew. It was directed from a central guide-beam at Jupiter. The beam carried it from the Sol System here, where, because of a mechanical error, a meteor penetrated the protection screen and the ship crashed.'

'And if it hadn't crashed?' Domgraf-Schwach asked faintly.

'Then we would have been taken to the main hospital at Fomalhaut IV.'

'Play the last tape again,' Tate urged.

The wall-speaker spluttered and then said smoothly: 'The distinction between paranoids and paranoiac syndromes in other psychotic personality disorders must be borne in mind when dealing with these patients. The paranoid retains his general personality structure unimpaired. Outside of the region of his complex, he is logical, rational, even brilliant. He can be talked to—he can discuss himself—he is aware of his surroundings.

'The paranoid differs from other psychotics in that he remains actively oriented to the outside world. He differs from so-called normal personality types in that he has a set of fixed ideas, false postulates from which he has relentlessly constructed an elaborate system of beliefs, logical and consistent with these false postulates.'

Shakily, Daniels interrupted the tape. 'These tapes were for the hospital authorities on Fomalhaut IV. Locked in a supply closet in the control cabin. The control cabin itself was sealed off from the rest of the ship. None of us was able to enter it.'

'The paranoid is totally rigid,' the calm voice of the Terran doctor continued. 'His fixed ideas cannot be shaken. They dominate his life. He logically weaves all events, all persons, all chance remarks and happenings, into his system. He is convinced the world is plotting against him—that he is a person of unusual importance and ability against whom endless machinations are directed. To thwart these plots, the paranoid goes to infinite lengths to protect himself. He repeatedly vidtapes the authorities, constantly moves from place to place and, in the dangerous final phases, may even become—'

Silberman snapped it off savagely and the chamber was silent. The nine leaders of the camp sat unmoving in their places.

'We're a bunch of nuts,' Tate said finally. 'A shipload of psychos who got wrecked by a chance meteor.'

'Don't kid yourself,' Horstokowski snapped. 'There wasn't anything chance about that meteor.'

Fisher giggled hysterically. 'More paranoid talk. Good God, all these attacks—hallucinations—all in our minds!'

Lanoir poked vaguely at the pile of tape. 'What are we to believe? *Are there any attackers?*'

'We've been defending ourselves against them for five years!' Portbane retorted. 'Isn't that proof enough?'

'Have you ever seen them?' Fisher asked slyly.

'We're up against the best agents in the Galaxy. Terran shock troops and military spies, carefully trained in subversion and sabotage. They're too clever to show themselves.'

'They wrecked the bridge-system,' O'Keefe said. 'It's true we didn't see them, but the bridge is sure as hell in ruins.'

'Maybe it was badly built,' Fisher pointed out. 'Maybe it just collapsed.'

'Things don't "just collapse"! There's a reason for all these things that have been happening.'

'Like what?' Tate demanded.

'Weekly poison gas attacks,' Portbane said. 'Metallic wastes in the water supply, to name only two.'

'And bacteriological crystals,' Daniels added.

'Maybe none of these things exist,' Lanoir argued. 'But how are we to prove it? If we're all insane, *how would we know?*'

'There are over a hundred of us,' Domgraf-Schwach said. 'We've all experienced these attacks. Isn't that proof enough?'

'A myth can be picked up by a whole society, believed and taught to the next generation. Gods, fairies, witches–believing a thing doesn't make it true. For centuries, Terrans believed the Earth was flat.'

'If all foot-rulers grow to thirteen inches,' Fisher asked, 'how would anybody know? One of them would have to stay twelve inches long, a nonvariable, a constant. We're a bunch of inaccurate rulers, each thirteen inches long. We need one nonparanoid for comparison.'

'Or maybe this is all part of their strategy,' Silberman said. 'Maybe they rigged up that control cabin and planted those tapes there.'

'This ought to be no different from trying to test any belief,' Portbane explained. 'What's the characteristic of a scientific test?'

'It can be duplicated,' Fisher said promptly. 'Look, we're going around in circles. *We're trying to measure ourselves*. You can't take your ruler, either twelve inches or thirteen inches long, and ask it to measure itself. No instrument can test its own accuracy.'

'Wrong,' Portbane answered calmly. 'I can put together a valid, objective test.'

'There's no such test!' Tate shouted excitedly.

'There sure as hell is. And inside of a week, I'll have it set up.'

'Gas!' the soldier shouted. On all sides, sirens wailed into life. Women and children scrambled for their masks. Heavy-duty cannon rumbled up from subsurface chambers and took up positions. Along the perimeter of the bog, the fusing bugs were searing away a ribbon of muck. Searchlights played out into the fern-thick darkness.

Portbane snapped off the cock of the steel tank and signaled the workmen. The tank was rolled quickly away from the sea of mud and seared weeds.

'All right,' Portbane gasped. 'Get it below.'

He emerged in the subsurface chamber as the cylinder was being rolled into position.

'That cylinder,' Portbane said, 'should contain hydrocyanic vapor. It's a sampling made at the site of the attack.'

'This is useless,' Fisher complained. 'They're attacking and here we stand!'

Portbane signaled the workmen and they began laying out the test apparatus. 'There will be two samples, precipitates of different vapors, each clearly marked and labeled A and B. One comes from the cylinder filled at the scene of the attack. The other is condensed from air taken out of this room.'

'Suppose we describe both as negative?' Silberman asked worriedly. 'Won't that throw your test off?'

'Then we'll take more tests. After a couple of months, if we still haven't got anything but negative findings, then the attack hypothesis is destroyed.'

'We may see both as positive,' Tate said, perplexed.

'In that case, we're dead right now. If we see both samples as positive, I think the case for the paranoid hypothesis has been proved.'

After a moment, Domgraf-Schwach reluctantly agreed. 'One is the control. If we maintain that it isn't possible to get a control sample that is free of hydrocyanic acid . . .'

'Pretty damn slick,' O'Keefe admitted. 'You start from the one known factor—our own existence. We can't very well doubt *that*.'

'Here are all the choices,' Portbane said. 'Both positive means we're psychotic. Both negative means either the attack was a false alarm or there are no attackers. One positive and one negative would indicate there are real attackers, that we're fully sane and rational.' He glanced around at the camp leads. '*But we'll all have to agree which sample is which.*'

'Our reactions will be recorded secretly?' Tate asked.

'Tabulated and punched by the mechanical eye. Tallied by machinery. Each of us will make an individual discrimination.'

After a pause, Fisher said, 'I'll try it.' He came forward, leaned over the colorimeter and studied the two samples intently. He alternated them for a time and then firmly grabbed the check-stylus.

'You're sure?' Domgraf-Schwach asked. 'You really know which is the negative control sample?'

'I know.' Fisher noted his findings on the punch sheet and moved away.

'I'm next,' Tate said, impatiently pushing up. 'Let's get this over with.'

One by one, the men examined the two samples, recorded their findings, and then moved off to stand waiting uneasily.

'All right,' Portbane said finally. 'I'm the last one.' He peered down briefly, scribbled his results, then pushed the equipment away. 'Give me the readings,' he told the workmen by the scanner.

A moment later, the findings were flashed up for everyone to see.

Fisher	A
Tate	A
O'Keefe	B
Horstokowski	B
Silberman	B
Daniels	B
Portbane	A
Domgraf-Schwach	B
Lanoir	A

'I'll be damned,' Silberman said softly. 'As simple as that. We're paranoids.'

'You cluck!' Tate shouted at Horstokowski. 'It was A, not B! How the hell could you get it wrong?'

'B was as bright as a searchlight!' Domgraf-Schwach answered furiously. 'A was completely colorless!'

O'Keefe pushed forward. 'Which was it, Portbane? Which was the positive sample?'

'I don't know,' Portbane confessed. 'How could any of us be sure?'

The buzzer on Domgraf-Schwach's desk clicked and he snapped on the vidscreen.

The face of a soldier-operator appeared. 'The attack's over, sir. We drove them away.'

Domgraf-Schwach smiled ironically. 'Catch any of them?'

'No, sir. They slipped back into the bog. I think we hit a couple, though. We'll go out tomorrow and try to find the corpses.'

'You think you'll find them?'

'Well, the bog usually swallows them up. But maybe this time—'

'All right,' Domgraf-Schwach interrupted. 'If this turns out to be an exception, let me know.' He broke the circuit.

'Now what?' Daniels inquired icily.

'There's no point in continuing work on the ship,' O'Keefe said. 'Why waste our time bombing empty bogs?'

'I suggest we keep working on the ship,' Tate contradicted.

'Why?' O'Keefe asked.

'So we can head for Fomalhaut and give ourselves up to the hospital station.'

Silberman stared at him incredulously. 'Turn ourselves in? Why not stay here? We're not harming anybody.'

'No, not yet. It's the future I'm thinking of, centuries from now.'

'We'll be dead.'

'Those of us in this room, sure, but what about our descendants?'

'He's right,' Lanoir conceded. 'Eventually our descendants will fill this whole solar system. Sooner or later, our ships might spread over the Galaxy.' He tried to smile, but his muscles would not respond. 'The tapes point out how tenacious paranoids are. They cling fanatically to their fixed beliefs. If our descendants expand into Terran regions, there'll be a fight and we might win because we're more one-track. We would never deviate.'

'Fanatics,' Daniels whispered.

'We'll have to keep this information from the rest of the camp,' O'Keefe said.

'Absolutely,' Fisher agreed. 'We'll have to keep them thinking the ship is for H-bomb attacks. Otherwise, we'll have one hell of a situation on our hands.'

They began moving numbly toward the sealed door.

'Wait a minute,' Domgraf-Schwach said urgently. 'The two workmen.' He started back, while some of them went out into the corridor, the rest back toward their seats.

And then it happened.

Silberman fired first. Fisher screamed as half of him vanished in swirling particles of radioactive ash. Silberman dropped to one knee and fired up at Tate. Tate leaped back and brought out his own B-pistol. Daniels stepped from the path of Lanoir's beam. It missed him and struck the first row of seats.

Lanoir calmly crept along the wall through the billowing clouds of smoke. A figure loomed ahead; he raised his gun and fired. The figure fell to one side and fired back. Lanoir staggered and collapsed like a deflated balloon and Silberman hurried on.

At his desk, Domgraf-Schwach was groping wildly for his escape button. His fingers touched it, but as he depressed the stud, a blast from Portbane's pistol removed the top of his head. The lifeless corpse stood momentarily, then was whisked to 'safety' by the intricate apparatus beneath the desk.

'This way!' Portbane shouted, above the sizzle of the B-blasts. 'Come on, Tate!'

Various beams were turned in his direction. Half the chamber burst apart and thundered down, disintegrating into rubble and flaming debris. He and Tate scrambled for one of the emergency exits. Behind them, the others hurried, firing savagely.

Horstokowski found the exit and slid past the jammed lock. He fired as the two figures raced up the passage ahead of him. One of them stumbled, but the other grabbed at him and they hobbled off together. Daniels was a better shot. As Tate and Portbane emerged on the surface, one of Daniels' blasts undercut the taller of the two.

Portbane continued running a little way, and then silently pitched face-forward against the side of a plastic house, a gloomy square of opaque blackness against the night sky.

'Where'd they go?' Silberman demanded hoarsely, as he appeared at the mouth of the passage. His right arm had been torn away by Lanoir's blast. The stump was seared hard.

'I got one of them.' Daniels and O'Keefe approached the inert figure warily. 'It's Portbane. That leaves Tate. We got three of the four. Not bad, on such short notice.'

'Tate's damn smart,' Silberman panted. 'I think he suspected.'

He scanned the darkness around them. Soldiers, returning from the gas attack, came hurrying up. Searchlights rumbled toward the scene of the shooting. Off in the distance, sirens wailed.

'Which way did he go?' Daniels asked.

'Over toward the bog.'

O'Keefe moved cautiously along the narrow street. The others came slowly behind.

'You were the first to realize,' Horstokowski said to Silberman. 'For a while, I believed the test. Then I realized we were being tricked—the four of them were plotting in unison.'

'I didn't expect four of them,' Silberman admitted. 'I knew there was at least one Terran spy among us. But Lanoir . . .'

'I always knew Lanoir was a Terran agent,' O'Keefe declared flatly. 'I wasn't surprised at the test results. They gave themselves away by faking their findings.'

Silberman waved over a group of soldiers. 'Have Tate picked up and brought here. He's somewhere at the periphery of the camp.'

The soldiers hurried away, dazed and muttering. Alarm bells dinned shrilly on all sides. Figures scampered back and forth. Like a disturbed ant colony, the whole camp was alive with excitement.

'In other words,' Daniels said, 'the four of them really saw the same as we. They saw B as the positive sample, but they put down A instead.'

'They knew we'd put down B,' O'Keefe said, 'since B was the positive sample taken from the attack site. All they had to do was record the opposite. The results seemed to substantiate Lanoir's paranoid theory, which was why Portbane set up the test in the first place. It was planned a long time ago—part of their overall job.'

'Lanoir dug up the tapes in the first place!' Daniels exclaimed. 'Fisher and he planted them down in the ruins of the ship. Portbane got us to accept his testing device.'

'What were they trying to do?' Silberman asked suddenly. 'Why were they trying to convince us we're paranoids?'

'Isn't it obvious?' O'Keefe replied. 'They wanted us to turn ourselves in. The Terran monkey men naturally are trying to choke off the race that's going to supplant them. We won't surrender, of course. The four of them were clever—they almost had me convinced. When the results flashed up five to four, I had a momentary doubt. But then I realized what an intricate strategy they had worked out.'

Horstokowski examined his B-pistol. 'I'd like to get hold of Tate and wring the whole story from him, the whole damn account of their planning, so we'd have it in black and white.'

'You're still not convinced?' Daniels inquired.

'Of course. But I'd like to hear him admit it.'

'I doubt if we'll see Tate again,' O'Keefe said. 'He must have reached the Terran lines by now. He's probably sitting in a big inter-system military transport, giving his story to gold-braid Terran officials. I'll bet they're moving up heavy guns and shock troops while we stand here.'

'We'd better get busy,' Daniels said sharply. 'We'll repair the ship and load it with H-bombs. After we wipe out their bases here, we'll carry the war to them. A few raids on the Sol System ought to teach them to leave us alone.'

Horstokowski grinned. 'It'll be an uphill fight—we're alone against a whole galaxy. But I think we'll take care of them. One of us is worth a million Terran monkey men.'

Tate lay trembling in the dark tangle of weeds. Dripping black stalks of nocturnal vegetables clutched and stirred around him. Poisonous night insects slithered across the surface of the fetid bog.

He was covered with slime. His clothing was torn and ripped. Somewhere along the way, he had lost his B-pistol. His right shoulder ached; he could hardly move his arm. Bones broken, probably. He was too numb and dazed to care. He lay facedown in the sticky muck and closed his eyes.

He didn't have a chance. Nobody survived in the bogs. He feebly smashed an insect oozing across his neck. It squirmed in his hand and then, reluctantly, died. For a long time, its dead legs kicked.

The probing stalk of a stinging snail began tracing webs across Tate's inert body. As the sticky pressure of the snail crept heavily onto him, he heard the first faint far-off sounds of the camp going into action. For a time, it meant nothing to him. Then he understood—and shuddered miserably, helplessly.

The first phase of the big offensive against Earth was already moving into high gear.

UPON THE DULL EARTH

Silvia ran laughing through the night brightness, between the roses and cosmos and Shasta daisies, down the gravel path and beyond the heaps of sweet-tasting grass swept from the lawns. Stars, caught in pools of water, glittered everywhere, as she brushed through them to the slope beyond the brick wall. Cedars supported the sky and ignored the slim shape squeezing past, her brown hair flying, her eyes flashing.

'Wait for me,' Rick complained, as he cautiously threaded his way after her, along the half familiar path. Silvia danced on without stopping. 'Slow down!' he shouted angrily.

'Can't—we're late.' Without warning, Silvia appeared in front of him, blocking the path. 'Empty your pockets,' she gasped, her gray eyes sparkling. 'Throw away all metal. You know they can't stand metal.'

Rick searched his pockets. In his overcoat were two dimes and a fifty-cent piece. 'Do these count?'

'Yes!' Silvia snatched the coins and threw them into the dark heaps of calla lilies. The bits of metal hissed into the moist depths and were gone. 'Anything else?' She caught hold of his arm anxiously. 'They're already on their way. Anything else, Rick?'

'Just my watch.' Rick pulled his wrist away as Silvia's wild fingers snatched for the watch. 'That's not going in the bushes.'

'Then lay it on the sundial—or the wall. Or in a hollow tree.' Silvia raced off again. Her excited, rapturous voice danced back to him. 'Throw away your cigarette case. And your keys, your belt buckle—everything metal. You know how they hate metal. Hurry, we're late!'

Rick followed sullenly after her. 'All right, *witch*.'

Silvia snapped at him furiously from the darkness. 'Don't *say* that! It isn't true. You've been listening to my sisters and my mother and–'

Her words were drowned out by the sound. Distant flapping, a long way off, like vast leaves rustling in a winter storm. The night sky was alive with the frantic poundings; they were coming very quickly this time. They were too greedy, too desperately eager to wait. Flickers of fear touched the man and he ran to catch up with Silvia.

Silvia was a tiny column of green skirt and blouse in the center of the thrashing mass. She was pushing them away with one arm and trying to manage the faucet with the other. The churning activity of wings and bodies twisted her like a reed. For a time she was lost from sight.

'Rick!' she called faintly. 'Come here and help!' She pushed them away and struggled up. 'They're suffocating me!'

Rick fought his way through the wall of flashing white to the edge of the trough. They were drinking greedily at the blood that spilled from the wooden faucet. He pulled Silvia close against him; she was terrified and trembling. He held her tight until some of the violence and fury around them had died down.

'They're hungry,' Silvia gasped feebly.

'You're a little cretin for coming ahead. They can sear you to ash!'

'I know. They can do anything.' She shuddered, excited and frightened. 'Look at them,' she whispered, her voice husky with awe. 'Look at the size of them–their wing-spread. And they're *white*, Rick. Spotless–perfect. There's nothing in our world as spotless as that. Great and clean and wonderful.'

'They certainly wanted the lamb's blood.'

Silvia's soft hair blew against his face as the wings fluttered on all sides. They were leaving now, roaring up into the sky. Not up, really–away. Back to their own world whence they had scented the blood. But it was not only the blood–they had come because of Silvia. *She* had attracted them.

The girl's gray eyes were wide. She reached up towards the rising white creatures. One of them swooped close. Grass and flowers sizzled as blinding white flames roared in a brief fountain. Rick scrambled away. The flaming figure hovered momentarily over Silvia and then there was a hollow *pop*. The last of the white-winged giants was gone. The air, the ground, gradually cooled into darkness and silence.

'I'm sorry,' Silvia whispered.

'Don't do it again,' Rick managed. He was numb with shock. 'It isn't safe.'

'Sometimes I forget. I'm sorry, Rick. I didn't mean to draw them so close.' She tried to smile. 'I haven't been that careless in months. Not since that other time, when I first brought you out here.' The avid, wild look slid across her face. 'Did you *see* him? Power and flames! And he didn't even touch us. He just—looked at us. That was all. And everything's burned up, all around.'

Rick grabbed hold of her. 'Listen,' he grated. 'You mustn't call them again. It's wrong. This isn't their world.'

'It's not wrong—it's beautiful.'

'It's not safe!' His fingers dug into her flesh until she gasped. 'Stop tempting them down here!'

Silvia laughed hysterically. She pulled away from him, out into the blasted circle that the horde of angels had seared behind them as they rose into the sky. 'I can't *help* it,' she cried. 'I belong with them. They're my family, my people. Generations of them, back into the past.'

'What do you mean?'

'They're my ancestors. And some day I'll join them.'

'You are a little witch!' Rick shouted furiously.

'No,' Silvia answered. 'Not a witch, Rick. Don't you see? I'm a saint.'

The kitchen was warm and bright. Silvia plugged in the Silex and got a big red can of coffee down from the cupboards over the sink. 'You mustn't listen to them,' she said, as she set out plates and cups and got cream from the refrigerator. 'You know they don't understand. Look at them in there.'

Silvia's mother and her sisters, Betty Lou and Jean, stood huddled together in the living room, fearful and alert, watching the young couple in the kitchen. Walter Everett was standing by the fireplace, his face blank, remote.

'Listen to *me*,' Rick said. 'You have this power to attract them. You mean you're not—isn't Walter your real father?'

'Oh, yes—of course he is. I'm completely human. Don't I look human?'

'But you're the only one who has the power.'

'I'm not physically different,' Silvia said thoughtfully. 'I have the ability to see, that's all. Others have had it before me—saints, martyrs. When I was a child, my mother read to me about St Bernadette. Remember where her cave was? Near a hospital. They were hovering there and she saw one of them.'

'But the blood! It's grotesque. There never was anything like that.'

'Oh, yes. The blood draws them, lamb's blood especially. They hover over battlefields. Valkyries—carrying off the dead to Valhalla. That's why saints and martyrs cut and mutilate themselves. You know where I got the idea?'

Silvia fastened a little apron around her waist and filled the Silex with coffee. 'When I was nine years old, I read of it in Homer, in the *Odyssey*. Ulysses dug a trench in the ground and filled it with blood to attract the spirits. The shades from the nether world.'

'That's right,' Rick admitted reluctantly. 'I remember.'

'The ghosts of people who died. They had lived once. Everybody lives here, then dies and goes there.' Her face glowed. 'We're all going to have wings! We're all going to fly. We'll all be filled with fire and power. We won't be worms any more.'

'Worms! That's what you always call me.'

'Of course you're a worm. We're all worms—grubby worms creeping over the crust of the Earth, through dust and dirt.'

'Why should blood bring them?'

'Because it's life and they're attracted by life. Blood is *uisge beatha*—the water of life.'

'Blood means death! A trough of spilled blood . . .'

'It's *not* death. When you see a caterpillar crawl into its cocoon, do you think it's dying?'

Walter Everett was standing in the doorway. He stood listening to his daughter, his face dark. 'One day,' he said hoarsely, 'they're going to grab her and carry her off. She wants to go with them. She's waiting for that day.'

'You see?' Silvia said to Rick. 'He doesn't understand either.' She shut off the Silex and poured coffee. 'Coffee for you?' she asked her father.

'No,' Everett said.

'Silvia,' Rick said, as if speaking to a child, 'if you went away with them, you know you couldn't come back to us.'

'We all have to cross sooner or later. It's all part of our life.'

'But you're only nineteen,' Rick pleaded. 'You're young and healthy and beautiful. And our marriage—what about our marriage?' He half rose from the table. 'Silvia, you've got to stop this!'

'I *can't* stop it. I was seven when I saw them first.' Silvia stood by the sink, gripping the Silex, a faraway look in her eyes. 'Remember, Daddy? We were living back in Chicago. It was winter. I fell, walking home from school.' She held up a slim arm. 'See the scar? I fell and cut myself on the gravel and slush. I came home crying—it was sleeting and the wind was howling around me. My arm was bleeding and my mitten was soaked with blood. And then I looked up and saw them.'

There was silence.

'They want you,' Everett said wretchedly. 'They're flies—blue-bottles, hovering around, waiting for you. Calling you to come along with them.'

'Why not?' Silvia's gray eyes were shining and her cheeks radiated joy and anticipation. 'You've seen them, Daddy. You know what it means. Transfiguration—from clay into gods!'

Rick left the kitchen. In the living room, the two sisters stood together, curious and uneasy. Mrs Everett stood by herself, her face granite-hard, eyes bleak behind her steel-rimmed glasses. She turned away as Rick passed them.

'What happened out there?' Betty Lou asked him in a taut whisper. She was fifteen, skinny and plain, hollow-cheeked, with mousy, sand-colored hair. 'Silvia never lets us come out with her.'

'Nothing happened,' Rick answered.

Anger stirred the girl's barren face. 'That's not true. You were both out in the garden, in the dark, and—'

'Don't talk to him!' her mother snapped. She yanked the two girls away and shot Rick a glare of hatred and misery. Then she turned quickly from him.

Rick opened the door to the basement and switched on the light. He descended slowly into the cold, damp room of concrete and dirt, with its unwinking yellow light hanging from the dust-covered wires overhead.

In one corner loomed the big floor furnace with its mammoth hot air pipes. Beside it stood the water heater and discarded bundles, boxes of books, newspapers and old furniture, thick with dust, encrusted with strings of spider webs.

At the far end were the washing machine and spin dryer. And Silvia's pump and refrigeration system.

From the work bench Rick selected a hammer and two heavy pipe wrenches. He was moving towards the elaborate tanks and pipes when Silvia appeared abruptly at the top of the stairs, her coffee cup in one hand.

She hurried quickly down to him. 'What are you doing down here?' she asked, studying him intently. 'Why that hammer and those two wrenches?'

Rick dropped the tools back onto the bench. 'I thought maybe this could be solved on the spot.'

Silvia moved between him and the tanks. 'I thought you understood. They've always been a part of my life. When I brought you with me the first time, you seemed to see what—'

'I don't want to lose you,' Rick said harshly, 'to anybody or anything—in this world or any other. I'*m not going to give you up*.'

'It's not giving me up!' Her eyes narrowed. 'You came down here to destroy and break everything. The moment I'm not looking you'll smash all this, won't you?'

'That's right.'

Fear replaced anger on the girl's face. 'Do you want me to be chained here? I have to go on—I'm through with this part of the journey. I've stayed here long enough.'

'Can't you wait?' Rick demanded furiously. He couldn't keep the ragged edge of despair out of his voice. 'Doesn't it come soon enough anyhow?'

Silvia shrugged and turned away, her arms folded, her red lips tight together. 'You want to be a worm always. A fuzzy, little creeping caterpillar.'

'I want *you*.'

'You can't *have* me!' She whirled angrily. 'I don't have any time to waste with this.'

'You have higher things in mind,' Rick said savagely.

'Of course.' She softened a little. 'I'm sorry, Rick. Remember Icarus? You want to fly, too. I know it.'

'In my time.'

'Why not now? Why wait? You're afraid.' She slid lithely away from him, cunning twisting her red lips. 'Rick, I want to show you something. Promise me first—you won't tell anybody.'

'What is it?'

'Promise?' She put her hand to his mouth. 'I have to be careful. It cost a lot of money. Nobody knows about it. It's what they do in China—everything goes towards it.'

'I'm curious,' Rick said. Uneasiness flicked at him. 'Show it to me.'

Trembling with excitement, Silvia disappeared behind the huge lumbering refrigerator, back into the darkness behind the web of frost-hard freezing coils. He could hear her tugging and pulling at something. Scraping sounds, sounds of something large being dragged out.

'See?' Silvia gasped. 'Give me a hand, Rick. It's heavy. Hardwood and brass—and metal lined. It's hand-stained and polished. And the carving—see the carving! Isn't it beautiful?'

'What is it?' Rick demanded huskily.

'It's my cocoon,' Silvia said simply. She settled down in a contented heap on the floor, and rested her head happily against the polished oak coffin.

Rick grabbed her by the arm and dragged her to her feet. 'You can't sit with that coffin, down here in the basement with—' He broke off. 'What's the matter?'

Silvia's face was twisting with pain. She backed away from him and put her finger quickly to her mouth. 'I cut myself—when you pulled me up—on a nail or something.' A thin trickle of blood oozed down her fingers. She groped in her pocket for a handkerchief.

'Let me see it.' He moved towards her, but she avoided him. 'Is it bad?' he demanded.

'Stay away from me,' Silvia whispered.

'What's wrong? Let me see it!'

'Rick,' Silvia said in a low intense voice, 'get some water and adhesive tape. As quickly as possible!' She was trying to keep down her rising terror. 'I have to stop the bleeding.'

'Upstairs?' He moved awkwardly away. 'It doesn't look too bad. Why don't you . . .'

'Hurry.' The girl's voice was suddenly bleak with fear. 'Rick, *hurry*!'

Confused, he ran a few steps.

Silvia's terror poured after him. 'No, it's too late,' she called thinly. 'Don't come back—keep away from me. It's my own fault. I trained them to come. *Keep away*! I'm sorry, Rick. *Oh*—' Her voice was lost to him, as the wall of the basement burst and shattered. A cloud of luminous white forced its way through and blazed out into the basement.

It was Silvia they were after. She ran a few hesitant steps towards Rick, halted uncertainly, then the white mass of bodies and wings settled around her. She shrieked once. Then a violent explosion blasted the basement into a shimmering dance of furnace heat.

He was thrown to the floor. The cement was hot and dry–the whole basement crackled with heat. Windows shattered as pulsing white shapes pushed out again. Smoke and flames licked up the walls. The ceiling sagged and rained plaster down.

Rick struggled to his feet. The furious activity was dying away. The basement was a littered chaos. All surfaces were scorched black, seared and crusted with smoking ash. Splintered wood, torn cloth and broken concrete were strewn everywhere. The furnace and washing machine were in ruins. The elaborate pumping and refrigeration system–now were a glittering mass of slag. One whole wall had been twisted aside. Plaster was rubbled over everything.

Silvia was a twisted heap, arms and legs doubled grotesquely. Shriveled, carbonized remains of fire-scorched ash, settling in a vague mound. What had been left were charred fragments, a brittle burned-out husk.

It was a dark night, cold and intense. A few stars glittered like ice from above his head. A faint, dank wind stirred through the dripping calla lilies and whipped gravel up in a frigid mist along the path between the black roses.

He crouched for a long time, listening and watching. Behind the cedars, the big house loomed against the sky. At the bottom of the slope a few cars slithered along the highway. Otherwise, there was no sound. Ahead of him jutted the squat outline of the porcelain trough and the pipe that had carried blood from the refrigerator in the basement. The trough was empty and dry, except for a few leaves that had fallen in it.

Rick took a deep breath of thin night air and held it. Then he got stiffly to his feet. He scanned the sky, but saw no movement. They were there, though, watching and waiting–dim shadows, echoing into the legendary past, a line of god-figures.

He picked up the heavy gallon drums, dragged them to the

trough and poured blood from a New Jersey abattoir, cheap-grade steer refuse, thick and clotted. It splashed against his clothes and he backed away nervously. But nothing stirred in the air above. The garden was silent, drenched with night fog and darkness.

He stood beside the trough, waiting and wondering if they were coming. They had come for Silvia, not merely for the blood. Without her there was no attraction but the raw food. He carried the empty metal cans over to the bushes and kicked them down the slope. He searched his pockets carefully, to make sure there was no metal in them.

Over the years, Silvia had nourished their habit of coming. Now she was on the other side. Did that mean they wouldn't come? Somewhere in the damp bushes something rustled. An animal or a bird?

In the trough the blood glistened, heavy and dull, like old lead. It was their time to come, but nothing stirred the great trees above. He picked out the rows of nodding black roses, the gravel path down which he and Silvia had run—violently he shut out the recent memory of her flashing eyes and deep red lips. The highway beyond the slope—the empty, deserted garden—the silent house in which her family huddled and waited. After a time, there was a dull, swishing sound. He tensed, but it was only a diesel truck lumbering along the highway, headlights blazing.

He stood grimly, his feet apart, his heels dug into the soft black ground. He wasn't leaving. He was staying there until they came. He wanted her back—at any cost.

Overhead, foggy webs of moisture drifted across the moon. The sky was a vast barren plain, without life or warmth. The deathly cold of deep space, away from suns and living things. He gazed up until his neck ached. Cold stars, sliding in and out of the matted layer of fog. Was there anything else? Didn't they want to come, or weren't they interested in him? It had been Silvia who had interested them—now they had her.

Behind him there was a movement without sound. He sensed it and started to turn, but suddenly, on all sides, the trees and undergrowth shifted. Like cardboard props they wavered and ran together, blending dully in the night shadows. Something moved through them, rapidly, silently, then was gone.

They had come. He could feel them. They had shut off their power and flame. Cold, indifferent statues, rising among the trees, dwarfing the cedars—remote from him and his world, attracted by curiosity and mild habit.

'Silvia,' he said clearly. 'Which are you?'

There was no response. Perhaps she wasn't among them. He felt foolish. A vague flicker of white drifted past the trough, hovered momentarily and then went on without stopping. The air above the trough vibrated, then died into immobility, as another giant inspected briefly and withdrew.

Panic breathed through him. They were leaving again, receding back into their own world. The trough had been rejected; they weren't interested.

'Wait,' he muttered thickly.

Some of the white shadows lingered. He approached them slowly, wary of their flickering immensity. If one of them touched him, he would sizzle briefly and puff into a dark heap of ash. A few feet away he halted.

'You know what I want,' he said. 'I want her back. She shouldn't have been taken yet.'

Silence.

'You were too greedy,' he said. 'You did the wrong thing. She was going to come over to you, eventually. She had it all worked out.'

The dark fog rustled. Among the trees the flickering shapes stirred and pulsed, responsive to his voice. 'True,' came a detached impersonal sound. The sound drifted around him, from tree to tree, without location or direction. It was swept off by the night wind to die into dim echoes.

Relief settled over him. They had paused—they were aware of him—listening to what he had to say.

'You think it's right?' he demanded. 'She had a long life here. We were to marry, have children.'

There was no answer, but he was conscious of a growing tension. He listened intently, but he couldn't make out anything. Presently he realized a struggle was taking place, a conflict among them. The tension grew—more shapes flickered—the clouds, the icy stars, were obscured by the vast presence swelling around him.

'Rick!' A voice spoke close by. Wavering, drifting back into the dim regions of the trees and dripping plants. He could hardly hear it—the words were gone as soon as they were spoken. 'Rick—help me get back.'

'Where are you?' He couldn't locate her. 'What can I do?'

'I don't know.' Her voice was wild with bewilderment and pain. 'I don't understand. Something went wrong. They must have thought I—wanted to come right away. I *didn't!*'

'I know,' Rick said. 'It was an accident.'

'They were waiting. The cocoon, the trough—but it was too soon.' Her terror came across to him, from the vague distances of another universe. 'Rick, I've changed my mind. I want to come back.'

'It's not as simple as that.'

'I know. Rick, time is different on this side. I've been gone so long—your world seems to creep along. It's been years, hasn't it?'

'One week,' Rick said.

'It was their fault. You don't blame me, do you? They know they did the wrong thing. Those who did it have been punished, but that doesn't help me.' Misery and panic distorted her voice so he could hardly understand her. 'How can I come back?'

'Don't they know?'

'They say it can't be done.' Her voice trembled. 'They say they destroyed the clay part—it was incinerated. There's nothing for me to go back to.'

Rick took a deep breath. 'Make them find some other way. It's up to them. Don't they have the power? They took you over too soon—they must send you back. It's *their* responsibility.'

The white shapes shifted uneasily. The conflict rose sharply; they couldn't agree. Rick warily moved back a few paces.

'They say it's dangerous,' Silvia's voice came from no particular spot. 'They say it was attempted once.' She tried to control her voice. 'The nexus between this world and yours is unstable. There are vast amounts of free-floating energy. The power we—on this side—have isn't really our own. It's a universal energy, tapped and controlled.'

'Why can't they . . .'

'This is a higher continuum. There's a natural process of energy from lower to higher regions. But the reverse process is risky. The blood—it's a sort of guide to follow—a bright marker.'

'Like moths around a light bulb,' Rick said bitterly.

'If they send me back and something goes wrong—' She broke off and then continued, 'If they make a mistake, I might be lost between the two regions. I might be absorbed by the free energy. It seems to be partly alive. It's not understood. Remember Prometheus and the fire . . .'

'I see,' Rick said, as calmly as he could.

'Darling, if they try to send me back, I'll have to find some shape to enter. You see, I don't exactly have a shape any more. There's no real material form on this side. What you see, the wings and the whiteness, are not really there. If I succeeded in making the trip back to your side . . .'

'You'd have to mold something,' Rick said.

'I'd have to take something there—something of clay. I'd have to enter it and reshape it. As He did a long time ago, when the original form was put on your world.'

'If they did it once, they can do it again.'

'The One who did that is gone. He passed on upward.' There was unhappy irony in her voice. 'There are regions beyond this. The ladder doesn't stop here. Nobody knows where it ends, it just seems to keep on going up and up. World after world.'

'Who decides about you?' Rick demanded.

'It's up to me,' Silvia said faintly. 'They say, if I want to take the chance, they'll try it.'

'What do you think you'll do?' he asked.

'I'm afraid. What if something goes wrong? You haven't seen it, the region between. The possibilities there are incredible—they terrify me. He was the only one with enough courage. Everyone else has been afraid.'

'It was their fault. They have to take responsibility.'

'They know that.' Silvia hesitated miserably. 'Rick, darling, please tell me what to do.'

'Come back!'

Silence. Then her voice, thin and pathetic. 'All right, Rick. If you think that's the right thing.'

'It is,' he said firmly. He forced his mind not to think, not to picture or imagine anything. *He had to have her back.* 'Tell them to get started now. Tell them—'

A deafening crack of heat burst in front of him. He was lifted up and tossed into a flaming sea of pure energy. They were leaving and the scalding lake of sheer power bellowed and thundered around him. For a split second he thought he glimpsed Silvia, her hands reaching imploringly towards him.

Then the fire cooled and he lay blinded in dripping, night-moistened darkness. Alone in the silence.

Walter Everett was helping him up. 'You damn fool!' he was saying, again and again. 'You shouldn't have brought them back. They've got enough from us.'

Then he was in the big, warm living room. Mrs Everett stood silently in front of him, her face hard and expressionless. The two daughters hovered anxiously around him, fluttering and curious, eyes wide with morbid fascination.

'I'll be all right,' Rick muttered. His clothing was charred and blackened. He rubbed black ash from his face. Bits of dried grass stuck to his hair—they had seared a circle around him as they'd ascended. He lay back against the couch and closed his eyes. When he opened them, Betty Lou Everett was forcing a glass of water into his hands.

'Thanks,' he muttered.

'You should never have gone out there,' Walter Everett repeated.

'Why? Why'd you do it? You know what happened to her. You want the same thing to happen to you?'

'I want her back,' Rick said quietly.

'Are you mad? You can't get her back. She's gone.' His lips twitched convulsively. 'You saw her.'

Betty Lou was gazing at Rick intently. 'What happened out there?' she demanded. 'You saw her.'

Rick got heavily to his feet and left the living room. In the kitchen he emptied the water in the sink and poured himself a drink. While he was leaning wearily against the sink, Betty Lou appeared in the doorway.

'What do you want?' Rick demanded.

The girl's face was flushed an unhealthy red. 'I know something happened out there. You were feeding them, weren't you?' She advanced towards him. 'You're trying to get her back?'

'That's right,' Rick said.

Betty Lou giggled nervously. 'But you can't. She's dead—her body's been cremated—I saw it.' Her face worked excitedly. 'Daddy always said that something bad would happen to her, and it did.' She leaned close to Rick. 'She was a witch! She got what she deserved!'

'She's coming back,' Rick said.

'No!' Panic stirred the girl's drab features. 'She can't come back. She's dead—like she always said—worm into butterfly—she's a butterfly!'

'Go inside,' Rick said.

'You can't order me around,' Betty Lou answered. Her voice rose hysterically. 'This is my house. We don't want you around here any more. Daddy's going to tell you. He doesn't want you and I don't want you and my mother and sister . . .'

The change came without warning. Like a film gone dead, Betty Lou froze, her mouth half open, one arm raised, her words dead on her tongue. She was suspended, an instantly lifeless thing raised off the floor, as if caught between two slides of glass. A vacant insect, without speech or sound, inert and hollow. Not dead, but abruptly thinned back to primordial inanimacy.

Into the captured shell filtered new potency and being. It settled over her, a rainbow of life that poured into place eagerly—like hot fluid—into every part of her. The girl stumbled and moaned; her body jerked violently and pitched against the wall. A china teacup tumbled from an overhead shelf and smashed on the floor. The girl retreated numbly, one hand to her mouth, her eyes wide with pain and shock.

'Oh!' she gasped. 'I cut myself.' She shook her head and gazed up mutely at him, appealing to him. 'On a nail or something.'

'*Silvia!*' He caught hold of her and dragged her to her feet, away from the wall. It was *her* arm he gripped, warm and full and mature. Stunned gray eyes, brown hair, quivering breasts—she was now as she had been those last moments in the basement.

'Let's see it,' he said. He tore her hand from her mouth and shakily examined her finger. There was no cut, only a thin white line rapidly dimming. 'It's all right, honey. You're all right. There's nothing wrong with you!'

'Rick, I was over *there*.' Her voice was husky and faint. 'They came and dragged me across with them.' She shuddered violently. 'Rick, am I actually *back*?'

He crushed her tight. 'Completely back.'

'It was so long. I was over there a century. Endless ages. I thought—' Suddenly she pulled away. 'Rick . . .'

'What is it?'

Silvia's face was wild with fear. 'There's something wrong.'

'There's nothing wrong. You've come back home and that's all that matters.'

Silvia retreated from him. 'But they took a living form, didn't they? Not discarded clay. They don't have the power, Rick. They altered His work instead.' Her voice rose in panic. 'A mistake—they should have known better than to alter the balance. It's unstable and none of them can control the . . .'

Rick blocked the doorway. 'Stop talking like that!' he said fiercely. 'It's worth it—*anything's* worth it. If they set things out of balance, it's their own fault.'

'We can't turn it back!' Her voice rose shrilly, thin and hard, like drawn wire. 'We've set it in motion, started the waves lapping out. The balance He set up is *altered*.'

'Come on, darling,' Rick said. 'Let's go and sit in the living room with your family. You'll feel better. You'll have to try to recover from this.'

They approached the three seated figures, two on the couch, one in the straight chair by the fireplace. The figures sat motionless, their faces blank, their bodies limp and waxen, dulled forms that did not respond as the couple entered the room.

Rick halted, uncomprehending. Walter Everett was slumped forward, newspaper in one hand, slippers on his feet; his pipe was still smoking in the deep ashtray on the arm of his chair. Mrs Everett sat with a lapful of sewing, her face grim and stern, but strangely vague. An unformed face, as if the material were melting and running together. Jean sat huddled in a shapeless heap, a ball of clay wadded up, more formless each moment.

Abruptly Jean collapsed. Her arms fell loose beside her. Her head sagged. Her body, her arms and legs filled out. Her features altered rapidly. Her clothing changed. Colors flowed in her hair, her eyes, her skin. The waxen pallor was gone.

Pressing her fingers to her lips she gazed up at Rick mutely. She blinked and her eyes focused. 'Oh,' she gasped. Her lips moved awkwardly; the voice was faint and uneven, like a poor soundtrack. She struggled up jerkily, with uncoordinated movements that propelled her stiffly to her feet and towards him—one awkward step at a time—like a wire dummy.

'Rick, I cut myself,' she said. 'On a nail or something.'

What had been Mrs Everett stirred. Shapeless and vague, it made dull sounds and flopped grotesquely. Gradually it hardened and shaped itself. 'My finger,' its voice gasped feebly. Like mirror echoes dimming off into darkness, the third figure in the easy chair took up the words. Soon, they were all of them repeating the phrase, four fingers, their lips moving in unison.

'My finger. I cut myself, Rick.'

Parrot reflections, receding mimicries of words and movement. And the settling shapes were familiar in every detail. Again and again, repeated around him, twice on the couch, in the easy chair, close beside him—so close he could hear her breath and see her trembling lips.

'What is it?' the Silvia beside him asked.

On the couch one Silvia resumed its sewing—she was sewing methodically, absorbed in her work. In the deep chair another took up its newspaper, its pipe and continued reading. One huddled, nervous and afraid. The one beside him followed as he retreated to the door. She was panting with uncertainty, her gray eyes wide, her nostrils flaring.

'Rick . . .'

He pulled the door open and made his way out onto the dark porch. Machine-like, he felt his way down the steps, through the pools of night collected everywhere, toward the driveway. In the yellow square of light behind him, Silvia was outlined, peering unhappily after him. And behind her, the other figures, identical, pure repetitions, nodding over their tasks.

He found his coupé and pulled out onto the road.

Gloomy trees and houses flashed past. He wondered how far it would go. Lapping waves spreading out—a widening circle as the imbalance spread.

He turned onto the main highway; there were soon more cars around him. He tried to see into them, but they moved too swiftly. The car ahead was a red Plymouth. A heavy-set man in a blue business suit was driving, laughing merrily with the woman beside him. He pulled his own coupé up close behind the Plymouth and followed it. The man flashed gold teeth, grinned, waved his plump hands. The girl was dark-haired, pretty. She smiled at the man, adjusted her white gloves, smoothed down her hair, then rolled up the window on her side.

He lost the Plymouth. A heavy diesel truck cut in between them. Desperately he swerved around the truck and nosed in beyond the swift-moving red sedan. Presently it passed him and, for a moment, the two occupants were clearly framed. The girl resembled Silvia. The same delicate line of her small chin—the same deep lips, parting slightly when she smiled—the same slender arms and hands. It was Silvia. The Plymouth turned off and there was no other car ahead of him.

He drove for hours through the heavy night darkness. The gas gauge dropped lower and lower. Ahead of him dismal rolling countryside spread out, blank fields between towns and unwinking stars suspended in the bleak sky. Once, a cluster of red and yellow lights gleamed. An intersection—filling stations and a big neon sign. He drove on past it.

At a single-pump stand, he pulled the car off the highway, onto the oil-soaked gravel. He climbed out, his shoes crunching the stone underfoot, as he grabbed the gas hose and unscrewed the cap of his car's tank. He had the tank almost full when the door of the drab station building opened and a slim woman in white overalls and navy shirt, with a little cap lost in her brown curls, stepped out.

'Good evening, Rick,' she said quietly.

He put back the gas hose. Then he was driving out onto the highway. Had he screwed the cap back on again? He didn't remember. He gained speed. He had gone over a hundred miles. He was nearing the state line.

At a little roadside cafe, warm, yellow light glowed in the chill gloom of early morning. He slowed the car down and parked at the edge of the highway in the deserted parking lot. Bleary-eyed he pushed the door open and entered.

Hot, thick smells of cooking ham and black coffee surrounded him, the comfortable sight of people eating. A jukebox blared in the corner. He threw himself onto a stool and hunched over, his head in his hands. A thin farmer next to him glanced at him curiously and then returned to his newspaper. Two hard-faced women across from him gazed at him momentarily. A handsome youth in denim jacket and jeans was eating red beans and rice, washing it down with steaming coffee from a heavy mug.

'What'll it be?' the pert blonde waitress asked, a pencil behind her ear, her hair tied back in a tight bun. 'Looks like you've got some hangover, mister.'

He ordered coffee and vegetable soup. Soon he was eating, his hands working automatically. He found himself devouring a ham and cheese sandwich; had he ordered it? The jukebox blared and people came and went. There was a little town sprawled beside the road, set back in some gradual hills. Gray sunlight, cold and sterile, filtered down as morning came. He ate hot apple pie and sat wiping dully at his mouth with a napkin.

The cafe was silent. Outside nothing stirred. An uneasy calm hung over everything. The jukebox had ceased. None of the people at the counter stirred or spoke. An occasional truck roared past, damp and lumbering, windows rolled up tight.

When he looked up, Silvia was standing in front of him. Her arms were folded and she gazed vacantly past him. A bright yellow pencil was behind her ear. Her brown hair was tied back in a hard bun. At the corner others were sitting, other Silvias, dishes in front of them, half dozing or eating, some of them reading. Each the same as the next, except for their clothing.

He made his way back to his parked car. In half an hour he had crossed the state line. Cold, bright sunlight sparkled off dew-moist roofs and pavements as he sped through tiny unfamiliar towns.

Along the shiny morning streets he saw them moving—early risers, on their way to work. In twos and threes they walked, their heels echoing in sharp silence. At bus stops he saw groups of them collected together. In the houses, rising from their beds, eating breakfast, bathing, dressing, were more of them—hundreds of them, legions without number. A town of them preparing for the day, resuming their regular tasks, as the circle widened and spread.

He left the town behind. The car slowed under him as his foot slid heavily from the gas pedal. Two of them walked across a level field together. They carried books—children on their way to school. Repetition, unvarying and identical. A dog circled excitedly after them, unconcerned, his joy untainted.

He drove on. Ahead a city loomed, its stern columns of office buildings sharply outlined against the sky. The streets swarmed with noise and activity as he passed through the main business section. Somewhere, near the center of the city, he overtook the expanding periphery of the circle and emerged beyond. Diversity took the place of the endless figures of Silvia. Gray eyes and brown hair gave way to countless varieties of men and women, children and adults, of all ages and appearances. He increased his speed and raced out on the far side, onto the wide four-lane highway.

He finally slowed down. He was exhausted. He had driven for hours; his body was shaking with fatigue.

Ahead of him a carrot-haired youth was cheerfully thumbing a ride, a thin bean-pole in brown slacks and light camel's-hair sweater. Rick pulled to a halt and opened the front door. 'Hop in,' he said.

'Thanks, buddy.' The youth hurried to the car and climbed in as Rick gathered speed. He slammed the door and settled gratefully back against the seat. 'It was getting hot, standing there.'

'How far are you going?' Rick demanded.

'All the way to Chicago.' The youth grinned shyly. 'Of course, I don't expect you to drive me that far. Anything at all is appreciated.' He eyed Rick curiously. 'Which way you going?'

'Anywhere,' Rick said. 'I'll drive you to Chicago.'

'It's two hundred miles!'

'Fine,' Rick said. He steered over into the left lane and gained speed. 'If you want to go to New York, I'll drive you there.'

'You feel all right?' The youth moved away uneasily. 'I sure appreciate a lift, but . . .' He hesitated. 'I mean, I don't want to take you out of your way.'

Rick concentrated on the road ahead, his hands gripping hard around the rim of the wheel. 'I'm going fast. I'm not slowing down or stopping.'

'You better be careful,' the youth warned, in a troubled voice. 'I don't want to get in an accident.'

'I'll do the worrying.'

'But it's dangerous. What if something happens? It's too risky.'

'You're wrong,' Rick muttered grimly, eyes on the road. 'It's worth the risk.'

'But if something goes wrong–' The voice broke off uncertainly and then continued, 'I might be lost. It would be so easy. It's all so unstable.' The voice trembled with worry and fear. 'Rick, please . . .'

Rick whirled. 'How do you know my name?'

The youth was crouched in a heap against the door. His face had a soft, molten look, as if it were losing its shape and sliding together in an unformed mass. 'I want to come back,' he was saying, from within himself, 'but I'm afraid. You haven't seen it–the region between. It's nothing but energy, Rick. He tapped it a long time ago, but nobody else knows how.'

The voice lightened, became clear and treble. The hair faded to a rich brown. Gray, frightened eyes flickered up at Rick. Hands frozen, he hunched over the wheel and forced himself not to move. Gradually he decreased speed and brought the car over into the right-hand lane.

'Are we stopping?' the shape beside him asked. It was Silvia's voice now. Like a new insect, drying in the sun, the shape hardened and locked into firm reality. Silvia struggled up on the seat and peered out. 'Where are we? We're between towns.'

He jammed on the brakes, reached past her and threw open the door. 'Get out!'

Silvia gazed at him uncomprehendingly. 'What do you mean?' she faltered. 'Rick, what is it? What's wrong?'

'*Get out!*'

'Rick, I don't understand.' She slid over a little. Her toes touched the pavement. 'Is there something wrong with the car? I thought everything was all right.'

He gently shoved her out and slammed the door. The car leaped ahead, out into the stream of mid-morning traffic. Behind him the small, dazed figure was pulling itself up, bewildered and injured. He forced his eyes from the rearview mirror and crushed down the gas pedal with all his weight.

The radio buzzed and clicked in vague static when he snapped it briefly on. He turned the dial and, after a time, a big network station came in. A faint, puzzled voice, a woman's voice. For a time he couldn't make out the words. Then he recognized it and, with a pang of panic, switched the thing off.

Her voice. Murmuring plaintively. Where was the station? Chicago. The circle had already spread that far.

He slowed down. There was no point hurrying. It had already passed him by and gone on. Kansas farms—sagging stores in little old Mississippi towns—along the bleak streets of New England manufacturing cities swarms of brown-haired gray-eyed women would be hurrying.

It would cross the ocean. Soon it would take in the whole world. Africa would be strange—kraals of white-skinned young women, all exactly alike, going about the primitive chores of hunting and fruit-gathering, mashing grain, skinning animals. Building fires and weaving cloth and carefully shaping razor-sharp knives.

In China . . . he grinned inanely. She'd look strange there, too. In the austere high-collar suit, the almost monastic robe of the young communist cadres. Parade marching up the main streets of Peiping. Row after row of slim-legged full-breasted girls, with heavy Russian-made rifles. Carrying spades, picks, shovels. Columns of cloth-booted soldiers. Fast-moving workers with their precious tools. Reviewed by an identical figure on the elaborate stand overlooking the street, one slender arm raised, her gentle, pretty face expressionless and wooden.

He turned off the highway onto a side road. A moment later he was on his way back, driving slowly, listlessly, the way he had come.

At an intersection a traffic cop waded out through traffic to his car. He sat rigid, hands on the wheel, waiting numbly.

'Rick,' she whispered pleadingly as she reached the window. 'Isn't everything all right?'

'Sure,' he answered dully.

She reached in through the open window and touched him imploringly on the arm. Familiar fingers, red nails, the hand he knew so well. 'I want to be with you so badly. Aren't we together again? Aren't I back?'

'Sure.'

She shook her head miserably. 'I don't understand,' she repeated. 'I thought it was all right again.'

Savagely he put the car into motion and hurtled ahead. The intersection was left behind.

It was afternoon. He was exhausted, riddled with fatigue. He guided the car towards his own town automatically. Along the streets she hurried everywhere, on all sides. She was omnipresent. He came to his apartment building and parked.

The janitor greeted him in the empty hall. Rick identified him by the greasy rag clutched in one hand, the big push-broom, the bucket of wood shavings. 'Please,' she implored, 'tell me what it is, Rick. Please tell me.'

He pushed past her, but she caught at him desperately. 'Rick, I'm back. Don't you understand? They took me too soon and then they sent me back again. It was a mistake. I won't ever call them again—that's all in the past.' She followed after him, down the hall to the stairs. 'I'm never going to call them again.'

He climbed the stairs. Silvia hesitated, then settled down on the bottom step in a wretched, unhappy heap, a tiny figure in thick workman's clothing and huge cleated boots.

He unlocked his apartment door and entered.

The late afternoon sky was a deep blue beyond the windows. The roofs of nearby apartment buildings sparkled white in the sun.

His body ached. He wandered clumsily into the bathroom—it seemed alien and unfamiliar, a difficult place to find. He filled the bowl with hot water, rolled up his sleeves and washed his face and hands in the swirling hot stream. Briefly, he glanced up.

It was a terrified reflection that showed out of the mirror above the bowl, a face, tear-stained and frantic. The face was difficult to

UPON THE DULL EARTH

catch—it seemed to waver and slide. Gray eyes, bright with terror. Trembling red mouth, pulse-fluttering throat, soft brown hair. The face gazed out pathetically—and then the girl at the bowl bent to dry herself.

She turned and moved wearily out of the bathroom into the living room.

Confused, she hesitated, then threw herself onto a chair and closed her eyes, sick with misery and fatigue.

'Rick,' she murmured pleadingly. 'Try to help me. I'm back, aren't I?' She shook her head, bewildered. 'Please, Rick, I thought everything was all right.'

FOSTER, YOU'RE DEAD

School was agony, as always. Only today it was worse. Mike Foster finished weaving his two watertight baskets and sat rigid, while all around him the other children worked. Outside the concrete-and-steel building the late-afternoon sun shone cool. The hills sparkled green and brown in the crisp autumn air. In the overhead sky a few NATS circled lazily above the town.

The vast, ominous shape of Mrs Cummings, the teacher, silently approached his desk. 'Foster, are you finished?'

'Yes, ma'am,' he answered eagerly. He pushed the baskets up. 'Can I leave now?'

Mrs Cummings examined his baskets critically. 'What about your trap-making?' she demanded.

He fumbled in his desk and brought out his intricate small-animal trap. 'All finished, Mrs Cummings. And my knife, it's done, too.' He showed her the razor-edged blade of his knife, glittering metal he had shaped from a discarded gasoline drum. She picked up the knife and ran her expert finger doubtfully along the blade.

'Not strong enough,' she stated. 'You've oversharpened it. It'll lose its edge the first time you use it. Go down to the main weapons-lab and examine the knives they've got there. Then hone it back some and get a thicker blade.'

'Mrs Cummings,' Mike Foster pleaded, 'could I fix it *tomorrow*? Could I leave right now, please?'

Everybody in the classroom was watching with interest. Mike Foster flushed; he hated to be singled out and made conspicuous, but he *had* to get away. He couldn't stay in school one minute more.

Inexorable, Mrs Cummings rumbled, 'Tomorrow is digging day. You won't have time to work on your knife.'

'I will,' he assured her quickly. 'After the digging.'

'No, you're not too good at digging.' The old woman was measuring the boy's spindly arms and legs. 'I think you better get your knife finished today. And spend all day tomorrow down at the field.'

'What's the use of digging?' Mike Foster demanded, in despair.

'Everybody has to know how to dig,' Mrs Cummings answered patiently. Children were snickering on all sides; she shushed them with a hostile glare. 'You all know the importance of digging. When the war begins the whole surface will be littered with debris and rubble. If we hope to survive we'll have to dig down, won't we? Have any of you ever watched a gopher digging around the roots of plants? The gopher knows he'll find something valuable down there under the surface of the ground. We're all going to be little brown gophers. We'll all have to learn to dig down in the rubble and find the good things, because that's where they'll be.'

Mike Foster sat miserably plucking his knife, as Mrs Cummings moved away from his desk and up the aisle. A few children grinned contemptuously at him, but nothing penetrated his haze of wretchedness. Digging wouldn't do him any good. When the bombs came he'd be killed instantly. All the vaccination shots up and down his arms, on his thighs and buttocks, would be of no use. He had wasted his allowance money: Mike Foster wouldn't be alive to catch any of the bacterial plagues. Not unless—

He sprang up and followed Mrs Cummings to her desk. In an agony of desperation he blurted, 'Please, I have to leave. I have to do something.'

Mrs Cummings' tired lips twisted angrily. But the boy's fearful eyes stopped her. 'What's wrong?' she demanded. 'Don't you feel well?'

The boy stood frozen, unable to answer her. Pleased by the tableau, the class murmured and giggled until Mrs Cummings rapped angrily on her desk with a writer. 'Be quiet,' she snapped. Her voice softened a shade. 'Michael, if you're not functioning properly, go downstairs to the psyche clinic. There's no point trying to work when your reactions are conflicted. Miss Groves will be glad to optimum you.'

'No,' Foster said.

'Then what is it?'

The class stirred. Voices answered for Foster; his tongue was stuck with misery and humiliation. 'His father's an anti-P,' the voices explained. 'They don't have a shelter and he isn't registered in Civic Defense. His father hasn't even contributed to the NATS. They haven't done anything.'

Mrs Cummings gazed up in amazement at the mute boy. 'You don't have a shelter?'

He shook his head.

A strange feeling filled the woman. 'But–' She had started to say, *But you'll die up here.* She changed it to 'But where'll you go?'

'Nowhere,' the mild voices answered for him. 'Everybody else'll be down in their shelters and he'll be up here. He even doesn't have a permit for the school shelter.'

Mrs Cummings was shocked. In her dull, scholastic way she had assumed every child in the school had a permit to the elaborate subsurface chambers under the building. But of course not. Only children whose parents were part of CD, who contributed to arming the community. And if Foster's father was an anti-P . . .

'He's afraid to sit here,' the voices chimed in calmly. 'He's afraid it'll come while he's sitting here, and everybody else will be safe down in the shelter.'

He wandered slowly along, hands deep in his pockets, kicking at dark stones on the sidewalk. The sun was setting. Snub-nosed commute rockets were unloading tired people, glad to be home from the factory strip a hundred miles to the west. On the distant hills something flashed: a radar tower revolving silently in the evening gloom. The circling NATS had increased in number. The twilight hours were the most dangerous; visual observers couldn't spot high-speed missiles coming in close to the ground. Assuming the missiles came.

A mechanical news-machine shouted at him excitedly as he passed. War, death, amazing new weapons developed at home and abroad. He hunched his shoulders and continued on, past the little concrete shells that served as houses, each exactly alike, sturdy reinforced pillboxes. Ahead of him bright neon signs glowed in the settling gloom: the business district, alive with traffic and milling people.

Half a block from the bright cluster of neons he halted. To his right was a public shelter, a dark tunnel-like entrance with a mechanical turnstile glowing dully. Fifty cents admission. If he was here, on the street, and he had fifty cents, he'd be all right. He had pushed down into public shelters many times, during the practice raids. But other times, hideous, nightmare times that never left his mind, he hadn't had the fifty cents. He had stood mute and terrified, while people pushed excitedly past him; and the shrill shrieks of the sirens thundered everywhere.

He continued slowly, until he came to the brightest blotch of light, the great, gleaming showrooms of General Electronics, two blocks long, illuminated on all sides, a vast square of pure color and radiation. He halted and examined for the millionth time the fascinating shapes, the display that always drew him to a hypnotized stop whenever he passed.

In the center of the vast room was a single object. An elaborate pulsing blob of machinery and support struts, beams and walls and sealed locks. All spotlights were turned on it; huge signs announced its hundred and one advantages—as if there could be any doubt.

THE NEW 1972 BOMBPROOF RADIATION-SEALED
SUBSURFACE SHELTER IS HERE! CHECK THESE
STAR-STUDDED FEATURES:

* automatic descent-lift—jam-proof, self-powered, e-z locking
* triple-layer hull guaranteed to withstand $5g$ pressure without buckling

FOSTER, YOU'RE DEAD

* A-powered heating and refrigeration system—self-servicing air-purification network
* three decontamination stages for food and water
* four hygienic stages for pre-burn exposure
* complete antibiotic processing
* e-z payment plan

He gazed at the shelter a long time. It was mostly a big tank, with a neck at one end that was the descent tube, and an emergency escape-hatch at the other. It was completely self-contained: a miniature world that supplied its own light, heat, air, water, medicines, and almost inexhaustible food. When fully stocked there were visual and audio tapes, entertainment, beds, chairs, vidscreen, everything that made up the above-surface home. It was, actually, a home below the ground. Nothing was missing that might be needed or enjoyed. A family would be safe, even comfortable, during the most severe H-bomb and bacterial-spray attack.

It cost twenty thousand dollars.

While he was gazing silently at the massive display, one of the salesmen stepped out onto the dark sidewalk, on his way to the cafeteria. 'Hi, sonny,' he said automatically, as he passed Mike Foster. 'Not bad, is it?'

'Can I go inside?' Foster asked quickly. 'Can I go down in it?'

The salesman stopped, as he recognized the boy. 'You're that kid,' he said slowly, 'that damn kid who's always pestering us.'

'I'd like to go down in it. Just for a couple minutes. I won't bust anything—I promise. I won't even touch anything.'

The salesman was young and blond, a good-looking man in his early twenties. He hesitated, his reactions divided. The kid was a pest. But he had a family, and that meant a reasonable prospect. Business was bad; it was late September and the seasonal slump was still on. There was no profit in telling the boy to go peddle his newstapes; but on the other hand it was bad business encouraging small fry to crawl around the merchandise. They wasted time; they broke things; they pilfered small stuff when nobody was looking.

'No dice,' the salesman said. 'Look, send your old man down here. Has he seen what we've got?'

'Yes,' Mike Foster said tightly.

'What's holding him back?' The salesman waved expansively up at the great gleaming display. 'We'll give him a good trade-in on his old one, allowing for depreciation and obsolescence. What model has he got?'

'We don't have any,' Mike Foster said.

The salesman blinked. 'Come again?'

'My father says it's a waste of money. He says they're trying to scare people into buying things they don't need. He says—'

'Your father's an anti-P?'

'Yes,' Mike Foster answered unhappily.

The salesman let out his breath. 'Okay, kid. Sorry we can't do business. It's not your fault.' He lingered. 'What the hell's wrong with him? Does he put on the NATS?'

'No.'

The salesman swore under his breath. A coaster, sliding along, safe because the rest of the community was putting up thirty per cent of its income to keep a constant-defense system going. There were always a few of them, in every town. 'How's your mother feel?' the salesman demanded. 'She go along with him?'

'She says—' Mike Foster broke off. 'Couldn't I go down in it for a little while? I won't bust anything. Just *once*.'

'How'd we ever sell it if we let kids run through it? We're not marking it down as a demonstration model—we've got roped into that too often.' The salesman's curiosity was aroused. 'How's a guy get to be anti-P? He always feel this way, or did he get stung with something?'

'He says they sold people as many cars and washing machines and television sets as they could use. He says NATS and bomb shelters aren't good for anything, so people never get all they can use. He says factories can keep turning out guns and gas masks forever, and as long as people are afraid they'll keep paying for them because they think if they don't they might get killed, and maybe a man gets tired of paying for a new car every year and stops, but he's never going to stop buying shelters to protect his children.'

'You believe that?' the salesman asked.

'I wish we had that shelter,' Mike Foster answered. 'If we had a shelter like that I'd go down and sleep in it every night. It'd be there when we needed it.'

'Maybe there won't be a war,' the salesman said. He sensed the boy's misery and fear, and he grinned good-naturedly down at him. 'Don't worry all the time. You probably watch too many vid-tapes—get out and play, for a change.'

'Nobody's safe on the surface,' Mike Foster said. 'We have to be down below. And there's no place I can go.'

'Send your old man around,' the salesman muttered uneasily. 'Maybe we can talk him into it. We've got a lot of time-payment plans. Tell him to ask for Bill O'Neill. Okay?'

Mike Foster wandered away, down the black evening street. He knew he was supposed to be home, but his feet dragged and his body was heavy and dull. His fatigue made him remember what the athletics coach had said the day before, during exercises. They were practicing breath suspension, holding a lungful of air and running. He hadn't done well; the others were still red-faced and racing when he halted, expelled his air, and stood gasping frantically for breath.

'Foster,' the coach said angrily, 'you're dead. You know that? If this had been a gas attack—' He shook his head wearily. 'Go over there and practice by yourself. You've got to do better, if you expect to survive.'

But he didn't expect to survive.

When he stepped up onto the porch of his home, he found the living room lights already on. He could hear his father's voice, and more faintly his mother's from the kitchen. He closed the door after him and began unpeeling his coat.

'Is that you?' his father demanded. Bob Foster sat sprawled out in his chair, his lap full of tapes and report sheets from his retail furniture store. 'Where have you been? Dinner's been ready half an hour.' He had taken off his coat and rolled up his sleeves. His arms were pale and thin, but muscular. He was tired; his eyes were large and dark, his hair thinning. Restlessly, he moved the tapes around, from one stack to another.

'I'm sorry,' Mike Foster said.

His father examined his pocket watch; he was surely the only man who still carried a watch. 'Go wash your hands. What have you been doing?' He scrutinized his son. 'You look odd. Do you feel all right?'

'I was downtown,' Mike Foster said.

'What were you doing?'

'Looking at the shelters.'

Wordless, his father grabbed up a handful of reports and stuffed them into a folder. His thin lips set; hard lines wrinkled his forehead. He snorted furiously as tapes spilled everywhere; he bent stiffly to pick them up. Mike Foster made no move to help him. He crossed to the closet and gave his coat to the hanger. When he turned away his mother was directing the table of food into the dining room.

They ate without speaking, intent on their food and not looking at each other. Finally his father said, 'What'd you see? Same old dogs, I suppose.'

'There's the new '72 models,' Mike Foster answered.

'They're the same as the '71 models.' His father threw down his fork savagely; the table caught and absorbed it. 'A few new gadgets, some more chrome. That's all.' Suddenly he was facing his son defiantly. 'Right?'

Mike Foster toyed wretchedly with his creamed chicken. 'The new ones have a jam-proof descent-lift. You can't get stuck halfway down. All you have to do is get in it, and it does the rest.'

'There'll be one next year that'll pick you up and carry you down. This one'll be obsolete as soon as people buy it. That's what they want—they want you to keep buying. They keep putting out new ones as fast as they can. This isn't 1972, it's still 1971. What's that thing doing out already? Can't they wait?'

Mike Foster didn't answer. He had heard it all before, many times. There was never anything new, only chrome and gadgets; yet the old ones became obsolete, anyhow. His father's argument was loud, impassioned, almost frenzied, but it made no sense. 'Let's get an old one, then,' he blurted out. 'I don't care, any one'll do. Even a secondhand one.'

'No, you want the *new* one. Shiny and glittery to impress the neighbors. Lots of dials and knobs and machinery. How much do they want for it?'

'Twenty thousand dollars.'

His father let his breath out. 'Just like that.'

'They've easy time-payment plans.'

'Sure. You pay for it the rest of your life. Interest, carrying charges, and how long is it guaranteed for?'

'Three months.'

'What happens when it breaks down? It'll stop purifying and decontaminating. It'll fall apart as soon as the three months are over.'

Mike Foster shook his head. 'No. It's big and sturdy.'

His father flushed. He was a small man, slender and light, brittle-boned. He thought suddenly of his lifetime of lost battles, struggling up the hard way, carefully collecting and holding on to something, a job, money, his retail store, bookkeeper to manager, finally owner. 'They're scaring us to keep the wheels going,' he yelled desperately at his wife and son. 'They don't want another depression.'

'Bob,' his wife said, slowly and quietly, 'you have to stop this. I can't stand any more.'

Bob Foster blinked. 'What're you talking about?' he muttered. 'I'm tired. These goddamn taxes. It isn't possible for a little store to keep open, not with the big chains. There ought to be a law.' His voice trailed off. 'I guess I'm through eating.' He pushed away from the table and got to his feet. 'I'm going to lie down on the couch and take a nap.'

His wife's thin face blazed. 'You have to get one! I can't stand the way they talk about us. All the neighbors and the merchants, everybody who knows. I can't go anywhere or do anything without hearing about it. Ever since that day they put up the flag. *Anti-P*. The last in the whole town. Those things circling around up there, and everybody paying for them but us.'

'No,' Bob Foster said. 'I can't get one.'

'Why not?'

'Because,' he answered simply, 'I can't afford it.'

There was silence.

'You've put everything in that store,' Ruth said finally. 'And it's failing anyhow. You're just like a pack-rat, hoarding everything down at that ratty little hole-in-the-wall. Nobody wants wood furniture anymore. You're a relic—a curiosity.' She slammed at the table and it leaped wildly to gather the empty dishes, like a startled animal. It dashed furiously from the room and back into the kitchen, the dishes churning in its washtank as it raced.

Bob Foster sighed wearily. 'Let's not fight. I'll be in the living room. Let me take a nap for an hour or so. Maybe we can talk about it later.'

'Always later,' Ruth said bitterly.

Her husband disappeared into the living room, a small, hunched-over figure, hair scraggly and gray, shoulder blades like broken wings.

Mike got to his feet. 'I'll go study my homework,' he said. He followed after his father, a strange look on his face.

The living room was quiet; the vidset was off and the lamp was down low. Ruth was in the kitchen setting the controls on the stove for the next month's meals. Bob Foster lay stretched out on the couch, his shoes off, his head on a pillow. His face was gray with fatigue. Mike hesitated for a moment and then said, 'Can I ask you something?'

His father grunted and stirred, opened his eyes. 'What?'

Mike sat down facing him. 'Tell me again how you gave advice to the President.'

His father pulled himself up. 'I didn't give any advice to the President. I just talked to him.'

'Tell me about it.'

'I've told you a million times. Every once in a while, since you were a baby. You were with me.' His voice softened, as he remembered. 'You were just a toddler—we had to carry you.'

'What did he look like?'

'Well,' his father began, slipping into a routine he had worked out and petrified over the years, 'he looked about like he does in the vidscreen. Smaller, though.'

'Why was he here?' Mike demanded avidly, although he knew every detail. The President was his hero, the man he most admired in all the world. 'Why'd he come all the way out here to *our* town?'

'He was on a tour.' Bitterness crept into his father's voice. 'He happened to be passing through.'

'What kind of a tour?'

'Visiting towns all over the country.' The harshness increased. 'Seeing how we were getting along. Seeing if we had bought enough NATS and bomb shelters and plague shots and gas masks and radar networks to repel attack. The General Electronics Corporation was just beginning to put up its big showrooms and displays—everything bright and glittering and expensive. The first defense equipment available for home purchase.' His lips twisted. 'All on easy-payment plans. Ads, posters, searchlights, free gardenias and dishes for the ladies.'

Mike Foster's breath panted in his throat. 'That was the day we got our Preparedness Flag,' he said hungrily. 'That was the day he came to give us our flag. And they ran it up on the flagpole in the middle of the town, and everybody was there yelling and cheering.'

'You remember that?'

'I—think so. I remember people and sounds. And it was hot. It was June, wasn't it?'

'June 10, 1965. Quite an occasion. Not many towns had the big green flag, then. People were still buying cars and TV sets. They hadn't discovered those days were over. TV sets and cars are good for something–you can only manufacture and sell so many of them.'

'He gave *you* the flag, didn't he?'

'Well, he gave it to all us merchants. The Chamber of Commerce had it arranged. Competition between towns, see who can buy the most the soonest. Improve our town and at the same time stimulate business. Of course, the way they put it, the idea was if we had to *buy* our gas masks and bomb shelters we'd take better care of them. As if we ever damaged telephones and sidewalks. Or highways, because the whole state provided them. Or armies. Haven't there always been armies? Hasn't the government always organized its people for defense? I guess defense costs too much. I guess they save a lot of money, cut down the national debt by this.'

'Tell me what he said,' Mike Foster whispered.

His father fumbled for his pipe and lit it with trembling hands. 'He said, *"Here's your flag, boys. You've done a good job."'* Bob Foster choked, as acrid pipe fumes guzzled up. 'He was red-faced, sunburned, not embarrassed. Perspiring and grinning. He knew how to handle himself. He knew a lot of first names. Told a funny joke.'

The boy's eyes were wide with awe. 'He came all the way out here, and you talked to him.'

'Yeah,' his father said. 'I talked to him. They were all yelling and cheering. The flag was going up, the big green Preparedness Flag.'

'You said–'

'I said to him, *"Is that all you brought us? A strip of green cloth?"'* Bob Foster dragged tensely on his pipe. 'That was when I became an anti-P. Only I didn't know it at the time. All I knew was we were on our own, except for a strip of green cloth. We should have been a country, a whole nation, one hundred and seventy million people working together to defend ourselves. And instead, we're a lot of separate little towns, little walled forts. Sliding and slipping back to the Middle Ages. Raising our separate armies–'

'Will the President ever come back?' Mike asked.

'I doubt it. He was—just passing through.'

'If he comes back,' Mike whispered, tense and not daring to hope, 'can we go *see* him? Can we *look* at him?'

Bob Foster pulled himself up to a sitting position. His bony arms were bare and white; his lean face was drab with weariness. And resignation. 'How much was the damn thing you saw?' he demanded hoarsely. 'That bomb shelter?'

Mike's heart stopped beating. 'Twenty thousand dollars.'

'This is Thursday. I'll go down with you and your mother next Saturday.' Bob Foster knocked out his smoldering, half-lit pipe. 'I'll get it on the easy-payment plan. The fall buying season is coming up soon. I usually do good—people buy wood furniture for Christmas gifts.' He got up abruptly from the couch. 'Is it a deal?'

Mike couldn't answer; he could only nod.

'Fine,' his father said, with desperate cheerfulness. 'Now you won't have to go down and look at it in the window.'

The shelter was installed—for an additional two hundred dollars— by a fast-working team of laborers in brown coats with the words GENERAL ELECTRONICS stitched across their backs. The back yard was quickly restored, dirt and shrubs spaded in place, the surface smoothed over, and the bill respectfully slipped under the front door. The lumbering delivery truck, now empty, clattered off down the street and the neighborhood was again silent.

Mike Foster stood with his mother and a small group of admiring neighbors on the back porch of the house. 'Well,' Mrs Carlyle said finally, 'now you've got a shelter. The best there is.'

'That's right,' Ruth Foster agreed. She was conscious of the people around her; it had been some time since so many had shown up at once. Grim satisfaction filled her gaunt frame, almost resentment. 'It certainly makes a difference,' she said harshly.

'Yes,' Mr Douglas from down the street agreed. 'Now you have some place to go.' He had picked up the thick book of instructions the laborers had left. 'It says here you can stock it for a whole year. Live down there twelve months without coming up once.' He shook his head admiringly. 'Mine's an old '69 model. Good for only six months. I guess maybe—'

'It's still good enough for us,' his wife cut in, but there was a longing wistfulness in her voice. 'Can we go down and peek at it, Ruth? It's all ready, isn't it?'

Mike made a strangled noise and moved jerkily forward. His mother smiled understandingly. 'He has to go down there first. He gets first look at it—it's really for him, you know.'

Their arms folded against the chill September wind, the group of men and women stood waiting and watching, as the boy approached the neck of the shelter and halted a few steps in front of it.

He entered the shelter carefully, almost afraid to touch anything. The neck was big for him; it was built to admit a full grown man. As soon as his weight was on the descent-lift it dropped beneath him. With a breathless *whoosk* it plummeted down the pitch-black tube to the body of the shelter. The lift slammed hard against its shock absorbers and the boy stumbled from it. The lift shot back to the surface, simultaneously sealing off the subsurface shelter, an impassable steel-and-plastic cork in the narrow neck.

Lights had come on around him automatically. The shelter was bare and empty; no supplies had yet been carried down. It smelled of varnish and motor grease: below him the generators were throbbing dully. His presence activated the purifying and decontamination systems; on the blank concrete wall meters and dials moved into sudden activity.

He sat down on the floor, knees drawn up, face solemn, eyes wide. There was no sound but that of the generators; the world above was completely cut off. He was in a little self-contained cosmos; everything needed was here—or would be here, soon: food, water, air, things to do. Nothing else was wanted. He could reach out and touch—whatever he needed. He could stay here forever, through all time, without stirring. Complete and entire. Not lacking, not fearing, with only the sound of the generators purring below him, and the sheer, ascetic walls around and above him on all sides, faintly warm, completely friendly, like a living container.

Suddenly he shouted, a loud jubilant shout that echoed and bounced from wall to wall. He was deafened by the reverberation. He shut his eyes tight and clenched his fists. Joy filled him. He shouted again—and let the roar of sound lap over him, his own voice reinforced by the near walls, close and hard and incredibly powerful.

The kids in school knew even before he showed up, the next morning. They greeted him as he approached, all of them grinning and nudging each other. 'Is it true your folks got a new General Electronics Model S-72ft?' Earl Peters demanded.

'That's right,' Mike answered. His heart swelled with a peaceful confidence he had never known. 'Drop around,' he said, as casually as he could. 'I'll show it to you.'

He passed on, conscious of their envious faces.

'Well, Mike,' Mrs Cummings said, as he was leaving the classroom at the end of the day. 'How does it feel?'

He halted by her desk, shy and full of quiet pride. 'It feels good,' he admitted.

'Is your father contributing to the NATS?'

'Yes.'

'And you've got a permit for our school shelter?'

He happily showed her the small blue seal clamped around his wrist. 'He mailed a check to the city for everything. He said, "As long as I've gone this far I might as well go the rest of the way."'

'Now you have everything everybody else has.' The elderly woman smiled across at him. 'I'm glad of that. You're now a pro-P, except there's no such term. You're just—like everyone else.'

The next day the news-machines shrilled out the news. The first revelation of the new Soviet bore-pellets.

Bob Foster stood in the middle of the living room, the newstape in his hands, his thin face flushed with fury and despair. 'Goddamn it, it's a plot!' His voice rose in baffled frenzy. 'We just bought the thing and now look. *Look!*' He shoved the tape at his wife. 'You see? I told you!'

'I've seen it,' Ruth said wildly. 'I suppose you think the whole world was just waiting with you in mind. They're always improving weapons, Bob. Last week it was those grain-impregnation flakes. This week it's bore-pellets. You don't expect them to stop the wheels of progress because you finally broke down and bought a shelter, do you?'

The man and woman faced each other. 'What the hell are we going to do?' Bob Foster asked quietly.

Ruth paced back into the kitchen. 'I heard they were going to turn out adaptors.'

'Adaptors! What do you mean?'

'So people won't have to buy new shelters. There was a commercial on the vidscreen. They're going to put some kind of metal grill on the market, as soon as the government approves it. They spread it over the ground and it intercepts the bore-pellets. It screens them, makes them explode on the surface, so they can't burrow down to the shelter.'

'How much?'

'They didn't say.'

Mike Foster sat crouched on the sofa, listening. He had heard the news at school. They were taking their test on berry-identification, examining encased samples of wild berries to distinguish the harmless ones from the toxic, when the bell had announced a general assembly. The principal read them the news about the bore-pellets and then gave a routine lecture on emergency treatment of a new variant of typhus, recently developed.

His parents were still arguing. 'We'll have to get one,' Ruth Foster said calmly. 'Otherwise it won't make any difference whether we've got a shelter or not. The bore-pellets were specifically designed to penetrate the surface and seek out warmth. As soon as the Russians have them in production—'

'I'll get one,' Bob Foster said. 'I'll get an anti-pellet grill and whatever else they have. I'll buy everything they put on the market. I'll never stop buying.'

'It's not as bad as that.'

'You know, this game has one real advantage over selling people cars and TV sets. With something like this we *have* to buy. It isn't a luxury, something big and flashy to impress the neighbors, something we could do without. If we don't buy this we die. They always said the way to sell something was create anxiety in people. Create a sense of insecurity—tell them they smell bad or look funny. But this makes a joke out of deodorant and hair oil. You can't escape this. If you don't buy, *they'll kill you.* The perfect sales-pitch. Buy or die—new slogan. Have a shiny new General Electronics H-bomb shelter in your back yard or be slaughtered.'

'Stop talking like that!' Ruth snapped.

Bob Foster threw himself down at the kitchen table. 'All right. I give up. I'll go along with it.'

'You'll get one? I think they'll be on the market by Christmas.'

'Oh, yes,' Foster said. 'They'll be out by Christmas.' There was a strange look on his face. 'I'll buy one of the damn things for Christmas, and so will everybody else.'

The GEC grill-screen adaptors were a sensation.

Mike Foster walked slowly along the crowd-packed December street, through the late-afternoon twilight. Adaptors glittered in every store window. All shapes and sizes, for every kind of shelter. All prices, for every pocketbook. The crowds of people were gay and excited, typical Christmas crowds, shoving good-naturedly, loaded down with packages and heavy overcoats. The air was white with gusts of sweeping snow. Cars nosed cautiously along the jammed streets. Lights and neon displays, immense glowing store windows gleamed on all sides.

His own house was dark and silent. His parents weren't home yet. Both of them were down at the store working; business had been bad and his mother was taking the place of one of the clerks. Mike held his hand up to the codekey, and the front door let him in. The automatic furnace had kept the house warm and pleasant. He removed his coat and put away his schoolbooks.

He didn't stay in the house long. His heart pounding with excitement, he felt his way out the back door and started onto the back porch.

He forced himself to stop, turn around, and reenter the house. It was better if he didn't hurry things. He had worked out every moment of the process, from the first instant he saw the low hinge of the neck reared up hard and firm against the evening sky. He had made a fine art of it; there was no wasted motion. His procedure had been shaped, molded until it was a beautiful thing. The first overwhelming sense of *presence* as the neck of the shelter came around him. Then the blood-freezing rush of air as the descent-lift hurtled down all the way to the bottom.

And the grandeur of the shelter itself.

Every afternoon, as soon as he was home, he made his way down into it, below the surface, concealed and protected in its steel silence, as he had done since the first day. Now the chamber was full, not empty. Filled with endless cans of food, pillows, books, vidtapes, audio-tapes, prints on the walls, bright fabrics, textures and colors, even vases of flowers. The shelter was his place, where he crouched curled up, surrounded by everything he needed.

Delaying things as long as possible, he hurried back through the house and rummaged in the audio-tape file. He'd sit down in the shelter until dinner, listening to *Wind in the Willows*. His parents knew where to find him; he was always down there. Two hours of uninterrupted happiness, alone by himself in the shelter. And then when dinner was over he would hurry back down, to stay until time for bed. Sometimes late at night, when his parents were sound asleep, he got quietly up and made his way outside, to the shelter-neck, and down into its silent depths. To hide until morning.

He found the audio-tape and hurried through the house, out onto the back porch and into the yard. The sky was a bleak gray, shot with streamers of ugly black clouds. The lights of the town were coming on here and there. The yard was cold and hostile. He made his way uncertainly down the steps—and froze.

A vast yawning cavity loomed. A gaping mouth, vacant and toothless, fixed open to the night sky. There was nothing else. The shelter was gone.

He stood for an endless time, the tape clutched in one hand, the other hand on the porch railing. Night came on; the dead hole dissolved in darkness. The whole world gradually collapsed into silence and abysmal gloom. Weak stars came out; lights in nearby houses came on fitfully, cold and faint. The boy saw nothing. He stood unmoving, his body rigid as stone, still facing the great pit where the shelter had been.

Then his father was standing beside him. 'How long have you been here?' his father was saying. 'How long, Mike? Answer me!'

With a violent effort Mike managed to drag himself back. 'You're home early,' he muttered.

'I left the store early on purpose. I wanted to be here when you—got home.'

'It's gone.'

'Yes.' His father's voice was cold, without emotion. 'The shelter's gone. I'm sorry, Mike. I called them and told them to take it back.'

'Why?'

'I couldn't pay for it. Not this Christmas, with those grills everyone's getting. I can't compete with them.' He broke off and then continued wretchedly, 'They were damn decent. They gave me back half the money I put in.' His voice twisted ironically. 'I knew if I made a deal with them before Christmas I'd come out better. They can resell it to somebody else.'

Mike said nothing.

'Try to understand,' his father went on harshly. 'I had to throw what capital I could scrape together into the store. I have to keep it running. It was either give up the shelter or the store. And if I gave up the store—'

'Then we wouldn't have anything.'

His father caught hold of his arm. 'Then we'd have to give up the shelter, too.' His thin, strong fingers dug in spasmodically. 'You're growing up—you're old enough to understand. We'll get one later, maybe not the biggest, the most expensive, but something. It was a mistake, Mike. I couldn't swing it, not with the goddamn adaptor things to buck. I'm keeping up the NAT payments, though. And your school tab. I'm keeping that going. This isn't a matter of principle,' he finished desperately. 'I can't help it. Do you understand, Mike? *I had to do it.*'

Mike pulled away.

'Where are you going?' His father hurried after him. 'Come back here!' He grabbed for his son frantically, but in the gloom he stumbled and fell. Stars blinded him as his head smashed into the edge of the house; he pulled himself up painfully and groped for some support.

When he could see again, the yard was empty. His son was gone.

'Mike!' he yelled. 'Where are you?'

There was no answer. The night wind blew clouds of snow around him, a thin bitter gust of chilled air. Wind and darkness, nothing else.

Bill O'Neill wearily examined the clock on the wall. It was nine thirty: he could finally close the doors and lock up the big dazzling store. Push the milling, murmuring throngs of people outside and on their way home.

'Thank God,' he breathed, as he held the door open for the last old lady, loaded down with packages and presents. He threw the code bolt in place and pulled down the shade. 'What a mob. I never saw so many people.'

'All done,' Al Conners said, from the cash register. 'I'll count the money—you go around and check everything. Make sure we got all of them out.'

O'Neill pushed his blond hair back and loosened his tie. He lit a cigarette gratefully, then moved around the store, checking light switches, turning off the massive GEC displays and appliances. Finally he approached the huge bomb shelter that took up the center of the floor.

He climbed the ladder to the neck and stepped onto the lift. The lift dropped with a *whoosh* and a second later he stepped out in the cavelike interior of the shelter.

In one corner Mike Foster sat curled up in a tight heap, his knees drawn up against his chin, his skinny arms wrapped around his ankles. His face was pushed down; only his ragged brown hair showed. He didn't move as the salesman approached him, astounded.

'Jesus!' O'Neill exclaimed. 'It's that kid.'

Mike said nothing. He hugged his legs tighter and buried his head as far down as possible.

'What the hell are you doing down here?' O'Neill demanded, surprised and angry. His outrage increased. 'I thought your folks got one of these.' Then he remembered. 'That's right. We had to repossess it.'

Al Conners appeared from the descent-lift. 'What's holding you up? Let's get out of here and–' He saw Mike and broke off. 'What's he doing down here? Get him out and let's go.'

'Come on, kid,' O'Neill said gently. 'Time to go home.'

Mike didn't move.

The two men looked at each other. 'I guess we're going to have to drag him out,' Conners said grimly. He took off his coat and tossed it over a decontamination fixture. 'Come on. Let's get it over with.'

It took both of them. The boy fought desperately, without sound, clawing and struggling and tearing at them with his fingernails, kicking them, slashing at them, biting them when they grabbed him. They half-dragged, half-carried him to the descent-lift and pushed him into it long enough to activate the mechanism. O'Neill rode up with him; Conners came immediately after. Grimly, efficiently, they bundled the boy to the front door, threw him out, and locked the bolts after him.

'Wow,' Conners gasped, sinking down against the counter. His sleeve was torn and his cheek was cut and gashed. His glasses hung from one ear; his hair was rumpled and he was exhausted. 'Think we ought to call the cops? There's something wrong with that kid.'

O'Neill stood by the door, panting for breath and gazing out into the darkness. He could see the boy sitting on the pavement. 'He's still out there,' he muttered. People pushed by the boy on both sides. Finally one of them stopped and got him up. The boy struggled away, and then disappeared into the darkness. The larger figure picked up its packages, hesitated a moment, and then went on. O'Neill turned away. 'What a hell of a thing.' He wiped his face with his handkerchief. 'He sure put up a fight.'

'What was the matter with him? He never said anything, not a goddamn word.'

'Christmas is a hell of a time to repossess something,' O'Neill said. He reached shakily for his coat. 'It's too bad. I wish they could have kept it.'

Conners shrugged. 'No tickie, no laundry.'

'Why the hell can't we give them a deal? Maybe—' O'Neill struggled to get the word out. 'Maybe sell the shelter wholesale, to people like that.'

Conners glared at him angrily. '*Wholesale?* And then everybody wants it wholesale. It wouldn't be fair—and how long would we stay in business? How long would GEC last that way?'

'I guess not very long,' O'Neill admitted moodily.

'Use your head.' Conners laughed sharply. 'What you need is a good stiff drink. Come on in the back closet—I've got a fifty of Haig and Haig in a drawer back there. A little something to warm you up, before you go home. That's what you need.'

Mike Foster wandered aimlessly along the dark street, among the crowds of shoppers hurrying home. He saw nothing; people pushed against him but he was unaware of them. Lights, laughing people, the honking of car horns, the clang of signals. He was blank, his mind empty and dead. He walked automatically, without consciousness or feeling.

To his right a garish neon sign winked and glowed in the deepening night shadows. A huge sign, bright and colorful.

PEACE ON EARTH   GOOD WILL TO MEN
PUBLIC SHELTER   ADMISSION 50C

FOSTER, YOU'RE DEAD   93

PAY FOR THE PRINTER

Ash, black and desolate, stretched out on both sides of the road. Uneven heaps extended as far as the eye could see—the dim ruins of buildings, cities, a civilization—a corroded planet of debris, wind-whipped black particles of bone and steel and concrete mixed together in an aimless mortar.

Allen Fergesson yawned, lit a Lucky Strike, and settled back drowsily against the shiny leather seat of his '57 Buick. 'Depressing damn sight,' he commented. 'The monotony—nothing but muti-lated trash. It gets you down.'

'Don't look at it,' the girl beside him said indifferently.

The sleek, powerful car glided silently over the rubble that made up the road. His hand barely touching the power-driven wheel, Fergesson relaxed comfortably to the soothing music of a Brahms Piano Quintet filtering from the radio, a transmission of the Detroit settlement. Ash blew up against the windows—a thick coat of black had already formed, though he had gone no more than a few miles. But it didn't matter. In the basement of her apart-ment, Charlotte had a green-plastic garden hose, a zinc bucket and a DuPont sponge.

'And you have a refrigerator full of good Scotch,' he added aloud. 'As I recall—unless that fast crowd of yours has finished it off.'

Charlotte stirred beside him. She had drifted into half-sleep, lulled by the purr of the motor and the heavy warmth of the air. 'Scotch?' she murmured. 'Well, I have a fifth of Lord Calvert.' She sat up and shook back her cloud of blonde hair. 'But it's a little puddinged.'

In the back seat, their thin-faced passenger responded. They had picked him up along the way, a bony, gaunt man in coarse gray work-pants and shirt. 'How puddinged?' he asked tautly.

'About as much as everything else,' she said.

Charlotte wasn't listening. She was gazing vacantly through the ash-darkened window at the scene outside. To the right of the road, the jagged, yellowed remains of a town jutted up like broken teeth against the sooty midday sky. A bathtub here, a couple of upright telephone poles, bones and bleak fragments, lost amid miles of pocked debris. A forlorn, dismal sight. Somewhere in the moldy cave-like cellars a few mangy dogs huddled against the chill. The thick fog of ash kept real sunlight from reaching the surface.

'Look there,' Fergesson said to the man in the back.

A mock-rabbit had bounded across the ribbon of road. He slowed the car to avoid it. Blind, deformed, the rabbit hurled itself with sickening force against a broken concrete slab and bounced off, stunned. It crawled feebly a few paces, then one of the cellar dogs rose and crunched it.

'*Ugh!*' said Charlotte, revolted. She shuddered and reached to turn up the car heater. Slim legs tucked under her, she was an attractive little figure in her pink wool sweater and embroidered skirt. 'I'll be glad when we get back to my settlement. It's not *nice* out here . . .'

Fergesson tapped the steel box on the seat between them. The firm metal felt good under his fingers. 'They'll be glad to get hold of these,' he said, 'if things are as bad as you say.'

'Oh, yes,' Charlotte agreed. 'Things are terrible. I don't know if this will help—he's just about useless.' Her small smooth face wrinkled with concern. 'I guess it's worth trying. But I can't see much hope.'

'We'll fix up your settlement,' Fergesson reassured her easily. The first item was to put the girl's mind at rest. Panic of this kind could get out of hand—*had* got out of hand, more than once. 'But it'll take a while,' he added, glancing at her. 'You should have told us sooner.'

'We thought it was just laziness. But he's really going, Allen.' Fear flickered in her blue eyes. 'We can't get anything good out of him anymore. He just sits there like a big lump, as if he's sick or dead.'

'He's old,' Fergesson said gently. 'As I recall, your Biltong dates back a hundred and fifty years.'

'But they're supposed to go on for centuries!'

'It's a terrible drain on them,' the man in the back seat pointed out. He licked his dry lips, leaned forward tensely, his dirt-cracked hands clenched. 'You're forgetting this isn't natural to them. On Proxima they worked together. Now they've broken up into separate units—and gravity is greater here.'

Charlotte nodded, but she wasn't convinced. 'Gosh!' she said plaintively. 'It's just terrible—look at this!' She fumbled in her sweater pocket and brought out a small bright object the size of a dime. 'Everything he prints is like this, now—or worse.'

Fergesson took the watch and examined it, one eye on the road. The strap broke like a dried leaf between his fingers into small brittle fragments of dark fiber without tensile strength. The face of the watch looked all right—but the hands weren't moving.

'It doesn't run,' Charlotte explained. She grabbed it back and opened it. 'See?' She held it up in front of his face, her crimson lips tight with displeasure. 'I stood in line half an hour for this, and it's just a blob!'

The works of the tiny Swiss watch were a fused, unformed mass of shiny steel. No separate wheels or jewels or springs, just a glitter of pudding.

'What did he have to go on?' the man in back asked. 'An original?'

'A print—but a good print. One he did thirty-five years ago—my mother's, in fact. How do you think I felt when I saw it? I can't use it.' Charlotte took the puddinged watch back and restored it to her sweater pocket. 'I was so mad I—' She broke off and sat up straight. 'Oh, we're here. See the red neon sign? That's the beginning of the settlement.'

The sign read STANDARD STATIONS INC. Its colors were blue,

red, and white—a spotlessly clean structure at the edge of the road. Spotless? Fergesson slowed the car as he came abreast of the station. All three of them peered out intently, stiffening for the shock they knew was coming.

'You see?' said Charlotte in a thin, clipped voice.

The gas station was crumbling away. The small white building was *old*—old and worn, a corroded, uncertain thing that sagged and buckled like an ancient relic. The bright red neon sign sputtered fitfully. The pumps were rusted and bent. The gas station was beginning to settle back into the ash, back into black, drifting particles, back to the dust from which it had come.

As Fergesson gazed at the sinking station, the chill of death touched him. In his settlement, there was no decay—yet. As fast as prints wore out, they were replaced by the Pittsburgh Biltong. New prints were made from the original objects preserved from the War. But here, the prints that made up the settlement were not being replaced.

It was useless to blame anyone. The Biltong were limited, like any race. They had done the best they could—and they were working in an alien environment.

Probably they were indigenous to the Centaurus system. They had appeared in the closing days of the War, attracted by the H-bomb flashes—and found the remnants of the human race creeping miserably through radioactive black ash, trying to salvage what they could of their destroyed culture.

After a period of analysis, the Biltong had separated into individual units, begun the process of duplicating surviving artifacts humans brought to them. That was their mode of survival—on their own planet, they had created an enclosing membrane of satisfactory environment in an otherwise hostile world.

At one of the gasoline pumps a man was trying to fill the tank of his '66 Ford. Cursing in futility, he tore the rotting hose away. Dull amber fluid poured on the ground and soaked into the grease-encrusted gravel. The pump itself spouted leaks in a dozen places. Abruptly, one of the pumps tottered and crashed in a heap.

Charlotte rolled down the car window. 'The Shell station is in better shape, Ben!' she called. 'At the other end of the settlement.'

The heavyset man clumped over, red-faced and perspiring. '*Damn!*' he muttered. 'I can't get a damn thing out of it. Give me a lift across town, and I'll fill me a bucket there.'

Fergesson shakily pushed open the car door. 'It's all like this here?'

'Worse.' Ben Untermeyer settled back gratefully with their other passenger as the Buick purred ahead. 'Look over there.'

A grocery store had collapsed in a twisted heap of concrete and steel supports. The windows had fallen in. Stacks of goods lay strewn everywhere. People were picking their way around, gathering up armloads, trying to clear some of the debris aside. Their faces were grim and angry.

The street itself was in bad repair, full of cracks, deep pits and eroded shoulders. A broken water main oozed slimy water in a growing pool. The stores and cars on both sides were dirty and run-down. Everything had a senile look. A shoe-shine parlor was boarded up, its broken windows stuffed with rags, its sign peeling and shabby. A filthy cafe next door had only a couple of patrons, miserable men in rumpled business suits, trying to read their newspapers and drink the mud-like coffee from cups that cracked and dribbled ugly brown fluid as they lifted them from the worm-eaten counter.

'It can't last much longer,' Untermeyer muttered, as he mopped his forehead. 'Not at this rate. People are even scared to go into the theatre. Anyhow, the film breaks and half the time it's upside-down.' He glanced curiously at the lean-jawed man sitting silently beside him. 'My name's Untermeyer,' he grunted.

They shook. 'John Dawes,' the gray-wrapped man answered. He volunteered no more information. Since Fergesson and Charlotte had picked him up along the road, he hadn't said fifty words.

Untermeyer got a rolled-up newspaper from his coat pocket and tossed it onto the front seat beside Fergesson. 'This is what I found on the porch, this morning.'

The newspaper was a jumble of meaningless words. A vague blur of broken type, watery ink that still hadn't dried, faint, streaked and uneven. Fergesson briefly scanned the text, but it was useless. Confused stories wandered off aimlessly, bold headlines proclaimed nonsense.

'Allen has some originals for us,' Charlotte said. 'In the box there.'

'They won't help,' Untermeyer answered gloomily. 'He didn't stir all morning. I waited in line with a pop-up toaster I wanted a print of. No dice. I was driving back home when my car began to break down. I looked under the hood, but who knows anything about motors? That's not *our* business. I poked around and got it to run as far as the Standard station . . . the damn metal's so weak I put my thumb through it.'

Fergesson pulled his Buick to a halt in front of the big white apartment building where Charlotte lived. It took him a moment to recognize it; there had been changes since he last saw it, a month before. A wooden scaffolding, clumsy and amateur, had been erected around it. A few workmen were poking uncertainly at the foundations; the whole building was sinking slowly to one side. Vast cracks yawned up and down the walls. Bits of plaster were strewn everywhere. The littered sidewalk in front of the building was roped off.

'There isn't anything we can do on our own,' Untermeyer complained angrily. 'All we can do is just sit and watch everything fall apart. If he doesn't come to life soon . . .'

'Everything he printed for us in the old days is beginning to wear out,' Charlotte said, as she opened the car door and slid onto the pavement. 'And everything he prints for us now is a pudding. So what are we going to do?' She shivered in the chill midday cold. 'I guess we're going to wind up like the Chicago settlement.'

The word froze all four of them. Chicago, the settlement that had collapsed! The Biltong printing there had grown old and died. Exhausted, he had settled into a silent, unmoving mound of inert matter. The buildings and streets around him, all the things he had printed, had gradually worn out and returned to black ash.

'He didn't spawn,' Charlotte whispered fearfully. 'He used himself up printing, and then he just—*died*.'

After a time, Fergesson said huskily, 'But the others noticed. They sent a replacement as soon as they could.'

'It was too late!' Untermeyer grunted. 'The settlement had already gone back. All that was left were maybe a couple of survivors wandering around with nothing on, freezing and starving, and the dogs devouring them. The damn dogs, flocking from everywhere, having a regular feast!'

They stood together on the corroded sidewalk, frightened and apprehensive. Even John Dawes' lean face had a look of bleak horror on it, a fear that cut to the bone. Fergesson thought yearningly of his own settlement, a dozen miles to the East. Thriving and virile—the Pittsburgh Biltong was in his prime, still young and rich with the creative powers of his race. Nothing like this!

The buildings in the Pittsburgh settlement were strong and spotless. The sidewalks were clean and firm underfoot. In the store windows, the television sets and mixers and toasters and autos and pianos and clothing and whiskey and frozen peaches were perfect prints of the originals—authentic, detailed reproductions that couldn't be told from the actual articles preserved in the vacuum-sealed subsurface shelters.

'If this settlement goes out,' Fergesson said awkwardly, 'maybe a few of you can come over with us.'

'Can your Biltong print for more than a hundred people?' John Dawes asked softly.

'Right now he can,' Fergesson answered. He proudly indicated his Buick. 'You rode in it—you know how good it is. Almost as good as the original it was printed from. You'd have to have them side by side to tell the difference.' He grinned and made an old joke. 'Maybe I got away with the original.'

'We don't have to decide now,' Charlotte said curtly. 'We still have *some* time, at least.' She picked up the steel box from the seat of the Buick and moved toward the steps of the apartment building. 'Come on up with us, Ben.' She nodded toward Dawes. 'You, too. Have a shot of whiskey. It's not too bad—tastes a little like anti-freeze, and the label isn't legible, but other than that it's not too puddinged.'

A workman caught her as she put a foot on the bottom step. 'You can't go up, miss.'

Charlotte pulled away angrily, her face pale with dismay. 'My apartment's up there! All my things—this is where I *live*!'

'The building isn't safe,' the workman repeated. He wasn't a real workman. He was one of the citizens of the settlement, who had volunteered to guard the buildings that were deteriorating. 'Look at the cracks, miss.'

'They've been there for weeks.' Impatiently, Charlotte waved Fergesson after her. 'Come on.' She stepped nimbly up onto the porch and reached to open the big glass-and-chrome front door.

The door fell from its hinges and burst. Glass shattered every-where, a cloud of lethal shards flying in all directions. Charlotte screamed and stumbled back. The concrete crumbled under her heels; with a groan the whole porch settled down in a heap of white powder, a shapeless mound of billowing particles.

Fergesson and the workman caught hold of the struggling girl. In the swirling clouds of concrete dust, Untermeyer searched fran-tically for the steel box; his fingers closed over it and he dragged it to the sidewalk.

Fergesson and the workman fought back through the ruins of the porch, Charlotte gripped between them. She was trying to speak, but her face jerked hysterically.

'My things!' she managed to whisper.

Fergesson brushed her off unsteadily. 'Where are you hurt? Are you all right?'

'I'm not hurt.' Charlotte wiped a trickle of blood and white powder from her face. Her cheek was cut, and her blonde hair was a sodden mass. Her pink wool sweater was torn and ragged. Her clothes were totally ruined. 'The box—have you got it?'

'It's fine,' John Dawes said impassively. He hadn't moved an inch from his position by the car.

Charlotte hung on tight to Fergesson—against him, her body shuddered with fear and despair. '*Look!*' she whispered. 'Look at my hands.' She held up her white-stained hands. 'It's beginning to turn black.'

The thick powder streaking her hands and arms had begun to darken. Even as they watched, the powder became gray, then black as soot. The girl's shredded clothing withered and shriveled up. Like a shrunken husk, her clothing cracked and fell away from her body.

'Get in the car,' Fergesson ordered. 'There's a blanket in there—from my settlement.'

Together, he and Untermeyer wrapped the trembling girl in the heavy wool blanket. Charlotte crouched against the seat, her eyes wide with terror, drops of bright blood sliding down her cheek onto the blue and yellow stripes of the blanket. Fergesson lit a cigarette and put it between her quivering lips.

'Thanks.' She managed a grateful half-whimper. She took hold of the cigarette shakily. 'Allen, what the hell are we going to do?'

Fergesson softly brushed the darkening powder from the girl's blonde hair. 'We'll drive over and show him the originals I brought. Maybe he can do something. They're always stimulated by the sight of new things to print from. Maybe this'll arouse some life in him.'

'He's not just asleep,' Charlotte said in a stricken voice. 'He's dead, Allen. I *know* it!'

'Not yet,' Untermeyer protested thickly. But the realization was in the minds of all of them.

'Has he spawned?' Dawes asked.

The look on Charlotte's face told them the answer. 'He tried to. There were a few that hatched, but none of them lived. I've seen eggs back there, but ...'

She was silent. They all knew. The Biltong had become sterile in their struggle to keep the human race alive. Dead eggs, progeny hatched without life ...

Fergesson slid in behind the wheel and harshly slammed the door. The door didn't close properly. The metal was sprung—or perhaps it was misshapen. His hackles rose. Here, too, was an imperfect print—a trifle, a microscopic element botched in the printing. Even his sleek, luxurious Buick was puddinged. The Biltong at his settlement was wearing out, too.

Sooner or later, what had happened to the Chicago settlement would happen to them all . . .

Around the park, rows of automobiles were lined up, silent and unmoving. The park was full of people. Most of the settlement was there. Everybody had something that desperately needed printing. Fergesson snapped off the motor and pocketed the keys.

'Can you make it?' he asked Charlotte. 'Maybe you'd better stay here.'

'I'll be all right,' Charlotte said, and tried to smile.

She had put on a sports shirt and slacks that Fergesson had picked up for her in the ruins of a decaying clothing store. He felt no qualms—a number of men and women were picking listlessly through the scattered stock that littered the sidewalk. The clothing would be good for perhaps a few days.

Fergesson had taken his time picking Charlotte's wardrobe. He had found a heap of sturdy-fibered shirts and slacks in the back storeroom, material still a long way from the dread black pulverization. Recent prints? Or, perhaps—incredible but possible—originals the store owners had used for printing. At a shoe store still in business, he found her a pair of low-heeled slippers. It was his own belt she wore—the one he had picked up in the clothing store rotted away in his hands while he was buckling it around her.

Untermeyer gripped the steel box with both hands as the four of them approached the center of the park. The people around them were silent and grim-faced. No one spoke. They all carried some article, originals carefully preserved through the centuries or good prints with only minor imperfections. On their faces were desperate hope and fear fused, in a taut mask.

'Here they are,' said Dawes, lagging behind. 'The dead eggs.'

In a grove of trees at the edge of the park was a circle of gray-brown pellets, the size of basketballs. They were hard, calcified. Some were broken. Fragments of shell were littered everywhere.

Untermeyer kicked at one egg; it fell apart, brittle and empty. 'Sucked dry by some animal,' he stated. 'We're seeing the end, Fergesson. I think dogs sneak in here at night, now, and get at them. He's too weak to protect them.'

A dull undercurrent of outrage throbbed through the waiting men and women. Their eyes were red-rimmed with anger as they stood clutching their objects, jammed in together in a solid mass, a circle of impatient, indignant humanity ringing the center of the park. They had been waiting a long time. They were getting tired of waiting.

'What the hell is this?' Untermeyer squatted down in front of a vague shape discarded under a tree. He ran his fingers over the indistinct blur of metal. The object seemed melted together like wax—nothing was distinguishable. 'I can't identify it.'

'That's a power lawnmower,' a man nearby said sullenly.

'How long ago did he print it?' Fergesson asked.

'Four days ago.' The man knocked at it in hostility. 'You can't even tell what it is—it could be anything. My old one's worn out. I wheeled the settlement's original up from the vault and stood in line all day—and look what I got.' He spat contemptuously. 'It isn't worth a damn. I left it sitting here—no point taking it home.'

His wife spoke up in a shrill, harsh wail. 'What are we going to do? We can't use the old one. It's crumbling away like everything else around here. If the new prints aren't any good, then what—'

'Shut up,' her husband snapped. His face was ugly and strained. His long-fingered hands gripped a length of pipe. 'We'll wait a little longer. Maybe he'll snap out of it.'

A murmur of hope rippled around them. Charlotte shivered and pushed on. 'I don't blame him,' she said to Fergesson. 'But . . .' She shook her head wearily. 'What good would it do? If he won't print copies for us that are any good . . .'

'He can't,' John Dawes said. 'Look at him!' He halted and held the rest of them back. 'Look at him and tell me how he could do better.'

The Biltong was dying. Huge and old, it squatted in the center of the settlement park, a lump of ancient yellow protoplasm, thick, gummy, opaque. Its pseudopodia were dried up, shriveled to blackened snakes that lay inert on the brown grass. The center of the mass looked oddly sunken. The Biltong was gradually settling, as the moisture was burned from its veins by the weak overhead sun.

'Oh, dear!' Charlotte whispered. 'How *awful* he looks!'

The Biltong's central lump undulated faintly. Sickly, restless heavings were noticeable as it struggled to hold onto its dwindling life. Flies clustered around it in dense swarms of black and shiny blue. A thick odor hung over the Biltong, a fetid stench of decaying organic matter. A pool of brackish waste liquid had oozed from it.

Within the yellow protoplasm of the creature, its solid core of nervous tissue pulsed in agony, with quick, jerky movements that sent widening waves across the sluggish flesh. Filaments were almost visibly degenerating into calcified granules. Age and decay —and suffering.

On the concrete platform, in front of the dying Biltong, lay a heap of originals to be duplicated. Beside them, a few prints had been commenced, unformed balls of black ash mixed with the moisture of the Biltong's body, the juice from which it laboriously constructed its prints. It had halted the work, pulled its still-functioning pseudopodia painfully back into itself. It was resting —and trying not to die.

'The poor damn thing!' Fergesson heard himself say. 'It can't keep on.'

'He's been sitting like that for six solid hours,' a woman snapped sharply in Fergesson's ear. 'Just sitting there! What does he expect us to do, get down on our hands and knees and *beg* him?'

Dawes turned furiously on her. 'Can't you see it's dying? For God's sake, *leave it alone!*'

An ominous rumble stirred through the ring of people. Faces turned toward Dawes—he icily ignored them. Beside him, Charlotte had stiffened to a frightened ramrod. Her eyes were pale with fear.

'Be careful,' Untermeyer warned Dawes softly. 'Some of these boys need things pretty bad. Some of them are waiting here for food.'

Time was running out. Fergesson grabbed the steel box from Untermeyer and tore it open. Bending down, he removed the originals and laid them on the grass in front of him.

At the sight, a murmur went up around him, a murmur blended of awe and amazement. Grim satisfaction knifed through Fergesson. These were originals lacking in this settlement. Only imperfect prints existed here. Printing had been done from defective duplicates. One by one, he gathered up the precious originals and moved toward the concrete platform in front of the Biltong. Men angrily blocked his way—until they saw the originals he carried.

He laid down a silver Ronson cigarette lighter. Then a Bausch and Lomb binocular microscope, still black and pebbled in its original leather. A high-fidelity Pickering phonograph cartridge. And a shimmering Steuben crystal cup.

'Those are fine-looking originals,' a man nearby said enviously. 'Where'd you get them?'

Fergesson didn't reply. He was watching the dying Biltong.

The Biltong hadn't moved. But it had seen the new originals added to the others. Inside the yellow mass, the hard fibers raced and blurred together. The front orifice shuddered and then split open. A violent wave lashed the whole lump of protoplasm. Then from the opening, rancid bubbles oozed. A pseudopodium twitched briefly, struggled forward across the slimy grass, hesitated, touched the Steuben glass.

It pushed together a heap of black ash, wadded it with fluid from the front orifice. A dull globe formed, a grotesque parody of the Steuben cup. The Biltong wavered and drew back to gather more strength. Presently it tried once more to form the blob. Abruptly, without warning, the whole mass shuddered violently, and the pseudopodium dropped, exhausted. It twitched, hesitated pathetically, and then withdrew, back into the central bulk.

'No use,' Untermeyer said hoarsely. 'He can't do it. It's too late.'

With stiff, awkward fingers, Fergesson gathered the originals together and shakily stuffed them back in the steel box. 'I guess I was wrong,' he muttered, climbing to his feet. 'I thought this might do it. I didn't realize how far it had gone.'

Charlotte, stricken and mute, moved blindly away from the platform. Untermeyer followed her through the coagulation of angry men and women, clustered around the concrete platform.

'Wait a minute,' Dawes said. 'I have something for him to try.'

Fergesson waited wearily, as Dawes groped inside his coarse gray shirt. He fumbled and brought out something wrapped in old newspaper. It was a cup, a wooden drinking cup, crude and ill-shaped. There was a strange wry smile on his face as he squatted down and placed the cup in front of the Biltong.

Charlotte watched, vaguely puzzled. 'What's the use? Suppose he does make a print of it.' She poked listlessly at the rough wooden object with the toe of her slipper. 'It's so simple you could duplicate it yourself.'

Fergesson started. Dawes caught his eye—for an instant the two men gazed at each other, Dawes smiling faintly, Fergesson rigid with burgeoning understanding.

'That's right,' Dawes said. 'I made it.'

Fergesson grabbed the cup. Trembling, he turned it over and over. 'You made it with *what*? I don't see how! What did you make it *out* of?'

'We knocked down some trees.' From his belt, Dawes slid something that gleamed metallically, dully, in the weak sunlight. 'Here— be careful you don't cut yourself.'

The knife was as crude as the cup—hammered, bent, tied together with wire. 'You made this knife?' Fergesson asked, dazed. 'I can't believe it. *Where do you start?* You have to have tools to make this. It's a paradox!' His voice rose with hysteria. 'It isn't *possible!*'

Charlotte turned despondently away. 'It's no good—you couldn't cut anything with that.' Wistfully, pathetically, she added, 'In my kitchen I had that whole set of stainless steel carving knives—the best Swedish steel. And now they're nothing but black ash.'

There were a million questions bursting in Fergesson's mind. 'This cup, this knife—there's a group of you? And that material you're wearing—you wove that?'

'Come on,' Dawes said brusquely. He retrieved the knife and cup, moved urgently away. 'We'd better get out of here. I think the end has about come.'

People were beginning to drift out of the park. They were giving up, shambling wretchedly off to forage in the decaying stores for food remnants. A few cars muttered into life and rolled hesitantly away.

Untermeyer licked his flabby lips nervously. His doughy flesh was mottled and grainy with fear. 'They're getting wild,' he muttered to Fergesson. 'This whole settlement's collapsing—in a few hours there won't be anything. No food, no place to stay!' His eyes darted toward the car, then faded to opaqueness.

He wasn't the only one who had noticed the car.

A group of men were slowly forming around the massive dusty Buick, their faces dark. Like hostile, greedy children, they poked at it intently, examining its fenders, hood, touching its headlights, its firm tires. The men had clumsy weapons—pipes, rocks, sections of twisted steel ripped from collapsing buildings.

'They know it isn't from this settlement,' Dawes said. 'They know it's going back.'

'I can take you to the Pittsburgh settlement,' Fergesson said to Charlotte. He headed toward the car. 'I'll register you as my wife. You can decide later on whether you want to go through with the legalities.'

'What about Ben?' Charlotte asked faintly.

'I can't marry him, too.' Fergesson increased his pace. 'I can take him there, but they won't let him stay. They have their quota system. Later on, when they realize the emergency . . .'

'Get out of the way,' Untermeyer said to the cordon of men. He lumbered toward them vengefully. After a moment, the men uncertainly retreated and finally gave way. Untermeyer stood by the door, his huge body drawn up and alert.

'Bring her through—and watch it!' he told Fergesson.

Fergesson and Dawes, with Charlotte between them, made their way through the line of men to Untermeyer. Fergesson gave the fat man the keys, and Untermeyer yanked the front door open. He pushed Charlotte in, then motioned Fergesson to hurry around to the other side.

The group of men came alive.

With his great fist, Untermeyer smashed the leader into those behind him. He struggled past Charlotte and got his bulk wedged behind the wheel of the car. The motor came on with a whirr. Untermeyer threw it into low gear and jammed savagely down on the accelerator. The car edged forward. Men clawed at it crazily, groping at the open door for the man and woman inside.

Untermeyer slammed the doors and locked them. As the car gained speed, Fergesson caught a final glimpse of the fat man's sweating, fear-distorted face.

Men grabbed vainly for the slippery sides of the car. As it gathered momentum, they slid away one by one. One huge red-haired man clung maniacally to the hood, pawing at the shattered windshield for the driver's face beyond. Untermeyer sent the car spinning into a sharp curve; the red-haired man hung on for a moment, then lost his grip and tumbled silently, face-forward, onto the pavement.

The car wove, careened, at last disappeared from view beyond a row of sagging buildings. The sound of its screaming tires faded. Untermeyer and Charlotte were on their way to safety at the Pittsburgh settlement.

Fergesson stared after the car until the pressure of Dawes' thin hand on his shoulder aroused him. 'Well,' he muttered, 'there goes the car. Anyhow, Charlotte got away.'

'Come on,' Dawes said tightly in his ear. 'I hope you have good shoes—we've got a long way to walk.'

Fergesson blinked. 'Walk? Where . . . ?'

'The nearest of our camps is thirty miles from here. We can make it, I think.' He moved away, and after a moment Fergesson followed him. 'I've done it before. I can do it again.'

Behind them, the crowd was collecting again, centering its interest upon the inert mass that was the dying Biltong. The hum of wrath sounded—frustration and impotence at the loss of the car pitched the ugly cacophony to a gathering peak of violence. Gradually, like water seeking its level, the ominous, boiling mass surged toward the concrete platform.

On the platform, the ancient dying Biltong waited helplessly. It was aware of them. Its pseudopodia were twisted in one last decrepit action, a final shudder of effort.

Then Fergesson saw a terrible thing—a thing that made shame rise inside him until his humiliated fingers released the metal box he carried, let it fall, splintering, to the ground. He retrieved it numbly, stood gripping it helplessly. He wanted to run off blindly, aimlessly, anywhere but here. Out into the silence and darkness and driving shadows beyond the settlement. Out in the dead acres of ash.

The Biltong was trying to print himself a defensive shield, a protective wall of ash, as the mob descended on him . . .

When they had walked a couple of hours, Dawes came to a halt and threw himself down in the black ash that extended everywhere. 'We'll rest awhile,' he grunted to Fergesson. 'I've got some food we can cook. We'll use that Ronson lighter you have there, if it's got any fluid in it.'

Fergesson opened the metal box and passed him the lighter. A cold, fetid wind blew around them, whipping ash into dismal clouds across the barren surface of the planet. Off in the distance, a few jagged walls of buildings jutted upward like splinters of bones. Here and there dark, ominous stalks of weeds grew.

'It's not as dead as it looks,' Dawes commented, as he gathered bits of dried wood and paper from the ash around them. 'You know about the dogs and the rabbits. And there's lots of plant seeds—all you have to do is water the ash, and up they spring.'

'Water? But it doesn't—rain. Whatever the word used to be.'

'We have to dig ditches. There's still water, but you have to dig for it.' Dawes got a feeble fire going—there was fluid in the lighter. He tossed it back and turned his attention to feeding the fire.

Fergesson sat examining the lighter. 'How can you build a thing like this?' he demanded bluntly.

'We can't.' Dawes reached into his coat and brought out a flat packet of food—dried, salted meat and parched corn. 'You can't start out building complex stuff. You have to work your way up slowly.'

'A healthy Biltong could print from this. The one in Pittsburgh could make a perfect print of this lighter.'

'I know,' Dawes said. 'That's what's held us back. We have to wait until they give up. They will, you know. They'll have to go back to their own star-system—it's genocide for them to stay here.'

Fergesson clutched convulsively at the lighter. 'Then our civilization goes with them.'

'That lighter?' Dawes grinned. 'Yes, that's going—for a long time, at least. But I don't think you've got the right slant. We're going to have to re-educate ourselves, every damn one of us. It's hard for me, too.'

'Where did you come from?'

Dawes said quietly, 'I'm one of the survivors from Chicago. After it collapsed, I wandered around—killed with a stone, slept in cellars, fought off the dogs with my hands and feet. Finally, I found my way to one of the camps. There were a few before me—you don't know it, my friend, but Chicago wasn't the first to fall.'

'And you're printing tools? Like that knife?'

Dawes laughed long and loud. 'The word isn't print—the word is *build*. We're building tools, making things.' He pulled out the crude wooden cup and laid it down on the ash. 'Printing means merely copying. I can't explain to you what building is; you'll have to try it yourself to find out. Building and printing are two totally different things.'

Dawes arranged three objects on the ash. The exquisite Steuben glassware, his own crude wooden drinking cup and the blob, the botched print the dying Biltong had attempted.

'This is the way it was,' he said, indicating the Steuben cup. 'Someday it'll be that way again . . . but we're going up the right way—the hard way—step by step, until we get back there.' He carefully replaced the glassware back in its metal box. 'We'll keep it—not to copy, but as a model, as a goal. You can't grasp the difference now, but you will.'

He indicated the crude wooden cup. 'That's where we are right now. Don't laugh at it. Don't say it's not civilization. It is—it's simple and crude, but it's the real thing. We'll go up from here.'

He picked up the blob, the print the Biltong had left behind. After a moment's reflection, he drew back and hurled it away from him. The blob struck, bounced once, then broke into fragments.

'That's nothing,' Dawes said fiercely. 'Better this cup. This wooden cup is closer to that Steuben glass than any print.'

'You're certainly proud of your little wooden cup,' Fergesson observed.

'I sure as hell am,' Dawes agreed, as he placed the cup in the metal box beside the Steuben glassware. 'You'll understand that, too, one of these days. It'll take a while, but you'll get it.' He began closing the box, then halted a moment and touched the Ronson lighter.

He shook his head regretfully. 'Not in our time,' he said, and closed the box. 'Too many steps in between.' His lean face glowed suddenly, a flicker of joyful anticipation. 'But by God, we're moving that way!'

WAR VETERAN

The old man sat on the park bench in the bright hot sunlight and watched the people moving back and forth.

The park was neat and clean; the lawns glittered wetly in the spray piped from a hundred shiny copper tubes. A polished robot gardener crawled here and there, weeding and plucking and gathering waste debris in its disposal slot. Children scampered and shouted. Young couples sat basking sleepily and holding hands. Groups of handsome soldiers strolled lazily along, hands in their pockets, admiring the tanned, naked girls sunbathing around the pool. Beyond the park the roaring cars and towering needle-spires of New York sparkled and gleamed.

The old man cleared his throat and spat sullenly into the bushes. The bright hot sun annoyed him; it was too yellow and it made perspiration stream through his seedy, ragged coat. It made him conscious of his grizzled chin and missing left eye. And the deep ugly burn-scar that had seared away the flesh of one cheek. He pawed fretfully at the h-loop around his scrawny neck. He unbuttoned his coat and pulled himself upright against the glowing metal slats of the bench. Bored, lonely, bitter, he twisted around and tried to interest himself in the pastoral scene of trees and grass and happily playing children.

Three blond-faced young soldiers sat down on the bench opposite him and began unrolling picnic lunch-cartons.

The old man's thin rancid breath caught in his throat. Painfully, his ancient heart thudded, and for the first time in hours he came fully alive. He struggled up from his lethargy and focused his dim sight on the soldiers. The old man got out his handkerchief, mopped his sweat-oozing face, and then spoke to them.

'Nice afternoon.'

The soldiers glanced up briefly. 'Yeah,' one said.

'They done a good job.' The old man indicated the yellow sun and the spires of the city. 'Looks perfect.'

The soldiers said nothing. They concentrated on their cups of boiling black coffee and apple pie.

'Almost fools you,' the old man went on plaintively. 'You boys with the seed teams?' he hazarded.

'No,' one of them said. 'We're rocketeers.'

The old man gripped his aluminum cane and said, 'I was in demolition. Back in the old Ba-3 Squad.'

None of the soldiers responded. They were whispering among themselves. The girls on a bench farther down had noticed them.

The old man reached into his coat pocket and brought out something wrapped in gray torn tissue-paper. He unfolded it with shaking fingers and then got to his feet. Unsteadily, he crossed the gravel path to the soldiers. 'See this?' He held out the object, a small square of glittering metal. 'I won that back in '87. That was before your time, I guess.'

A flicker of interest momentarily roused the young soldiers. 'Hey,' one whistled appreciatively. 'That's a Crystal Disc—first class.' He raised his eyes questioningly. 'You won that?'

The old man cackled proudly, as he wrapped up the medal and restored it to his coat pocket. 'I served under Nathan West, in the *Wind Giant*. It wasn't until the final jump they took against us I got mine. But I was out there with my d-squad. You probably remember the day we set off our network, rigged all the way from—'

'Sorry,' one of the soldiers said vaguely. 'We don't go back that far. That must have been before our time.'

'Sure,' the old man agreed eagerly. 'That was more than sixty years ago. You heard of Major Perati, haven't you? How he rammed their covering fleet into a meteor cloud as they were converging for their final attack? And how the Ba-3 was able to hold them back months before they finally slammed us?' He swore bitterly. 'We held them off. Until there wasn't more'n a couple of us left. And then they came in like vultures. And what they found they–'

'Sorry, Pop.' The soldiers had got lithely up, collected their lunches, and were moving toward the bench of girls. The girls glanced at them shyly and giggled in anticipation. 'We'll see you some other time.'

The old man turned and hobbled furiously back to his own bench. Disappointed, muttering under his breath and spitting into the wet bushes, he tried to make himself comfortable. But the sun irritated him; and the noises of people and cars made him sick.

He sat on the park bench, eye half shut, wasted lips twisted in a snarl of bitterness and defeat. Nobody was interested in a decrepit half-blind old man. Nobody wanted to hear his garbled, rambling tales of the battles he had fought and strategies he had witnessed. Nobody seemed to remember the war that still burned like a twisting, corroding fire in the decaying old man's brain. A war he longed to speak of, if he could only find listeners.

Vachel Patterson jerked his car to a halt and slammed on the emergency brake. 'That's that,' he said over his shoulder. 'Make yourselves comfortable. We're going to have a short wait.'

The scene was familiar. A thousand Earthmen in gray caps and armbands streamed along the street, chanting slogans, waving immense crude banners that were visible for blocks.

NO NEGOTIATION! TALK IS FOR TRAITORS!
ACTION IS FOR MEN!
DON'T TELL THEM SHOW THEM!
A STRONG EARTH IS THE BEST GUARANTEE OF PEACE!

In the back seat of the car Edwin LeMarr put aside his report tapes with a grunt of near-sighted surprise. 'Why have we stopped? What is it?'

'Another demonstration,' Evelyn Cutter said distantly. She leaned back and disgustedly lit a cigarette. 'Same as all of them.'

The demonstration was in full swing. Men, women, youths out of school for the afternoon, marched wild-faced, excited and intense, some with signs, some with crude weapons and in partial uniform. Along the sidewalks more and more watching spectators were being tugged along. Blue-clad policemen had halted surface traffic; they stood watching indifferently, waiting for somebody to try to interfere. Nobody did, of course. Nobody was that foolish.

'Why doesn't the Directorate put a stop to this?' LeMarr demanded. 'A couple of armored columns would finish this once and for all.'

Beside him, John V-Stephens laughed coldly. 'The Directorate finances it, organizes it, gives it free time on the vidnet, even beats up people who complain. Look at those cops standing over there. Waiting for somebody to beat up.'

LeMarr blinked. 'Patterson, is that true?'

Rage-distorted faces loomed up beyond the hood of the sleek '64 Buick. The tramp of feet made the chrome dashboard rattle; Doctor LeMarr tugged his tapes nervously into their metal case and peered around like a frightened turtle.

'What are you worried about?' V-Stephens said harshly. 'They wouldn't touch you—you're an Earthman. I'm the one who should be sweating.'

'They're crazy,' LeMarr muttered. 'All those morons chanting and marching—'

'They're not morons,' Patterson answered mildly. 'They're just too trusting. They believe what they're told, like the rest of us. The only trouble is, what *they're* told isn't true.'

He indicated one of the gigantic banners, a vast 3-D photograph that twisted and turned as it was carried forward. 'Blame *him*. He's the one who thinks up the lies. He's the one who puts the pressure on the Directorate, fabricates the hate and violence—and has the funds to sell it.'

The banner showed a stern-browed white-haired gentleman, clean-shaven and dignified. A scholarly man, heavy-set, in his late fifties. Kindly blue eyes, firm jawline, an impressive and respected dignitary. Under his handsome portrait was his personal slogan, coined in a moment of inspiration.

ONLY TRAITORS COMPROMISE!

'That's Francis Gannet,' V-Stephens said to LeMarr. 'Fine figure of a man, isn't he?' He corrected himself. 'Of an *Earth*man.'

'He looks so genteel,' Evelyn Cutter protested. 'How could an intelligent-looking man like that have anything to do with this?'

V-Stephens bellowed with taut laughter. 'His nice clean white hands are a lot filthier than any of those plumbers and carpenters marching out there.'

'But why—'

'Gannet and his group own Transplan Industries, a holding company that controls most of the export–import business of the inner worlds. If my people and the Martian people are given their independence they'll start cutting into his trade. They'll be competition. But as it stands, they're bottled up in a cold-decked mercantile system.'

The demonstrators had reached an intersection. A group of them dropped their banners and sprouted clubs and rocks. They shouted orders, waved the others on, and then headed grimly for a small modern building that blinked the word COLOR-AD in neon lights.

'Oh, God,' Patterson said. 'They're after the Color-Ad office.' He grabbed at the door handle, but V-Stephens stopped him.

'You can't do anything,' V-Stephens said. 'Anyhow, nobody's in there. They usually get advance warning.'

The rioters smashed the plate-plastic windows and poured into the swank little store. The police sauntered over, arms folded, enjoying the spectacle. From the ruined front office, smashed furniture was tossed out onto the sidewalks. Files, desks, chairs, vidscreens, ashtrays, even gay posters of happy life on the inner worlds. Acrid black fingers of smoke curled up as the store room was ignited by a hot-beam. Presently the rioters came streaming back out, satiated and happy.

Along the sidewalk, people watched with a variety of emotions. Some showed delight. Some a vague curiosity. But most showed fear and dismay. They backed hurriedly away as the wild-faced rioters pushed brutally past them, loaded down with stolen goods.

'See?' Patterson said. 'This stuff is done by a few thousand, a Committee Gannet's financing. Those in front are employees of Gannet's factories, goon squads on extracurricular duty. They try to sound like Mankind, but they aren't. They're a noisy minority, a small bunch of hard-working fanatics.'

The demonstration was breaking up. The Color-Ad office was a dismal fire-gutted ruin; traffic had been stopped; most of downtown New York had seen the lurid slogans and heard the tramp of feet and shouted hate. People began drifting back into offices and shops, back to their daily routine.

And then the rioters saw the Venusian girl, crouched in the locked and bolted doorway.

Patterson gunned the car forward. Bucking and grinding savagely, it hurtled across the street and up on the sidewalk, toward the running knot of dark-faced hoods. The nose of the car caught the first wave of them and tossed them like leaves. The rest collided with the metal hull and tumbled down in a shapeless mass of struggling arms and legs.

The Venusian girl saw the car sliding toward her—and the Earth-people in the front seat. For a moment she crouched in paralyzed terror. Then she turned and scurried off in panic, down the sidewalk and into the milling throng that filled up the street. The rioters regrouped themselves and in an instant were after her in full cry.

'Get the webfoot!'

'Webfoots back to their own planet!'

'Earth for Earthmen!'

And beneath the chanted slogans, the ugly undercurrent of unverbalized lust and hate.

Patterson backed the car up and onto the street. His fist clamped savagely over the horn, he gunned the car after the girl, abreast with the loping rioters and then past them. A rock crashed off the rear-view window and for an instant a hail of rubbish banged and clattered. Ahead, the crowd separated aimlessly, leaving an open path for the car and the rioters. No hand was lifted against the desperately running girl as she raced sobbing and panting between parked cars and groups of people. And nobody made a move to help her. Everybody watched dull-eyed and detached. Remote spectators viewing an event in which they had no part.

'I'll get her,' V-Stephens said. 'Pull up in front of her and I'll head her off.'

Patterson passed the girl and jammed on the brakes. The girl doubled off the street like a terrified hare. V-Stephens was out of the car in a single bound. He sprinted after her as she darted mindlessly back toward the rioters. He swept her up and then plunged back to the car. LeMarr and Evelyn Cutter dragged the two of them in; and Patterson sent the car bucking ahead.

A moment later he turned a corner, snapped a police rope, and passed beyond the danger zone. The roar of people, the flap-flap of feet against the pavement, died down behind them.

'It's all right,' V-Stephens was saying gently and repeatedly to the girl. 'We're friends. Look, I'm a webfoot, too.'

The girl was huddled against the door of the car, green eyes wide with terror, thin face convulsed, knees pulled up against her stomach. She was perhaps seventeen years old. Her webbed fingers scrabbled aimlessly with the torn collar of her blouse. One shoe was missing. Her face was scratched, dark hair disheveled. From her trembling mouth only vague sounds came.

LeMarr took her pulse. 'Her heart's about to pop out of her,' he muttered. From his coat he took an emergency capsule and shot a narcotic into the girl's trembling forearm. 'That'll relax her. She's not harmed—they didn't get to her.'

'It's all right,' V-Stephens murmured. 'We're doctors from the City Hospital, all but Miss Cutter, who manages the files and records. Doctor LeMarr is a neurologist, Doctor Patterson is a cancer specialist, I'm a surgeon—see my hand?' He traced the girl's forehead with his surgeon's hand. 'And I'm a Venusian, like you. We'll take you to the hospital and keep you there for a while.'

'Did you see them?' LeMarr sputtered. 'Nobody lifted a finger to help her. They just stood there.'

'They were afraid,' Patterson said. 'They want to avoid trouble.'

'They can't,' Evelyn Cutter said flatly. 'Nobody can avoid this kind of trouble. They can't keep standing on the sidelines watching. This isn't a football game.'

'What's going to happen?' the girl quavered.

'You better get off Earth,' V-Stephens said gently. 'No Venusian is safe here. Get back to your own planet and stay there until this thing dies down.'

'Will it?' the girl gasped.

'Eventually.' V-Stephens reached down and passed her Evelyn's cigarette. 'It can't go on like this. We have to be free.'

'Take it easy,' Evelyn said in a dangerous voice. Her eyes faded to hostile coals. 'I thought you were above all this.'

V-Stephens' dark green face flushed. 'You think I can stand idly by while my people are killed and insulted, and our interests passed over, ignored so paste-faces like Gannet can get rich on blood squeezed from—'

'Paste-face,' LeMarr echoed wonderingly. 'What's that mean, Vachel?'

'That's their word for Earthmen,' Patterson answered. 'Can it, V-Stephens. As far as we're concerned it's not your people and our people. We're all the same race. Your ancestors were Earthmen who settled Venus back in the late twentieth century.'

'The changes are only minor adaptive alterations,' LeMarr assured V-Stephens. 'We can still interbreed—that proves we're the same race.'

'We can,' Evelyn Cutter said thinly. 'But who wants to marry a webfoot or a crow?'

Nobody said anything for a while. The air in the car was tense with hostility as Patterson sped toward the hospital. The Venusian girl sat crouched, smoking silently, her terrified eyes on the vibrating floor.

Patterson slowed down at the check-point and showed his i.d. tab. The hospital guard signaled the car ahead and he picked up speed. As he put his tab away his fingers touched something clipped to the inside of his pocket. Sudden memory returned.

'Here's something to take your mind off your troubles,' he said to V-Stephens. He tossed the sealed tube back to the webfoot. 'Military fired it back this morning. Clerical error. When you're through with it hand it over to Evelyn. It's supposed to go to her, but I got interested.'

V-Stephens slit open the tube and spilled out the contents. It was a routine application for admission to a Government hospital, stamped with the number of a war veteran. Old sweat-grimed tapes, papers torn and mutilated throughout the years. Greasy bits of metal foil that had been folded and refolded, stuffed in a shirt pocket, carried next to some filthy, hair-matted chest. 'Is this important?' V-Stephens asked impatiently. 'Do we have to worry over clerical trifles?'

Patterson halted the car in the hospital parking lot and turned off the motor. 'Look at the number of the application,' he said, as he pushed open the car door. 'When you have time to examine it you'll find something unusual. The applicant is carrying around an old veteran's i.d. card—with a number that hasn't been issued yet.'

LeMarr, hopelessly baffled, looked from Evelyn Cutter to V-Stephens, but got no explanation.

The old man's h-loop awoke him from a fitful slumber. 'David Unger,' the tinny female voice repeated. 'You are wanted back at the hospital. It is requested that you return to the hospital immediately.'

The old man grunted and pulled himself up with an effort. Grabbing his aluminum cane he hobbled away from his sweat-shiny bench, toward the escape ramp of the park. Just when he was getting to sleep, shutting out the too-bright sun and the shrill laughter of children and girls and young soldiers . . .

At the edge of the park two shapes crept furtively into the bushes. David Unger halted and stood in disbelief, as the shapes glided past him along the path.

His voice surprised him. He was screaming at the top of his lungs, shrieks of rage and revulsion that echoed through the park, among the quiet trees and lawns. '*Webfoots!*' he wailed. He began to run clumsily after them. 'Webfoots and crows! Help! Somebody help!'

Waving his aluminum cane, he hobbled after the Martian and Venusian, panting wildly. People appeared, blank-faced with astonishment. A crowd formed, as the old man hurried after the terrified pair. Exhausted, he stumbled against a drinking fountain and half-fell, his cane sliding from his fingers. His shrunken face was livid; the burn-scar stood out sick and ugly against the mottled skin. His good eye was red with hate and fury. From his wasted lips saliva drooled. He waved his skinny claw-like hands futilely, as the two altereds crept into the grove of cedars toward the far end of the park.

'Stop them!' David Unger slobbered. 'Don't let them get away! What's the matter with you? You bunch of lily-white cowards. What kind of men are you?'

'Take it easy, Pop,' a young soldier said good-naturedly. 'They're not hurting anybody.'

Unger retrieved his cane and whooshed it past the soldier's head. 'You–*talker*,' he snapped. 'What kind of a soldier are you?' A fit of coughing choked off his words; he bent double, struggling to breathe. 'In my day,' he managed to gasp, 'we poured rocket fuel on them and strung them up. We mutilated them. We cut up the dirty webfoots and crows. We showed them.'

A looming cop had stopped the pair of altereds. 'Get going,' he ordered ominously. 'You things got no right here.'

The two altereds scuttled past him. The cop leisurely raised his stick and cracked the Martian across the eyes. The brittle, thin-shelled head splintered, and the Martian careened on, blinded and in agony.

'That's more like it,' David Unger gasped, in weak satisfaction.

'You evil dirty old man,' a woman muttered at him, face white with horror. 'It's people like you that make all this trouble.'

'What are you?' Unger snapped. 'A crow-lover?'

The crowd melted and broke. Unger, grasping his cane, stumbled toward the exit ramp, muttering curses and abuse, spitting violently into the bushes and shaking his head.

He arrived at the hospital grounds still trembling with rage and resentment. 'What do you want?' he demanded, as he came up to the big receiving desk in the center of the main lobby. 'I don't know what's going on around here. First you wake me out of the first real sleep I've had since I got here, and then what do I see but two web-foots walking around in broad daylight, sassy as—'

'Doctor Patterson wants you,' the nurse said patiently. 'Room 301.' She nodded to a robot. 'Take Mr Unger down to 301.'

The old man hobbled sullenly after the smoothly-gliding robot. 'I thought all you tinmen were used up in the Europa battle of '88,' he complained. 'It don't make sense, all these lily-white boys in uniforms. Everybody wandering around having a good time, laughing and diddling girls with nothing better to do than lie around on the grass naked. Something's the matter. Something must be—'

'In here, sir,' the robot said, and the door of 301 slid away.

Vachel Patterson rose slightly as the old man entered and stood fuming and gripping his aluminum cane in front of the work-desk. It was the first time he had seen David Unger face to face. Each of them sized the other up intently; the thin hawk-faced old soldier and the well-dressed young doctor, black thinning hair, horn-rimmed glasses and good-natured face. Beside his desk Evelyn Cutter stood watching and listening impassively, a cigarette between her red lips, blond hair swept back.

'I'm Doctor Patterson, and this is Miss Cutter.' Patterson toyed with the dog-eared, eroded tape strewn across his desk. 'Sit down, Mr Unger. I want to ask you a couple of questions. Some uncertainty

has come up regarding one of your papers. A routine error, probably, but they've come back to me.'

Unger seated himself warily. 'Questions and red tape. I've been
here a week and every day it's something. Maybe I should have just
laid there in the street and died.'

'You've been here eight days, according to this.'

'I suppose so. If it says so there, must be true.' The old man's
thin sarcasm boiled out viciously. 'Couldn't put it down if it wasn't
true.'

'You were admitted as a war veteran. All costs of care and maintenance are covered by the Directorate.'

Unger bristled. 'What's wrong with that? I earned a little care.'
He leaned toward Patterson and jabbed a crabbed finger at him. 'I
was in the Service when I was sixteen. Fought and worked for
Earth all my life. Would be there yet, if I hadn't been half killed by
that dirty mop-up attack of theirs. Lucky to be alive at all.' He
self-consciously rubbed the livid ruin of his face. 'Looks like you
weren't even in it. Didn't know there *was* any place got by.'

Patterson and Evelyn Cutter looked at each other. 'How old are
you?' Evelyn asked suddenly.

'Don't it say?' Unger muttered furiously. 'Eighty-nine.'

'And the year of your birth?'

'2154. Can't you figure that?'

Patterson made a faint notation on the metal foil reports. 'And
your unit?'

At that, Unger broke loose. 'The Ba-3, if maybe you've heard of
it. Although the way things are around here, I wonder if you know
there was ever a war.'

'The Ba-3,' Patterson repeated. 'And you served with them how
long?'

'Fifty years. Then I retired. The first time, I mean. I was sixty-six
years old. Usual age. Got my pension and bit of land.'

'And they called you back?'

'Of course they called me back! Don't you remember how the
Ba-3 went back into the line, all us old guys, and damn near stopped

them, the last time? You must have been just a kid, but everybody knows what we did.' Unger fumbled out his Crystal Disc first class and slammed it on the desk. 'I got *that*. All us survivors did. All ten of us, out of thirty thousand.' He gathered the medal up with shaking fingers. 'I was hurt bad. You see my face. Burned, when Nathan West's battleship blew up. I was in the military hospital for a couple years. That was when they cracked Earth wide open.' The ancient hands clenched into futile fists. 'We had to sit there, watching them turn Earth into a smoking ruin. Nothing but slag and ash, miles of death. No towns, no cities. We sat there, while their C-missiles whizzed by. Finally they got finished—and got us on Luna, too.'

Evelyn Cutter tried to speak, but no words came. At his workdesk Patterson's face had turned chalk-white. 'Continue,' he managed to mutter. 'Go on talking.'

'We hung on there, subsurface, down under the Copernicus crater, while they slammed their C-missiles into us. We held out maybe five years. Then they started landing. Me and those still left took off in high-speed attack torpedoes, set up pirate bases among the outer planets.' Unger twitched restlessly. 'I hate to talk about that part. Defeat, the end of everything. Why do you ask me? I helped build 3-4-9-5, the best artibase of the lot. Between Uranus and Neptune. Then I retired again. Until the dirty rats slid in and *leisurely* blew it to bits. Fifty thousand men, women, kids. The whole colony.'

'You escaped?' Evelyn Cutter whispered.

'Of course I escaped! I was on patrol. I got one of those webfoot ships. Shot it down and watched them die. It made me feel a little better. I moved over to 3-6-7-7 for a few years. Until it was attacked. That was early this month. I was fighting with my back to the wall.' The dirty yellow teeth glinted in agony. 'No place to escape to, that time. None that I knew of.' The red-rimmed eye surveyed the luxurious office. 'Didn't know about this. You people sure done a good job fixing up your artibase. Looks almost like I remember the real Earth. A little too fast and bright; not so peaceful as Earth really was. But you even got the smell of the air the same.'

There was silence.

'Then you came here after—that colony was destroyed?' Patterson asked hoarsely.

'I guess so.' Unger shrugged wearily. 'Last I remember was the bubble shattering and the air and heat and grav leaking out. Crow and webfoot ships landing everywhere. Men dying around me. I was knocked out by the concussion. The next thing I knew I was lying out in the street here, and some people were getting me to my feet. A tinman and one of your doctors took me here.'

Patterson let out a deep shuddering breath. 'I see.' His fingers plucked aimlessly at the eroded, sweat-grimed i.d. papers. 'Well, that explains this irregularity.'

'Ain't it all there? Is something missing?'

'All your papers are here. Your tube was hanging around your wrist when they brought you in.'

'Naturally.' Unger's bird-like chest swelled with pride. 'I learned that when I was sixteen. Even when you're dead you have to have that tube with you. Important to keep the records straight.'

'The records are straight,' Patterson admitted thickly. 'You can go back to your room. Or the park. Anywhere.' He waved and the robot calmly escorted the withered old man from the office and out into the hall.

As the door slid shut Evelyn Cutter began swearing slowly and monotonously. She crushed out her cigarette with her sharp heel and paced wildly back and forth. 'Good God what have we got ourselves into?'

Patterson snatched up the intervid, dialed outside, and said to the supra-plan monitor, 'Get me military headquarters. Right away.'

'At Luna, sir?'

'That's right,' Patterson said. 'At the main base on Luna.'

On the wall of the office, past the taut, pacing figure of Evelyn Cutter, the calendar read August 4, 2169. If David Unger was born in 2154 he would be a boy of fifteen. And he *had* been born in 2154. It said so on his battered, yellowed, sweat-stained cards. On the i.d. papers carried through a war that hadn't yet happened.

*

'He's a veteran, all right,' Patterson said to V-Stephens. 'Of a war that won't begin for another month. No wonder his application was turned back by the IBM machines.'

V-Stephens licked his dark green lips. 'This war will be between Earth and the two colony planets. And Earth will lose?'

'Unger fought through the whole war. He saw it from the start to finish—to the total destruction of Earth.' Patterson paced over to the window and gazed out. 'Earth lost the war and the race of Earthmen was wiped out.'

From the window of V-Stephens' office, Patterson could see the city spread out. Miles of buildings, white and gleaming in the late-afternoon sun. Eleven million people. A gigantic center of commerce and industry, the economic hub of the system. And beyond it, a world of cities and farms and highways, three billion men and women. A thriving, healthy planet, the mother world from which the altereds had originally sprung, the ambitious settlers of Venus and Mars. Endless cargo carriers lumbered between Earth and the colonies, weighed down with minerals and ores and produce. And already, survey teams were poking around the outer planets, laying claim in the Directorate's name to new sources of raw materials.

'He saw all this go up in radioactive dust,' Patterson said. 'He saw the final attack on Earth that broke our defenses. And then they wiped out the Lunar base.'

'You say some brass hats are on their way here from Luna?'

'I gave them enough of the story to start them moving. It usually takes weeks to stir up those fellows.'

'I'd like to see this Unger,' V-Stephens said thoughtfully. 'Is there some way I can—'

'You've seen him. You revived him, remember? When he was originally found and brought in.'

'Oh,' V-Stephens said softly. 'That filthy old man?' His dark eyes flickered. 'So that's Unger . . . the veteran of the war we're going to fight.'

'The war you're going to win. The war Earth is going to lose.' Patterson abruptly left the window. 'Unger thinks this is an artificial satellite someplace between Uranus and Neptune. A reconstruction of a small part of New York—a few thousand people and machines under a plastic dome. He has no conception of what's actually happened to him. Somehow, he must have been hurled back along his time-track.'

'I suppose the release of energy . . . and maybe his frantic desire to escape. But even so, the whole thing is fantastic. It has a sort of—' V-Stephens groped for the word. '—a sort of mystic ring to it. What the hell is this, a visitation? A prophet from heaven?'

The door opened and V-Rafia slid in. 'Oh,' she said, as she saw Patterson. 'I didn't know—'

'That's all right.' V-Stephens nodded her inside his office. 'You remember Patterson. He was with us in the car when we picked you up.'

V-Rafia looked much better than she had a few hours before. Her face was no longer scratched, her hair was back in place, and she had changed to a crisp gray sweater and skirt. Her green skin sparkled as she moved over beside V-Stephens, still nervous and apprehensive. 'I'm staying here,' she said defensively to Patterson. 'I can't go back out there, not for a while.' She darted a quick glance of appeal at V-Stephens.

'She has no family on Earth,' V-Stephens explained. 'She came here as a Class-2 biochemist. She's been working over at a Westinghouse lab outside Chicago. She came to New York on a shopping trip, which was a mistake.'

'Can't she join the V-colony at Denver?' Patterson asked.

V-Stephens flushed. 'You don't want another webfoot around here?'

'What can she do? We're not an embattled fortress. There's no reason why we can't shoot her to Denver in a fast freight rocket. Nobody'll interfere with that.'

'We can discuss it later,' V-Stephens said irritably. 'We've got more important things to talk about. You've made a check of Unger's papers? You're certain they're not forgeries? I suppose it's possible this is on the level, but we have to be certain.'

'This has to be kept quiet,' Patterson said urgently, with a glance at V-Rafia. 'Nobody on the outside should be brought in.'

'You mean me?' V-Rafia asked hesitantly. 'I guess I better leave.'

'Don't leave,' V-Stephens said, grabbing hold of her arm roughly. 'Patterson, you can't keep this quiet. Unger's probably told it to fifty people; he sits out there on his park bench all day, buttonholing everybody who passes.'

'What is this?' V-Rafia asked curiously.

'Nothing important,' Patterson said warningly.

'Nothing important?' V-Stephens echoed. 'Just a little war. Programs for sale in advance.' Across his face a spasm of emotion passed, excitement and yearning hunger pouring up from inside him. 'Place your bets *now*. Don't take chances. Bet on a sure thing, sweetheart. After all, it's history. Isn't that right?' He turned toward Patterson, his expression demanding confirmation. 'What do you say? I can't stop it—you can't stop it. Right?'

Patterson nodded slowly. 'I guess you're right,' he said unhappily. And swung with all his strength.

He caught V-Stephens slightly to one side, as the Venusian scrambled away. V-Stephens' cold-beam came out; he aimed with shaky fingers. Patterson kicked it from his hands and dragged him to his feet. 'It was a mistake, John,' he panted. 'I shouldn't have showed you Unger's i.d. tube. I shouldn't have let you know.'

'That's right,' V-Stephens managed to whisper. His eyes were blank with sorrow as he focused on Patterson. 'Now I know. Now we both know. *You're going to lose the war*. Even if you lock Unger up in a box and sink him to the center of the Earth, it's too late. Color-Ad will know as soon as I'm out of here.'

'They burned down the Color-Ad office in New York.'

'Then I'll find the one in Chicago. Or Baltimore. I'll fly back to Venus, if I have to. I'm going to spread the good news. It'll be hard and long, but we'll win. And you can't do anything about it.'

'I can kill you,' Patterson said. His mind was racing frantically. It wasn't too late. If V-Stephens were contained, and David Unger turned over to the Military—

'I know what you're thinking,' V-Stephens gasped. 'If Earth doesn't fight, if you avoid war, you may still have a chance.' His green lips twisted savagely. 'You think we'd *let* you avoid war? Not now! Only traitors compromise, according to you. Now it's too late!'

'Only too late,' Patterson said, 'if you get out of here.' His hand groped on the desk and found a steel paper weight. He drew it to him—and felt the smooth tip of the cold-beam in his ribs.

'I'm not sure how this thing works,' V-Rafia said slowly, 'but I guess there's only this one button to press.'

'That's right,' V-Stephens said, with relief. 'But don't press it yet. I want to talk to him a few minutes more. Maybe he can be brought around to rationality.' He pulled himself gratefully out of Patterson's grip and moved back a few paces, exploring his cut lip and broken front teeth. 'You brought this on yourself, Vachel.'

'This is insane,' Patterson snapped, his eyes on the snout of the cold-beam as it wavered in V-Rafia's uncertain fingers. 'You expect us to fight a war we know we're going to lose?'

'You won't have a choice.' V-Stephens' eyes gleamed. 'We'll make you fight. When we attack your cities you'll come back at us. It's—human nature.'

The first blast of the cold-beam missed Patterson. He floundered to one side and grabbed for the girl's slim wrist. His fingers caught air, and then he was down, as the beam hissed again. V-Rafia retreated, eyes wide with fright and dismay, aiming blindly for his rising body. He leaped up, hands extended for the terrified girl. He saw her fingers twist, saw the snout of the tube darken as the field clicked on. And that was all.

From the kicked-open door, the blue-clad soldiers caught V-Rafia in a crossfire of death. A chill breath mushroomed in Patterson's face. He collapsed back, arms up frantically, as the frigid whisper glided past him.

V-Rafia's trembling body danced briefly, as the cloud of absolute cold glowed around her. Then abruptly she halted as rigid as if the tape-track of her life had stopped in the projector. All color drained from her body. The bizarre imitation of a still-standing human figure stood silently, one arm raised, caught in the act of futile defense.

Then the frozen pillar burst. The expanded cells ruptured in a shower of crystalline particles that were hurled sickeningly into every part of the office.

Francis Gannet moved cautiously in behind the troops, red-faced and perspiring. 'You're Patterson?' he demanded. He held out his heavy hand, but Patterson didn't take it. 'The Military people notified me as a matter of course. Where's this old man?'

'Somewhere around,' Patterson muttered. 'Under guard.' He turned toward V-Stephens and briefly their eyes met. 'You see?' he said huskily. 'This is what happens. Is this what you really want?'

'Come on, Mr Patterson,' Francis Gannet boomed impatiently. 'I don't have much time to waste. From your description this sounds like something important.'

'It is,' V-Stephens answered calmly. He wiped at the trickle of mouth-blood with his pocket handkerchief. 'It's worth the trip from Luna. Take my word for it—I *know*.'

The man who sat on Gannet's right was a lieutenant. He gazed in mute awe at the vidscreen. His young, handsome blond face was alive with amazement as from the bank of gray haze a huge battle-ship lumbered, one reactor smashed, its forward turrets crumpled, hull twisted open.

'Good God,' Lieutenant Nathan West said faintly. 'That's the *Wind Giant*. The biggest battleship we have. Look at it—it's out of commission. Totally disabled.'

'That will be your ship,' Patterson said. 'You'll be commander of it in '87 when it's destroyed by the combined Venusian and Martian fleets. David Unger will be serving under you. You'll be killed, but Unger will escape. The few survivors of your ship will watch from Luna as Earth is systematically demolished by C-missiles from Venus and Mars.'

On the screen, the figures leaped and swirled like fish in the bottom of a dirt-saturated tank. A violent maelstrom surged in the center, a vortex of energy that lashed the ships on vast spasms of motion. The silver Earth ships hesitated, then broke. Flashing black Mars battleships swept through the wide breach—and the Earth flank was turned simultaneously by the waiting Venusians. Together, they caught the remnants of the Earth ships in a steel pincers and crunched them out of existence. Brief puffs of light, as the ships winked out of being. In the distance, the solemn blue and green orb that was Earth slowly and majestically revolved.

Already, it showed ugly pocks. Bomb craters from the C-missiles that had penetrated the defense network.

LeMarr snapped off the projector and the screen died. 'That ends that brain-sequence. All we can get are visual fragments like this, brief instants that left strong impressions on him. We can't get continuity. The next one takes up years later, on one of the artificial satellites.'

The lights came on, and the group of spectators moved stiffly to their feet. Gannet's face was a sickly putty-gray. 'Doctor LeMarr, I want to see that shot again. The one of Earth.' He gestured helplessly. 'You know which one I mean.'

The lights dimmed and again the screen came to life. This time it showed only Earth, a receding orb that fell behind as the high-velocity torpedo on which David Unger rode hurtled toward outer space. Unger had placed himself so his dead world would be visible to the last.

Earth was a ruin. Involuntarily, a gasp rose from the group of watching officers. Nothing lived. Nothing moved. Only dead clouds of radioactive ash billowed aimlessly over the crater-pocked surface. What had been a living planet of three billion people was a charred cinder of ash. Nothing remained but heaps of debris, dispersed and blown dismally across vacant seas by the howling, ceaseless wind.

'I suppose some kind of vegetable life will take over,' Evelyn

Cutter said harshly, as the screen faded and the overhead lights returned. She shuddered violently and turned away.

'Weeds, maybe,' LeMarr said. 'Dark dry weeds poking up through the slag. Maybe some insects, later on. Bacteria, of course. I suppose in time bacterial action will transform the ash into usable soil. And it'll rain for a billion years.'

'Let's face it,' Gannet said. 'The webfoots and crows will resettle it. They'll be living here on Earth after we're all dead.'

'Sleeping in our beds?' LeMarr inquired mildly. 'Using our bathrooms and sitting rooms and transports?'

'I don't understand you,' Gannet answered impatiently. He waved Patterson over. 'You're sure nobody knows but we here in this room?'

'V-Stephens knows,' Patterson said. 'But he's locked up in the psychotic ward. V-Rafia knew. She's dead.'

Lieutenant West came over to Patterson. 'Could we interview him?'

'Yes, where's Unger?' Gannet demanded. 'My staff is eager to meet him face to face.'

'You have all the essential facts,' Patterson answered. 'You know how the war is going to come out. You know what's going to happen to Earth.'

'What do you suggest?' Gannet asked warily.

'Avoid the war.'

Gannet shrugged his plump well-fed body. 'After all, you can't change history. And this is future history. We have no choice but to go ahead and fight.'

'At least we'll get our share of them,' Evelyn Cutter said icily.

'What are you talking about?' LeMarr stuttered excitedly. 'You work in a hospital and you talk like that?'

The woman's eyes blazed. 'You saw what they did to Earth. You saw them cut us to ribbons.'

'We have to stand above this,' LeMarr protested. 'If we allow ourselves to get dragged into this hate and violence—' He appealed to Patterson. 'Why is V-Stephens locked up? He's no crazier than she is.'

'True,' Patterson agreed. 'But she's crazy on *our* side. We don't lock up that kind of lunatic.'

LeMarr moved away from him. 'Are you going out to fight, too? Alongside Gannet and his soldiers?'

'I want to avoid the war,' Patterson said dully.

'Can it be done?' Gannet demanded. An avid glow winked briefly behind his pale, blue eyes and then faded out.

'Maybe it can be done. Why not? Unger coming back here adds a new element.'

'If the future can be changed,' Gannet said slowly, 'then maybe we have a choice of various possibilities. If there's two possible futures there may be an infinite number. Each branching off at a different point.' A granite mask slid over his face. 'We can use Unger's knowledge of the battles.'

'Let me talk to him,' Lieutenant West interrupted excitedly. 'Maybe we can get a clear idea of the webfoot battle-strategy. He's probably gone over the battles in his mind a thousand times.'

'He'd recognize you,' Gannet said. 'After all, he served under your command.'

Patterson was deep in thought. 'I don't think so,' he said to West. 'You're a lot older than David Unger.'

West blinked. 'What do you mean? He's a broken-down old man and I'm still in my twenties.'

'David Unger is fifteen,' Patterson answered. 'At this point you're almost twice his age. You're already a commissioned officer on the Lunar policy-level staff. Unger isn't even in the Military Service. He'll volunteer when war breaks out, as a buck private without experience or training. When you're an old man, commanding the *Wind Giant*, David Unger will be a middle-aged nonentity working one of the gun turrets, a name you won't even know.'

'Then Unger is already alive?' Gannet said, puzzled.

'Unger is someplace around, waiting to step onto the stage.' Patterson filed the thought away for future study; it might have valuable possibilities. 'I don't think he'll recognize you, West. He may never even have seen you. The *Wind Giant* is a big ship.'

West quickly agreed. 'Put a bug-system on me, Gannet. So the command staff can have the aud and vid images of what Unger says.'

In the bright mid-morning sunlight, David Unger sat moodily on his park bench, gnarled fingers gripping his aluminum cane, gazing dully at the passers-by.

To his right a robot gardener worked over the same patch of grass again and again, its metallic eye-lenses intently fastened on the wizened, hunched-over figure of the old man. Down the gravel path a group of loitering men sent random comments to the various monitors scattered through the park, keeping the relay system open. A bare-bosomed young woman sunbathing by the pool nodded faintly to a pair of soldiers pacing around the park, within constant sight of David Unger.

That morning there were a hundred people in the park. All were integrated elements of the screen surrounding the half-dozing, resentful old man.

'All right,' Patterson said. His car was parked at the edge of the plot of green trees and lawns. 'Remember not to overexcite him. V-Stephens revived him originally. If something goes wrong with his heart we can't get V-Stephens to pump him back.'

The blond young lieutenant nodded, straightened his immaculate blue tunic and slid onto the sidewalk. He pushed his helmet back and briskly strode down the gravel path, toward the center of the park. As he approached, the lounging figures moved imperceptibly. One by one they took up positions on the lawns, on the benches, in groups here and there around the pool.

Lieutenant West stopped at a drinking-fountain and allowed the robot water-brain to find his mouth with a jet of ice-cold spray. He wandered slowly away and stood for a moment, arms loose at his sides, vacantly watching a young woman as she removed her clothes and stretched out languidly on a multi-colored blanket. Her eyes shut, red lips parted, the woman relaxed with a grateful sigh.

'Let him speak to you first,' she said faintly, to the lieutenant standing a few feet from her, one black boot on the edge of a bench. 'Don't start the conversation.'

Lieutenant West watched her a moment longer and then continued along the path. A passing heavy-set man said swiftly in his ear, 'Not so fast. Take your time and don't appear to hurry.'

'You want to give the impression you have all day,' a hatchet-faced nurse grated, as she passed him wheeling a baby carriage.

Lieutenant West slowed almost to a halt. He aimlessly kicked a bit of gravel from the path into the wet bushes. Hands deep in his pockets he wandered over to the central pool and stood gazing absently into its depths. He lit a cigarette, then bought an ice cream bar from a passing robot salesman.

'Spill some on your tunic, sir,' the robot's speaker instructed faintly. 'Swear and start dabbing at it.'

Lieutenant West let the ice cream melt in the warm summer sun. When some had dripped down his wrist onto his starched blue tunic he scowled, dug out his handkerchief, dipped it in the pool, and began clumsily to wipe the ice cream away.

On his bench, the scar-faced old man watched with his one good eye, gripping his aluminum cane and cackling happily. 'Watch out,' he wheezed. 'Look out there!'

Lieutenant West glanced up in annoyance.

'You're dripping more,' the old man cackled, and lay back in weak amusement, toothless mouth slack with pleasure.

Lieutenant West grinned good-naturedly. 'I guess so,' he admitted. He dropped the melting half-eaten ice cream bar into a disposal slot and finished cleaning his tunic. 'Sure is warm,' he observed, wandering vaguely over.

'They do a good job,' Unger agreed, nodding his bird-like head. He peered and craned his neck, trying to make out the insignia markings on the young soldier's shoulder. 'You with the rocketeers?'

'Demolition,' Lieutenant West said. As of that morning his insignia had been changed. 'Ba-3.'

The old man shuddered. He hawked and spat feverishly into

the nearby bushes. 'That so?' He half-rose, excited and fearful, as the lieutenant started to move away. 'Say, you know, I was in the Ba-3 years ago.' He tried to make his voice sound calm and casual. 'Long before your time.'

Amazement and disbelief slid over Lieutenant West's handsome blond face. 'Don't kid me. Only a couple guys from the old group are still alive. You're pulling my leg.'

'I was, I was,' Unger wheezed, fumbling with trembling haste at his coat pocket. 'Say, look at this. Stop a minute and I'll show you something.' Reverent and awed, he held out his Crystal Disc. 'See? You know what this is?'

Lieutenant West gazed down at the metal a long time. Real emotion welled up inside him; he didn't have to counterfeit it. 'Can I examine it?' he asked finally.

Unger hesitated. 'Sure,' he said. 'Take it.'

Lieutenant West took the medal and held it for a long moment, weighing it and feeling its cold surface against his smooth skin. Finally he returned it. 'You got that back in '87?'

'That's right,' Unger said. 'You remember?' He returned it to his pocket. 'No, you weren't even alive, then. But you heard about it, haven't you?'

'Yes,' West said. 'I've heard about it many times.'

'And you haven't forgotten? A lot of people forgot that, what we did there.'

'I guess we took a beating that day,' West said. He sat down slowly on the bench beside the old man. 'That was a bad day for Earth.'

'We lost,' Unger agreed. 'Only a few of us got out of there. I got to Luna. I saw Earth go, piece by piece, until there was nothing left. It broke my heart. I cried until I lay like a dead thing. We were all weeping, soldiers, workmen, standing there helpless. And then they turned their missiles on us.'

The lieutenant licked his dry lips. 'Your Commander didn't get out, did he?'

'Nathan West died on his ship,' Unger said. 'He was the finest commander in the line. They didn't give him the *Wind Giant* for nothing.' His ancient, withered features dimmed in recollection. 'There'll never be another man like West. I saw him, once. Big stern-faced man, wide-shouldered. A giant himself. He was a great old man. Nobody could have done better.'

West hesitated. 'You think if somebody else had been in command—'

'*No!*' Unger shrieked. 'Nobody could have done better! I've heard it said—I know what some of those fat-bottomed armchair strategists say. But they're wrong! Nobody could have won that battle. We didn't have a chance. We were outnumbered five to one—two huge fleets, one straight at our middle and the other waiting to chew us up and swallow us.'

'I see,' West said thickly. Reluctantly he continued, in an agony of turmoil, 'These armchair men, what the hell is it they say? I never listen to the brass.' He tried to grin but his face refused to respond. 'I know they're always saying we could have won the battle and maybe even saved the *Wind Giant,* but I—'

'Look here,' Unger said fervently, his sunken eye wild and glittering. With the point of his aluminum cane he began gouging harsh, violent ditches in the gravel by his feet. 'This line is our fleet. Remember how West had it drawn up? It was a mastermind arranged our fleet, that day. A genius. We held them off for twelve hours before they busted through. Nobody thought we'd have a chance of even doing that.' Savagely, Unger gouged another line. 'That's the crow fleet.'

'I see,' West muttered. He leaned over so his chest-lens would vid the rough lines in the gravel back to the scanning center in the mobile unit circling lazily overhead. And from there to main headquarters on Luna. 'And the webfoot fleet?'

Unger glanced cagily at him, suddenly shy. 'I'm not boring you, am I? I guess an old man likes to talk. Sometimes I bother people, trying to take up their time.'

'Go on,' West answered. He meant what he said. 'Keep drawing—I'm watching.'

*

Evelyn Cutter paced restlessly around her softly-lit apartment, arms folded, red lips tight with anger. 'I don't understand you!' She paused to lower the heavy drapes. 'You were willing to kill V-Stephens a little while ago. Now you won't even help block LeMarr. You know LeMarr doesn't grasp what's happening. He dislikes Gannet and he prattles about the interplan community of scientists, our duty to all mankind and that sort of stuff. Can't you see if V-Stephens gets hold of him–'

'Maybe LeMarr is right,' Patterson said. 'I don't like Gannet either.'

Evelyn exploded. 'They'll destroy us! We can't fight a war with them—we don't have a chance.' She halted in front of him, eyes blazing. 'But they don't know that yet. We've got to neutralize LeMarr, at least for a while. Every minute he's walking around free puts our world in jeopardy. Three billion lives depend on keeping this suppressed.'

Patterson was brooding. 'I suppose Gannet briefed you on the initial exploration West conducted today.'

'No results so far. The old man knows every battle by heart, and we lost them all.' She rubbed her forehead wearily. 'I mean, we *will* lose them all.' With numb fingers she gathered up the empty coffee cups. 'Want some more coffee?'

Patterson didn't hear her; he was intent on his own thoughts. He crossed over to the window and stood gazing out until she returned with fresh coffee, hot and black and steaming.

'You didn't see Gannet kill that girl,' Patterson said.

'What girl? That webfoot?' Evelyn stirred sugar and cream into her coffee. 'She was going to kill you. V-Stephens would have lit out for Color-Ad and the war would begin.' Impatiently, she pushed his coffee cup to him. 'Anyhow, that was the girl we saved.'

'I know,' Patterson said. 'That's why it bothers me.' He took the coffee automatically and sipped without tasting. 'What was the point of dragging her from the mob? Gannet's work. We're employees of Gannet.'

'So?'

'You know what kind of game he's playing!'

Evelyn shrugged. 'I'm just being practical. I don't want Earth destroyed. Neither does Gannet—he wants to avoid the war.'

'He wanted war a few days ago. When he expected to win.'

Evelyn laughed sharply. 'Of course! Who'd fight a war they knew they'd lose? That's irrational.'

'Now Gannet will hold off the war,' Patterson admitted slowly. 'He'll let the colony planets have their independence. He'll recognize Color-Ad. He'll destroy David Unger and everybody who knows. He'll pose as a benevolent peacemaker.'

'Of course. He's already making plans for a dramatic trip to Venus. A last-minute conference with Color-Ad officials, to prevent war. He'll put pressure on the Directorate to back down and let Mars and Venus sever. He'll be the idol of the system. But isn't that better than Earth destroyed and our race wiped out?'

'Now the big machine turns around and roars *against* war.' Patterson's lips twisted ironically. 'Peace and compromise instead of hate and destructive violence.'

Evelyn perched on the arm of a chair and made rapid calculations. 'How old was David Unger when he joined the Military?'

'Fifteen or sixteen.'

'When a man joins the Service he gets his i.d. number, doesn't he?'

'That's right. So?'

'Maybe I'm wrong, but according to my figures—' She glanced up. 'Unger should appear and claim his number, soon. That number will be coming up any day, according to how fast the enlistments pour in.'

A strange expression crossed Patterson's face. 'Unger is already alive ... a fifteen-year-old kid. Unger the youth and Unger the senile old war veteran. Both alive at once.'

Evelyn shuddered. 'It's weird. Suppose they ran into each other? There'd be a lot of difference between them.'

In Patterson's mind a picture of a bright-eyed youth of fifteen formed. Eager to get into the fight. Ready to leap in and kill webfoots and crows with idealistic enthusiasm. At this moment, Unger was moving inexorably toward the recruiting office . . . and the half-blind, crippled old relic of eighty-nine wretched years was creeping hesitantly from his hospital room to his park bench, hugging his aluminum cane, whispering in his raspy, pathetic voice to anyone who would listen.

'We'll have to keep our eyes open,' Patterson said. 'You better have somebody at Military notify you when that number comes up. When Unger appears to claim it.'

Evelyn nodded. 'It might be a good idea. Maybe we should request the Census Department to make a check for us. Maybe we can locate–'

She broke off. The door of the apartment had swung silently open. Edwin LeMarr stood gripping the knob, blinking red-eyed in the half-light. Breathing harshly, he came into the room. 'Vachel, I have to talk to you.'

'What is it?' Patterson demanded. 'What's going on?'

LeMarr shot Evelyn a look of pure hate. 'He found it. I knew he would. As soon as he can get it analyzed and the whole thing down on tape–'

'Gannet?' Cold fear knifed down Patterson's spine. 'Gannet found what?'

'The moment of crisis. The old man's babbling about a five-ship convoy. Fuel for the crow warfleet. Unescorted and moving toward the battle line. Unger says our scouts will miss it.' LeMarr's breathing was hoarse and frenzied. 'He says if we knew in advance–' He pulled himself together with a violent effort. 'Then we could destroy it.'

'I see,' Patterson said. 'And throw the balance in Earth's favor.'

'If West can plot the convoy route,' LeMarr finished, 'Earth will win the war. That means Gannet will fight–as soon as he gets the exact information.'

V-Stephens sat crouched on the single-piece bench that served as chair and table and bed for the psychotic ward. A cigarette dangled between his dark green lips. The cube-like room was ascetic, barren. The walls glittered dully. From time to time V-Stephens examined his wristwatch and then turned his attention back to the object crawling up and down the sealed edges of the entrance-lock.

The object moved slowly and cautiously. It had been exploring the lock for twenty-nine hours straight; it had traced down the power leads that kept the heavy plate fused in place. It had located the terminals at which the leads joined the magnetic rind of the door. During the last hour it had cut its way through the rexeroid surface to within an inch of the terminals. The crawling, exploring object was V-Stephens' surgeon-hand, a self-contained robot of precision quality usually joined to his right wrist.

It wasn't joined there now. He had detached it and sent it up the face of the cube to find a way out. The metal fingers clung precariously to the smooth dull surface, as the cutting-thumb laboriously dug its way in. It was a big job for the surgeon-hand; after this it wouldn't be of much use at the operating table. But V-Stephens could easily get another—they were for sale at any medical supply house on Venus.

The forefinger of the surgeon-hand reached the anode terminal and paused questioningly. All four fingers rose erect and waved like insect antennae. One by one they fitted themselves into the cut slot and probed for the nearby cathode lead.

Abruptly there was a blinding flash. A white acrid cloud billowed out, and then came a sharp *pop*. The entrance-lock remained motionless as the hand dropped to the floor, its work done. V-Stephens put out his cigarette, got leisurely to his feet, and crossed the cube to collect it.

With the hand in place and acting as part of his own neuromuscular system again, V-Stephens gingerly grasped the lock by its perimeter and after a moment pulled inward. The lock came without resistance and he found himself facing a deserted corridor. There was no sound or motion. No guards. No check-system on the psych patients. V-Stephens loped quickly ahead, around a turn, and through a series of connecting passages.

In a moment he was at a wide view-window, overlooking the street, the surrounding buildings, and the hospital grounds.

He assembled his wristwatch, cigarette lighter, fountain pen, keys and coins. From them his agile flesh and metal fingers rapidly formed an intricate gestalt of wiring and plates. He snapped off the cutting-thumb and screwed a heat-element in its place. In a brief flurry he had fused the mechanism to the underside of the window ledge, invisible from the hall, too far from ground level to be noticed.

He was starting back down the corridor when a sound stopped him rigid. Voices, a routine hospital guard and somebody else. A familiar somebody else.

He raced back to the psych ward and into his sealed cube. The magnetic lock fitted reluctantly in place; the heat generated by the short had sprung its clamps. He got it shut as footsteps halted outside. The magnetic field of the lock was dead, but of course the visitors didn't know that. V-Stephens listened with amusement as the visitor carefully negated the supposed magnetic field and then pushed the lock open.

'Come in,' V-Stephens said.

Doctor LeMarr entered, briefcase in one hand, cold-beam in the other. 'Come along with me. I have everything arranged. Money, fake identification, passport, tickets and clearance. You'll go as a webfoot commercial agent. By the time Gannet finds out you'll be past the Military monitor and out of Earth jurisdiction.'

V-Stephens was astounded. 'But—'

'Hurry up!' LeMarr waved him into the corridor with his cold-beam. 'As a staff member of the hospital I have authority over psych prisoners. Technically, you're listed as a mental patient. As far as I'm concerned you're no more crazy than the rest of them. If not less. That's why I'm here.'

V-Stephens eyed him doubtfully. 'You sure you know what you're doing?' He followed LeMarr down the corridor, past the blank-faced guard and into the elevator. 'They'll destroy you as a traitor, if they catch you. That guard saw you—how are you going to keep this quiet?'

'I don't expect to keep this quiet. Gannet is here, you know. He and his staff have been working over the old man.'

'Why are you telling me this?' The two of them strode down the descent ramp to the subsurface garage. An attendant rolled out LeMarr's car and they climbed into it, LeMarr behind the wheel. 'You know why I was thrown in the psych-cube in the first place.'

'Take this.' LeMarr tossed V-Stephens the cold-beam and steered up the tunnel to the surface, into the bright mid-day New York traffic. 'You were going to contact Color-Ad and inform them Earth will absolutely lose the war.' He spun the car from the mainstream of traffic and onto a side lane, toward the interplan spacefield. 'Tell them to stop working for compromise and strike hard—immediately. Full scale war. Right?'

'Right,' V-Stephens said. 'After all, if we're certain to win—'

'You're not certain.'

V-Stephens raised a green eyebrow. 'Oh? I thought Unger was a veteran of total defeat.'

'Gannet is going to change the course of the war. He's found a critical point. As soon as he gets the exact information he'll pressure the Directorate into an all-out attack on Venus and Mars. War can't be avoided, not now.' LeMarr slammed his car to a halt at the edge of the interplan field. 'If there has to be war at least nobody's going to be taken by a sneak attack. You can tell your Colonial Organization and Administration our warfleet is on its way. Tell them to get ready. Tell them—'

LeMarr's voice trailed off. Like an unwound toy he sagged against the seat, slid silently down, and lay quietly with his head against the steering wheel. His glasses dropped from his nose onto the floor and after a moment V-Stephens replaced them. 'I'm sorry,' he said softly. 'You meant well, but you sure fouled everything up.'

He briefly examined the surface of LeMarr's skull. The impulse from the cold-beam had not penetrated into brain tissue; LeMarr would regain consciousness in a few hours with nothing worse than a severe headache. V-Stephens pocketed the cold-beam, grabbed up the briefcase, and pushed the limp body of LeMarr away from the wheel. A moment later he was turning on the motor and backing the car around.

As he sped back to the hospital he examined his watch. It wasn't too late. He leaned forward and dropped a quarter in the pay vidphone mounted on the dashboard. After a mechanical dialing process the Color-Ad receptionist flickered into view.

'This is V-Stephens,' he said. 'Something went wrong. I was taken out of the hospital building. I'm heading back there now. I can make it in time, I think.'

'Is the vibrator-pack assembled?'

'Assembled, yes. But not with me. I had already fused it into polarization with the magnetic flux. It's ready to go—if I can get back there and at it.'

'There's a hitch at this end,' the green-skinned girl said. 'Is this a closed circuit?'

'It's open,' V-Stephens admitted. 'But it's public and probably random. They couldn't very well have a bug on it.' He checked the power meter on the guarantee seal fastened to the unit. 'It shows no drain. Go ahead.'

'The ship won't be able to pick you up in the city.'

'Hell,' V-Stephens said.

'You'll have to get out of New York on your own power; we can't help you there. Mobs destroyed our New York port facilities. You'll have to go by surface car to Denver. That's the nearest place the ship can land. That's our last protected spot on Earth.'

V-Stephens groaned. 'Just my luck. You know what'll happen if they catch me?'

The girl smiled faintly. 'All webfoots look alike to Earthmen. They'll be stringing us up indiscriminately. We're in this together. Good luck; we'll be waiting for you.'

V-Stephens angrily broke the circuit and slowed the car. He parked in a public parking lot on a dingy side street and got quickly out. He was at the edge of the green expanse of park. Beyond it, the hospital buildings rose. Gripping the briefcase tightly he ran toward the main entrance.

*

David Unger wiped his mouth on his sleeve, then lay back weakly against his chair. 'I don't know,' he repeated, his voice faint and dry. 'I told you I don't remember any more. It was so long ago.'

Gannet signaled, and the officers moved away from the old man. 'It's coming,' he said wearily. He mopped his perspiring forehead. 'Slowly and surely. We should have what we want inside another half hour.'

One side of the therapy house had been turned into a Military table-map. Counters had been laid out across the surface to represent units of the webfoot and crow fleets. White luminous chips represented Earth ships lined up against them in a tight ring around the third planet.

'It's someplace near here,' Lieutenant West said to Patterson. Red-eyed, stubble-chinned, hands shaking with fatigue and tension, he indicated a section of the map. 'Unger remembers hearing officers talking about this convoy. The convoy took off from a supply base on Ganymede. It disappeared on some kind of deliberate random course.' His hands swept the area. 'At the time, nobody on Earth paid any attention to it. Later, they realized what they'd lost. Some military expert charted the thing in retrospect and it was taped and passed around. Officers got together and analyzed the incident. Unger *thinks* the convoy route took it close to Europa. But maybe it was Callisto.'

'That's not good enough,' Gannet snapped. 'So far we don't have any more route data than Earth tacticians had at that time. We need to add exact knowledge, material released after the event.'

David Unger fumbled with a glass of water. 'Thanks,' he muttered gratefully, as one of the young officers handed it to him. 'I sure wish I could help you fellows out better,' he said plaintively. 'I'm trying to remember. But I don't seem able to think clear, like I used to.' His wizened face twisted with futile concentration. 'You know, it seems to me that convoy was stopped near Mars by some kind of meteor swarm.'

Gannet moved forward. 'Go on.'

Unger appealed to him pathetically. 'I want to help you all I can, mister. Most people go to write a book about a war, they just scan 'stuff from other books.' There was a pitiful gratitude on the eroded face. 'I guess you'll mention my name in your book, someplace.'

'Sure,' Gannet said expansively. 'Your name'll be on the first page. Maybe we could even get in a picture of you.'

'I know all about the war,' Unger muttered. 'Give me time and I'll have it straight. *Just give me time.* I'm trying as best I can.'

The old man was deteriorating rapidly. His wrinkled face was an unhealthy gray. Like drying putty, his flesh clung to his brittle, yellowed bones. His breath rattled in his throat. It was obvious to everyone present that David Unger was going to die—and soon.

'If he croaks before he remembers,' Gannet said softly to Lieutenant West, 'I'll—'

'What's that?' Unger asked sharply. His one good eye was suddenly keen and wary. 'I can't hear so good.'

'Just fill in the missing elements,' Gannet said wearily. He jerked his head. 'Get him over to the map where he can see the setup. Maybe that'll help.'

The old man was yanked to his feet and propelled to the table. Technicians and brass hats closed in around him and the dim-eyed stumbling figure was lost from sight.

'He won't last long,' Patterson said savagely. 'If you don't let him rest his heart's going to give out.'

'We must have the information,' Gannet retorted. He eyed Patterson. 'Where's the other doctor? LeMarr, I think he's called.'

Patterson glanced briefly around. 'I don't see him. He probably couldn't stand it.'

'LeMarr never came,' Gannet said, without emotion. 'I wonder if we should have somebody round him up.' He indicated Evelyn Cutter, who had just arrived, white-faced, her black eyes wide, breathing quickly. 'She suggests—'

'It doesn't matter now,' Evelyn said frigidly. She shot a quick, urgent glance at Patterson. 'I want nothing to do with you and your war.'

Gannet shrugged. 'I'll send out a routine net, in any case. Just to be on the safe side.' He moved off, leaving Evelyn and Patterson standing alone together.

'Listen to me,' Evelyn said harshly, her lips hot and close to his ear. '*Unger's number has come up.*'

'When did they notify you?' Patterson demanded.

'I was on my way here. I did what you said—I fixed it up with a clerk at Military.'

'How long ago?'

'Just now.' Evelyn's face trembled. 'Vachel, *he's here.*'

It was a moment before Patterson understood. 'You mean they sent him over here? To the hospital?'

'I told them to. I told them when he came to volunteer, when his number came to the top—'

Patterson grabbed her and hurried her from the therapy house, outside into the bright sunlight. He pushed her onto an ascent ramp and crowded in after her. 'Where are they holding him?'

'In the public reception room. They told him it was a routine physical check. A minor test of some kind.' Evelyn was terrified. 'What are we going to do? *Can* we do something?'

'Gannet thinks so.'

'Suppose we—stopped him? Maybe we could turn him aside?' She shook her head, dazed. 'What would happen? What would the future be like if we stopped him here? You could keep him out of the Service—you're a doctor. A little red check on his health card.' She began to laugh wildly. 'I see them all the time. A little red check, and no more David Unger. Gannet never sees him, Gannet never knows Earth can't win and then Earth will win, and V-Stephens doesn't get locked up as a psychotic and that webfoot girl—'

Patterson's open hand smashed across the woman's face. 'Shut up and snap out of it! We don't have time for that!'

Evelyn shuddered; he caught hold of her and held on tight to her until finally she raised her face. A red welt was rising slowly on her cheek. 'I'm sorry,' she managed to murmur. 'Thanks. I'll be all right.'

The lift had reached the main floor. The door slid back and Patterson led her out into the hall. 'You haven't seen him?'

'No. When they told me the number had come up and he was

on his way'—Evelyn hurried breathlessly after Patterson—'I came as quickly as I could. Maybe it's too late. Maybe he got tired of waiting and left. He's a fifteen-year-old boy. He wants to get into the fight. Maybe he's gone!'

Patterson halted a robot attendant. 'Are you busy?'

'No sir,' the robot answered.

Patterson gave the robot David Unger's i.d. number. 'Get this man from the main reception room. Send him out here and then close off this hall. Seal it at both ends so nobody can enter or leave.'

The robot clicked uncertainly. 'Will there be further orders? This syndrome doesn't complete a—'

'I'll instruct you later. Make sure nobody comes out with him. I want to meet him here alone.'

The robot scanned the number and then disappeared into the reception room.

Patterson gripped Evelyn's arm. 'Scared?'

'I'm terrified.'

'I'll handle it. You just stand there.' He passed her his cigarettes. 'Light one for both of us.'

'Three, maybe. One for Unger.'

Patterson grinned. 'He's too young, remember? He's not old enough to smoke.'

The robot returned. With it was a blond boy, plump and blue-eyed, his face wrinkled with perplexity. 'You wanted me, Doc?' He came uncertainly up to Patterson. 'Is there something wrong with me? They told me to come here, but they didn't say what for.' His anxiety increased with a tidal rush. 'There's nothing to keep me out of the Service, is there?'

Patterson grabbed the boy's newly stamped i.d. card, glanced at it, and then passed it to Evelyn. She accepted it with paralyzed fingers, her eyes on the blond youth.

He was not David Unger.

'What's your name?' Patterson demanded.

The boy stammered out his name shyly. 'Bert Robinson. Doesn't it say there on my card?'

Patterson turned to Evelyn. 'It's the right number. But this isn't Unger. Something's happened.'

'Say, Doc,' Robinson asked plaintively, 'is there something going to keep me out of the Service or not? Give me the word.'

Patterson signaled the robot. 'Open up the hall. It's all over with. You can go back to what you were doing.'

'I don't understand,' Evelyn murmured. 'It doesn't make sense.'

'You're all right,' Patterson said to the youth. 'You can report for induction.'

The boy's face sagged with relief. 'Thanks a lot, Doc.' He edged toward the descent ramp. 'I sure appreciate it. I'm dying to get a crack at those webfoots.'

'Now what?' Evelyn said tightly, when the youth's broad back had disappeared. 'Where do we go from here?'

Patterson shook himself alive. 'We'll get the Census Department to make their check. *We've got to locate Unger.*'

The transmission room was a humming blur of vid and aud reports. Patterson elbowed his way to an open circuit and placed the call.

'That information will take a short time, sir,' the girl at Census told him. 'Will you wait, or shall we return your call?'

Patterson grabbed up an h-loop and clipped it around his neck. 'As soon as you have any information on Unger let me know. Break into this loop immediately.'

'Yes, sir,' the girl said dutifully, and broke the circuit.

Patterson headed out of the room and down the corridor. Evelyn hurried after him. 'Where are we going?' she asked.

'To the therapy house. I want to talk to the old man. I want to ask him some things.'

'Gannet's doing that,' Evelyn gasped, as they descended to the ground level. 'Why do you—'

'I want to ask him about the present, not the future.' They emerged in the blinding afternoon sunlight. 'I want to ask him about things going on right now.'

Evelyn stopped him. 'Can't you explain it to me?'

'I have a theory.' Patterson pushed urgently past her. 'Come on, before it's too late.'

They entered the therapy house. Technicians and officers were standing around the huge map-table, examining the counters and indicator lines. 'Where's Unger?' Patterson demanded.

'He's gone,' one of the officers answered. 'Gannet gave up for today.'

'Gone where?' Patterson began to swear savagely. 'What happened?'

'Gannet and West took him back to the main building. He was too worn out to continue. We almost had it. Gannet's ready to burst a blood vessel, but we'll have to wait.'

Patterson grabbed Evelyn Cutter. 'I want you to set off a general emergency alarm. Have the building surrounded. And *hurry*!'

Evelyn gaped at him. 'But—'

Patterson ignored her and raced out of the therapy house, toward the main hospital building. Ahead of him were three slowly moving figures. Lieutenant West and Gannet walked on each side of the old man, supporting him as he crept forward.

'Get away!' Patterson shouted at them.

Gannet turned. 'What's going on?'

'Get him away!' Patterson dived for the old man—but it was too late.

The burst of energy seared past him; an ignited circle of blinding white flame lapped everywhere. The hunched-over figure of the old man wavered, then charred. The aluminum cane fused and ran down in a molten mass. What had been the old man began to smoke. The body cracked open and shriveled. Then very slowly, the dried, dehydrated fragment of ash crumpled in a weightless heap. Gradually the circle of energy faded out.

Gannet kicked aimlessly at it, his heavy face numb with shock and disbelief. 'He's dead. And we didn't get it.'

Lieutenant West stared at the still-smoking ash. His lips twisted into words. 'We'll never find out. We can't change it. We can't win.'

Suddenly his fingers grabbed at his coat. He tore the insignia from it and hurled the square of cloth savagely away. 'I'll be damned if I'm going to give up my life so you can corner the system. I'm not getting into that death trap. Count me out!'

The wail of the general emergency alarm dinned from the hospital building. Scampering figures raced toward Gannet, soldiers and hospital guards scurrying in confusion. Patterson paid no attention to them; his eyes were on the window directly above.

Someone was standing there. A man, his hands deftly at work removing an object that flashed in the afternoon sun. The man was V-Stephens. He got the object of metal and plastic loose and disappeared with it, away from the window.

Evelyn hurried up beside Patterson. 'What–' She saw the remains and screamed. 'Oh, God. Who did it? *Who?*'

'V-Stephens.'

'LeMarr must have let him out. I knew it would happen.' Tears filled her eyes and her voice rose in shrill hysteria. 'I told you he'd do it! I warned you!'

Gannet appealed childishly to Patterson. 'What are we going to do? He's been murdered.' Rage suddenly swept away the big man's fear. 'I'll kill every webfoot on the planet. I'll burn down their homes and string them up. I'll–' He broke off raggedly. 'But it's too late, isn't it? There's nothing we can do. We've lost. We're beaten, and the war hasn't even begun.'

'That's right,' Patterson said. 'It's too late. Your chance is gone.'

'If we could have got him to talk–' Gannet snarled helplessly.

'You couldn't. It wasn't possible.'

Gannet blinked. 'Why not?' Some of his innate animal cunning filtered back. 'Why do you say that?'

Around Patterson's neck his h-loop buzzed loudly. 'Doctor Patterson,' the monitor's voice came, 'there is a rush call for you from Census.'

'Put it through,' Patterson said.

The voice of the Census clerk came tinnily in his ears. 'Doctor Patterson, I have the information you requested.'

'What is it?' Patterson demanded. But he already knew the answer.

'We have cross-checked our results to be certain. There is no person such as you described. There is no individual at this time or in our past records named David L. Unger with the identifying characteristics you outlined. The brain, teeth, and fingerprints do not refer to anything extant in our files. Do you wish us to—'

'No,' Patterson said. 'That answers my question. Let it go.' He cut off the h-loop switch.

Gannet was listening dully. 'This is completely over my head, Patterson. Explain it to me.'

Patterson ignored him. He squatted down and poked at the ash that had been David Unger. After a moment he snapped the h-loop on again. 'I want this taken upstairs to the analytical labs,' he ordered quietly. 'Get a team out here at once.' He got slowly to his feet and added even more softly, 'Then I'm going to find V-Stephens—if I can.'

'He's undoubtedly on his way to Venus by now,' Evelyn Cutter said bitterly. 'Well, that's that. There's nothing we can do about it.'

'We're going to have war,' Gannet admitted. He came slowly back to reality. With a violent effort he focused on the people around him. He smoothed down his mane of white hair and adjusted his coat. A semblance of dignity was restored to his once-impressive frame. 'We might as well meet it like men. There's no use trying to escape it.'

Patterson moved aside as a group of hospital robots approached the charred remains and began gingerly to collect them in a single heap. 'Make a complete analysis,' he said to the technician in charge of the work-detail. 'Break down the basic cell-units, especially the neurological apparatus. Report what you find to me as soon as you possibly can.'

It took just about an hour.

'Look for yourself,' the lab technician said. 'Here, take hold of some of the material. It doesn't even *feel* right.'

Patterson accepted a sample of dry, brittle organic matter. It might have been the smoked skin of some sea creature. It broke apart easily in his hands; as he put it down among the test equipment it crumbled into powdery fragments. 'I see,' he said slowly.

'It's good, considering. But it's weak. Probably it wouldn't have stood up another couple of days. It was deteriorating rapidly; sun, air, everything was breaking it down. There was no innate repair-system involved. Our cells are constantly reprocessed, cleaned and maintained. This thing was set up and then pushed into motion. Obviously, somebody's a long way ahead of us in biosynthetics. This is a masterpiece.'

'Yes, it's a good job,' Patterson admitted. He took another sample of what had been the body of David Unger and thoughtfully broke it into small dry pieces. 'It fooled us completely.'

'You knew, didn't you?'

'Not at first.'

'As you can see we're reconstructing the whole system, getting the ash back into one piece. Parts are missing, of course, but we can get the general outlines. I'd like to meet the manufacturers of this thing. This really worked. This was no machine.'

Patterson located the charred ash that had been reconstructed into the android's face. Withered, blackened paper-thin flesh. The dead eye gazed out lusterless and blind. Census had been right. There was never a David Unger. Such a person had never lived on Earth or anywhere else. What they had called 'David Unger' was a man-made synthetic.

'We were really taken in,' Patterson admitted. 'How many people know, besides the two of us?'

'Nobody else.' The lab technician indicated his squad of work-robots. 'I'm the only human on this detail.'

'Can you keep it quiet?'

'Sure. You're my boss, you know.'

'Thanks,' Patterson said. 'But if you want, this information would get you another boss any time.'

'Gannet?' The lab technician laughed. 'I don't think I'd like to work for him.'

'He'd pay you pretty well.'

'True,' said the lab technician. 'But one of these days I'd be in the front lines. I like it better here in the hospital.'

Patterson started toward the door. 'If anybody asks, tell them there wasn't enough left to analyze. Can you dispose of these remains?'

'I'd hate to, but I guess I can.' The technician eyed him curiously. 'You have any idea who put this thing together? I'd like to shake hands with them.'

'I'm interested in only one thing right now,' Patterson said obliquely. 'V-Stephens has to be found.'

LeMarr blinked, as dull late-afternoon sunlight filtered into his brain. He pulled himself upright—and banged his head sharply on the dashboard of the car. Pain swirled around him and for a time he sank back down into agonized darkness. Then slowly, gradually, he emerged. And peered around him.

His car was parked in the rear of a small, dilapidated public lot. It was about five-thirty. Traffic swarmed noisily along the narrow street onto which the lot fed. LeMarr reached up and gingerly explored the side of his skull. There was a numb spot the size of a silver dollar, an area totally without sensation. The spot radiated a chill breath, the utter absence of heat, as if somehow he had bumped against a nexus of outer space.

He was still trying to collect himself and recollect the events that had preceded his period of unconsciousness, when the swift-moving form of Doctor V-Stephens appeared.

V-Stephens ran lithely between the parked surface cars, one hand in his coat pocket, eyes alert and wary. There was something strange about him, a difference that LeMarr in his befuddled state couldn't pin down. V-Stephens had almost reached the car before he realized what it was—and at the same time was lashed by the full surge of memory. He sank down and lay against the door, as limp and inert as possible. In spite of himself he started slightly, as V-Stephens yanked the door open and slid behind the wheel.

V-Stephens was no longer green.

The Venusian slammed the door, jabbed the car key in the lock, and started up the motor. He lit a cigarette, examined his pair of heavy gloves, glanced briefly at LeMarr, and pulled out of the lot into the early-evening traffic. For a moment he drove with one gloved hand on the wheel, the other still inside his coat. Then, as he gained full speed, he slid his cold-beam out, gripped it briefly, and dropped it on the seat beside him.

LeMarr pounced on it. From the corner of his eye, V-Stephens saw the limp body swing into life. He slammed on the emergency brake and forgot the wheel; the two of them struggled silently, furiously. The car shrieked to a halt and immediately became the center of an angry mass of honking car-horns. The two men fought with desperate intensity, neither of them breathing, locked almost immobile as momentarily all forces balanced. Then LeMarr yanked away, the cold-beam aimed at V-Stephens' colorless face.

'What happened?' he croaked hoarsely. 'I'm missing five hours. *What did you do?*'

V-Stephens said nothing. He released the brake and began driving slowly with the swirl of traffic. Gray cigarette smoke dribbled from between his lips; his eyes were half-closed, filmed over and opaque.

'You're an Earthman,' LeMarr said, wonderingly. 'You're not a webfoot after all.'

'I'm a Venusian,' V-Stephens answered indifferently. He showed his webbed fingers, then replaced his heavy driving gloves.

'But how—'

'You think we can't pass over the color line when we want to?' V-Stephens shrugged. 'Dyes, chemical hormones, a few minor surgical operations. A half hour in the men's room with a hypodermic and salve . . . This is no planet for a man with green skin.'

Across the street a hasty barricade had been erected. A group of sullen-faced men stood around with guns and crude hand-clubs, some of them wearing gray Home Guard caps. They were flagging down cars one by one and searching them. A beefy-faced man waved V-Stephens to a halt. He strolled over and gestured for the window to be rolled down.

'What's going on?' LeMarr demanded nervously.

'Looking for webfoots,' the man growled, a thick odor of garlic and perspiration steaming from his heavy canvas shirt. He darted quick, suspicious glances into the car. 'Seen any around?'

'No,' V-Stephens said.

The man ripped open the luggage compartment and peered in. 'We caught one a couple minutes ago.' He jerked his thick thumb. 'See him up there?'

The Venusian had been strung up to a street lamp. His green body dangled and swayed with the early-evening wind. His face was a mottled, ugly mass of pain. A crowd of people stood around the pole, grim, mean-looking. Waiting.

'There'll be more,' the man said, as he slammed the luggage compartment. 'Plenty more.'

'What happened?' LeMarr managed to ask. He was nauseated and horrified; his voice came out almost inaudible. 'Why all this?'

'A webfoot killed a man. An *Earth*man.' The man pulled back and slapped the car. 'Okay—you can go.'

V-Stephens moved the car forward. Some of the loitering people had whole uniforms, combinations of the Home Guard gray and Terran blue. Boots, heavy belt-buckles, caps, pistols, and armbands. The armbands read DC in bold black letters against a red background.

'What's that?' LeMarr asked faintly.

'Defense Committee,' V-Stephens answered. 'Gannet's front outfit. To defend Earth against the webfoots and crows.'

'But—' LeMarr gestured helplessly. 'Is Earth being attacked?'

'Not that I know of.'

'Turn the car around. Head back to the hospital.'

V-Stephens hesitated, then did as he was told. In a moment the car was speeding back toward the center of New York. 'What's this for?' V-Stephens asked. 'Why do you want to go back?'

LeMarr didn't hear him; he was gazing with fixed horror at the people along the street. Men and women prowling like animals, looking for something to kill. 'They've gone crazy,' LeMarr muttered. 'They're beasts.'

'No,' V-Stephens said. 'This'll die down, soon. When the Committee gets its financial support jerked out from under it. It's still going full blast, but pretty soon the gears will change around and the big engine will start grinding in reverse.'

'Why?'

'Because Gannet doesn't want war, now. It takes a while for the new line to trickle down. Gannet will probably finance a movement called PC. Peace Committee.'

The hospital was surrounded by a wall of tanks and trucks and heavy mobile guns. V-Stephens slowed the car to a halt and stubbed out his cigarette. No cars were being passed. Soldiers moved among the tanks with gleaming heavy-duty weapons that were still shiny with packing grease.

'Well?' V-Stephens said. 'What now? You have the gun. It's your hot potato.'

LeMarr dropped a coin in the vidphone mounted on the dashboard. He gave the hospital number, and when the monitor appeared, asked hoarsely for Vachel Patterson.

'Where are you?' Patterson demanded. He saw the cold-beam in LeMarr's hand, and then his eyes fastened on V-Stephens. 'I see you got him.'

'Yes,' LeMarr agreed, 'but I don't understand what's happening.' He appealed helplessly to Patterson's miniature vidimage. 'What'll I do? What is all this?'

'Give me your location,' Patterson said tensely.

LeMarr did so. 'You want me to bring him to the hospital? Maybe I should—'

'Just hold onto that cold-beam. I'll be right there.' Patterson broke the connection and the screen died.

LeMarr shook his head in bewilderment. 'I was trying to get you away,' he said to V-Stephens. 'Then you cold-beamed me. *Why?*' Suddenly LeMarr shuddered violently. Full understanding came to him. 'You killed David Unger!'

'That's right,' V-Stephens answered.

The cold-beam trembled in LeMarr's hand. 'Maybe I ought to kill you right now. Maybe I ought to roll down the window and yell to those madmen to come and get you. I don't know.'

'Do whatever you think best,' V-Stephens said.

LeMarr was still trying to decide, when Patterson appeared beside the car. He rapped on the window and LeMarr unlocked the door. Patterson climbed quickly in, and slammed the door after him.

'Start up the car,' he said to V-Stephens. 'Keep moving, away from downtown.'

V-Stephens glanced briefly at him, and then slowly started up the motor. 'You might as well do it here,' he said to Patterson. 'Nobody'll interfere.'

'I want to get out of the city,' Patterson answered. He added in explanation, 'My lab staff analyzed the remains of David Unger. They were able to reconstruct most of the synthetic.'

V-Stephens' face registered a surge of frantic emotion. 'Oh?'

Patterson reached out his hand. 'Shake,' he said grimly.

'Why?' V-Stephens asked, puzzled.

'Somebody told me to do this. Somebody who agrees you Venusians did one hell of a good job when you made that android.'

The car purred along the highway, through the evening gloom. 'Denver is the last place left,' V-Stephens explained to the two Earthmen. 'There're too many of us, there. Color-Ad says a few Committee men started shelling our offices, but the Directorate put a sudden stop to it. Gannet's pressure, probably.'

'I want to hear more,' Patterson said. 'Not about Gannet; I know where he stands. I want to know what you people are up to.'

'Color-Ad engineered the synthetic,' V-Stephens admitted. 'We don't know any more about the future than you do—which is absolutely nothing. There never was a David Unger. We forged the i.d. papers, built up a whole false personality, history of a non-existent war—everything.'

'Why?' LeMarr demanded.

'To scare Gannet into calling off the dogs. To terrify him into letting Venus and Mars become independent. To keep him from fanning up a war to preserve his economic strangle-hold. The fake history we constructed in Unger's mind has Gannet's nine-world empire broken and destroyed. Gannet's a realist. He'd take a risk when he had odds—but our history put the odds one hundred per-cent against him.'

'So Gannet pulls out,' Patterson said slowly. 'And you?'

'We were always out,' V-Stephens said quietly. 'We were never in this war game. All we want is our freedom and independence. I don't know what the war would really be like, but I can guess. Not very pleasant. Not worth it for either of us. And as things were going, war was in the cards.'

'I want to get a few things straight,' Patterson said. 'You're a Color-Ad agent?'

'Right.'

'And V-Rafia?'

'She was also Color-Ad. Actually, all Venusians and Martians are Color-Ad agents as soon as they hit Earth. We wanted to get V-Rafia into the hospital to help me out. There was a chance I'd be pre-vented from destroying the synthetic at the proper time. If I hadn't been able to do it, V-Rafia would have. But Gannet killed her.'

'Why didn't you simply cold-beam Unger?'

'For one thing we wanted the synthetic body completely des-troyed. That isn't possible, of course. Reduced to ash was the next best thing. Broken down small enough so a cursory examination wouldn't show anything.' He glanced up at Patterson. 'Why'd you order such a radical examination?'

'Unger's i.d. number had come up. And Unger didn't appear to claim it.'

'Oh,' V-Stephens said uneasily. 'That's bad. We had no way to tell when it would appear. We tried to pick a number due in a few months—but enlistment rose sharply the last couple of weeks.'

'Suppose you hadn't been able to destroy Unger?'

'We had the demolition machinery phased in such a way that

the synthetic didn't have a chance. It was tuned to his body; all I had to do was activate it with Unger in the general area. If I had been killed, or I hadn't been able to set off the mechanism, the synthetic would have died naturally before Gannet got the information he wanted. Preferably, I was to destroy it in plain view of Gannet and his staff. It was important they think we knew about the war. The psychological shock-value of seeing Unger murdered outweighs the risk of my capture.'

'What happens next?' Patterson asked presently.

'I'm supposed to join with Color-Ad. Originally, I was to grab a ship at the New York office, but Gannet's mobs took care of that. Of course, this is assuming you won't stop me.'

LeMarr had begun to sweat. 'Suppose Gannet finds out he was tricked? If he discovers there never was a David Unger—'

'We're patching that up,' V-Stephens said. 'By the time Gannet checks, there will be a David Unger. Meanwhile—' He shrugged. 'It's up to you two. You've got the gun.'

'Let him go,' LeMarr said fervently.

'That's not very patriotic,' Patterson pointed out. 'We're helping the webfoots put over something. Maybe we ought to call in one of those Committee men.'

'The devil with them,' LeMarr grated. 'I wouldn't turn anybody over to those lynch-happy lunatics. Even a—'

'Even a webfoot?' V-Stephens asked.

Patterson was gazing up at the black, star-pocked sky. 'What's finally going to happen?' he asked V-Stephens. 'You think this stuff will end?'

'Sure,' V-Stephens said promptly. 'One of these days we'll be moving out into the stars. Into other systems. We'll bump into other races—and I mean *real* other races. Non-human in the true sense of the word. Then people will see we're all of the same stem. It'll be obvious, when we've got something to compare ourselves to.'

'Okay,' Patterson said. He took the cold-beam and handed it to V-Stephens. 'That was all that worried me. I'd hate to think this stuff might keep on going.'

'It won't,' V-Stephens answered quietly. 'Some of those non-human races ought to be pretty hideous. After a look at them, Earthmen will be *glad* to have their daughters marry men with green skin.' He grinned briefly. 'Some of the non-human races may not have any skin at all ...'

THE CHROMIUM FENCE

Earth tilted toward six o'clock, the work-day almost over. Commute discs rose in dense swarms and billowed away from the industrial zone toward the surrounding residential rings. Like nocturnal moths, the thick clouds of discs darkened the evening sky. Silent, weightless, they whisked their passengers toward home and waiting families, hot meals and bed.

Don Walsh was the third man on his disc; he completed the load. As he dropped the coin in the slot the carpet rose impatiently. Walsh settled gratefully against the invisible safety-rail and unrolled the evening newspaper. Across from him the other two commuters were doing the same.

HORNEY AMENDMENT STIRS UP FIGHT

Walsh reflected on the significance of the headline. He lowered the paper from the steady windcurrents and perused the next column.

HUGE TURNOUT EXPECTED MONDAY
ENTIRE PLANET TO GO TO POLLS

On the back of the single sheet was the day's scandal.

WIFE MURDERS HUSBAND OVER POLITICAL TIFF

And an item that made strange chills up and down his spine.

He had seen it crop up repeatedly, but it always made him feel uncomfortable.

PURIST MOB LYNCHES NATURALIST IN BOSTON
WINDOWS SMASHED—GREAT DAMAGE DONE

And in the next column:

NATURALIST MOB LYNCHES PURIST IN CHICAGO
BUILDINGS BURNED—GREAT DAMAGE DONE

Across from Walsh, one of his companions was beginning to mumble aloud. He was a big heavy-set man, middle-aged, with red hair and beer-swollen features. Suddenly he wadded up his newspaper and hurled it from the disc. 'They'll never pass it!' he shouted. 'They won't get away with it!'

Walsh buried his nose in his paper and desperately ignored the man. It was happening again, the thing he dreaded every hour of the day. A political argument. The other commuter had lowered his newspaper; briefly, he eyed the red-haired man and then continued reading.

The red-haired man addressed Walsh. 'You signed the Butte Petition?' He yanked a metal foil tablet from his pocket and pushed it in Walsh's face. 'Don't be afraid to put down your name for liberty.'

Walsh clutched his newspaper and peered frantically over the side of the disc. The Detroit residential units were spinning by; he was almost home. 'Sorry,' he muttered. 'Thanks, no thanks.'

'Leave him alone,' the other commuter said to the red-haired man. 'Can't you see he doesn't want to sign it?'

'Mind your own business.' The red-haired man moved close to Walsh, the tablet extended belligerently. 'Look, friend. You know what it'll mean to you and yours if this thing gets passed? You think you'll be safe? Wake up, friend. When the Horney Amendment comes in, freedom and liberty go out.'

The other commuter quietly put his newspaper away. He was slim, well-dressed, a gray-haired cosmopolitan. He removed his glasses and said, 'You smell like a Naturalist, to me.'

The red-haired man studied his opponent. He noticed the wide plutonium ring on the slender man's hand; a jaw-breaking band of heavy metal. 'What are you?' the red-haired man muttered, 'a sissy-kissing Purist? Agh.' He made a disgusting spitting motion and returned to Walsh. 'Look, friend, you know what these Purists are after. They want to make us degenerates. They'll turn us into a race of women. If God made the universe the way it is, it's good enough for me. They're going against God when they go against nature. This planet was built up by red-blooded *men*, who were proud of their bodies, proud of the way they looked and smelled.' He tapped his own heavy chest. 'By God, I'm proud of the way *I* smell!'

Walsh stalled desperately. 'I—' he muttered. 'No, I can't sign it.'

'You already signed?'

'No.'

Suspicion settled over the red-haired man's beefy features. 'You mean you're *for* the Horney Amendment?' His thick voice rose wrathfully. 'You want to see an end to the natural order of—'

'This is where I get off,' Walsh interrupted; he hurriedly yanked the stop-cord of the disc. It swept down toward the magnetic grapple at the end of his unit-section, a row of white squares set across the green and brown hillside.

'Wait a minute, friend.' The red-haired man reached ominously for Walsh's sleeve, as the disc slid to a halt on the flat surface of the grapple. Surface cars were parked in rows; wives waiting to cart their husbands home. 'I don't like your attitude. You afraid to stand up and be counted? You ashamed to be a part of your race? By God, if you're not man enough to—'

The lean, gray-haired man smashed him with his plutonium ring, and the grip on Walsh's sleeve loosened. The petition clattered to the ground and the two of them fought furiously, silently.

Walsh pushed aside the safety-rail and jumped from the disc, down the three steps of the grapple and onto the ashes and cinders of the parking lot. In the gloom of early evening he could make out his wife's car; Betty sat watching the dashboard TV, oblivious of him and the silent struggle between the red-haired Naturalist and the gray-haired Purist.

'Beast,' the gray-haired man gasped, as he straightened up. 'Stinking animal!'

The red-haired man lay semi-conscious against the safety-rail. 'God damn—lily!' he grunted.

The gray-haired man pressed the release, and the disc rose above Walsh and on its way. Walsh waved gratefully. 'Thanks,' he called up. 'I appreciate that.'

'Not at all,' the gray-haired man answered, cheerfully examining a broken tooth. His voice dwindled, as the disc gained altitude. 'Always glad to help out a fellow . . .' The final words came drifting to Walsh's ears. '. . . A fellow Purist.'

'I'm not!' Walsh shouted futilely 'I'm not a Purist and I'm not a Naturalist! You hear me?'

Nobody heard him.

'I'm not,' Walsh repeated monotonously, as he sat at the dinner table spooning up creamed corn, potatoes, and rib steak. 'I'm not a Purist and I'm not a Naturalist. Why do I have to be one or the other? Isn't there any place for a man who has his *own* opinion?'

'Eat your food, dear,' Betty murmured.

Through the thin walls of the bright little dining room came the echoing clink of other families eating, other conversations in progress. The tinny blare of TV sets. The purr of stoves and freezers and air conditioners and wall-heaters. Across from Walsh his brother-in-law Carl was gulping down a second plateful of steaming food. Beside him, Walsh's fifteen-year-old son Jimmy was scanning a paper-bound edition of *Finnegans Wake* he had bought in the downramp store that supplied the self-contained housing unit.

'Don't read at the table,' Walsh said angrily to his son.

Jimmy glanced up. 'Don't kid me. I know the unit rules; that one sure as hell isn't listed. And anyhow, I have to get this read before I leave.'

'Where are you going tonight, dear?' Betty asked.

'Official party business,' Jimmy answered obliquely. 'I can't tell you any more than that.'

Walsh concentrated on his food and tried to brake the tirade of thoughts screaming through his mind. 'On the way home from work,' he said, 'there was a fight.'

Jimmy was interested. 'Who won?'

'The Purist.'

A glow of pride slowly covered the boy's face; he was a sergeant in the Purist Youth League. 'Dad, you ought to get moving. Sign up now and you'll be eligible to vote next Monday.'

'I'm going to vote.'

'Not unless you're a member of one of the two parties.'

It was true. Walsh gazed unhappily past his son, into the days that lay ahead. He saw himself involved in endless wretched situations like the one today; sometimes it would be Naturalists who attacked him, and other times (like last week) it would be enraged Purists.

'You know,' his brother-in-law said, 'you're helping the Purists by just sitting around here doing nothing.' He belched contentedly and pushed his empty plate away. 'You're what *we* class as unconsciously pro-Purist.' He glared at Jimmy. 'You little squirt! If you were legal age I'd take you out and whale the tar out of you.'

'Please,' Betty sighed. 'No quarreling about politics at the table. Let's have peace and quiet, for a change. I'll certainly be glad when the election is over.'

Carl and Jimmy glared at each other and continued eating warily. 'You should eat in the kitchen,' Jimmy said to him. 'Under the stove. That's where you belong. Look at you—there's sweat all over you.' A nasty sneer interrupted his eating. 'When we get the Amendment passed, you better get rid of that, if you don't want to get hauled off to jail.'

Carl flushed. 'You creeps won't get it passed.' But his gruff voice lacked conviction. The Naturalists were scared; Purists had control of the Federal Council. If the election moved in their favor it was really possible the legislation to compel forced observation of the five-point Purist code might get on the books. 'Nobody is going to remove my sweat glands,' Carl muttered. 'Nobody is going to make me submit to breath-control and teeth-whitening and hair-restorer. It's part of life to get dirty and bald and fat and old.'

'Is it true?' Betty asked her husband. 'Are you really unconsciously pro-Purist?'

Don Walsh savagely speared a remnant of rib steak. 'Because I don't join either party I'm called unconsciously pro-Purist and unconsciously pro-Naturalist. I claim they balance. If I'm everybody's enemy then I'm nobody's enemy.' He added, 'Or friend.'

'You Naturalists have nothing to offer the future,' Jimmy said to Carl. 'What can you give the youth of the planet—like me? Caves and raw meat and a bestial existence. You're anti-civilization.'

'Slogans,' Carl retorted.

'You want to carry us back to a primitive existence, away from social integration.' Jimmy waved an excited skinny finger in his uncle's face. 'You're thalamically oriented!'

'I'll break your head,' Carl snarled, half out of his chair. 'You Purist squirts have no respect for your elders.'

Jimmy giggled shrilly. 'I'd like to see you try. It's five years in prison for striking a minor. Go ahead—hit me.'

Don Walsh got heavily to his feet and left the dining room.

'Where are you going?' Betty called peevishly after him. 'You're not through eating.'

'The future belongs to youth,' Jimmy was informing Carl. 'And the youth of the planet is firmly Purist. You don't have a chance; the Purist revolution is coming.'

Don Walsh left the apartment and wandered down the common corridor toward the ramp. Closed doors extended in rows on both sides of him. Noise and light and activity radiated around him, the close presence of families and domestic interaction. He pushed past a boy and girl making love in the dark shadows and reached the ramp. For a moment he halted, then abruptly he moved forward and descended to the lowest level of the unit.

The level was deserted and cool and slightly moist. Above him the sounds of people had faded to dull echoes against the concrete ceiling. Conscious of his sudden plunge into isolation and silence he advanced thoughtfully between the dark grocery and dry goods stores, past the beauty shop and the liquor store, past the laundry and medical supply store, past the dentist and physical doctor, to the ante-room of the unit analyst.

He could see the analyst within the inner chamber. It sat immobile and silent, in the dark shadows of evening. Nobody was consulting it; the analyst was turned off. Walsh hesitated, then crossed the check-frame of the ante-room and knocked on the transparent inner door. The presence of his body closed relays and switches; abruptly the lights of the inner office winked on and the analyst itself sat up, smiled and half-rose to its feet.

'Don,' it called heartily. 'Come on in and sit down.'

He entered and wearily seated himself. 'I thought maybe I could talk to you, Charley,' he said.

'Sure, Don.' The robot leaned forward to see the clock on its wide mahogany desk. 'But, isn't it dinner time?'

'Yes,' Walsh admitted. 'I'm not hungry. Charley, you know what we were talking about last time . . . you remember what I was saying. You remember what's been bothering me.'

'Sure, Don.' The robot settled back in its swivel chair, rested its almost-convincing elbows on the desk, and regarded its patient kindly. 'How's it been going, the last couple of days?'

'Not so good. Charley, I've got to do something. You can help me; you're not biased.' He appealed to the quasi-human face of metal and plastic. 'You can see this undistorted, Charley. *How can I join one of the parties?* All their slogans and propaganda, it seems so damn—silly. How the hell can I get excited about clean teeth and underarm odor? People kill each other over these trifles . . . it doesn't make sense. There's going to be suicidal civil war, if that

Amendment passes, and I'm supposed to join one side or the other.'

Charley nodded. 'I have the picture, Don.'

'Am I supposed to go out and knock some fellow over the head because he does or doesn't smell? Some man I never saw before? I won't do it. I refuse. Why can't they let me alone? Why can't I have my own opinions? Why do I have to get in on this—insanity?'

The analyst smiled tolerantly. 'That's a little harsh, Don. You're out of phase with your society, you know. So the cultural climate and mores seem a trifle unconvincing to you. But this is your society; you have to live in it. You can't withdraw.'

Walsh forced his hands to relax. 'Here's what I think. Any man who wants to smell should be allowed to smell. Any man who doesn't want to smell should go and get his glands removed. What's the matter with that?'

'Don, you're avoiding the issue.' The robot's voice was calm, dispassionate. 'What you're saying is that neither side is right. And that's foolish, isn't it? One side must be right.'

'Why?'

'Because the two sides exhaust the practical possibilities. Your position isn't really a position . . . it's a sort of description. You see, Don, you have a psychological inability to come to grips with an issue. You don't want to commit yourself for fear you'll lose your freedom and individuality. You're sort of an intellectual virgin; you want to stay pure.'

Walsh reflected. 'I want,' he said, 'to keep my integrity.'

'You're not an isolated individual, Don. You're a part of society . . . ideas don't exist in a vacuum.'

'I have a right to hold my own ideas.'

'No, Don,' the robot answered gently. 'They're not your ideas; you didn't create them. You can't turn them on and off when you feel like it. They operate through you . . . they're conditionings deposited by your environment. What you believe is a reflection of certain social forces and pressures. In your case the two mutually-exclusive social trends have produced a sort of stalemate. You're at

THE CHROMIUM FENCE

war with yourself . . . you can't decide which side to join because elements of both exist in you.' The robot nodded wisely. 'But you've got to make a decision. You've got to resolve this conflict and act. You can't remain a spectator . . . you've got to be a participant. Nobody can be a spectator to life . . . and this is life.'

'You mean there's no other world but this business about sweat and teeth and hair?'

'Logically, there are other societies. But this is the one you were born into. This is your society . . . the only one you will ever have. You either live in it, or you don't live.'

Walsh got to his feet. 'In other words, I have to make the adjustment. Something has to give, and it's got to be me.'

'Afraid so, Don. It would be silly to expect everybody else to adjust to you, wouldn't it? Three and a half billion people would have to change just to please Don Walsh. You see, Don, you're not quite out of your infantile-selfish stage. You haven't quite got to the point of facing reality.' The robot smiled. 'But you will.'

Walsh started moodily from the office. 'I'll think it over.'

'It's for your own good, Don.'

At the door, Walsh turned to say something more. But the robot had clicked off; it was fading into darkness and silence, elbows still resting on the desk. The dimming overhead lights caught something he hadn't noticed before. The powercord that was the robot's umbilicus had a white-plastic tag wired to it. In the semi-gloom he could make out the printed words.

PROPERTY OF THE FEDERAL COUNCIL
FOR PUBLIC USE ONLY

The robot, like everything else in the multi-family unit, was supplied by the controlling institutions of society. The analyst was a creature of the state, a bureaucrat with a desk and job. Its function was to equate people like Don Walsh with the world as it was.

But if he didn't listen to the unit analyst, who was he supposed to listen to? Where else could he go?

*

Three days later the election took place. The glaring headline told him nothing he didn't already know; his office had buzzed with the news all day. He put the paper away in his coat pocket and didn't examine it until he got home.

PURISTS WIN BY LANDSLIDE

HORNEY AMENDMENT CERTAIN TO PASS

Walsh lay back wearily in his chair. In the kitchen Betty was briskly preparing dinner. The pleasant clink of dishes and the warm odor of cooking food drifted through the bright little apartment.

'The Purists won,' Walsh said, when Betty appeared with an armload of silver and cups. 'It's all over.'

'Jimmy will be happy,' Betty answered vaguely. 'I wonder if Carl will be home in time for dinner.' She calculated silently. 'Maybe I ought to run downramp for some more coffee.'

'Don't you understand?' Walsh demanded. 'It's happened! The Purists have complete power!'

'I understand,' Betty answered peevishly. 'You don't have to shout. Did you sign that petition thing? That Butte Petition the Naturalists have been circulating?'

'No.'

'Thank God. I didn't think so; you never sign anything anybody brings around.' She lingered at the kitchen door. 'I hope Carl has sense enough to do something. I never did like him sitting around guzzling beer and smelling like a pig in summer.'

The door of the apartment opened and Carl hurried in, flushed and scowling. 'Don't fix dinner for me, Betty. I'll be at an emergency meeting.' He glanced briefly at Walsh. 'Now are you satisfied? If you'd put your back to the wheel, maybe this wouldn't have happened.'

'How soon will they get the Amendment passed?' Walsh asked.

Carl bellowed with nervous laughter. 'They've already passed it.' He grabbed up an armload of papers from his desk and stuffed them in a waste-disposal slot. 'We've got informants at Purist head-

THE CHROMIUM FENCE

quarters. As soon as the new councilmen were sworn in they rammed the Amendment through. They want to catch us unawares.' He grinned starkly. 'But they won't.'

The door slammed and Carl's hurried footsteps diminished down the public hall.

'I've never seen him move so fast,' Betty remarked wonderingly.

Horror rose in Don Walsh as he listened to the rapid, lumbering footsteps of his brother-in-law. Outside the unit, Carl was climbing quickly into his surface car. The motor gunned, and Carl drove off. 'He's afraid,' Walsh said. 'He's in danger.'

'I guess he can take care of himself. He's pretty big.'

Walsh shakily lit a cigarette. 'Even your brother isn't that big. It doesn't seem possible they really mean this. Putting over an Amendment like this, forcing everybody to conform to their idea of what's right. But it's been in the cards for years . . . this is the last step on a large road.'

'I wish they'd get it over with, once and for all,' Betty complained. 'Was it always this way? I don't remember always hearing about politics when I was a child.'

'They didn't call it politics, back in those days. The industrialists hammered away at the people to buy and consume. It centered around this hair-sweat-teeth purity; the city people got it and developed an ideology around it.'

Betty set the table and brought in the dishes of food. 'You mean the Purist political movement was deliberately started?'

'They didn't realize what a hold it was getting on them. They didn't know their children were growing up to take such things as underarm perspiration and white teeth and nice-looking hair as the most important things in the world. Things worth fighting and dying for. Things important enough to kill those who didn't agree.'

'The Naturalists were country people?'

'People who lived outside the cities and weren't conditioned by the stimuli.' Walsh shook his head irritably. 'Incredible, that one man will kill another over trivialities. All through history men murdering each other over verbal nonsense, meaningless slogans instilled in them by somebody else—who sits back and benefits.'

'It isn't meaningless if they believe in it.'

'It's meaningless to kill another man because he has halitosis! It's meaningless to beat up somebody because he hasn't had his sweat glands removed and artificial waste-excretion tubes installed. There's going to be senseless warfare; the Naturalists have weapons stored up at party headquarters. Men'll be just as dead as if they died for something real.'

'Time to eat, dear,' Betty said, indicating the table.

'I'm not hungry.'

'Stop sulking and eat. Or you'll have indigestion, and you know what that means.'

He knew what it meant, all right. It meant his life was in danger. One belch in the presence of a Purist and it was a life and death struggle. There was no room in the same world for men who belched and men who wouldn't tolerate men who belched. Something had to give ... and it had already given. The Amendment had been passed: the Naturalists' days were numbered.

'Jimmy will be late tonight,' Betty said, as she helped herself to lamb chops, green peas, and creamed corn. 'There's some sort of Purist celebration. Speeches, parades, torch-light rallies.' She added wistfully, 'I guess we can't go down and watch, can we? It'll be pretty, all the lights and voices, and marching.'

'Go ahead.' Listlessly, Walsh spooned up his food. He ate without tasting. 'Enjoy yourself.'

They were still eating, when the door burst open and Carl entered briskly. 'Anything left for me?' he demanded.

Betty half-rose, astonished. 'Carl! You don't—smell any more.'

Carl seated himself and grabbed for the plate of lamb chops. Then he recollected, and daintily selected a small one, and a tiny portion of peas. 'I'm hungry,' he admitted, 'but not too hungry.' He ate carefully, quietly.

Walsh gazed at him dumbfounded. 'What the hell happened?' he demanded. 'Your hair—and your teeth and breath. *What did you do?*'

Without looking up, Carl answered, 'Party tactics. We're beating a strategical retreat. In the face of this Amendment, there's no point in doing something foolhardy. Hell, we don't intend to get slaughtered.' He sipped some luke-warm coffee. 'As a matter of fact, we've gone underground.'

Walsh slowly lowered his fork. 'You mean you're not going to fight?'

'Hell, no. It's suicide.' Carl glanced furtively around. 'Now listen to me. I'm completely in conformity with the provisions of the Horney Amendment; nobody can pin a thing on me. When the cops come snooping around, keep your mouths shut. The Amendment gives the right to recant, and that's technically what we've done. We're clean; they can't touch us. But let's just not say anything.' He displayed a small blue card. 'A Purist membership card. Backdated; we planned for any eventuality.'

'Oh, Carl!' Betty cried delightedly. 'I'm so glad. You look just—wonderful!'

Walsh said nothing.

'What's the matter?' Betty demanded. 'Isn't this what you wanted? You didn't want them to fight and kill each other—' Her voice rose shrilly. 'Won't anything satisfy you? This is what you wanted and you're still dissatisfied. What on earth more do you want?'

There was noise below the unit. Carl sat up straight, and for an instant color left his face. He would have begun sweating if it were still possible. 'That's the conformity police,' he said thickly. 'Just sit tight; they'll make a routine check and keep on going.'

'Oh, dear,' Betty gasped. 'I hope they don't break anything. Maybe I better go and freshen up.'

'Just sit still,' Carl grated. 'There's no reason for them to suspect anything.'

When the door opened, Jimmy stood dwarfed by the green-tinted conformity police.

'There he is!' Jimmy shrilled, indicating Carl. 'He's a Naturalist official! *Smell* him!'

The police spread efficiently into the room. Standing around the immobile Carl, they examined him briefly, then moved away. 'No body odor,' the police sergeant disagreed. 'No halitosis. Hair thick and well-groomed.' He signalled, and Carl obediently opened his mouth. 'Teeth white, totally brushed. Nothing nonacceptable. No, this man is all right.'

Jimmy glared furiously at Carl. 'Pretty smart.'

Carl picked stoically at his plate of food and ignored the boy and the police.

'Apparently we've broken the core of Naturalist resistance,' the sergeant said into his neck-phone. 'At least in this area there's no organized opposition.'

'Good,' the phone answered. 'Your area was a stronghold. We'll go ahead and set up the compulsory purification machinery, though. It should be implemented as soon as possible.'

One of the cops turned his attention to Don Walsh. His nostrils twitched and then a harsh, oblique expression settled over his face. 'What's your name?' he demanded.

Walsh gave his name.

The police came cautiously around him. 'Body odor,' one noted. 'But hair fully restored and groomed. Open your mouth.'

Walsh opened his mouth.

'Teeth clean and white. But—' The cop sniffed. 'Faint halitosis . . . stomach variety. I don't get it. Is he a Naturalist or isn't he?'

'He's not a Purist,' the sergeant said. 'No Purist would have body odor. So he must be a Naturalist.'

Jimmy pushed forward. 'This man,' he explained, 'is only a fellow hiker. He's not a party member.'

'You know him?'

'He's—related to me,' Jimmy admitted.

The police took notes. 'He's been playing around with Naturalists, but he hasn't gone the whole way?'

'He's on the fence,' Jimmy agreed. 'A quasi-Naturalist. He can be salvaged; this shouldn't be a criminal case.'

'Remedial action,' the sergeant noted. 'All right, Walsh,' he addressed Walsh. 'Get your things and let's go. The Amendment provides compulsory purification for your type of person; let's not waste time.'

Walsh hit the sergeant in the jaw.

The sergeant sprawled foolishly, arms flapping, dazed with disbelief. The cops drew their guns hysterically and milled around the room shouting and knocking into each other. Betty began to scream wildly. Jimmy's shrill voice was lost in the general uproar.

Walsh grabbed up a table lamp and smashed it over a cop's head. The lights in the apartment flickered and died out; the room was a chaos of yelling blackness. Walsh encountered a body; he kicked with his knee and with a groan of pain the body settled down. For a moment he was lost in the seething din; then his fingers found the door. He pried it open and scrambled out into the public corridor.

One shape followed, as Walsh reached the descent lift. '*Why?*' Jimmy wailed unhappily. 'I had it all fixed—you didn't have to worry!'

His thin, metallic voice faded as the lift plunged down the well to the ground floor. Behind Walsh, the police were coming cautiously out into the hall; the sound of their boots echoed dismally after him.

He examined his watch. Probably, he had fifteen or twenty minutes. They'd get him, then; it was inevitable. Taking a deep breath, he stepped from the lift and as calmly as possible walked down the dark, deserted commercial corridor, between the rows of black store-entrances.

Charley was lit up and animate, when Walsh entered the antechamber. Two men were waiting, and a third was being interviewed. But at the sight of the expression on Walsh's face the robot waved him instantly in.

'What is it, Don?' it asked seriously, indicating a chair. 'Sit down and tell me what's on your mind.'

Walsh told it.

When he was finished, the analyst sat back and gave a low, soundless whistle. 'That's a felony, Don. They'll freeze you for that; it's a provision of the new Amendment.'

'I know,' Walsh agreed. He felt no emotion. For the first time in years the ceaseless swirl of feelings and thoughts had been purged from his mind. He was a little tired and that was all.

The robot shook its head. 'Well, Don, you're finally off the fence. That's something, at least; you're finally moving.' It reached thoughtfully into the top drawer of its desk and got out a pad. 'Is the police pick-up van here, yet?'

'I heard sirens as I came in the ante-room. It's on its way.'

The robot's metal fingers drummed restlessly on the surface of the big mahogany desk. 'Your sudden release of inhibition marks the moment of psychological integration. You're not undecided any more, are you?'

'No,' Walsh said.

'Good. Well, it had to come sooner or later. I'm sorry it had to come this way, though.'

'I'm not,' Walsh said. 'This was the only way possible. It's clear to me, now. Being undecided isn't necessarily a negative thing. Not seeing anything in slogans and organized parties and beliefs and dying can be a belief worth dying for, in itself. I thought I was without a creed . . . now I realize I have a very strong creed.'

The robot wasn't listening. It scribbled something on its pad, signed it, and then expertly tore it off. 'Here.' It handed the paper briskly to Walsh.

'What's this?' Walsh demanded.

'I don't want anything to interfere with your therapy. You're finally coming around—and we want to keep moving.' The robot got quickly to its feet. 'Good luck, Don. Show that to the police; if there's any trouble have them call me.'

The slip was a voucher from the Federal Psychiatric Board. Walsh turned it over numbly. 'You mean this'll get me off?'

'You were acting compulsively; you weren't responsible. There'll be a cursory examination, of course, but nothing to worry about.'

The robot slapped him good-naturedly on the back. 'It was your final neurotic act ... now you're free. That was the pent-up stuff; strictly a symbolic assertion of libido—with no political significance.'

'I see,' Walsh said.

The robot propelled him firmly toward the external exit. 'Now go on out there and give the slip to them.' From its metal chest the robot popped a small bottle. 'And take one of these capsules before you go to sleep. Nothing serious, just a mild sedative to quiet your nerves. Everything will be all right; I'll expect to see you again, soon. And keep this in mind: we're finally making some real progress.'

Walsh found himself outside in the night darkness. A police van was pulled up at the entrance of the unit, a vast ominous black shape against the dead sky. A crowd of curious people had collected at a safe distance, trying to make out what was going on.

Walsh automatically put the bottle of pills away in his coat pocket. He stood for a time breathing the chill night air, the cold clear smell of darkness and evening. Above his head a few bright pale stars glittered remotely.

'Hey,' one of the policemen shouted. He flashed his light suspiciously in Walsh's face. 'Come over here.'

'That looks like him,' another said. 'Come on, buddy. Make it snappy.'

Walsh brought out the voucher Charley had given him. 'I'm coming,' he answered. As he walked up to the policeman he carefully tore the paper to shreds and tossed the shreds to the night wind. The wind picked the shreds up and scattered them away.

'What the hell did you do?' one of the cops demanded.

'Nothing,' Walsh answered. 'I just threw away some waste paper. Something I won't be needing.'

'What a strange one this one is,' a cop muttered, as they froze Walsh with their cold beams. 'He gives me the creeps.'

'Be glad we don't get more like him,' another said. 'Except for a few guys like this, everything's going fine.'

THE CHROMIUM FENCE

Walsh's inert body was tossed in the van and the doors slammed shut. Disposal machinery immediately began consuming his body and reducing it to basic mineral elements. A moment later, the van was on its way to the next call.

MISADJUSTMENT

When Richards got home from work he had a secret little routine he went through, a pleasant series of actions that brought him more satisfaction than his ten-hour workday at the Commerce Institute. He tossed his briefcase into a chair, rolled up his sleeves, grabbed a squirt-tank of liquid fertilizer, and kicked open the back door. Cool late-evening sunlight filtered down on him as he stepped gingerly across the moist black soil to the center of the garden. His heart thudded excitedly; how was it coming?

Fine. Growing bigger every day.

He watered it, tore off a few old leaves, spaded up the soil, killed a weed that had edged in, squirted fertilizer at random, and then stepped back to survey it. There was no satisfaction like that of creative activity. On the job he was a high-paid cog in the niplan economic system; he worked with verbal signs, and somebody else's signs at that. Here, he dealt directly with reality.

Richards squatted on his haunches and surveyed what he had accomplished. It was a good sight; almost ready, almost fully grown. He leaned forward to poke cautiously at the firm sides.

In the dwindling light of day the high-velocity transport glittered dully. Its windows had already formed: four pale squares in the tapered metal hull. The control bubble was just starting to burgeon from the center of the chassis. The jet flanges were full and developed. The input hatch and emergency locks hadn't grown into existence, yet; but it wouldn't be long.

Richards' satisfaction rose to fever-pitch. No doubt about it:

the transport was almost ripe. Any day now he could pick it . . . and start flying it around.

At nine the waiting room had been full of people and cigarette smoke; now, at three-thirty, it was almost empty. One by one the visitors had given up and departed. Discarded tapes, bulging ashtrays, empty chairs surrounded the robot desk industriously grinding out its mechanical business. But in one corner, sitting bolt upright, her small hands clasped around her purse, remained a last young woman the desk hadn't been able to discourage.

The desk tried once more. It was getting close to four; Eggerton would soon be leaving. The gross irrationality of waiting for a man about to put on his hat and coat and go home grated against the desk's sensitive nerves. And the girl had been sitting there since nine, eyes large and wide, gazing at nothing, not smoking or examining tapes, only sitting and waiting.

'Look, lady,' the desk said aloud, 'there's nobody going to see Mr Eggerton today.'

The girl smiled slightly. 'It'll only take a minute.'

The desk sighed. 'You're persistent. What do you want? Your firm must do a spectacular business with jobbers like you—but as I said, Mr Eggerton never buys anything. That's how he got where he is, by throwing people like you out. I suppose you think that figure of yours is going to get you a big order.' The desk added peevishly, 'You ought to be ashamed, wearing a dress like that. A nice girl like you.'

'He'll see me,' the girl answered faintly.

The desk whizzed forms through its scanner and searched for a double-entendre on the word *see*. 'Yes, I suppose with a dress like that,' it began, but at that moment the inner door lifted and John Eggerton appeared.

'Turn yourself off,' he ordered the desk; 'I'm going home. Set yourself for ten; I'll be late tomorrow. The id bloc is holding a policy level conference in Pittsburgh, and I have a few things to say to them while they're together.'

The girl slid to her feet. John Eggerton was a huge, ape-shouldered man, shaggy and unkempt, his jacket hanging open and food-stained, sleeves rolled up, eyes deep-set and dark with industrial cunning. He peered at her warily as she approached.

'Mr Eggerton,' she said, 'do you have a moment? There's something I want to discuss with you.'

'I'm not buying and I'm not hiring.' Eggerton's voice was gruff with fatigue. 'Young lady, go back to your employer and tell them if they want to show me something to send around an experienced representative, not a kid just out of . . .'

Eggerton was nearsighted. It wasn't until the girl was almost to him that he saw the card between her fingers. For a man of his size he moved with astonishing agility; with one leap he knocked the girl aside, dashed around the robot desk, and disappeared through a side exit from the office. The girl's purse clattered to the floor, its contents spilling wildly. She hesitated between them and the door, then with an exasperated hiss, rushed from the office and out into the hall. The express elevator to the roof showed red; it was already on its way up fifty stories to the building's private field.

'Damn,' the girl said. She turned and reentered the office, seething with disgust.

The desk had begun to recover. 'Why didn't you tell me you're an Immune?' it demanded. Its outrage grew—the indignation of a bureaucrat. 'I gave you form so45 to fill out and line six distinctly asked for specific information on your occupation. You—*deceived* me!'

The girl ignored the desk and knelt down to collect her things. Gun, magnetic bracelet, intercom neck-mike, lipstick, keys, mirror, small change, handkerchief, the twenty-four-hour notice intended for John Eggerton . . . she was going to get hell when she appeared back at the Agency. Eggerton had even managed to avoid oral acknowledgment: the spool of recording tape spilled from her purse was blank and useless.

'You've got a clever boss,' she said to the desk, in a burst of wrath. 'All day sitting here in this reeking office with all these salesmen for nothing.'

'I wondered why you were so persistent,' the desk said. 'I never saw a saleswoman so persistent; I should have known something was wrong. You almost got him.'

'We'll get him,' the girl said, on her way out of the office. 'Tell him that tomorrow, when he shows up.'

'He won't show up,' the desk answered; to itself, since the girl was gone. 'He won't ever come back here, not now. Not with you Immunes hanging around. A man's life is worth more than his business, even a business this size.'

The girl entered a public vid booth and dialed the Agency. 'He skipped,' she said to the grim-faced woman who was her immediate superior. 'He didn't touch the summons-card; I guess I'm not much of a server.'

'Did he see the card?'

'Of course; that's why he bolted.'

The older woman scratched a few tentative lines on a note pad. 'Technically, we have him. I'll let our lawyers battle it out with his heirs; I'm going ahead with the twenty-four-hour notice, just as if he accepted it. If he was wary before, he'll be impossible from now on; we'll never get closer than this. It's too bad you muffed this . . .' The woman decided. 'Call his home and give his personal staff the notice of culpability. Tomorrow morning we'll release it over the regular newsmachines.'

Doris broke the circuit, held her hand over the screen to clear it, and then dialed Eggerton's personal number. To the attendant she gave the formal notice that Eggerton was legal prey for any niplan citizen. The attendant—mechanical—dutifully took the information as if it had been an order for so many dozen yards of cloth. Somehow, the machine's calmness made her more discouraged than ever. She left the booth and wandered gloomily down-ramp to the cocktail bar to wait for her husband.

John Eggerton didn't seem like a parakineticist. Doris's mind imagined small wan-faced youths, withdrawn and agonized, buried in out-of-the-way towns and farms, hidden away from urban areas. Eggerton was prominent ... but of course that didn't affect his chance of being picked up in the random check-net. As she sipped her Tom Collins, she tried to think of other reasons why John Eggerton would ignore his initial check notice, then his warning—fine and possible imprisonment—and now this, his last notice.

Was Eggerton really P-K?

Her face in the dark mirror behind the bar wavered, rings of half-shadows, nebulous succubi, a gloom of fog like that which lay over the niplan system. Her reflection might have been that of a young female parakineticist: black circles for eyes, moist lashes, dank hair around her thin shoulders, fingers too tapered and too sharp. But it was only the mirror; there were no distaff parakineticists. At least, none reported *yet*.

Unnoticed, her husband came up behind her, tossed his coat over a stool, and seated himself. 'How did it come off?' Harvey asked sympathetically.

Doris started in surprise. 'You scared me!'

Harvey lit a cigarette and attracted the attention of the bartender. 'Bourbon and water.' He turned mildly to his wife. 'Cheer up—there're other mutants to track down.' He tossed her the foil from the afternoon newsmachines. 'You probably know already, but your San Francisco office picked up four in a row. All of them unique; there was one party who had a sweet little talent of speeding up metabolic processes in those he didn't care for.'

Doris nodded absently. 'We heard through the Agency memos. And one could walk through walls, without falling through floors. And one animated stones.'

'Eggerton got away?'

'Like lightning—I wouldn't think a man that big would react that fast. But maybe he isn't a man.' She spun her tall cold glass between her fingers. 'The Agency is going to give the public twenty-four-hour notice. I've already called his home ... that gives his personal staff a head start.'

'They ought to have it. After all, they've been working for him;

they ought to have first crack at the bounty.' Harvey was trying to be funny, but his wife didn't respond. 'You think a man that big can hide out?'

Doris shrugged. The problem was simple with the ones who hid; they gave themselves away by departing more and more from the behavior norm. It was the ones unaware of their innate difference, those who kept on functioning until discovered by accident . . . the so-called *unconscious* P-Ks had forced into existence the random check system and its Agency of female Immunes. In Doris's mind, the weird thought crept that a man might not be P-K and think he was—the timeless neurotic fear that one was somehow different, oddball, when in fact one was quite normal. Eggerton, for all his industrial power and influence, might be an ordinary human being suffering from a gnawing phobia that he was P-K. Such had happened . . . and there were genuine P-Ks wandering around blithely unaware of their alienness.

'We need a sure-fire test,' Doris said aloud. 'Something an individual can apply on himself. So he can be *certain*.'

'Don't you have it? Can't you be positive when you get hold of them in your net?'

'*If* we get hold of them. One out of ten thousand. Too damn small a number come up in the nets.' Abruptly she pushed away her drink and got to her feet. 'Let's go home. I'm hungry and tired; I want to go to bed.'

Harvey gathered up his coat as he paid the tab. 'Sorry, honey, we're going out for dinner tonight. A fellow in the Commerce Institute, a man named Jay Richards. I met him at luncheon . . . as a matter of fact, you were along. We're all invited over to celebrate something.'

'Celebrate what?' Doris demanded irritably. 'What do we have to celebrate?'

'Something secret of his,' Harvey answered, as he pushed open the wide street door. 'He's going to spring it on us after dinner. Cheer up—it may be good for an evening's entertainment.'

*

Eggerton did not fly directly home. At high velocity he circled aimlessly near the first ring of residential syndromes at the edge of New York, his mind ebbing first with terror, then with outrage. His natural impulse was to head for his own lands and houses, but fear of running into more Agency servers paralyzed his will. While he was trying to make up his mind, his neck-mike came on with the relay of the Agency's call.

He was lucky. The girl had given the twenty-four-hour notice to one of his robots; and robots weren't interested in bounty.

He landed on a randomly-selected roof field within the industrial area of Pittsburgh. No one saw him: lucky again. He was trembling as he entered the descent elevator, and began the trip down to the street level. With him were crowded a blank-faced clerk, two elderly women, a serious young man, and the pretty daughter of some minor official. A harmless clump of people, but he wasn't fooled; at the end of twenty-four hours any and all of them would be panting for his hide. And he couldn't blame them: ten million dollars was a lot of money.

Theoretically, he had a one-day grace period; but final notices were badly-kept secrets. Most higher-ups were undoubtedly in on it; he'd approach an old friend, be welcomed, wined and dined, given a cabin-shelter on Ganymede and plenty of supplies—and be shot between the eyes as soon as the day was up.

He had remote units of his own industrial combine, of course; but they'd be checked off systematically. He had a variety of holding companies, dummy corporations, but the Agency would run through them if they considered it worth their time. The intuitive realization that he could easily become an object lesson to the niplan system, manipulated and exploited by the Agency, drove him to a frenzy. The female Immunes had always tripped deep-buried complexes built up in his mind from early infancy; the thought of a matriarchal culture was vitally abhorrent to him. And to pick off Eggerton was to unfasten a basic pivot of the bloc: now it occurred to him that his number on the random check might not really be random after all.

Clever—compile the identifying serial numbers of the id bloc leaders, revolve them in the check-nets from time to time, gradually eliminate them one by one.

He reached the street level and stood undecided, as urban traffic flowed around him noisily. Suppose the id bloc leaders simply cooperated with the check-nets? Compliance with the initial notice meant only a routine mind-probe by the protected corps of mutants society sanctioned, the telepathic *castrati* tolerated because of their usefulness against other mutants. Pulled at random or by design, the victim could simply permit the probe, lay his mind bare to the Agency, let the battleaxes claw and peck over the contents of his psyche, and then return to his office, cleared and safe. But this posited one item: that the industrial leader could pass the probe, that he was not P-K.

Sweat stood out on Eggerton's heavy forehead. Wasn't he, in a roundabout way, telling himself that he *was* P-K? No, that wasn't it. The issue was a principle; the Agency had no moral right to probe the half-dozen men whose industrial bloc was the mainstay of the niplan system. On that point every id bloc leader agreed with him . . . an attack on Eggerton was an assault on the bloc itself.

Fervently, he prayed they *would* see it that way. He hailed a robot taxi and ordered: 'Get me over to the id bloc hall. And if anybody tries to halt you, fifty dollars says keep going.'

The vast, echoing hall was dark and gloomy when he reached it. The meeting wouldn't begin for several days, yet; Eggerton wandered aimlessly up and down the aisles, between the rows of seats where the technological and clerical staffs of the various industrial units would be placed, past the steel and plastic benches where the leaders themselves sat, up finally to the vacant speaker's stand. Faint lights glowed for him as he halted vaguely before the marble stand. The futility of his position came to him with a rush: standing here in this empty hall, he momentarily comprehended how completely he had made himself an outcast. He could yell and shout and nobody would appear. He could summon up nobody and nothing; the Agency was the legal government of the niplan system. In

MISADJUSTMENT

tilting with it he had placed himself against all organized society—powerful as he was he couldn't hope to defeat society itself.

He left the hall hurriedly, located an expensive restaurant, and enjoyed a lavish dinner. Almost feverishly, he downed immense quantities of scarce imported delicacies; at least he could enjoy his last twenty-four hours. As he ate he gazed apprehensively at the waiters and the other diners. Bland, indifferent faces—but very soon they would see his number and image in every newsmachine. The great hunt would be on; billions of hunters after one quarry. Abruptly, he finished his meal, examined his watch, and left the restaurant. It was six in the evening.

For an hour he squandered himself furiously in a swank bed girl mart, going from one apartment to the next, only half-seeing the occupants. He left behind a chaos—for which he paid; and then abandoned the frenetic turmoil for the fresh air of the evening streets. Until eleven he wandered through the dark star-lit parks that surrounded the residential area of the city, among other dim shadows, his hands stuffed miserably in his pockets, hunched over, wretched. Somewhere far off a city clock-tower radiated an audio time signal. The twenty-four hours were leaking out and no one could stop them.

At eleven-thirty he halted his purposeless wanderings and pulled himself together long enough to analyze his situation. He had to face it: his only chance lay back at the id bloc hall. The technological and clerical staffs wouldn't have begun to show, but most of the leaders would be staking out preferred living quarters. His wristmap showed that he had drifted five miles from the hall. Suddenly terrified, he made his decision.

He flew directly back to the hall, landed on the deserted roof field, and descended to the floor of living quarters. It couldn't be put off: it was now or never.

'Come in, John,' Townsand invited good-naturedly, and then his expression changed as Eggerton briefly outlined what had taken place in his office.

'You say they've already sent the final notice to your home?' Laura Townsand asked quickly. She had got up from the couch where she had been sitting and came immediately to the door. 'Then it's too late!'

Eggerton tossed his overcoat to the closet and sank down in an easy chair. 'Too late? Maybe . . . too late to avoid the notice; but I'm not giving up.'

Townsand and the other id bloc leaders came around Eggerton, faces showing curiosity, sympathy, and traces of cold amusement. 'You've really got yourself into something,' one of the leaders said. 'If you'd let us know before the final notice was sent out maybe we could have done something. But this late . . .'

Eggerton strangled as he felt the boom being lowered down around him. 'Wait,' he said thickly, 'let's get this straight. We're all in this together; it's me today and you tomorrow. If I fold under this—'

'Take it easy,' murmured voices came. 'Let's work this out rationally or not at all.'

Eggerton lay back against the chair as it adjusted to his tired body. Yes, he was glad to work it out rationally.

'As I see it,' Townsand said quietly, leaning forward, his fingers pressed together, 'it's not really a question of *can* we neutralize the Agency. Collectively, we're the economic battery of the niplan system; if we draw the props out from under the Agency it collapses. The real question is—do we *want* to write off the Agency?'

Eggerton croaked wildly: 'Good God, it's either us or them! Can't you see they're using this net-check and probe system to undermine us?'

Townsand glanced at him and then continued for the benefit of the other leaders. 'Perhaps we're forgetting something. *We* set up the Agency in the first place; that is, the id bloc before us worked out the fundamentals of random net-check inspection, use of tame telepaths, the final notice and hunt—the whole works. *The Agency is for our protection*; otherwise parakineticists would grow like weeds and finally choke us off. Of course, we must keep control of the Agency . . . it's our instrument.'

'Yes,' another leader agreed. 'We can't let it get on our backs; Eggerton is certainly right, there.'

'We can assume,' Townsand continued, 'that some mechanism must exist at all times to detect P-Ks. If the Agency goes, something must be constructed in its place. Now I tell you what, John.' He gazed thoughtfully at Eggerton. 'If you can think of a substitute, then maybe we'll be interested. But if not, then the Agency stands. Since the first P-K back in 2045, only females have shown immunity. Whatever we set up will have to be operated from a female policy-board . . . and that's the Agency all over again.'

There was silence.

Dimly, in Eggerton's mind, the ghosts of hope flickered. 'You agree the Agency is on our backs?' he demanded huskily. 'All right, we have to assert ourselves.' He gestured around the room futilely; the leaders were watching stonily and Laura Townsand was quietly pouring coffee into half-empty cups. She shot him a glance of mute sympathy and then turned back to the kitchen. Cold silence cut down around Eggerton; he settled unhappily back in his chair and listened to Townsand drone on.

'I'm sorry you didn't inform us that your number had come up,' Townsand was saying. 'On the first notice we could have done something, but not now. Not unless we want to have a showdown at this time—and I don't think we're prepared for that.' He pointed his authoritative finger at Eggerton. 'You know, John, I don't think you really understand what these P-K individuals are. You probably think of them as lunatics, people with delusions.'

'I know what they are,' Eggerton answered stiffly. But he couldn't keep himself from saying, '*Aren't* they people with delusions?'

'They're lunatics who have the power to actualize their delusional systems in space–time. They warp a limited area around them to conform to their eccentric notions—understand? *The P-K makes his delusion work.* Therefore in a sense it isn't a delusion . . . not unless you can stand far enough back, get a long way off and compare his warped area with the world proper. But how can the P-K himself do that? He has no objective standard; he can't very well get away from himself, and the warp follows him wherever he goes. The really dangerous P-Ks are the ones who think everybody can animate stones, or change themselves into animals, or transmute base minerals. If we let a P-K get away, if we let him grow up, reproduce, have a family, a wife and children, we let this inherited parafaculty spread . . . it becomes a group belief . . . it becomes a socially institutionalized practice.

'Any given P-K is capable of spawning a society of P-Ks built around his particular power. The great danger is this: eventually we non-P-Ks may become the minority . . . our rational world-view may come to be considered eccentric.'

Eggerton licked his lips. The dry, languid voice made him sick; as Townsand spoke the ominous chill of death settled over him. 'In other words,' he muttered, 'you're not going to help me.'

'That's right,' Townsand said. 'But not because we don't *want* to help you. We feel that the danger from the Agency is less than you imagine; we consider the P-Ks the real menace. Find us some way we can detect them without the Agency, and we'll go along with you—but not until then.' He leaned close to Eggerton and tapped him on the shoulder with a lean, bony finger. 'If females weren't clear of this stuff, we wouldn't stand a chance. We're lucky . . . we could be a lot worse off than we are.'

Eggerton got slowly to his feet.

'Goodnight.'

Townsand also rose. There was a moment of strained, awkward silence. 'However,' Townsand said, 'we can beat this hunt and chase rap they have on you. There's still time; the public notice hasn't been put out, yet.'

'What'll I do?' Eggerton asked hopelessly.

'You have the written copy of your twenty-four-hour notice?'

'No!' Eggerton's voice cracked hysterically. 'I ran out of the office before the girl could give it to me!'

Townsand pondered. 'You know who she is? You know where you can find her?'

'No.'

'Make inquiries. Trace her down, accept the notice, then throw yourself on the mercy of the Agency.'

Eggerton spread his hands numbly. 'But that means I'll be bonded to them for the rest of my life.'

'You'll be alive,' Townsand said mildly, without emotion of any kind.

Laura Townsand brought steaming black coffee over to Eggerton. 'Cream or sugar?' she asked gently, when she was able to attract his attention. 'Or both? John, you must get something hot under your belt before you go; it's such a long trip back.'

The girl's name was Doris Sorrel. Her apartment was listed under the name Harvey Sorrel, her husband. There was no one there; Eggerton carbonized the door-lock, then entered and searched the four small rooms. He rooted through the dresser drawers, tossed clothing and personal articles aside one after another, systematically rifled the closets and cupboards. In the waste disposal slot by the work desk he found what he was looking for: a not-yet incinerated note, crumpled and discarded, a jotted notation with the name Jay Richards, the date and the time, the address, and the words, *if Doris isn't too tired.* Eggerton put the note in his coat pocket and departed.

It was three-thirty in the morning when he found them. He landed on the roof of the squat Commerce Institute Building and descended the ramp to the residential floors. From the north wing light and noise came: the party was still in session. Praying silently, Eggerton raised his hand to the door and tripped the analyzer.

The man who opened the door was handsome, gray-haired, a heavy man in his late thirties. A glass in one hand, he gazed blankly at Eggerton, his eyes blurred with fatigue and alcohol. 'I don't remember inviting–' he began, but Eggerton pushed past him and into the apartment.

There were plenty of people. Sitting, standing, keeping up a low murmur of talk and laughter. Liquor, soft couches, thick perfumes and fabrics, shifting color-walls, robots serving hors d'oeuvres, the muted cacophony of feminine giggles from darkened siderooms . . . Eggerton slid off his coat and moved aimlessly around. She was there somewhere; he glanced from face to face, saw only vacant, half-glazed eyes and slack mouths, and abruptly left the living room and entered a bedroom.

Doris Sorrel was standing at a window gazing silently out at the lights of the city, her back to him, one arm resting on the window sill. 'Oh,' she murmured, turning a little. 'Already?' And then she saw who it was.

'I want it,' Eggerton said. 'The twenty-four-hour notice; I'll take it, now.'

'You scared me.' Trembling she moved away from the wide expanse of window. 'How—long have you been here?'

'I just came.'

'But—why? You're a strange person, Mr Eggerton. You don't make sense.' She laughed nervously. 'I don't understand you at all.'

From the gloom the figure of a man emerged, briefly outlined in the doorway. 'Darling, here's your martini.' The man made out Eggerton, and an ugly expression settled over his half-stupefied face. 'Move on, buddy; this isn't for you.'

Shakily, Doris caught his arm. 'Harvey, this is the man I tried to serve today. Mr Eggerton, this is my husband.'

They shook hands icily. 'Where is it?' Eggerton demanded bluntly. 'You have it with you?'

'Yes . . . it's in my purse.' Doris moved away. 'I'll get it. You can come along, if you want.' She was regaining her composure. 'I think I left it around here somewhere. Harvey, where the hell's my purse?' In the darkness she fumbled for something small and vaguely shiny. 'Yes, here it is. On the bed.'

She stood lighting a cigarette and watching, as Eggerton examined the twenty-four-hour notice. 'Why did you come back?' she asked. For the party she had changed to a knee-length silk shirt, copper bracelets, sandals, and a luminous flower in her hair. Now the flower drooped miserably; her shirt was wrinkled and unbuttoned, and she looked dead-tired. Leaning against the bedroom

MISADJUSTMENT

wall, cigarette between her stained lips, she said: 'I don't see that it makes any difference what you do. The notice will be out publicly in half an hour—your personal staff has already been notified. God, I'm exhausted.' She looked around impatiently for her husband. 'Let's get out of here,' she said to him, as he wandered up. 'I have to go to work tomorrow.'

'We haven't seen it,' Harvey Sorrel answered sullenly.

'The hell with it!' Doris grabbed her coat from the closet. 'Why all this mystery? My God, we've been here five hours and he hasn't trotted it out *yet*. Even if he's perfected time travel or squared the circle I'm not interested, not this late.'

As she pushed her way through the crowded living room, Eggerton hurried to catch up with her. 'Listen to me,' he gasped. Holding onto her shoulder he continued rapidly, 'Townsand said if I came back I could throw myself on the mercy of the Agency. He said—'

The girl shook loose. 'Yes, of course; it's the law.' She turned angrily to her husband who had scrambled after them. 'Are you coming?'

'I'm coming,' Harvey answered, bloodshot eyes blazing with indignation. 'But I'm saying goodnight to Richards. And you're going to tell him it's *your* idea to leave; I'm not going to pretend it's my fault we're walking out. If you haven't got the social decency at least to say goodnight to your host . . .'

The gray-haired man who had let Eggerton in broke away from a circle of guests and came smilingly over. 'Harvey! Doris! Are you leaving? But you haven't seen it.' Dismay flooded his heavy face. 'You *can't* leave.'

Doris opened her mouth to say that she damn well could. 'Look,' Harvey cut in desperately, 'can't you show it to us now? Come on, Jay; we've waited long enough.'

Richards hesitated. More people were wearily getting up and clustering over. 'Come on,' voices demanded, 'let's get it over with.'

After a moment of indecision Richards conceded. 'All right,' he agreed; he knew he had stalled long enough. Into the tired, experience-satiated guests a measure of anticipation trickled back. Richards raised his arms dramatically; he was still going to milk what he could from the moment. 'This is it, folks! Come on along with me—it's out back.'

'I wondered where it was,' Harvey said, following after his host. 'Come on, Doris.' He seized her arm and dragged her after him. The others crowded along, through the dining room, the kitchen, to the back door.

The night was ice chill. Frigid wind blew around them as they shivered and stumbled uncertainly down the black steps, into the hyperborean gloom. John Eggerton felt a small shape push into him: as Doris savagely yanked away from her husband, Eggerton managed to follow after her. She rapidly shoved through the mass of guests, along the concrete walk to the fence that enclosed the yard. 'Wait,' Eggerton gasped, 'listen to me. Then the Agency will take me?' He was powerless to keep the thin edge of pleading from his voice. 'I can count on that? The notice will be voided?'

Doris sighed wearily. 'That's right. Okay, if you want, I'll take you over to the Agency and get action on your papers; otherwise they'll sit there for a month. You know what it means, I suppose. You're indentured to the Agency for the balance of your natural life; you know that, I suppose. Do you?'

'I know.'

'Do you want that?' She was distantly curious. 'A man like you . . . I would have thought otherwise.'

Eggerton twisted miserably. 'Townsand said—' he began pathetically.

'What I want to know,' Doris interrupted, 'is why you didn't respond to your first notice? If only you'd come around . . . this never would have happened.'

Eggerton opened his mouth to answer. He was going to say something about the principle involved, the concept of a free society, the rights of the individual, liberty and due process, the encroachment of the state. It was at that moment that Richards snapped on the powerful outdoor searchlights he had rigged up especially for the occasion; for the first time, his great achievement was revealed for everyone to see.

For a moment there was stunned silence. Then all at once they were screaming and milling from the yard. Wild-faced, dazed with terror, they scrambled over the fence, burst through the plastic wall surrounding the yard, crashed into the next yard and onto the public street.

Richards stood dumbfounded beside his masterpiece, bewildered and not yet understanding. In the artificial white glare of the searchlights the high-velocity transport was a thing of utter beauty. It was fully formed, completely ripe. Half an hour before, Richards had slipped outside with a flashlight, inspected it, and then, trembling with excitement, had cut the stem from which the ship had grown. It was now separate from the plant on which it had formed; he had rolled it to the edge of the yard, filled the fuel tank, slid back the hatch, and made it ready for flight.

On the plant were the embryonic buds of other transports, in various stages of growth. He had watered and fertilized with skill: the plant was going to turn out a dozen jet transports before the end of the summer.

Tears dribbled down Doris's tired cheeks. 'You see it?' she whispered wretchedly to Eggerton. 'It's—lovely. Look at it; see it sitting there?' Agonized, she turned away. 'Poor Jay . . . when he understands . . .'

Richards stood, feet planted apart, gazing around at the deserted, trampled remains of his yard. He made out the shapes of Eggerton and Doris; after a moment he started hesitantly toward them. 'Doris,' he choked brokenly, '*what is it?* What did I do?'

Suddenly his expression changed. Bewilderment vanished; first came brute, naked terror as finally he understood what he was, and why his guests had fled. And then crazed cunning fell into place. Richards turned clumsily and began lumbering across the yard toward his ship.

Eggerton killed him with a single shot at the base of the skull. As Doris began screaming shrilly, he shot out the searchlights one by one. The yard, Richards' body, the gleaming metal transport, dissolved in the frigid gloom. He shoved the girl down and forced her face into the wet, cold vines growing up the wall of the garden.

She was able to get hold of herself, after a time. Shuddering, she lay pressed against the mashed grass and vines, arms clutched around her waist, trembling back and forth in an aimless rocking motion that gradually drained itself away.

Eggerton helped her up. 'All these years and nobody suspected. He was saving it up—big secret.'

'You'll be all right,' Doris was saying, so low and faint that he could hardly hear her. 'The Agency will be willing to write you off; you stopped him.' Weak with shock, she groped blindly in the darkness for her scattered purse and cigarettes. 'He would have got away. And that *plant*. What are we going to do with it?' She found her cigarettes and lit up wildly. 'What about it?'

Their eyes were growing accustomed to the night gloom. Under the faint sheen of starlight the outline of the plant came dimly into focus. 'It won't live,' Eggerton said. 'It's part of his delusion; now he's dead.'

Frightened and subdued, the other guests were beginning to filter back into the yard. Harvey Sorrel crept drunkenly from the shadows and apologetically approached his wife. Somewhere far off the wail of a siren sounded; the automatic police had been called. 'Do you want to come with us?' Doris asked Eggerton shakily. She indicated her husband. 'We'll all drive over to the Agency together and get you straightened out; it can be fixed up. There'll be some kind of indenture, a few years at the most. Nothing more than that.'

Eggerton moved away from her. 'No thanks,' he said. 'I have something else to do. Maybe later.'

'But—'

'I think I have what I want.' Eggerton fumbled for the back door and entered Richards' deserted quarters. 'This is what we've been looking for.'

He put through his emergency call immediately. In Townsand's apartment the buzzer was sounding within thirty seconds. Sleepily, Laura roused her husband; Eggerton began talking as soon as the two men were facing each other's image.

'We have our standard,' he said; 'we don't need the Agency. We can pull the rug out from under them because we don't really need them to watch us.'

'What?' Townsand demanded angrily, his mind fuzzy with sleep. 'What are you talking about?'

Eggerton repeated what he had said, as calmly as possible.

'Then who *will* watch us?' Townsand growled. 'What the hell is this?'

'We'll watch each other,' Eggerton continued patiently. 'Nobody will be exempt. Each of us will be the standard for the next man. Richards couldn't see himself objectively, but I could—*even though I'm not immune*. We don't need anybody over us, because we can do the job ourselves.'

Townsand reflected resentfully. He yawned, pulled his nightrobe around him, glanced sleepily at his wristwatch. 'Lord, it's late. Maybe you have something, maybe not. Tell me more about this Richards . . . what sort of P-K talent did he have?'

Eggerton told him. 'You see? All these years . . . and he couldn't tell. But we could tell instantly.' Eggerton's voice rose excitedly. 'We can run our own society, again! Consensus gentium—we've had our measuring standard all the time and none of us has realized it. Individually, each of us is fallible; *but as a group we can't go wrong*. All we have to do is make sure the random check-nets get everybody; we'll have to step the process up, get more people and get them oftener. It has to be accelerated so that everybody, sooner or later, gets hauled in.'

'I see,' Townsand agreed.

'We'll keep the tame telepaths, of course; so we can get out all the thoughts and subliminal material. The teeps won't evaluate; we'll handle that ourselves.'

Townsand nodded dully. 'Sounds good, John.'

'It came to me as soon as I saw Richards' plant. It was instantaneous—I had complete certitude. How could there be error? A delusional system like his simply doesn't fit into our world.' Eggerton's hand slammed down on the table in front of him; a book that had belonged to Jay Richards slipped off and landed soundlessly on the thick carpet of the apartment. 'You understand? There's no equation between a P-K world and ours; all we have to do is get the P-K material up where we can see it. Where we can compare it to our own reality.'

Townsand was silent a moment. 'All right,' he said at last. 'Come on over. If you convince the rest of the id bloc then we'll act.' He made his decision. 'I'll get them out of bed and over here.'

'Fine.' Eggerton reached quickly for the cut-off switch. 'I'll hurry over; and thanks!'

He rushed from the littered, bottle-strewn apartment, now dismal and deserted without the celebrating guests. In the back yard, the police were already picking around, examining the dying plant that Jay Richards' delusional talent had brought into momentary existence.

The night air was cold and crisp, as Eggerton emerged from the ascent ramp, onto the roof field of the Commerce Building. A few voices drifted up from far below; the roof itself was deserted. He buttoned his heavy overcoat around him, extended his arms, and rose from the roof. He gained altitude and speed; in a few moments he was on his way toward Pittsburgh.

As he flew silently through the night he gulped vast lungfuls of the clean, fresh air. Satisfaction and rising excitement raced through him. He had spotted Richards immediately—and why not? How could he miss? A man who grew jet transports from a plant in his back yard was clearly a lunatic.

It was so much simpler just to flap one's arms.

A WORLD OF TALENT

I

When he entered the apartment, a great number of people were making noises and flashing colors. The sudden cacophony confused him. Aware of the surge of shapes, sounds, smells, three-dimensional oblique patches, but trying to peer through and beyond, he halted at the door. With an act of will, he was able to clear the blur somewhat; the meaningless frenzy of human activity settled gradually into a quasi-orderly pattern.

'What's the matter?' his father asked sharply.

'This is what we previewed a half-hour ago,' his mother said when the eight-year-old boy failed to answer. 'I wish you'd let me get a Corpsman to probe him.'

'I don't fully trust the Corps. And we have twelve years to handle this ourselves. If we haven't cracked it by then—'

'Later.' She bent down and ordered in a crisp tone, 'Go on in, Tim. Say hello to people.'

'Try to hold an objective orientation,' his father added gently. 'At least for this evening, to the end of the party.'

Tim passed silently through the crowded living room ignoring the various oblique shapes, his body tilted forward, head turned to one side. Neither of his parents followed him; they were intercepted by the host and then surrounded by Norm and Psi guests.

In the melee, the boy was forgotten. He made a brief circuit of the living room, satisfied himself that nothing existed there, and then sought a side hall. A mechanical attendant opened a bedroom door for him and he entered.

The bedroom was deserted; the party had only begun. He allowed the voices and movement behind him to fade into an indiscriminate blur. Faint perfumes of women drifted through the swank apartment, carried by the warm, Terran-like, artificial air pumped from the central ducts of the city. He raised himself up and inhaled the sweet scents, flowers, fruits, spices—and something more.

He had to go all the way into the bedroom to isolate it. There it was—sour, like spoiled milk—the warning he counted on. And it *was* in the bedroom.

Cautiously, he opened a closet. The mechanical selector tried to present him with clothing, but he ignored it. With the closet open, the scent was stronger. The Other was somewhere near the closet, if not actually in it.

Under the bed?

He crouched down and peered. Not there. He lay outstretched and stared under Fairchild's metal workdesk, typical furniture of a Colonial official's quarters. Here, the scent was stronger. Fear and excitement touched him. He jumped to his feet and pushed the desk away from the smooth plastic surface of the wall.

The Other clung against the wall in the dark shadow where the desk had rested.

It was a Right Other, of course. He had only identified one Left and that for no more than a split second. The Other hadn't managed to phase totally. He retreated warily from it, conscious that, without his cooperation, it had come as far as it could. The Other watched him calmly, aware of his negative actions, but there was little it could do. It made no attempt to communicate, for that had always failed.

Tim was safe. He halted and spent a long moment scrutinizing the Other. This was his chance to learn more about it. A space separated the two of them, across which only the visual image and odor—small vaporized particles—of the Other crossed.

It was not possible to identify this Other; many were so similar, they appeared to be multiples of the same unit. But sometimes the Other was radically different. Was it possible that various selections were being tried, alternate attempts to get across?

Again the thought struck him. The people in the living room, both Norm- and Psi-classes—and even the Mute-class of which he was a part—seemed to have reached a workable stalemate with their own Others. It was strange, since their Lefts would be advanced over his own . . . unless the procession of Rights diminished as the Left group increased.

Was there a finite total of Others?

He went back to the frenetic living room. People murmured and swirled on all sides, gaudy opaque shapes everywhere, warm smells overpowering him with their closeness. It was clear that he would have to get information from his mother and father. He had already spun the research indices hooked to the Sol System educational transmission—spun them without results, since the circuit was not working.

'Where did you wander off to?' his mother asked him, pausing in the animated conversation that had grown up among a group of Norm-class officials blocking one side of the room. She caught the expression on his face.

'Oh,' she said. 'Even here?'

He was surprised at her question. Location made no difference. Didn't she know that? Floundering, he withdrew into himself to consider. He needed help; he couldn't understand without outside assistance. But a staggering verbal block existed. Was it only a problem of terminology or was it more?

As he wandered around the living room, the vague musty odor filtered to him through the heavy curtain of people-smells. The Other was still there, crouched in the darkness where the desk had been, in the shadows of the deserted bedroom. Waiting to come over. Waiting for him to take two more steps.

Julie watched her eight-year-old son move away, an expression of concern on her petite face. 'We'll have to keep our eyes on him,' she said to her husband. 'I preview a mounting situation built around this thing of his.'

Curt had caught it, too, but he kept on talking to the Norm-class officials grouped around the two Precogs. 'What would you do,' he demanded, 'if they really opened up on us? You know Big Noodle can't handle a stepped-up shower of robot projectiles. The handful now and then are in the nature of experiments . . . and he has the half-hour warnings from Julie and me.'

'True.' Fairchild scratched his gray nose, rubbed the stubble of beard showing below his lip. 'But I don't think they'll swing to overt war operations. It would be an admission that we're getting somewhere. It would legalize us and open things up. We might collect you Psi-class people together and–' he grinned wearily–'and think the Sol System far out past the Andromache Nebula.'

Curt listened without resentment, since the man's words were no surprise. As he and Julie had driven over, they had both previewed the party, its unfruitful discussions, the growing aberrations of their son. His wife's precog span was somewhat greater than his own. She was seeing, at this moment, ahead of his own vision. He wondered what the worried expression on her face indicated.

'I'm afraid,' Julie said tightly, 'that we're going to have a little quarrel before we get home tonight.'

Well, he had also seen that. 'It's the situation,' he said, rejecting the topic. 'Everybody here is on edge. It isn't only you and I who're going to be fighting.'

Fairchild listened sympathetically. 'I can see some drawbacks to being a Precog. But knowing you're going to have a spat, can't you alter things before it begins?'

'Sure,' Curt answered, 'the way we give you pre-information and you use it to alter the situation with Terra. But neither Julie nor I particularly care. It takes a huge mental effort to stave off something like this . . . and neither of us has that much energy.'

'I just wish you'd let me turn him over to the Corps,' Julie said in a low voice. 'I can't stand him wandering around, peering under things, looking in closets for God knows what!'

'For Others,' Curt said.

'Whatever that might be.'

Fairchild, a natural-born moderator, tried intercession. 'You've got twelve years,' he began. 'It's no disgrace to have Tim stay in the Mute-class; every one of you starts out that way. If he has Psi powers, he'll show.'

'You talk like an infinite Precog,' Julie said, amused. 'How do you know they'll show?'

Fairchild's good-natured face twisted with effort. Curt felt sorry for him. Fairchild had too much responsibility, too many decisions to make, too many lives on his hands. Before the Separation with Terra, he had been an appointed official, a bureaucrat with a job and clearly defined routine. Now there was nobody to tap out an inter-system memo to him early Monday morning. Fairchild was working without instructions.

'Let's see that doodad of yours,' Curt said. 'I'm curious about how it works.'

Fairchild was astonished. 'How the hell—' Then he remembered. 'Sure, you must have already previewed it.' He dug around in his coat. 'I was going to make it the surprise of the party, but we can't have surprises with you two Precogs around.'

The other Norm-class officials crowded around as their boss unwrapped a square of tissue paper and from it lifted a small glittering stone. An interested silence settled over the room as Fairchild examined the stone, his eyes close to it, like a jeweler studying a precious gem.

'An ingenious thing,' Curt admitted.

'Thanks,' Fairchild said. 'They should start arriving any day, now. The glitter is to attract children and lower-class people who would go out for a bauble—possible wealth, you know. And women, of course. Anybody who would stop and pick up what they thought was a diamond, everybody but the Tech-classes. I'll show you.'

He glanced around the hushed living room at the guests in their gay party clothes. Off to one side, Tim stood with his head turned at an angle. Fairchild hesitated, then tossed the stone across the carpet in front of the boy, almost at his feet. The boy's eyes didn't flicker. He was gazing absently through the people, unaware of the bright object at his feet.

Curt moved forward, ready to take up the social slack. 'You'd have to produce something the size of a jet transport.' He bent down and retrieved the stone. 'It's not your fault that Tim doesn't respond to such mundane things as fifty-carat diamonds.'

Fairchild was crestfallen at the collapse of his demonstration. 'I forgot.' He brightened. 'But there aren't any Mutes on Terra any more. Listen and see what you think of the spiel. I had a hand at writing it.'

In Curt's hand, the stone rested coldly. In his ears, a tiny gnat-like buzz sounded, a controlled, modulated cadence that caused a stir of murmurs around the room.

'My friends,' the canned voice stated, 'the causes of the conflict between Terra and the Centaurian colonies have been grossly mis-stated in the press.'

'Is this seriously aimed at children?' Julie asked.

'Maybe he thinks Terran children are advanced over our own,' a Psi-class official said as a rustle of amusement drifted through the room.

The tiny whine droned on, turning out its mixture of legalistic arguments, idealism and an almost pathetic pleading. The begging quality grated on Curt. Why did Fairchild have to get down on his knees and plead with the Terrans? As he listened, Fairchild puffed confidently on his pipe, arms folded, heavy face thick with satisfaction. Evidently Fairchild wasn't aware of the precarious *thinness* of his canned words.

It occurred to Curt that none of them—including himself—was facing how really fragile their Separation movement was. There was no use blaming the weak words wheezing from the pseudo-gem. Any description of their position was bound to reflect the querulous half-fear that dominated the Colonies.

'It has long been established,' the stone asserted, 'that freedom is the natural condition of Man. Servitude, the bondage of one man or one group of men to another, is a remnant of the past, a vicious anachronism. Men must govern themselves.'

'Strange to hear a stone saying that,' Julie said, half amused. 'An inert lump of rock.'

'You have been told that the Colonial Secessionist movement will jeopardize your lives and your standard of living. *This is not true*. The standard of living of all mankind will be raised if the colony planets are allowed to govern themselves and find their own economic markets. The mercantile system practiced by the Terran government on Terrans living outside the Sol group—'

'The children will bring this thing home,' Fairchild said. 'The parents will pick it up from them.'

The stone droned on. 'The Colonies could not remain mere supply bases for Terra, sources of raw materials and cheap labor. The Colonists could not remain second-class citizens. Colonists have as much right to determine their own society as those remaining in the Sol group. Thus, the Colonial Government has petitioned the Terran Government for a severance of those bonds to keep us from realizing our manifest destinies.'

Curt and Julie exchanged glances. The academic text-book dissertation hung like a dead weight in the room. Was this the man the Colony had elected to manage the resistance movement? A pedant, a salaried official, a bureaucrat and—Curt couldn't help thinking—a man without Psi powers. A Normal.

Fairchild had probably been moved to break with Terra over some trivial miswording of a routine directive. Nobody, except perhaps the telepathic Corps, knew his motives or how long he could keep going.

'What do you think of it?' Fairchild asked when the stone had finished its monologue and had started over. 'Millions of them showering down all over the Sol group. You know what the Terran press is saying about us—vicious lies—that we want to take over Sol, that we're hideous invaders from outer space, monsters, mutants, freaks. We have to counter such propaganda.'

'Well,' Julie said, 'a third of us are freaks, so why not face it? I know my son is a useless freak.'

Curt took her arm. 'Nobody's calling Tim a freak, not even you!'

'But it's true!' She pulled away. 'If we were back in the Sol System—if we hadn't separated—you and I would be in detention camps, waiting to be—you know.' She fiercely jabbed in the direction of their son. 'There wouldn't be any Tim.'

From the corner a sharp-faced man spoke up. 'We wouldn't be in the Sol System. We'd have broken out on our own without anybody's help. Fairchild had nothing to do with it; we brought him along. Don't ever forget that!'

Curt eyed the man hostilely. Reynolds, chief of the telepathic Corps, was drunk again. Drunk and spilling over his load of vitriolic hate for Norms.

'Possibly,' Curt agreed, 'but we would have had a hell of a time doing it.'

'You and I know what keeps this Colony alive,' Reynolds answered, his flushed face arrogant and sneering. 'How long could these bureaucrats keep on going without Big Noodle and Sally, you two Precogs, the Corps and all the rest of us? Face facts—we don't need this legalistic window-dressing. We're not going to win because of any pious appeals for freedom and equality. We're going to win because there are no Psis on Terra.'

The geniality of the room dwindled. Angry murmurs rose from the Norm-class guests.

'Look here,' Fairchild said to Reynolds, 'you're still a human being, even if you can read minds. Having a talent doesn't—'

'Don't lecture me,' Reynolds said. 'No numbskull is going to tell me what to do.'

'You're going too far,' Curt told Reynolds. 'Somebody's going to smack you down some day. If Fairchild doesn't do it, maybe I will.'

'You and your meddling Corps,' a Psi-class Resurrector said to Reynolds, grabbing hold of his collar. 'You think you're above us because you can merge your minds. You think—'

'Take your hands off me,' Reynolds said in an ugly voice. A glass crashed to the floor; one of the women became hysterical. Two men struggled; a third joined and, in a flash, a wild turmoil of resentment was boiling in the center of the room.

Fairchild shouted for order. 'For God's sake, if we fight each other, we're finished. Don't you understand—*we have to work together!*'

It took a while before the uproar subsided. Reynolds pushed past Curt, white-faced and muttering under his breath. 'I'm getting out of here.' The other Telepaths trailed belligerently after him.

As he and Julie drove slowly home through the bluish darkness, one section of Fairchild's propaganda repeated itself in Curt's brain over and over again.

'You've been told a victory by the Colonists means a victory of Psis over Normal human beings. This is not true! The Separation was not planned and is not conducted by either Psis or Mutants. The revolt was a spontaneous reaction by Colonists of all classes.'

'I wonder,' Curt mused. 'Maybe Fairchild's wrong. Maybe he's being operated by Psis without knowing it. Personally, I like him, stupid as he is.'

'Yes, he's stupid,' Julie agreed. In the darkness of the car's cabin, her cigarette was a bright burning coal of wrath. In the back seat, Tim lay curled up asleep, warmed by the heat from the motor. The barren, rocky landscape of Proxima III rolled out ahead of the small surface-car, a dim expanse, hostile and alien. A few Man-made roads and buildings lay here and there among crop-tanks and fields.

'I don't trust Reynolds,' Curt continued, knowing he was opening the previewed scene between them, yet not willing to sidestep it. 'Reynolds is smart, unscrupulous and ambitious. What he wants is prestige and status. But Fairchild is thinking of the welfare of the Colony. He means all that stuff he dictated into his stones.'

'That drivel,' Julie was scornful. 'The Terrans will laugh their heads off. Listening to it with a straight face was more than I could manage, and God knows our lives depend on this business.'

'Well,' Curt said carefully, knowing what he was getting into, 'there may be Terrans with more sense of justice than you and

Reynolds.' He turned toward her. 'I can see what you're going to do and so can you. Maybe you're right, maybe we ought to get it over with. Ten years is a long time when there's no feeling. And it wasn't our idea in the first place.'

'No,' Julie agreed. She crushed her cigarette out and shakily lit another. 'If there had been another male Precog besides you, just *one*. That's something I can't forgive Reynolds for. It was his idea, you know. I never should have agreed. For the glory of the race! Onward and upward with the Psi banner! The mystical mating of the first real Precogs in history . . . and look what came of it!'

'Shut up,' Curt said. 'He's not asleep and he can hear you.'

Julie's voice was bitter. 'Hear me, yes. Understand, no. We wanted to know what the second generation would be like—well, now we know. Precog plus Precog equals freak. Useless mutant. Monster—let's face it, the M on his card stands for monster.'

Curt's hands tightened on the wheel. 'That's a word neither you nor anybody else is going to use.'

'Monster!' She leaned close to him, teeth white in the light from the dashboard, eyes glowing. 'Maybe the Terrans are right—maybe we Precogs ought to be sterilized and put to death. Erased. I think . . .' She broke off abruptly, unwilling to finish.

'Go ahead,' Curt said. 'You think perhaps when the revolt is successful and we're in control of the Colonies, we should go down the line selectively. With the Corps on top naturally.'

'Separate the wheat from the chaff,' Julie said. 'First the Colonies from Terra. Then us from them. And when he comes up, even if he is my son . . .'

'What you're doing,' Curt interrupted, 'is passing judgment on people according to their use. Tim isn't useful, so there's no point in letting him live, right?' His blood pressure was on the way up, but he was past caring. 'Breeding people like cattle. A human hasn't a right to live; that's a privilege we dole out according to our whim.'

Curt raced the car down the deserted highway. 'You heard Fairchild prattle about freedom and equality. He believes it and so do I. And I believe Tim—or anybody else—has a right to exist whether we can make use of his talent or whether he even has a talent.'

'He has a right to live,' Julie said, 'but remember he's not one of us. He's an oddity. He doesn't have our ability, our—' she ground out the words triumphantly—'superior ability.'

Curt pulled the car over to the edge of the highway. He brought it to a halt and pushed open the door. Dismal, arid air billowed into the car.

'You drive on home.' He leaned over the back seat and prodded Tim into wakefulness. 'Come on, kid. We're getting out.'

Julie reached over to get the wheel. 'When will you be home? Or have you got it completely set up now? Better make sure. She might be the kind that has a few others on the string.'

Curt stepped from the car and the door slammed behind him. He took his son's hand and led him down the roadway to the black square of a ramp that rose darkly in the night gloom. As they started up the steps, he heard the car roar off down the highway through the darkness toward home.

'Where are we?' Tim asked.

'You know this place. I bring you here every week. This is the school where they train people like you and me—where we Psis get our education.'

II

Lights came on around them. Corridors branched off the main entrance ramp like metal vines.

'You may stay here for a few days,' Curt said to his son. 'Can you stand not seeing your mother for a while?'

Tim didn't answer. He had lapsed back into his usual silence as he followed along beside his father. Curt again wondered how the boy could be so withdrawn—as he obviously was—and yet be so terribly alert. The answer was written over each inch of the taut, young body. Tim was only withdrawn from contact with human beings. He maintained an almost compulsive tangency with the outside world—or, rather, an outside world. Whatever it was, it didn't include humans, although it was made up of real, external objects.

As he had already previewed, his son suddenly broke away from him. Curt let the boy hurry down a side corridor. He watched as Tim stood tugging anxiously at a supply locker, trying to get it open.

'Okay,' Curt said resignedly. He followed after him and unlocked the locker with his pass key. 'See? There's nothing in it.'

How completely the boy lacked precog could be seen by the flood of relief that swept his face. Curt's heart sank at the sight. The precious talent that both he and Julie possessed simply hadn't been passed on. Whatever the boy was, he was not a Precog.

It was past two in the morning, but the interior departments of the School Building were alight with activity. Curt moodily greeted a couple of Corpsmen lounging around the bar, surrounded by beers and ashtrays.

'Where's Sally?' he demanded. 'I want to go in and see Big Noodle.'

One of the Telepaths lazily jerked a thumb. 'She's around somewhere. Over that way, in the kids' quarters, probably asleep. It's late.' He eyed Curt, whose thoughts were on Julie. 'You ought to get rid of a wife like that. She's too old and thin, anyhow. What you'd really like is a plump young dish—'

Curt lashed a blast of mental dislike and was satisfied to see the grinning young face go hard with antagonism. The other Telepath pulled himself upright and shouted after Curt, 'When you're through with your wife, send her around to us.'

'I'd say you're after a girl of about twenty,' another Telepath said as he admitted Curt to the sleeping quarters of the children's wing. 'Dark hair—correct me if I'm wrong—and dark eyes. You have a fully formed image. Maybe there's a specific girl. Let's see, she's short, fairly pretty and her name is—'

Curt cursed at the situation that required them to turn their minds over to the Corps. Telepaths were interlaced throughout the Colonies and, in particular, throughout the School and the offices of the Colonial Government. He tightened his grip around Tim's hand and led him through the doorway.

'This kid of yours,' the Telepath said as Tim passed close to him, 'sure probes queer. Mind if I go down a little?'

'Keep out of his mind,' Curt ordered sharply. He slammed the door shut after Tim, knowing it made no difference, but enjoying the feel of the heavy metal sliding in place. He pushed Tim down a narrow corridor and into a small room. Tim pulled away, intent on a side door; Curt savagely yanked him back. 'There's nothing in there!' he reprimanded harshly. 'That's only a bathroom.'

Tim continued to tug away. He was still tugging when Sally appeared, fastening a robe around her, face puffy with sleep. 'Hello, Mr Purcell,' she greeted Curt. 'Hello, Tim.' Yawning, she turned on a floor lamp and tossed herself down on a chair. 'What can I do for you this time of night?'

She was thirteen, tall and gangling, with yellow cornsilk hair and freckled skin. She picked sleepily at her thumbnail and yawned again as the boy sat down across from her. To amuse him, she animated a pair of gloves lying on a sidetable. Tim laughed with delight as the gloves groped their way to the edge of the table, waved their fingers blindly and began a cautious descent to the floor.

'Fine,' Curt said. 'You're getting good. I'd say you're not cutting any classes.'

Sally shrugged. 'Mr Purcell, the School can't teach me anything. You know I'm the most advanced Psi with the power of animation. They just let me work alone. In fact, I'm instructing a bunch of little kids, still Mutes, who might have something. I think a couple of them could work out, with practice. All they can give me is encouragement; you know, psychological stuff and lots of vitamins and fresh air. But they can't teach me anything.'

'They can teach you how important you are,' Curt said. He had previewed this, of course. During the last half-hour, he had selected a number of possible approaches, discarded one after another, finally ended with this. 'I came over to see Big Noodle. That meant I had to wake you. Do you know why?'

'Sure,' Sally answered. 'You're afraid of him. And since Big Noodle is afraid of me, you need me to come along.' She allowed the gloves to sag into immobility as she got to her feet. 'Well, let's go.'

He had seen Big Noodle many times in his life, but he had never got used to the sight. Awed, in spite of his preview of this scene, Curt stood in the open space before the platform, gazing up, silent and impressed as always.

'He's fat,' Sally said practically. 'If he doesn't get thinner, he won't live long.'

Big Noodle slumped like a gray, sickly pudding in the immense chair the Tech Department had built for him. His eyes were half-closed; his pulpy arms lay slack and inert at his sides. Wads of oozing dough hung in folds over the arms and sides of the chair. Big Noodle's egglike skull was fringed with damp, stringy hair, matted like decayed seaweed. His nails were lost in the sausage fingers. His teeth were rotting and black. His tiny plate-blue eyes flickered dully as he identified Curt and Sally, but the obese body did not stir.

'He's resting,' Sally explained. 'He just ate.'

'Hello,' Curt said.

From the swollen mouth, between rolls of pink flesh lips, a grumbled response came.

'He doesn't like to be bothered this late,' Sally said, yawning. 'I don't blame him.'

She wandered around the room, amusing herself by animating light brackets along the wall. The brackets struggled to pull free from the hot-pour plastic in which they were set.

'This seems so dumb, if you don't mind my saying so, Mr Purcell. The Telepaths keep Terran infiltrators from coming in here, and all this business of yours is against them. That means you're helping Terra, doesn't it? If we didn't have the Corps to watch out for us—'

'I keep out Terrans,' Big Noodle mumbled. 'I have my wall and I turn back everything.'

'You turn back projectiles,' Sally said, 'but you can't keep out infiltrators. A Terran infiltrator could come in here this minute and you wouldn't know. You're just a big stupid lump of lard.'

Her description was accurate. But the vast mound of fat was the nexus of the Colony's defense, the most talented of the Psis. Big Noodle was the core of the Separation movement . . . and the living symbol of its problem.

Big Noodle had almost infinite parakinetic power and the mind of a moronic three-year-old. He was, specifically, an idiot savant. His legendary powers had absorbed his whole personality, withered and degenerated it, rather than expanded it. He could have swept the Colony aside years ago if his bodily lusts and fears had been accompanied by cunning. But Big Noodle was helpless and inert, totally dependent on the instructions of the Colonial Government, reduced to sullen passivity by his terror of Sally.

'I ate a whole pig.' Big Noodle struggled to a quasi-sitting position, belched, wiped feebly at his chin. 'Two pigs, in fact. Right here in this room, just a little while ago. I could get more if I wanted.'

The diet of the Colonist consisted mainly of tank-grown artificial protein. Big Noodle was amusing himself at their expense.

'The pig,' Big Noodle continued grandly, 'came from Terra. The night before, I had a flock of wild ducks. And before that, I brought over some kind of animal from Betelgeuse IV. It doesn't have any name; it just runs around and eats.'

'Like you,' Sally said. 'Only you don't run around.'

Big Noodle giggled. Pride momentarily overcame his fear of the girl. 'Have some candy,' he offered. A shower of chocolate rattled down like hail. Curt and Sally retreated as the floor of the chamber disappeared under the deluge. With the chocolate came fragments of machinery, cardboard boxes, sections of display counter, a jagged chunk of concrete floor. 'Candy factory on Terra,' Big Noodle explained happily. 'I've got it pinpointed pretty good.'

Tim had awakened from his contemplation. He bent down and eagerly picked up a handful of chocolates.

'Go ahead,' Curt said to him. 'You might as well take them.'

'I'm the only one that gets the candy,' Big Noodle thundered, outraged. The chocolate vanished. 'I sent it back,' he explained peevishly. 'It's mine.'

There was nothing malevolent in Big Noodle, only an infinite childish selfishness. Through his power, every object in the Universe had become his possession. There was nothing outside the reach of his bloated arms; he could reach for the Moon and get it. Fortunately, most things were outside his span of comprehension. He was uninterested.

'Let's cut out these games,' Curt said. 'Can you say if any Telepaths are within probe range of us?'

Big Noodle made a begrudging search. He had a consciousness of objects wherever they were. Through his talent, he was in contact with the physical contents of the Universe.

'None near here,' he declared after a time. 'One about a hundred feet off . . . I'll move him back. I hate Teeps getting into my privacy.'

'Everybody hates Teeps,' Sally said. 'It's a nasty, dirty talent. Looking into other people's minds is like watching them when they're bathing or dressing or eating. It isn't natural.'

Curt grinned. 'Is it any different from precog? You wouldn't call that natural.'

'Precog has to do with events, not people,' Sally said. 'Knowing what's going to happen isn't any worse than knowing what's already happened.'

'It might even be better,' Curt pointed out.

'No,' Sally said emphatically. 'It's got us into this trouble. I have to watch what I think all the time because of you. Every time I see a Teep, I get goose bumps, and no matter how hard I try, I can't keep from thinking about *her*, just because I know I'm not supposed to.'

'My precog faculty has nothing to do with Pat,' Curt said. 'Precog doesn't introduce fatality. Locating Pat was an intricate job. It was a deliberate choice I made.'

'Aren't you sorry?' Sally demanded.

'No.'

'If it wasn't for me,' Big Noodle interrupted, 'you never would have got across to Pat.'

'I wish we hadn't,' Sally said fervently. 'If it wasn't for Pat, we wouldn't be mixed up in all this business.' She shot a hostile glance at Curt. 'And I don't think she's pretty.'

'What would you suggest?' Curt asked the child with more patience than he felt. He had previewed the futility of making a child and an idiot understand about Pat. 'You know we can't pretend we never found her.'

'I know,' Sally admitted. 'And the Teeps have got something from our minds already. That's why there're so many of them hanging around here. It's a good thing we don't know where she is.'

'I know where she is,' Big Noodle said. 'I know exactly where.'

'No, you don't,' Sally answered. 'You just know how to get to her and that's not the same thing. You can't explain it; you just send us over there and back.'

'It's a planet,' Big Noodle said angrily, 'with funny plants and a lot of green things. And the air's thin. She lives in a camp. People go out and farm all day. There's only a few people there. A lot of dopey animals live there. It's cold.'

'Where is it?' Curt asked.

Big Noodle sputtered. 'It's . . .' His pulpy arms waved. 'It's some place near . . .' He gave up, wheezed resentfully at Sally and then brought a tank of filthy water into being above the girl's head. As the water flowed toward her, the child made a few brief motions with her hands.

Big Noodle shrieked in terror and the water vanished. He lay panting with fright, body quivering, as Sally mopped at a wet spot on her robe. She had animated the fingers of his left hand.

'Better not do that again,' Curt said to her. 'His heart might give out.'

'The big slob.' Sally rummaged around in a supply closet. 'Well, if you've made up your mind, we might as well get it over with. Only let's not stay so long. You get to talking with Pat and then the two of you go off, and you don't come back for hours. At night, it's freezing and they don't have any heating plants.' She pulled down a coat from the closet. 'I'll take this with me.'

'We're not going,' Curt told her. 'This time is going to be different.'

Sally blinked. 'Different? How?'

Even Big Noodle was surprised. 'I was just getting ready to move you across,' he complained.

'I know,' Curt said firmly. 'But this time I want you to bring Pat here. Bring her to this room, understand? This is the time we've been talking about. The big moment's arrived.'

There was only one person with Curt as he entered Fairchild's office. Sally was now in bed, back at the School. Big Noodle never stirred from his chamber. Tim was still at the School, in the hands of Psi-class authorities, not Telepaths.

Pat followed hesitantly, frightened and nervous as the men sitting around the office glanced up in annoyance.

She was perhaps nineteen, slim and copper-skinned, with large dark eyes. She wore a canvas workshirt and jeans, heavy shoes caked with mud. Her tangle of black curls was tied back and knotted with a red bandana. Her rolled-up sleeves showed tanned, competent arms. At her leather belt she carried a knife, a field telephone and an emergency pack of rations and water.

'This is the girl,' Curt said. 'Take a good look at her.'

'Where are you from?' Fairchild asked Pat. He pushed aside a heap of directives and memotapes to find his pipe.

Pat hesitated. 'I–' she began. She turned uncertainly to Curt. 'You told me never to say, even to you.'

'It's okay,' Curt said gently. 'You can tell us now.' He explained to Fairchild, 'I can preview what she's going to say, but I never knew before. I didn't want to get it probed out of me by the Corps.'

'I was born on Proxima VI,' Pat said in a low voice. 'I grew up there. This is the first time I've left the planet.'

Fairchild's eyes widened. 'That's a wild place. In fact, about our most primitive region.'

Around the office, his group of Norm and Psi consultants moved closer to watch. One wide-shouldered old man, face weathered as stone, eyes shrewd and alert, raised his hand. 'Are we to understand that Big Noodle brought you here?'

Pat nodded. 'I didn't know. I mean it was unexpected.' She tapped her belt. 'I was working, clearing the brush . . . we've been trying to expand, develop more usable land.'

'What's your name?' Fairchild asked her.

'Patricia Ann Connley.'

'What class?'

The girl's sun-cracked lips moved. 'Mute-class.'

A stir moved through the officials. 'You're a Mutant,' the old man asked her, 'without Psi powers? Exactly how do you differ from the Norm?'

Pat glanced at Curt and he moved forward to answer for her. 'This girl will be twenty-one in two years. You know what that means. If she's still in the Mute-class, she'll be sterilized and put in a camp. That's our Colonial policy. And if Terra whips us, she'll be sterilized in any case, as will all of us Psis and Mutants.'

'Are you trying to say she has a talent?' Fairchild asked. 'You want us to lift her from Mute to Psi?' His hands fumbled at the papers on the table. 'We get a thousand petitions a day like this. You came down here at four in the morning just for this? There's a routine form you can fill out, a common office procedure.'

The old man cleared his throat and blurted, 'This girl is close to you?'

'That's right,' Curt said. 'I have a personal interest.'

'How did you meet her?' the old man asked. 'If she's never been off Proxima VI . . .'

'Big Noodle shuttled me there and back,' Curt answered. 'I've made the trip about twenty times. I didn't know it was Prox VI, of course. I only knew it was a Colony planet, primitive, still wild. Originally, I came across an analysis of her personality and neural characteristics in our Mute-class files. As soon as I understood, I gave Big Noodle the identifying brain pattern and had him send me across.'

'What is that pattern?' Fairchild asked. 'What's different about her?'

'Pat's talent has never been acknowledged as Psi,' Curt said. 'In a way, it isn't, but it's going to be one of the most useful talents we've discovered. We should have known it would arise. Wherever some organism develops, so does another to prey on it.'

'Get to the point,' Fairchild said. He rubbed the blue stubble on his chin. 'When you called me, all you said was that—'

'Consider the various Psi talents as survival weapons,' Curt said. 'Consider telepathic ability as evolving for the defense of an organism. It puts the Telepath head and shoulders above his enemies. Is this going to continue? Don't these things usually balance out?'

It was the old man who understood. 'I see,' he said with a grin of wry admiration. 'This girl is opaque to telepathic probes.'

'That's right,' Curt said. 'The first, but there'll likely be others. And not only defenses to telepathic probes. There are going to be organisms resistant to Parakineticists, to Precogs like myself, to Resurrectors, to Animators, to every and all Psi powers. Now we have a fourth class. The Anti-Psi class. It was bound to come into existence.'

III

The coffee was artificial, but hot and satisfying. Like the eggs and bacon it was synthetically compounded from tank-grown meals and proteins, with a carefully regulated mix of native-grown plant fiber. As they ate, the morning sun rose outside. The barren gray landscape of Proxima III was touched with a faint tint of red.

'It looks nice,' Pat said shyly, glancing out the kitchen window. 'Maybe I can examine your farming equipment. You have a lot we don't have.'

'We've had more time,' Curt reminded her. 'This planet was settled a century before your own. You'll catch up with us. In many ways Prox VI is richer and more fertile.'

Julie wasn't sitting at the table. She stood leaning against the refrigerator, arms folded, her face hard and frigid. 'Is she really staying here?' she demanded in a thin, clipped voice. 'In this house with us?'

'That's right,' Curt answered.

'How long?'

'A few days. A week. Until I can get Fairchild moving.'

Faint sounds stirred beyond the house. Here and there in the residential syndrome people were waking up and preparing for the day. The kitchen was warm and cheerful; a window of clear plastic separated it from the landscape of tumbled rocks, thin trees and plants that stretched to a few hundred miles off. Cold morning wind whipped around the rubbish that littered the deserted inter-system field at the rim of the syndrome.

'That field was the link between us and the Sol System,' Curt said. 'The umbilical cord. Gone now, for a while at least.'

'It's beautiful,' Pat stated.

'The field?'

She gestured at the towers of an elaborate mining and smelting combine partly visible beyond the rows of houses. 'Those, I mean. The landscape is like ours; bleak and awful. It's all the installations that mean something . . . where you've pushed the landscape back.' She shivered. 'We've been fighting trees and rocks all my life, trying to get the soil usable, trying to make a place to live. We don't have any heavy equipment on Prox VI, just hand tools and our own backs. You know, you've seen our villages.'

Curt sipped his coffee. 'Are there many Psis on Prox VI?'

'A few. Mostly minor. A few Resurrectors, a handful of Animators. No one even as good as Sally.' She laughed, showing her teeth.

'We're rustic hicks, compared to this urban metropolis. You saw how we live. Villages stuck here and there, farms, a few isolated supply centers, one miserable field. You saw my family, my brothers and my father, our home life, if you can call that log shack a home. Three centuries behind Terra.'

'They taught you about Terra?'

'Oh, yes. Tapes came direct from the Sol System until the Separation. Not that I'm sorry we separated. We should have been out working anyhow, instead of watching the tapes. But it was interesting to see the mother world, the big cities, all the billions of people. And the earlier colonies on Venus and Mars. It was amazing.' Her voice throbbed with excitement. 'Those colonies were like ours, once. They had to clear Mars the same way we're clearing Prox VI. We'll get Prox VI cleared, cities built up and fields laid out. And we'll all go on doing our part.'

Julie detached herself from the refrigerator and began gathering dishes from the table without looking at Pat. 'Maybe I'm being naive,' she said to Curt, 'but where's she going to sleep?'

'You know the answer,' Curt answered patiently. 'You've previewed all this. Tim's at the School so she can have his room.'

'What am I supposed to do? Feed her, wait on her, be her maid? What am I supposed to tell people when they see her?' Julie's voice rose to a shrill. 'Am I supposed to say she's my sister?'

Pat smiled across at Curt, toying with a button on her shirt. It was apparent that she was untouched, remote from Julie's harsh voice. Probably that was why the Corps couldn't probe her. Detached, almost aloof, she seemed unaffected by rancor and violence.

'She won't need any supervision,' Curt said to his wife. 'Leave her alone.'

Julie lit a cigarette with rapid, jerky fingers. 'I'll be glad to leave her alone. But she can't go around in those work clothes looking like a convict.'

'Find her something of yours,' Curt suggested.

Julie's face twisted. 'She couldn't wear my things; she's too heavy.' To Pat she said with deliberate cruelty, 'What are you, about a size 30 waist? My God, what have you been doing, dragging a plow? Look at her neck and shoulders . . . she looks like a fieldhorse.'

Curt got abruptly to his feet and pushed his chair back from the table. 'Come on,' he said to Pat. It was vital to show her something besides this undercurrent of resentment. 'I'll show you around.'

Pat leaped up, her cheeks flushed. 'I want to see everything. This is all so new.' She hurried after him as he grabbed his coat and headed for the front door. 'Can we see the School where you train the Psis? I want to see how you develop their abilities. And can we see how the Colonial Government is organized? I want to see how Fairchild works with the Psis.'

Julie followed the two of them out onto the front porch. Cool, chill morning air billowed around them, mixed with the sounds of cars heading from the residential syndrome toward the city. 'In my room you'll find skirts and blouses,' she said to Pat. 'Pick out something light. It's warmer here than on Prox VI.'

'Thank you,' Pat said. She hurried back into the house.

'She's pretty,' Julie said to Curt. 'When I get her washed and dressed, I guess she'll look all right. She's got a figure—in a healthy sort of way. But is there anything to her mind? To her personality?'

'Sure,' Curt answered.

Julie shrugged. 'Well, she's young. A lot younger than I am.' She smiled wanly. 'Remember when we first met? Ten years ago . . . I was so curious to see you, talk to you. The only other Precog besides myself. I had so many dreams and hopes about both of us. I was her age, perhaps a little younger.'

'It was hard to see how it would work out,' Curt said. 'Even for us. A half-hour preview isn't much, in a thing like this.'

'How long has it been?' Julie asked.

'Not long.'

'Have there been other girls?'

'No. Only Pat.'

'When I realized there was somebody else, I hoped she was good enough for you. If I could be sure this girl had something to offer. I suppose it's her remoteness that gives an impression of emptiness. And you have more rapport with her than I do. Probably you don't feel the lack, if it is a lack. And it may be tied in with her talent, her opaqueness.'

Curt fastened the cuffs of his coat. 'I think it's a kind of innocence. She's not touched by a lot of things we have here in our urban, industrial society. When you were talking about her it didn't seem to reach her.'

Julie touched his arm lightly. 'Then take care of her. She's going to need it around here. I wonder what Reynolds' reaction is going to be.'

'Do you see anything?'

'Nothing about her. You're going off . . . I'm by myself for the next interval, as far as I can preview, working around the house. As for now, I'm going into town to do some shopping, to pick up some new clothes. Maybe I can get something for her to wear.'

'We'll get her things,' Curt said. 'She should get her clothes first-hand.'

Pat appeared in a cream-colored blouse and ankle-length yellow skirt, black eyes sparkling, hair moist with morning mist. 'I'm ready! Can we go now?'

Sunlight glittered down on them as they stepped eagerly onto the level ground. 'We'll go over to the School first and pick up my son.'

The three of them walked slowly along the gravel path that led by the white concrete School Building, by the faint sheen of wet lawn that was carefully maintained against the hostile weather of the planet. Tim scampered on ahead of Pat and Curt, listening and peering intently past the objects around him, body tensed forward, lithe and alert.

'He doesn't speak much,' Pat observed.

'He's too busy to pay any attention to us.'

Tim halted to gaze behind a shrub. Pat followed a little after him, curious. 'What's he looking for? He's a beautiful child . . . he has Julie's hair. She has nice hair.'

'Look over there,' Curt said to his son. 'There are plenty of children to sort over. Go play with them.'

At the entrance to the main School Building, parents and their children swarmed in restless, anxious groups. Uniformed School Officials moved among them, sorting, checking, dividing the children into various sub-groups. Now and then a small sub-group was admitted through the check-system into the School Building. Apprehensive, pathetically hopeful, the mothers waited outside.

Pat said, 'It's like that on Prox VI, when the School Teams come to make their census and inspection. Everybody wants to get the unclassified children put up into the Psi-class. My father tried for years to get me out of Mute. He finally gave up. That report you saw was one of his periodic requests. It was filed away somewhere, wasn't it? Gathering dust in a drawer.'

'If this works out,' Curt said, 'many more children will have a chance to get out of the Mute-class. You won't be the only one. You're the first of many, we hope.'

Pat kicked at a pebble. 'I don't feel so new, so astonishingly different. I don't feel anything at all. You say I'm opaque to telepathic invasion, but I've only been scanned one or two times in my life.' She touched her head with her copper-colored fingers and smiled. 'If no Corpsman is scanning me, I'm just like anybody else.'

'Your ability is a counter-talent,' Curt pointed out. 'It takes the original talent to call it into being. Naturally, you're not conscious of it during your ordinary routine of living.'

'A counter-talent. It seems so—so negative. I don't do anything, like you do . . . I don't move objects or turn stones into bread or give birth without impregnation or bring dead people back to life. I just negate somebody else's ability. It seems like a hostile, stultifying sort of ability—to cancel out the telepathic factor.'

'That could be as useful as the telepathic factor itself. Especially for all of us non-teeps.'

'Suppose somebody comes along who balances your ability, Curt.' She had turned dead serious, sounding discouraged and unhappy. 'People will arise who balance out *all* Psi talents. We'll be back where we started from. It'll be like not having Psi at all.'

'I don't think so,' Curt answered. 'The Anti-Psi factor is a natural restoration of balance. One insect learns to fly, so another learns to build a web to trap him. Is that the same as no flight? Clams developed hard shells to protect them; therefore birds learn to fly the clam up high in the air and drop him on a rock. In a sense you're a life-form preying on the Psis and the Psis are life-forms that prey on the Norms. That makes you a friend of the Norm-class. Balance, the full circle, predator and prey. It's an eternal system and frankly I can't see how it could be improved.'

'You might be considered a traitor.'

'Yes,' Curt agreed. 'I suppose so.'

'Doesn't it bother you?'

'It bothers me that people will feel hostile toward me. But you can't live very long without arousing hostility. Julie feels hostility toward you. Reynolds feels hostility for me already. You can't please everybody, because people want different things. Please one and you displease another. In this life you have to decide which of them you want to please. I'd prefer to please Fairchild.'

'He should be glad.'

'If he's aware of what's going on. Fairchild's an overworked bureaucrat. He may decide I exceeded my authority in acting on your father's petition. He may want it filed back where it was, and you returned to Prox VI. He may even fine me a penalty.'

They left the School and drove down the long highway to the shore of the ocean. Tim shouted with happiness at the vast stretch of deserted beach as he raced off, arms waving, his yells lost in the ceaseless lapping of the ocean waves. The red-tinted sky warmed above them. The three of them were completely isolated by the bowl of ocean and sky and beach. No other humans were visible, only a flock of indigenous birds strolling around in search of sand crustaceans.

'It's wonderful,' Pat said, awed. 'I guess the oceans of Terra are like this, big and bright and red.'

'Blue,' Curt corrected. He lay sprawled out on the warm sand, smoking his pipe and gazing moodily at the probing waves that oozed up on the beach a few yards away. The waves left heaps of steaming seaplants stranded.

Tim came hurrying back with his arms full of the dripping, slimy weeds. He dumped the coils of still quivering vegetable life in front of Pat and his father.

'He likes the ocean,' Pat said.

'No hiding places for Others,' Curt answered. 'He can see for miles, so he knows they can't creep up on him.'

'Others?' She was curious. 'He's such a strange boy. So worried and busy. He takes his alternate world so seriously. Not a pleasant world, I guess. Too many responsibilities.'

The sky turned hot. Tim began building an intricate structure out of wet sand lugged from the water's edge.

Pat scampered barefooted to join Tim. The two of them labored, adding infinite walls and side-buildings and towers. In the hot glare of the water, the girl's bare shoulders and back dripped perspiration. She sat up finally, gasping and exhausted, pushed her hair from her eyes and struggled to her feet.

'It's too hot,' she gasped, throwing herself down beside Curt. 'The weather's so different here. I'm sleepy.'

Tim continued building the structure. The two of them watched him languidly, crumbling bits of dry sand between their fingers.

'I guess,' Pat said after a while, 'there isn't much left to your marriage. I've made it impossible for you and Julie to live together.'

'It's not your fault. We were never really together. All we had in common was our talent and that has nothing to do with over-all personality. The total individual.'

Pat slid off her skirt and waded down to the ocean's edge. She curled up in the swirling pink foam and began washing her hair. Half-buried in the piles of foam and seakelp, her sleek, tanned body glowed wet and healthy in the overhead sun.

'Come on!' she called to Curt. 'It's so cool.'

Curt knocked the ashes from his pipe into the dry sand. 'We have to get back. Sooner or later I've got to have it out with Fairchild. We need a decision.'

Pat strode from the water, body streaming, head tossed back, hair dripping down her shoulders. Tim attracted her attention and she halted to study his sand building.

'You're right,' she said to Curt. 'We shouldn't be here wading and dozing and building sand castles. Fairchild's trying to keep the Separation working, and we have real things to build up in the backward Colonies.'

As she dried herself with Curt's coat she told him about Proxima VI.

'It's like the Middle Ages back on Terra. Most of our people think Psi powers are miracles. They think the Psis are saints.'

'I suppose that's what the saints were,' Curt agreed. 'They raised the dead, turned inorganic material into organic and moved objects around. The Psi ability has probably always been present in the human race. The Psi-class individual isn't new; he's always been with us, helping here and there, sometimes doing harm when he exploited his talent against mankind.'

Pat tugged on her sandals. 'There's an old woman near our village, a first-rate Resurrector. She won't leave Prox VI; she won't go with the Government Teams or get mixed up with the School. She wants to stay where she is, being a witch and wise woman. People come to her and she heals the sick.'

Pat fastened her blouse and started toward the car. 'When I was seven I broke my arm. She put her old withered hands on it and the break repaired itself. Apparently her hands radiate some kind of generative field that affects the growth-rate of the cells. And I remember one time when a boy was drowned and she brought him back to life.'

'Get an old woman who can heal, another who can precog the future, and your village is set up. We Psis have been helping longer than we realize.'

'Come on, Tim!' Pat called, tanned hands to her lips. 'Time to go back!'

The boy bent down one last time to peer into the depths of his structure, the elaborate inner sections and his sand building.

Suddenly he screamed, leaped back and came racing frantically toward the car.

Pat caught hold of him and he clung to her, face distorted with terror. 'What is it?' Pat was frightened. 'Curt, *what was it?*'

Curt came over and squatted down beside the boy. 'What was in there?' he asked gently. 'You built it.'

The boy's lips moved. 'A *Left*,' he muttered almost inaudibly. 'There was a Left, I know it. The first real Left. And it hung on.'

Pat and Curt glanced at each other uneasily. 'What's he talking about?' Pat asked.

Curt got behind the wheel of the car and pushed open the doors for the two of them. 'I don't know. But I think we'd better get back to town. I'll talk to Fairchild and get this business of Anti-Psi cleared up. Once that's out of the way, you and I can devote ourselves to Tim for the rest of our lives.'

Fairchild was pale and tired as he sat behind his desk in his office, hands folded in front of him, a few Norm-class advisors here and there, listening intently. Dark circles mooned under his eyes. As he listened to Curt he sipped at a glass of tomato juice.

'In other words,' Fairchild muttered, 'you're saying we can't really trust you Psis. It's a paradox.' His voice broke with despair. 'A Psi comes here and says *all Psis lie*. What the hell am I supposed to do?'

'Not all Psis.' Being able to preview the scene gave Curt remarkable calmness. 'I'm saying that in a way Terra is right . . . the existence of super-talented humans poses a problem for those without super-talents. But Terra's answer is wrong; sterilization is vicious and senseless. But cooperation isn't as easy as you imagine. You're dependent on our talents for survival and that means we have you where we want you. We can dictate to you because, without us, Terra would come in and clap you all into military prison.'

'And destroy you Psis,' the old man said. 'Don't forget that.'

Curt eyed the old man. It was the same wide-shouldered, gray-faced individual of the night before. There was something familiar about him. Curt peered closer and gasped, in spite of his preview.

'You're a Psi,' he said.

The old man bowed slightly. 'Evidently.'

'Come on,' Fairchild said. 'All right, we've seen this girl and we'll accept your theory of Anti-Psi. *What do you want us to do?*' He wiped his forehead miserably. 'I know Reynolds is a menace. But damn it, Terran infiltrators would be running all around here without the Corps!'

'I want you to create a legal fourth class,' Curt stated. 'The Anti-Psi class. I want you to give it status-immunity from sterilization. I want you to publicize it. Women come in here with their children from all parts of the Colonies, trying to convince you they've got Psis to offer, not Mutes. I want you to set up the Anti-Psi talents out where we can utilize them.'

Fairchild licked his dry lips. 'You think more exist already?'

'Very possibly. I came on Pat by accident. But get the flow started! Get the mothers hovering anxiously over their cribs for Anti-Psis . . . We'll need all we can get.'

There was silence.

'Consider what Mr Purcell is doing,' the old man said at last. 'An Anti-Precog may arise, a person whose actions in the future can't be previewed. A sort of Heisenberg's indeterminate particle . . . a man who throws off all precog prediction. And yet Mr Purcell has come here to make his suggestions. He's thinking of Separation, not himself.'

Fairchild's fingers twitched. 'Reynolds is going to be mad as hell.'

'He's already mad,' Curt said. 'He undoubtedly knows about this right now.'

'He'll protest!'

Curt laughed, some of the officials smiled. 'Of course he'll protest. Don't you understand? *You're being eliminated.* You think Norms are going to be around much longer? Charity is damn scarce in this universe. You Norms gape at Psis like rustics at a carnival. Wonderful . . . magical. You encouraged Psis, built the School, gave us our chance here in the Colonies. In fifty years you'll be slave laborers for us. You'll be doing our manual labor—unless you have sense enough to create the fourth class, the Anti-Psi class. You've got to stand up to Reynolds.'

'I hate to alienate him,' Fairchild muttered. 'Why the hell can't we all work together?' He appealed to the others around the room. 'Why can't we all be brothers?'

'Because,' Curt answered, 'we're not. Face facts. Brotherhood is a fine idea, but it'll come into existence sooner if we achieve a balance of social forces.'

'Is it possible,' the old man suggested, 'that once the concept of Anti-Psi reaches Terra the sterilization program will be modified? This idea may erase the irrational terror the non-mutants have, their phobia that we're monsters about to invade and take over their world. Sit next to them in theaters. Marry their sisters.'

'All right,' Fairchild agreed. 'I'll construct an official directive. Give me an hour to word it—I want to get all the loopholes out.'

Curt got to his feet. It was over. As he had previewed, Fairchild had agreed. 'We should start getting reports almost at once,' he said. 'As soon as routine checking of the files begins.'

Fairchild nodded. 'Yes, almost at once.'

'I assume you'll keep me informed.' Apprehension moved through Curt. He had succeeded . . . or had he? He scanned the next half-hour. There was nothing negative he could preview. He caught a quick scene of himself and Pat, himself and Julie and Tim. But still his uneasiness remained, an intuition deeper than his precog.

Everything looked fine, but he knew better. Something basic and chilling had gone wrong.

IV

He met Pat in a small out-of-the-way bar at the rim of the city. Darkness flickered around their table. The air was thick and pungent with the presence of people. Bursts of muted laughter broke out, muffled by the steady blur of conversation.

'How'd it go?' she asked, eyes large and dark, as he seated himself across from her. 'Did Fairchild agree?'

Curt ordered a Tom Collins for her and bourbon and water for himself. Then he outlined what had taken place.

'So everything's all right.' Pat reached across the table to touch his hand. 'Isn't it?'

Curt sipped at his drink. 'I guess so. The Anti-Psi class is being formed. But it was too easy. Too simple.'

'You can see ahead, can't you? Is anything going to happen?'

Across the dark room the music machine was creating vague patterns of sound, random harmonics and rhythms in a procession of soft clusters that drifted through the room. A few couples moved languidly together in response to the shifting patterns.

Curt offered her a cigarette and the two of them lit up from the candle in the center of the table. 'Now you have your status.'

Pat's dark eyes flickered. 'Yes, that's so. The new Anti-Psi class. I don't have to worry now. That's all over.'

'We're waiting for others. If no others show, you're a member of a unique class. The only Anti-Psi in the Universe.'

For a moment Pat was silent. Then she asked, 'What do you see after that?' She sipped her drink. 'I mean, I'm going to stay here, aren't I? Or will I be going back?'

'You'll stay here.'

'With you?'

'With me. And with Tim.'

'What about Julie?'

'The two of us signed mutual releases a year ago. They're on file, somewhere. Never processed. It was an agreement we made, so neither of us could block the other later on.'

'I think Tim likes me. He won't mind, will he?'

'Not at all,' Curt said.

'It ought to be nice, don't you think? The three of us. We can work with Tim, try to find out about his talent, what he is and what he's thinking. I'd enjoy that . . . he responds to me. And we have a long time; there's no hurry.'

Her fingers clasped around his. In the shifting darkness of the bar her features swam close to his own. Curt leaned forward, hesitated a moment as her warm breath stained his lips and then kissed her.

Pat smiled up at him. 'There're so many things for us to do. Here, and perhaps later on Prox VI. I want to go back there, sometime. Could we? Just for a while; we wouldn't have to stay. So I can see that it's still going on, all the things I worked at all my life. So I could see my world.'

'Sure,' Curt said. 'Yes, we'll go back there.'

Across from them a nervous little man had finished his garlic bread and wine. He wiped his mouth, glanced at his wristwatch and got to his feet. As he squeezed past Curt he reached into his pocket, jangled change and jerkily brought out his hand. Gripping a slender tube, he turned around, bent over Pat, and depressed the tube.

A single pellet dribbled from the tube, clung for a split second to the shiny surface of her hair, and then was gone. A dull echo of vibration rolled up toward the nearby tables. The nervous little man continued on.

Curt was on his feet, numb with shock. He was still gazing down, paralyzed, when Reynolds appeared beside him and firmly pulled him away.

'She's dead,' Reynolds was saying. 'Try to understand. She died instantly; there was no pain. It goes directly to the central nervous system. She wasn't even aware of it.'

Nobody in the bar had stirred. They sat at their tables, faces impassive, watching as Reynolds signaled for more light. The darkness faded and the objects of the room leaped into clarity.

'Stop that machine,' Reynolds ordered sharply. The music machine stumbled into silence. 'These people here are Corpsmen,' he explained to Curt. 'We probed your thoughts about this place as you entered Fairchild's office.'

'But I didn't catch it,' Curt muttered. 'There was no warning. No preview.'

'The man who killed her is an Anti-Psi,' Reynolds said. 'We've known of the category for a number of years; remember, it took an initial probe to uncover Patricia Connley's shield.'

'Yes,' Curt agreed. 'She was probed years ago. By one of you.'

'We don't like the Anti-Psi idea. We wanted to keep the class out of existence, but we were interested. We've uncovered and neutralized fourteen Anti-Psis over the past decade. On this, we have virtually the whole Psi-class behind us—except you. The problem, of course, is that no Anti-Psi talent can be brought out unless matched against the Psionic talent it negates.'

Curt understood. 'You had to match this man against a Precog. And there's only one Precog other than myself.'

'Julie was cooperative. We brought the problem to her a few months ago. We had definite proof to give her concerning your affair with this girl. I don't understand how you expected to keep Telepaths from knowing your plans, but apparently you did. In any case, the girl is dead. And there won't be any Anti-Psi class. We waited as long as possible, for we don't like to destroy talented individuals. But Fairchild was on the verge of signing the enabling legislation, so we couldn't hold off any longer.'

Curt hit out frantically, knowing even as he did so that it was futile. Reynolds slid back; his foot tangled with the table and he staggered. Curt leaped on him, smashed the tall cold glass that had held Pat's drink and lifted the jagged edges over Reynolds' face.

Corpsmen pulled him off.

Curt broke away. He reached down and gathered up Pat's body. She was still warm; her face was calm, expressionless, an empty burned-out shell that mirrored nothing. He carried her from the bar and out into the frigid night-dark street. A moment later he lowered her into his car and crept behind the wheel.

He drove to the School, parked the car, and carried her into the main building. Pushing past astonished officials, he reached the children's quarters and forced open the door to Sally's room with his shoulder.

She was wide-awake and fully dressed. Seated on a straight-back chair the child faced him defiantly. 'You see?' she shrilled. 'See what you did?'

He was too dazed to answer.

'It's all your fault! You made Reynolds do it. He *had* to kill her.' She leaped to her feet and ran toward him screaming hysterically. 'You're an enemy! You're against us! You want to make trouble for all of us. I told Reynolds what you were doing and he—'

Her voice trailed off as he moved out of the room with his heavy armload. As he lumbered up the corridor the hysterical girl followed him.

'You want to go across—you want me to get Big Noodle to take you across!' She ran in front of him, darting here and there like a maniacal insect. Tears ran down her cheeks; her face was distorted beyond recognition. She followed him all the way to Big Noodle's chamber. 'I'm not going to help you! You're against all of us and I'm never going to help you again! I'm *glad* she's dead. I wish you were dead, too. And you're going to be dead when Reynolds catches you. He told me so. He said there wasn't going to be any more like you and we would have things the way they ought to be, and nobody, not you nor any of those *numbskulls* can stop us!'

He lowered Pat's body onto the floor and moved out of the chamber. Sally raced after him.

'You know what he did to Fairchild? He had him fixed so he can't do anything ever again.'

Curt tripped a locked door and entered his son's room. The door closed after him and the girl's frenzied screams died to a muffled vibration. Tim sat up in bed, surprised and half-stupefied by sleep.

'Come on,' Curt said. He dragged the boy from his bed, dressed him, and hurried him outside into the hall.

Sally stopped them as they re-entered Big Noodle's chamber. 'He won't do it,' she screamed. 'He's afraid of me and I told him not to. You understand?'

*

Big Noodle lay slumped in his massive chair. He lifted his great hand as Curt approached him. 'What do you want?' he muttered. 'What's the matter with her?' He indicated Pat's inert body. 'She pass out or something?'

'Reynolds killed her!' Sally shrilled, dancing around Curt and his son. 'And he's going to kill Mr Purcell! He's going to kill everybody that tries to stop us!'

Big Noodle's thick features darkened. The wattles of bristly flesh turned a flushed, mottled crimson. 'What's going on, Curt?' he muttered.

'The Corps is taking over,' Curt answered.

'They killed your girl?'

'Yes.'

Big Noodle strained to a sitting position and leaned forward. 'Reynolds is after you?'

'Yes.'

Big Noodle licked his thick lips hesitantly. 'Where do you want to go?' he asked hoarsely. 'I can move you out of here, to Terra, maybe. Or—'

Sally made frantic motions with her hands. Part of Big Noodle's chair writhed and became animate. The arms twisted around him, cut viciously into his puddinglike paunch. He retched and closed his eyes.

'I'll make you sorry!' Sally chanted. 'I can do terrible things to you!'

'I don't want to go to Terra,' Curt said. He gathered up Pat's body and motioned Tim over beside him. 'I want to go to Proxima VI.'

Big Noodle struggled to make up his mind. Outside the room officials and Corpsmen were in cautious motion. A bedlam of sound and uncertainty rang up and down the corridors.

Sally's shrill voice rose over the rumble of sound as she tried to attract Big Noodle's attention. 'You know what I'll do! You know what will happen to you!'

Big Noodle made his decision. He tried an abortive stab at Sally before turning to Curt; a ton of molten plastic transported from some Terran factory cascaded down on her in a hissing torrent. Sally's body dissolved, one arm raised and twitching, the echo of her voice still hanging in the air.

Big Noodle had acted, but the warp directed at him from the dying girl was already in existence. As Curt felt the air of space-transformation all around him, he caught a final glimpse of Big Noodle's torment. He had never known precisely what it was Sally dangled over the big idiot's head. Now he saw it and understood Big Noodle's hesitation. A high-pitched scream rattled from Big Noodle's throat and around Curt as the chamber ebbed away. Big Noodle altered and flowed as Sally's change engulfed him.

Curt realized, then, the amount of courage buried in the vegetable rolls of fat. Big Noodle had known the risk, taken it, and accepted—more or less—the consequences.

The vast body had become a mass of crawling spiders. What had been Big Noodle was now a mound of hairy, quivering beings, thousands of them, spiders without number, dropping off and clinging again, clustering and separating and reclustering.

And then the chamber was gone. He was across.

It was early afternoon. He lay for a time, half-buried in tangled vines. Insects hummed around him, seeking moisture from the stalks of foul-smelling flowers. The red-tinted sky baked in the mounting sunlight. Far off, an animal of some kind called mournfully.

Nearby, his son stirred. The boy got to his feet, wandered about aimlessly and finally approached his father.

Curt pulled himself up. His clothes were torn. Blood oozed down his cheek, into his mouth. He shook his head, shuddered, and looked around.

Pat's body lay a few feet off. A crumpled and broken thing, it was without life of any kind. A hollow husk, abandoned and deserted.

He made his way over to her. For a time he squatted on his

haunches, gazing vacantly down at her. Then he leaned over, picked her up, and struggled to his feet.

'Come on,' he said to Tim. 'Let's get started.'

They walked a long time. Big Noodle had dropped them between villages, in the turgid chaos of the Proxima VI forests. Once he stopped in an open field and rested. Against the line of drooping trees a waver of blue smoke drifted. A kiln, perhaps. Or somebody clearing away the brush. He lifted Pat up in his arms again and continued on.

When he crashed from the underbrush and out into the road, the villagers were paralyzed with fright. Some of them raced off, a few remained, staring blankly at the man and the boy beside him.

'Who are you?' one of them demanded as he fumbled for a hack-knife. 'What have you got there?'

They got a work-truck for him, allowed him to dump Pat in with the rough-cut lumber and then drove him and his son to the nearest village. He wasn't far off, only a hundred miles. From the common store of the village he was given heavy work clothes and fed. Tim was bathed and cared for, and a general conference was called.

He sat at a huge, rough table, littered with remains of the midday meal. He knew their decision; he could preview it without trouble.

'She can't fix up anybody that far gone,' the leader of the village explained to him. 'The girl's whole upper ganglia and brain are gone, and most of the spinal column.'

He listened, but didn't speak. Afterwards, he wangled a battered truck, loaded Pat and Tim in, and started on.

Her village had been notified by short-wave radio. He was pulled from the truck by savage hands; a pandemonium of noise and fury boiled around him, excited faces distorted by grief and horror. Shouts, outraged shoves, questions, a blur of men and women milling and pushing until finally her brothers cleared a path for him to their home.

'It's useless,' her father was saying to him. 'And the old woman's gone, I think. That was years ago.' The man gestured toward the mountains. 'She lived up there—used to come down. Not for years.' He grabbed Curt roughly. 'It's too late, God damn it! She's dead! You can't bring her back!'

He listened to the words, still said nothing. He had no interest in predictions of any kind. When they had finished talking to him, he gathered up Pat's body, carried it back to the truck, called his son and continued on.

It grew cold and silent as the truck wheezily climbed the road into the mountains. Frigid air plucked at him; the road was obscured by dense clouds of mist that billowed up from the chalky soil. At one point a lumbering animal barred his way until he drove it off by throwing rocks at it. Finally the truck ran out of fuel and stopped. He got out, stood for a time, then woke up his son and continued on foot.

It was almost dark when he found the hut perched on a lip of rock. A fetid stench of offal and drying hides stung his nose as he staggered past heaps of discarded rubble, tin cans and boxes, rotting fabric and vermin-infested lumber.

The old woman was watering a patch of wretched vegetables. As he approached, she lowered her sprinkling can and turned toward him, wrinkled face tight with suspicion and wonder.

'I can't do it,' she said flatly as she crouched over Pat's inert body. She ran her dry, leathery hands over the dead face, pulled aside the girl's shirt and kneaded the cold flesh at the base of the neck. She pushed aside the tangle of black hair and gripped the skull with her strong fingers. 'No, I can't do a thing.' Her voice was rusty and harsh in the night fog that billowed around them. 'She's burned out. No tissue left to repair.'

Curt made his cracked lips move. 'Is there another?' he grated. 'Any more Resurrectors here?'

The old woman struggled to her feet. 'Nobody can help you, don't you understand? She's dead!'

He remained. He asked the woman again and again. Finally

there was a begrudging answer. Somewhere on the other side of the planet there was supposed to be a competitor. He gave the old woman his cigarettes and lighter and fountain pen, picked up the cold body and started back. Tim trailed after him, head drooping, body bent with fatigue.

'Come on,' Curt ordered harshly. The old woman watched silently as they threaded their way down by the light of Proxima VI's two sullen, yellowed moons.

He got only a quarter mile. In some way, without warning, her body was gone. He had lost her, dropped her along the way. Somewhere among the rubbish-littered rocks and weeds that fingered their way over the trail. Probably into one of the deep gorges that cut into the jagged side of the mountain.

He sat down on the ground and rested. There was nothing left. Fairchild had dwindled into the hands of the Corps. Big Noodle was destroyed by Sally. Sally was gone, too. The Colonies were open to the Terrans; their wall against projectiles had dissolved when Big Noodle died. And Pat.

There was a sound behind him. Panting with despair and fatigue, he turned only slightly. For a brief second he thought it was Tim catching up with him. He strained to see; the shape that emerged from the half-light was too tall, too sure-footed. A familiar shape.

'You're right,' the old man said, the ancient Psi who had stood beside Fairchild. He came up, vast and awesome in the aged yellow moonlight. 'There's no use trying to bring her back. It could be done, but it's too difficult. And there are other things for you and me to think about.'

Curt scrambled off. Falling, sliding, slashed by the stones under him, he made his way blindly down the trail. Dirt rattled after him while, choking, he struggled onto the level ground.

When he halted again, it was Tim who came after him. For an instant he thought it had been an illusion, a figment of his imagination. The old man was gone; he hadn't been there.

He didn't fully understand until he saw the change take place in front of him. And this time it went the other way. He realized that this one was a *Left*. And it was a familiar figure, but in a different way. A figure he remembered from the past.

Where the boy of eight had stood, a wailing, fretful baby of sixteen months struggled and groped. Now the substitution had gone in the other direction . . . and he couldn't deny what his eyes saw.

'All right,' he said, when the eight-year-old Tim reappeared and the baby was gone. But the boy remained only a moment. He vanished almost at once, and this time a new shape stood on the trail. A man in his middle thirties, a man Curt had never seen before.

A familiar man.

'*You're my son*,' Curt said.

'That's right.' The man appraised him in the dim light. 'You realize that she can't be brought back, don't you? We have to get that out of the way before we can proceed.'

Curt nodded wearily. 'I know.'

'Fine.' Tim advanced toward him, hand out. 'Then let's get back down. We have a lot to do. We middle and extreme Rights have been trying to get through for some time. It's been difficult to come back without the approval of the Center one. And in these cases the Center is too young to understand.'

'So that's what he meant,' Curt murmured as the two of them made their way along the road, toward the village. 'The Others are himself, along his time-track.'

'Left is previous Others,' Tim answered. 'Right, of course, is the future. You said that Precog and Precog made nothing. Now you know. They make the ultimate Precog—the ability to move through time.'

'You Others were trying to get over. He'd see you and be frightened.'

'It was very hard, but we knew eventually he'd grow old enough to comprehend. He built up an elaborate mythology. That is, we did. I did.' Tim laughed. 'You see, there still isn't an adequate terminology. There never is for a unique happening.'

'I could change the future,' Curt said, 'because I could see into it. But I couldn't change the present. You can change the present by going back into the past. That's why that extreme Right Other, the old man, hung around Fairchild.'

'That was our first successful crossing. We were finally able to induce the Center to take his two steps Right. That switched the two, but it took time.'

'What's going to happen now?' Curt asked. 'The war? The Separation? All this about Reynolds?'

'As you realized before, we can alter it by going back. It's dangerous. A simple change in the past may completely alter the present. The time-traveling talent is the most critical—and the most Promethean. Every other talent, without exception, can change only what's going to happen. I could wipe out everything that stands. I precede everyone and everything. Nothing can be used against me. I am always there first. I have always been there.'

Curt was silent as they passed the abandoned, rusting truck. Finally he asked, 'What is Anti-Psi? What did you have to do with that?'

'Not much,' his son said. 'You can take credit for bringing it out into the open, since we didn't begin operating until the last few hours. We came along in time to aid it—you saw us with Fairchild. We're *sponsoring* Anti-Psi. You'd be surprised to see some of the alternate time-paths on which Anti-Psi fails to get pushed forward. Your precog was right—they're not very pleasant.'

'So I've had help lately.'

'We're behind you, yes. And from now on, our help will increase. Always, we try to introduce balances. Stalemates, such as Anti-Psi. Right now, Reynolds is a little out of balance, but he can easily be checked. Steps are being taken. We're not infinite in power, of course. We're limited by our life-span, about seventy years. It's a strange feeling to be outside of time. You're outside of change, subject to no laws.

242 A WORLD OF TALENT

'It's like suddenly being lifted off the chess board and seeing everybody as pieces—seeing the whole Universe as a game of black and white squares—with everybody and every object stuck on his space-time spot. We're off the board; we can reach down from above. Adjust, alter the position of the men, change the game without the pieces knowing. From outside.'

'And you won't bring her back?' Curt appealed.

'You can't expect me to be too sympathetic toward the girl,' his son said. 'After all, Julie is my mother. I know now what they used to mean by *mill of the gods*. I wish we could grind less small . . . I wish we could spare some of those who get caught in the gears. But if you could see it as we do, you'd understand. We have a universe hanging in the balance; it's an awfully big board.'

'A board so big that one person doesn't count?' Curt asked, agonized.

His son looked concerned. Curt remembered looking like that himself when trying to explain something to the boy that was beyond the child's comprehension. He hoped Tim would do a better job than he'd been able to do.

'Not that,' Tim said. 'To us, she isn't gone. She's still there, on another part of the board that you can't see. She always was there. She always will be. No piece ever falls off the board . . . no matter how small.'

'For you,' said Curt.

'Yes. We're outside the board. It may be that our talent will be shared by everybody. When that happens, there will be no misunderstanding of tragedy and death.'

'And meanwhile?' Curt ached with the tension of *willing* Tim to agree. 'I don't have the talent. To me, she's dead. The place she occupied on the board is empty. Julie can't fill it. Nobody can.'

Tim considered. It looked like deep thought, but Curt could sense that his son was moving restlessly along the time-paths, seeking a rebuttal. His eyes focused again on his father and he nodded sadly.

'I can't show you where she is on the board,' he said. 'And your life is vacant along every path except one.'

Curt heard someone coming through the brush. He turned– and then Pat was in his arms.

'This one,' Tim said.

PSI-MAN HEAL MY CHILD!

He was a lean man, middle-aged, with grease-stained hair and skin, a crumpled cigarette between his teeth, his left hand clamped around the wheel of his car. The car, an ex-commercial surface truck, rumbled noisily but smoothly as it ascended the outgoing ramp and approached the check-gate that terminated the commune area.

'Slow down,' his wife said. 'There's the guard sitting on that pile of crates.'

Ed Garby rode the brake; the car settled grimly into a long glide that ended directly in front of the guard. In the back seat of the car the twins fretted restlessly, already bothered by the gummy heat oozing through the top and windows of the car. Down his wife's smooth neck great drops of perspiration slid. In her arms the baby twisted and struggled feebly.

'How's she?' Ed muttered to his wife, indicating the wad of gray, sickly flesh that poked from the soiled blanket. 'Hot—like me.'

The guard came strolling over indifferently, sleeves rolled up, rifle slung over his shoulder. 'What say, mac?' Resting his big hands in the open window, he gazed dully into the interior of the car, observing the man and wife, the children, the dilapidated upholstery. 'Going outside awhile? Let's see your pass.'

Ed got out the crumpled pass and handed it over. 'I got a sick child.'

The guard examined the pass and returned it. 'Better take her down to the sixth level. You got a right to use the infirmary; you live in this dump like the rest of us.'

'No,' Ed said. 'I'm taking no child of mine down to that butchery.'

The guard shook his head in disagreement. 'They got good equipment, mac. High-powered stuff left over from the war. Take her down there and they'll fix her up.' He waved toward the desolate expanse of dry trees and hills that lay beyond the check-gate. 'What do you think you'll find out there? You going to dump her somewhere? Toss her in a creek? Down a well? It's none of my business, but I wouldn't take a dog out there, let alone a sick child.'

Ed started up the motor. 'I'm getting help out there. Take a child down to sixth and they make her a laboratory animal. They experiment, cut her up, throw her away and say they couldn't save her. They got used to doing that in the war; they never stopped.'

'Suit yourself,' the guard said, moving away from the car. 'Myself, I'd sooner trust military doctors with equipment than some crazy old quack living out in the ruins. Some savage heathen tie a bag of stinking dung around her neck, mumble nonsense and wave and dance around.' He shouted furiously after the car: 'Damn fools— going back to barbarism, when you got doctors and X-rays and serums down on sixth! Why the hell do you want to go out in the ruins when you've got a civilization here?'

He wandered glumly back to his crates. And added, 'What there is left of it.'

Arid land, as dry and parched as dead skin, lay on both sides of the rutted tracks that made up the road. A harsh rattle of noonday wind shook the gaunt trees jutting here and there from the cracked, baking soil. An occasional drab bird fluttered in the thick underbrush, heavy-set gray shapes that scratched peevishly in search of grubs.

Behind the car the white concrete walls of the commune faded and were lost in the distance. Ed Garby watched them go apprehensively; his hands convulsively jerked as a twist in the road cut off the radar towers posted on the hills overlooking the commune.

'Damn it,' he muttered thickly, 'maybe he was right; maybe

　　　　　　　　　　　PSI-MAN HEAL MY CHILD!

we're making a mistake.' Doubts shivered through his mind. The trip was dangerous; even heavily-armed scavenger parties were attacked by predatory animals and by the wild bands of quasi-humans living in the abandoned ruins littered across the planet. All he had to protect himself and his family was his hand-operated cutting tool. He knew how to use it, of course; didn't he grind it into a moving belt of reclaimed wreckage ten hours a day every day of the week? But if the motor of the car failed . . .

'Stop worrying,' Barbara said quietly. 'I've been along here before, and there's nothing ever gone wrong.'

He felt shame and guilt: his wife had crept outside the commune many times, along with other women and wives; and with some of the men, too. A good part of the proletariat left the commune, with and without passes . . . anything to break the monotony of work and educational lectures. But his fear returned. It wasn't the physical menace that bothered him, or even unfamiliar separation from the vast submerged tank of steel and concrete in which he had been born and in which he had grown up, spent his life, worked and married. It was the realization that the guard had been right, that he was sinking into ignorance and superstition, that made his skin turn cold and clammy, in spite of the baking midsummer heat.

'Women always lead it,' he said aloud. 'Men built machines, organized science, cities. Women have their potions and brews. I guess we're seeing the end of reason. We're seeing the last remnants of rational society.'

'What's a city?' one of the twins asked.

'You're seeing one now,' Ed answered. He pointed beyond the road. 'Take a good look.'

The trees had ended. The baked surface of brown earth had faded to a dull metallic glint. An uneven plain stretched out, bleak and dismal, a pocked surface of jagged heaps and pits. Dark weeds grew here and there. An occasional wall remained standing; at one point a bathtub lay on its side like a dead, toothless mouth, deprived of face and head.

The region had been picked over countless times. Everything of value had been loaded up and trucked to the various communes in the area. Along the road were neat heaps of bones, collected but never utilized. Use had been found for cement rubble, iron scrap, wiring, plastic tubing, paper and cloth—but not for bones.

'You mean people lived *there*?' the twins protested simultaneously. Disbelief and horror showed on their faces. 'It's—awful.'

The road divided. Ed slowed the car down and waited for his wife to direct him. 'Is it far?' he demanded hoarsely. 'This place gives me the creeps. You can't tell what's hanging around in those cellars. We gassed them back in '09, but it's probably worn off by now.'

'To the right,' Barbara said. 'Beyond that hill, there.'

Ed shifted into low-low and edged the car past a ditch, onto a side road. 'You really think this old woman has the power?' he asked helplessly. 'I hear so damn much stuff—I never know what's true and what's hogwash. There's always supposed to be some old hag that can raise the dead and read the future and cure the sick. People've been reporting that stuff for five thousand years.'

'And for five thousand years such things have been happening.' His wife's voice was placid, confident. 'They're always there to help us. All we have to do is go to them. I saw her heal Mary Fulsome's son; remember, he had that withered leg and couldn't walk. The medics wanted to destroy him.'

'According to Mary Fulsome,' Ed muttered harshly.

The car nosed its way between dead branches of ancient trees. The ruins fell behind; abruptly the road plunged into a gloomy thicket of vines and shrubs that shut out the sunlight. Ed blinked, then snapped on the dim headlights. They flickered on as the car ground its way up a rutted hill, around a narrow curve . . . and then the road ceased.

They had reached their destination. Four rusty cars blocked the road; others were parked on the shoulders and among the twisted trees. Beyond the cars stood a group of silent people, men and their families, in the drab uniforms of commune workers. Ed pulled on the brake and fumbled for the ignition key; he was astounded at the variety of communes represented. All the nearby communes, and distant ones he had never encountered. Some of the waiting people had come hundreds of miles.

'There's always people waiting,' Barbara said. She kicked open the bent door and carefully slid out, the baby in her arms. 'People come here for all kinds of help, whenever they're in need.'

Beyond the crowd was a crude wooden building, shabby and dilapidated, a patched-together shelter of the war years. A gradual line of waiting persons was being conducted up the rickety steps and into the building; for the first time Ed caught sight of those whom he had come to consult.

'Is that the old woman?' he demanded, as a thin, withered shape appeared briefly at the top of the steps, glanced over the waiting people, and selected one. She conferred with a plump man, and then a muscular giant joined the discussion. 'My God,' Ed said, 'is there an *organization* of them?'

'Different ones do different things,' Barbara answered. Clutching the baby tight, she edged her way forward into the waiting mass of people. 'We want to see the healer—we'll have to stand with that group over to the right, waiting by that tree.'

Porter sat in the kitchen of the shelter, smoking and drinking coffee, his feet up on the windowsill, vaguely watching the shuffling line of people moving through the front door and into the various rooms.

'A lot of them, today,' he said to Jack. 'What we need is a flat cover-charge.'

Jack grunted angrily and shook back his mane of blond hair. 'Why aren't you out helping instead of sitting here guzzling coffee?'

'Nobody wants to peep into the future.' Porter belched noisily; he was plump and flabby, blue-eyed, with thin, damp hair. 'When somebody wants to know if they're going to strike it rich or marry a beautiful woman I'll be there in my booth to advise them.'

'Fortune-telling,' Jack muttered. He stood restlessly by the window, great arms folded, face stern with worry. 'That's what we're down to.'

'I can't help that they ask me. One old geezer asked me when he was going to die; when I told him thirty-one days he turned red as a beet and started screaming at me. One thing, I'm honest. I tell them the truth, not what they want to hear.' Porter grinned. 'I'm not a quack.'

'How long has it been since somebody asked you something important?'

'You mean something of abstract significance?' Porter lazily searched his mind. 'Last week a fellow asked me if there'd ever be interplanetary ships again. I told him not that I could see.'

'Did you also tell him you can't see worth a damn? A half year at the most?'

Porter's toad-like face bloomed contentedly. 'He didn't ask me that.'

The thin, withered old woman entered the kitchen briefly. 'Lord,' Thelma gasped, sinking down in a chair and pouring herself coffee. 'I'm exhausted. And there must be fifty of them out there waiting to get healed.' She examined her shaking hands. 'Two bone cancers in one day about finishes me. I think the baby will survive, but the other's too far gone even for me. The baby will have to come back.' Her voice trailed off wearily. 'Back again next week.'

'It'll be slower tomorrow,' Porter predicted. 'Ash storm down from Canada will keep most of them at their communes. Of course, after that—' He broke off and eyed Jack curiously. 'What are you upset about? Everybody's growling around, today.'

'I just came from Butterford,' Jack answered moodily. 'I'm going back later and try again.'

Thelma shuddered. Porter looked away uneasily; he disliked hearing about conversations with a man whose bones were piled in the basement of the shelter. An almost superstitious fear drifted through the plump body of the precog. It was one thing to preview the future; seeing ahead was a positive, progressive talent. But returning to the past, to men already dead, to cities now turned to ash and rubble, places erased from the maps, participating in events long since forgotten—it was a sickly, neurotic rehashing of what had already been. Picking and stirring among the bones—literally bones—of the past.

'What did he say?' Thelma asked.

'The same as always,' Jack answered.

'How many times is this?'

Jack's lips twisted. 'Eleven times. And he knows it—I told him.'

Thelma moved from the kitchen, out into the hall. 'Back to work.' She lingered at the door. 'Eleven times and always the same. I've been making computations. How old are you, Jack?'

'How old do I look?'

'About thirty. You were born in 1946. This is 2017. That makes you seventy-one years old. I'd say I'm talking to an entity about a third of the way along. Where's your current entity?'

'You should be able to figure that out. Back in '76.'

'Doing what?'

Jack didn't answer. He knew perfectly well what his entity of this date, 2017, was doing back in the past. The old man of seventy-one years was lying in a medical hospital at one of the military centers, receiving treatment for a gradually worsening nephritis. He shot a quick glance at Porter to see if the precog was going to volunteer information previewed from the future. There was no expression on Porter's languid features, but that proved nothing. He'd have to get Stephen to probe into Porter if he really wanted to be sure.

Like the common workers who filed in daily to learn if they were going to strike it rich and marry happily, he wanted vitally to know the date of his own death. He *had* to know—it went beyond mere wanting.

He faced Porter squarely. 'Let's have it. What do you see about me in the next six months?'

Porter yawned. 'Am I supposed to orate the whole works? It'll take hours.'

Jack relaxed, weak with relief. Then he would survive another six months, at least. In that he could bring to a successful completion his discussions with General Ernest Butterford, chief of staff of the armed forces of the United States. He pushed past Thelma and out of the kitchen.

'Where are you going?' she demanded.

'Back to Butterford again. I'm going to make one more try.'

'You always say that,' Thelma complained peevishly.

'And I always am,' Jack said. *Until I'm dead*, he thought bitterly, resentfully. Until the half-conscious old man lying in the hospital bed at Baltimore, Maryland, passes away or is destroyed to make room for some wounded private carted by boxcar from the front lines, charged by Soviet napalm, crippled by nerve gas, insane from metallic ash-particles. When the ancient corpse was thrown out—and it wouldn't be long—there would be no more discussion with General Butterford.

First, he descended the stairs to the supply lockers in the basement of the shelter. Doris lay asleep on her bed in the corner, dark hair like cobwebs over her coffee-colored features, one bare arm raised, a heap of clothing strewn on the chair beside the bed. She awoke sleepily, stirred, and half sat up.

'What time is it?'

Jack glanced at his wristwatch. 'One-thirty in the afternoon.' He began opening one of the intricate locks that sealed in their supplies. Presently he slid a metal case down a rail and onto the cement floor. He swung an overhead light around and clicked it on.

The girl watched with interest. 'What are you doing?' She tossed her covers back and got to her feet, stretched, and padded barefoot over to him. 'I could have brought it out for you without all that work.'

From the lead-lined case Jack removed the carefully stacked heap of bones and remnants of personal possessions: wallet, identification papers, photographs, fountain pen, bits of tattered uniform, a gold wedding ring, some silver coins. 'He died under difficulties,' Jack murmured. He examined the data-tape, made sure it was complete, and then slammed shut the case. 'I told him I would bring this. Of course, he won't remember.'

'Each time erases the last?' Doris wandered over to get her clothes. 'It's really the same time again and again, isn't it?'

'The same interval,' Jack admitted, 'but there's no repetition of material.'

Doris eyed him slyly as she struggled into her jeans. '*Some* repetition . . . it always comes out the same, no matter what you do. Butterford goes ahead and presents his recommendations to the President.'

Jack didn't hear her. He had already moved back, taken his series of steps along the time-path. The basement, Doris' half-dressed figure, wavered and receded, as if seen through the bottom of a glass gradually filled with opaque liquid. Darkness, mixed with shifting textures of density, wavered around him as he walked sternly forward, the metal case gripped. *Backward*, actually. He was retreating along the direction in which the flow itself moved. Changing places with an earlier John Tremaine, the pimple-faced boy of sixteen who had trudged dutifully to high school, in the year 1962 A D in the city of Chicago, Illinois. This was a switch he had made many times. His younger entity should be resigned, by now . . . but he hoped idly that Doris would be finished dressing when the boy emerged.

The darkness that was no-time dwindled, and he blinked in a sudden torrent of yellow sunlight. Still gripping his metal case he made the final step backward and found himself in the center of a vast murmuring room. People drifted on all sides; several gaped at him, paralyzed with astonishment. For a moment he couldn't place the spatial location—and then memory came, a swift bitter flood of nostalgia.

He was back in the high school library where he had spent much time. The familiar place of books and bright-faced youths, gaily-dressed girls giggling and studying and flirting . . . young people totally oblivious of the approaching war. The mass death that would leave nothing of this city but dead, drifting ash.

He hurried from the library, conscious of the circle of bewilderment he had left behind. It was awkward to make a switch in which the passive entity was near other people; the abrupt transformation of a sixteen-year-old high school boy into the stern, towering figure of a thirty-year-old man was difficult to assimilate, even in a society theoretically aware of Psionic powers.

Theoretically—because at this date public consciousness was minimal. Awe and disbelief were the primary emotions; the surge of hopefulness hadn't begun. Psi-powers seemed miraculous only; the realization that these powers were at the disposal of the public wouldn't set in for a number of years.

He emerged on the busy Chicago street and hailed a taxi. The roar of buses, autos, the metallic swirl of buildings and people and signs, dazed him. Activity on all sides: the ordinary harmless routines of the common citizen, remote from the lethal planning at top levels. The people on all sides of him were about to be traded for the chimera of international prestige . . . human life for metaphysical phantoms. He gave the cabdriver the address of Butterford's hotel suite and settled back to prepare himself for the familiar encounter.

The first steps were routine. He gave his identification to the battery of armed guards, was checked, searched, and processed into the suite. For fifteen minutes he sat in a luxurious anteroom smoking and restlessly waiting—as always. There were no alterations he could make here: the changes, if they were to materialize, came later.

'Do you know who I am?' he began bluntly, when the tiny, suspicious head of General Butterford was stuck from an inner office. He advanced grimly, case gripped. 'This is the twelfth visit; there had better be results, this time.'

Butterford's deep-set little eyes danced hostilely behind his thick glasses. 'You're one of those supermen,' he squeaked. 'Those Psionics.' He blocked the door with his wizened, uniformed body. 'Well? What do you want? My time's valuable.'

Jack seated himself facing the general's desk and corps of aides. 'You have the analysis of my talent and history in your hands. You know what I can do.'

Butterford glanced hostilely at the report. 'You move into time. So?' His eyes narrowed. 'What do you mean, *twelfth* time?' He grabbed up a heap of memoranda. 'I've never seen you before. State what you have to say and then get out; I'm busy.'

'I have a present for you,' Jack said grimly. He carried the metal case to the desk, unsnapped it, and exposed the contents. 'They belong to you—go ahead, take them out and run your hands over them.'

Butterford gazed with revulsion at the bones. 'What is this, some sort of anti-war exhibit? Are you Psis mixed up with those Jehovah's Witnesses?' His voice rose shrilly, resentfully. 'Is this something you expect to pressure me with?'

'These are your goddamn bones!' Jack shouted in the man's face. He overturned the case; the contents spilled out on the desk and floor. '*Touch them!* You're going to die in this war, like everybody else. You're going to suffer and die hideously—they're going to get you with bacterial poisons one year and six days from this date. You'll live long enough to see the total destruction of organized society and then you'll go the way of everybody else!'

It would have been easier if Butterford were a coward. He sat gazing down at the tattered remains, the coins and pictures and rusting possessions, his face white, body stiff as metal. 'I don't know whether to believe you,' he said finally. 'I never really believed any of this Psi-stuff.'

'That's totally untrue,' Jack answered hotly. 'There isn't a government on the planet ignorant of us. You and the Soviet Union have been trying to organize us since '58, when we made ourselves known.'

The discussion was on ground that Butterford understood. His eyes blazed furiously. 'That's the whole point! If you Psis co-operated there wouldn't be those bones.' He jabbed wildly at the pale heap on the desk. 'You come here and blame me for the war.

Blame yourself—you won't put your shoulders to the wheel. How can we hope to come out of this war unless everybody does his part?' He leaned meaningfully toward Jack. 'You came from the future, you say. Tell me what you Psis are going to do in the war. Tell me the part you're going to play.'

'No part.'

Butterford settled back triumphantly. 'You're going to stand idly by?'

'Absolutely.'

'And you came here to blame *me*?'

'If we help,' Jack said carefully, 'we help at policy level, not as hired servants. Otherwise, we will stand on the sidelines, waiting. We're available, but if winning the war depends on us, we want to say how that war will be won. Or whether there'll be a war at all.' He slammed the metal case shut. 'Otherwise, we might become apprehensive, as the scientists did in the middle fifties. We might begin to lose *our* enthusiasm . . . and also become bad security risks.'

In Jack's mind a voice spoke, thin and bitter. A telepathic member of the Guild, a Psi of the present, monitoring the discussion from the New York office. 'Very well-spoken. But you've lost. You lack the ability to maneuver him . . . all you've done is defend our position. You haven't even brought up the possibility of changing his.'

It was true. Desperately, Jack said: 'I didn't come back here to state the Guild's position—you know our position! I came here to lay the facts out in front of you. I came here from 2017. The war is over. Only a remnant survives. These are the facts, events that have taken place. You're going to recommend to the President that the United States call Russia's bluff on Java.' His words came out individually, icily. 'It's not a bluff. It means total war. Your recommendation is in error.'

Butterford bristled. 'You want us to back down? Let them take over the free world?'

Twelve times: impasse. He had accomplished nothing. 'You'd go into the war knowing you can't win?'

'We'll fight,' Butterford said. 'Better an honorable war than a dishonorable peace.'

'No war is honorable. War means death, barbarism, and mass destruction.'

'What does peace mean?'

'Peace means the growth of the Guild. In fifty years our presence will shift the ideology of both blocs. We're above the war; we straddle both worlds. There're Psis here and in Russia; we're part of no country. The scientists could have been that, once. But they chose to cooperate with national governments. Now it's up to us.'

Butterford shook his head. 'No,' he said firmly. 'You're not going to influence us. *We* make policy . . . if you act, you act in line with our directives. Or you don't act. You stay out.'

'We'll stay out.'

Butterford leaped up. '*Traitors!*' he shouted as Jack left the office. 'You don't have a choice! We demand your abilities! We'll hunt you out and grab you one by one. You've got to cooperate—everybody's got to cooperate. This is total war!'

The door closed, and he was in the anteroom.

'No, there isn't any hope,' the voice in his mind stated bleakly. 'I can prove that you've done this twelve times. And you're contemplating a thirteenth. Give up. The withdrawal order has been given out already. When the war begins we'll be aloof.'

'We ought to help!' Jack said futilely. 'Not the war—we ought to help *them*, the people who're going to be killed by the millions.'

'We can't. We're not gods. We're only humans with paratalents. We can help, if they accept us, allow us to help. We can't force our views on them. We can't force the Guild in, if the governments don't want us.'

Gripping the metal case, Jack headed numbly down the stairs, toward the street. Back to the high school library.

At the dinner table, with black night lying outside the shelter, he faced the other surviving Guild members. 'So here we are. Outside society—doing nothing. Not harming and not helping. *Useless!*' He smashed his fist convulsively against the rotting wooden wall. 'Peripheral and useless, and while we sit here the communes fall apart and what's left collapses.'

Thelma spooned up her soup impassively. 'We heal the sick, read the future, offer advice, and perform miracles.'

'We've been doing that thousands of years,' Jack answered bitterly. 'Sibyls, witches, perched on deserted hills outside towns. *Can't we get in and help?* Do we always have to be on the outside, we who understand what's going on? Watching the blind fools lead mankind to destruction! Couldn't we have stopped the war, forced peace on them?'

Porter said languidly, 'We don't want to force anything on them, Jack. You know that. We're not their masters. We want to help them, not control them.'

The meal continued in gloomy silence. Doris said presently, 'The trouble is with the governments. It's the politicians who're jealous of us.' She smiled mournfully across the table at Jack. 'They know if we had our way, a time would come when politicians wouldn't be needed.'

Thelma attacked her plate of dried beans and broiled rabbit in a thin paste of gravy. 'There isn't much of a government, these days. It isn't like it was before the war. You can't really call a few majors sitting around in commune offices a *government*.'

'They make the decisions,' Porter pointed out. 'They decide what commune policy will be.'

'I know of a commune up north,' Stephen said, 'in which the workers killed the officers and took over. They're dying out. It won't be long before they're extinct.'

Jack pushed his plate away and got to his feet. 'I'm going out on the porch.' He left the kitchen, crossed through the deserted living room and opened the steel-reinforced front door. Cold evening wind swirled around him as he blindly felt his way to the railing and stopped, hands in his pockets, gazing sightlessly out at the vacant field.

The rusty fleet of cars was gone. Nothing stirred except the withered trees along the road, dry rustles in the restless night wind. A dismal sight; overhead a few stars glowed fitfully. Far off somewhere an animal crashed after its prey, a wild dog or perhaps a quasi-human living down in the ruined cellars of Chicago.

After a time Doris appeared behind him. Silently, she came up and stood next to him, a slim dark shape in the night gloom, her arms folded against the cold. 'You're not going to try again?' she asked softly.

'Twelve is enough. I—can't change him. I don't have the ability. I'm not adroit enough.' Jack spread his massive hands miserably. 'He's a clever little chicken of a thing. Like Thelma—scrawny and full of talk. Again and again I get back there—and what can I do?'

Doris touched his arm wistfully. 'How does it look? I never saw cities full of life, before the war. Remember, I was born in a military camp.'

'You'd like it. People laughing and hurrying. Cars, signs, life everywhere. It drives me crazy. I wish I couldn't see it—to be able to step from here to there.' He indicated the twisted trees. 'Ten steps back from those trees, and there it is. And yet it's gone forever . . . even for me. There'll be a time when I can't step there either, like the rest of you.'

Doris failed to understand him. 'Isn't it strange?' she murmured. 'I can move anything in the world, but I can't move myself back, the way you do.' She made a slight flutter of her hands; in the darkness something slapped against the rail of the porch and she bent over to retrieve it. 'See the pretty bird? Stunned, not dead.' She tossed the bird up and it managed to struggle off into the shrubs. 'I've got so I only stun them.'

Jack wasn't pleased. 'That's what we do with our talents. Tricks, games. Nothing more.'

'That isn't so!' Doris objected. 'Today when I got up, there was a bunch of doubters. Stephen caught their thoughts and sent me out.' Pride tingled in her voice. 'I brought an underground spring up to the surface—it burst out everywhere and got them all soaked, before I sent it back. They were convinced.'

'Did it ever occur to you,' Jack said, 'that you could make it possible for them to rebuild their cities?'

'They don't want to rebuild their cities.'

'They don't think they can. They've given up the idea of rebuilding. It's a lost concept.' He brooded unhappily. 'There's too many millions of miles of ruined ash, and too few people. They don't even try to unify the communes.'

'They have radios,' Doris pointed out. 'They can talk to each other, if they want.'

'If they use them, the war will start up again. They know there're pockets of fanatics left who'd be happy to start the war, given half the chance. They'd rather sink into barbarism than get that started.' He spat into the weedy bushes growing beneath the porch. 'I don't blame them.'

'If we controlled the communes,' Doris said thoughtfully, 'we wouldn't start up the war. We'd unify them on a peaceful basis.'

'You're playing all sides at once,' Jack said angrily. 'A minute ago you were performing miracles—where'd this thought come from?'

Doris hesitated. 'Well, I was just passing it on. I guess Stephen really said it, or thought it. I just spoke it out loud.'

'You enjoy being a mouthpiece for Stephen?'

Doris fluttered fearfully. 'My God, Jack—he can probe you. Don't say things like that!'

Jack stepped away from her and down the porch steps. He rapidly crossed the dark, silent field, away from the shelter. The girl hurried after him.

'Don't walk off,' she gasped breathlessly. 'Stephen's just a kid. He's not like you, grown-up and big. Mature.'

Jack laughed upward at the black sky. 'You damn fool. Do you know how old I am?'

'No,' Doris said, 'and don't say. I know you're older than I am. You've always been around; I remember you when I was just a kid. You were always big and strong and blond.' She giggled nervously. 'Of course, all those *others* . . . those different persons, old and young.

I don't really understand, but they're all you, I guess. Different yous along your time-path.'

'That's right,' Jack said tightly. 'They're all me.'

'That one today, when you switched down in the basement, when I was sleeping.' Doris caught his arm and tucked her cold fingers around his wrist. 'Just a kid, with books under his arm, in a green sweater and brown slacks.'

'Sixteen years old,' Jack muttered.

'He was cute. Shy, flustered. Younger than I am. We went upstairs and he watched the crowd; that was when Stephen called me to do the miracle. He—I mean, *you*—stood around so interested. Porter kidded him. Porter doesn't mean any harm—he likes to eat and sleep and that's about all. He's all right. Stephen kidded him, too. I don't think Stephen liked him.'

'You mean he doesn't like me.'

'I—guess you know how we feel. All of us, to some degree . . . we wonder why you keep going back again and again, trying to patch up the past. The past is over! Maybe not to you . . . but it really is over. You can't change it; the war came, this is all ruined, only remnants are left. You said it yourself: *why are we on the outside?* We could so easily be on the inside.' Childish excitement thrilled through her; she pushed against him eagerly, carried away by her flow of words. 'Forget the past—let's work with the present! The material is here; the people, the objects. Let's move it all around. Pick it up, set it down.' She lifted a grove of trees a mile away; the whole top of a line of hills burst loose, rose high in the air, and then dissolved in booming fragments. 'We can take things apart and put them back together!'

'I'm seventy-one years old,' Jack said. 'There isn't going to be any putting together for me. And I'm through picking over the past. I'm not going to try anymore. You can all rejoice . . . I'm finished.'

She tugged at him fiercely. 'Then it's up to the rest of us!'

If he had Porter's talent he could see beyond his death. Porter would, at some future time, view his own corpse stretched out, view his burial, continue to live month after month, while his plump corpse rotted underground. Porter's bovine contentedness was possible in a man who could preview the future . . . Jack twisted wretchedly as anguished uncertainty ached through him. After the dying old man in the military hospital reached the inevitable end of his life-span—then what? What happened *here*, among the survivors of the Guild?

Beside him, the girl babbled on. The possibilities he had suggested: real material to work with, not tricks or miracles. For her, the possibilities of social action were swimming into existence. They were all restless, except perhaps Porter. Tired of standing idle. Impatient with the anachronistic officers who kept the communes alive, misguided remnants of a past order of incompetents who had proved their unfitness to rule by leading their bloc to almost total destruction.

Rule by the Guild couldn't be worse.

Or could it? Something had survived rule by power-oriented politicians, professional spellbinders recruited from smoke-dingy city halls and cheap law offices. If Psionic rule failed, if analogues of the struggle of national states arose, there might be nothing spared. The collective power of the Guild reached into all dimensions of life; for the first time a genuine totalitarian society could arise. Dominated by telepaths, precogs, healers with the power to animate inorganic matter and to wither organic matter, what ordinary person could survive?

There would be no recourse against the Guild. Man controlled by Psionic organizers would be powerless. It was merely a question of time before the maintenance of non-Psis would be seriously scrutinized, with an eye toward greater efficiency, toward the elimination of useless material. Rule by super-competents could be worse than rule by incompetents.

'Worse for whom?' Stephen's clear, treble thoughts came into his mind. Cold, confident, utterly without doubt. 'You can see they're dying out. It's not a question of our eliminating them; it's a question of how long are we going to maintain their artificial preservation? We're running a zoo, Jack. We're keeping alive an extinct species. And the cage is too large . . . it takes up all the world. Give them some space, if you want. A subcontinent. But we deserve the balance for our own use.'

Porter sat scooping up baked rice pudding from his dish. He continued eating even after Stephen had begun screaming. It wasn't until Thelma clawed his hand loose from his spoon that he gave up and turned his attention to what was happening.

Surprise was totally unknown to him; six months earlier he had examined the scene, reflected on it, and turned his attention to later events. Reluctantly, he pushed back his chair and dragged his heavy body upright.

'He's going to kill me!' Stephen was wailing. 'Why didn't you tell me?' he shouted at Porter. 'You know—he's coming to kill me right now.'

'For God's sake,' Thelma shrilled in Porter's ear, 'is it true? Can't you do something? You're a man—stop him!'

While Porter gathered a reply, Jack entered the kitchen. Stephen's shrill wails grew frantic. Doris hurried wild-eyed after Jack, her talent forgotten in the abrupt explosion of excitement. Thelma hurried around the table, between Jack and the boy, scrawny arms out, dried-up face contorted with outrage.

'I can see it!' Stephen screamed. 'In his mind—he's going to kill me because he knows I want to—' He broke off. 'He doesn't want us to do anything. He wants us to stay here in this old ruin, doing tricks for people.' Fury broke through his terror. 'I'm not going to do it. I'm through doing mind-reading tricks. Now he's thinking about killing all of us! He wants us all dead!'

Porter settled down in his chair and pawed for his spoon. He pulled his plate under his chin; eyes intently on Jack and Stephen, he continued slowly eating.

'I'm sorry,' Jack said. 'You shouldn't have told me your thoughts, I couldn't have read them. You could have kept them to yourself.' He moved forward.

Thelma grabbed him with her skinny claws and hung on tight. The wail and babble rose in hysteria; Porter winced and bobbed his thick neck-wattles. Impassively, he watched Jack and the old woman struggle together; beyond them, Stephen stood paralyzed with childish terror, face waxen, youthful body rigid.

Doris moved forward, and Porter stopped eating. A kind of tension settled over him; but it was a finality that made him forget eating, not doubt or uncertainty. Knowing what was going to happen didn't diminish the awesomeness of it. He couldn't be surprised . . . but he could be sobered.

'Leave him alone,' Doris gasped. 'He's just a boy. Go sit down and behave yourself.' She caught hold of Jack around the waist; the two women swayed back and forth, trying to hold the immense muscular figure. 'Stop it! Leave him alone!'

Jack broke away. He tottered, tried to regain his balance. The two women fluttered and clawed after him like furious birds; he reached back to push them away . . .

'Don't look,' Porter said sharply.

Doris turned in his direction. And didn't see, as he anticipated. Thelma saw, and her voice suddenly died into silence. Stephen choked off, horrified, then screeched in stricken dismay.

They had seen the last entity along Jack's time-path once before. Briefly one night the withered old man had appeared, as the more youthful entity inspected the military hospital to analyze its resources. The younger Jack had returned at once, satisfied that the dying old man would be given the best treatment available. In that moment they had seen his gaunt, fever-ridden face. This time the eyes weren't bright. Lusterless, the eyes of a dead object gazed blankly at them, as the hunched figure remained briefly upright.

Thelma tried vainly to catch it as it pitched forward. Like a sack of meal it crashed into the table, scattering cups and silver. It wore a faded blue robe, knotted at the waist. Its pale-white feet were bare. From it oozed the pungent hygienic scent of the hospital, of age and illness and death.

'You did it,' Porter said. 'Both of you together. Doris, especially.

But it would have come in the next few days, anyhow.' He added, 'Jack's dead. We'll have to bury him, unless you think any of you can bring him back.'

Thelma stood wiping at her eyes. Tears dribbled down her shrunken cheeks, into her mouth. 'It was my fault. I wanted to destroy him. My hands.' She held up her claws. 'He never trusted me; he never put himself in my care. And he was right.'

'We both did it,' Doris muttered, shaken. 'Porter's telling the truth. I wanted him to go away . . . I wanted him to leave. I never moved anything into time, before.'

'You never will again,' Porter said. 'He left no descendants. He was the first and last man to move through time. It was a unique talent.'

Stephen was recovering slowly, still white-faced and shaken, eyes fixed on the withered shape in its frayed blue pajamas, spread out under the table. 'Anyhow,' he muttered finally, 'there won't be any more picking over the past.'

'I believe,' Thelma said tightly, 'you can follow my thoughts. Are you aware of what I'm thinking?'

Stephen blinked. 'Yes.'

'Now listen carefully. I'm going to put them into words so everybody will hear them.'

Stephen nodded without speaking. His eyes darted frantically around the room, but he didn't stir.

'There are now four Guild members,' Thelma said. Her voice was flat and low, without expression. 'Some of us want to leave this place and enter the communes. Some of us think this would be a good time to impose ourselves on the communes, whether they like it or not.'

Stephen nodded.

'I would say,' Thelma continued, examining her ancient, dried-up hands, 'that if any of us tries to leave here, I will do what Jack tried to do.' She pondered. 'But I don't know if I can. Maybe I'll fail, too.'

'Yes,' Stephen said. His voice trembled, then gained strength. 'You're not strong enough. There's somebody here a lot stronger than you. She can pick you up and put you down anywhere she wants. On the other side of the world—on the moon—in the middle of the ocean.'

Doris made a faint strangled sound. 'I—'

'That's true,' Thelma agreed. 'But I'm standing only three feet from her. If I touch her first she'll be drained.' She studied the smooth, frightened face of the girl. 'But you're right. What happens depends not on you or me, but on what Doris wants to do.'

Doris breathed rapidly, huskily. 'I don't know,' she said, faintly. 'I don't want to stay here, just sitting around in this old ruin, day after day, doing—tricks. But Jack always said we shouldn't force ourselves on the communes.' Her voice trailed off uncertainly. 'All my life, as long as I can remember, when I was a little girl growing up, there was Jack saying over and over again we shouldn't force them. If they didn't want us . . .'

'She won't move you now,' Stephen said to Thelma, 'but she will eventually. Sooner or later she'll move you away from here, some night when you're sleeping. Eventually she'll make up her mind.' He grinned starkly. 'Remember, I can talk to her, silently in her mind. Any time I want.'

'Will you?' Thelma asked the girl.

Doris faltered miserably. 'I—don't know. Will I? . . . Maybe so. It's so—bewildering.'

Porter sat up straight in his chair, leaned back, and belched loudly. 'It's strange to hear you all conjecturing,' he said. 'As a matter of fact, you won't touch Thelma.' To the old woman he said, 'There's nothing to worry about. I can see this stalemate going on. The four of us balance each other—we'll stay where we are.'

Thelma sagged. 'Maybe Stephen's right. If we have to keep on living this way, doing nothing—'

'We'll be here,' Porter said, 'but we won't be living the way we've been living.'

'What do you mean?' Thelma demanded. 'How will we be living? What's going to happen?'

'It's hard to probe you,' Stephen said to Porter peevishly. 'These are things you've seen, not things you're thinking. Have the commune governments changed their position? Are they finally going to call us in?'

'The governments won't call us in,' Porter said. 'We'll never be invited into Washington and Moscow. We've had to stand outside waiting.' He glanced up and stated enigmatically, 'That waiting is about over.'

It was early morning. Ed Garby brought the rumbling, battered truck into line behind the other surface cars leaving the commune. Cold, fitful sunlight filtered down on the concrete squares that made up the commune installations; today was going to be another cloudy day, exactly like the last. Even so, the exit check-gate ahead was already clogged with outgoing traffic.

'A lot of them, this morning,' his wife murmured. 'I guess they can't wait any longer for the ash to lift.'

Ed clutched for his pass, buried in his sweat-gummed shirt pocket. 'The gate's a bottleneck,' he muttered resentfully. 'What are they doing, getting into the cars?'

There were four guards, today, not the usual one. A squad of armed troops that moved back and forth among the stalled cars, peering and murmuring, reporting through their neck-mikes to the commune officers below surface. A massive truck loaded with workers pulled suddenly away from the line and onto a side road. Roaring and belching clouds of foul blue gas, it made a complete circle and lumbered back toward the center of the commune, away from the exit gate. Ed watched it uneasily.

'What's it doing, turning back?' Fear clutched him. 'They're turning us back!'

'No, they're not,' Barbara said quietly. 'Look—there goes a car through.'

An ancient wartime pleasure car precariously edged through the gate and out onto the plain beyond the commune. A second followed it and the two cars gathered speed to climb the long low ridge that became the first tangle of trees.

A horn honked behind Ed. Convulsively, he moved the car forward. In Barbara's lap the baby wailed anxiously; she wound its seedy cotton blanket around it and rolled up the window. 'It's an awful day. If we didn't have to go–' She broke off. 'Here come the guards. Get the pass out.'

Ed greeted the guards apprehensively. 'Morning.'

Curtly, one of the guards took his pass, examined it, punched it, and filed it away in a steel-bound notebook. 'Each of you prepare your thumb for prints,' he instructed. A black, oozing pad was passed up. 'Including the baby.'

Ed was astounded. 'Why? What the hell's going on?'

The twins were too terrified to move. Numbly, they allowed the guards to take their prints. Ed protested weakly, as the pad was pushed against his thumb. His wrist was grabbed and yanked forward. As the guards walked around the truck to get at Barbara, the squad leader placed his boot on the running board and addressed Ed briefly.

'Five of you. Family?'

Ed nodded mutely. 'Yeah, my family.'

'Complete. Any more?'

'No. Just us five.'

The guard's dark eyes bored down at him. 'When are you coming back?'

'Tonight.' Ed indicated the metal notebook in which his pass had been filed. 'It says before six.'

'If you go through that gate,' the guard said, 'you won't be coming back. That gate only goes one way.'

'Since when?' Barbara whispered, face ashen.

'Since last night. It's your choice. Go ahead out there, get your business done, consult your soothsayer. But don't come back.' The guard pointed to the side road. 'If you want to turn around, that road takes you to the descent ramps. Follow the truck ahead–it's turning back.'

Ed licked his dry lips. 'I can't. My kid–she's got bone cancer. The old woman started her healing, but she isn't well, not yet. The old woman says today she can finish.'

The guard examined a dog-eared directory. 'Ward 9, sixth level. Go down there and they'll fix up your kid. The docs have all the equipment.' He closed the book and stepped back from the car, a heavy-set man, red-faced, with bristled, beefy skin. 'Let's get started, buddy. One way or the other. It's your choice.'

Automatically, Ed moved the car forward. 'They must have decided,' he muttered, dazed. 'Too many people going out. They want to scare us . . . they know we can't live out there. We'd die out there!'

Barbara quietly clutched the baby. 'We'll die here eventually.'

'But it's nothing but ruins out there!'

'Aren't *they* out there?'

Ed choked helplessly. 'We can't come back—suppose it's a mistake?'

The truck ahead wavered toward the side road. An uncertain hand signal was made; suddenly the driver yanked his hand in and wobbled the truck back toward the exit gate. A moment of confusion took place. The truck slowed almost to a stop; Ed slammed on his brakes, cursed, and shifted into low. Then the truck ahead gained speed. It rumbled through the gate and out onto the barren ground. Without thinking, Ed followed it. Cold, ash-heavy air swept into the cabin as he gained speed and pulled up beside the truck. Even with it, he leaned out and shouted, 'Where you going? They won't let you back!'

The driver, a skinny little man, bald and bony, shouted angrily back, 'Goddamn it, I'm not coming back! The hell with them—I got all my food and bedding in here—I got every damn thing I own. Let them try to get me back!' He gunned up his truck and pulled ahead of Ed.

'Well,' Barbara said quietly, 'it's done. We're outside.'

'Yeah,' Ed agreed shakily. 'We are. A yard, a thousand miles—it's all the same.' In panic, he turned wildly to his wife. 'What if they don't take us? I mean, what if we get there and they don't want us. All they got is that old broken-down wartime shelter. There isn't room for anybody—and look behind us.'

A line of hesitant, lumbering trucks and cars was picking its way uncertainly from the gate, streaming rustily out onto the parched plain. A few pulled out and swung back; one pulled over to the side of the road and halted while its passengers argued with bitter desperation.

'They'll take us,' Barbara said. 'They want to help us—they always wanted to.'

'But suppose they *can't!*'

'I think they can. There's a lot of power there, if we ask for it. They couldn't come to us, but we can go to them. We've been held back too long, separated from them too many years. If the government won't let them in, then we'll have to go outside.'

'Can we live outside?' Ed asked hoarsely.

'Yes.'

Behind them a horn honked excitedly. Ed gained speed. 'It's a regular exodus. Look at them pouring out. Who'll be left?'

'There'll be plenty left,' Barbara answered. 'All the big shots will stay behind.' She laughed breathlessly. 'Maybe they'll be able to get the war going again. It'll give them something to do, while we're away.'

AUTOFAC

I

Tension hung over the three waiting men. They smoked, paced back and forth, kicked aimlessly at weeds growing by the side of the road. A hot noonday sun glared down on brown fields, rows of neat plastic houses, the distant line of mountains to the west.

'Almost time,' Earl Perine said, knotting his skinny hands together. 'It varies according to the load, a half second for every additional pound.'

Bitterly, Morrison answered, 'You've got it plotted? You're as bad as it is. Let's pretend it just *happens* to be late.'

The third man said nothing. O'Neill was visiting from another settlement; he didn't know Perine and Morrison well enough to argue with them. Instead, he crouched down and arranged the papers clipped to his aluminum checkboard. In the blazing sun, O'Neill's arms were tanned, furry, glistening with sweat. Wiry, with tangled gray hair, horn-rimmed glasses, he was older than the other two. He wore slacks, a sports shirt and crepe-soled shoes. Between his fingers, his fountain pen glittered, metallic and efficient.

'What're you writing?' Perine grumbled.

'I'm laying out the procedure we're going to employ,' O'Neill said mildly. 'Better to systemize it now, instead of trying at random. We want to know what we tried and what didn't work. Otherwise we'll go around in a circle. The problem we have here is one of communication; that's how I see it.'

'Communication,' Morrison agreed in his deep, chesty voice.

'Yes, we can't get in touch with the damn thing. It comes, leaves off its load and goes on—there's no contact between us and it.'

'It's a machine,' Perine said excitedly. 'It's dead—blind and deaf.'

'But it's in contact with the outside world,' O'Neill pointed out. 'There has to be some way to get to it. Specific semantic signals are meaningful to it; all we have to do is find those signals. Rediscover, actually. Maybe half a dozen out of a billion possibilities.'

A low rumble interrupted the three men. They glanced up, wary and alert. The time had come.

'Here it is,' Perine said. 'Okay, wise guy, let's see you make one single change in its routine.'

The truck was massive, rumbling under its tightly packed load. In many ways, it resembled conventional human-operated transportation vehicles, but with one exception—there was no driver's cabin. The horizontal surface was a loading stage, and the part that would normally be the headlights and radiator grill was a fibrous spongelike mass of receptors, the limited sensory apparatus of this mobile utility extension.

Aware of the three men, the truck slowed to a halt, shifted gears and pulled on its emergency brake. A moment passed as relays moved into action; then a portion of the loading surface tilted and a cascade of heavy cartons spilled down onto the roadway. With the objects fluttered a detailed inventory sheet.

'You know what to do,' O'Neill said rapidly. 'Hurry up, before it gets out of here.'

Expertly, grimly, the three men grabbed up the deposited cartons and ripped the protective wrappers from them. Objects gleamed: a binocular microscope, a portable radio, heaps of plastic dishes, medical supplies, razor blades, clothing, food. Most of the shipment, as usual, was food. The three men systematically began smashing objects. In a few minutes, there was nothing but a chaos of debris littered around them.

'That's that,' O'Neill panted, stepping back. He fumbled for his check-sheet. 'Now let's see what it does.'

The truck had begun to move away; abruptly it stopped and backed toward them. Its receptors had taken in the fact that the three men had demolished the dropped-off portion of the load. It spun in a grinding half circle and came around to face its receptor bank in their direction. Up went its antenna; it had begun communicating with the factory. Instructions were on the way.

A second, identical load was tilted and shoved off the truck.

'We failed,' Perine groaned as a duplicate inventory sheet fluttered after the new load. 'We destroyed all that stuff for nothing.'

'What now?' Morrison asked O'Neill. 'What's the next stratagem on our board?'

'Give me a hand.' O'Neill grabbed up a carton and lugged it back to the truck. Sliding the carton onto the platform, he turned for another. The other two men followed clumsily after him. They put the load back onto the truck. As the truck started forward, the last square box was again in place.

The truck hesitated. Its receptors registered the return of its load. From within its works came a low sustained buzzing.

'This may drive it crazy,' O'Neill commented, sweating. 'It went through its operation and accomplished nothing.'

The truck made a short, abortive move toward going on. Then it swung purposefully around and, in a blur of speed, again dumped the load onto the road.

'Get them!' O'Neill yelled. The three men grabbed up the cartons and feverishly reloaded them. But as fast as the cartons were shoved back on the horizontal stage, the truck's grapples tilted them down its far-side ramps and onto the road.

'No use,' Morrison said, breathing hard. 'Water through a sieve.'

'We're licked,' Perine gasped in wretched agreement, 'like always. We humans lose every time.'

The truck regarded them calmly, its receptors blank and impassive. It was doing its job. The planetwide network of automatic factories was smoothly performing the task imposed on it five years before, in the early days of the Total Global Conflict.

'There it goes,' Morrison observed dismally. The truck's antenna had come down; it shifted into low gear and released its parking brake.

'One last try,' O'Neill said. He swept up one of the cartons and ripped it open. From it he dragged a ten-gallon milk tank and unscrewed the lid. 'Silly as it seems.'

'This is absurd,' Perine protested. Reluctantly, he found a cup among the littered debris and dipped it into the milk. 'A kid's game!'

The truck had paused to observe them.

'Do it,' O'Neill ordered sharply. 'Exactly the way we practiced it.'

The three of them drank quickly from the milk tank, visibly allowing the milk to spill down their chins; there had to be no mistaking what they were doing.

As planned, O'Neill was the first. His face twisting in revulsion, he hurled the cup away and violently spat the milk into the road.

'God's sake!' he choked.

The other two did the same; stamping and loudly cursing, they kicked over the milk tank and glared accusingly at the truck.

'It's no good!' Morrison roared.

Curious, the truck came slowly back. Electronic synapses clicked and whirred, responding to the situation; its antenna shot up like a flagpole.

'I think this is it,' O'Neill said, trembling. As the truck watched, he dragged out a second milk tank, unscrewed its lid and tasted the contents. 'The same!' he shouted at the truck. 'It's just as bad!'

From the truck popped a metal cylinder. The cylinder dropped at Morrison's feet; he quickly snatched it up and tore it open.

STATE NATURE OF DEFECT

The instruction sheets listed rows of possible defects, with neat boxes by each; a punch-stick was included to indicate the particular deficiency of the product.

'What'll I check?' Morrison asked. 'Contaminated? Bacterial?

Sour? Rancid? Incorrectly labeled? Broken? Crushed? Cracked? Bent? Soiled?'

Thinking rapidly, O'Neill said, 'Don't check any of them. The factory's undoubtedly ready to test and resample. It'll make its own analysis and then ignore us.' His face glowed as frantic inspiration came. 'Write in that blank at the bottom. It's an open space for further data.'

'Write what?'

O'Neill said, 'Write: *the product is thoroughly pizzled.*'

'What's that?' Perine demanded, baffled.

'Write it! It's a semantic garble—the factory won't be able to understand it. Maybe we can jam the works.'

With O'Neill's pen, Morrison carefully wrote that the milk was pizzled. Shaking his head, he resealed the cylinder and returned it to the truck. The truck swept up the milk tanks and slammed its railing tidily into place. With a shriek of tires, it hurtled off. From its slot, a final cylinder bounced; the truck hurriedly departed, leaving the cylinder lying in the dust.

O'Neill got it open and held up the paper for the others to see.

A FACTOR REPRESENTATIVE
WILL BE SENT OUT.
BE PREPARED TO SUPPLY COMPLETE DATA
ON PRODUCT DEFICIENCY.

For a moment, the three men were silent. Then Perine began to giggle. 'We did it. We contacted it. We got across.'

'We sure did,' O'Neill agreed. 'It never heard of a product being pizzled.'

Cut into the base of the mountains lay the vast metallic cube of the Kansas City factory. Its surface was corroded, pitted with radiation pox, cracked and scarred from the five years of war that had swept over it. Most of the factory was buried subsurface, only its entrance stages visible. The truck was a speck rumbling at high speed toward the expanse of black metal. Presently an opening formed in the uniform surface; the truck plunged into it and disappeared inside. The entrance snapped shut.

'Now the big job remains,' O'Neill said. 'Now we have to persuade it to close down operations—to shut itself off.'

II

Judith O'Neill served hot black coffee to the people sitting around the living room. Her husband talked while the others listened. O'Neill was as close to being an authority on the autofac system as could still be found.

In his own area, the Chicago region, he had shorted out the protective fence of the local factory long enough to get away with data tapes stored in its posterior brain. The factory, of course, had immediately reconstructed a better type of fence. But he had shown that the factories were not infallible.

'The Institute of Applied Cybernetics,' O'Neill explained, 'had complete control over the network. Blame the war. Blame the big noise along the lines of communication that wiped out the knowledge we need. In any case, the Institute failed to transmit its information to us, so we can't transmit our information to the factories—the news that the war is over and we're ready to resume control of industrial operations.'

'And meanwhile,' Morrison added sourly, 'the damn network expands and consumes more of our natural resources all the time.'

'I get the feeling,' Judith said, 'that if I stamped hard enough, I'd fall right down into a factory tunnel. They must have mines everywhere by now.'

'Isn't there some limiting injunction?' Perine asked nervously. 'Were they set up to expand indefinitely?'

'Each factory is limited to its own operational area,' O'Neill said, 'but the network itself is unbounded. It can go on scooping up our resources forever. The Institute decided it gets top priority; we mere people come second.'

'Will there be *anything* left for us?' Morrison wanted to know.

'Not unless we can stop the network's operations. It's already used up half a dozen basic minerals. Its search teams are out all the time, from every factory, looking everywhere for some last scrap to drag home.'

'What would happen if tunnels from two factories crossed each other?'

O'Neill shrugged. 'Normally, that won't happen. Each factory has its own special section of our planet, its own private cut of the pie for its exclusive use.'

'But it *could* happen.'

'Well, they're raw material-tropic; as long as there's anything left, they'll hunt it down.' O'Neill pondered the idea with growing interest. 'It's something to consider. I suppose as things get scarcer—'

He stopped talking. A figure had come into the room; it stood silently by the door, surveying them all.

In the dull shadows, the figure looked almost human. For a brief moment, O'Neill thought it was a settlement latecomer. Then, as it moved forward, he realized that it was only quasi-human: a functional upright biped chassis, with data-receptors mounted at the top, effectors and proprioceptors mounted in a downward worm that ended in floor-grippers. Its resemblance to a human being was testimony to nature's efficiency; no sentimental imitation was intended.

The factory representative had arrived.

It began without preamble. 'This is a data-collecting machine capable of communicating on an oral basis. It contains both broadcasting and receiving apparatus and can integrate facts relevant to its line of inquiry.'

The voice was pleasant, confident. Obviously it was a tape, recorded by some Institute technician before the war. Coming from the quasi-human shape, it sounded grotesque; O'Neill could vividly imagine the dead young man whose cheerful voice now issued from the mechanical mouth of this upright construction of steel and wiring.

'One word of caution,' the pleasant voice continued. 'It is

fruitless to consider this receptor human and to engage it in discussions for which it is not equipped. Although purposeful, it is not capable of conceptual thought; it can only reassemble material already available to it.'

The optimistic voice clicked out and a second voice came on. It resembled the first, but now there were no intonations or personal mannerisms. The machine was utilizing the dead man's phonetic speech-pattern for its own communication.

'Analysis of the rejected product,' it stated, 'shows no foreign elements or noticeable deterioration. The product meets the continual testing-standards employed throughout the network. Rejection is therefore on a basis outside the test area; standards not available to the network are being employed.'

'That's right,' O'Neill agreed. Weighing his words with care, he continued, 'We found the milk substandard. We want nothing to do with it. We insist on more careful output.'

The machine responded presently. 'The semantic content of the term "pizzled" is unfamiliar to the network. It does not exist in the taped vocabulary. Can you present a factual analysis of the milk in terms of specific elements present or absent?'

'No,' O'Neill said warily; the game he was playing was intricate and dangerous. '"Pizzled" is an overall term. It can't be reduced to chemical constituents.'

'What does "pizzled" signify?' the machine asked. 'Can you define it in terms of alternate semantic symbols?'

O'Neill hesitated. The representative had to be steered from its special inquiry to more general regions, to the ultimate problem of closing down the network. If he could pry it open at any point, get the theoretical discussion started . . .

'"Pizzled,"' he stated, 'means the condition of a product that is manufactured when no need exists. It indicates the rejection of objects on the grounds that they are no longer wanted.'

The representative said, 'Network analysis shows a need of high-grade pasteurized milk-substitute in this area. There is no alternate source; the network controls all the synthetic mammary-type equipment in existence.' It added, 'Original taped instructions describe milk as an essential to human diet.'

O'Neill was being outwitted; the machine was returning the discussion to the specific. 'We've decided,' he said desperately, 'that we don't *want* any more milk. We'd prefer to go without it, at least until we can locate cows.'

'That is contrary to the network tapes,' the representative objected. 'There are no cows. All milk is produced synthetically.'

'Then we'll produce it synthetically ourselves,' Morrison broke in impatiently. 'Why can't we take over the machines? My God, we're not children! We can run our own lives!'

The factory representative moved toward the door. 'Until such time as your community finds other sources of milk supply, the network will continue to supply you. Analytical and evaluating apparatus will remain in this area, conducting the customary random sampling.'

Perine shouted futilely, 'How can we find other sources? You have the whole setup! You're running the whole show!' Following after it, he bellowed, 'You say we're not ready to run things—you claim we're not capable. How do you know? You don't give us a chance! We'll never have a chance!'

O'Neill was petrified. The machine was leaving; its one-track mind had completely triumphed.

'Look,' he said hoarsely, blocking its way. 'We want you to shut down, understand. We want to take over your equipment and run it ourselves. The war's over with. Damn it, you're not needed anymore!'

The factory representative paused briefly at the door. 'The inoperative cycle,' it said, 'is not geared to begin until network production merely duplicates outside production. There is at this time, according to our continual sampling, no outside production. Therefore network production continues.'

Without warning, Morrison swung the steel pipe in his hand. It slashed against the machine's shoulder and burst through the elaborate network of sensory apparatus that made up its chest.

The tank of receptors shattered; bits of glass, wiring and minute parts showered everywhere.

'It's a paradox!' Morrison yelled. 'A word game—a semantic game they're pulling on us. The Cyberneticists have it rigged.' He raised the pipe and again brought it down savagely on the unprotesting machine. 'They've got us hamstrung. We're completely helpless.'

The room was in uproar. 'It's the only way,' Perine gasped as he pushed past O'Neill. 'We'll have to destroy them—it's the network or us.' Grabbing down a lamp, he hurled it in the 'face' of the factory representative. The lamp and the intricate surface of plastic burst; Perine waded in, groping blindly for the machine. Now all the people in the room were closing furiously around the upright cylinder, their impotent resentment boiling over. The machine sank down and disappeared as they dragged it to the floor.

Trembling, O'Neill turned away. His wife caught hold of his arm and led him to the side of the room.

'The idiots,' he said dejectedly. 'They can't destroy it; they'll only teach it to build more defenses. They're making the whole problem worse.'

Into the living room rolled a network repair team. Expertly, the mechanical units detached themselves from the half-track mother-bug and scurried toward the mound of struggling humans. They slid between people and rapidly burrowed. A moment later, the inert carcass of the factory representative was dragged into the hopper of the mother-bug. Parts were collected, torn remnants gathered up and carried off. The plastic strut and gear was located. Then the units restationed themselves on the bug and the team departed.

Through the open door came a second factory representative, an exact duplicate of the first. And outside in the hall stood two more upright machines. The settlement had been combed at random by a corps of representatives. Like a horde of ants, the mobile data-collecting machines had filtered through the town until, by chance, one of them had come across O'Neill.

'Destruction of network mobile data-gathering equipment is detrimental to best human interests,' the factory representative informed the roomful of people. 'Raw material intake is at a dangerously low ebb; what basic materials still exist should be utilized in the manufacture of consumer commodities.'

O'Neill and the machine stood facing each other.

'Oh?' O'Neill said softly. 'That's interesting. I wonder what you're lowest on—and what you'd really be willing to fight for.'

Helicopter rotors whined tinnily above O'Neill's head; he ignored them and peered through the cabin window at the ground not far below.

Slag and ruins stretched everywhere. Weeds poked their way up, sickly stalks among which insects scuttled. Here and there, rat colonies were visible: matted hovels constructed of bone and rubble. Radiation had mutated the rats, along with most insects and animals. A little farther, O'Neill identified a squadron of birds pursuing a ground squirrel. The squirrel dived into a carefully prepared crack in the surface of slag and the birds turned, thwarted.

'You think we'll ever have it rebuilt?' Morrison asked. 'It makes me sick to look at it.'

'In time,' O'Neill answered. 'Assuming, of course, that we get industrial control back. And assuming that anything remains to work with. At best, it'll be slow. We'll have to inch out from the settlements.'

To the right was a human colony, tattered scarecrows, gaunt and emaciated, living among the ruins of what had once been a town. A few acres of barren soil had been cleared; drooping vegetables wilted in the sun, chickens wandered listlessly here and there, and a fly-bothered horse lay panting in the shade of a crude shed.

'Ruins-squatters,' O'Neill said gloomily. 'Too far from the network—not tangent to any of the factories.'

'It's their own fault,' Morrison told him angrily. 'They could come into one of the settlements.'

'That was their town. They're trying to do what *we're* trying to do—build up things again on their own. But they're starting now, without tools or machines, with their bare hands, nailing together bits of rubble. And it won't work. We need machines. We can't repair ruins; we've got to start industrial production.'

Ahead lay a series of broken hills, chipped remains that had once been a ridge. Beyond stretched out the titanic ugly sore of an H-bomb crater, half filled with stagnant water and slime, a disease-ridden inland sea.

And beyond that—a glitter of busy motion.

'There,' O'Neill said tensely. He lowered the helicopter rapidly. 'Can you tell which factory they're from?'

'They all look alike to me,' Morrison muttered, leaning over to see. 'We'll have to wait and follow them back, when they get a load.'

'*If* they get a load,' O'Neill corrected.

The autofac exploring crew ignored the helicopter buzzing overhead and concentrated on its job. Ahead of the main truck scuttled two tractors; they made their way up mounds of rubble, probes burgeoning like quills, shot down the far slope and disappeared into a blanket of ash that lay spread over the slag. The two scouts burrowed until only their antennas were visible. They burst up to the surface and scuttled on, their treads whirring and clanking.

'What are they after?' Morrison asked.

'God knows.' O'Neill leafed intently through the papers on his clipboard. 'We'll have to analyze all our back-order slips.'

Below them, the autofac exploring crew disappeared behind. The helicopter passed over a deserted stretch of sand and slag on which nothing moved. A grove of scrub-brush appeared and then, far to the right, a series of tiny moving dots.

A procession of automatic ore carts was racing over the bleak slag, a string of rapidly moving metal trucks that followed one another nose to tail. O'Neill turned the helicopter toward them and a few minutes later it hovered above the mine itself.

Masses of squat mining equipment had made their way to the operations. Shafts had been sunk; empty carts waited in patient rows. A steady stream of loaded carts hurried toward the horizon, dribbling ore after them. Activity and the noise of machines hung over the area, an abrupt center of industry in the bleak wastes of slag.

'Here comes that exploring crew,' Morrison observed, peering back the way they had come. 'You think maybe they'll tangle?' He grinned. 'No, I guess it's too much to hope for.'

'It is this time,' O'Neill answered. 'They're looking for different substances, probably. And they're normally conditioned to ignore each other.'

The first of the exploring bugs reached the line of ore carts. It veered slightly and continued its search; the carts traveled in their inexorable line as if nothing had happened.

Disappointed, Morrison turned away from the window and swore. 'No use. It's like each doesn't exist for the other.'

Gradually the exploring crew moved away from the line of carts, past the mining operations and over a ridge beyond. There was no special hurry; they departed without having reacted to the ore-gathering syndrome.

'Maybe they're from the same factory,' Morrison said hopefully.

O'Neill pointed to the antennas visible on the major mining equipment. 'Their vanes are turned at a different vector, so these represent two factories. It's going to be hard; we'll have to get it exactly right or there won't be any reaction.' He clicked on the radio and got hold of the monitor at the settlement. 'Any results on the consolidated back-order sheets?'

The operator put him through to the settlement governing offices.

'They're starting to come in,' Perine told him. 'As soon as we get sufficient samplings, we'll try to determine which raw materials which factories lack. It's going to be risky, trying to extrapolate from complex products. There may be a number of basic elements common to the various sublots.'

'What happens when we've identified the missing element?' Morrison asked O'Neill. 'What happens when we've got two tangent factories short on the same material?'

'Then,' O'Neill said grimly, 'we start collecting the material ourselves—even if we have to melt down every object in the settlements.'

III

In the moth-ridden darkness of night, a dim wind stirred, chill and faint. Dense underbrush rattled metallically. Here and there a nocturnal rodent prowled, its senses hyper-alert, peering, planning, seeking food.

The area was wild. No human settlements existed for miles; the entire region had been seared flat, cauterized by repeated H-bomb blasts. Somewhere in the murky darkness, a sluggish trickle of water made its way among slag and weeds, dripping thickly into what had once been an elaborate labyrinth of sewer mains. The pipes lay cracked and broken, jutting up into the night darkness, overgrown with creeping vegetation. The wind raised clouds of black ash that swirled and danced among the weeds. Once an enormous mutant wren stirred sleepily, pulled its crude protective night coat of rags around it and dozed off.

For a time, there was no movement. A streak of stars showed in the sky overhead, glowing starkly, remotely. Earl Perine shivered, peered up and huddled closer to the pulsing heat-element placed on the ground between the three men.

'Well?' Morrison challenged, teeth chattering.

O'Neill didn't answer. He finished his cigarette, crushed it against a mound of decaying slag and, getting out his lighter, lit another. The mass of tungsten—the bait—lay a hundred yards directly ahead of them.

During the last few days, both the Detroit and Pittsburgh factories had run short of tungsten. And in at least one sector, their apparatus overlapped. This sluggish heap represented precision cutting tools, parts ripped from electrical switches, high-quality surgical equipment, sections of permanent magnets, measuring devices—tungsten from every possible source, gathered feverishly from all the settlements.

Dark mist lay spread over the tungsten mound. Occasionally, a night moth fluttered down, attracted by the glow of reflected starlight. The moth hung momentarily, beat its elongated wings futilely against the interwoven tangle of metal and then drifted off, into the shadows of the thick-packed vines that rose up from the stumps of sewer pipes.

'Not a very damn pretty spot,' Perine said wryly.

'Don't kid yourself,' O'Neill retorted. 'This is the prettiest spot on Earth. This is the spot that marks the grave of the autofac network. People are going to come around here looking for it someday. There's going to be a plaque here a mile high.'

'You're trying to keep your morale up,' Morrison snorted. 'You don't believe they're going to slaughter themselves over a heap of surgical tools and light-bulb filaments. They've probably got a machine down in the bottom level that sucks tungsten out of rock.'

'Maybe,' O'Neill said, slapping at a mosquito. The insect dodged cannily and then buzzed over to annoy Perine. Perine swung viciously at it and squatted sullenly down against the damp vegetation.

And there was what they had come to see.

O'Neill realized with a start that he had been looking at it for several minutes without recognizing it. The search-bug lay absolutely still. It rested at the crest of a small rise of slag, its anterior end slightly raised, receptors fully extended. It might have been an abandoned hulk; there was no activity of any kind, no sign of life or consciousness. The search-bug fitted perfectly into the wasted, fire-drenched landscape. A vague tub of metal sheets and gears and flat treads, it rested and waited. And watched.

It was examining the heap of tungsten. The bait had drawn its first bite.

'Fish,' Perine said thickly. 'The line moved. I think the sinker dropped.'

'What the hell are you mumbling about?' Morrison grunted. And then he, too, saw the search-bug. 'Jesus,' he whispered. He half rose to his feet, massive body arched forward. 'Well, there's *one* of them. Now all we need is a unit from the other factory. Which do you suppose it is?'

O'Neill located the communication vane and traced its angle. 'Pittsburgh, so pray for Detroit . . . pray like mad.'

Satisfied, the search-bug detached itself and rolled forward. Cautiously approaching the mound, it began a series of intricate maneuvers, rolling first one way and then another. The three watching men were mystified—until they glimpsed the first probing stalks of other search-bugs.

'Communication,' O'Neill said softly. 'Like bees.'

Now five Pittsburgh search-bugs were approaching the mound of tungsten products. Receptors waving excitedly, they increased their pace, scurrying in a sudden burst of discovery up the side of the mound to the top. A bug burrowed and rapidly disappeared. The whole mound shuddered; the bug was down inside, exploring the extent of the find.

Ten minutes later, the first Pittsburgh ore carts appeared and began industriously hurrying off with their haul.

'Damn it!' O'Neill said, agonized. 'They'll have it all before Detroit shows up.'

'Can't we do anything to slow them down?' Perine demanded helplessly. Leaping to his feet, he grabbed up a rock and heaved it at the nearest cart. The rock bounced off and the cart continued its work, unperturbed.

O'Neill got to his feet and prowled around, body rigid with impotent fury. Where were they? The autofacs were equal in all respects and the spot was the exact same linear distance from each center. Theoretically, the parties should have arrived simultaneously. Yet there was no sign of Detroit—and the final pieces of tungsten were being loaded before his eyes.

But then something streaked past him.

He didn't recognize it, for the object moved too quickly. It shot like a bullet among the tangled vines, raced up the side of the hill-crest, poised for an instant to aim itself and hurtled down the far side. It smashed directly into the lead cart. Projectile and victim shattered in an abrupt burst of sound.

Morrison leaped up. 'What the hell?'

'That's it!' Perine screamed, dancing around and waving his skinny arms. 'It's Detroit!'

A second Detroit search-bug appeared, hesitated as it took in the situation, and then flung itself furiously at the retreating Pittsburgh carts. Fragments of tungsten scattered everywhere—parts, wiring, broken plates, gears and springs and bolts of the two antagonists flew in all directions. The remaining carts wheeled screechingly; one of them dumped its load and rattled off at top speed. A second followed, still weighed down with tungsten. A Detroit search-bug caught up with it, spun directly in its path and neatly overturned it. Bug and cart rolled down a shallow trench, into a stagnant pool of water. Dripping and glistening, the two of them struggled, half submerged.

'Well,' O'Neill said unsteadily, 'we did it. We can start back home.' His legs felt weak. 'Where's our vehicle?'

As he gunned the truck motor, something flashed a long way off, something large and metallic, moving over the dead slag and ash. It was a dense clot of carts, a solid expanse of heavy-duty ore carriers racing to the scene. Which factory were they from?

It didn't matter, for out of the thick tangle of black dripping vines, a web of counter-extensions was creeping to meet them. Both factories were assembling their mobile units. From all directions, bugs slithered and crept, closing in around the remaining heap of tungsten. Neither factory was going to let needed raw material get away; neither was going to give up its find. Blindly, mechanically, in the grip of inflexible directives, the two opponents labored to assemble superior forces.

'Come on,' Morrison said urgently. 'Let's get out of here. All hell is bursting loose.'

O'Neill hastily turned the truck in the direction of the settlement. They began rumbling through the darkness on their way back. Every now and then, a metallic shape shot by them, going in the opposite direction.

'Did you see the load in that last cart?' Perine asked, worried. 'It wasn't empty.'

Neither were the carts that followed it, a whole procession of bulging supply carriers directed by an elaborate high-level surveying unit.

'Guns,' Morrison said, eyes wide with apprehension. 'They're taking in weapons. But who's going to use them?'

'They are,' O'Neill answered. He indicated a movement to their right. 'Look over there. This is something we hadn't expected.'

They were seeing the first factory representative move into action.

As the truck pulled into the Kansas City settlement, Judith hurried breathlessly toward them. Fluttering in her hand was a strip of metal-foil paper.

'What is it?' O'Neill demanded, grabbing it from her.

'Just come.' His wife struggled to catch her breath. 'A mobile car—raced up, dropped it off—and left. Big excitement. Golly, the factory's—a blaze of lights. You can see it for miles.'

O'Neill scanned the paper. It was a factory certification for the last group of settlement-placed orders, a total tabulation of requested and factory-analyzed needs. Stamped across the list in heavy black type were six foreboding words:

ALL SHIPMENTS SUSPENDED UNTIL FURTHER NOTICE

Letting out his breath harshly, O'Neill handed the paper over to Perine. 'No more consumer goods,' he said ironically, a nervous grin twitching across his face. 'The network's going on a wartime footing.'

'Then we did it?' Morrison asked haltingly.

'That's right,' O'Neill said. Now that the conflict had been sparked, he felt a growing, frigid terror. 'Pittsburgh and Detroit are in it to the finish. It's too late for us to change our minds, now—they're lining up allies.'

IV

Cool morning sunlight lay across the ruined plain of black metallic ash. The ash smoldered a dull, unhealthy red; it was still warm.

'Watch your step,' O'Neill cautioned. Grabbing hold of his wife's arm, he led her from the rusty, sagging truck, up onto the top of a pile of strewn concrete blocks, the scattered remains of a pillbox installation. Earl Perine followed, making his way carefully, hesitantly.

Behind them, the dilapidated settlement lay spread out, a disorderly checkerboard of houses, buildings and streets. Since the autofac network had closed down its supply and maintenance, the human settlements had fallen into semibarbarism. The commodities that remained were broken and only partly usable. It had been over a year since the last mobile factory truck had appeared, loaded with food, tools, clothing and repair parts. From the flat expanse of dark concrete and metal at the foot of the mountains, nothing had emerged in their direction.

Their wish had been granted—they were cut off, detached from the network.

On their own.

Around the settlement grew ragged fields of wheat and tattered stalks of sun-baked vegetables. Crude handmade tools had been distributed, primitive artifacts hammered out with great labor by the various settlements. The settlements were linked only by horsedrawn carts and by the slow stutter of the telegraph key.

They had managed to keep their organization, though. Goods and services were exchanged on a slow, steady basis. Basic commodities were produced and distributed. The clothing that O'Neill and his wife and Earl Perine wore was coarse and unbleached, but sturdy. And they had managed to convert a few of the trucks from gasoline to wood.

'Here we are,' O'Neill said. 'We can see from here.'

'Is it worth it?' Judith asked, exhausted. Bending down, she plucked aimlessly at her shoe, trying to dig a pebble from the soft hide sole. 'It's a long way to come, to see something we've seen every day for thirteen months.'

'True,' O'Neill admitted, his hand briefly resting on his wife's limp shoulder. 'But this may be the last. And that's what we want to see.'

In the gray sky above them, a swift circling dot of opaque black moved. High, remote, the dot spun and darted, following an intricate and wary course. Gradually, its gyrations moved it toward the mountains and the bleak expanse of bomb-rubbled structure sunk in their base.

'San Francisco,' O'Neill explained. 'One of those long-range hawk projectiles, all the way from the West Coast.'

'And you think it's the last?' Perine asked.

'It's the only one we've seen this month.' O'Neill seated himself and began sprinkling dried bits of tobacco into a trench of brown paper. 'And we used to see hundreds.'

'Maybe they have something better,' Judith suggested. She found a smooth rock and tiredly seated herself. 'Could it be?'

Her husband smiled ironically. 'No. They don't have anything better.'

The three of them were tensely silent. Above them, the circling dot of black drew closer. There was no sign of activity from the flat surface of metal and concrete; the Kansas City factory remained inert, totally unresponsive. A few billows of warm ash drifted across it and one end was partly submerged in rubble. The factory had taken numerous direct hits. Across the plain, the furrows of its subsurface tunnels lay exposed, clogged with debris and the dark, water-seeking tendrils of tough vines.

'Those damn vines,' Perine grumbled, picking at an old sore on his unshaven chin. 'They're taking over the world.'

Here and there around the factory, the demolished ruin of a mobile extension rusted in the morning dew. Carts, trucks, search-bugs, factory representatives, weapons carriers, guns, supply trains, subsurface projectiles, indiscriminate parts of machinery mixed and fused together in shapeless piles. Some had been destroyed returning to the factory; others had been contacted as they emerged, fully loaded, heavy with equipment. The factory itself— what remained of it—seemed to have settled more deeply into the earth. Its upper surface was barely visible, almost lost in drifting ash.

In four days, there had been no known activity, no visible movement of any sort.

'It's dead,' Perine said. 'You can see it's dead.'

O'Neill didn't answer. Squatting down, he made himself comfortable and prepared to wait. In his own mind, he was sure that some fragment of automation remained in the eroded factory. Time would tell. He examined his wristwatch; it was eight thirty. In the old days, the factory would be starting its daily routine. Processions of trucks and varied mobile units would be coming to the surface, loaded with supplies, to begin their expeditions to the human settlement.

Off to the right, something stirred. He quickly turned his attention to it.

A single battered ore-gathering cart was creeping clumsily toward the factory. One last damaged mobile unit trying to complete its task. The cart was virtually empty; a few meager scraps of metal lay strewn in its hold. A scavenger . . . the metal was sections ripped from destroyed equipment encountered on the way. Feebly, like a blind metallic insect, the cart approached the factory. Its progress was incredibly jerky. Every now and then, it halted, bucked and quivered, and wandered aimlessly off the path.

'Control is bad,' Judith said, with a touch of horror in her voice. 'The factory's having trouble guiding it back.'

Yes, he had seen that. Around New York, the factory had lost its high-frequency transmitter completely. Its mobile units had floundered in crazy gyrations, racing in random circles, crashing against rocks and trees, sliding into gullies, overturning, finally unwinding and becoming reluctantly inanimate.

The ore cart reached the edge of the ruined plain and halted briefly. Above it, the dot of black still circled the sky. For a time, the cart remained frozen.

'The factory's trying to decide,' Perine said. 'It needs the material, but it's afraid of that hawk up there.'

The factory debated and nothing stirred. Then the ore cart again resumed its unsteady crawl. It left the tangle of vines and started out across the blasted open plain. Painfully, with infinite caution, it headed toward the slab of dark concrete and metal at the base of the mountains.

The hawk stopped circling.

'Get down!' O'Neill said sharply. 'They've got those rigged with the new bombs.'

His wife and Perine crouched down beside him and the three of them peered warily at the plain and the metal insect crawling laboriously across it. In the sky, the hawk swept in a straight line until it hung directly over the cart. Then, without a sound or warning, it came down in a straight dive. Hands to her face, Judith shrieked, 'I can't watch! It's awful! Like wild animals!'

'It's not after the cart,' O'Neill grated.

As the airborne projectile dropped, the cart put on a burst of desperate speed. It raced noisily toward the factory, clanking and rattling, trying in a last futile attempt to reach safety. Forgetting the menace above, the frantically eager factory opened up and guided its mobile unit directly inside. And the hawk had what it wanted.

Before the barrier could close, the hawk swooped down in a long glide parallel with the ground. As the cart disappeared into the depths of the factory, the hawk shot after it, a swift shimmer of metal that hurtled past the clanking cart. Suddenly aware, the factory snapped the barrier shut. Grotesquely, the cart struggled; it was caught fast in the half-closed entrance.

But whether it freed itself didn't matter. There was a dull rumbling stir. The ground moved, billowed, then settled back. A deep shock wave passed beneath the three watching human beings. From the factory rose a single column of black smoke. The surface of concrete split like a dried pod; it shriveled and broke, and dribbled shattered bits of itself in a shower of ruin. The smoke hung for a while, drifting aimlessly away with the morning wind.

The factory was a fused, gutted wreck. It had been penetrated and destroyed.

O'Neill got stiffly to his feet. 'That's all. All over with. We've got what we set out after—we've destroyed the autofac network.' He glanced at Perine. 'Or was that what we were after?'

They looked toward the settlement that lay behind them. Little remained of the orderly rows of houses and streets of the previous years. Without the network, the settlement had rapidly decayed. The original prosperous neatness had dissipated; the settlement was shabby, ill-kept.

'Of course,' Perine said haltingly. 'Once we get into the factories and start setting up our own assembly lines . . .'

'Is there anything left?' Judith inquired.

'There must be something left. My God, there were levels going down miles!'

'Some of those bombs they developed toward the end were awfully big,' Judith pointed out. 'Better than anything we had in our war.'

'Remember that camp we saw? The ruins-squatters?'

'I wasn't along,' Perine said.

'They were like wild animals. Eating roots and larvae. Sharpening rocks, tanning hides. Savagery, bestiality.'

'But that's what people like that want,' Perine answered defensively.

'Do they? Do we want this?' O'Neill indicated the straggling settlement. 'Is this what we set out looking for, that day we collected the tungsten? Or that day we told the factory truck its milk was—' He couldn't remember the word.

'Pizzled,' Judith supplied.

'Come on,' O'Neill said. 'Let's get started. Let's see what's left of that factory—left for us.'

They approached the ruined factory late in the afternoon. Four trucks rumbled shakily up to the rim of the gutted pit and halted, motors steaming, tailpipes dripping. Wary and alert, workmen scrambled down and stepped gingerly across the hot ash.

'Maybe it's too soon,' one of them objected.

O'Neill had no intention of waiting. 'Come on,' he ordered. Grabbing up a flashlight, he stepped down into the crater.

The sheltered hull of the Kansas City factory lay directly ahead. In its gutted mouth, the ore cart still hung caught, but it was no longer struggling. Beyond the cart was an ominous pool of gloom. O'Neill flashed his light through the entrance; the tangled, jagged remains of upright supports were visible.

'We want to get down deep,' he said to Morrison, who prowled cautiously beside him. 'If there's anything left, it's at the bottom.'

Morrison grunted. 'Those boring moles from Atlanta got most of the deep layers.'

'Until the others got their mines sunk.' O'Neill stepped carefully through the sagging entrance, climbed a heap of debris that had been tossed against the slit from inside, and found himself within the factory—an expanse of confused wreckage, without pattern or meaning.

'Entropy,' Morrison breathed, oppressed. 'The thing it always hated. The thing it was built to fight. Random particles everywhere. No purpose to it.'

'Down underneath,' O'Neill said stubbornly, 'we may find some sealed enclaves. I know they got so they were dividing up into autonomous sections, trying to preserve repair units intact, to re-form the composite factory.'

'The moles got most of them, too,' Morrison observed, but he lumbered after O'Neill.

Behind them, the workmen came slowly. A section of wreckage shifted ominously and a shower of hot fragments cascaded down.

'You men get back to the trucks,' O'Neill said. 'No sense endangering any more of us than we have to. If Morrison and I don't come back, forget us—don't risk sending a rescue party.' As they left, he pointed out to Morrison a descending ramp still partially intact. 'Let's get below.'

Silently, the two men passed one dead level after another. Endless miles of dark ruin stretched out, without sound or activity. The vague shapes of darkened machinery, unmoving belts and conveyer equipment were partially visible, and the partially completed husks of war projectiles, bent and twisted by the final blast.

'We can salvage some of that,' O'Neill said, but he didn't actually believe it. The machinery was fused, shapeless. Everything in the factory had run together, molten slag without form or use. 'Once we get it to the surface . . .'

'We can't,' Morrison contradicted bitterly. 'We don't have hoists or winches.' He kicked at a heap of charred supplies that had stopped along its broken belt and spilled halfway across the ramp.

'It seemed like a good idea at the time,' O'Neill said as the two of them continued past vacant levels of machines. 'But now that I look back, I'm not so sure.'

They had penetrated a long way into the factory. The final level lap spread out ahead of them. O'Neill flashed the light here and there, trying to locate undestroyed sections, portions of the assembly process still intact.

It was Morrison who felt it first. He suddenly dropped to his hands and knees; heavy body pressed against the floor, he lay listening, face hard, eyes wide. 'For God's sake—'

'What is it?' O'Neill cried. Then he, too, felt it. Beneath them, a faint, insistent vibration hummed through the floor, a steady hum of activity. They had been wrong; the hawk had not been totally successful. Below, in a deeper level, the factory was still alive. Closed, limited operations still went on.

'On its own,' O'Neill muttered, searching for an extension of the descent lift. 'Autonomous activity, set to continue after the rest is gone. How do we get down?'

The descent lift was broken off, sealed by a thick section of metal. The still-living layer beneath their feet was completely cut off; there was no entrance.

Racing back the way they had come, O'Neill reached the surface and hailed the first truck. 'Where the hell's the torch? Give it here!'

The precious blowtorch was passed to him and he hurried back, puffing, into the depths of the ruined factory where Morrison waited. Together, the two of them began frantically cutting through the warped metal flooring, burning apart the sealed layers of protective mesh.

'It's coming,' Morrison gasped, squinting in the glare of the torch. The plate fell with a clang, disappearing into the level below. A blaze of white light burst up around them and the two men leaped back.

In the sealed chamber, furious activity boomed and echoed, a steady process of moving belts, whirring machine-tools, fast-moving mechanical supervisors. At one end, a steady flow of raw materials entered the line; at the far end, the final product was whipped off, inspected and crammed into a conveyer tube.

All this was visible for a split second; then the intrusion was discovered. Robot relays came into play. The blaze of lights flickered and dimmed. The assembly line froze to a halt, stopped in its furious activity.

The machines clicked off and became silent.

At one end, a mobile unit detached itself and sped up the wall toward the hole O'Neill and Morrison had cut. It slammed an emergency seal in place and expertly welded it tight. The scene below was gone. A moment later the floor shivered as activity resumed.

Morrison, white-faced and shaking, turned to O'Neill. 'What are they doing? What are they making?'

'Not weapons,' O'Neill said.

'That stuff is being sent up'—Morrison gestured convulsively—'to the surface.'

Shakily, O'Neill climbed to his feet. 'Can we locate the spot?'

'I—think so.'

'We better.' O'Neill swept up the flashlight and started toward the ascent ramp. 'We're going to have to see what those pellets are that they're shooting up.'

The exit valve of the conveyer tube was concealed in a tangle of vines and ruins a quarter of a mile beyond the factory. In a slot of rock at the base of the mountains the valve poked up like a nozzle. From ten yards away, it was invisible; the two men were almost on top of it before they noticed it.

Every few moments, a pellet burst from the valve and shot up into the sky. The nozzle revolved and altered its angle of deflection; each pellet was launched in a slightly varied trajectory.

'How far are they going?' Morrison wondered.

'Probably varies. It's distributing them at random.' O'Neill advanced cautiously, but the mechanism took no note of him. Plastered against the towering wall of rock was a crumpled pellet; by accident, the nozzle had released it directly at the mountainside. O'Neill climbed up, got it and jumped down.

The pellet was a smashed container of machinery, tiny metallic elements too minute to be analyzed without a microscope.

'Not a weapon,' O'Neill said.

The cylinder had split. At first he couldn't tell if it had been the impact or deliberate internal mechanisms at work. From the rent, an ooze of metal bits was sliding. Squatting down, O'Neill examined them.

The bits were in motion. Microscopic machinery, smaller than ants, smaller than pins, working energetically, purposefully—constructing something that looked like a tiny rectangle of steel.

'They're building,' O'Neill said, awed. He got up and prowled on. Off to the side, at the far edge of the gully, he came across a downed pellet far advanced on its construction. Apparently it had been released some time ago.

This one had made great enough progress to be identified. Minute as it was, the structure was familiar. The machinery was building a miniature replica of the demolished factory.

'Well,' O'Neill said thoughtfully, 'we're back where we started from. For better or worse . . . I don't know.'

'I guess they must be all over Earth by now,' Morrison said, 'landing everywhere and going to work.'

A thought struck O'Neill. 'Maybe some of them are geared to escape velocity. That would be neat—autofac networks throughout the whole universe.'

Behind him, the nozzle continued to spurt out its torrent of metal seeds.

SERVICE CALL

It would be wise to explain what Courtland was doing just before the doorbell rang.

In his swank apartment on Leavenworth Street where Russian Hill drops to the flat expanse of North Beach and finally to the San Francisco Bay itself, David Courtland sat hunched over a series of routine reports, a week's file of technical data dealing with the results of the Mount Diablo tests. As research director for Pesco Paints, Courtland was concerning himself with the comparative durability of various surfaces manufactured by his company. Treated shingles had baked and sweated in the California heat for five hundred and sixty-four days. It was now time to see which pore-filler withstood oxidation, and to adjust production schedules accordingly.

Involved with his intricate analytical data, Courtland at first failed to hear the bell. In the corner of the living room his high-fidelity Bogen amplifier, turntable, and speaker were playing a Schumann symphony. His wife, Fay, was doing the dinner dishes in the kitchen. The two children, Bobby and Ralf, were already in their bunk beds, asleep. Reaching for his pipe, Courtland leaned back from the desk a moment, ran a heavy hand through his thinning gray hair . . . and heard the bell.

'Damn,' he said. Vaguely, he wondered how many times the demure chimes had sounded; he had a dim subliminal memory of repeated attempts to attract his attention. Before his tired eyes the mass of report sheets wavered and receded. Who the hell was it? His watch read only nine-thirty; he couldn't really complain, yet.

'Want me to get it?' Fay called brightly from the kitchen.

'I'll get it.' Wearily, Courtland got to his feet, stuffed his feet into his shoes, and plodded across the room, past the couch, floor lamp, magazine rack, the phonograph, the bookcase, to the door. He was a heavy-set middle-aged technologist, and he didn't like people interrupting his work.

In the hall stood an unfamiliar visitor. 'Good evening, sir,' the visitor said, intently examining a clipboard; 'I'm sorry to bother you.'

Courtland glared sourly at the young man. A salesman, probably. Thin, blond-haired, in a white shirt, bow tie, single-breasted blue suit, the young man stood gripping his clipboard in one hand and a bulging black suitcase with the other. His bony features were set in an expression of serious concentration. There was an air of studious confusion about him; brow wrinkled, lips tight together, the muscles of his cheeks began to twitch into overt worry. Glancing up he asked, 'Is this 1846 Leavenworth? Apartment 3A?'

'That's right,' Courtland said, with the infinite patience due a dumb animal.

The taut frown on the young man's face relaxed a trifle. 'Yes, sir,' he said, in his urgent tenor. Peering past Courtland into the apartment, he said, 'I'm sorry to bother you in the evening when you're working, but as you probably know we've been pretty full up the last couple of days. That's why we couldn't answer your call sooner.'

'My call?' Courtland echoed. Under his unbuttoned collar, he was beginning to glow a dull red. Undoubtedly something Fay had got him mixed up in; something she thought he should look into, something vital to gracious living. 'What the hell are you talking about?' he demanded. 'Come to the point.'

The young man flushed, swallowed noisily, tried to grin, and then hurried on huskily, 'Sir, I'm the repairman you asked for; I'm here to fix your swibble.'

The facetious retort that came to Courtland's mind was one that later on he wished he had used. 'Maybe,' he wished he had said, 'I don't want my swibble fixed. Maybe I like my swibble the way it is.' But he didn't say that. Instead, he blinked, pulled the door in slightly, and said, 'My *what?*'

'Yes, sir,' the young man persisted. 'The record of your swibble installation came to us as a matter of course. Usually we make an automatic adjustment inquiry, but your call preceded that—so I'm here with complete service equipment. Now, as to the nature of your particular complaint . . .' Furiously, the young man pawed through the sheaf of papers on his clipboard. 'Well, there's no point in looking for that; you can tell me orally. As you probably know, sir, we're not officially a part of the vending corporation . . . we have what is called an *insurance*-type coverage that comes into existence automatically, when your purchase is made. Of course, you can cancel the arrangement with us.' Feebly, he tried a joke. 'I have heard there're a couple of competitors in the service business.'

Stern morality replaced humor. Pulling his lank body upright, he finished, 'But let me say that we've been in the swibble repair business ever since old R. J. Wright introduced the first A-driven experimental model.'

For a time, Courtland said nothing. Phantasmagoria swirled through his mind: random quasi-technological thoughts, reflex evaluations and notations of no importance. So swibbles broke right down, did they? Big-time business operations . . . send out a repairman as soon as the deal is closed. Monopoly tactics . . . squeeze out the competition before they have a chance. Kickback to the parent company, probably. Interwoven books.

But none of his thoughts got down to the basic issue. With a violent effort he forced his attention back onto the earnest young man who waited nervously in the hall with his black service kit and clipboard. 'No,' Courtland said emphatically, 'no, you've got the wrong address.'

'Yes, sir?' the young man quavered politely, a wave of stricken dismay crossing his features. 'The wrong address? Good Lord, has dispatch got another route fouled up with that new-fangled—'

'Better look at your paper again,' Courtland said, grimly pulling the door toward him. 'Whatever the hell a swibble is, I haven't got one; and I didn't call you.'

As he shut the door, he perceived the final horror on the young man's face, his stupefied paralysis. Then the brightly painted wood surface cut off the sight, and Courtland turned wearily back to his desk.

A swibble. What the hell was a swibble? Seating himself moodily, he tried to take up where he had left off . . . but the direction of his thoughts had been totally shattered.

There was no such thing as a swibble. And he was on the in, industrially speaking. He read *US News*, the *Wall Street Journal*. If there was a swibble he would have heard about it—unless a swibble was some pip-squeak gadget for the home. Maybe that was it.

'Listen,' he yelled at his wife as Fay appeared momentarily at the kitchen door, dishcloth and blue-willow plate in her hands. 'What is this business? You know anything about swibbles?'

Fay shook her head. 'It's nothing of mine.'

'You didn't order a chrome-and-plastic a.c.-d.c. swibble from Macy's?'

'Certainly not.'

Maybe it was something for the kids. Maybe it was the latest grammar-school craze, the contemporary bolo or flip cards or knock-knock-who's-there? But nine-year-old kids didn't buy things that needed a service man carrying a massive black tool kit—not on fifty cents a week allowance.

Curiosity overcame aversion. He had to know, just for the record, what a swibble was. Springing to his feet, Courtland hurried to the hall door and yanked it open.

The hall was empty, of course. The young man had wandered off. There was a faint smell of men's cologne and nervous perspiration, nothing more.

Nothing more, except a wadded-up fragment of paper that had come unclipped from the man's board. Courtland bent down and retrieved it from the carpet. It was a carbon copy of a route-instruction, giving code-identification, the name of the service company, the address of the caller.

> 1846 Leavenworth Street S.F. v-call rec'd Ed Fuller 9:20 PM.
> 5-28. Swibble 30s15H (deluxe). Suggest check lateral feedback
> & neural replacement bank. AAw3-6.

The numbers, the information, meant nothing to Courtland. He closed the door and slowly returned to his desk. Smoothing out the crumpled sheet of paper, he reread the dull words again, trying to squeeze some meaning from them. The printed letterhead was:

ELECTRONIC SERVICE INDUSTRIES
455 Montgomery Street, San Francisco 14. Ri8-4456n
Est. 1963

That was it. The meager printed statement: Established in 1963. Hands trembling, Courtland reached mechanically for his pipe. Certainly, it explained why he had never heard of swibbles. It explained why he didn't own one ... and why, no matter how many doors in the apartment building he knocked on, the young repairman wouldn't find anybody who did.

Swibbles hadn't been invented yet.

After an interval of hard, furious thought Courtland picked up the phone and dialed the home number of his subordinate at the Pesco labs.

'I don't care,' he said carefully, 'what you're doing this evening. I'm going to give you a list of instructions and I want them carried out right away.'

At the other end of the line Jack Hurley could be heard pulling himself angrily together. 'Tonight? Listen, Dave, the company isn't my mother—I have some life of my own. If I'm supposed to come running down—'

'This has nothing to do with Pesco. I want a tape recorder and a movie camera with infrared lens. I want you to round up a legal stenographer. I want one of the company electricians—you pick him out, but get the best. And I want Anderson from the engineering room. If you can't get him, get any of our designers. And I want somebody off the assembly line; get me some old mechanic who knows his stuff. Who really knows machines.'

Doubtfully, Hurley said, 'Well, you're the boss; at least, you're boss of research. But I think this will have to be cleared with the company. Would you mind if I went over your head and got an okay from Pesbroke?'

'Go ahead.' Courtland made a quick decision. 'Better yet, I'll call him myself; he'll probably have to know what's going on.'

'What *is* going on?' Hurley demanded curiously. 'I never heard you sound this way before . . . has somebody brought out a self-spraying paint?'

Courtland hung up the phone, waited out a torturous interval, and then dialed his superior, the owner of Pesco Paint.

'You have a minute?' he asked tightly, when Pesbroke's wife had roused the white-haired old man from his after-dinner nap and got him to the phone. 'I'm mixed up in something big; I want to talk to you about it.'

'Has it got to do with paint?' Pesbroke muttered, half humorously, half seriously. 'If not—'

Courtland interrupted him. Speaking slowly, he gave a full account of his contact with the swibble repairman.

When Courtland had finished, his employer was silent. 'Well,' Pesbroke said finally, 'I guess I could go through some kind of routine. But you've got me interested. All right, I'll buy it. But,' he added quietly, 'if this is an elaborate time-waster, I'm going to bill you for the use of the men and equipment.'

'By time-waster, you mean if nothing profitable comes out of this?'

'No,' Pesbroke said. 'I mean, if you *know* it's a fake; if you're consciously going along with a gag. I've got a migraine headache and I'm not going along with a gag. If you're serious, if you really think this might be something, I'll put the expenses on the company books.'

'I'm serious,' Courtland said. 'You and I are both too damn old to play games.'

'Well,' Pesbroke reflected, 'the older you get, the more you're apt to go off the deep end; and this sounds pretty deep.' He could be heard making up his mind. 'I'll telephone Hurley and give him the okay. You can have whatever you want . . . I suppose you're going to try to pin this repairman down and find out what he really is.'

'That's what I want to do.'

'Suppose he's on the level . . . what then?'

'Well,' Courtland said cautiously, 'then I want to find out what a swibble is. As a starter. Maybe after that—'

'You think he'll be back?'

'He might be. He won't find the right address; I know that. Nobody in *this* neighborhood called for a swibble repairman.'

'What do you care what a swibble is? Why don't you find out how he got from his period back here?'

'I think he knows what a swibble is—and I don't think he knows how he got here. He doesn't even know he's here.'

Pesbroke agreed. 'That's reasonable. If I come over, will you let me in? I'd sort of enjoy watching.'

'Sure,' Courtland said, perspiring, his eye on the closed door to the hall. 'But you'll have to watch from the other room. I don't want anything to foul this up . . . we may never have another chance like this.'

Grumpily, the jury-rigged company team filed into the apartment and stood waiting for Courtland to instruct. Jack Hurley, in aloha sports shirt, slacks, and crepe-soled shoes, clodded resentfully over to Courtland and waved his cigar in his face. 'Here we are; I don't know what you told Pesbroke, but you certainly pulled him along.' Glancing around the apartment, he asked, 'Can I assume we're going to get the pitch now? There's not much these people can do unless they understand what they're after.'

In the bedroom doorway stood Courtland's two sons, eyes half-shut with sleep. Fay nervously swept them up and herded them back into the bedroom. Around the living room the various men and women took up uncertain positions, their faces registering outrage, uneasy curiosity, and bored indifference. Anderson, the designing engineer, acted aloof and blasé. MacDowell, the stoop-shouldered, pot-bellied lathe operator, glared with proletarian resentment at the expensive furnishings of the apartment, and then sank into embarrassed apathy as he perceived his own work boots and grease-saturated pants. The recording specialist was trailing wire from his microphones to the tape recorder set up in the kitchen. A slim young woman, the legal stenographer, was trying to make herself comfortable in a chair in the corner. On the couch, Parkinson, the plant emergency electrician, was glancing idly through a copy of *Fortune*.

'Where's the camera equipment?' Courtland demanded.

'Coming,' Hurley answered. 'Are you trying to catch somebody trying out the old Spanish Treasure bunco?'

'I wouldn't need an engineer and an electrician for that,' Courtland said dryly. Tensely, he paced around the living room. 'Probably he won't even show up; he's probably back in his own time, by now, or wandering around God knows where.'

'Who?' Hurley shouted, puffing gray cigar smoke in growing agitation. 'What's going on?'

'A man knocked on my door,' Courtland told him briefly. 'He talked about some machinery, equipment I never heard of. Something called a swibble.'

Around the room blank looks passed back and forth.

'Let's guess what a swibble is,' Courtland continued grimly. 'Anderson, you start. What would a swibble be?'

Anderson grinned. 'A fish hook that chases down fish.'

Parkinson volunteered a guess. 'An English car with only one wheel.'

Grudgingly, Hurley came next. 'Something dumb. A machine for house-breaking pets.'

'A new plastic bra,' the legal stenographer suggested.

'I don't know,' MacDowell muttered resentfully. 'I never heard of anything like that.'

'All right,' Courtland agreed, again examining his watch. He was getting close to hysteria; an hour had passed and there was no sign of the repairman. 'We don't know; we can't even guess. But someday, nine years from now, a man named Wright is going to invent a swibble, and it's going to become big business. People are going to make them; people are going to buy them and pay for them; repairmen are going to come around and service them.'

The door opened and Pesbroke entered the apartment, overcoat over his arm, crushed Stetson hat clamped over his head. 'Has he showed up again?' His ancient, alert eyes darted around the room. 'You people look ready to go.'

'No sign of him,' Courtland said drearily. 'Damn it—I sent him off; I didn't grasp it until he was gone.' He showed Pesbroke the crumpled carbon.

'I see,' Pesbroke said, handing it back. 'And if he comes back you're going to tape what he says, and photograph everything he has in the way of equipment.' He indicated Anderson and MacDowell. 'What about the rest of them? What's the need of them?'

'I want people here who can ask the right questions,' Courtland explained. 'We won't get answers any other way. The man, if he shows up at all, will stay only a finite time. During that time, we've got to find out—' He broke off as his wife came up beside him. 'What is it?'

'The boys want to watch,' Fay explained. 'Can they? They promise they won't make any noise.' She added wistfully, 'I'd sort of like to watch, too.'

'Watch, then,' Courtland answered gloomily. 'Maybe there won't be anything to see.'

While Fay served coffee around, Courtland went on with his explanation. 'First of all, we want to find out if this man is on the level. Our first questions will be aimed at tripping him up; I want these specialists to go to work on him. If he's a fake, they'll probably find it out.'

'And if he isn't?' Anderson asked, an interested expression on his face. 'If he isn't, you're saying . . .'

'If he isn't, then he's from the next decade, and I want him pumped for all he's worth. But–' Courtland paused. 'I doubt if we'll get much theory. I had the impression that he's a long way down on the totem pole. The best we probably can do is get a run-down on his specific work. From that, we may have to assemble our picture, make our own extrapolations.'

'You think he can tell us what he does for a living,' Pesbroke said cannily, 'but that's about it.'

'We'll be lucky if he shows up at all,' Courtland said. He settled down on the couch and began methodically knocking his pipe against the ashtray. 'All we can do is wait. Each of you think over what you're going to ask. Try to figure out the questions you want answered by a man from the future who doesn't know he's from the future, who's trying to repair equipment that doesn't yet exist.'

'I'm scared,' the legal stenographer said, white-faced and wide-eyed, her coffee cup trembling.

'I'm about fed up,' Hurley muttered, eyes fixed sullenly on the floor. 'This is all a lot of hot air.'

It was just about that time that the swibble repairman came again, and once more timidly knocked on the hall door.

The young repairman was flustered. And he was getting perturbed. 'I'm sorry, sir,' he began without preamble. 'I can see you have company, but I've rechecked my route-instructions and this is *absolutely* the right address.' He added plaintively, 'I tried some other apartments; nobody knew what I was talking about.'

'Come in,' Courtland managed. He stepped aside, got himself between the swibble repairman and the door, and ushered him into the living room.

'Is this the person?' Pesbroke rumbled doubtfully, his gray eyes narrowing.

Courtland ignored him. 'Sit down,' he ordered the swibble repairman. Out of the corner of his eye he could see Anderson and Hurley and MacDowell moving in closely; Parkinson threw down his *Fortune* and got quickly to his feet. In the kitchen, the sound of tape running through the recording head was audible . . . the room had begun moving into activity.

'I could come some other time,' the repairman said apprehensively, eyeing the closing circle of people. 'I don't want to bother you, sir, when you have guests.'

Perched grimly on the arm of the couch, Courtland said, 'This is as good a time as any. In fact, this is the best time.' A wild flood of relief spilled over him: now they had a chance. 'I don't know what got into me,' he went on rapidly. 'I was confused. Of course I have a swibble; it's set up in the dining room.'

The repairman's face twitched with a spasm of laughter. 'Oh, really,' he choked. 'In the dining room? That's about the funniest joke I've heard in weeks.'

Courtland glanced at Pesbroke. What the hell was so funny about that? Then his flesh began to crawl; cold sweat broke out on his forehead and the palms of his hands. What the hell was a swibble? Maybe they had better find out right away—or not at all. Maybe they were getting into something deeper than they knew. Maybe—and he didn't like the thought—they were better off where they were.

'I was confused,' he said, 'by your nomenclature. I don't think of it as a swibble.' Cautiously, he finished, 'I know that's the popular jargon, but with that much money involved, I like to think of it by its legitimate title.'

The swibble repairman looked completely confused; Courtland realized that he had made another mistake; apparently *swibble* was its correct name.

Pesbroke spoke up. 'How long have you been repairing swibbles, Mr . . .' He waited, but there was no response from the thin, blank face. 'What's your name, young man?' he demanded.

'My *what*?' The swibble repairman pulled jerkily away. 'I don't understand you, sir.'

Good Lord, Courtland thought. It was going to be a lot harder than he had realized—than any of them had realized.

Angrily, Pesbroke said, 'You must have a name. Everybody has a name.'

The young repairman gulped and stared down red-faced at the carpet. 'I'm still only in service group four, sir. So I don't have a name yet.'

'Let it go,' Courtland said. What kind of a society gave out names as a status privilege? 'I want to make sure you're a competent repairman,' he explained. 'How long have you been repairing swibbles?'

'For six years and three months,' the repairman asserted. Pride took the place of embarrassment. 'In junior high school I showed a straight-A record in swibble-maintenance aptitude.' His meager chest swelled. 'I'm a born swibble-man.'

'Fine,' Courtland agreed uneasily; he couldn't believe the industry was that big. They gave tests in junior high school? Was swibble maintenance considered a basic talent, like symbol manipulation and manual dexterity? Had swibble work become as fundamental as musical talent, or as the ability to conceive spatial relationships?

'Well,' the repairman said briskly, gathering up his bulging tool kit, 'I'm all ready to get started. I have to be back at the shop before long . . . I've got a lot of other calls.'

Bluntly, Pesbroke stepped up squarely in front of the thin young man. 'What is a swibble?' he demanded. 'I'm tired of this damn fooling around. You say you work on these things—*what are they?* That's a simple enough question; they must be something.'

'Why,' the young man said hesitantly, 'I mean, that's hard to say. Suppose—well, suppose you ask me what a cat or a dog is. How can I answer that?'

'We're getting nowhere,' Anderson spoke up. 'The swibble is manufactured, isn't it? You must have schematics, then; hand them over.'

The young repairman gripped his tool kit defensively. 'What in the world is the matter, sir? If this is your idea of a joke—' He turned back to Courtland. 'I'd like to start work; I really don't have much time.'

Standing in the corner, hands shoved deep in his pockets,

MacDowell said slowly, 'I've been thinking about getting a swib-ble. The missus thinks we ought to have one.'

'Oh, certainly,' the repairman agreed. Color rising in his cheeks, he rushed on, 'I'm surprised you don't have a swibble already; in fact, I can't imagine what's wrong with you people. You're all act-ing—oddly. Where, if I may ask, do you come from? Why are you so—well, so uninformed?'

'These people,' Courtland explained, 'come from a part of the country where there aren't any swibbles.'

Instantly, the repairman's face hardened with suspicion. 'Oh?' he said sharply. 'Interesting. What part of the country is that?'

Again, Courtland had said the wrong thing; he knew that. While he floundered for a response, MacDowell cleared his throat and inexorably went on. 'Anyhow,' he said, 'we've been meaning to get one. You have any folders with you? Pictures of different models?'

The repairman responded. 'I'm afraid not, sir. But if you'll give me your address I'll have the sales department send you informa-tion. And if you want, a qualified representative can call on you at your convenience and describe the advantages of owning a swibble.'

'The first swibble was developed in 1963?' Hurley asked.

'That's right.' The repairman's suspicions had momentarily lulled. 'And just in time, too. Let me say this—if Wright hadn't got his first model going, there wouldn't be any human beings left alive. You people here who don't own swibbles—you may not know it—and you certainly act as if you didn't know it—but you're alive right now because of old R. J. Wright. It's swibbles that keep the world going.'

Opening his black case, the repairman briskly brought out a complicated apparatus of tubes and wiring. He filled a drum with clear fluid, sealed it, tried the plunger, and straightened up. 'I'll start out with a shot of dx—that usually puts them back into operation.'

'What is dx?' Anderson asked quickly.

Surprised at the question, the repairman answered, 'It's a high-protein food concentrate. We've found that ninety per cent of our early service calls are the result of improper diet. People just don't know how to care for their new swibble.'

'My God,' Anderson said feebly. 'It's alive.'

Courtland's mind took a nose dive. He had been wrong; it wasn't precisely a repairman who had stood gathering his equipment together. The man had come to fix the swibble, all right, but his capacity was slightly different than Courtland had supposed. He wasn't a repairman; he was a veterinarian.

Laying out instruments and meters, the young man explained: 'The new swibbles are a lot more complex than the early models; I need all this before I can even get started. But blame the War.'

'The War?' Fay Courtland echoed apprehensively.

'Not the early war. The big one, in '75. That little war in '61 wasn't really much. You know, I suppose, that Wright was originally an Army engineer, stationed over in—well, I guess it was called Europe. I believe the idea came to him because of all those refugees pouring across the border. Yes, I'm sure that's how it was. During that little war, back in '61, they came across by the millions. And they went the other way, too. My goodness, people were shifting back and forth between the two camps—it was revolting.'

'I'm not clear on my history,' Courtland said thickly. 'I never paid much attention in school . . . the '61 war, that was between Russia and America?'

'Oh,' the repairman said, 'it was between everybody. Russia headed the Eastern side, of course. And America the West. But everybody was in it. That was the little war, though; that didn't count.'

'Little?' Fay demanded, horrified.

'Well,' the repairman admitted, 'I suppose it looked like a lot at the time. But I mean, there were buildings still standing, afterward. And it only lasted a few months.'

'Who—won?' Anderson croaked.

The repairman tittered. 'Won? What an odd question. Well,

there were more people left in the Eastern bloc, if that's what you mean. Anyhow, the importance of the '61 war—and I'm *sure* your history teachers made that clear—was that swibbles appeared. R. J. Wright got his idea from the camp-changers that appeared in that war. So by '75, when the *real* war came along, we had plenty of swibbles.' Thoughtfully, he added, 'In fact, I'd say the real war was a war over swibbles. I mean, it was the last war. It was the war between the people who wanted swibbles and those who didn't.' Complacently, he finished, 'Needless to say, *we* won.'

After a time Courtland managed to ask, 'What happened to the others? Those who—didn't want swibbles?'

'Why,' the repairman said gently, 'the swibbles got them.'

Shakily, Courtland started his pipe going. 'I didn't know about that.'

'What do you mean?' Pesbroke demanded hoarsely. 'How did they get them? What did they do?'

Astonished, the repairman shook his head. 'I didn't know there was such ignorance in lay circles.' The position of pundit obviously pleased him; sticking out his bony chest, he proceeded to lecture the circle of intent faces on the fundamentals of history. 'Wright's first A-driven swibble was crude, of course. But it served its purpose. Originally, it was able to differentiate the camp-shifters into two groups: those who had really seen the light, and those who were insincere. Those who were going to shift back . . . who weren't really loyal. The authorities wanted to know which of the shifters had really come over to the West and which were spies and secret agents. That was the original swibble function. But that was nothing compared to now.'

'No,' Courtland agreed, paralyzed. 'Nothing at all.'

'Now,' the repairman said sleekly, 'we don't deal with such crudities. It's absurd to wait until an individual has accepted a contrary ideology, and then hope he'll shift away from it. In a way, it's ironic, isn't it? After the '61 war there was really only one contrary ideology: those who opposed the swibbles.'

He laughed happily. 'So the swibbles differentiated those who didn't want to be differentiated by swibbles. My, that was quite a war. Because that wasn't a messy war, with a lot of bombs and jellied gasoline. That was a *scientific* war—none of that random pulverizing. That was just swibbles going down into cellars and ruins and hiding places and digging out those Contrapersons one by one. Until we had all of them. So now,' he finished, gathering up his equipment, 'we don't have to worry about wars or anything of that sort. There won't be any more conflicts, because we don't have any contrary ideologies. As Wright showed, it doesn't really matter what ideology we have; it isn't important whether it's Communism or Free Enterprise or Socialism or Fascism or Slavery. What's important is that every one of us agrees completely; that we're all absolutely loyal. And as long as we have our swibbles–' He winked knowingly at Courtland. 'Well, as a new swibble owner, you've found out the advantages. You know the sense of security and satisfaction in being *certain* that your ideology is exactly congruent with that of everybody else in the world. That there's no possibility, no chance whatsoever that you'll go astray—and that some passing swibble will feed on you.'

It was MacDowell who managed to pull himself together first. 'Yeah,' he said ironically. 'It certainly sounds like what the missus and I want.'

'Oh, you ought to have a swibble of your own,' the repairman urged. 'Consider–if you have your own swibble, it'll adjust you automatically. It'll keep you on the right track without strain or fuss. You'll always know you're not going wrong—remember the swibble slogan: Why be *half* loyal? With your own swibble, your outlook will be corrected by painless degrees . . . but if you wait, if you just *hope* you're on the right track, why, one of these days you may walk into a friend's living room and his swibble may just simply crack you open and drink you down. Of course,' he reflected, 'a passing swibble may still get you in time to straighten you out. But usually it's too late. Usually–' He smiled. 'Usually people go beyond redemption, once they get started.'

'And your job,' Pesbroke muttered, 'is to keep the swibbles working?'

'They do get out of adjustment, left to themselves.'

'Isn't it a kind of paradox?' Pesbroke pursued. 'The swibbles keep us in adjustment, and we keep them in adjustment . . . it's a closed circle.'

The repairman was intrigued. 'Yes, that's an interesting way of putting it. But we must keep control over the swibbles, of course. So they don't die.' He shivered. 'Or worse.'

'Die?' Hurley said, still not understanding. 'But if they're built—' Wrinkling his brows he said, 'Either they're machines or they're alive. Which is it?'

Patiently, the repairman explained elementary physics. 'Swibble-culture is an organic phenotype evolved in a protein medium under controlled conditions. The directing neurological tissue that forms the basis of the swibble is alive, certainly, in the sense that it grows, thinks, feeds, excretes waste. Yes, it's definitely alive. But the swibble, as a functioning whole, is a manufactured item. The organic tissue is inserted in the master tank and then sealed. I certainly don't repair *that*; I give it nutriments to restore a proper balance of diet, and I try to deal with parasitic organisms that find their way into it. I try to keep it adjusted and healthy. The balance of the organism is, of course, totally mechanical.'

'The swibble has direct access to human minds?' Anderson asked, fascinated.

'Naturally. It's an artificially evolved telepathic metazoan. And with it, Wright solved the basic problem of modern times: the existence of diverse, warring ideological factions, the presence of disloyalty and dissent. In the words of General Steiner's famous aphorism: War is an extension of the disagreement from the voting booth to the battlefield. And the preamble of the World Service Charter: war, if it is to be eliminated, must be eliminated from the minds of men, for it is in the minds of men that disagreement begins. Up until 1963, we had no way to get into the minds of men. Up until 1963, the problem was unsolvable.'

'Thank God,' Fay said clearly.

The repairman failed to hear her; he was carried away by his own enthusiasm. 'By means of the swibble, we've managed to transform the basic sociological problem of loyalty into a routine technical matter: to the mere matter of maintenance and repair. Our only concern is keep the swibbles functioning correctly; the rest is up to them.'

'In other words,' Courtland said faintly, 'you repairmen are the only controlling influence over the swibbles. You represent the total human agency standing above these machines.'

The repairman reflected. 'I suppose so,' he admitted modestly. 'Yes, that's correct.'

'Except for you, they pretty damn well manage the human race.'

The bony chest swelled with complacent, confident pride. 'I suppose you could say that.'

'Look,' Courtland said thickly. He grabbed hold of the man's arm. 'How the hell can you be sure? Are you really in control?' A crazy hope was rising up inside him: as long as men had power over the swibbles there was a chance to roll things back. The swibbles could be disassembled, taken apart piece by piece. As long as swibbles had to submit to human servicing it wasn't quite hopeless.

'What, sir?' the repairman inquired. 'Of course we're in control. Don't you worry.' Firmly, he disengaged Courtland's fingers. 'Now, where is your swibble?' He glanced around the room. 'I'll have to hurry; there isn't much time left.'

'I haven't got a swibble,' Courtland said.

For a moment it didn't register. Then a strange, intricate expression crossed the repairman's face. 'No swibble? But you told me—'

'Something went wrong,' Courtland said hoarsely. 'There aren't any swibbles. It's too early—they haven't been invented. Understand? You came too soon!'

The young man's eyes popped. Clutching his equipment, he stumbled back two steps, blinked, opened his mouth and tried to speak. 'Too—soon?' Then comprehension arrived. Suddenly he looked older, much older. 'I wondered. All the undamaged buildings . . . the archaic furnishings. The transmission machinery must have misphased!' Rage flashed over him. 'That instantaneous service—I knew dispatch should have stuck to the old mechanical system. I told them to make better tests. Lord, there's going to be hell to pay; if we ever get this mix-up straightened out I'll be surprised.'

Bending down furiously, he hastily dropped his equipment back in the case. In a single motion he slammed and locked it, straightened up, bowed briefly at Courtland.

'Good evening,' he said frigidly. And vanished.

The circle of watchers had nothing to watch. The swibble repairman had gone back to where he came from.

After a time Pesbroke turned and signaled to the man in the kitchen. 'Might as well shut off the tape recorder,' he muttered bleakly. 'There's nothing more to record.'

'Good Lord,' Hurley said, shaken. 'A world run by machines.'

Fay shivered. 'I couldn't believe that little fellow had so much power; I thought he was just a minor official.'

'He's completely in charge,' Courtland said harshly.

There was silence.

One of the two children yawned sleepily. Fay turned abruptly to them and herded them efficiently into the bedroom. 'Time for you two to be in bed,' she commanded, with false gaiety.

Protesting sullenly, the two boys disappeared, and the door closed. Gradually, the living room broke into motion. The tape-recorder man began rewinding his reel. The legal stenographer shakily collected her notes and put away her pencils. Hurley lit up a cigar and stood puffing moodily, his face dark and somber.

'I suppose,' Courtland said finally, 'that we've all accepted it; we assume it's not a fake.'

'Well,' Pesbroke pointed out, 'he vanished. That ought to be proof enough. And all the junk he took out of his kit—'

'It's only nine years,' Parkinson, the electrician, said thoughtfully. 'Wright must be alive already. Let's look him up and stick a shiv into him.'

'Army engineer,' MacDowell agreed. 'R. J. Wright. It ought to be possible to locate him. Maybe we can keep it from happening.'

'How long would you guess people like him can keep the swibbles under control?' Anderson asked.

Courtland shrugged wearily. 'No telling. Maybe years . . . maybe a century. But sooner or later something's going to come up, something they didn't expect. And then it'll be predatory machinery preying on all of us.'

Fay shuddered violently. 'It sounds awful; I'm certainly glad it won't be for a while.'

'You and the repairman,' Courtland said bitterly. 'As long as it doesn't affect you—'

Fay's overwrought nerves flared up. 'We'll discuss it later on.' She smiled jerkily at Pesbroke. 'More coffee? I'll put some on.' Turning on her heel, she rushed from the living room into the kitchen.

While she was filling the Silex with water, the doorbell quietly rang.

The roomful of people froze. They looked at each other, mute and horrified.

'He's back,' Hurley said thickly.

'Maybe it's not him,' Anderson suggested weakly. 'Maybe it's the camera people, finally.'

But none of them moved toward the door. After a time the bell rang again, longer, and more insistently.

'We have to answer it,' Pesbroke said woodenly.

'Not me,' the legal stenographer quavered.

'This isn't my apartment,' MacDowell pointed out.

Courtland moved rigidly toward the door. Even before he took hold of the knob he knew what it was. Dispatch, using its newfangled instantaneous transmission. Something to get work crews and repairmen directly to their stations. So control of the swibbles would be absolute and perfect; so nothing would go wrong.

But something had gone wrong. The control had fouled itself up. It was working upside down, completely backward. Self-defeating, futile: it was too perfect. Gripping the knob, he tore the door open.

Standing in the hall were four men. They wore plain gray uniforms and caps. The first of them whipped off his cap, glanced at a written sheet of paper, and then nodded politely at Courtland.

'Evening, sir,' he said cheerfully. He was a husky man, wide-shouldered, with a shock of thick brown hair hanging over his sweat-shiny forehead. 'We—uh—got a little lost, I guess. Took a while to get here.'

Peering into the apartment, he hitched up his heavy leather belt, stuffed his route sheet into his pocket, and rubbed his large, competent hands together.

'It's downstairs in the trunk,' he announced, addressing Courtland and the whole living room of people. 'Tell me where you want it, and we'll bring it right up. We should have a good-sized space—that side over there by the window should do.' Turning away, he and his crew moved energetically toward the service elevator. 'These late-model swibbles take up a lot of room.'

CAPTIVE MARKET

Saturday morning, about eleven o'clock, Mrs Edna Berthelson was ready to make her little trip. Although it was a weekly affair, consuming four hours of her valuable business time, she made the profitable trip alone, preserving for herself the integrity of her find.

Because that was what it was. A find, a stroke of incredible luck. There was nothing else like it, and she had been in business fifty-three years. More, if the years in her father's store were counted—but they didn't really count. That had been for the experience (her father made that clear); no pay was involved. But it gave her the understanding of business; the feel of operating a small country store, dusting pencils and unwrapping fly paper and serving up dried beans and chasing the cat out of the cracker barrel where he liked to sleep.

Now the store was old, and so was she. The big heavy-set, black-browed man who was her father had died long ago; her own children and grandchildren had been spawned, had crept out over the world, were everywhere. One by one they had appeared, lived in Walnut Creek, sweated through the dry, sun-baked summers, and then gone on, leaving one by one as they had come. She and the store sagged and settled a little more each year, became a little more frail and stern and grim. A little more themselves.

That morning very early Jackie said: 'Grandmaw, where are you going?' Although he knew, of course, where she was going. She was going out in her truck as she always did; this was the Saturday trip. But he liked to ask; he was pleased by the stability of the answer. He liked having it always the same.

To another question there was another unvarying answer, but this one didn't please him so much. It came in answer to the question: 'Can I come along?'

The answer to that was always *no*.

Edna Berthelson laboriously carried packages and boxes from the back of the store to the rusty, upright pickup truck. Dust lay over the truck; its red-metal sides were bent and corroded. The motor was already on; it was wheezing and heating up in the mid-day sun. A few drab chickens pecked in the dust around its wheels. Under the porch of the store a plump white shaggy sheep squatted, its face vapid, indolent, indifferently watching the activity of the day. Cars and trucks rolled along Mount Diablo Boulevard. Along Lafayette Avenue a few shoppers strolled, farmers and their wives, petty businessmen, farm hands, some city women in their gaudy slacks and print shirts, sandals, bandanas. In the front of the store the radio tinnily played popular songs.

'I asked you a question,' Jackie said righteously. 'I asked you where you're going.'

Mrs Berthelson bent stiffly over to lift the last armload of boxes. Most of the loading had been done the night before by Arnie the Swede, the hulking white-haired man who did the heavy work around the store. 'What?' she murmured vaguely, her gray, wrinkled face twisting with concentration. 'You know perfectly well where I'm going.'

Jackie trailed plaintively after her, as she re-entered the store to look for her order book. 'Can I come? Please, can I come along? You never let me come—you never let *anybody* come.'

'Of course not,' Mrs Berthelson said sharply. 'It's nobody's business.'

'But I *want* to come along,' Jackie explained.

Slyly, the little old woman turned her gray head and peered back at him, a worn, colorless bird taking in a world perfectly understood. 'So does everybody else.' Thin lips twitching in a secret smile, Mrs Berthelson said softly: 'But nobody can.'

Jackie didn't like the sound of that. Sullenly, he retired to a corner, hands stuck deep in the pockets of his jeans, not taking part in something that was denied him, not approving of something in which he could not share. Mrs Berthelson ignored him. She pulled her frayed blue sweater around her thin shoulders, located her sunglasses, pulled the screen door shut after her, and strode briskly to the truck.

Getting the truck into gear was an intricate process. For a time she sat tugging crossly at the shift, pumping the clutch up and down, waiting impatiently for the teeth to fall into place. At last, screeching and chattering, the gears meshed; the truck leaped a little, and Mrs Berthelson gunned the motor and released the hand brake.

As the truck roared jerkily down the highway, Jackie detached himself from the shade by the house and followed along after it. His mother was nowhere in sight. Only the dozing sheep and the two scratching chickens were visible. Even Arnie the Swede was gone, probably getting a cold Coke. Now was a fine time. Now was the best time he had ever had. And it was going to be sooner or later anyhow, because he was determined to come along.

Grabbing hold of the tailboard of the truck, Jackie hoisted himself up and landed face-down on the tightly-packed heaps of packages and boxes. Under him the truck bounced and bumped. Jackie hung on for dear life; clutching at the boxes he pulled his legs under him, crouched down, and desperately sought to keep from being flung off. Gradually the truck righted itself, and the torque diminished. He breathed a sigh of relief and settled gratefully down.

He was on his way. He was along, finally. Accompanying Mrs Berthelson on her secret weekly trip, her strange covert enterprise from which—he had heard—she made a fabulous profit. A trip which nobody understood, and which he knew, in the deep recesses of his child's mind, was something awesome and wonderful, something that would be well worth the trouble.

He had hoped fervently that she wouldn't stop to check her load along the way.

*

CAPTIVE MARKET

With infinite care, Tellman prepared himself a cup of 'coffee.' First, he carried a tin cup of roasted grain over to the gasoline drum the colony used as a mixing bowl. Dumping it in, he hurried to add a handful of chicory and a few fragments of dried bran. Dirt-stained hands trembling, he managed to get a fire started among the ashes and coals under the pitted metal grate. He set a pan of tepid water on the flames and searched for a spoon.

'What are you up to?' his wife demanded from behind him.

'Uh,' Tellman muttered. Nervously, he edged between Gladys and the meal. 'Just fooling around.' In spite of himself, his voice took on a nagging whine. 'I have a right to fix myself something, don't I? As much right as anybody else.'

'You ought to be over helping.'

'I was. I wrenched something in my back.' The wiry middle-aged man ducked uneasily away from his wife; tugging at the remains of his soiled white shirt, he retreated toward the door of the shack. 'Damn it, a person has to rest, sometimes.'

'Rest when we get there.' Gladys wearily brushed back her thick dark-blonde hair. 'Suppose everybody was like you.'

Tellman flushed resentfully. 'Who plotted our trajectory? Who's done all the navigation work?'

A faint ironic smile touched his wife's chapped lips. 'We'll see how your charts work out,' she said. 'Then we'll talk about it.'

Enraged, Tellman plunged out of the shack, into the blinding late-afternoon sunlight.

He hated the sun, the sterile white glare that began at five in the morning and lasted until nine in the evening. The Big Blast had sizzled the water vapor from the air; the sun beat down piti-lessly, sparing nobody. But there were few left to care.

To his right was the cluster of shacks that made up the camp. An eclectic hodge-podge of boards, sheets of tin, wire and tar paper, upright concrete blocks, anything and everything dragged from the San Francisco ruins, forty miles west. Cloth blankets flapped dismally in doorways, protection against the vast hosts of insects that swept across the camp site from time to time. Birds, the natural enemy of insects, were gone. Tellman hadn't seen a bird in two years—and he didn't expect to see one again. Beyond the camp began the eternal dead black ash, the charred face of the world, without features, without life.

The camp had been set up in a natural hollow. One side was sheltered by the tumbled ruins of what had once been a minor mountain range. The concussion of the blast had burst the towering cliffs; rock had cascaded into the valley for days. After San Francisco had been fired out of existence, survivors had crept into the heaps of boulders, looking for a place to hide from the sun. That was the hardest part: the unshielded sun. Not the insects, not the radioactive clouds of ash, not the flashing white fury of the blasts, but the sun. More people had died of thirst and dehydration and blind insanity than from toxic poisons.

From his breast pocket, Tellman got a precious package of cigarettes. Shakily, he lit up. His thin, claw-like hands were trembling, partly from fatigue, partly from rage and tension. How he hated the camp. He loathed everybody in it, his wife included. Were they worth saving? He doubted it. Most of them were barbarians, already; what did it matter if they got the ship off or not? He was sweating away his mind and life, trying to save them. The hell with them.

But then, his own safety was involved with theirs.

He stalked stiff-legged over to where Barnes and Masterson stood talking. 'How's it coming?' he demanded gruffly.

'Fine,' Barnes answered. 'It won't be long, now.'

'One more load,' Masterson said. His heavy features twitched uneasily. 'I hope nothing gets fouled up. She ought to be here any minute.'

Tellman loathed the sweaty, animal-like scent that rolled from Masterson's beefy body. Their situation wasn't an excuse to creep around filthy as a pig . . . on Venus, things would be different. Masterson was useful, now; he was an experienced mechanic, invaluable in servicing the turbine and jets of the ship. But when the ship had landed and been pillaged . . .

Satisfied, Tellman brooded over the re-establishment of the rightful order. The hierarchy had collapsed in the ruins of the cities, but it would be back strong as ever. Take Flannery, for example. Flannery was nothing but a foul-mouthed shanty-Irish stevedore . . . but he was in charge of loading the ship, the greatest job at the moment. Flannery was top dog, for the time being . . . but that would change.

It had to change. Consoled, Tellman strolled away from Barnes and Masterson, over to the ship itself.

The ship was huge. Across its muzzle the stenciled identification still remained, not yet totally obliterated by drifting ash and the searing heat of the sun.

US ARMY ORDNANCE

SERIES A-3 (B)

Originally, it had been a high-velocity 'massive retaliation' weapon, loaded with an H-warhead, ready to carry indiscriminate death to the enemy. The projectile had never been launched. Soviet toxic crystals had blown quietly into the windows and doors of the local command barracks. When launching day arrived, there was no crew to send it off. But it didn't matter—there was no enemy, either. The rocket had stood on its buttocks for months . . . it was still there when the first refugees straggled into the shelter of the demolished mountains.

'Nice, isn't it?' Patricia Shelby said. She glanced up from her work and smiled blearily at Tellman. Her small, pretty face was streaked with fatigue and eye-strain. 'Sort of like the trylon at the New York World's Fair.'

'My God,' Tellman said, 'you remember that?'

'I was only eight,' Patricia answered. In the shadow of the ship she was carefully checking the automatic relays that would maintain the air, temperature, and humidity of the ship. 'But I'll never forget it. Maybe I was a precog—when I saw it sticking up I knew someday it would mean a lot to everybody.'

'A lot to the twenty of us,' Tellman corrected. Suddenly he offered her the remains of his cigarette. 'Here—you look like you could use it.'

'Thanks.' Patricia continued with her work, the cigarette between her lips. 'I'm almost done—Boy, some of these relays are tiny. Just think.' She held up a microscopic wafer of transparent plastic. 'While we're all out cold, this makes the difference between life and death.' A strange, awed look crept into her dark-blue eyes. 'To the human race.'

Tellman guffawed. 'You and Flannery. He's always spouting idealistic twaddle.'

Professor John Crowley, once head of the history department at Stanford, now the nominal leader of the colony, sat with Flannery and Jean Dobbs, examining the suppurating arm of a ten-year-old boy. 'Radiation,' Crowley was saying emphatically. 'The overall level is rising daily. It's settling ash that does it. If we don't get out soon, we're done.'

'It's not radiation,' Flannery corrected in his ultimately-certain voice. 'It's toxic crystalline poisoning; that stuff's knee-deep up in the hills. He's been playing around up there.'

'Is that so?' Jean Dobbs demanded. The boy nodded his head, not daring to look at her. 'You're right,' she said to Flannery.

'Put some salve on it,' Flannery said. 'And hope he'll live. Outside of sulfathiazole there's not much we have.' He glanced at his watch, suddenly tense. 'Unless she brings the penicillin, today.'

'If she doesn't bring it today,' Crowley said, 'she'll never bring it. This is the last load; as soon as it's stored, we're taking off.'

Rubbing his hands, Flannery suddenly bellowed: 'Then get out the money!'

Crowley grinned. 'Right.' He fumbled in one of the steel storage lockers and yanked out a handful of paper bills. Holding a sheaf of bills up to Tellman he fanned them out invitingly. 'Take your pick. Take them all.'

Nervously, Tellman said, 'Be careful with that. She's probably raised the price on everything, again.'

'We've got plenty.' Flannery took some and stuffed it into a partly-filled load being wheeled by, on its way to the ship. 'There's money blowing all over the world, along with the ash and particles of bone. On Venus we won't need it—she might as well have it all.'

On Venus, Tellman thought, savagely, things would revert to their legitimate order—with Flannery digging sewers where he belonged. 'What's she bringing mostly?' he asked Crowley and Jean Dobbs, ignoring Flannery. 'What's the last load made up of?'

'Comic books,' Flannery said dreamily, wiping perspiration from his balding forehead; he was a lean, tall, dark-haired young man. 'And harmonicas.'

Crowley winked at him. 'Uke picks, so we can lie in our hammocks all day, strumming "Someone's in the Kitchen with Dinah."'

'And swizzle sticks,' Flannery reminded him. 'In order that we may all the more properly flatten the bubbles of our vintage '38 champagne.'

Tellman boiled. 'You—degenerate!'

Crowley and Flannery roared with laughter, and Tellman stalked off, smoldering under this new humiliation. What kind of morons and lunatics were they? Joking at a time like this . . . He peered miserably, almost accusingly, at the ship. Was this the kind of world they were going to found?

In the pitiless white-hot sun, the huge ship shimmered and glowed. A vast upright tube of alloy and protective fiber mesh rising up above the tumble of wretched shacks. One more load, and they were off. One more truckful of supplies from their only source, the meager trickle of uncontaminated goods that meant the difference between life and death.

Praying that nothing would go wrong, Tellman turned to await the arrival of Mrs Edna Berthelson and her battered red pickup truck. Their fragile umbilical cord, connecting them with the opulent, undamaged past.

On both sides of the road lay groves of lush apricot trees. Bees and flies buzzed sleepily among the rotting fruit scattered over the soil;

every now and then a roadside stand appeared, operated by somnambulistic children. In driveways stood parked Buicks and Oldsmobiles. Rural dogs wandered here and there. At one intersection stood a swank tavern, its neon sign blinking on and off, ghostly pale in the mid-morning sun.

Mrs Edna Berthelson glared hostilely at the tavern, and at the cars parked around it. City people were moving out into the valley, cutting down the old oak trees, the ancient fruit orchards, setting up suburban homes, stopping in the middle of the day for a whiskey sour and then driving cheerfully on. Driving at seventy-five miles an hour in their swept-back Chryslers. A column of cars that had piled up behind her truck suddenly burst forth and swung past her. She let them go, stony-faced, indifferent. Served them right for being in such a hurry. If she always hurried like that, she would never have had time to pay attention to that odd ability she had found in her introspective, lonely drives; never have discovered that she could look 'ahead,' never have discovered that hole in the warp of time which enabled her to trade so easily at her own exorbitant prices. Let them hurry if they wanted. The heavy load in the back of the truck jogged rhythmically. The motor wheezed. Against the back window a half-dead fly buzzed.

Jackie lay stretched out among the cartons and boxes, enjoying the ride, gazing complacently at the apricot trees and cars. Against the hot sky the peak of Mount Diablo rose, blue and white, an expanse of cold rock. Trails of mist clung to the peak; Mount Diablo went a long way up. He made a face at a dog standing indolently at the side of the road, waiting to cross. He waved gaily at a Pacific Telephone Co. repairman, stringing wire from a huge reel.

Abruptly the truck turned off the state highway and onto a black-surfaced side road. Now there were fewer cars. The truck began to climb . . . the rich orchards fell behind and gave way to flat brown fields. A dilapidated farm house lay to the right; he watched it with interest, wondering how old it was. When it was out of sight, no other man-made structures followed. The fields became unkempt. Broken, sagging fences were visible occasionally. Torn signs, no longer legible. The truck was approaching the base of Mount Diablo . . . almost nobody came this way.

Idly, the boy wondered why Mrs Berthelson's little trip took her in this direction. Nobody lived here; suddenly there were no fields, only scrub grass and bushes, wild countryside, the tumbled slope of the mountain. A rabbit hopped skillfully across the half-decayed road. Rolling hills, a broad expanse of trees and strewn boulders . . . there was nothing here but a State fire tower, and maybe a water shed. And an abandoned picnic area, once maintained by the State, now forgotten.

An edge of fear touched the boy. No customers lived out this way . . . he had been positive the battered red pickup truck would head directly into town, take him and the load to San Francisco or Oakland or Berkeley, a city where he could get out and run around, see the interesting sights. There was nothing here, only abandoned emptiness, silent and foreboding. In the shadow of the mountain, the air was chill. He shivered. All at once he wished he hadn't come.

Mrs Berthelson slowed the truck and shifted noisily into low. With a roar and an explosive belch of exhaust gases, the truck crept up a steep ascent, among jagged boulders, ominous and sharp. Somewhere far off a bird cried shrilly; Jackie listened to its thin sounds echoing dismally away and wondered how he could attract his grandmother's attention. It would be nice to be in front, in the cabin. It would be nice—

And then he noticed it. At first he didn't believe it . . . but he *had* to believe it.

Under him, the truck was beginning to fade away.

It faded slowly, almost imperceptibly. Dimmer and dimmer the truck grew; its rusty red sides became gray, then colorless. The black road was visible underneath. In wild panic, the boy clutched at the piles of boxes. His hands passed through them; he was riding precariously on an uneven sea of dim shapes, among almost invisible phantoms.

He lurched and slid down. Now—hideously—he was suspended

momentarily halfway *through* the truck, just above the tail pipe. Groping desperately, he struggled to catch hold of the boxes directly above him. 'Help!' he shouted. His voice echoed around him; it was the only sound . . . the roar of the truck was fading. For a moment he clutched at the retreating shape of the truck; then, gently, gradually, the last image of the truck faded, and with a sickening crunch, the boy dropped to the road.

The impact sent him rolling into the dry weeds beyond the drainage ditch. Stunned, dazed with disbelief and pain, he lay gasping, trying feebly to pull himself up. There was only silence; the truck, Mrs Berthelson, had vanished. He was totally alone. He closed his eyes and lay back, stupefied with fright.

Sometime later, probably not much later, he was aroused by the squeal of brakes. A dirty, orange State maintenance truck had lurched to a stop; two men in khaki work clothes were climbing down and hurrying over.

'What's the matter?' one yelled at him. They grabbed him up, faces serious and alarmed. 'What are you doing here?'

'Fell,' he muttered. 'Off the truck.'

'What truck?' they demanded. 'How?'

He couldn't tell them. All he knew was that Mrs Berthelson had gone. He hadn't made it, after all. Once again, she was making her trip alone. He would never know where she went; he would never find out who her customers were.

Gripping the steering wheel of the truck, Mrs Berthelson was conscious that the transition had taken place. Vaguely, she was aware that the rolling brown fields, rocks and green scrub bushes had faded out. The first time she had gone 'ahead' she had found the old truck floundering in a sea of black ash. She had been so excited by her discovery that day that she had neglected to 'scan' conditions on the other side of the hole. She had known there were customers . . . and dashed headlong through the warp to get there first. She smiled complacently . . . she needn't have hurried, there was no competition here. In fact, the customers were so eager to deal with her, they had done virtually everything in their power to make things easier for her.

The men had built a crude strip of road out into the ash, a sort of wooden platform onto which the truck now rolled. She had learned the exact moment to 'go ahead'; it was the instant that the truck passed the drainage culvert a quarter mile inside the State park. Here, 'ahead,' the culvert also existed ... but there was little left of it, only a vague jumble of shattered stone. And the road was utterly buried. Under the wheels of the truck the rough boards thumped and banged. It would be bad if she had a flat tire ... but some of them could fix it. They were always working; one little additional task wouldn't make much difference. She could see them, now; they stood at the end of the wooden platform, waiting impatiently for her. Beyond them was their jumble of crude, smelly shacks and beyond that, their ship.

A lot she cared about their ship. She knew what it was: stolen Army property. Setting her bony hand rigidly around the gearshift knob, she threw the truck into neutral and coasted to a stop. As the men approached, she began pulling on the hand brake.

'Afternoon,' Professor Crowley muttered, his eyes sharp and keen as he peered eagerly into the back of the truck.

Mrs Berthelson grunted a noncommittal answer. She didn't like any of them ... dirty men, smelling of sweat and fear, their bodies and clothes streaked with grime, and the ancient coating of desperation that never seemed to leave them. Like awed, pitiful children they clustered around the truck, poking hopefully at the packages, already beginning to pluck them out onto the black ground.

'Here now,' she said sharply. 'You leave those alone.'

Their hands darted back as if seared. Mrs Berthelson sternly climbed from the truck, grabbed up her inventory sheet, and plodded up to Crowley.

'You just wait,' she told him. 'Those have to be checked off.'

He nodded, glanced at Masterson, licked his dry lips, and waited. They all waited. It had always been that way; they knew, and she knew, that there was no other way they could get their supplies. And if they didn't get their supplies, their food and medicine and clothing and instruments and tools and raw materials, they wouldn't be able to leave in their ship.

In this world, in the 'ahead,' such things didn't exist. At least, not so anybody could use them. A cursory glance had told her that; she could see the ruin with her own eyes. They hadn't taken very good care of their world. They had wasted it all, turned it into black ash and ruin. Well, it was their business, not hers.

She had never been much interested in the relationship between their world and hers. She was content to know that both existed, and that she could go from one to the other and back. And she was the *only* one who knew how. Several times, people from this world, members of this group, had tried to go 'back there' with her. It had always failed. As she made the transition, they were left behind. It was her power, her faculty. Not a shared faculty—she was glad of that. And for a person in business, quite a valuable faculty.

'All right,' she said crisply. Standing where she could keep her eye on them, she began checking off each box as it was carried from the truck. Her routine was exact and certain; it was a part of her life. As long as she could remember she had transacted business in a distinct way. Her father had taught her how to live in a business world; she had learned his stern principles and rules. She was following them now.

Flannery and Patricia Shelby stood together at one side; Flannery held the money, payment for the delivery. 'Well,' he said, under his breath, 'now we can tell her to go leap in the river.'

'Are you sure?' Pat asked nervously.

'The last load's here.' Flannery grinned starkly and ran a trembling hand through his thinning black hair. 'Now we can get rolling. With this stuff, the ship's crammed to the gills. We may even have to sit down and eat some of that *now*.' He indicated a bulging paste-board carton of groceries. 'Bacon, eggs, milk, real coffee. Maybe we won't shove it in deep-freeze. Maybe we ought to have a last-meal-before-the-flight orgy.'

Wistfully, Pat said, 'It would be nice. It's been a long time since we've had food like that.'

Masterson strode over. 'Let's kill her and boil her in a big kettle. Skinny old witch—she might make good soup.'

'In the oven,' Flannery corrected. 'Some gingerbread, to take along with us.'

'I wish you wouldn't talk like that,' Pat said apprehensively. 'She's so—well, maybe she *is* a witch. I mean, maybe that's what witches were . . . old women with strange talents. Like her—being able to pass through time.'

'Damn lucky for us,' Masterson said briefly.

'But she doesn't understand it. Does she? Does she know what she's doing? That she could save us all by sharing her ability. Does she know what's happened to our world?'

Flannery considered. 'Probably she doesn't know—or care. A mind like hers, business and profit—getting exorbitant rates from us, selling this stuff to us at an incredible premium. And the joke is that money's worth nothing to us. If she could see, she'd know that. It's just paper, in this world. But she's caught in a narrow little routine. Business, profit.' He shook his head. 'A mind like that, a warped, miserable flea-sized mind . . . and *she* has that unique talent.'

'But she can *see*,' Pat persisted. 'She can see the ash, the ruin. How can she not know?'

Flannery shrugged. 'She probably doesn't connect it with her own life. After all, she'll be dead in a couple of years . . . she won't see the war in her real time. She'll only see it this way, as a region into which she can travel. A sort of travelogue of strange lands. She can enter and leave—but we're stuck. It must give you a damn fine sense of security to be able to walk out of one world, into another. God, what I'd give to be able to go back with her.'

'It's been tried,' Masterson pointed out. 'That lizard-head Tellman tried it. And he came walking *back*, covered with ash. He said the truck faded out.'

'Of course it did,' Flannery said mildly. 'She drove it back to Walnut Creek. Back to 1965.'

The unloading had been completed. The members of the colony were toiling up the slope, lugging the cartons to the check-area beneath the ship. Mrs Berthelson strode over to Flannery, accompanied by Professor Crowley.

'Here's the inventory,' she said briskly. 'A few items couldn't be found. You know, I don't stock all that in my store. I have to send out for most of it.'

'We know,' Flannery said, coldly amused. It would be interesting to see a country store that stocked binocular microscopes, turret lathes, frozen packs of antibiotics, high-frequency radio transmitters, advanced text books in all fields.

'So that's why I have to charge you a little dearer,' the old woman continued, the inflexible routine of squeeze. 'On items I bring in—' She examined her inventory, then returned the ten-page typewritten list that Crowley had given her on the previous visit. 'Some of these weren't available. I marked them "back order." That bunch of metals from those laboratories back East—they said maybe later.' A cunning look slid over the ancient gray eyes. 'And they'll be very expensive.'

'It doesn't matter,' Flannery said, handing her the money. 'You can cancel all the back orders.'

At first her face showed nothing. Only a vague inability to understand.

'No more shipments,' Crowley explained. A certain tension faded from them; for the first time, they weren't afraid of her. The old relationship had ended. They weren't dependent on the rusty red truck. They had their shipment; they were ready to leave.

'We're taking off,' Flannery said, grinning starkly. 'We're full up.'

Comprehension came. 'But I placed orders for those things.' Her voice was thin, bleak. Without emotion. 'They'll be shipped to me. I'll have to pay for them.'

'Well,' Flannery said softly, 'isn't that too damn bad.'

Crowley shot him a warning glance. 'Sorry,' he said to the old woman. 'We can't stick around—this place is getting hot. We've got to take off.'

On the withered face, dismay turned to growing wrath. 'You ordered those things! You *have* to take them!' Her shrill voice rose to a screech of fury. 'What am I supposed to do with them?'

As Flannery framed his bitter answer, Pat Shelby intervened. 'Mrs Berthelson,' she said quietly, 'you've done a lot for us, even if you wouldn't help us through the hole into your time. And we're very grateful. If it wasn't for you, we couldn't have got together enough supplies. But we really have to go.' She reached out her hand to touch the frail shoulder, but the old woman jerked furiously away. 'I mean,' Pat finished awkwardly, 'we can't stay any longer, whether we want to or not. Do you see all that black ash? It's radioactive, and more of it sifts down all the time. The toxic level is rising—if we stay any longer it'll start destroying us.'

Mrs Edna Berthelson stood clutching her inventory list. There was an expression on her face that none of the group had ever seen before. The violent spasm of wrath had vanished; now a cold, chill glaze lay over the aged features. Her eyes were like gray rocks, utterly without feeling.

Flannery wasn't impressed. 'Here's your loot,' he said, thrusting out the handful of bills. 'What the hell.' He turned to Crowley. 'Let's toss in the rest. Let's stuff it down her goddamn throat.'

'Shut up,' Crowley snapped.

Flannery sank resentfully back. 'Who are you talking to?'

'Enough's enough.' Crowley, worried and tense, tried to speak to the old woman. 'My God, you can't expect us to stay around here forever, can you?'

There was no response. Abruptly, the old woman turned and strode silently back to her truck.

Masterson and Crowley looked uneasily at each other. 'She sure is mad,' Masterson said apprehensively.

Tellman hurried up, glanced at the old woman getting into her truck, and then bent down to root around in one of the cartons of groceries. Childish greed flushed across his thin face. 'Look,' he gasped. 'Coffee—fifteen pounds of it. Can we open some? Can we get one tin open, to celebrate?'

'Sure,' Crowley said tonelessly, his eyes on the truck. With a muffled roar, the truck turned in a wide arc and rumbled off down the crude platform, toward the ash. It rolled off into the ash, slithered for a short distance, and then faded out. Only the bleak, sun-swept plain of darkness remained.

'Coffee!' Tellman shouted gleefully. He tossed the bright metal can high in the air and clumsily caught it again. 'A celebration! Our last night—last meal on Earth!'

It was true.

As the red pickup truck jogged metallically along the road, Mrs Berthelson scanned 'ahead' and saw that the men were telling the truth. Her thin lips writhed; in her mouth an acid taste of bile rose. She had taken it for granted that they would continue to buy—there was no competition, no other source of supply. But they were leaving. And when they left, there would be no more market.

She would never find a market that satisfactory. It was a perfect market; the group was a perfect customer. In the locked box at the back of the store, hidden down under the reserve sacks of grain, was almost two hundred and fifty thousand dollars. A fortune, taken in over the months, received from the imprisoned colony as it toiled to construct its ship.

And *she* had made it possible. She was responsible for letting them get away after all. Because of her short-sightedness, they were able to escape. She hadn't used her head.

As she drove back to town she meditated calmly, rationally. It was totally because of her: she was the only one who had possessed the power to bring them their supplies. Without her, they were helpless.

Hopefully, she cast about, looking this way and that, peering with her deep inner sense, into the various 'aheads.' There was more than one, of course. The 'aheads' lay like a pattern of squares, an intricate web of worlds into which she could step, if she cared. But all were empty of what she wanted.

All showed bleak plains of black ash, devoid of human habitation. What she wanted was lacking: they were each without customers.

The patterns of 'aheads' were complex. Sequences were connected like beads on a string; there were chains of 'aheads' which formed interwoven links. One step led to the next . . . but not to alternate chains.

Carefully, with great precision, she began the job of searching through each of the chains. There were many of them . . . a virtual infinity of possible 'aheads.' And it was her power to select; she had stepped into that one, the particular chain in which the huddled colony had labored to construct its ship. She had, by entering it, made it manifest. Frozen it into reality. Dredged it up from among the many, from among the multitude of possibilities.

Now she needed to dredge another. That particular 'ahead' had proven unsatisfactory. The market had petered out.

The truck was entering the pleasant town of Walnut Creek, passing bright stores and houses and supermarkets, before she located it. There were so many, and her mind was old . . . but now she had picked it out. And as soon as she found it, she knew it was the one. Her innate business instinct certified it; the particular 'ahead' clicked.

Of the possibilities, this one was unique. The ship was well-built, and thoroughly tested. In 'ahead' after 'ahead' the ship rose, hesitated as automatic machinery locked, and then burst from the jacket of atmosphere, toward the morning star. In a few 'aheads,' the wasted sequences of failure, the ship exploded into white-hot fragments. Those, she ignored; she saw no advantage in that.

In a few 'aheads' the ship failed to take off at all. The turbines lashed; exhaust poured out . . . and the ship remained as it was. But then the men scampered out, and began going over the turbines, searching for the faulty parts. So nothing was gained. In later segments along the chain, in subsequent links, the damage was repaired, and the take-off was satisfactorily completed.

But one chain was correct. Each element, each link, developed perfectly. The pressure-locks closed, and the ship was sealed. The turbines fired, and the ship, with a shudder, rose from the plain of black ash. Three miles up, the rear jets tore loose. The ship floundered, dropped in a screaming dive, and plunged back toward the Earth. Emergency landing jets, designed for Venus, were frantically thrown on. The ship slowed, hovered for an agonizing instant, and then crashed into the heap of rubble that had been Mount Diablo. There the remains of the ship lay, twisted metal sheets, smoking in the dismal silence.

From the ship the men emerged, shaken and mute, to inspect the damage. To begin the miserable, futile task all over again. Collecting supplies, patching the rocket up . . . The old woman smiled to herself.

That was what she wanted. That would do perfectly. And all she had to do—such a little thing—was select that sequence when she made her next trip. When she took her little business trip, the following Saturday.

Crowley lay half buried in the black ash, pawing feebly at a deep gash in his cheek. A broken tooth throbbed. A thick ooze of blood dripped into his mouth, the hot salty taste of his own body-fluids leaking helplessly out. He tried to move his leg, but there was no sensation. Broken. His mind was too dazed, too bewildered with despair, to comprehend.

Somewhere in the half-darkness, Flannery stirred. A woman groaned; scattered among the rocks and buckled sections of the ship lay the injured and dying. An upright shape rose, stumbled, and pitched over. An artificial light flickered. It was Tellman, making his way clumsily over the tattered remains of their world. He gaped foolishly at Crowley; his glasses hung from one ear and part of his lower jaw was missing. Abruptly he collapsed face-forward into a smoking mound of supplies. His skinny body twitched aimlessly.

Crowley managed to pull himself to his knees. Masterson was bending over him, saying something again and again.

'I'm all right,' Crowley rasped.

'We're down. Wrecked.'

'I know.'

On Masterson's shattered face glittered the first stirrings of hysteria. 'Do you think—'

'No,' Crowley muttered. 'It isn't possible.'

Masterson began to giggle. Tears streaked the grime of his cheeks; drops of thick moisture dripped down his neck into his charred collar. 'She did it. She fixed us. She wants us to stay here.'

'No,' Crowley repeated. He shut out the thought. It couldn't be. It just couldn't. 'We'll get away,' he said. 'We'll assemble the remains—start over.'

'She'll be back,' Masterson quavered. 'She knows we'll be here waiting for her. Customers!'

'No,' Crowley said. He didn't believe it; he made himself not believe it. 'We'll get away. We've *got* to get away!'

THE MOLD OF YANCY

Leon Sipling groaned and pushed away his work papers. In an organization of thousands he was the only employee not putting out. Probably he was the only yance-man on Callisto not doing his job. Fear, and the quick pluckings of desperation, made him reach up and wave on the audio circuit to Babson, the over-all office controller.

'Say,' Sipling said hoarsely, 'I think I'm stuck, Bab. How about running the gestalt through, up to my spot? Maybe I can pick up the rhythm . . .' He grinned weakly. 'The hum of other creative minds.'

After a speculative moment, Babson reached for the impulse synapsis, his massive face unsympathetic. 'You holding up progress, Sip? This has to be integrated with the daily by six tonight. The schedule calls for the works to be on the vidlines during the dinner-hour stretch.'

The visual side of the gestalt had already begun to form on the wall screen; Sipling turned his attention to it, grateful of a chance to escape Babson's cold glare.

The screen showed a 3-D of Yancy, the usual three quarter view, from the waist up. John Edward Yancy in his faded workshirt, sleeves rolled up, arms brown and furry. A middle-aged man in his late fifties, his face sunburned, neck slightly red, a good-natured smile on his face, squinting because he was looking into the sun. Behind Yancy was a still of his yard, his garage, his flower garden, lawn, the back of his neat little white plastic house. Yancy grinned at Sipling: a neighbor pausing in the middle of a summer day, perspiring from the heat and the exertion of mowing his lawn, about to launch into a few harmless remarks about the weather, the state of the planet, the condition of the neighborhood.

'Say,' Yancy said, in the audio phones propped up on Sipling's desk. His voice was low, personal. 'The darndest thing happened to my grandson Ralf, the other morning. You know how Ralf is; he's always getting to school half an hour early . . . says he likes to be in his seat before anybody else.'

'That eager-beaver,' Joe Pines, at the next desk, cat-called.

From the screen, Yancy's voice rolled on, confident, amiable, undisturbed. 'Well, Ralf saw this squirrel; it was just sitting there on the sidewalk. He stopped for a minute and watched.' The look on Yancy's face was so real that Sipling almost believed him. He could, almost, see the squirrel and the tow-headed youngest grandson of the Yancy family, the familiar child of the familiar son of the planet's most familiar—and beloved—person.

'This squirrel,' Yancy explained, in his homey way, 'was collecting nuts. And by golly, this was just the other day, only the middle of June. And here was this little squirrel—' with his hands he indicated the size, 'collecting these nuts and carrying them off for winter.'

And then, the amused, anecdote-look on Yancy's face faded. A serious, thoughtful look replaced it: the meaningful-look. His blue eyes darkened (good color work). His jaw became more square, more imposing (good dummy-switch by the android crew). Yancy seemed older, more solemn and mature, more impressive. Behind him, the garden-scene had been jerked and a slightly different backdrop filtered in; Yancy now stood firmly planted in a cosmic landscape, among mountains and winds and huge old forests.

'I got to thinking,' Yancy said, and his voice was deeper, slower. 'There was that little squirrel. How did he know winter was coming? There he was, working away, getting prepared for it.' Yancy's voice rose. 'Preparing for a winter he'd never seen.'

Sipling stiffened and prepared *himself*; it was coming. At his desk, Joe Pines grinned and yelled: 'Get set!'

'That squirrel,' Yancy said solemnly, 'had faith. No, he never saw any sign of winter. But he knew winter was coming.' The firm jaw moved; one hand came slowly up . . .

And then the image stopped. It froze, immobile, silent. No words came from it; abruptly the sermon ended, in the middle of a paragraph.

'That's it,' Babson said briskly, filtering the Yancy out. 'Help you any?'

Sipling pawed jerkily at his work papers. 'No,' he admitted, 'actually it doesn't. But—I'll get it worked out.'

'I hope so.' Babson's face darkened ominously and his small mean eyes seemed to grow smaller. 'What's the matter with you? Home problems?'

'I'll be okay,' Sipling muttered, sweating. 'Thanks.'

On the screen a faint impression of Yancy remained, still poised at the word *coming*. The rest of the gestalt was in Sipling's head: the continuing slice of words and gestures hadn't been worked out and fed to the composite. Sipling's contribution was missing, so the entire gestalt was stopped cold in its tracks.

'Say,' Joe Pines said uneasily, 'I'll be glad to take over, today. Cut your desk out of the circuit and I'll cut myself in.'

'Thanks,' Sipling muttered, 'but I'm the only one who can get this damn part. It's the central gem.'

'You ought to take a rest. You've been working too hard.'

'Yes,' Sipling agreed, on the verge of hysteria. 'I'm a little under the weather.'

That was obvious: everybody in the office could see that. But only Sipling knew why. And he was fighting with all his strength to keep from screaming out the reason at the top of his lungs.

Basic analysis of the political milieu at Callisto was laid out by Niplan computing apparatus at Washington, DC; but the final evaluations were done by human technicians. The Washington computers could ascertain that the Callisto political structure was moving toward a totalitarian make-up, but they couldn't say what

THE MOLD OF YANCY

that indicated. Human beings were required to class the drift as malign.

'It isn't possible,' Taverner protested. 'There's constant industrial traffic in and out of Callisto; except for the Ganymede syndicate they've got out-planet commerce bottled up. We'd know as soon as anything phony got started.'

'How would we know?' Police Director Kellman inquired.

Taverner indicated the data-sheets, graphs and charts of figures and percentages that covered the walls of the Niplan Police offices. 'It would show up in hundreds of ways. Terrorist raids, political prisons, extermination camps. We'd hear about political recanting, treason, disloyalty . . . all the basic props of a dictatorship.'

'Don't confuse a totalitarian society with a dictatorship,' Kellman said dryly. 'A totalitarian state reaches into every sphere of its citizens' lives, forms their opinions on every subject. The government can be a dictatorship, *or* a parliament, *or* an elected president, *or* a council of priests. That doesn't matter.'

'All right,' Taverner said, mollified. 'I'll go. I'll take a team there and see what they're doing.'

'Can you make yourselves look like Callistotes?'

'What are they like?'

'I'm not sure,' Kellman admitted thoughtfully, with a glance at the elaborate wall charts. 'But whatever it is, they're all beginning to turn out alike.'

Among its passengers the interplan commercial liner that settled down at Callisto carried Peter Taverner, his wife, and their two children. With a grimace of concern, Taverner made out the shapes of local officials waiting at the exit hatch. The passengers were going to be carefully screened; as the ramp descended, the clot of officials moved forward.

Taverner got to his feet and collected his family. 'Ignore them,' he told Ruth. 'Our papers will get us by.'

Expertly prepared documents identified him as a speculator in nonferric metals, looking for a wholesale outlet to handle his jobbing. Callisto was a clearing-point for land and mineral operations; a constant flood of wealth-hungry entrepreneurs streamed back and forth, carting raw materials from the underdeveloped moons, hauling mining equipment from the inner planets.

Cautiously, Taverner arranged his topcoat over his arm. A heavyset man, in his middle thirties, he could have passed for a successful business operator. His double-breasted business suit was expensive, but conservative. His big shoes were brightly shined. All things considered, he'd probably get by. As he and his family moved toward the exit ramp, they presented a perfect and exact imitation of the out-planet business-class.

'State your business,' a green-uniformed official demanded, pencil poised. I-d tabs were being checked, photographed, recorded. Brain pattern comparisons were being made: the usual routine.

'Nonferric enterprises,' Taverner began, but a second official cut him abruptly off.

'You're the third cop this morning. What's biting you people on Terra?' The official eyed Taverner intently. 'We're getting more cops than ministers.'

Trying to maintain his poise, Taverner answered evenly: 'I'm here to take a rest. Acute alcoholism—nothing official.'

'That's what your cohorts said.' The official grinned humorously. 'Well, what's one more Terran cop?' He slid the lockbars aside and waved Taverner and his family through. 'Welcome to Callisto. Have fun—enjoy yourselves. Fastest-growing moon in the system.'

'Practically a planet,' Taverner commented ironically.

'Any day now.' The official examined some reports. 'According to our friends in your little organization, you've been pasting up wall graphs and charts about us. Are we that important?'

'Academic interest,' Taverner said; if three spots had been made, then the whole team had been netted. The local authorities were obviously primed to detect infiltration ... the realization chilled him.

But they were letting him through. Were they *that* confident?

Things didn't look good. Peering around for a cab, he grimly prepared to undertake the business of integrating the scattered team members into a functioning whole.

That evening, at the Stay-Lit bar on the main street of the commercial district of town, Taverner met with his two team members. Hunched over their whiskey sours, they compared notes.

'I've been here almost twelve hours,' Eckmund stated, gazing impassively at the rows of bottles in the gloomy depths of the bar. Cigar smoke hovered in the air; the automatic music box in the corner banged away metallically. 'I've been walking around town, looking at things, making observations.'

'Me,' Dorser said, 'I've been at the tape-library. Getting official myth, comparing it to Callistote reality. And talking to the scholars —educated people hanging around the scanning rooms.'

Taverner sipped his drink. 'Anything of interest?'

'You know the primitive rule-of-thumb test,' Eckmund said wryly. 'I loafed around on a slum street corner until I got in a conversation with some people waiting for a bus. I started knocking the authorities: complaining about the bus service, the sewage disposal, taxes, everything. They chimed right in. Heartily. No hesitation. And no fear.'

'The legal government,' Dorser commented, 'is set up in the usual archaic fashion. Two-party system, one a little more conservative than the other—no fundamental difference of course. But both elect candidates at open primaries, ballots circulated to all registered voters.' A spasm of amusement touched him. 'This is a model democracy. I read the text books. Nothing but idealistic slogans: freedom of speech, assembly, religion—the works. Same old grammar school stuff.'

The three of them were temporarily silent.

'There are jails,' Taverner said slowly. 'Every society has law violations.'

'I visited one,' Eckmund said, belching. 'Petty thieves, murderers, claim-jumpers, strong-arm hoods—the usual.'

THE MOLD OF YANCY

'No political prisoners?'

'No.' Eckmund raised his voice. 'We might as well discuss this at the top of our lungs. Nobody cares—the authorities don't care.'

'Probably after we're gone they'll clap a few thousand people into prison,' Dorser murmured thoughtfully.

'My God,' Eckmund retorted, 'people can leave Callisto any time they want. If you're operating a police state you have to keep your borders shut. And these borders are wide open. People pour in and out.'

'Maybe it's a chemical in the drinking water,' Dorser suggested.

'How the hell can they have a totalitarian society without terrorism?' Eckmund demanded rhetorically. 'I'll swear to it—there are no thought-control cops here. There is absolutely no fear.'

'Somehow, pressure is being exerted,' Taverner persisted.

'Not by cops,' Dorser said emphatically. 'Not by force and brutality. Not by illegal arrest and imprisonment and forced labor.'

'If this were a police state,' Eckmund said thoughtfully, 'there'd be some kind of resistance movement. Some sort of "subversive" group trying to overthrow the authorities. But in this society you're free to complain; you can buy time on the TV and radio stations, you can buy space in the newspapers—anything you want.' He shrugged. 'So how can there be a clandestine resistance movement? It's silly.'

'Nevertheless,' Taverner said, 'these people are living in a one-party society with a party line, with an official ideology. They show the effects of a carefully controlled totalitarian state. They're guinea pigs—whether they realize it or not.'

'Wouldn't they realize it?'

Baffled, Taverner shook his head. 'I would have thought so. There must be some mechanism we don't understand.'

'It's all open. We can look everything over.'

'We must be looking for the wrong thing.' Idly, Taverner gazed at the television screen above the bar. The nude girlie song-and-dance routine had ended; now the features of a man faded into view. A genial, round-faced man in his fifties, with guileless blue

THE MOLD OF YANCY

eyes, an almost childish twitch to his lips, a fringe of brown hair playing around his slightly prominent ears.

'Friends,' the TV image rumbled, 'it's good to be with you again, tonight. I thought I might have a little chat with you.'

'A commercial,' Dorser said, signalling the bartending machine for another drink.

'Who is that?' Taverner asked curiously.

'That kindly-looking geezer?' Eckmund examined his notes. 'A sort of popular commentator. Name of Yancy.'

'Is he part of the government?'

'Not that I know of. A kind of home-spun philosopher. I picked up a biography of him on a magazine stand.' Eckmund passed the gaily-colored pamphlet to his boss. 'Totally ordinary man, as far as I can see. Used to be a soldier; in the Mars–Jupiter War he distinguished himself—battlefield commission. Rose to the rank of major.' He shrugged indifferently. 'A sort of talking almanac. Pithy sayings on every topic. Wise old saws: how to cure a chest cold. What the trouble is back on Terra.'

Taverner examined the booklet. 'Yes, I saw his picture around.'

'Very popular figure. Loved by the masses. Man of the people—speaks for them. When I was buying cigarettes I noticed he endorses one particular brand. Very popular brand, now; just about driven the others off the market. Same with beer. The Scotch in this glass is probably the brand Yancy endorses. The same with tennis balls. Only he doesn't play tennis—he plays croquet. All the time, every weekend.' Accepting his fresh drink Eckmund finished, 'So now everybody plays croquet.'

'How can croquet be a planet-wide sport?' Taverner demanded.

'This isn't a planet,' Dorser put in. 'It's a pipsqueak moon.'

'Not according to Yancy,' Eckmund said. 'We're supposed to think of Callisto as a planet.'

'How?' Taverner asked.

'Spiritually, it's a planet. Yancy likes people to take a spiritual view of matters. He's strong on God and honesty in government and being hard-working and clean-cut. Warmed-over truisms.'

The expression on Taverner's face hardened. 'Interesting,' he murmured. 'I'll have to drop by and meet him.'

'Why? He's the dullest, most mediocre man you could dream up.'

'Maybe,' Taverner answered, 'that's why I'm interested.'

Babson, huge and menacing, met Taverner at the entrance of the Yancy Building. 'Of course you can meet Mr Yancy. But he's a busy man—it'll take a while to squeeze in an appointment. Everybody wants to meet Mr Yancy.'

Taverner was unimpressed. 'How long do I have to wait?'

As they crossed the main lobby to the elevators, Babson made a computation. 'Oh, say four months.'

'Four *months*!'

'John Yancy is just about the most popular man alive.'

'Around here, maybe,' Taverner commented angrily, as they entered the packed elevator. 'I never heard of him before. If he's got so much on the ball, why isn't he piped all around Niplan?'

'Actually,' Babson admitted, in a hoarse, confidential whisper, 'I can't imagine what people see in Yancy. As far as I'm concerned he's just a big bag of wind. But people around here enjoy him. After all, Callisto is—provincial. Yancy appeals to a certain type of rural mind—to people who like their world simple. I'm afraid Terra would be too sophisticated for Yancy.'

'Have you tried?'

'Not yet,' Babson said. Reflectively, he added: 'Maybe later.'

While Taverner was pondering the meaning of the big man's words, the elevator ceased climbing. The two of them stepped off into a luxurious, carpeted hall, illuminated by recessed lights. Babson pushed open a door, and they entered a large, active office.

Inside, a screening of a recent Yancy gestalt was in progress. A group of yance-men watched it silently, faces alert and critical. The gestalt showed Yancy sitting at his old-fashioned oak desk, in his study. It was obvious that he had been working on some philosophical thoughts: spread out over the desk were books and papers.

On Yancy's face was a thoughtful expression; he sat with his hand against his forehead, features screwed up into a solemn study of concentration.

'This is for next Sunday morning,' Babson explained.

Yancy's lips moved, and he spoke. 'Friends,' he began, in his deep, personal, friendly, man-to-man voice, 'I've been sitting here at my desk—well, about the way you're sitting around your living rooms.' A switch in camera work occurred; it showed the open door of Yancy's study. In the living room was the familiar figure of Yancy's sweet-faced middle-aged homey wife; she was sitting on the comfortable sofa, primly sewing. On the floor their grandson Ralf played the familiar game of jacks. The family dog snoozed in the corner.

One of the watching yance-men made a note on his pad. Taverner glanced at him curiously, baffled.

'Of course, I was in there with them,' Yancy continued, smiling briefly. 'I was reading the funnies to Ralf. He was sitting on my knee.' The background faded, and a momentary phantom scene of Yancy sitting with his grandson on his knee floated into being. Then the desk and the book-lined study returned. 'I'm mighty grateful for my family,' Yancy revealed. 'In these times of stress, it's my family that I turn to, as my pillar of strength.' Another notation was made by a watching yance-man.

'Sitting here, in my study, this wonderful Sunday morning,' Yancy rumbled on, 'I realize how lucky we are to be alive, and to have this lovely planet, and the fine cities and houses, all the things God has given us to enjoy. But we've got to be careful. We've got to make sure we don't lose these things.'

A change had come over Yancy. It seemed to Taverner that the image was subtly altering. It wasn't the same man; the good humor was gone. This was an older man, and larger. A firm-eyed father, speaking to his children.

'My friends,' Yancy intoned, 'there are forces that could weaken this planet. Everything we've built up for our loved ones, for our children, *could be taken away from us overnight*. We must learn to be vigilant. We must protect our liberties, our possessions, our way of life. If we become divided, and fall to bickering among each other, we will be easy prey for our enemies. We must work together, my friends.

'That's what I've been thinking about this Sunday morning. *Cooperation. Teamwork.* We've got to be secure, and to be secure, we must be one united people. That's the key, my friends, the key to a more abundant life.' Pointing out the window at the lawn and garden, Yancy said: 'You know, I was . . .'

The voice trailed off. The image froze. Full room lights came on, and the watching yance-men moved into muttering activity.

'Fine,' one of them said. 'So far, at least. But where's the rest?'

'Sipling, again,' another answered. 'His slice still hasn't come through. What's wrong with that guy?'

Scowling, Babson detached himself. 'Pardon me,' he said to Taverner. 'I'll have to excuse myself—technical matters. You're free to look around, if you care to. Help yourself to any of the literature—anything you want.'

'Thanks,' Taverner said uncertainly. He was confused; everything *seemed* harmless, even trivial. But something basic was wrong.

Suspiciously, he began to prowl.

It was obvious that John Yancy had pontificated on every known subject. A Yancy opinion on every conceivable topic was available . . . modern art, or garlic in cooking, or the use of intoxicating beverages, or eating meat, or socialism, or war, or education, or open-front dresses on women, or high taxes, or atheism, or divorce, or patriotism—every shade and nuance of opinion possible.

Was there any subject that Yancy *hadn't* expressed himself on?

Taverner examined the voluminous tapes that lined the walls of the offices. Yancy's utterances had run into billions of tape feet . . . could one man have an opinion on everything in the universe?

Choosing a tape at random, he found himself being addressed on the topic of table manners.

'You know,' the miniature Yancy began, his voice tinny in Taverner's ears, 'at dinner the other night I happened to notice how my grandson Ralf was cutting his steak.' Yancy grinned at the viewer, as an image of the six-year-old boy sawing grimly away floated briefly into sight. 'Well, I got to thinking, there was Ralf working away at that steak, not having any luck with it. And it seemed to me—'

Taverner snapped the tape off and returned it to the slot. Yancy had definite opinions on everything ... or *were* they so definite?

A strange suspicion was growing in him. On some topics, yes. On minor issues, Yancy had exact rules, specific maxims drawn from mankind's rich storehouse of folklore. But major philosophical and political issues were something else again.

Getting out one of the many tapes listed under War, Taverner ran it through at random.

'... I'm against war,' Yancy pronounced angrily. 'And I ought to know; I've done my share of fighting.'

There followed a montage of battle scenes: the Jupiter–Mars War in which Yancy had distinguished himself by his bravery, his concern for his comrades, his hatred of the enemy, his variety of proper emotions.

'But,' Yancy continued staunchly, 'I feel a planet must be strong. We must not surrender ourselves meekly ... weakness invites attack and fosters aggression. By being weak we promote war. We must gird ourselves and protect those we love. With all my heart and soul I'm against useless wars; but I say again, as I've said many times before, a man must come forward and fight a *just* war. He must not shrink from his responsibility. War is a terrible thing. But sometimes we must ...'

As he restored the tape, Taverner wondered just what the hell Yancy *had* said. What were his views on war? They took up a hundred separate reels of tape; Yancy was always ready to hold forth on such vital and grandiose subjects as War, the Planet, God, Taxation. But did he *say* anything?

A cold chill crawled up Taverner's spine. On specific—and

trivial—items there were absolute opinions: dogs are better than cats, grapefruit is too sour without a dash of sugar, it's good to get up early in the morning, too much drinking is bad. But on big topics . . . an empty vacuum, filled with the vacant roll of high-sounding phrases. A public that agreed with Yancy on war and taxes and God and planet agreed with absolutely nothing. And with everything.

On topics of importance, they had no opinion at all. They only *thought* they had an opinion.

Rapidly, Taverner scanned tapes on various major subjects. It was the same all down the line. With one sentence Yancy gave; with the next he took away. The total effect was a neat cancellation, a skillful negation. But the viewer was left with the illusion of having consumed a rich and varied intellectual feast. It was amazing. And it was professional: the ends were tied up too slickly to be mere accident.

Nobody was as harmless and vapid as John Edward Yancy. He was just too damn good to be true.

Sweating, Taverner left the main reference room and poked his way toward the rear offices, where busy yance-men worked away at their desks and assembly tables. Activity whirred on all sides. The expression on the faces around him was benign, harmless, almost bored. The same friendly, trivial expression that Yancy himself displayed.

Harmless—and in its harmlessness, diabolical. And there wasn't a damn thing he could do. If people liked to listen to John Edward Yancy, if they wanted to model themselves after him—what could the Niplan Police do about it?

What crime was being committed?

No wonder Babson didn't care if the police prowled around. No wonder the authorities had freely admitted them. There weren't any political jails or labor gangs or concentration camps . . . there didn't have to be.

Torture chambers and extermination camps were needed only when persuasion failed. And persuasion was working perfectly. A police state, rule by terror, came about when the totalitarian apparatus began to break down. The earlier totalitarian societies had been incomplete; the authorities hadn't really gotten into every sphere of life. But techniques of communication had improved.

The first really successful totalitarian state was being realized before his eyes: harmless and trivial, it emerged. And the last stage—nightmarish, but perfectly logical—was when all the new-born boys were happily and voluntarily named John Edward.

Why not? They already lived, acted, and thought like John Edward. And there was Mrs Margaret Ellen Yancy, for the women. She had her full range of opinions, too; she had her kitchen, her taste in clothes, her little recipes and advice, for all the women to imitate.

There were even Yancy children for the youth of the planet to imitate. The authorities hadn't overlooked anything.

Babson strolled over, a genial expression on his face. 'How's it going, officer?' he chuckled wetly, putting his hand on Taverner's shoulder.

'Fine,' Taverner managed to answer; he evaded the hand.

'You like our little establishment?' There was genuine pride in Babson's thick voice. 'We do a good job. An artistic job—we have real standards of excellence.'

Shaking with helpless anger, Taverner plunged out of the office and into the hall. The elevator took too long; furiously, he turned toward the stairs. He had to get out of the Yancy Building; he had to get away.

From the shadows of the hall a man appeared, face pale and taut. 'Wait. Can—I talk to you?'

Taverner pushed past him. 'What do you want?'

'You're from the Terran Niplan Police? I—' The man's Adam's apple bobbed. 'I work here. My name's Sipling, Leon Sipling. I have to do something—I can't stand it anymore.'

'Nothing can be done,' Taverner told him. 'If they want to be like Yancy—'

'But there isn't any Yancy,' Sipling broke in, his thin face twitching spasmodically. 'We made him up . . . we invented him.'

Taverner halted. 'You *what?*'

'I've decided.' Voice quavering excitedly, Sipling rushed on: 'I'm going to do something—and I know exactly what.' Catching hold of Taverner's sleeve he grated: 'You've got to help me. I can stop all this, but I can't do it alone.'

In Leon Sipling's attractive, well-furnished living room, the two of them sat drinking coffee and watching their children scramble around on the floor, playing games. Sipling's wife and Ruth Taverner were in the kitchen, drying the dishes.

'Yancy is a synthesis,' Sipling explained. 'A sort of composite person. No such individual actually exists. We drew on basic prototypes from sociological records; we based the gestalt on various typical persons. So it's true to life. But we stripped off what we didn't want, and intensified what we did want.' Broodingly, he added: 'There could be a Yancy. There are a lot of Yancy-like people. In fact, that's the problem.'

'You deliberately set out with the idea of remolding people along Yancy's line?' Taverner inquired.

'I can't precisely say what the idea is, at top level. I was an ad writer for a mouth wash company. The Callisto authorities hired me and outlined what they wanted me to do. I've had to guess as to the purpose of the project.'

'By authorities, you mean the governing council?'

Sipling laughed sharply. 'I mean the trading syndicates that own this moon: lock, stock, and barrel. But we're not supposed to call it a moon. It's a planet.' His lips twitched bitterly. 'Apparently, the authorities have a big program built up. It involves absorbing their trade rivals on Ganymede—when that's done, they'll have the out-planets sewed up tight.'

'They can't get at Ganymede without open war,' Taverner protested. 'The Medean companies have their own population behind them.' And then it dawned. 'I see,' he said softly. 'They'd actually start a war. It would be worth a war, to them.'

'You're damn right it would. And to start a war, they have to get the public lined up. Actually, the people here have nothing to gain. A war would wipe out all the small operators—it would concentrate power in fewer hands—and they're few enough already. To get the eighty million people here behind the war, they need an indifferent, sheep-like public. *And they're getting that.* When this Yancy campaign is finished, the people here on Callisto will accept anything. Yancy does all their thinking for them. He tells them how to wear their hair. What games to play. He tells the jokes the men repeat in their back rooms. His wife whips up the meal they all have for dinner. All over this little world—millions of duplicates of Yancy's day. Whatever he does, whatever he believes. We've been conditioning the public for eleven straight years. The important thing is the unvarying monotony of it. A whole generation is growing up looking to Yancy for an answer to everything.'

'It's a big business, then,' Taverner observed. 'This project of creating and maintaining Yancy.'

'Thousands of people are involved in just writing the material. You only saw the first stage—and it goes into every city. Tapes, films, books, magazines, posters, pamphlets, dramatic visual and audio shows, plants in the newspapers, sound trucks, kids' comic strips, word-of-mouth report, elaborate ads . . . the works. A steady stream of Yancy.' Picking up a magazine from the coffee table he indicated the lead article. '"How is John Yancy's Heart?" Raises the question of what would we do without Yancy? Next week, an article on Yancy's stomach.' Acidly, Sipling finished: 'We know a million approaches. We turn it out of every pore. We're called yance-men; it's a new art-form.'

'How do you—the corps, feel about Yancy?'

'He's a big sack of hot air.'

'None of you is convinced?'

'Even Babson has to laugh. And Babson is at the top; after him come the boys who sign the checks. God, if we ever started believing in Yancy . . . if we got started thinking that trash *meant* something—' An expression of acute agony settled over Sipling's face. 'That's it. That's why I can't stand it.'

'Why?' Taverner asked, deeply curious. His throat-mike was taking it all in, relaying it back to the home office at Washington. 'I'm interested in finding out why you broke away.'

Sipling bent down and called his son. 'Mike, stop playing and come on over here.' To Taverner he explained: 'Mike's nine years old. Yancy's been around as long as he's been alive.'

Mike came dully over. 'Yes, sir?'

'What kind of marks do you get in school?' his father asked.

The boy's chest stuck out proudly; he was a clear-eyed little miniature of Leon Sipling. 'All A's and B's.'

'He's a smart kid,' Sipling said to Taverner. 'Good in arithmetic, geography, history, all that stuff.' Turning to the boy he said: 'I'm going to ask you some questions; I want this gentleman to hear your answers. Okay?'

'Yes, sir,' the boy said obediently.

His thin face grim, Sipling said to his son: 'I want to know what you think about war. You've been told about war in school; you know about all the famous wars in history. Right?'

'Yes, sir. We learned about the American Revolution, and the First Global War, and then the Second Global War, and then the First Hydrogen War, and the War between the colonists on Mars and Jupiter.'

'To the schools,' Sipling explained tightly to Taverner, 'we distribute Yancy material—educational subsidies in packet form. Yancy takes children through history, explains the meaning of it all. Yancy explains natural science. Yancy explains good posture and astronomy and every other thing in the universe. But I never thought my own son . . .' His voice trailed off unhappily, then picked up life. 'So you know all about war. Okay, what do you think of war?'

Promptly, the boy answered: 'War is bad. War is the most terrible thing there is. It almost destroyed mankind.'

Eying his son intently, Sipling demanded: 'Did anybody tell you to say that?'

The boy faltered uncertainly. 'No, sir.'

THE MOLD OF YANCY

'You really believe those things?'

'Yes, sir. It's true, isn't it? Isn't war bad?'

Sipling nodded. 'War is bad. But what about *just* wars?'

Without hesitation the boy answered: 'We have to fight just wars, of course.'

'Why?'

'Well, we have to protect our way of life.'

'Why?'

Again, there was no hesitation in the boy's reedy answer. 'We can't let them walk over us, sir. That would encourage aggressive war. We can't permit a world of brute power. We have to have a world of–' He searched for the exact word. 'A world of *law*.'

Wearily, half to himself, Sipling commented: 'I wrote those meaningless, contradictory words myself, eight years ago.' Pulling himself together with a violent effort he asked: 'So war is bad. But we have to fight just wars. Well, maybe this–*planet*, Callisto, will get into a war with . . . let's pick Ganymede, at random.' He was unable to keep the harsh irony from his voice. 'Just at random. Now, we're at war with Ganymede. Is it a *just* war? Or only a war?'

This time, there was no answer. The boy's smooth face was screwed up in a bewildered, struggling frown.

'No answer?' Sipling inquired icily.

'Why, uh,' the boy faltered. 'I mean . . .' He glanced up hopefully. 'When the time comes won't somebody say?'

'Sure,' Sipling choked. 'Somebody will say. Maybe even Mr Yancy.'

Relief flooded the boy's face. 'Yes, sir. Mr Yancy will say.' He retreated back toward the other children. 'Can I go now?'

As the boy scampered back to his game, Sipling turned miserably to Taverner. 'You know what game they're playing? It's called Hippo-Hoppo. Guess whose grandson just loves it. Guess who invented the game.'

There was silence.

'What do you suggest?' Taverner asked. 'You said you thought something could be done.'

A cold expression appeared on Sipling's face, a flash of deeply-felt cunning. 'I know the project . . . I know how it can be pried apart. But somebody has to stand with a gun at the head of the authorities. In nine years I've come to see the essential key to the Yancy character . . . the key to the new type of person we're growing, here. It's simple. It's the element that makes that person malleable enough to be led around.'

'I'll bite,' Taverner said patiently, hoping the line to Washington was good and clear.

'All Yancy's beliefs are insipid. The key is *thinness*. Every part of his ideology is diluted: nothing excessive. We've come as close as possible to *no* beliefs . . . you've noticed that. Wherever possible we've cancelled attitudes out, left the person apolitical. Without a viewpoint.'

'Sure,' Taverner agreed. 'But with the illusion of a viewpoint.'

'All aspects of personality have to be controlled; we want the total person. So a specific attitude has to exist for each concrete question. In every respect, our rule is: *Yancy believes the least troublesome possibility*. The most shallow. The simple, effortless view, the view that fails to go deep enough to stir any real thought.'

Taverner got the drift. 'Good solid lulling views.' Excitedly he hurried on, 'But if an extreme original view got in, one that took real effort to work out, something that was hard to live . . .'

'Yancy plays croquet. So everybody fools around with a mallet.' Sipling's eyes gleamed. 'But suppose Yancy had a preference for— Kriegspiel.'

'For *what?*'

'Chess played on two boards. Each player has his own board, with a complete set of men. He never sees the other board. A moderator sees both; he tells each player when he's taken a piece, or lost a piece, or moved into an occupied square, or made an impossible move, or checked, or is in check himself.'

'I see,' Taverner said quickly. 'Each player tries to infer his opponent's location on the board. He plays blind. Lord, it would take every mental faculty possible.'

'The Prussians taught their officers military strategy that way. It's more than a game: it's a cosmic wrestling match. What if Yancy sat down in the evening with his wife and grandson, and played a nice lively six-hour game of Kriegspiel? Suppose his favorite books—instead of being western gun-toting anachronisms—were Greek tragedy? Suppose his favorite piece of music was Bach's *Art of the Fugue*, not "My Old Kentucky Home"?'

'I'm beginning to get the picture,' Taverner said, as calmly as possible. 'I think we can help.'

Babson squeaked once. 'But this is—illegal!'

'Absolutely,' Taverner acknowledged. 'That's why we're here.' He waved the squad of Niplan secret-servicemen into the offices of the Yancy Building, ignoring the stunned workers sitting bolt-upright at their desks. Into his throat-mike he said, 'How's it coming with the big-shots?'

'Medium,' Kellman's faint voice came, strengthened by the relay system between Callisto and Earth. 'Some slipped out of bounds to their various holdings, of course. But the majority never thought we'd take action.'

'You can't!' Babson bleated, his great face hanging down in wattles of white dough. 'What have we done? What law—'

'I think,' Taverner interrupted, 'we can get you on purely commercial grounds alone. You've used the name Yancy to endorse various manufactured products. There's no such person. That's a violation of statutes governing ethical presentation of advertising.'

Babson's mouth closed with a snap, then slid feebly open. 'No—such—person? But everybody knows John Yancy. Why, he's—' Stammering, gesturing, he finished, 'He's everywhere.'

Suddenly a wretched little pistol appeared in his pulpy hand; he was waving it wildly as Dorser stepped up and quietly knocked it skidding across the floor. Babson collapsed into fumbling hysterics.

Disgusted, Dorser clamped handgrapples around him. 'Act like a man,' he ordered. But there was no response; Babson was too far gone to hear him.

Satisfied, Taverner plunged off, past the knot of stunned officials and workers, into the inner offices of the project. Nodding curtly, Taverner made his way up to the desk where Leon Sipling sat surrounded by his work.

The first of the altered gestalts was already flickering through the scanner. Together, the two men stood watching it.

'Well?' Taverner said, when it was done. 'You're the judge.'

'I believe it'll do,' Sipling answered nervously. 'I hope we don't stir up too much . . . it's taken eleven years to build it up; we want to tear it down by degrees.'

'Once the first crack is made, it should start swaying.' Taverner moved toward the door. 'Will you be all right on your own?'

Sipling glanced at Eckmund who lounged at the end of the office, eyes fixed on the uneasily working yance-men. 'I suppose so. Where are you going?'

'I want to watch this as it's released. I want to be around when the public gets its first look at it.' At the door, Taverner lingered. 'It's going to be a big job for you, putting out the gestalt on your own. You may not get much help, for a while.'

Sipling indicated his co-workers; they were already beginning to pick up their tempo where they had left off. 'They'll stay on the job,' he disagreed. 'As long as they get full salaries.'

Taverner walked thoughtfully across the hall to the elevator. A moment later he was on his way downstairs.

At a nearby street corner, a group of people had collected around a public vid-screen. Anticipating the late-afternoon TV cast of John Edward Yancy.

The gestalt began in the regular way. There was no doubt about it: when Sipling wanted to, he could put together a good slice. And in this case he had done practically the whole pie.

In rolled-up shirt sleeves and dirt-stained trousers, Yancy crouched in his garden, a trowel in one hand, straw hat pulled down over his eyes, grinning into the warm glare of the sun. It was

THE MOLD OF YANCY

so real that Taverner could hardly believe no such person existed. But he had watched Sipling's sub-crews laboriously and expertly constructing the thing from the ground up.

'Afternoon,' Yancy rumbled genially. He wiped perspiration from his steaming, florid face and got stiffly to his feet. 'Man,' he admitted, 'it's a hot day.' He indicated a flat of primroses. 'I was setting them out. Quite a job.'

So far so good. The crowd watched impassively, taking their ideological nourishment without particular resistance. All over the moon, in every house, schoolroom, office, on each street corner, the same gestalt was showing. And it would be shown again.

'Yes,' Yancy repeated, 'it's really hot. Too hot for those primroses—they like shade.' A fast pan-up showed he had carefully planted his primroses in the shadows at the base of his garage. 'On the other hand,' Yancy continued, in his smooth, good-natured, over-the-back-fence conversational voice, 'my dahlias need lots of sun.'

The camera leaped to show the dahlias blooming frantically in the blazing sunlight.

Throwing himself down in a striped lawnchair, Yancy removed his straw hat and wiped his brow with a pocket handkerchief. 'So,' he continued genially, 'if anybody asked me which is better, shade or sun, I'd have to reply it depends on whether you're a primrose or a dahlia.' He grinned his famous guileless boyish grin into the camera. 'I guess I must be a primrose—I've had all the sun I can stand for today.'

The audience was taking it in without complaint. An inauspicious beginning, but it was going to have long-term consequences. And Yancy was starting to develop them right now.

His genial grin faded. That familiar look, that awaited serious frown showing that deep thoughts were coming, faded into place. Yancy was going to hold forth: wisdom was on the way. But it was nothing ever uttered by him before.

'You know,' Yancy said slowly, seriously, 'that makes a person do some thinking.' Automatically, he reached for his glass of gin and tonic—a glass which up until now would have contained beer. And the magazine beside it wasn't *Dog Stories Monthly*; it was *The Journal of Psychological Review*. The alteration of peripheral props would sink in subliminally; right now, all conscious attention was riveted on Yancy's words.

'It occurs to me,' Yancy orated, as if the wisdom were fresh and brand-new, arriving just now, 'that some people might maintain that, say, sunlight is *good* and shade is *bad*. But that's down-right silly. Sunlight is good for roses and dahlias, but it would darn well finish off my fuchsias.'

The camera showed his ubiquitous prize fuchsias.

'Maybe you know people like that. They just don't understand that—' And as was his custom, Yancy drew on folklore to make his point. 'That one man's meat,' he stated profoundly, 'is another man's poison. Like for instance, for breakfast I like a couple of eggs done sunny-side up, maybe a few stewed prunes, and a piece of toast. But Margaret, she prefers a bowl of cereal. And Ralf, he won't take either. He likes flapjacks. And the fellow down the street, the one with the big front lawn, he likes a kidney pie and a bottle of stout.'

Taverner winced. Well, they would have to feel their way along. But still the audience stood absorbing it, word after word. The first feeble stirrings of a radical idea: that each person had a different set of values, a unique style of life. That each person might believe, enjoy, and approve of different things.

It would take time, as Sipling said. The massive library of tapes would have to be replaced; injunctions built up in each area would have to be broken down. A new type of thinking was being introduced, starting with a trite observation about primroses. When a nine-year-old-boy wanted to find out if a war was just or unjust, he would have to inquire into his own mind. There would be no ready answer from Yancy; a gestalt was already being prepared on that, showing that every war had been called just by some, unjust by others.

There was one gestalt Taverner wished he could see. But it wouldn't be around for a long time; it would have to wait. Yancy was going to change his taste in art, slowly but steadily. One of these days, the public would learn that Yancy no longer enjoyed pastoral calendar scenes.

That now he preferred the art of that fifteenth-century Dutch master of macabre and diabolical horror, Hieronymus Bosch.

THE MINORITY REPORT

I

The first thought Anderton had when he saw the young man was: *I'm getting bald. Bald and fat and old.* But he didn't say it aloud. Instead, he pushed back his chair, got to his feet, and came resolutely around the side of his desk, his right hand rigidly extended. Smiling with forced amiability, he shook hands with the young man.

'Witwer?' he asked, managing to make this query sound gracious.

'That's right,' the young man said. 'But the name's Ed to you, of course. That is, if you share my dislike for needless formality.' The look on his blond, overly-confident face showed that he considered the matter settled. It would be Ed and John: everything would be agreeably cooperative right from the start.

'Did you have much trouble finding the building?' Anderton asked guardedly, ignoring the too-friendly overture. *Good God, he had to hold on to something.* Fear touched him and he began to sweat. Witwer was moving around the office as if he already owned it— as if he were measuring it for size. Couldn't he wait a couple of days—a decent interval?

'No trouble,' Witwer answered blithely, his hands in his pockets. Eagerly, he examined the voluminous files that lined the wall. 'I'm not coming into your agency blind, you understand. I have quite a few ideas of my own about the way Precrime is run.'

Shakily, Anderton lit his pipe. 'How is it run? I should like to know.'

'Not badly,' Witwer said. 'In fact, quite well.'

Anderton regarded him steadily. 'Is that your private opinion? Or is it just cant?'

Witwer met his gaze guilelessly. 'Private and public. The Senate's pleased with your work. In fact, they're enthusiastic.' He added, 'As enthusiastic as very old men can be.'

Anderton winced, but outwardly he remained impassive. It cost him an effort, though. He wondered what Witwer *really* thought. What was actually going on in that closecropped skull? The young man's eyes were blue, bright—and disturbingly clever. Witwer was nobody's fool. And obviously he had a great deal of ambition.

'As I understand it,' Anderton said cautiously, 'you're going to be my assistant until I retire.'

'That's my understanding, too,' the other replied, without an instant's hesitation.

'Which may be this year, or next year—or ten years from now.' The pipe in Anderton's hand trembled. 'I'm under no compulsion to retire. I founded Precrime and I can stay on here as long as I want. It's purely *my* decision.'

Witwer nodded, his expression still guileless. 'Of course.'

With an effort, Anderton cooled down a trifle. 'I merely wanted to get things straight.'

'From the start,' Witwer agreed. 'You're the boss. What you say goes.' With every evidence of sincerity, he asked: 'Would you care to show me the organization? I'd like to familiarize myself with the general routine as soon as possible.'

As they walked along the busy, yellow-lit tiers of offices, Anderton said: 'You're acquainted with the theory of precrime, of course. I presume we can take that for granted.'

'I have the information publicly available,' Witwer replied. 'With the aid of your precog mutants, you've boldly and successfully abolished the post-crime punitive system of jails and fines. As we all realize, punishment was never much of a deterrent, and could scarcely have afforded comfort to a victim already dead.'

They had come to the descent lift. As it carried them swiftly downward, Anderton said: 'You've probably grasped the basic legalistic drawback to precrime methodology. We're taking in individuals who have broken no law.'

'But they surely will,' Witwer affirmed with conviction.

'Happily they *don't*—because we get them first, before they can commit an act of violence. So the commission of the crime itself is absolute metaphysics. We claim they're culpable. They, on the other hand, eternally claim they're innocent. And, in a sense, they *are* innocent.'

The lift let them out, and they again paced down a yellow corridor. 'In our society we have no major crimes,' Anderton went on, 'but we do have a detention camp full of would-be criminals.'

Doors opened and closed, and they were in the analytical wing. Ahead of them rose impressive banks of equipment—the data-receptors, and the computing mechanisms that studied and restructured the incoming material. And beyond the machinery sat the three precogs, almost lost to view in the maze of wiring.

'There they are,' Anderton said dryly. 'What do you think of them?'

In the gloomy half-darkness the three idiots sat babbling. Every incoherent utterance, every random syllable, was analyzed, compared, reassembled in the form of visual symbols, transcribed on conventional punchcards, and ejected into various coded slots. All day long the idiots babbled, imprisoned in their special high-backed chairs, held in one rigid position by metal bands, and bundles of wiring, clamps. Their physical needs were taken care of automatically. They had no spiritual needs. Vegetable-like, they muttered and dozed and existed. Their minds were dull, confused, lost in shadows.

But not the shadows of today. The three gibbering, fumbling creatures, with their enlarged heads and wasted bodies, were contemplating the future. The analytical machinery was recording prophecies, and as the three precog idiots talked, the machinery carefully listened.

THE MINORITY REPORT

For the first time Witwer's face lost its breezy confidence. A sick, dismayed expression crept into his eyes, a mixture of shame and moral shock. 'It's not—pleasant,' he murmured. 'I didn't realize they were so—' He groped in his mind for the right word, gesticulating. 'So—deformed.'

'Deformed and retarded,' Anderton instantly agreed. 'Especially the girl, there. Donna is forty-five years old. But she looks about ten. The talent absorbs everything; the esp-lobe shrivels the balance of the frontal area. But what do we care? We get their prophecies. They pass on what we need. They don't understand any of it, but *we* do.'

Subdued, Witwer crossed the room to the machinery. From a slot he collected a stack of cards. 'Are these names that have come up?' he asked.

'Obviously.' Frowning, Anderton took the stack from him. 'I haven't had a chance to examine them,' he explained, impatiently concealing his annoyance.

Fascinated, Witwer watched the machinery pop a fresh card into the now empty slot. It was followed by a second—and a third. From the whirring disks came one card after another. 'The precogs must see quite far into the future,' Witwer exclaimed.

'They see a quite limited span,' Anderton informed him. 'One week or two ahead at the very most. Much of their data is worthless to us—simply not relevant to our line. We pass it on to the appropriate agencies. And they in turn trade data with us. Every important bureau has its cellar of treasured *monkeys*.'

'Monkeys?' Witwer stared at him uneasily. 'Oh, yes, I understand. See no evil, speak no evil, et cetera. Very amusing.'

'Very *apt*.' Automatically, Anderton collected the fresh cards which had been turned up by the spinning machinery. 'Some of these names will be totally discarded. And most of the remainder record petty crimes: thefts, income tax evasion, assault, extortion. As I'm sure you know, Precrime has cut down felonies by ninety-nine and decimal point eight percent. We seldom get actual murder or treason. After all, the culprit knows we'll confine him in the detention camp a week before he gets a chance to commit the crime.'

'When was the last time an actual murder was committed?' Witwer asked.

'Five years ago,' Anderton said, pride in his voice.

'How did it happen?'

'The criminal escaped our teams. We had his name—in fact, we had all the details of the crime, including the victim's name. We knew the exact moment, the location of the planned act of violence. But in spite of us he was able to carry it out.' Anderton shrugged. 'After all, we can't get all of them.' He riffled the cards. 'But we do get most.'

'One murder in five years.' Witwer's confidence was returning. 'Quite an impressive record . . . something to be proud of.'

Quietly Anderton said: 'I *am* proud. Thirty years ago I worked out the theory—back in the days when the self-seekers were thinking in terms of quick raids on the stock market. I saw something legitimate ahead—something of tremendous social value.'

He tossed the packet of cards to Wally Page, his subordinate in charge of the monkey block. 'See which ones we want,' he told him. 'Use your own judgment.'

As Page disappeared with the cards, Witwer said thoughtfully: 'It's a big responsibility.'

'Yes, it is,' agreed Anderton. 'If we let one criminal escape—as we did five years ago—we've got a human life on our conscience. We're solely responsible. If we slip up, somebody dies.' Bitterly, he jerked three new cards from the slot. 'It's a public trust.'

'Are you ever tempted to—' Witwer hesitated. 'I mean, some of the men you pick up must offer you plenty.'

'It wouldn't do any good. A duplicate file of cards pops out at Army GHQ. It's check and balance. They can keep their eye on us as continuously as they wish.' Anderton glanced briefly at the top card. 'So even if we wanted to accept a—'

He broke off, his lips tightening.

'What's the matter?' Witwer asked curiously.

Carefully, Anderton folded up the top card and put it away in his pocket. 'Nothing,' he muttered. 'Nothing at all.'

The harshness in his voice brought a flush to Witwer's face. 'You really don't like me,' he observed.

'True,' Anderton admitted. 'I don't. But—'

He couldn't believe he disliked the young man that much. It didn't seem possible: it *wasn't* possible. Something was wrong. Dazed, he tried to steady his tumbling mind.

On the card was his name. Line one—an already accused future murderer! According to the coded punches, Precrime Commissioner John A. Anderton was going to kill a man—and within the next week.

With absolute, overwhelming conviction, he didn't believe it.

II

In the outer office, talking to Page, stood Anderton's slim and attractive young wife, Lisa. She was engaged in a sharp, animated discussion of policy, and barely glanced up as Witwer and her husband entered.

'Hello, darling,' Anderton said.

Witwer remained silent. But his pale eyes flickered slightly as they rested on the brown-haired woman in her trim police uniform. Lisa was now an executive official of Precrime but once, Witwer knew, she had been Anderton's secretary.

Noticing the interest on Witwer's face Anderton paused and reflected. To plant the card in the machines would require an accomplice on the inside—someone who was closely connected with Precrime and had access to the analytical equipment. Lisa was an improbable element. But the possibility did exist.

Of course, the conspiracy could be large-scale and elaborate, involving far more than a 'rigged' card inserted somewhere along the line. The original data itself might have been tampered with. Actually, there was no telling how far back the alteration went.

A cold fear touched him as he began to see the possibilities. His original impulse—to tear open the machines and remove all the data—was uselessly primitive. Probably the tapes agreed with the card: he would only incriminate himself further.

He had approximately twenty-four hours. Then, the Army people would check over their cards and discover the discrepancy. They would find in their files a duplicate of the card he had appropriated. He had only one of two copies, which meant that the folded card in his pocket might just as well be lying on Page's desk in plain view of everyone.

From outside the building came the drone of police cars starting out on their routine round-ups. How many hours would elapse before one of them pulled up in front of *his* house?

'What's the matter, darling?' Lisa asked him uneasily. 'You look as if you've just seen a ghost. Are you all right?'

'I'm fine,' he assured her.

Lisa suddenly seemed to become aware of Ed Witwer's admiring scrutiny. 'Is this gentleman your new co-worker, darling?' she asked.

Warily, Anderton introduced his new associate. Lisa smiled in friendly greeting. Did a covert awareness pass between them? He couldn't tell. God, he was beginning to suspect everybody—not only his wife and Witwer, but a dozen members of his staff.

'Are you from New York?' Lisa asked.

'No,' Witwer replied. 'I've lived most of my life in Chicago. I'm staying at a hotel—one of the big downtown hotels. Wait—I have the name written on a card somewhere.'

While he self-consciously searched his pockets, Lisa suggested: 'Perhaps you'd like to have dinner with us. We'll be working in close cooperation, and I really think we ought to get better acquainted.'

Startled, Anderton backed off. What were the chances of his wife's friendliness being benign, accidental? Witwer would be present the balance of the evening, and would now have an excuse to trail along to Anderton's private residence. Profoundly disturbed, he turned impulsively, and moved toward the door.

'Where are you going?' Lisa asked, astonished.

'Back to the monkey block,' he told her. 'I want to check over some rather puzzling data tapes before the Army sees them.' He was out in the corridor before she could think of a plausible reason for detaining him.

Rapidly, he made his way to the ramp at its far end. He was striding down the outside stairs toward the public sidewalk, when Lisa appeared breathlessly behind him.

'What on earth has come over you?' Catching hold of his arm, she moved quickly in front of him. 'I *knew* you were leaving,' she exclaimed, blocking his way. 'What's wrong with you? Everybody thinks you're—' She checked herself. 'I mean, you're acting so erratically.'

People surged by them—the usual afternoon crowd. Ignoring them, Anderton pried his wife's fingers from his arm. 'I'm getting out,' he told her. 'While there's still time.'

'But—*why?*'

'I'm being framed—deliberately and maliciously. This creature is out to get my job. The Senate is getting at me *through* him.'

Lisa gazed up at him, bewildered. 'But he seems like such a nice young man.'

'Nice as a water moccasin.'

Lisa's dismay turned to disbelief. 'I don't believe it. Darling, all this strain you've been under—' Smiling uncertainly, she faltered: 'It's not really credible that Ed Witwer is trying to frame you. How could he, even if he wanted to? Surely Ed wouldn't—'

'Ed?'

'That's his name, isn't it?'

Her brown eyes flashed in startled, wildly incredulous protest. 'Good heavens, you're suspicious of everybody. You actually believe I'm mixed up with it in some way, don't you?'

He considered. 'I'm not sure.'

She drew closer to him, her eyes accusing. 'That's not true. You really believe it. Maybe you *ought* to go away for a few weeks. You desperately need a rest. All this tension and trauma, a younger man coming in. You're acting paranoiac. Can't you see that? People plotting against you. Tell me, do you have any actual proof?'

Anderton removed his wallet and took out the folded card. 'Examine this carefully,' he said, handing it to her.

The color drained out of her face, and she gave a little harsh, dry gasp.

'The set-up is fairly obvious,' Anderton told her, as levelly as he could. 'This will give Witwer a legal pretext to remove me right now. He won't have to wait until I resign.' Grimly, he added: 'They know I'm good for a few years yet.'

'But–'

'It will end the check and balance system. Precrime will no longer be an independent agency. The Senate will control the police, and after that–' His lips tightened. 'They'll absorb the Army too. Well, it's outwardly logical enough. *Of course* I feel hostility and resentment toward Witwer–*of course* I have a motive.

'Nobody likes to be replaced by a younger man, and find himself turned out to pasture. It's all really quite plausible–except that I haven't the remotest intention of killing Witwer. But I can't prove that. So what can I do?'

Mutely, her face very white, Lisa shook her head. 'I–I don't know. Darling, if only–'

'Right now,' Anderton said abruptly, 'I'm going home to pack my things. That's about as far ahead as I can plan.'

'You're really going to–to try to hide out?'

'I am. As far as the Centaurian-colony planets, if necessary. It's been done successfully before, and I have a twenty-four-hour start.' He turned resolutely. 'Go back inside. There's no point in your coming with me.'

'Did you imagine I would?' Lisa asked huskily.

Startled, Anderton stared at her. 'Wouldn't you?' Then with amazement, he murmured: 'No, I can see you don't believe me. You still think I'm imagining all this.' He jabbed savagely at the card. 'Even with that evidence you still aren't convinced.'

'No,' Lisa agreed quickly, 'I'm not. You didn't look at it closely enough, darling. Ed Witwer's name isn't on it.'

Incredulous, Anderton took the card from her.

'Nobody says you're going to kill Ed Witwer,' Lisa continued rapidly, in a thin, brittle voice. 'The card *must* be genuine, understand? And it has nothing to do with Ed. He's not plotting against you and neither is anybody else.'

Too confused to reply, Anderton stood studying the card. She was right. Ed Witwer was not listed as his victim. On line five, the machine had neatly stamped another name.

LEOPOLD KAPLAN

Numbly, he pocketed the card. He had never heard of the man in his life.

III

The house was cool and deserted, and almost immediately Anderton began making preparations for his journey. While he packed, frantic thoughts passed through his mind.

Possibly he was wrong about Witwer—but how could he be sure? In any event, the conspiracy against him was far more complex than he had realized. Witwer, in the over-all picture, might be merely an insignificant puppet animated by someone else—by some distant, indistinct figure only vaguely visible in the background.

It had been a mistake to show the card to Lisa. Undoubtedly, she would describe it in detail to Witwer. He'd never get off Earth, never have an opportunity to find out what life on a frontier planet might be like.

While he was thus preoccupied, a board creaked behind him. He turned from the bed, clutching a weather-stained winter sports jacket, to face the muzzle of a gray-blue A-pistol.

'It didn't take you long,' he said, staring with bitterness at the tight-lipped, heavyset man in a brown overcoat who stood holding the gun in his gloved hand. 'Didn't she even hesitate?'

The intruder's face registered no response. 'I don't know what you're talking about,' he said. 'Come along with me.'

Startled, Anderton laid down the sports jacket. 'You're not from my agency? You're not a police officer?'

Protesting and astonished, he was hustled outside the house to a waiting limousine. Instantly three heavily armed men closed in behind him. The door slammed and the car shot off down the highway, away from the city. Impassive and remote, the faces around him jogged with the motion of the speeding vehicle as open fields, dark and somber, swept past.

Anderton was still trying futilely to grasp the implications of what had happened, when the car came to a rutted side road, turned off, and descended into a gloomy sub-surface garage. Someone shouted an order. The heavy metal lock grated shut and overhead lights blinked on. The driver turned off the car motor.

'You'll have reason to regret this,' Anderton warned hoarsely, as they dragged him from the car. 'Do you realize who I am?'

'We realize,' the man in the brown overcoat said.

At gun-point, Anderton was marched upstairs, from the clammy silence of the garage into a deep-carpeted hallway. He was, apparently, in a luxurious private residence, set out in the war-devoured rural area. At the far end of the hallway he could make out a room—a book-lined study simply but tastefully furnished. In a circle of lamplight, his face partly in shadows, a man he had never met sat waiting for him.

As Anderton approached, the man nervously slipped a pair of rimless glasses in place, snapped the case shut, and moistened his dry lips. He was elderly, perhaps seventy or older, and under his arm was a slim silver cane. His body was thin, wiry, his attitude curiously rigid. What little hair he had was dusty brown—a carefully-smoothed sheen of neutral color above his pale, bony skull. Only his eyes seemed really alert.

'Is this Anderton?' he inquired querulously, turning to the man in the brown overcoat. 'Where did you pick him up?'

'At his home,' the other replied. 'He was packing—as we expected.'

The man at the desk shivered visibly. 'Packing.' He took off his glasses and jerkily returned them to their case. 'Look here,' he said bluntly to Anderton, 'what's the matter with you? Are you hopelessly insane? How could you kill a man you've never met?'

The old man, Anderton suddenly realized, was Leopold Kaplan.

'First, I'll ask you a question,' Anderton countered rapidly. 'Do you realize what you've done? I'm Commissioner of Police. I can have you sent up for twenty years.'

He was going to say more, but a sudden wonder cut him short.

'*How did you find out?*' he demanded. Involuntarily, his hand went to his pocket, where the folded card was hidden. 'It won't be for another—'

'I wasn't notified through your agency,' Kaplan broke in, with angry impatience. 'The fact that you've never heard of me doesn't surprise me too much. Leopold Kaplan, General of the Army of the Federated Westbloc Alliance.' Begrudgingly, he added. 'Retired, since the end of the Anglo-Chinese War, and the abolishment of AFWA.'

It made sense. Anderton had suspected that the Army processed its duplicate cards immediately, for its own protection. Relaxing somewhat, he demanded: 'Well? You've got me here. What next?'

'Evidently,' Kaplan said, 'I'm not going to have you destroyed, or it would have shown up on one of those miserable little cards. I'm curious about you. It seemed incredible to me that a man of your stature could contemplate the cold-blooded murder of a total stranger. There must be something more here. Frankly, I'm puzzled. If it represented some kind of police strategy—' He shrugged his thin shoulders. 'Surely you wouldn't have permitted the duplicate card to reach us.'

'Unless,' one of his men suggested, 'it's a deliberate plant.'

Kaplan raised his bright, bird-like eyes and scrutinized Anderton. 'What do you have to say?'

'That's exactly what it is,' Anderton said, quick to see the advantage of stating frankly what he believed to be the simple truth. 'The prediction on the card was deliberately fabricated by a clique inside the police agency. The card is prepared and I'm netted. I'm relieved of my authority automatically. My assistant steps in and claims he prevented the murder in the usual efficient Precrime manner. Needless to say, there is no murder or intent to murder.'

'I agree with you that there will be no murder,' Kaplan affirmed grimly. 'You'll be in police custody. I intend to make certain of that.'

Horrified, Anderton protested: 'You're taking me back there? If I'm in custody I'll never be able to prove—'

'I don't care what you prove or don't prove,' Kaplan interrupted. 'All I'm interested in is having you out of the way.' Frigidly, he added: 'For my own protection.'

'He was getting ready to leave,' one of the men asserted.

'That's right,' Anderton said, sweating. 'As soon as they get hold of me I'll be confined in the detention camp. Witwer will take over—lock, stock and barrel.' His face darkened. 'And my wife. They're acting in concert, apparently.'

For a moment Kaplan seemed to waver. 'It's possible,' he conceded, regarding Anderton steadily. Then he shook his head. 'I can't take the chance. If this is a frame against you, I'm sorry. But it's simply not my affair.' He smiled slightly. 'However, I wish you luck.' To the men he said: 'Take him to the police building and turn him over to the highest authority.' He mentioned the name of the acting Commissioner, and waited for Anderton's reaction.

'Witwer!' Anderton echoed, incredulous.

Still smiling slightly, Kaplan turned and clicked on the console radio in the study. 'Witwer has already assumed authority. Obviously, he's going to create quite an affair out of this.'

There was a brief static hum, and then, abruptly, the radio blared out into the room—a noisy professional voice, reading a prepared announcement.

'. . . all citizens are warned not to shelter or in any fashion aid or assist this dangerous marginal individual. The extraordinary circumstance of an escaped criminal at liberty and in a position to commit an act of violence is unique in modern times. All citizens are hereby notified that legal statutes still in force implicate any and all persons failing to cooperate fully with the police in their task of apprehending John Allison Anderton. To repeat: the Precrime Agency of the Federal Westbloc Government is in the process of locating and neutralizing its former Commissioner, John Allison Anderton, who, through the methodology of the Precrime system, is hereby declared a potential murderer and as such forfeits his rights to freedom and all its privileges.'

'It didn't take him long,' Anderton muttered, appalled. Kaplan snapped off the radio and the voice vanished.

'Lisa must have gone directly to him,' Anderton speculated bitterly.

'Why should he wait?' Kaplan asked. 'You made your intentions clear.'

He nodded to his men. 'Take him back to town. I feel uneasy having him so close. In that respect I concur with Commissioner Witwer. I want him neutralized as soon as possible.'

IV

Cold, light rain beat against the pavement, as the car moved through the dark streets of New York City toward the police building.

'You can see his point,' one of the men said to Anderton. 'If you were in his place you'd act just as decisively.'

Sullen and resentful, Anderton stared straight ahead.

'Anyhow,' the man went on, 'you're just one of many. Thousands of people have gone to that detention camp. You won't be lonely. As a matter of fact, you may not want to leave.'

Helplessly, Anderton watched pedestrians hurrying along the rain-swept sidewalks. He felt no strong emotion. He was aware only of an overpowering fatigue. Dully, he checked off the street numbers: they were getting near the police station.

'This Witwer seems to know how to take advantage of an opportunity,' one of the men observed conversationally. 'Did you ever meet him?'

'Briefly,' Anderton answered.

'He wanted your job—so he framed you. Are you sure of that?'

Anderton grimaced. 'Does it matter?'

'I was just curious.' The man eyed him languidly. 'So you're the ex-Commissioner of Police. People in the camp will be glad to see you coming. They'll remember you.'

'No doubt,' Anderton agreed.

'Witwer sure didn't waste any time. Kaplan's lucky—with an official like that in charge.' The man looked at Anderton almost pleadingly. 'You're really convinced it's a plot, eh?'

'Of course.'

'You wouldn't harm a hair of Kaplan's head? For the first time in history, Precrime goes wrong? An innocent man is framed by one of those cards. Maybe there've been other innocent people—right?'

'It's quite possible,' Anderton admitted listlessly.

'Maybe the whole system can break down. Sure, you're not going to commit a murder—and maybe none of them were. Is that why you told Kaplan you wanted to keep yourself outside? Were you hoping to prove the system wrong? I've got an open mind, if you want to talk about it.'

Another man leaned over, and asked, 'Just between the two of us, is there really anything to this plot stuff? Are you really being framed?'

Anderton sighed. At that point he wasn't certain, himself. Perhaps he was trapped in a closed, meaningless time-circle with no motive and no beginning. In fact, he was almost ready to concede that he was the victim of a weary, neurotic fantasy, spawned by growing insecurity. Without a fight, he was willing to give himself up. A vast weight of exhaustion lay upon him. He was struggling against the impossible—and all the cards were stacked against him.

The sharp squeal of tires roused him. Frantically, the driver struggled to control the car, tugging at the wheel and slamming on the brakes, as a massive bread truck loomed up from the fog and ran directly across the lane ahead. Had he gunned the motor instead he might have saved himself. But too late he realized his error. The car skidded, lurched, hesitated for a brief instant, and then smashed head on into the bread truck.

Under Anderton the seat lifted up and flung him face-forward against the door. Pain, sudden, intolerable, seemed to burst in his brain as he lay gasping and trying feebly to pull himself to his knees. Somewhere the crackle of fire echoed dismally, a patch of hissing brilliance winking in the swirls of mist making their way into the twisted hulk of the car.

Hands from outside the car reached for him. Slowly he became aware that he was being dragged through the rent that had been the door. A heavy seat cushion was shoved brusquely aside, and all at once he found himself on his feet, leaning heavily against a dark shape and being guided into the shadows of an alley a short distance from the car.

In the distance, police sirens wailed.

'You'll live,' a voice grated in his ear, low and urgent. It was a voice he had never heard before, as unfamiliar and harsh as the rain beating into his face. 'Can you hear what I'm saying?'

'Yes,' Anderton acknowledged. He plucked aimlessly at the ripped sleeve of his shirt. A cut on his cheek was beginning to throb. Confused, he tried to orient himself. 'You're not—'

'Stop talking and listen.' The man was heavyset, almost fat. Now his big hands held Anderton propped against the wet brick wall of the building, out of the rain and the flickering light of the burning car. 'We had to do it that way,' he said. 'It was the only alternative. We didn't have much time. We thought Kaplan would keep you at his place longer.'

'Who are you?' Anderton managed.

The moist, rain-streaked face twisted into a humorless grin. 'My name's Fleming. You'll see me again. We have about five seconds before the police get here. Then we're back where we started.' A flat packet was stuffed into Anderton's hands. 'That's enough loot to keep you going. And there's a full set of identification in there. We'll contact you from time to time.' His grin increased and became a nervous chuckle. 'Until you've proved your point.'

Anderton blinked. 'It is a frameup, then?'

'Of course.' Sharply, the man swore. 'You mean they got you to believe it, too?'

'I thought—' Anderton had trouble talking, one of his front teeth seemed to be loose. 'Hostility toward Witwer . . . replaced, my wife and a younger man, natural resentment . . .'

'Don't kid yourself,' the other said. 'You know better than that. This whole business was worked out carefully. They had every phase of it under control. The card was set to pop the day Witwer appeared. They've already got the first part wrapped up. Witwer is Commissioner, and you're a hunted criminal.'

'Who's behind it?'

'Your wife.'

Anderton's head spun. 'You're positive?'

The man laughed. 'You bet your life.' He glanced quickly around. 'Here come the police. Take off down this alley. Grab a bus, get yourself into the slum section, rent a room and buy a stack of magazines to keep you busy. Get other clothes—You're smart enough to take care of yourself. Don't try to leave Earth. They've got all the inter-system transports screened. If you can keep low for the next seven days, you're made.'

'Who are you?' Anderton demanded.

Fleming let go of him. Cautiously, he moved to the entrance of the alley and peered out. The first police car had come to rest on

THE MINORITY REPORT

the damp pavement; its motor spinning tinnily, it crept suspiciously toward the smoldering ruin that had been Kaplan's car. Inside the wreck the squad of men were stirring feebly, beginning to creep painfully through the tangle of steel and plastic out into the cold rain.

'Consider us a protective society,' Fleming said softly, his plump, expressionless face shining with moisture. 'A sort of police force that watches the police. To see,' he added, 'that everything stays on an even keel.'

His thick hand shot out. Stumbling, Anderton was knocked away from him, half-falling into the shadows and damp debris that littered the alley.

'Get going,' Fleming told him sharply. 'And don't discard that packet.' As Anderton felt his way hesitantly toward the far exit of the alley, the man's last words drifted to him. 'Study it carefully and you may still survive.'

V

The identification cards described him as Ernest Temple, an unemployed electrician, drawing a weekly subsistence from the State of New York, with a wife and four children in Buffalo and less than a hundred dollars in assets. A sweat-stained green card gave him permission to travel and to maintain no fixed address. A man looking for work needed to travel. He might have to go a long way.

As he rode across town in the almost empty bus, Anderton studied the description of Ernest Temple. Obviously, the cards had been made out with him in mind, for all the measurements fitted. After a time he wondered about the fingerprints and the brain-wave pattern. They couldn't possibly stand comparison. The walletful of cards would get him past only the most cursory examinations.

But it was something. And with the ID cards came ten thousand dollars in bills. He pocketed the money and cards, then turned to the neatly-typed message in which they had been enclosed.

At first he could make no sense of it. For a long time he studied it, perplexed.

The existence of a majority logically implies
a corresponding minority.

The bus had entered the vast slum region, the tumbled miles of cheap hotels and broken-down tenements that had sprung up after the mass destruction of the war. It slowed to a stop, and Anderton got to his feet. A few passengers idly observed his cut cheek and damaged clothing. Ignoring them, he stepped down onto the rain-swept curb.

Beyond collecting the money due him, the hotel clerk was not interested. Anderton climbed the stairs to the second floor and entered the narrow, musty-smelling room that now belonged to him. Gratefully, he locked the door and pulled down the window shades. The room was small but clean. Bed, dresser, scenic calendar, chair, lamp, a radio with a slot for the insertion of quarters.

He dropped a quarter into it and threw himself heavily down on the bed. All main stations carried the police bulletin. It was novel, exciting, something unknown to the present generation. An escaped criminal! The public was avidly interested.

'. . . this man has used the advantage of his high position to carry out an initial escape,' the announcer was saying, with professional indignation. 'Because of his high office he had access to the previewed data and the trust placed in him permitted him to evade the normal process of detection and re-location. During the period of his tenure he exercised his authority to send countless potentially guilty individuals to their proper confinement, thus sparing the lives of innocent victims. This man, John Allison Anderton, was instrumental in the original creation of the Pre-crime system, the prophylactic pre-detection of criminals through the ingenious use of mutant precogs, capable of previewing future events and transferring orally that data to analytical machinery. These three precogs, in their vital function . . .'

The voice faded out as he left the room and entered the tiny bathroom. There, he stripped off his coat, and shirt, and ran hot water in the wash bowl. He began bathing the cut on his cheek. At the drugstore on the corner he had bought iodine and Band-aids, a razor, comb, toothbrush, and other small things he would need. The next morning he intended to find a second-hand clothing store and buy more suitable clothing. After all, he was now an unemployed electrician, not an accident-damaged Commissioner of Police.

In the other room the radio blared on. Only subconsciously aware of it, he stood in front of the cracked mirror, examining a broken tooth.

'. . . the system of three precogs finds its genesis in the computers of the middle decades of this century. How are the results of an electronic computer checked? By feeding the data to a second computer of identical design. But two computers are not sufficient. If each computer arrived at a different answer it is impossible to tell *a priori* which is correct. The solution, based on a careful study of statistical method, is to utilize a third computer to check the results of the first two. In this manner, a so-called majority report is obtained. It can be assumed with fair probability that the agreement of two out of three computers indicates which of the alternative results is accurate. It would not be likely that two computers would arrive at identically incorrect solutions—'

Anderton dropped the towel he was clutching and raced into the other room. Trembling, he bent to catch the blaring words of the radio.

'. . . unanimity of all three precogs is a hoped-for but seldom-achieved phenomenon, acting Commissioner Witwer explains. It is much more common to obtain a collaborative majority report of two precogs, plus a minority report of some slight variation, usually with reference to time and place, from the third mutant. This is explained by the theory of *multiple-futures*. If only one time-path existed, precognitive information would be of no importance, since no possibility would exist, in possessing this information, of altering the future. In the Precrime Agency's work we must first of all assume–'

Frantically, Anderton paced around the tiny room. Majority report–only two of the precogs had concurred on the material underlying the card. That was the meaning of the message enclosed with the packet. The report of the third precog, the minority report, was somehow of importance.

Why?

His watch told him that it was after midnight. Page would be off duty. He wouldn't be back in the monkey block until the next afternoon. It was a slim chance, but worth taking. Maybe Page would cover for him, and maybe not. He would have to risk it.

He had to see the minority report.

VI

Between noon and one o'clock the rubbish-littered streets swarmed with people. He chose that time, the busiest part of the day, to make his call. Selecting a phonebooth in a patron-teeming super drugstore, he dialed the familiar police number and stood holding the cold receiver to his ear. Deliberately, he had selected the aud, not the vid line: in spite of his second-hand clothing and seedy, unshaven appearance, he might be recognized.

The receptionist was new to him. Cautiously, he gave Page's extension. If Witwer were removing the regular staff and putting in his satellites, he might find himself talking to a total stranger.

'Hello,' Page's gruff voice came.

Relieved, Anderton glanced around. Nobody was paying any attention to him. The shoppers wandered among the merchandise, going about their daily routines. 'Can you talk?' he asked. 'Or are you tied up?'

There was a moment of silence. He could picture Page's mild

face torn with uncertainty as he wildly tried to decide what to do. At last came halting words. 'Why—are you calling here?'

Ignoring the question, Anderton said, 'I didn't recognize the receptionist. New personnel?'

'Brand-new,' Page agreed, in a thin, strangled voice. 'Big turnover, these days.'

'So I hear.' Tensely, Anderton asked, 'How's your job? Still safe?'

'Wait a minute.' The receiver was put down and the muffled sound of steps came in Anderton's ear. It was followed by the quick slam of a door being hastily shut. Page returned. 'We can talk better now,' he said hoarsely.

'How much better?'

'Not a great deal. Where are you?'

'Strolling through Central Park,' Anderton said. 'Enjoying the sunlight.' For all he knew, Page had gone to make sure the line-tap was in place. Right now, an airborne police team was probably on its way. But he had to take the chance. 'I'm in a new field,' he said curtly. 'I'm an electrician these days.'

'Oh?' Page said, baffled.

'I thought maybe you had some work for me. If it can be arranged, I'd like to drop by and examine your basic computing equipment. Especially the data and analytical banks in the monkey block.'

After a pause, Page said: 'It—might be arranged. If it's really important.'

'It is,' Anderton assured him. 'When would be best for you?'

'Well,' Page said, struggling. 'I'm having a repair team come in to look at the intercom equipment. The acting Commissioner wants it improved, so he can operate quicker. You might trail along.'

'I'll do that. About when?'

'Say four o'clock. Entrance B, level 6. I'll—meet you.'

'Fine,' Anderton agreed, already starting to hang up. 'I hope you're still in charge, when I get there.'

He hung up and rapidly left the booth. A moment later he was pushing through the dense pack of people crammed into the nearby cafeteria. Nobody would locate him there.

He had three and a half hours to wait. And it was going to seem a lot longer. It proved to be the longest wait of his life before he finally met Page as arranged.

The first thing Page said was: 'You're out of your mind. Why in hell did you come back?'

'I'm not back for long.' Tautly, Anderton prowled around the monkey block, systematically locking one door after another. 'Don't let anybody in. I can't take chances.'

'You should have quit when you were ahead.' In an agony of apprehension, Page followed after him. 'Witwer is making hay, hand over fist. He's got the whole country screaming for your blood.'

Ignoring him, Anderton snapped open the main control bank of the analytical machinery. 'Which of the three monkeys gave the minority report?'

'Don't question me—I'm getting out.' On his way to the door Page halted briefly, pointed to the middle figure, and then disappeared. The door closed; Anderton was alone.

The middle one. He knew that one well. The dwarfed, hunched-over figure had sat buried in its wiring and relays for fifteen years. As Anderton approached, it didn't look up. With eyes glazed and blank, it contemplated a world that did not yet exist, blind to the physical reality that lay around it.

'Jerry' was twenty-four years old. Originally, he had been classified as a hydrocephalic idiot but when he reached the age of six the psych testers had identified the precog talent, buried under the layers of tissue corrosion. Placed in a government-operated training school, the latent talent had been cultivated. By the time he was nine the talent had advanced to a useful stage. 'Jerry,' however, remained in the aimless chaos of idiocy; the burgeoning faculty had absorbed the totality of his personality.

Squatting down, Anderton began disassembling the protective shields that guarded the tape-reels stored in the analytical machinery. Using schematics, he traced the leads back from the final stages of the integrated computers, to the point where 'Jerry's' individual equipment branched off. Within minutes he was shakily lifting out two half-hour tapes: recent rejected data not fused with majority reports. Consulting the code chart, he selected the section of tape which referred to his particular card.

A tape scanner was mounted nearby. Holding his breath, he inserted the tape, activated the transport, and listened. It took only a second. From the first statement of the report it was clear what had happened. He had what he wanted; he could stop looking.

'Jerry's' vision was misphased. Because of the erratic nature of precognition, he was examining a time-area slightly different from that of his companions. For him, the report that Anderton would commit a murder was an event to be integrated along with everything else. That assertion—and Anderton's reaction—was one more piece of datum.

Obviously, 'Jerry's' report superseded the majority report. Having been informed that he would commit a murder, Anderton would change his mind and not do so. The preview of the murder had cancelled out the murder; prophylaxis had occurred simply in his being informed. Already, a new time-path had been created. But 'Jerry' was outvoted.

Trembling, Anderton rewound the tape and clicked on the recording head. At high speed he made a copy of the report, restored the original, and removed the duplicate from the transport. Here was the proof that the card was invalid: *obsolete*. All he had to do was show it to Witwer . . .

His own stupidity amazed him. Undoubtedly, Witwer had seen the report; and in spite of it, had assumed the job of Commissioner, had kept the police teams out. Witwer didn't intend to back down; he wasn't concerned with Anderton's innocence.

What, then, could he do? Who else would be interested?

'You damn fool!' a voice behind him grated, wild with anxiety.

Quickly, he turned. His wife stood at one of the doors, in her police uniform, her eyes frantic with dismay. 'Don't worry,' he told her briefly, displaying the reel of tape. 'I'm leaving.'

Her face distorted, Lisa rushed frantically up to him. 'Page said you were here, but I couldn't believe it. He shouldn't have let you in. He just doesn't understand what you are.'

'What am I?' Anderton inquired caustically. 'Before you answer, maybe you better listen to this tape.'

'I don't want to listen to it! I just want you to get out of here! Ed Witwer knows somebody's down here. Page is trying to keep him occupied, but–' She broke off, her head turned stiffly to one side. 'He's here now! He's going to force his way in.'

'Haven't you got any influence? Be gracious and charming. He'll probably forget about me.'

Lisa looked at him in bitter reproach. 'There's a ship parked on the roof. If you want to get away . . .' Her voice choked and for an instant she was silent. Then she said, 'I'll be taking off in a minute or so. If you want to come–'

'I'll come,' Anderton said. He had no other choice. He had secured his tape, his proof, but he hadn't worked out any method of leaving. Gladly, he hurried after the slim figure of his wife as she strode from the block, through a side door and down a supply corridor, her heels clicking loudly in the deserted gloom.

'It's a good fast ship,' she told him over her shoulder. 'It's emergency-fueled–ready to go. I was going to supervise some of the teams.'

VII

Behind the wheel of the high-velocity police cruiser, Anderton outlined what the minority report tape contained. Lisa listened without comment, her face pinched and strained, her hands clasped tensely in her lap. Below the ship, the war-ravaged rural countryside spread out like a relief map, the vacant regions between cities crater-pitted and dotted with the ruins of farms and small industrial plants.

'I wonder,' she said, when he had finished, 'how many times this has happened before.'

'A minority report? A great many times.'

'I mean, one precog misphased. Using the report of the others as data—superseding them.' Her eyes dark and serious, she added, 'Perhaps a lot of the people in the camps are like you.'

'No,' Anderton insisted. But he was beginning to feel uneasy about it, too. 'I was in a position to see the card, to get a look at the report. That's what did it.'

'But—' Lisa gestured significantly. 'Perhaps all of them would have reacted that way. We could have told them the truth.'

'It would have been too great a risk,' he answered stubbornly.

Lisa laughed sharply. 'Risk? Chance? Uncertainty? With precogs around?'

Anderton concentrated on steering the fast little ship. 'This is a unique case,' he repeated. 'And we have an immediate problem. We can tackle the theoretical aspects later on. I have to get this tape to the proper people—before your bright young friend demolishes it.'

'You're taking it to Kaplan?'

'I certainly am.' He tapped the reel of tape which lay on the seat between them. 'He'll be interested. Proof that his life isn't in danger ought to be of vital concern to him.'

From her purse, Lisa shakily got out her cigarette case. 'And you think he'll help you.'

'He may—or he may not. It's a chance worth taking.'

'How did you manage to go underground so quickly?' Lisa asked. 'A completely effective disguise is difficult to obtain.'

'All it takes is money,' he answered evasively.

As she smoked, Lisa pondered. 'Probably Kaplan will protect you,' she said. 'He's quite powerful.'

'I thought he was only a retired general.'

'Technically—that's what he is. But Witwer got out the dossier on him. Kaplan heads an unusual kind of exclusive veterans' organization. It's actually a kind of club, with a few restricted members. High officers only—an international class from both sides of the war. Here in New York they maintain a great mansion of a house, three glossy-paper publications, and occasional TV coverage that costs them a small fortune.'

'What are you trying to say?'

'Only this. You've convinced me that you're innocent. I mean, it's obvious that you *won't* commit a murder. But you must realize now that the original report, the majority report, *was not a fake*. Nobody falsified it. Ed Witwer didn't create it. There's no plot against you, and there never was. If you're going to accept this minority report as genuine you'll have to accept the majority one, also.'

Reluctantly, he agreed. 'I suppose so.'

'Ed Witwer,' Lisa continued, 'is acting in complete good faith. He really believes you're a potential criminal—and why not? He's got the majority report sitting on his desk, but you have that card folded up in your pocket.'

'I destroyed it,' Anderton said, quietly.

Lisa leaned earnestly toward him. 'Ed Witwer isn't motivated by any desire to get your job,' she said. 'He's motivated by the same desire that has always dominated you. He believes in Precrime. He wants the system to continue. I've talked to him and I'm convinced he's telling the truth.'

Anderton asked, 'Do you want me to take this reel to Witwer? If I do—he'll destroy it.'

'Nonsense,' Lisa retorted. 'The originals have been in his hands from the start. He could have destroyed them any time he wished.'

'That's true,' Anderton conceded. 'Quite possibly he didn't know.'

'Of course he didn't. Look at it this way. If Kaplan gets hold of that tape, the police will be discredited. Can't you see why? It would prove that the majority report was an error. Ed Witwer is absolutely right. You have to be taken in—if Precrime is to survive. You're thinking of your own safety. But think, for a moment, about the system.' Leaning over, she stubbed out her cigarette and fumbled in her purse for another. 'Which means more to you—your own personal safety or the existence of the system?'

'My safety,' Anderton answered, without hesitation.

'You're positive?'

'If the system can survive only by imprisoning innocent people, then it deserves to be destroyed. My personal safety is important because I'm a human being. And furthermore—'

From her purse, Lisa got out an incredibly tiny pistol. 'I believe,' she told him huskily, 'that I have my finger on the firing release. I've never used a weapon like this before. But I'm willing to try.'

After a pause, Anderton asked: 'You want me to turn the ship around? Is that it?'

'Yes, back to the police building. I'm sorry. If you could put the good of the system above your own selfish—'

'Keep your sermon,' Anderton told her. 'I'll take the ship back. But I'm not going to listen to your defense of a code of behavior no intelligent man could subscribe to.'

Lisa's lips pressed into a thin, bloodless line. Holding the pistol tightly, she sat facing him, her eyes fixed intently on him as he swung the ship in a broad arc. A few loose articles rattled from the glove compartment as the little craft turned on a radical slant, one wing rising majestically until it pointed straight up.

Both Anderton and his wife were supported by the constraining metal arms of their seats. But not so the third member of the party.

Out of the corner of his eye, Anderton saw a flash of motion. A sound came simultaneously, the clawing struggle of a large man as he abruptly lost his footing and plunged into the reinforced wall of the ship. What followed happened quickly. Fleming scrambled instantly to his feet, lurching and wary, one arm lashing out for the woman's pistol. Anderton was too startled to cry out. Lisa turned, saw the man—and screamed. Fleming knocked the gun from her hand, sending it clattering to the floor.

Grunting, Fleming shoved her aside and retrieved the gun. 'Sorry,' he gasped, straightening up as best he could. 'I thought she might talk more. That's why I waited.'

'You were here when—' Anderton began—and stopped. It was obvious that Fleming and his men had kept him under surveillance. The existence of Lisa's ship had been duly noted and factored in, and while Lisa had debated whether it would be wise to fly him to safety, Fleming had crept into the storage compartment of the ship.

'Perhaps,' Fleming said, 'you'd better give me that reel of tape.' His moist, clumsy fingers groped for it. 'You're right—Witwer would have melted it down to a puddle.'

'Kaplan, too?' Anderton asked numbly, still dazed by the appearance of the man.

'Kaplan is working directly with Witwer. That's why his name showed on line five of the card. Which one of them is the actual boss, we can't tell. Possibly neither.' Fleming tossed the tiny pistol away and got out his own heavy-duty military weapon. 'You pulled a real flub in taking off with this woman. I told you she was back of the whole thing.'

'I can't believe that,' Anderton protested. 'If she—'

'You've got no sense. This ship was warmed up by Witwer's order. They wanted to fly you out of the building so that we couldn't get to you. With you on your own, separated from us, you didn't stand a chance.'

A strange look passed over Lisa's stricken features. 'It's not true,' she whispered. 'Witwer never saw this ship. I was going to supervise—'

'You almost got away with it,' Fleming interrupted inexorably. 'We'll be lucky if a police patrol ship isn't hanging on us. There wasn't time to check.' He squatted down as he spoke, directly behind the woman's chair. 'The first thing is to get this woman out of the way. We'll have to drag you completely out of this area. Page tipped off Witwer on your new disguise, and you can be sure it has been widely broadcast.'

Still crouching, Fleming seized hold of Lisa. Tossing his heavy gun to Anderton, he expertly tilted her chin up until her temple was shoved back against the seat. Lisa clawed frantically at him; a thin, terrified wail rose in her throat. Ignoring her, Fleming closed his great hands around her neck and began relentlessly to squeeze.

'No bullet wound,' he explained, gasping. 'She's going to fall out—natural accident. It happens all the time. But in this case, her neck will be broken *first*.'

It seemed strange that Anderton waited so long. As it was, Fleming's thick fingers were cruelly embedded in the woman's pale flesh before he lifted the butt of the heavy-duty pistol and brought it down on the back of Fleming's skull. The monstrous hands relaxed. Staggered, Fleming's head fell forward and he sagged against the wall of the ship. Trying feebly to collect himself, he began dragging his body upward. Anderton hit him again, this time above the left eye. He fell back, and lay still.

Struggling to breathe, Lisa remained for a moment huddled over, her body swaying back and forth. Then, gradually, the color crept back into her face.

'Can you take the controls?' Anderton asked, shaking her, his voice urgent.

'Yes, I think so.' Almost mechanically she reached for the wheel. 'I'll be all right. Don't worry about me.'

'This pistol,' Anderton said, 'is Army ordnance issue. But it's not from the war. It's one of the useful new ones they've developed. I could be a long way off but there's just a chance—'

He climbed back to where Fleming lay spread out on the deck. Trying not to touch the man's head, he tore open his coat and rummaged in his pockets. A moment later Fleming's sweat-sodden wallet rested in his hands.

Tod Fleming, according to his identification, was an Army Major attached to the Internal Intelligence Department of Military Information. Among the various papers was a document signed by General Leopold Kaplan, stating that Fleming was under the special protection of his own group—the International Veterans' League.

Fleming and his men were operating under Kaplan's orders. The bread truck, the accident, had been deliberately rigged.

It meant that Kaplan had deliberately kept him out of police hands. The plan went back to the original contact in his home, when Kaplan's men had picked him up as he was packing. Incredulous, he realized what had really happened. Even then, they were making sure they got him before the police. From the start, it had been an elaborate strategy to make certain that Witwer would fail to arrest him.

'You were telling the truth,' Anderton said to his wife, as he climbed back in the seat. 'Can we get hold of Witwer?'

Mutely, she nodded. Indicating the communications circuit of the dashboard, she asked: 'What—did you find?'

'Get Witwer for me. I want to talk to him as soon as I can. It's very urgent.'

Jerkily, she dialed, got the closed-channel mechanical circuit, and raised police headquarters in New York. A visual panorama of petty police officials flashed by before a tiny replica of Ed Witwer's features appeared on the screen.

'Remember me?' Anderton asked him.

Witwer blanched. 'Good God. What happened? Lisa, are you bringing him in?' Abruptly his eyes fastened on the gun in Anderton's hands. 'Look,' he said savagely, 'don't do anything to her. Whatever you may think, she's not responsible.'

'I've already found that out,' Anderton answered. 'Can you get a fix on us? We may need protection getting back.'

'*Back!*' Witwer gazed at him unbelievingly. 'You're coming in? You're giving yourself up?'

'I am, yes.' Speaking rapidly, urgently, Anderton added, 'There's something you must do immediately. Close off the monkey block. Make certain nobody gets in—Page or anyone else. *Especially Army people.*'

'Kaplan,' the miniature image said.

'What about him?'

'He was here. He—he just left.'

Anderton's heart stopped beating. 'What was he doing?'

'Picking up data. Transcribing duplicates of our precog reports on you. He insisted he wanted them solely for his protection.'

'Then he's already got it,' Anderton said. 'It's too late.'

Alarmed, Witwer almost shouted: 'Just what do you mean? What's happening?'

'I'll tell you,' Anderton said heavily, 'when I get back to my office.'

VIII

Witwer met him on the roof of the police building. As the small ship came to rest, a cloud of escort ships dipped their fins and sped off. Anderton immediately approached the blond-haired young man.

'You've got what you wanted,' he told him. 'You can lock me up, and send me to the detention camp. But that won't be enough.'

Witwer's blue eyes were pale with uncertainty. 'I'm afraid I don't understand—'

'It's not my fault. I should never have left the police building. Where's Wally Page?'

'We've already clamped down on him,' Witwer replied. 'He won't give us any trouble.'

Anderton's face was grim.

'You're holding him for the wrong reason,' he said. 'Letting me into the monkey block was no crime. But passing information to Army is. You've had an Army plant working here.' He corrected himself, a little lamely, 'I mean, I have.'

'I've called back the order on you. Now the teams are looking for Kaplan.'

'Any luck?'

'He left here in an Army truck. We followed him, but the truck got into a militarized Barracks. Now they've got a big wartime R-3 tank blocking the street. It would be civil war to move it aside.'

Slowly, hesitantly, Lisa made her way from the ship. She was still pale and shaken and on her throat an ugly bruise was forming.

'What happened to you?' Witwer demanded. Then he caught sight of Fleming's inert form lying spread out inside. Facing

Anderton squarely, he said: 'Then you've finally stopped pretending this is some conspiracy of mine.'

'I have.'

'You don't think I'm–' He made a disgusted face. '*Plotting* to get your job.'

'Sure you are. Everybody is guilty of that sort of thing. And I'm plotting to keep it. But this is something else–and you're not responsible.'

'Why do you assert,' Witwer inquired, 'that it's too late to turn yourself in? My God, we'll put you in the camp. The week will pass and Kaplan will still be alive.'

'He'll be alive, yes,' Anderton conceded. 'But he can prove he'd be just as alive if I were walking the streets. He has the information that proves the majority report obsolete. He can break the Pre-crime system.' He finished, 'Heads or tails, he wins–and we lose. The Army discredits us; their strategy paid off.'

'But why are they risking so much? What exactly do they want?'

'After the Anglo-Chinese War, the Army lost out. It isn't what it was in the good old AFWA days. They ran the complete show, both military and domestic. And they did their own police work.'

'Like Fleming,' Lisa said faintly.

'After the war, the Westbloc was demilitarized. Officers like Kaplan were retired and discarded. Nobody likes that.' Anderton grimaced. 'I can sympathize with him. He's not the only one. But we couldn't keep on running things that way. We had to divide up the authority.'

'You say Kaplan has won,' Witwer said. 'Isn't there anything we can do?'

'I'm not going to kill him. We know it and he knows it. Probably he'll come around and offer us some kind of deal. We'll continue to function, but the Senate will abolish our real pull. You wouldn't like that, would you?'

'I should say not,' Witwer answered emphatically. 'One of these days I'm going to be running this agency.' He flushed. 'Not immediately, of course.'

Anderton's expression was somber. 'It's too bad you publicized the majority report. If you had kept it quiet, we could cautiously draw it back in. But everybody's heard about it. We can't retract it now.'

'I guess not,' Witwer admitted awkwardly. 'Maybe I—don't have this job down as neatly as I imagined.'

'You will, in time. You'll be a good police officer. You believe in the status quo. But learn to take it easy.' Anderton moved away from them. 'I'm going to study the data tapes of the majority report. I want to find out exactly how I was supposed to kill Kaplan.' Reflectively, he finished: 'It might give me some ideas.'

The data tapes of the precogs 'Donna' and 'Mike' were separately stored. Choosing the machinery responsible for the analysis of 'Donna,' he opened the protective shield and laid out the contents. As before, the code informed him which reels were relevant and in a moment he had the tape-transport mechanism in operation.

It was approximately what he had suspected. This was the material utilized by 'Jerry'—the superseded time-path. In it Kaplan's Military Intelligence agents kidnapped Anderton as he drove home from work. Taken to Kaplan's villa, the organization GHQ of the International Veterans' League, Anderton was given an ultimatum: voluntarily disband the Precrime system or face open hostilities with Army.

In this discarded time-path, Anderton, as Police Commissioner, had turned to the Senate for support. No support was forthcoming. To avoid civil war, the Senate had ratified the dismemberment of the police system, and decreed a return to military law 'to cope with the emergency.' Taking a corps of fanatic police, Anderton had located Kaplan and shot him, along with other officials of the Veterans' League. Only Kaplan had died. The others had been patched up. And the coup had been successful.

This was 'Donna.' He rewound the tape and turned to the material previewed by 'Mike.' It would be identical; both precogs had combined to present a unified picture. 'Mike' began as 'Donna' had begun: Anderton had become aware of Kaplan's plot against the police. But something was wrong. Puzzled, he ran the tape back to the beginning. Incomprehensibly, it didn't jibe. Again he replayed the tape, listening intently.

The 'Mike' report was quite different from the 'Donna' report.

An hour later, he had finished his examination, put away the tapes, and left the monkey block. As soon as he emerged, Witwer asked. 'What's the matter? I can see something's wrong.'

'No,' Anderton answered slowly, still deep in thought. 'Not exactly wrong.' A sound came to his ears. He walked vaguely over to the window and peered out.

The street was crammed with people. Moving down the center lane was a four-column line of uniformed troops. Rifles, helmets ... marching soldiers in their dingy wartime uniforms, carrying the cherished pennants of AFWA flapping in the cold afternoon wind.

'An Army rally,' Witwer explained bleakly. 'I was wrong. They're not going to make a deal with us. Why should they? Kaplan's going to make it public.'

Anderton felt no surprise. 'He's going to read the minority report?'

'Apparently. They're going to demand the Senate disband us, and take away our authority. They're going to claim we've been arresting innocent men—nocturnal police raids, that sort of thing. Rule by terror.'

'You suppose the Senate will yield?'

Witwer hesitated. 'I wouldn't want to guess.'

'I'll guess,' Anderton said. 'They will. That business out there fits with what I learned downstairs. We've got ourselves boxed in and there's only one direction we can go. Whether we like it or not, we'll have to take it.' His eyes had a steely glint.

Apprehensively, Witwer asked: 'What is it?'

'Once I say it, you'll wonder why you didn't invent it. Very obviously, I'm going to have to fulfill the publicized report. I'm going to have to kill Kaplan. That's the only way we can keep them from discrediting us.'

'But,' Witwer said, astonished, 'the majority report has been superseded.'

'I can do it,' Anderton informed him, 'but it's going to cost. You're familiar with the statutes governing first-degree murder?'

'Life imprisonment.'

'At least. Probably, you could pull a few wires and get it commuted to exile. I could be sent to one of the colony planets, the good old frontier.'

'Would you—prefer that?'

'Hell, no,' Anderton said heartily. 'But it would be the lesser of the two evils. And it's got to be done.'

'I don't see how you can kill Kaplan.'

Anderton got out the heavy-duty military weapon Fleming had tossed to him. 'I'll use this.'

'They won't stop you?'

'Why should they? They've got that minority report that says I've changed my mind.'

'Then the minority report is incorrect?'

'No,' Anderton said, 'it's absolutely correct. But I'm going to murder Kaplan anyhow.'

IX

He had never killed a man. He had never even seen a man killed. And he had been Police Commissioner for thirty years. For this generation, deliberate murder had died out. It simply didn't happen.

A police car carried him to within a block of the Army rally. There, in the shadows of the back seat, he painstakingly examined the pistol Fleming had provided him. It seemed to be intact. Actually, there was no doubt of the outcome. He was absolutely certain of what would happen within the next half hour. Putting the pistol back together, he opened the door of the parked car and stepped warily out.

Nobody paid the slightest attention to him. Surging masses of people pushed eagerly forward, trying to get within hearing distance of the rally. Army uniforms predominated, and at the perimeter of the cleared area, a line of tanks and major weapons was displayed—formidable armament still in production.

Army had erected a metal speaker's stand and ascending steps. Behind the stand hung the vast AFWA banner, emblem of the combined powers that had fought in the war. By a curious corrosion of time, the AFWA Veterans' League included officers from the wartime enemy. But a general was a general and fine distinctions had faded over the years.

Occupying the first rows of seats sat the high brass of the AFWA command. Behind them came junior commissioned officers. Regimental banners swirled in a variety of colors and symbols. In fact, the occasion had taken on the aspect of a festive pageant. On the raised stand itself sat stern-faced dignitaries of the Veterans' League, all of them tense with expectancy. At the extreme edges, almost unnoticed, waited a few police units, ostensibly to keep order. Actually, they were informants making observations. If order were kept, the Army would maintain it.

The late-afternoon wind carried the muffled booming of many people packed tightly together. As Anderton made his way through the dense mob he was engulfed by the solid presence of humanity. An eager sense of anticipation held everybody rigid. The crowd seemed to sense that something spectacular was on the way. With difficulty, Anderton forced his way past the rows of seats and over to the tight knot of Army officials at the edge of the platform.

Kaplan was among them. But he was now General Kaplan.

The vest, the gold pocket watch, the cane, the conservative business suit—all were gone. For this event, Kaplan had got his old uniform from its mothballs. Straight and impressive, he stood surrounded by what had been his general staff. He wore his service bars, his medals, his boots, his decorative short-sword, and his visored cap. It was amazing how transformed a bald man became under the stark potency of an officer's peaked and visored cap.

Noticing Anderton, General Kaplan broke away from the group and strode to where the younger man was standing. The expression on his thin, mobile countenance showed how incredulously glad he was to see the Commissioner of Police.

'This is a surprise,' he informed Anderton, holding out his small gray-gloved hand. 'It was my impression you had been taken in by the acting Commissioner.'

'I'm still out,' Anderton answered shortly, shaking hands. 'After all, Witwer has that same reel of tape.' He indicated the package Kaplan clutched in his steely fingers and met the man's gaze confidently.

In spite of his nervousness, General Kaplan was in good humor. 'This is a great occasion for the Army,' he revealed. 'You'll be glad to hear I'm going to give the public a full account of the spurious charge brought against you.'

'Fine,' Anderton answered noncommittally.

'It will be made clear that you were unjustly accused.' General Kaplan was trying to discover what Anderton knew. 'Did Fleming have an opportunity to acquaint you with the situation?'

'To some degree,' Anderton replied. 'You're going to read only the minority report? That's all you've got there?'

'I'm going to compare it to the majority report.' General Kaplan signalled an aide and a leather briefcase was produced. 'Everything is here—all the evidence we need,' he said. 'You don't mind being an example, do you? Your case symbolizes the unjust arrests of countless individuals.' Stiffly, General Kaplan examined his wrist-watch. 'I must begin. Will you join me on the platform?'

'Why?'

Coldly, but with a kind of repressed vehemence, General Kaplan said: 'So they can see the living proof. You and I together—the killer and his victim. Standing side by side, exposing the whole sinister fraud which the police have been operating.'

'Gladly,' Anderton agreed. 'What are we waiting for?'

Disconcerted, General Kaplan moved toward the platform. Again, he glanced uneasily at Anderton, as if visibly wondering why he had appeared and what he really knew. His uncertainty grew as Anderton willingly mounted the steps of the platform and found himself a seat directly beside the speaker's podium.

'You fully comprehend what I'm going to be saying?' General Kaplan demanded. 'The exposure will have considerable repercussions. It may cause the Senate to reconsider the basic validity of the Precrime system.'

'I understand,' Anderton answered, arms folded. 'Let's go.'

A hush had descended on the crowd. But there was a restless, eager stirring when General Kaplan obtained the briefcase and began arranging his material in front of him.

'The man sitting at my side,' he began, in a clean, clipped voice, 'is familiar to you all. You may be surprised to see him, for until recently he was described by the police as a dangerous killer.'

The eyes of the crowd focused on Anderton. Avidly, they peered at the only potential killer they had ever been privileged to see at close range.

'Within the last few hours, however,' General Kaplan continued, 'the police order for his arrest has been cancelled; because former Commissioner Anderton voluntarily gave himself up? No, that is not strictly accurate. He is sitting here. He has not given himself up, but the police are no longer interested in him. John Allison Anderton is innocent of any crime in the past, present, and future. The allegations against him were patent frauds, diabolical distortions of a contaminated penal system based on a false premise—a vast, impersonal engine of destruction grinding men and women to their doom.'

Fascinated, the crowd glanced from Kaplan to Anderton. Everyone was familiar with the basic situation.

'Many men have been seized and imprisoned under the so-called prophylactic Precrime structure,' General Kaplan continued, his voice gaining feeling and strength. 'Accused not of crimes they have committed, *but of crimes they will commit*. It is asserted that these men, if allowed to remain free, will at some future time commit felonies.

'But there can be no valid knowledge about the future. As soon as precognitive information is obtained, *it cancels itself out*. The assertion that this man will commit a future crime is paradoxical. The very act of possessing this data renders it spurious. In every case, without exception, the report of the three police precogs has invalidated their own data. If no arrests had been made, there would still have been no crimes committed.'

Anderton listened idly, only half-hearing the words. The crowd, however, listened with great interest. General Kaplan was now gathering up a summary made from the minority report. He explained what it was and how it had come into existence.

From his coat pocket, Anderton slipped out his gun and held it in his lap. Already, Kaplan was laying aside the minority report, the precognitive material obtained from 'Jerry.' His lean, bony fingers groped for the summary of, first, 'Donna,' and after that, 'Mike.'

'This was the original majority report,' he explained. 'The assertion, made by the first two precogs, that Anderton would commit a murder. Now here is the automatically invalidated material. I shall read it to you.' He whipped out his rimless glasses, fitted them to his nose, and started slowly to read.

A queer expression appeared on his face. He halted, stammered, and abruptly broke off. The papers fluttered from his hands. Like a cornered animal, he spun, crouched, and dashed from the speaker's stand.

For an instant his distorted face flashed past Anderton. On his feet now, Anderton raised the gun, stepped quickly forward, and fired. Tangled up in the rows of feet projecting from the chairs that filled the platform, Kaplan gave a single shrill shriek of agony and fright. Like a ruined bird, he tumbled, fluttering and flailing, from the platform to the ground below. Anderton stepped to the railing, but it was already over.

Kaplan, as the majority report had asserted, was dead. His thin chest was a smoking cavity of darkness, crumbling ash that broke loose as the body lay twitching.

Sickened, Anderton turned away, and moved quickly between the rising figures of stunned Army officers. The gun, which he still held, guaranteed that he would not be interfered with. He leaped from the platform and edged into the chaotic mass of people at its base. Stricken, horrified, they struggled to see what had happened. The incident, occurring before their very eyes, was incomprehensible. It would take time for acceptance to replace blind terror.

At the periphery of the crowd, Anderton was seized by the waiting police. 'You're lucky to get out,' one of them whispered to him as the car crept cautiously ahead.

'I guess I am,' Anderton replied remotely. He settled back and tried to compose himself. He was trembling and dizzy. Abruptly, he leaned forward and was violently sick.

'The poor devil,' one the cops murmured sympathetically.

Through the swirls of misery and nausea, Anderton was unable to tell whether the cop was referring to Kaplan or to himself.

X

Four burly policemen assisted Lisa and John Anderton in the packing and loading of their possessions. In fifty years, the ex-Commissioner of Police had accumulated a vast collection of material goods. Somber and pensive, he stood watching the procession of crates on their way to the waiting trucks.

By truck they would go directly to the field—and from there to Centaurus X by inter-system transport. A long trip for an old man. But he wouldn't have to make it back.

'There goes the second from the last crate,' Lisa declared, absorbed and preoccupied by the task. In sweater and slacks, she roamed through the barren rooms, checking on last-minute details. 'I suppose we won't be able to use these new atronic appliances. They're still using electricity on Centten.'

'I hope you don't care too much,' Anderton said.

'We'll get used to it,' Lisa replied, and gave him a fleeting smile. 'Won't we?'

'I hope so. You're positive you'll have no regrets. If I thought—'

'No regrets,' Lisa assured him. 'Now suppose you help me with this crate.'

As they boarded the lead truck, Witwer drove up in a patrol car. He leaped out and hurried up to them, his face looking strangely haggard. 'Before you take off,' he said to Anderton, 'you'll have to give me a break-down on the situation with the precogs. I'm getting inquiries from the Senate. They want to find out if the middle report, the retraction, was an error—or what.' Confusedly, he finished: 'I still can't explain it. The minority report was wrong, wasn't it?'

'Which minority report?' Anderton inquired, amused.

Witwer blinked. 'Then that *is* it. I might have known.'

Seated in the cabin of the truck, Anderton got out his pipe and shook tobacco into it. With Lisa's lighter he ignited the tobacco and began operations. Lisa had gone back to the house, wanting to be sure nothing vital had been overlooked.

'There were three minority reports,' he told Witwer, enjoying the young man's confusion. Someday, Witwer would learn not to wade into situations he didn't fully understand. Satisfaction was Anderton's final emotion. Old and worn-out as he was, he had been the only one to grasp the real nature of the problem.

'The three reports were consecutive,' he explained. 'The first was "Donna." In that time-path, Kaplan told me of the plot, and I promptly murdered him. "Jerry," phased slightly ahead of "Donna," used her report as data. He factored in my knowledge of the report. In that, the second time-path, all I wanted to do was to keep my job. It wasn't Kaplan I wanted to kill. It was my own position and life I was interested in.'

'And "Mike" was the third report? That came *after* the minority report?' Witwer corrected himself. 'I mean, it came last?'

'"Mike" was the last of the three, yes. Faced with the knowledge of the first report, I had decided *not* to kill Kaplan. That produced report two. But faced with *that* report, I changed my mind back. Report two, situation two, was the situation Kaplan wanted to create. It was to the advantage of the police to recreate position one. And by that time I was thinking of the police. I had figured out what Kaplan was doing. The third report invalidated the second one in the same way the second one invalidated the first. That brought us back where we started from.'

Lisa came over, breathless and gasping. 'Let's go—we're all finished here.' Lithe and agile, she ascended the metal rungs of the truck and squeezed in beside her husband and the driver. The latter obediently started up his truck and the others followed.

'Each report was different,' Anderton concluded. 'Each was unique. But two of them agreed on one point. If left free, I *would kill Kaplan*. That created the illusion of a majority report. Actually, that's all it was—an illusion. "Donna" and "Mike" previewed the same event—but in two totally different time-paths, occurring under totally different situations. "Donna" and "Jerry," the so-called minority report and half of the majority report, were incorrect. Of the three, "Mike" was correct—since no report came after his, to invalidate him. That sums it up.'

Anxiously, Witwer trotted along beside the truck, his smooth, blond face creased with worry. 'Will it happen again? Should we overhaul the set-up?'

'It can happen in only one circumstance,' Anderton said. 'My case was unique, since I had access to the data. It *could* happen again—but only to the next Police Commissioner. So watch your step.' Briefly, he grinned, deriving no inconsiderable comfort from Witwer's strained expression. Beside him, Lisa's red lips twitched and her hand reached out and closed over his.

'Better keep your eyes open,' he informed young Witwer. 'It might happen to you at any time.'

RECALL MECHANISM

The analyst said: 'I'm Humphrys, the man you came to see.' There were fear and hostility on the patient's face, so Humphrys said: 'I could tell a joke about analysts. Would that make you feel better? Or I could remind you that the National Health Trust is paying my fee; it's not going to cost you a cent. Or I could cite the case of Psychoanalyst Y, who committed suicide last year because of overburdening anxiety resulting from a fraudulently filled out income tax.'

Grudgingly, the patient smiled. 'I heard about that. So psychologists are fallible.' He got to his feet and held out his hand. 'My name is Paul Sharp. My secretary made the arrangements with you. I have a little problem, nothing important, but I'd like to clear it up.'

The expression on his face showed that it was no small problem, and that, if he didn't clear it up, it would probably destroy him.

'Come inside,' Humphrys said genially, opening the door to his office, 'so we can both sit down.'

Sinking down in a soft easy chair, Sharp stretched his legs out in front of him. 'No couch,' he observed.

'The couch vanished back around 1980,' Humphrys said. 'Post-war analysts feel enough confidence to face their patients on an equal level.' He offered a pack of cigarettes to Sharp and then lit up himself. 'Your secretary gave me no details; she just said you wanted a conference.'

Sharp said: 'I can talk frankly?'

'I'm bonded,' Humphrys said, with pride. 'If any of the material you tell me gets into the hands of security organizations, I forfeit approximately ten thousand dollars in Westbloc silver—hard cash, not paper stuff.'

'That's good enough for me,' Sharp said, and began. 'I'm an economist, working for the Department of Agriculture—the Division of War Destruction Salvage. I poke around H-bomb craters seeing what's worth rebuilding.' He corrected himself. 'Actually, I analyze reports on H-bomb craters and make recommendations. It was my recommendation to reclaim the farm lands around Sacramento and the industrial ring here at Los Angeles.'

In spite of himself, Humphrys was impressed. Here was a man in the policy-planning level of the Government. It gave him an odd feeling to realize that Sharp, like any other anxiety-ridden citizen, had come to the Psych Front for therapy.

'My sister-in-law got a nice advantage from the Sacramento reclamation,' Humphrys commented. 'She had a small walnut orchard up there. The Government hauled off the ash, rebuilt the house and outbuildings, even staked her to a few dozen new trees. Except for her leg injury, she's as well off as before the war.'

'We're pleased with our Sacramento project,' Sharp said. He had begun to perspire; his smooth, pale forehead was streaked, and his hands, as he held his cigarette, shook. 'Of course, I have a personal interest in Northern California. I was born there myself, up around Petaluma, where they used to turn out hens' eggs by the million . . .' His voice trailed off huskily. 'Humphrys,' he muttered, 'what am I going to do?'

'First,' Humphrys said, 'give me more information.'

'I—' Sharp grinned inanely. 'I have some kind of hallucination. I've had it for years, but it's getting worse. I've tried to shake it, but—' he gestured—'it comes back, stronger, bigger, more often.'

Beside Humphrys' desk the vid and aud recorders were scanning covertly. 'Tell me what the hallucination is,' he instructed. 'Then maybe I can tell you why you have it.'

*

He was tired. In the privacy of his living room, he sat dully examining a series of reports on carrot mutation. A variety, externally indistinguishable from the norm, was sending people in Oregon and Mississippi to the hospital with convulsions, fever and partial blindness. Why Oregon and Mississippi? Here with the report were photographs of the feral mutation; it *did* look like an ordinary carrot. And with the report came an exhaustive analysis of the toxic agent and recommendation for a neutralizing antidote.

Sharp wearily tossed the report aside and selected the next in order.

According to the second report, the notorious Detroit rat had shown up in St Louis and Chicago, infesting the industrial and agricultural settlements replacing the destroyed cities. The Detroit rat—he had seen one once. That was three years ago; coming home one night, he had unlocked the door and seen, in the darkness, something scuttle away to safety. Arming himself with a hammer, he had pushed furniture around until he found it. The rat, huge and gray, had been in the process of building itself a wall-to-wall web. As it leaped up, he killed it with the hammer. A rat that spun webs . . .

He called an official exterminator and reported its presence.

A Special Talents Agency had been set up by the Government to utilize parabilities of wartime mutants evolved from the various radiation-saturated areas. But, he reflected, the Agency was equipped to handle only human mutants and their telepathic, precog, parakinetic and related abilities. There should have been a Special Talents Agency for vegetables and rodents, too.

From behind his chair came a stealthy sound. Turning quickly, Sharp found himself facing a tall, thin man wearing a drab raincoat and smoking a cigar.

'Did I scare you?' Giller asked, and snickered. 'Take it easy, Paul. You look as if you're going to pass out.'

'I was working,' Sharp said defensively, partially recovering his equilibrium.

'So I see,' said Giller.

'And thinking about rats.' Sharp pushed his work to one side. 'How'd you get in?'

'Your door was unlocked.' Giller removed his raincoat and tossed it on the couch. 'That's right—you killed a Detroit. Right here in this room.' He gazed around the neat, unostentatious living room. 'Are those things fatal?'

'Depends where they get you.' Going into the kitchen, Sharp found two beers in the refrigerator. As he poured, he said: 'They shouldn't waste grain making this stuff . . . but as long as they do, it's a shame not to drink it.'

Giller accepted his beer greedily. 'Must be nice to be a big wheel and have luxuries like this.' His small, dark eyes roved speculatively around the kitchen. 'Your own stove, and your own refrigerator.' Smacking his lips, he added: 'And beer. I haven't had a beer since last August.'

'You'll live,' Sharp said, without compassion. 'Is this a business call? If so, get to the point; I've got plenty of work to do.'

Giller said: 'I just wanted to say hello to a fellow Petaluman.'

Wincing, Sharp answered: 'It sounds like some sort of synthetic fuel.'

Giller wasn't amused. 'Are you ashamed to have come from the very section that was once—'

'I know. The egg-laying capital of the universe. Sometimes I wonder—how many chicken feathers do you suppose were drifting around, the day the first H-bomb hit our town?'

'Billions,' Giller said morosely. 'And some of them were mine. My chickens, I mean. Your family had a farm, didn't they?'

'No,' Sharp said, refusing to be identified with Giller. 'My family operated a drug store facing on Highway 101. A block from the park, near the sporting goods shop.' And, he added under his breath: You can go to hell. Because I'm not going to change my mind. You can camp on my doorstep the rest of your life and it still won't do any good. Petaluma isn't that important. And anyhow, the chickens are dead.

'How's the Sac rebuild coming?' Giller inquired.

'Fine.'

'Plenty of those walnuts again?'

'Walnuts coming out of people's ears.'

'Mice getting in the shell heaps?'

'Thousands of them.' Sharp sipped his beer; it was good quality, probably as good as pre-war. He wouldn't know, because in 1961, the year the war broke out, he had been only six years old. But the beer tasted the way he remembered the old days: opulent and carefree and satisfying.

'We figure,' Giller said hoarsely, an avid gleam in his face, 'that the Petaluma-Sonoma area can be built up again for about seven billion Westbloc. That's nothing compared to what you've been doling out.'

'And the Petaluma-Sonoma area is nothing compared with the areas we've been rebuilding,' Sharp said. 'You think we need eggs and wine? What we need is machinery. It's Chicago and Pittsburgh and Los Angeles and St Louis and—'

'You've forgotten,' Giller droned on, 'that you're a Petaluman. You're turning your back on your origin—and on your duty.'

'Duty! You suppose the Government hired me to be a lobbyist for one trivial farm area?' Sharp flushed with outrage. 'As far as I'm concerned—'

'We're your people,' Giller said inflexibly. 'And your people come first.'

When he had got rid of the man, Sharp stood for a time in the night darkness, gazing down the road after Giller's receding car. Well, he said to himself, there goes the way of the world—me first and to hell with everybody else.

Sighing, he turned and made his way up the path toward the front porch of his house. Lights gleamed friendlily in the window. Shivering, he put his hand out and groped for the railing.

And then, as he clumsily mounted the stairs, the terrible thing happened.

With a rush, the lights of the window winked out. The porch railing dissolved under his fingers. In his ears a shrill scream-ing whine rose up and deafened him. He was falling. Struggling frantically, he tried to get hold of something, but there was only empty darkness around him, no substance, no reality, only the depth beneath him and the din of his own terrified shrieks.

'Help!' he shouted, and the sound beat futilely back at him. 'I'm falling!'

And then, gasping, he was outstretched on the damp lawn, clutching handfuls of grass and dirt. Two feet from the porch—he had missed the first step in the darkness and had slipped and fallen. An ordinary event: the window lights had been blocked by the concrete railing. The whole thing had happened in a split second and he had fallen only the length of his own body. There was blood on his forehead; he had cut himself as he struck.

Silly. A childish, infuriating event.

Shakily, he climbed to his feet and mounted the steps. Inside the house, he stood leaning against the wall, shuddering and panting. Gradually the fear faded out and rationality returned.

Why was he so afraid of falling?

Something had to be done. This was worse than ever before, even worse than the time he had stumbled coming out of the elevator at the office—and had instantly been reduced to screaming terror in front of a lobbyful of people.

What would happen to him if he *really* fell? If, for example, he were to step off one of the overhead ramps connecting the major Los Angeles office buildings? The fall would be stopped by safety screens; no physical harm was ever done, though people fell all the time. But for him—the psychological shock might be fatal. *Would* be fatal; to his mind, at least.

He made a mental note: no more going out on the ramps. Under no circumstances. He had been avoiding them for years, but from now on, ramps were in the same class as air travel. Since 1982 he hadn't left the surface of the planet. And, in the last few years, he seldom visited offices more than ten flights up.

But if he stopped using the ramps, how was he going to get into his own research files? The file room was accessible only by ramp: the narrow metallic path leading up from the office area.

Perspiring, terrified, he sank down on the couch and sat huddled over, wondering how he was going to keep his job, do his work.

And how he was going to stay alive.

Humphrys waited, but his patient seemed to have finished.

'Does it make you feel any better,' Humphrys asked, 'to know that fear of falling is a common phobia?'

'No,' Sharp answered.

'I guess there's no reason why it should. You say it's shown up before? When was the first time?'

'When I was eight. The war had been going on two years. I was on the surface, examining my vegetable garden.' Sharp smiled weakly. 'Even when I was a kid, I grew things. The San Francisco network picked up exhaust trails of a Soviet missile and all the warning towers went off like Roman candles. I was almost on top of the shelter. I raced to it, lifted the lid and started down the stairs. At the bottom were my mother and father. They yelled for me to hurry. I started to run down the stairs.'

'And fell?' Humphrys asked expectantly.

'I didn't fall; I suddenly got afraid. I couldn't go any farther; I just stood there. And they were yelling up at me. They wanted to get the bottom plate screwed in place. And they couldn't until I was down.'

With a touch of aversion, Humphrys acknowledged: 'I remember those old two-stage shelters. I wonder how many people got shut between the lid and the bottom plate.' He eyed his patient. 'As a child, had you heard of that happening? People being trapped on the stairs, not able to get back up, not able to get down . . .'

'I wasn't scared of being trapped! I was scared of falling—afraid I'd pitch head-forward off the steps.' Sharp licked his dry lips. 'Well, so I turned around—' His body shuddered. 'I went back up and outside.'

'During the attack?'

'They shot down the missile. But I spent the alert tending my vegetables. Afterward, my family beat me nearly unconscious.'

Humphrys' mind formed the words: origin of guilt.

'The next time,' Sharp continued, 'was when I was fourteen. The war had been over a few months. We started back to see what was left of our town. Nothing was left, only a crater of radioactive slag several hundred feet deep. Work teams were creeping down into the crater. I stood on the edge watching them. The fear came.' He put out his cigarette and sat waiting until the analyst found him another. 'I left the area after that. Every night I dreamed about that crater, that big dead mouth. I hitched a ride on a military truck and rode to San Francisco.'

'When was the next time?' asked Humphrys.

Irritably, Sharp said: 'Then it happened all the time, every time I was up high, every time I had to walk up or down a flight of steps— any situation where I was high and might fall. But to be afraid to walk up the steps of my own house—' He broke off temporarily. 'I can't walk up three steps,' he said wretchedly. 'Three concrete steps.'

'Any particular bad episodes, outside of those you've mentioned?'

'I was in love with a pretty brown-haired girl who lived on the top floor of the Atcheson Apartments. Probably she still lives there; I wouldn't know. I got five or six floors up and then—I told her good night and came back down.' Ironically, he said: 'She must have thought I was crazy.'

'Others?' Humphrys asked, mentally noting the appearance of the sexual element.

'One time I couldn't accept a job because it involved travel by air. It had to do with inspecting agricultural projects.'

Humphrys said: 'In the old days, analysts looked for the origin of a phobia. Now we ask: *what does it do?* Usually it gets the individual out of situations he unconsciously dislikes.'

A slow, disgusted flush appeared on Sharp's face. 'Can't you do better than that?'

Disconcerted, Humphrys murmured: 'I don't say I agree with the theory or that it's necessarily true in your case. I'll say this much though: it's not falling you're afraid of. It's something that falling reminds you of. With luck we ought to be able to dig up the prototype experience—what they used to call the original traumatic incident.' Getting to his feet, he began to drag over a stemmed tower of electronic mirrors. 'My lamp,' he explained. 'It'll melt the barriers.'

Sharp regarded the lamp with apprehension. 'Look,' he muttered nervously, 'I don't want my mind reconstructed. I may be a neurotic, but I take pride in my personality.'

'This won't affect your personality.' Bending down, Humphrys plugged in the lamp. 'It will bring up material not accessible to your rational center. I'm going to trace your life-track back to the incident at which you were done great harm—and find out what you're *really* afraid of.'

Black shapes drifted around him. Sharp screamed and struggled wildly, trying to pry loose the fingers closing over his arms and legs. Something smashed against his face. Coughing, he slumped forward, dribbling blood and saliva and bits of broken teeth. For an instant, blinding light flashed; he was being scrutinized.

'Is he dead?' a voice demanded.

'Not yet.' A foot poked experimentally into Sharp's side. Dimly, in his half-consciousness, he could hear ribs cracking. 'Almost, though.'

'Can you hear me, Sharp?' a voice rasped, close to his ear.

He didn't respond. He lay trying not to die, trying not to associate himself with the cracked and broken thing that had been his body.

'You probably imagine,' the voice said, familiar, intimate, 'that I'm going to say you've got one last chance. But you don't, Sharp. Your chance is gone. I'm telling you what we're going to do with you.'

Gasping, he tried not to hear. And, futilely, he tried not to feel what they were systematically doing to him.

'All right,' the familiar voice said finally, when it had been done. 'Now throw him out.'

What remained of Paul Sharp was lugged to a circular hatch. The nebulous outline of darkness rose up around him and then—hideously—he was pitched into it. Down he fell, but this time he didn't scream.

No physical apparatus remained with which to scream.

Snapping the lamp off, Humphrys bent over and methodically roused the slumped figure.

'Sharp!' he ordered loudly. 'Wake up! Come out of it!'

The man groaned, blinked his eyes, stirred. Over his face settled a glaze of pure, unmitigated torment.

'God,' he whispered, eyes blank, body limp with suffering. 'They—'

'You're back here,' Humphrys said, shaken by what had been dredged up. 'There's nothing to worry about; you're absolutely safe. It's over with—happened years ago.'

'Over,' Sharp murmured pathetically.

'You're back in the present. Understand?'

'Yes,' Sharp muttered. 'But—what was it? They pushed me out—through and into something. And I went on down.' He trembled violently. 'I fell.'

'You fell through a hatch,' Humphrys told him calmly. 'You were beaten up and badly injured—fatally, they assumed. But you *did* survive. You are alive. You got out of it.'

'Why did they do it?' Sharp asked brokenly. His face, sagging and gray, twitched with despair. 'Help me, Humphrys . . .'

'Consciously, you don't remember when it happened?'

'No.'

'Do you remember where?'

'No.' Sharp's face jerked spasmodically. 'They tried to kill me—they *did* kill me!' Struggling upright, he protested: 'Nothing like that happened to me. I'd remember if it had. It's a false memory—my mind's been tampered with!'

'It's been repressed,' Humphrys said firmly, 'deeply buried because of the pain and shock. A form of amnesia—it's been filtering indirectly up in the form of your phobia. But now that you recall it consciously—'

'Do I have to go back?' Sharp's voice rose hysterically. 'Do I have to get under that damn lamp again?'

'It's got to come out on a conscious level,' Humphrys told him, 'but not all at once. You've had your limit for today.'

Sagging with relief, Sharp settled back in the chair. 'Thanks,' he said weakly. Touching his face, his body, he whispered: 'I've been carrying that in my mind all these years. Corroding, eating away—'

'There should be some diminution of the phobia,' the analyst told him, 'as you grapple with the incident itself. We've made progress; we now have some idea of the real fear. It involves bodily injury at the hands of professional criminals. Ex-soldiers in the early post-war years . . . gangs of bandits. I remember.'

A measure of confidence returned to Sharp. 'It isn't hard to understand a falling fear, under the circumstances. Considering what happened to me . . .' Shakily, he started to his feet.

And screamed shrilly.

'What is it?' Humphrys demanded, hastily coming over and grabbing hold of his arm. Sharp leaped violently away, staggered, and collapsed inertly in the chair. 'What happened?'

Face working, Sharp managed: 'I can't get up.'

'What?'

'I can't stand up.' Imploringly, he gazed up at the analyst, stricken and terrified. 'I'm—afraid I'll fall. Doctor, now I can't even get to my feet.'

For an interval neither man spoke. Finally, his eyes on the floor, Sharp whispered: 'The reason I came to you, Humphrys, is because your office is on the ground floor. That's a laugh, isn't it? I couldn't go any higher.'

'We're going to have to turn the lamp back on you,' Humphrys said.

'I realize it. I'm scared.' Gripping the arms of the chair, he continued: 'Go ahead. What else can we do? I can't leave here. Humphrys, this thing is going to kill me.'

'No, it isn't.' Humphrys got the lamp into position. 'We'll get you out of this. Try to relax; try to think of nothing in particular.' Clicking the mechanism on, he said softly: 'This time I don't want the traumatic incident itself. I want the envelope of experience that surrounds it. I want the broader segment of which it's a part.'

Paul Sharp walked quietly through the snow. His breath, in front of him, billowed outward and formed a sparkling cloud of white. To his left lay the jagged ruins of what had been buildings. The ruins, covered with snow, seemed almost lovely. For a moment he paused, entranced.

'Interesting,' a member of his research team observed, coming up. 'Could be anything—absolutely anything—under there.'

'It's beautiful, in a way,' Sharp commented.

'See that spire?' The young man pointed with one heavily gloved finger; he still wore his lead-shielded suit. He and his group had been poking around the still-contaminated crater. Their boring bars were lined up in an orderly row. 'That was a church,' he informed Sharp. 'A nice one, by the looks of it. And over there—' he indicated an indiscriminate jumble of ruin—'that was the main civic center.'

'The city wasn't directly hit, was it?' Sharp asked.

'It was bracketed. Come on down and see what we've run into. The crater to our right—'

'No, thanks,' Sharp said, pulling back with intense aversion. 'I'll let you do the crawling around.'

The youthful expert glanced curiously at Sharp, then forgot the matter. 'Unless we run into something unexpected, we should be able to start reclamation within a week. The first step, of course, is to clear off the slag-layer. It's fairly well cracked—a lot of plant growth has perforated it, and natural decay has reduced a great deal of it to semi-organic ash.'

'Fine,' Sharp said, with satisfaction. 'I'll be glad to see something here again, after all these years.'

The expert asked: 'What was it like before the war? I never saw that; I was born after the destruction began.'

'Well,' Sharp said, surveying the fields of snow, 'this was a thriving agricultural center. They grew grapefruit here. Arizona grapefruit. The Roosevelt Dam was along this way.'

'Yes,' the expert said, nodding. 'We located the remnants of it.'

'Cotton was grown here. So was lettuce, alfalfa, grapes, olives, apricots—the thing I remember most, the time I came through Phoenix with my family, was the eucalyptus trees.'

'We won't have all that back,' the expert said regretfully. 'What the heck—eucalyptus? I never heard of that.'

'There aren't any left in the United States,' Sharp said. 'You'd have to go to Australia.'

Listening, Humphrys jotted down a notation. 'Okay,' he said aloud, switching off the lamp. 'Come back, Sharp.'

With a grunt, Paul Sharp blinked and opened his eyes. 'What—' Struggling up, he yawned, stretched, peered blankly around the office. 'Something about reclamation. I was supervising a team of recon men. A young kid.'

'When did you reclaim Phoenix?' Humphrys asked. 'That seems to be included in the vital time-space segment.'

Sharp frowned. 'We never reclaimed Phoenix. That's still projected. We hope to get at it sometime in the next year.'

'Are you positive?'

'Naturally. That's my job.'

'I'm going to have to send you back,' Humphrys said, already reaching for the lamp.

'What happened?'

The lamp came on. 'Relax,' Humphrys instructed briskly, a trifle too briskly for a man supposed to know exactly what he was doing. Forcing himself to slow down, he said carefully: 'I want your perspective to broaden. Take in an earlier incident, one preceding the Phoenix reclamation.'

In an inexpensive cafeteria in the business district, two men sat facing each other across a table.

'I'm sorry,' Paul Sharp said, with impatience. 'I've got to get back to my work.' Picking up his cup of ersatz coffee, he gulped the contents down.

The tall, thin man carefully pushed away his empty dishes and, leaning back, lit a cigar.

'For two years,' Giller said bluntly, 'you've been giving us the runaround. Frankly, I'm a little tired of it.'

'Runaround?' Sharp had started to rise. 'I don't get your drift.'

'You're going to reclaim an agricultural area—you're going to tackle Phoenix. So don't tell me you're sticking to industrial. How long do you imagine those people are going to keep on living? Unless you reclaim their farms and lands—'

'What people?'

Harshly, Giller said: 'The people living at Petaluma. Camped around the craters.'

With vague dismay, Sharp murmured: 'I didn't realize there was anybody living there. I thought you all headed for the nearest reclaimed regions, San Francisco and Sacramento.'

'You never read the petitions we presented,' Giller said softly.

Sharp colored. 'No, as a matter of fact. Why should I? If there're people camping in the slag, it doesn't alter the basic situation; you should leave, get out of there. That area is through.' He added: 'I got out.'

Very quietly, Giller said: 'You would have stuck around if you'd farmed there. If your family had farmed there for over a century. It's different from running a drug store. Drug stores are the same everywhere in the world.'

'So are farms.'

'No,' Giller said dispassionately. 'Your land, your family's land, has a unique feeling. We'll keep on camping there until we're dead or until you decide to reclaim.' Mechanically collecting the checks, he finished: 'I'm sorry for you, Paul. You never had roots like we have. And I'm sorry you can't be made to understand.' As he reached into his coat for his wallet, he asked: 'When can you fly out there?'

'Fly!' Sharp echoed, shuddering. 'I'm not flying anywhere.'

'You've got to see the town again. You can't decide without having seen those people, seen how they're living.'

'No,' Sharp said emphatically. 'I'm not flying out there. I can decide on the basis of reports.'

Giller considered. 'You'll come,' he declared.

'Over my dead body!'

Giller nodded. 'Maybe so. But you're going to come. You can't let us die without looking at us. You've got to have the courage to see what it is you're doing.' He got out a pocket calendar and scratched a mark by one of the dates. Tossing it across the table to Sharp, he informed him: 'We'll come by your office and pick you up. We have the plane we flew down here. It's mine. It's a sweet ship.'

Trembling, Sharp examined the calendar. And, standing over his mumbling, supine patient, so did Humphrys.

He had been right. Sharp's traumatic incident, the repressed material, didn't lie in the past.

Sharp was suffering from a phobia based on an event six months in the future.

'Can you get up?' Humphrys inquired.

In the chair, Paul Sharp stirred feebly. 'I–' he began, and then sank into silence.

'No more for a while,' Humphrys told him reassuringly. 'You've had enough. But I wanted to get you away from the trauma itself.'

'I feel better now.'

'Try to stand.' Humphrys approached and stood waiting, as the man crept unsteadily to his feet.

'Yes,' Sharp breathed. 'It has receded. What was that last? I was in a cafe or something. With Giller.'

From his desk Humphrys got a prescription pad. 'I'm going to write you out a little comfort. Some round white pills to take every four hours.' He scribbled and then handed the slip to his patient. 'So you will relax. It'll take away some of the tension.'

'Thanks,' Sharp said, in a weak, almost inaudible voice. Presently, he asked: 'A lot of material came up, didn't it?'

'It certainly did,' Humphrys admitted tightly.

There was nothing he could do for Paul Sharp. The man was very close to death now—in six short months, Giller would go to work on him. And it was too bad, because Sharp was a nice guy, a nice, conscientious, hard-working bureaucrat who was only trying to do his job as he saw it.

'What do you think?' Sharp asked pathetically. 'Can you help me?'

'I'll—try,' Humphrys answered, not able to look directly at him. 'But it goes very deep.'

'It's been a long time growing,' Sharp admitted humbly. Standing by the chair, he seemed small and forlorn; not an important official but only one isolated, unprotected individual. 'I'd sure appreciate your help. If this phobia keeps up, no telling where it'll end.'

Humphrys asked suddenly, 'Would you consider changing your mind and granting Giller's demands?'

'I can't,' Sharp said. 'It's bad policy. I'm opposed to special pleading, and that's what it is.'

'Even if you come from the area? Even if the people are friends and former neighbors of yours?'

'It's my job,' Sharp said. 'I have to do it without regard for my feelings or anybody else's.'

'You're not a bad fellow,' Humphrys said involuntarily. 'I'm sorry—' He broke off.

'Sorry what?' Sharp moved mechanically toward the exit door. 'I've taken enough of your time. I realize how busy you analysts are. When shall I come back. *Can* I come back?'

'Tomorrow.' Humphrys guided him outside and into the corridor. 'About this same time, if it's convenient.'

'Thanks a lot,' Sharp said, with relief. 'I really appreciate it.'

As soon as he was alone in his office, Humphrys closed the door and strode back to his desk. Reaching down, he grabbed the telephone and unsteadily dialed.

'Give me somebody on your medical staff,' he ordered curtly when he had been connected with the Special Talents Agency.

'This is Kirby,' a professional-sounding voice came presently. 'Medical research.'

Humphrys briefly identified himself. 'I have a patient here,' he said, 'who seems to be a latent precog.'

Kirby was interested. 'What area does he come from?'

'Petaluma. Sonoma County, north of San Francisco Bay. It's east of—'

'We're familiar with the area. A number of precogs have showed up there. That's been a gold mine for us.'

'Then I was right,' Humphrys said.

'What's the date of the patient's birth?'

'He was six years old when the war began.'

'Well,' Kirby said, disappointed, 'then he didn't really get enough of a dose. He'll never develop a full precog talent, such as we work with here.'

'In other words, you won't help?'

'Latents—people with a touch of it—outnumber the real carriers. We don't have time to fool with them. You'll probably run into dozens like your patient, if you stir around. When it's imperfect, the talent isn't valuable; it's going to be a nuisance for the man, probably nothing else.'

'Yes, it's a nuisance,' Humphrys agreed caustically. 'The man is only months away from a violent death. Since he was a child, he's been getting advanced phobic warnings. As the event gets closer, the reactions intensify.'

'He's not conscious of the future material?'

'It operates strictly on a sub-rational level.'

'Under the circumstances,' Kirby said thoughtfully, 'maybe it's just as well. These things appear to be fixed. If he knew about it, he still couldn't change it.'

Dr Charles Bamberg, consulting psychiatrist, was just leaving his office when he noticed a man sitting in the waiting room.

Odd, Bamberg thought. I have no patients left for today.

Opening the door, he stepped into the waiting room. 'Did you wish to see me?'

The man sitting on the chair was tall and thin. He wore a wrinkled tan raincoat, and, as Bamberg appeared, he began tensely stubbing out a cigar.

'Yes,' he said, getting clumsily to his feet.

'Do you have an appointment?'

'No appointment.' The man gazed at him in appeal. 'I picked you–' He laughed with confusion. 'Well, you're on the top floor.'

'The top floor?' Bamberg was intrigued. 'What's that got to do with it?'

'I–well, Doc, I feel much more comfortable when I'm up high.'

'I see,' Bamberg said. A compulsion, he thought to himself. Fascinating. 'And,' he said aloud, 'when you're up high, how do you feel? Better?'

'Not better,' the man answered. 'Can I come in? Do you have a second to spare me?'

Bamberg looked at his watch. 'All right,' he agreed, admitting the man. 'Sit down and tell me about it.'

Gratefully, Giller seated himself. 'It interferes with my life,' he said rapidly, jerkily. 'Every time I see a flight of stairs, I have an irresistible compulsion to go up it. And plane flight–I'm always flying around. I have my own ship; I can't afford it, but I've got to have it.'

'I see,' Bamberg said. 'Well,' he continued genially, 'that's not really so bad. After all, it isn't exactly a fatal compulsion.'

Helplessly, Giller replied: 'When I'm up there–' He swallowed wretchedly, his dark eyes gleaming. 'Doctor, when I'm up high, in an office building, or in my plane–I feel another compulsion.'

'What is it?'

'I–' Giller shuddered. 'I have an irresistible urge to push people.'

'To push people?'

'Toward windows. Out.' Giller made a gesture. 'What am I going to do, Doc? I'm afraid I'll kill somebody. There was a little shrimp of a guy I pushed once—and one day a girl was standing ahead of me on an escalator—I shoved her. She was injured.'

'I see,' Bamberg said, nodding. Repressed hostility, he thought to himself. Interwoven with sex. Not unusual.

He reached for his lamp.

THE UNRECONSTRUCTED M

I

The machine was a foot wide and two feet long; it looked like an oversized box of crackers. Silently, with great caution, it climbed the side of a concrete building; it had lowered two rubberized rollers and was now beginning the first phase of its job.

From its rear, a flake of blue enamel was exuded. The machine pressed the flake firmly against the rough concrete and then continued on. Its upward path carried it from vertical concrete to vertical steel: it had reached a window. The machine paused and produced a microscopic fragment of cloth fabric. The cloth, with great care, was embedded in the fitting of the steel window frame.

In the chill darkness, the machine was virtually invisible. The glow of a distant tangle of traffic briefly touched it, illuminated its polished hull, and departed. The machine resumed its work.

It projected a plastic pseudopodium and incinerated the pane of window glass. There was no response from within the gloomy apartment: nobody was home. The machine, now dulled with particles of glass-dust, crept over the steel frame and raised an inquisitive receptor.

While it received, it exerted precisely two hundred pounds' pressure on the steel window frame; the frame obediently bent. Satisfied, the machine descended the inside of the wall to the moderately thick carpet. There it began the second phase of its job.

One single human hair—follicle and speck of scalp included—was deposited on the hardwood floor by the lamp. Not far from the piano, two dried grains of tobacco were ceremoniously laid out. The machine waited an interval of ten seconds and then, as an internal section of magnetic tape clicked into place, it suddenly said, 'Ugh! Damn it . . .'

Curiously, its voice was husky and masculine.

The machine made its way to the closet door, which was locked. Climbing the wood surface, the machine reached the lock mechanism, and, inserting a thin section of itself, caressed the tumblers back. Behind the row of coats was a small mound of batteries and wires: a self-powered video recorder. The machine destroyed the reservoir of film—which was vital—and then, as it left the closet, expelled a drop of blood on the jagged tangle that had been the lens-scanner. The drop of blood was even more vital.

While the machine was pressing the artificial outline of a heel mark into the greasy film that covered the flooring of the closet, a sharp sound came from the hallway. The machine ceased its work and became rigid. A moment later a small, middle-aged man entered the apartment, coat over one arm, briefcase in the other.

'Good God,' he said, stopping instantly as he saw the machine. 'What are you?'

The machine lifted the nozzle of its front section and shot an explosive pellet at the man's half-bald head. The pellet traveled into the skull and detonated. Still clutching his coat and briefcase, a bewildered expression on his face, the man collapsed to the rug. His glasses, broken, lay twisted beside his ear. His body stirred a little, twitched, and then was satisfactorily quiet.

Only two steps remained to the job, now that the main part was done. The machine deposited a bit of burnt match in one of the spotless ashtrays resting on the mantel, and entered the kitchen to search for a water glass. It was starting up the side of the sink when the noise of human voices startled it.

'This is the apartment,' a voice said, clear and close.

'Get ready—he ought to still be here.' Another voice, a man's voice, like the first. The hall door was pushed open and two individuals in heavy overcoats sprinted purposefully into the apartment. At their approach, the machine dropped to the kitchen floor, the water glass forgotten. Something had gone wrong. Its rectangular outline flowed and wavered; pulling itself into an upright package it fused its shape into that of a conventional TV unit.

It was holding that emergency form when one of the men—tall, red-haired—peered briefly into the kitchen.

'Nobody in here,' the man declared, and hurried on.

'The window,' his companion said, panting. Two more figures entered the apartment, an entire crew. 'The glass is gone—missing. He got in that way.'

'But he's gone.' The red-haired man reappeared at the kitchen door; he snapped on the light and entered, a gun visible in his hand. 'Strange . . . we got here right away, as soon as we picked up the rattle.' Suspiciously, he examined his wristwatch. 'Rosenburg's been dead only a few seconds . . . how could he have got out again so fast?'

Standing in the street entrance, Edward Ackers listened to the voice. During the last half hour the voice had taken on a carping, nagging whine; sinking almost to inaudibility, it plodded along, mechanically turning out its message of complaint.

'You're tired,' Ackers said. 'Go home. Take a hot bath.'

'No,' the voice said, interrupting its tirade. The locus of the voice was a large illuminated blob on the dark sidewalk, a few yards to Acker's right. The revolving neon sign read:

BANISH IT!

Thirty times—he had counted—within the last few minutes the sign had captured a passerby and the man in the booth had begun his harangue. Beyond the booth were several theaters and restaurants: the booth was well-situated.

THE UNRECONSTRUCTED M

But it wasn't for the crowd that the booth had been erected. It was for Ackers and the offices behind him; the tirade was aimed directly at the Interior Department. The nagging racket had gone on so many months that Ackers was scarcely aware of it. Rain on the roof. Traffic noises. He yawned, folded his arms, and waited.

'Banish it,' the voice complained peevishly. 'Come on, Ackers. Say something; do something.'

'I'm waiting,' Ackers said complacently.

A group of middle-class citizens passed the booth and were handed leaflets. The citizens scattered the leaflets after them, and Ackers laughed.

'Don't laugh,' the voice muttered. 'It's not funny; it costs us money to print those.'

'Your personal money?' Ackers inquired.

'Partly.' Garth was lonely, tonight. 'What are you waiting for? What's happened? I saw a police team leave your roof a few minutes ago . . . ?

'We may take in somebody,' Ackers said, 'there's been a killing.'

Down the dark sidewalk the man stirred in his dreary propaganda booth. 'Oh?' Harvey Garth's voice came. He leaned forward and the two looked directly at each other: Ackers, carefully-groomed, well-fed, wearing a respectable overcoat . . . Garth, a thin man, much younger, with a lean, hungry face composed mostly of nose and forehead.

'So you see,' Ackers told him, 'we do need the system. Don't be utopian.'

'A man is murdered; and you rectify the moral imbalance by killing the killer.' Garth's protesting voice rose in a bleak spasm. 'Banish it! Banish the system that condemns men to certain extinction!'

'Get your leaflets here,' Ackers parodied dryly. 'And your slogans. Either or both. What would you suggest in place of the system?'

Garth's voice was proud with conviction. 'Education.'

Amused, Ackers asked: 'Is that all? You think that would stop anti-social activity? Criminals just don't—*know* better?'

'And psychotherapy, of course.' His projected face bony and intense, Garth peered out of his booth like an aroused turtle. 'They're sick ... that's why they commit crimes, healthy men don't commit crimes. And you compound it; you create a sick society of punitive cruelty.' He waggled an accusing finger. 'You're the real culprit, you and the whole Interior Department. You and the whole Banishment System.'

Again and again the neon sign blinked BANISH IT! Meaning, of course, the system of compulsory ostracism for felons, the machinery that projected a condemned human being into some random backwater region of the sidereal universe, into some remote and out-of-the-way corner where he would be of no harm.

'No harm to us, anyhow,' Ackers mused aloud.

Garth spoke the familiar argument. 'Yes, but what about the local inhabitants?'

Too bad about the local inhabitants. Anyhow, the banished victim spent his energy and time trying to find a way back to the Sol System. If he got back before old age caught up with him he was readmitted by society. Quite a challenge ... especially to some cosmopolite who had never set foot outside Greater New York. There were—probably—many involuntary expatriates cutting grain in odd fields with primitive sickles. The remote sections of the universe seemed composed mostly of dank rural cultures, isolated agrarian enclaves typified by small-time bartering of fruit and vegetables and handmade artifacts.

'Did you know,' Ackers said, 'that in the Age of Monarchs, a pickpocket was usually hanged?'

'Banish it,' Garth continued monotonously, sinking back into his booth. The sign revolved; leaflets were passed out. And Ackers impatiently watched the late-evening street for sign of the hospital truck.

He knew Heimie Rosenburg. A sweeter little guy there never was ... although Heimie had been mixed up in one of the sprawling slave combines that illegally transported settlers to out-system fertile planets. Between them, the two largest slavers had settled virtually the entire Sirius System. Four out of six emigrants were hustled out in carriers registered as 'freighters.' It was hard to picture gentle little Heimie Rosenburg as a business agent for Tirol Enterprises, but there it was.

As he waited, Ackers conjectured on Heimie's murder. Probably one element of the incessant subterranean war going on between Paul Tirol and his major rival. David Lantano was a brilliant and energetic newcomer . . . but murder was anybody's game. It all depended on how it was done; it could be commercial hack or the purest art.

'Here comes something,' Garth's voice sounded, carried to his inner ear by the delicate output transformers of the booth's equipment. 'Looks like a freezer.'

It was; the hospital truck had arrived. Ackers stepped forward as the truck halted and the back was let down.

'How soon did you get there?' he asked the cop who jumped heavily to the pavement.

'Right away,' the cop answered, 'but no sign of the killer. I don't think we're going to get Heimie back . . . they got him dead-center, right in the cerebellum. Expert work, no amateur stuff.'

Disappointed, Ackers clambered into the hospital truck to inspect for himself.

Very tiny and still, Heimie Rosenburg lay on his back, arms at his sides, gazing sightlessly up at the roof of the truck. On his face remained the expression of bewildered wonder. Somebody—one of the cops—had placed his bent glasses in his clenched hand. In falling he had cut his cheek. The destroyed portion of his skull was covered by a moist plastic web.

'Who's back at the apartment?' Ackers asked presently.

'The rest of my crew,' the cop answered. 'And an independent researcher. Leroy Beam.'

'Him,' Ackers said, with aversion. 'How is it he showed up?'

'Caught the rattle, too, happened to be passing with his rig. Poor

Heimie had an awful big booster on that rattle . . . I'm surprised it wasn't picked up here at the main offices.'

'They say Heimie had a high anxiety level,' Ackers said. 'Bugs all over his apartment. You're starting to collect evidence?'

'The teams are moving in,' the cop said. 'We should begin getting specifications in half an hour. The killer knocked out the vid bug set up in the closet. But—' He grinned. 'He cut himself breaking the circuit. A drop of blood, right on the wiring; it looks promising.'

At the apartment, Leroy Beam watched the Interior police begin their analysis. They worked smoothly and thoroughly, but Beam was dissatisfied.

His original impression remained: he was suspicious. Nobody could have gotten away so quickly. Heimie had died, and his death—the cessation of his neural pattern—had triggered off an automatic squawk. A rattle didn't particularly protect its owner, but its existence ensured (or usually ensured) detection of the murderer. Why had it failed Heimie?

Prowling moodily, Leroy Beam entered the kitchen for the second time. There, on the floor by the sink, was a small portable TV unit, the kind popular with the sporting set: a gaudy little packet of plastic and knobs and multi-tinted lenses.

'Why this?' Beam asked, as one of the cops plodded past him. 'This TV unit sitting here on the kitchen floor. It's out of place.'

The cop ignored him. In the living room, elaborate police detection equipment was scraping the various surfaces inch by inch. In the half hour since Heimie's death, a number of specifications had been logged. First, the drop of blood on the damaged vid wiring. Second, a hazy heel mark where the murderer had stepped. Third, a bit of burnt match in the ashtray. More were expected; the analysis had only begun.

It usually took nine specifications to delineate the single individual.

Leroy Beam glanced cautiously around him. None of the cops was watching, so he bent down and picked up the TV unit; it felt ordinary. He clicked the *on* switch and waited. Nothing happened; no image formed. Strange.

He was holding it upside down, trying to see the inner chassis, when Edward Ackers from Interior entered the apartment. Quickly, Beam stuffed the TV unit into the pocket of his heavy overcoat.

'What are you doing here?' Ackers said.

'Seeking,' Beam answered, wondering if Ackers noticed his tubby bulge. 'I'm in business, too.'

'Did you know Heimie?'

'By reputation,' Beam answered vaguely. 'Tied in with Tirol's combine, I hear; some sort of front man. Had an office on Fifth Avenue.'

'Swank place, like the rest of those Fifth Avenue feather merchants.' Ackers went on into the living room to watch detectors gather up evidence.

There was a vast nearsightedness to the wedge grinding ponderously across the carpet. It was scrutinizing at a microscopic level, and its field was sharply curtailed. As fast as material was obtained, it was relayed to the Interior offices, to the aggregate file banks where the civil population was represented by a series of punch cards, cross-indexed infinitely.

Lifting the telephone, Ackers called his wife. 'I won't be home,' he told her. 'Business.'

A lag and then Ellen responded. 'Oh?' she said distantly. 'Well, thanks for letting me know.'

Over in the corner, two members of the police crew were delightedly examining a new discovery, valid enough to be a specification. 'I'll call you again,' he said hurriedly to Ellen, 'before I leave. Goodbye.'

'Goodbye,' Ellen said curtly, and managed to hang up before he did.

The new discovery was the undamaged aud bug, which was mounted under the floor lamp. A continuous magnetic tape—still in motion—gleamed amiably; the murder episode had been recorded sound-wise in its entirety.

'Everything,' a cop said gleefully to Ackers. 'It was going before Heimie got home.'

'You played it back?'

'A portion. There's a couple words spoken by the murderer, should be enough.'

Ackers got in touch with Interior. 'Have the specifications on the Rosenburg case been fed, yet?'

'Just the first,' the attendant answered. 'The file discriminates the usual massive category—about six billion names.'

Ten minutes later the second specification was fed to the files. Persons with type O blood, with size 11½ shoes, numbered slightly over a billion. The third specification brought in the element of smoker-nonsmoker. That dropped the number to less than a billion, but not much less. Most adults smoked.

'The aud tape will drop it fast,' Leroy Beam commented, standing beside Ackers, his arms folded to conceal his bulging coat. 'Ought to be able to get age, at least.'

The aud tape, analyzed, gave thirty to forty years as the conjectured age. And—timbre analysis—a man of perhaps two hundred pounds. A little later the bent steel window frame was examined, and the warp noted. It jibed with the specification of the aud tape. There were now six specifications, including that of sex (male). The number of persons in the in-group was falling rapidly.

'It won't be long,' Ackers said genially. 'And if he tacked one of those little buckets to the building side, we'll have a paint scrape.'

Beam said: 'I'm leaving. Good luck.'

'Stick around.'

'Sorry.' Beam moved toward the hall door. 'This is yours, not mine. I've got my own business to attend to . . . I'm doing research for a hot-shot nonferrous mining concern.'

Ackers eyed his coat. 'Are you pregnant?'

'Not that I know of,' Beam said, coloring. 'I've led a good clean life.' Awkwardly, he patted his coat. 'You mean this?'

By the window, one of the police gave a triumphant yap. The

two bits of pipe tobacco had been discovered: a refinement for the third specification. 'Excellent,' Ackers said, turning away from Beam and momentarily forgetting him.

Beam left.

Very shortly he was driving across town toward his own labs, the small and independent research outfit that he headed, unsupported by a government grant. Resting on the seat beside him was the portable TV unit, it was still silent.

'First of all,' Beam's gowned technician declared, 'it has a power supply approximately seventy times that of a portable TV pack. We picked up the Gamma radiation.' He displayed the usual detector. 'So you're right, it's not a TV set.'

Gingerly, Beam lifted the small unit from the lab bench. Five hours had passed, and still he knew nothing about it. Taking firm hold of the back he pulled with all his strength. The back refused to come off. It wasn't stuck: there were no seams. The back was not a back; it only looked like a back.

'Then what is it?' he asked.

'Could be lots of things,' the technician said noncommittally; he had been roused from the privacy of his home, and it was now two-thirty in the morning. 'Could be some sort of scanning equipment. A bomb. A weapon. Any kind of gadget.'

Laboriously, Beam felt the unit all over, searching for a flaw in the surface. 'It's uniform,' he murmured. 'A single surface.'

'You bet. The breaks are false—it's a poured substance. And,' the technician added, 'it's hard. I tried to chip off a representative sample but—' He gestured. 'No results.'

'Guaranteed not to shatter when dropped,' Beam said absently. 'New extra-tough plastic.' He shook the unit energetically; the muted noise of metal parts in motion reached his ear. 'It's full of guts.'

'We'll get it open,' the technician promised, 'but not tonight.'

Beam replaced the unit on the bench. He could, with bad luck, work days on this one item—to discover, after all, that it had nothing to do with the murder of Heimie Rosenburg. On the other hand . . .

'Drill me a hole in it,' he instructed. 'So we can see it.'

His technician protested: 'I drilled, the drill broke. I've sent out for an improved density. This substance is imported; somebody hooked it from a white dwarf system. It was conceived under stupendous pressure.'

'You're stalling,' Beam said, irritated. 'That's how they talk in the advertising media.'

The technician shrugged. 'Anyhow, it's extra hard. A naturally-evolved element, or an artificially-processed product from somebody's labs. Who has funds to develop a metal like this?'

'One of the big slavers,' Beam said. 'That's where the wealth winds up. And they hop around to various systems . . . they'd have access to raw materials. Special ores.'

'Can't I go home?' the technician asked. 'What's so important about this?'

'This device either killed or helped kill Heimie Rosenburg. We'll sit here, you and I, until we get it open.' Beam seated himself and began examining the check sheet showing which tests had been applied. 'Sooner or later it'll fly open like a clam—if you can remember that far back.'

Behind them, a warning bell sounded.

'Somebody in the anteroom,' Beam said, surprised and wary. 'At two-thirty?' He got up and made his way down the dark hall to the front of the building. Probably it was Ackers. His conscience stirred guiltily: somebody had logged the absence of the TV unit.

But it was not Ackers.

Waiting humbly in the cold, deserted anteroom was Paul Tirol, with him was an attractive young woman unknown to Beam. Tirol's wrinkled face broke into smiles, and he extended a hearty hand. 'Beam,' he said. They shook. 'Your front door said you were down here. Still working?'

Guardedly, wondering who the woman was and what Tirol wanted, Beam said: 'Catching up on some slipshod errors. Whole firm's going broke.'

Tirol laughed indulgently. 'Always a japer.' His deep-set eyes darted; Tirol was a powerfully-built person, older than most, with a somber, intensely-creased face. 'Have room for a few contracts? I thought I might slip a few jobs your way . . . if you're open.'

'I'm always open,' Beam countered, blocking Tirol's view of the lab proper. The door, anyhow, had slid itself shut. Tirol had been Heimie's boss . . . he no doubt felt entitled to all extant information on the murder. Who did it? When? How? Why? But that didn't explain why he was *here*.

'Terrible thing,' Tirol said crudely. He made no move to introduce the woman; she had retired to the couch to light a cigarette. She was slender, with mahogany-colored hair; she wore a blue coat, and a kerchief tied around her head.

'Yes,' Beam agreed. 'Terrible.'

'You were there, I understand.'

That explained some of it. 'Well,' Beam conceded, 'I showed up.'

'But you didn't actually see it?'

'No,' Beam admitted, 'nobody saw it. Interior is collecting specification material. They should have it down to one card before morning.'

Visibly, Tirol relaxed. 'I'm glad of that. I'd hate to see the vicious criminal escape. Banishment's too good for him. He ought to be gassed.'

'Barbarism,' Beam murmured dryly. 'The days of the gas chamber. Medieval.'

Tirol peered past him. 'You're working on—' Now he was overtly beginning to pry. 'Come now, Leroy. Heimie Rosenburg—God bless his soul—was killed tonight and tonight I find you burning the midnight oil. You can talk openly with me; you've got something relevant to his death, haven't you?'

'That's Ackers you're thinking of.'

Tirol chuckled. 'Can I take a look?'

'Not until you start paying me; I'm not on your books yet.'

In a strained, unnatural voice, Tirol bleated: 'I want it.'

Puzzled, Beam said: 'You want what?'

With a grotesque shudder, Tirol blundered forward, shoved Beam aside, and groped for the door. The door flew open and Tirol started noisily down the dark corridor, feeling his way by instinct toward the research labs.

'Hey!' Beam shouted, outraged. He sprinted after the older man, reached the inner door, and prepared to fight it out. He was shaking, partly with amazement, partly with anger. 'What the hell?' he demanded breathlessly. 'You don't own me!'

Behind him the door mysteriously gave way. Foolishly, he sprawled backward, half-falling into the lab. There, stricken with helpless paralysis, was his technician. And, coming across the floor of the lab was something small and metallic. It looked like an over-sized box of crackers, and it was going lickety-split toward Tirol. The object—metal and gleaming—hopped up into Tirol's arms, and the old man turned and lumbered back up the hall to the anteroom.

'What was it?' the technician said, coming to life.

Ignoring him, Beam hurried after Tirol. 'He's got it!' he yelled futilely.

'It—' the technician mumbled. 'It was the TV set. And it *ran*.'

II

The file banks at Interior were in agitated flux.

The process of creating a more and more restricted category was tedious, and it took time. Most of the Interior staff had gone home to bed; it was almost three in the morning, and the corridors and offices were deserted. A few mechanical cleaning devices crept here and there in the darkness. The sole source of life was the study chamber of the file banks. Edward Ackers sat patiently waiting for the results, waiting for specifications to come in, and for the file machinery to process them.

To his right a few Interior police played a benign lottery and waited stoically to be sent out for the pick-up. The lines of communication to Heimie Rosenburg's apartment buzzed ceaselessly. Down the street, along the bleak sidewalk, Harvey Garth was still at his propaganda booth, still flashing his BANISH IT! sign and muttering in people's ears. There were virtually no passersby, now, but Garth went on. He was tireless; he never gave up.

'Psychopath,' Ackers said resentfully. Even where he sat, six floors up, the tinny, carping voice reached his middle ear.

'Take him in,' one of the game-playing cops suggested. The game, intricate and devious, was a version of a Centaurian III practice. 'We can revoke his vendor's license.'

Ackers had, when there was nothing else to do, concocted and refined an indictment of Garth, a sort of lay analysis of the man's mental aberrations. He enjoyed playing the psychoanalytic game; it gave him a sense of power.

> Garth, Harvey
> Prominent compulsive syndrome. Has assumed role of ideological anarchist, opposing legal and social system. No rational expression, only repetition of key words and phrases. Idée fixe is *Banish the banishment system*. Cause dominates life. Rigid fanatic, probably of manic type, since . . .

Ackers let the sentence go, since he didn't really know what the structure of the manic type was. Anyhow, the analysis was excellent, and someday it would be resting in an official slot instead of merely drifting through his mind. And, when that happened, the annoying voice would conclude.

'Big turmoil,' Garth droned. 'Banishment system in vast upheaval . . . crisis moment has arrived.'

'Why crisis?' Ackers asked aloud.

Down below on the pavement Garth responded. 'All your machines are humming. Grand excitement reigns. Somebody's head will be in the basket before sun-up.' His voice trailed off in a weary blur.

'Intrigue and murder. Corpses . . . the police scurry and a beautiful woman lurks.'

To his analysis Ackers added an amplifying clause.

> . . . Garth's talents are warped by his compulsive sense of *mission*. Having designed an ingenious communication device he sees only its propaganda possibility. Whereas Garth's voice-ear mechanism could be put to work for All Humanity.

That pleased him. Ackers got up and wandered over to the attendant operating the file. 'How's it coming?' he asked.

'Here's the situation,' the attendant said. There was a line of gray stubble smeared over his chin, and he was bleary-eyed. 'We're gradually paring it down.'

Ackers, as he resumed his seat, wished he were back in the days of the almighty fingerprint. But a print hadn't shown up in months, a thousand techniques existed for print-removal and print alteration. There was no single specification capable, in itself, of delineating the individual. A composite was needed, a gestalt of the assembled data.

1) blood sample (type O) 6,139,481,601
2) shoe size (11½) 1,268,303,431
3) smoker 791,992,386
3a) smoker (pipe) 52,774,853
4) sex (male) 26,449,094
5) age (30–40 years) 9,221,397
6) weight (200 lbs) 488,290
7) fabric of clothing 17,459
8) hair variety 866
9) ownership of utilized weapon 40

A vivid picture was emerging from the data. Ackers could see him clearly. The man was practically standing there, in front of his desk. A fairly young man, somewhat heavy, a man who smoked a pipe and wore an extremely expensive tweed suit. An individual created by nine specifications; no tenth had been listed because no more data of specification level had been found.

Now, according to the report, the apartment had been thoroughly searched. The detection equipment was going outdoors.

'One more should do it,' Ackers said, returning the report to the attendant. He wondered if it would come in and how long it would take.

To waste time he telephoned his wife, but instead of getting Ellen he got the automatic response circuit. 'Yes, sir,' it told him. 'Mrs Ackers has retired for the night. You may state a thirty-second message which will be transcribed for her attention tomorrow morning. Thank you.'

Ackers raged at the mechanism futilely and then hung up. He wondered if Ellen were really in bed; maybe she had, as often before, slipped out. But, after all, it was almost three o'clock in the morning. Any sane person would be asleep: only he and Garth were still at their little stations, performing their vital duties.

What had Garth meant by a *beautiful woman*?

'Mr Ackers,' the attendant said, 'there's a tenth specification coming in over the wires.'

Hopefully, Ackers gazed up at the file bank. He could see nothing, of course; the actual mechanism occupied the underground levels of the building, and all that existed here was the input receptors and throw-out slots. But just looking at the machinery was in itself comforting. At this moment the bank was accepting the tenth piece of material. In a moment he would know how many citizens fell into the ten categories . . . he would know if already he had a group small enough to be sorted one by one.

'Here it is,' the attendant said, pushing the report to him.

Type of utilized vehicle (color) 7

'My God,' Ackers said mildly. 'That's low enough. Seven persons—we can go to work.'

'You want the seven cards popped?'

'Pop them,' Ackers said.

A moment later, the throw-out slot deposited seven neat white cards in the tray. The attendant passed them to Ackers and he quickly riffled them. The next step was personal motive and proximity: items that had to be gotten from the suspects themselves.

Of the seven names six meant nothing to him. Two lived on Venus, one in the Centaurus System, one was somewhere in Sirius, one was in the hospital, and one lived in the Soviet Union. The seventh, however, lived within a few miles, on the outskirts of New York.

LANTANO, DAVID

That clinched it. The gestalt, in Ackers' mind, locked clearly in place, the image hardened to reality. He had half-expected, even prayed to see Lantano's card brought up.

'Here's your pick-up,' he said shakily to the game-playing cops. 'Better get as large a team together as possible, this one won't be easy.' Momentously, he added: 'Maybe I'd better come along.'

Beam reached the anteroom of his lab as the ancient figure of Paul Tirol disappeared out the street door and onto the dark sidewalk. The young woman, trotting ahead of him, had climbed into a parked car and started it forward; as Tirol emerged, she swept him up and at once departed.

Panting, Beam stood impotently collecting himself on the deserted pavement. The ersatz TV unit was gone; now he had nothing. Aimlessly, he began to run down the street. His heels echoed loudly in the cold silence. No sign of them; no sign of anything.

'I'll be damned,' he said, with almost religious awe. The unit—a robot device of obvious complexity—clearly belonged to Paul Tirol; as soon as it had identified his presence it had sprinted gladly to him. For ... protection?

It had killed Heimie; and it belonged to Tirol. So, by a novel and indirect method, Tirol had murdered his employee, his Fifth Avenue front man. At a rough guess, such a highly-organized robot would cost in the neighborhood of a hundred thousand dollars.

A lot of money, considering that murder was the easiest of criminal acts. Why not hire an itinerant goon with a crowbar?

Beam started slowly back toward his lab. Then, abruptly, he changed his mind and turned in the direction of the business area. When a free-wheeling cab came by, he hailed it and clambered in.

'Where to, sport?' the starter at cab relay asked. City cabs were guided by remote control from one central source.

He gave the name of a specific bar. Settling back against the seat he pondered. Anybody could commit a murder; an expensive, complicated machine wasn't necessary.

The machine had been built to do something else. The murder of Heimie Rosenburg was incidental.

Against the nocturnal skyline, a huge stone residence loomed. Ackers inspected it from a distance. There were no lights burning; everything was locked up tight. Spread out before the house was an acre of grass. David Lantano was probably the last person on Earth to own an acre of grass outright; it was less expensive to buy an entire planet in some other system.

'Let's go,' Ackers commanded; disgusted by such opulence, he deliberately trampled through a bed of roses on his way up the wide porch steps. Behind him flowed the team of shock-police.

'Gosh,' Lantano rumbled, when he had been roused from his bed. He was a kindly-looking, rather youthful fat man, wearing now an abundant silk dressing robe. He would have seemed more in place as director of a boys' summer camp; there was an expression of perpetual good humor on his soft, sagging face. 'What's wrong, officer?'

Ackers loathed being called officer. 'You're under arrest,' he stated.

'Me?' Lantano echoed feebly. 'Hey, officer, I've got lawyers to take care of these things.' He yawned voluminously. 'Care for some coffee?' Stupidly, he began puttering around his front room, fixing a pot.

It had been years since Ackers had splurged and bought himself a cup of coffee. With Terran land covered by dense industrial and residential installations there was no room for crops, and coffee had refused to 'take' in any other system. Lantano probably grew his somewhere on an illicit plantation in South America—the pickers probably believed they had been transported to some remote colony.

'No thanks,' Ackers said. 'Let's get going.'

Still dazed, Lantano plopped himself down in an easy chair and regarded Ackers with alarm. 'You're serious.' Gradually his expression faded; he seemed to be drifting back to sleep. 'Who?' he murmured distantly.

'Heimie Rosenburg.'

'No kidding.' Lantano shook his head listlessly. 'I always wanted him in my company. Heimie's got real charm. Had, I mean.'

It made Ackers nervous to remain here in the vast lush mansion. The coffee was heating, and the smell of it tickled his nose. And, heaven forbid—there on the table was a basket of *apricots*.

'Peaches,' Lantano corrected, noticing his fixed stare. 'Help yourself.'

'Where—did you get them?'

Lantano shrugged. 'Synthetic dome. Hydroponics. I forget where . . . I don't have a technical mind.'

'You know what the fine is for possessing natural fruit?'

'Look,' Lantano said earnestly, clasping his mushy hands together. 'Give me the details on this affair, and I'll prove to you I had nothing to do with it. Come on, officer.'

'Ackers,' Ackers said.

'Okay, Ackers. I thought I recognized you, but I wasn't sure; didn't want to make a fool of myself. When was Heimie killed?'

Grudgingly, Ackers gave him the pertinent information.

For a time Lantano was silent. Then, slowly, gravely, he said: 'You better look at those seven cards again. One of those fellows isn't in the Sirius System . . . he's back here.'

Ackers calculated the chances of successfully banishing a man of David Lantano's importance. His organization—Interplay Export—had fingers all over the galaxy; there'd be search crews going out like bees. But nobody went out banishment distance. The condemned, temporarily ionized, rendered in terms of charged particles of energy, radiated outward at the velocity of light. This was an experimental technique that had failed; it worked only one way.

'Consider,' Lantano said thoughtfully. 'If I *was* going to kill Heimie—*would I do it myself?* You're not being logical, Ackers. I'd send somebody.' He pointed a fleshy finger at Ackers. 'You imagine I'd risk my own life? I know you pick up everybody . . . you usually turn up enough specifications.'

'We have ten on you,' Ackers said briskly.

'So you're going to banish me?'

'If you're guilty, you'll have to face banishment like anyone else. Your particular prestige has no bearing.'

Nettled, Ackers said: 'Obviously, you'll be released. You'll have plenty of opportunity to prove your innocence; you can question each of the ten specifications in turn.'

He started to go on and describe the general process of court procedure employed in the twenty-first century, but something made him pause. David Lantano and his chair seemed to be gradually sinking into the floor. Was it an illusion? Blinking, Ackers rubbed his eyes and peered. At the same time, one of the policemen yelped a warning of dismay; Lantano was quietly leaving them.

'Come back!' Ackers demanded; he leaped forward and grabbed hold of the chair. Hurriedly, one of his men shorted out the power supply of the building; the chair ceased descending and groaned to a halt. Only Lantano's head was visible above the floor level. He was almost entirely submerged in a concealed escape shaft.

'What seedy, useless—' Ackers began.

'I know,' Lantano admitted, making no move to drag himself up. He seemed resigned; his mind was again off in clouds of contemplation. 'I hope we can clear all this up. Evidently I'm being framed. Tirol got somebody who looks like me, somebody to go in and murder Heimie.'

Ackers and the police crew helped him up from his depressed chair. He gave no resistance; he was too deep in his brooding.

The cab let Leroy Beam off in front of the bar. To his right, in the next block, was the Interior Building . . . and, on the sidewalk, the opaque blob that was Harvey Garth's propaganda booth.

Entering the bar, Beam found a table in the back and seated himself. Already he could pick up the faint, distorted murmur of Garth's reflections. Garth, speaking to himself in a directionless blur, was not yet aware of him.

'Banish it,' Garth was saying. 'Banish all of them. Bunch of crooks and thieves.' Garth, in the miasma of his booth, was rambling vitriolically.

'What's going on?' Beam asked. 'What's the latest?'

Garth's monologue broke off as he focussed his attention on Beam. 'You in there? In the bar?'

'I want to find out about Heimie's death.'

'Yes,' Garth said. 'He's dead; the files are moving, kicking out cards.'

'When I left Heimie's apartment,' Beam said, 'they had turned up six specifications.' He punched a button on the drink selector and dropped in a token.

'That must have been earlier,' Garth said; 'they've got more.'

'How many?'

'Ten in all.'

Ten. That was usually enough. And all ten of them laid out by a robot device . . . a little procession of hints strewn along its path: between the concrete side of the building and the dead body of Heimie Rosenburg.

'That's lucky,' he said speculatively. 'Helps out Ackers.'

'Since you're paying me,' Garth said, 'I'll tell you the rest. They've already gone out on their pick-up: Ackers went along.'

Then the device had been successful. Up to a point, at least. He was sure of one thing: the device should have been out of the apartment. Tirol hadn't known about Heimie's death rattle; Heimie had been wise enough to do the installation privately.

Had the rattle not brought persons into the apartment, the device would have scuttled out and returned to Tirol. Then, no doubt, Tirol would have detonated it. Nothing would remain to indicate that a machine could lay down a trail of synthetic clues: blood type, fabric, pipe tobacco, hair . . . all the rest, and all spurious.

'Who's the pick-up on?' Beam asked.

'David Lantano.'

Beam winced. 'Naturally. That's what the whole thing's about; he's being framed!'

Garth was indifferent; he was a hired employee, stationed by the pool of independent researchers to siphon information from the Interior Department. He had no actual interest in politics; his *Banish It!* was sheer window-dressing.

'I know it's a frame,' Beam said, 'and so does Lantano. But neither of us can prove it . . . unless Lantano has an absolutely airtight alibi.'

'Banish it,' Garth murmured, reverting to his routine. A small group of late-retiring citizens had strolled past his booth, and he was masking his conversation with Beam. The conversation, directed to the one listener, was inaudible to everyone else; but it was better not to take risks. Sometimes, very close to the booth, there was an audible feedback of the signal.

Hunched over his drink, Leroy Beam contemplated the various items he could try. He could inform Lantano's organization, which existed relatively intact . . . but the result would be epic civil war. And, in addition, he didn't really care if Lantano was framed; it was all the same to him. Sooner or later one of the big slavers had to absorb the other: cartel is the natural conclusion of big business.

With Lantano gone, Tirol would painlessly swallow his organization; everybody would be working at his desk as always.

On the other hand, there might someday be a device—now half-completed in Tirol's basement—that left a trail of *Leroy Beam* clues. Once the idea caught on, there was no particular end.

'And I had the damn thing,' he said fruitlessly. 'I hammered on it for five hours. It was a TV unit, then, but it was still the device that killed Heimie.'

'You're positive it's gone?'

'It's not only gone—it's out of existence. Unless she wrecked the car driving Tirol home.'

'She?' Garth asked.

'The woman.' Beam pondered. 'She saw it. Or she knew about it; she was with him.' But, unfortunately, he had no idea who the woman might be.

'What'd she look like?' Garth asked.

'Tall, mahogany hair. Very nervous mouth.'

'I didn't realize she was working with him openly. They must have really needed the device.' Garth added: 'You didn't identify her? I guess there's no reason why you should; she's kept out of sight.'

'Who is she?'

'That's Ellen Ackers.'

Beam laughed sharply. 'And she's driving Paul Tirol around?'

'She's—well, she's driving Tirol around, yes. You can put it that way.'

'How long?'

'I thought you were in on it. She and Ackers split up; that was last year. But he wouldn't let her leave; he wouldn't give her a divorce. Afraid of the publicity. Very important to keep up respectability . . . keep the shirt fully stuffed.'

'He knows about Paul Tirol and her?'

'Of course not. He knows she's—spiritually hooked up. But he doesn't care . . . as long as she keeps it quiet. It's his position he's thinking about.'

'If Ackers found out,' Beam murmured. 'If he saw the link between his wife and Tirol . . . he'd ignore his ten interoffice memos. He'd

THE UNRECONSTRUCTED M

want to haul in Tirol. The hell with the evidence; he could always collect that later.' Beam pushed away his drink; the glass was empty anyhow. 'Where is Ackers?'

'I told you. Out at Lantano's place, picking him up.'

'He'd come back here? He wouldn't go home?'

'Naturally he'd come back here.' Garth was silent a moment. 'I see a couple of Interior vans turning into the garage ramp. That's probably the pick-up crew returning.'

Beam waited tensely. 'Is Ackers along?'

'Yes, he's there. *Banish It!*' Garth's voice rose in stentorian frenzy. '*Banish the system of Banishment! Root out the crooks and pirates!*'

Sliding to his feet, Beam left the bar.

A dull light showed in the rear of Edward Ackers' apartment: probably the kitchen light. The front door was locked. Standing in the carpeted hallway, Beam skillfully tilted with the door mechanism. It was geared to respond to specific neural patterns: those of its owners and a limited circle of friends. For him there was no activity.

Kneeling down, Beam switched on a pocket oscillator and started sine wave emission. Gradually, he increased the frequency. At perhaps 150,000 cps the lock guiltily clicked; that was all he needed. Switching the oscillator off, he rummaged through his supply of skeleton patterns until he located the closet cylinder. Slipped into the turret of the oscillator, the cylinder emitted a synthetic neural pattern close enough to the real thing to affect the lock.

The door swung open. Beam entered.

In half-darkness the living room seemed modest and tasteful. Ellen Ackers was an adequate housekeeper. Beam listened. Was she home at all? And if so, where? Awake? Asleep?

He peeped into the bedroom. There was the bed, but nobody was in it.

If she wasn't here she was at Tirol's. But he didn't intend to follow her; this was as far as he cared to risk.

He inspected the dining room. Empty. The kitchen was empty, too. Next came an upholstered general-purpose rumpus room; on one side was a gaudy bar and on the other a wall-to-wall couch. Tossed on the couch was a woman's coat, purse, gloves. Familiar clothes: Ellen Ackers had worn them. So she had come here after leaving his research lab.

The only room left was the bathroom. He fumbled with the knob; it was locked from the inside. There was no sound, but somebody was on the other side of the door. He could sense her in there.

'Ellen,' he said, against the panelling. 'Mrs Ellen Ackers; is that you?'

No answer. He could sense her not making any sound at all: a stifled, frantic silence.

While he was kneeling down, fooling with his pocketful of magnetic lock-pullers, an explosive pellet burst through the door at head level and splattered into the plaster of the wall beyond.

Instantly the door flew open; there stood Ellen Ackers, her face distorted with fright. One of her husband's government pistols was clenched in her small, bony hand. She was less than a foot from him. Without getting up, Beam grabbed her wrist; she fired over his head, and then the two of them deteriorated into harsh, labored breathing.

'Come on,' Beam managed finally. The nozzle of the gun was literally brushing the top of his head. To kill him, she would have to pull the pistol back against her. But he didn't let her; he kept hold of her wrist until finally, reluctantly, she dropped the gun. It clattered to the floor and he got stiffly up.

'You were sitting down,' she whispered, in a stricken, accusing voice.

'Kneeling down: picking the lock. I'm glad you aimed for my brain.' He picked up the gun and succeeded in getting it into his overcoat pocket; his hands were shaking.

Ellen Ackers gazed at him starkly; her eyes were huge and dark, and her face was an ugly white. Her skin had a dead cast, as if it were artificial, totally dry, thoroughly sifted with talc. She seemed on the verge of hysteria; a harsh, muffled shudder struggled up inside her, lodging finally in her throat. She tried to speak but only a rasping noise came out.

'Gee, lady,' Beam said, embarrassed. 'Come in the kitchen and sit down.'

She stared at him as if he had said something incredible or obscene or miraculous; he wasn't sure which.

'Come on.' He tried to take hold of her arm but she jerked frantically away. She had on a simple green suit, and in it she looked very nice; a little too thin and terribly tense, but still attractive. She had on expensive earrings, an imported stone that seemed always in motion . . . but otherwise her outfit was austere.

'You—were the man at the lab,' she managed, in a brittle, choked voice.

'I'm Leroy Beam. An independent.' Awkwardly guiding her, he led her into the kitchen and seated her at the table. She folded her hands in front of her and studied them fixedly; the bleak boniness of her face seemed to be increasing rather than receding. He felt uneasy.

'Are you all right?' he asked.

She nodded.

'Cup of coffee?' He began searching the cupboards for a bottle of Venusian-grown coffee substitute. While he was looking, Ellen Ackers said tautly: 'You better go in there. In the bathroom. I don't think he's dead, but he might be.'

Beam raced into the bathroom. Behind the plastic shower curtain was an opaque shape. It was Paul Tirol, lying wadded up in the tub, fully clothed. He was not dead but he had been struck behind the left ear and his scalp was leaking a slow, steady trickle of blood. Beam took his pulse, listened to his breathing, and then straightened up.

At the doorway Ellen Ackers materialized, still pale with fright. 'Is he? Did I kill him?'

'He's fine.'

Visibly, she relaxed. 'Thank God. It happened so fast—he stepped ahead of me to take the M inside his place, and then I did it. I hit him as lightly as I could. He was so interested in it . . . he forgot about me.' Words spilled from her, quick, jerky sentences, punctuated by rigid tremors of her hands. 'I lugged him back in the car and drove here; it was all I could think of.'

'What are you in this for?'

Her hysteria rose in a spasm of convulsive muscle-twitching. 'It was all planned—I had *everything* worked out. As soon as I got hold of it I was going to—' She broke off.

'Blackmail Tirol?' he asked, fascinated.

She smiled weakly. 'No, not Paul. It was Paul who gave me the idea . . . it was his first idea, when his researchers showed him the thing. The—*unreconstructed M*, he calls it. *M* stands for machine. He means it can't be educated, morally corrected.'

Incredulous, Beam said: 'You were going to blackmail your husband.'

Ellen Ackers nodded. 'So he'd let me leave.'

Suddenly Beam felt sincere respect for her. 'My God—the rattle. Heimie didn't arrange that; *you* did. So the device would be trapped in the apartment.'

'Yes,' she agreed. 'I was going to pick it up. But Paul showed up with other ideas; he wanted it, too.'

'What went haywire? You have it, don't you?'

Silently she indicated the linen closet. 'I stuffed it away when I heard you.'

Beam opened the linen closet. Resting primly on the neatly-folded towels was a small, familiar, portable TV unit.

'It's reverted,' Ellen said, from behind him, in an utterly defeated monotone. 'As soon as I hit Paul it changed. For half an hour I've been trying to get it to shift. It won't. It'll stay that way forever.'

III

Beam went to the telephone and called a doctor. In the bathroom, Tirol groaned and feebly thrashed his arms. He was beginning to return to consciousness.

'Was that necessary?' Ellen Ackers demanded. 'The doctor—did you have to call?'

Beam ignored her. Bending, he lifted the portable TV unit and held it in his hands; he felt its weight move up his arms like a slow, leaden fatigue. The ultimate adversary, he thought; too stupid to be defeated. It was worse than an animal. It was a rock, solid and dense, lacking all qualities. Except, he thought, the quality of determination. It was determined to persist, to survive; a rock with will. He felt as if he were holding up the universe, and he put the unreconstructed M down.

From behind him Ellen said: 'It drives you crazy.' Her voice had regained tone. She lit a cigarette with a silver cigarette lighter and then shoved her hands in the pockets of her suit.

'Yes,' he said.

'There's nothing you can do, is there? You tried to get it open before. They'll patch Paul up, and he'll go back to his place, and Lantano will be banished–' She took a deep shuddering breath. 'And the Interior Department will go on as always.'

'Yes,' he said. Still kneeling, he surveyed the M. Now, with what he knew, he did not waste time struggling with it. He considered it impassively; he did not even bother to touch it.

In the bathroom, Paul Tirol was trying to crawl from the tub. He slipped back, cursed and moaned, and started his laborious ascent once again.

'Ellen?' his voice quavered, a dim and distorted sound, like dry wires rubbing.

'Take it easy,' she said between her teeth; not moving she stood smoking rapidly on her cigarette.

'Help me, Ellen,' Tirol muttered. 'Something happened to me . . . I don't remember what. Something hit me.'

'He'll remember,' Ellen said.

Beam said: 'I can take this thing to Ackers as it is. You can tell him what it's for—what it did. That ought to be enough; he won't go through with Lantano.'

But he didn't believe it, either. Ackers would have to admit a mistake, a basic mistake, and if he had been wrong to pick up Lantano, he was ruined. And so, in a sense, was the whole system of delineation. It could be fooled; it had been fooled. Ackers was rigid, and he would go right on in a straight line: the hell with Lantano. The hell with abstract justice. Better to preserve cultural continuity and keep society running on an even keel.

'Tirol's equipment,' Beam said. 'Do you know where it is?'

She shrugged wildly. 'What equipment?'

'This thing—' he jabbed at the M—'was made somewhere.'

'Not here, Tirol didn't make it.'

'All right,' he said reasonably. They had perhaps six minutes more before the doctor and the emergency medical carrier arrived on rooftop. 'Who did make it?'

'The alloy was developed on Bellatrix.' She spoke jerkily, word by word. 'The rind ... forms a skin on the outside, a bubble that gets sucked in and out of a reservoir. That's its rind, the TV shape. It sucks it back and becomes the M; it's ready to act.'

'What made it?' he repeated.

'A Bellatrix machine tool syndicate ... a subsidiary of Tirol's organization. They're made to be watchdogs. The big plantations on outplanets use them; they patrol. They get poachers.'

Beam said: 'Then originally they're not set for one person.'

'No.'

'Then *who* set this for Heimie? Not a machine tool syndicate.'

'That was done here.'

He straightened up and lifted the portable TV unit. 'Let's go. Take me there, where Tirol had it altered.'

For a moment the woman did not respond. Grabbing her arm he hustled her to the door. She gasped and stared at him mutely.

'Come on,' he said, pushing her out into the hall. The portable TV unit bumped against the door as he shut it; he held the unit tight and followed after Ellen Ackers.

The town was slatternly and run-down, a few retail stores, fuel station, bars and dance halls. It was two hours' flight from Greater New York and it was called Olum.

'Turn right,' Ellen said listlessly. She gazed out at the neon signs and rested her arm on the window sill of the ship.

They flew above warehouses and deserted streets. Lights were few. At an intersection Ellen nodded and he set the ship down on a roof.

Below them was a sagging, fly-specked wooden frame store. A peeling sign was propped up in the window: FULTON BROTHERS LOCKSMITHS. With the sign were doorknobs, locks, keys, saws, and spring-wound alarm clocks. Somewhere in the interior of the store a yellow night light burned fitfully.

'This way,' Ellen said. She stepped from the ship and made her way down a flight of rickety wooden stairs. Beam laid the portable TV unit on the floor of the ship, locked the doors, and then followed after the woman. Holding onto the railing, he descended to a back porch on which were trash cans and a pile of sodden newspapers tied with string. Ellen was unlocking a door and feeling her way inside.

First he found himself in a musty, cramped storeroom. Pipe and rolls of wire and sheets of metal were heaped everywhere; it was like a junkyard. Next came a narrow corridor and then he was standing in the entrance of a workshop. Ellen reached overhead and groped to find the hanging string of a light. The light clicked on. To the right was a long and littered workbench with a hand grinder at one end, a vise, a keyhole saw; two wooden stools were before the bench and half-assembled machinery was stacked on the floor in no apparent order. The workshop was chaotic, dusty, and archaic. On the wall was a threadbare blue coat hung from a nail: the workcoat of a machinist.

'Here,' Ellen said, with bitterness. 'This is where Paul had it brought. This outfit is owned by the Tirol organization; this whole slum is part of their holdings.'

Beam walked to the bench. 'To have altered it,' he said, 'Tirol must have had a plate of Heimie's neural pattern.' He overturned a heap of glass jars; screws and washers poured onto the pitted surface of the bench.

'He got it from Heimie's door,' Ellen said. 'He had Heimie's lock analyzed and Heimie's pattern inferred from the setting of the tumblers.'

'And he had the M opened?'

'There's an old mechanic,' Ellen said. 'A little dried-up old man; he runs this shop. Patrick Fulton. He installed the bias on the M.'

'A bias,' Beam said, nodding.

'A bias against killing people. Heimie was the exception, for everybody else it took its protective form. Out in the wilds they would have set it for something else, not a TV unit.' She laughed, a sudden ripple close to hysteria. 'Yes, that would have looked odd, it sitting out in a forest somewhere, a TV unit. They would have made it into a rock or a stick.'

'A rock,' Beam said. He could imagine it. The M waiting, covered with moss, waiting for months, years, and then weathered and cor-roded, finally picking up the presence of a human being. Then the M ceasing to be a rock, becoming, in a quick blur of motion, a box one foot wide and two feet long. An oversized cracker box that started forward—

But there was something missing. 'The fakery,' he said. 'Emit-ting flakes of paint and hair and tobacco. How did that come in?'

In a brittle voice Ellen said: 'The landowner murdered the poacher, and he was culpable in the eyes of the law. So the M left clues. Claw marks. Animal blood. Animal hair.'

'God,' he said, revolted. 'Killed by an animal.'

'A bear, a wildcat—whatever was indigenous, it varied. The predator of the region, a natural death.' With her toe she touched a cardboard carton under the workbench. 'It's in there, it used to be, anyhow. The neural plate, the transmitter, the discarded parts of the M, the schematics.'

The carton had been a shipping container for power packs. Now the packs were gone, and in their place was a carefully-wrapped inner box, sealed against moisture and insect infestation. Beam tore away the metal foil and saw that he had found what he wanted. He gingerly carried the contents out and spread them on the workbench among the soldering irons and drills.

'It's all there,' Ellen said, without emotion.

'Maybe,' he said, 'I can leave you out of this. I can take this and the TV unit to Ackers and try it without your testimony.'

'Sure,' she said wearily.

'What are you going to do?'

'Well,' she said, 'I can't go back to Paul, so I guess there's not much I can do.'

'The blackmail bit was a mistake,' he said.

Her eyes glowed. 'Okay.'

'If he releases Lantano,' Beam said, 'he'll be asked to resign. Then he'll probably give you your divorce, it won't be important to him one way or another.'

'I—' she began. And then she stopped. Her face seemed to fade, as if the color and texture of her flesh was vanishing from within. She lifted one hand and half-turned, her mouth open and the sentence still unfinished.

Beam, reaching, slapped the overhead light out; the workroom winked into darkness. He had heard it too, had heard it at the same time as Ellen Ackers. The rickety outside porch had creaked and now the slow, ponderous motion was past the storeroom and into the hall.

A heavy man, he thought. A slow-moving man, sleepy, making his way step by step, his eyes almost shut, his great body sagging beneath his suit. Beneath, he thought, his expensive tweed suit. In the darkness the man's shape was looming; Beam could not see it but he could sense it there, filling up the doorway as it halted. Boards creaked under its weight. In a daze he wondered if Ackers already knew, if his order had already been rescinded. Or had the man got out on his own, worked through his own organization?

The man, starting forward again, spoke in a deep, husky voice. 'Ugh,' Lantano said. 'Damn it.'

Ellen began to shriek. Beam still did not realize what it was; he was still fumbling for the light and wondering stupidly why it did not come on. He had smashed the bulb, he realized. He lit a match. The match went out and he grabbed for Ellen Ackers' cigarette lighter. It was in her purse, and it took him an agonized second to get it out.

The unreconstructed M was approaching them slowly, one receptor stalk extended. Again it halted, swiveled to the left until it was facing the workbench. It was not now in the shape of a portable TV unit; it had retaken its cracker-box shape.

'The plate,' Ellen Ackers whispered. 'It responded to the plate.'

The M had been roused by Heimie Rosenburg's looking for it. But Beam still felt the presence of David Lantano. The big man was still here in the room; the sense of heaviness, the proximity of weight and ponderousness had arrived with the machine, as it moved, sketching Lantano's existence. As he fixedly watched, the machine produced a fragment of cloth fabric and pressed it into a nearby heap of grid-mesh. Other elements, blood and tobacco and hair, were being produced, but they were too small for him to see. The machine pressed a heel mark into the dust of the floor and then projected a nozzle from its anterior section.

Her arm over her eyes, Ellen Ackers ran away. But the machine was not interested in her; revolving in the direction of the workbench it raised itself and fired. An explosive pellet, released by the nozzle, traveled across the workbench and entered the debris heaped across the bench. The pellet detonated; bits of wire and nails showered in particles.

Heimie's dead, Beam thought, and went on watching. The machine was searching for the plate, trying to locate and destroy the synthetic neural emission. It swiveled, lowered its nozzle hesitantly, and then fired again. Behind the workbench, the wall burst and settled into itself.

Beam, holding the cigarette lighter, walked toward the M. A receptor stalk waved toward him and the machine retreated. Its lines wavered, flowed, and then painfully reformed. For an interval, the device struggled with itself; then, reluctantly, the portable TV unit again became visible. From the machine a high-pitched whine emerged, an anguished squeal. Conflicting stimuli were present; the machine was unable to make a decision.

The machine was developing a situation neurosis and the ambivalence of its response was destroying it. In a way its anguish had a human quality, but he could not feel sorry for it. It was a mechanical contraption trying to assume a posture of disguise and attack at the same time; the breakdown was one of relays and tubes, not of a living brain. And it had been a living brain into which it had fired its original pellet. Heimie Rosenburg was dead, and there were no more like him and no possibility that more could be assembled. He went over to the machine and nudged it onto its back with his foot.

The machine whirred snake-like and spun away. 'Ugh, damn it!' it said. It showered bits of tobacco as it rolled off; drops of blood and flakes of blue enamel fell from it as it disappeared into the corridor. Beam could hear it moving about, bumping into the walls like a blind, damaged organism. After a moment he followed after it.

In the corridor, the machine was traveling in a slow circle. It was erecting around itself a wall of particles: cloth and hairs and burnt matches and bits of tobacco, the mass cemented together with blood.

'Ugh, damn it,' the machine said in its heavy masculine voice. It went on working, and Beam returned to the other room.

'Where's a phone?' he said to Ellen Ackers.

She stared at him vacantly.

'It won't hurt you,' he said. He felt dull and worn-out. 'It's in a closed cycle. It'll go on until it runs down.'

'It went crazy,' she said, she shuddered.

'No,' he said. 'Regression. It's trying to hide.'

From the corridor the machine said, 'Ugh. Damn it.' Beam found the phone and called Edward Ackers.

Banishment for Paul Tirol meant first a procession of bands of darkness and then a protracted, infuriating interval in which empty matter drifted randomly around him, arranging itself into first one pattern and then another.

The period between the time Ellen Ackers attacked him and the time banishment sentence had been pronounced was vague and dim in his mind. Like the present shadows, it was hard to pin down.

He had—he thought—awakened in Ackers' apartment. Yes, that was it; and Leroy Beam was there, too. A sort of transcendental Leroy Beam who hovered robustly around, arranging everybody in configurations of his choice. A doctor had come. And finally Edward Ackers had shown up to face his wife and the situation.

Bandaged, and on his way into Interior, he had caught a glimpse of a man going out. The ponderous, bulbous shape of David Lantano, on his way home to his luxurious stone mansion and acre of grass.

At sight of him Tirol had felt a goad of fear. Lantano hadn't even noticed him; an acutely thoughtful expression on his face, Lantano padded into a waiting car and departed.

'You have one thousand dollars,' Edward Ackers was saying wearily, during the final phase. Distorted, Ackers' face bloomed again in the drifting shadows around Tirol, an image of the man's last appearance. Ackers, too, was ruined, but in a different way. 'The law supplies you with one thousand dollars to meet your immediate needs, also you'll find a pocket dictionary of representative out-system dialects.'

Ionization itself was painless. He had no memory of it; only a blank space darker than the blurred images on either side.

'You hate me,' he had declared accusingly, his last words to Ackers. 'I destroyed you. But . . . it wasn't you.' He had been confused. 'Lantano. Maneuvered but not. How? You did . . .'

But Lantano had had nothing to do with it. Lantano had shambled off home, a withdrawn spectator throughout. The hell with Lantano. The hell with Ackers and Leroy Beam and—reluctantly—the hell with Mrs Ellen Ackers.

'Wow,' Tirol babbled, as his drifting body finally collected physical shape. 'We had a lot of good times . . . didn't we, Ellen?'

And then a roaring hot field of sunlight was radiating down on him. Stupefied, he sat slumped over, limp and passive. Yellow, scalding sunlight . . . everywhere. Nothing but the dancing heat of it, blinding him, cowing him into submission.

*

He was sprawled in the middle of a yellow clay road. To his right was a baking, drying field of corn wilted in the midday heat. A pair of large, disreputable-looking birds wheeled silently overhead. A long way off was a line of blunted hills: ragged troughs and peaks that seemed nothing more than heaps of dust. At their base was a meager lump of man-made buildings.

At least he *hoped* they were man-made.

As he climbed shakily to his feet, a feeble noise drifted to his ears. Coming down the hot, dirty road was a car of some sort. Apprehensive and cautious, Tirol walked to meet it.

The driver was human, a thin, almost emaciated youth with pebbled black skin and a heavy mass of weed-colored hair. He wore a stained canvas shirt and overalls. A bent, unlit cigarette hung from his lower lip. The car was a combustion-driven model and had rolled out of the twentieth century; battered and twisted, it rattled to a halt as the driver critically inspected Tirol. From the car's radio yammered a torrent of tinny dance music.

'You a tax collector?' the driver asked.

'Certainly not,' Tirol said, knowing the bucolic hostility toward tax collectors. But—he floundered. He couldn't confess that he was a banished criminal from Earth; that was an invitation to be massacred, usually in some picturesque way. 'I'm an inspector,' he announced, 'Department of Health.'

Satisfied, the driver nodded. 'Lots of scuttly cutbeetle, these days. You fellows got a spray, yet? Losing one crop after another.'

Tirol gratefully climbed into the car. 'I didn't realize the sun was so hot,' he murmured.

'You've got an accent,' the youth observed, starting up the engine. 'Where you from?'

'Speech impediment,' Tirol said cagily. 'How long before we reach town?'

'Oh, maybe an hour,' the youth answered, as the car wandered lazily forward.

Tirol was afraid to ask the name of the planet. It would give him away. But he was consumed with the need to know. He might be two star-systems away or two million; he might be a month out of Earth or seventy years. Naturally, he had to get back; he had no intention of becoming a sharecropper on some backwater colony planet.

'Pretty swip,' the youth said, indicating the torrent of noxious jazz pouring from the car radio. 'That's Calamine Freddy and his Woolybear Creole Original Band. Know that tune?'

'No,' Tirol muttered. The sun and dryness and heat made his head ache, and he wished to God he knew where he was.

The town was miserably tiny. The houses were dilapidated; the streets were dirt. A kind of domestic chicken roamed here and there, pecking in the rubbish. Under a porch a bluish quasi-dog lay sleeping. Perspiring and unhappy, Paul Tirol entered the bus station and located a schedule. A series of meaningless entries flashed by: names of towns. The name of the planet, of course, was not listed.

'What's the fare to the nearest port?' he asked the indolent official behind the ticket window.

The official considered. 'Depends on what sort of port you want. Where you planning to go?'

'Toward Center,' Tirol said. 'Center' was the term used in out-systems for the Sol Group.

Dispassionately, the official shook his head. 'No inter-system port around here.'

Tirol was baffled. Evidently, he wasn't on the hub planet of this particular system. 'Well,' he said, 'then the nearest interplan port.'

The official consulted a vast reference book. 'You want to go to which system-member?'

'Whichever one has the inter-system port,' Tirol said patiently. He would leave from there.

'That would be Venus.'

Astonished, Tirol said: 'Then this system—' He broke off, chagrined, as he remembered. It was the parochial custom in many out-systems, especially those a long way out, to name their member planets after the original nine. This one was probably called 'Mars' or 'Jupiter' or 'Earth,' depending on its position in the group. 'Fine,' Tirol finished. 'One-way ticket to—Venus.'

Venus, or what passed for Venus, was a dismal orb no larger than an asteroid. A bleak cloud of metallic haze hung over it, obscuring the sun. Except for mining and smelting operations the planet was deserted. A few dreary shacks dotted the barren countryside. A perpetual wind blew, scattering debris and trash.

But the inter-system port was here, the field which linked the planet to its nearest star-neighbor and, ultimately, with the balance of the universe. At the moment a giant freighter was taking ore.

Tirol entered the ticket office. Spreading out most of his remaining money he said: 'I want a one-way ticket taking me toward Center. As far as I can go.'

The clerk calculated. 'You care what class?'

'No,' he said, mopping his forehead.

'How fast?'

'No.'

The clerk said: 'That'll carry you as far as the Betelgeuse System.'

'Good enough,' Tirol said, wondering what he did then. But at least he could contact his organization from there; he was already back in the charted universe. But now he was almost broke. He felt a prickle of icy fear, despite the heat.

The hub planet of the Betelgeuse System was called Plantagenet III. It was a thriving junction for passenger carriers transporting settlers to undeveloped colony planets. As soon as Tirol's ship landed he hurried across the field to the taxi stand.

'Take me to Tirol Enterprises,' he instructed, praying there was an outlet here. There had to be, but it might be operating under a front name. Years ago he lost track of the particulars of his sprawling empire.

'Tirol Enterprises,' the cab driver repeated thoughtfully. 'Nope, no such outfit, mister.'

Stunned, Tirol said: 'Who does the slaving around here?'

The driver eyed him. He was a wizened, dried-up little man with glasses; he peered turtle-wise, without compassion. 'Well,' he said, 'I've been told you can get carried out-system without papers. There's a shipping contractor . . . called—' He reflected. Tirol, trembling, handed him a last bill.

'The Reliable Export–Import,' the driver said.

That was one of Lantano's fronts. In horror Tirol said: 'And that's it?'

The driver nodded.

Dazed, Tirol moved away from the cab. The buildings of the field danced around him; he settled down on a bench to catch his breath. Under his coat his heart pounded unevenly. He tried to breathe, but his breath caught painfully in his throat. The bruise on his head where Ellen Ackers had hit him began to throb. It was true, and he was gradually beginning to understand and believe it. He was not going to get to Earth; he was going to spend the rest of his life here on this rural world, cut off from his organization and everything he had built up over the years.

And, he realized, as he sat struggling to breathe, the rest of his life was not going to be very long.

He thought about Heimie Rosenburg.

'Betrayed,' he said, and coughed wrackingly. 'You betrayed me. You hear that? Because of you I'm here. It's your fault; I never should have hired you.'

He thought about Ellen Ackers. 'You too,' he gasped, coughing. Sitting on the bench he alternately coughed and gasped and thought about the people who had betrayed him. There were hundreds of them.

The living room of David Lantano's house was furnished in exquisite taste. Priceless late nineteenth-century Blue Willow dishes lined the walls in a rack of wrought iron. At his antique yellow plastic and chrome table, David Lantano was eating dinner, and the spread of food amazed Beam even more than the house.

Lantano was in good humor and he ate with enthusiasm. His linen napkin was tucked under his chin and once, as he sipped coffee, he dribbled and belched. His brief period of confinement was over; he ate to make up for the ordeal.

He had been informed, first by his own apparatus and now by Beam, that banishment had successfully carried Tirol past the point of return. Tirol would not be coming back and for that Lantano was thankful. He felt expansive toward Beam; he wished Beam would have something to eat.

Moodily, Beam said: 'It's nice here.'

'You could have something like this,' Lantano said.

On the wall hung a framed folio of ancient paper protected by helium-filled glass. It was the first printing of a poem of Ogden Nash, a collector's item that should have been in a museum. It aroused in Beam a mixed feeling of longing and aversion.

'Yes,' Beam said. 'I could have this.' This, he thought, or Ellen Ackers or the job at Interior or perhaps all three at once. Edward Ackers had been retired on pension and he had given his wife a divorce. Lantano was out of jeopardy. Tirol had been banished. He wondered what he did want.

'You could go a long way,' Lantano said sleepily.

'As far as Paul Tirol?'

Lantano chuckled and yawned.

'I wonder if he left any family,' Beam said. 'Any children.' He was thinking about Heimie.

Lantano reached across the table toward the bowl of fruit. He selected a peach and carefully brushed it against the sleeve of his robe. 'Try a peach,' he said.

'No thanks,' Beam said irritably.

Lantano examined the peach but he did not eat it. The peach was made of wax; the fruit in the bowl was imitation. He was not really as rich as he pretended, and many of the artifacts about the living room were fakes. Each time he offered fruit to a visitor he took a calculated risk. Returning the peach to the bowl he leaned back in his chair and sipped his coffee.

If Beam did not have plans, at least *he* had, and with Tirol gone the plans had a better than even chance of working out. He felt peaceful. Someday, he thought, and not too far off, the fruit in the bowl would be real.

EXPLORERS WE

'Golly,' Parkhurst gasped, his red face tingling with excitement. 'Come here, you guys. Look!'

They crowded around the viewscreen.

'There she is,' Barton said. His heart beat strangely. 'She sure looks good.'

'Damn right she looks good,' Leon agreed. He trembled. 'Say—I can make out New York.'

'The hell you can.'

'I can! The gray. By the water.'

'That's not even the United States. We're looking at it upside down. That's Siam.'

The ship hurtled through space, meteoroid shields shrieking. Below it, the blue-green globe swelled. Clouds drifted around it, hiding the continents and oceans.

'I never expected to see her again,' Merriweather said. 'I thought sure as hell we were stuck up there.' His face twisted. 'Mars. That damned red waste. Sun and flies and ruins.'

'Barton knows how to repair jets,' Captain Stone said. 'You can thank *him*.'

'You know what I'm going to do, first thing I'm back?' Parkhurst yelled.

'What?'

'Go to Coney Island.'

'Why?'

'People. I want to see people again. Lots of them. Dumb, sweaty, noisy. Ice cream and water. The ocean. Beer bottles, milk cartons, paper napkins—'

'And gals,' Vecchi said, eyes shining. 'Long time, six months. I'll go with you. We'll sit on the beach and watch the gals.'

'I wonder what kind of bathing suits they got now,' Barton said.

'Maybe they don't wear any!' Parkhurst cried.

'Hey!' Merriweather shouted. 'I'm going to see my wife again.' He was suddenly dazed. His voice sank to a whisper. 'My wife.'

'I got a wife, too,' Stone said. He grinned. 'But I been married a long time.' Then he thought of Pat and Jean. A stabbing ache choked his windpipe. 'I bet they have grown.'

'Grown?'

'My kids,' Stone said huskily.

They looked at each other, six men, ragged, bearded, eyes bright and feverish.

'How long?' Vecchi whispered.

'An hour,' Stone said. 'We'll be down in an hour.'

The ship struck with a crash that threw them on their faces. It leaped and bucked, brake jets screaming, tearing through rocks and soil. It came to rest, nose buried in a hillside.

Silence.

Parkhurst got unsteadily to his feet. He caught hold of the safety rail. Blood dripped down his face from a cut over his eye.

'We're down,' he said.

Barton stirred. He groaned, forced himself up on his knees. Parkhurst helped him. 'Thanks. Are we . . .'

'We're down. We're back.'

The jets were off. The roaring had ceased . . . there was only the faint trickle of wall fluids leaking out on the ground.

The ship was a mess. The hull was cracked in three places. It billowed in, bent and twisted. Papers and ruined instruments were strewn everywhere.

Vecchi and Stone got slowly up. 'Everything all right?' Stone muttered, feeling his arm.

'Give me a hand,' Leon said. 'My damn ankle's twisted or something.'

They got him up. Merriweather was unconscious. They revived him and got him to his feet.

'We're down,' Parkhurst repeated, as if he couldn't believe it. 'This is Earth. We're back—alive!'

'I hope the specimens are all right,' Leon said.

'The hell with the specimens!' Vecchi shouted excitedly. He worked the port bolts frantically, unscrewing the heavy hatch lock. 'Let's get out and walk around.'

'Where are we?' Barton asked Captain Stone.

'South of San Francisco. On the peninsula.'

'San Francisco! Hey—we can ride the cable cars!' Parkhurst helped Vecchi unscrew the hatch. 'San Francisco. I was through Frisco once. They got a big park. Golden Gate Park. We can go to the funhouse.'

The hatch opened, swinging wide. Talk ceased abruptly. The men peered out, blinking in the white-hot sunlight.

A green field stretched down and away from them. Hills rose in the distance, sharp in the crystal air. Along a highway below, a few cars moved, tiny dots, the sun glinting on them. Telephone poles.

'What's that sound?' Stone said, listening intently.

'A train.'

It was coming along the distant track, black smoke pouring from its stack. A faint wind moved across the field, stirring the grass. Over to the right lay a town. Houses and trees. A theater marquee. A Standard gas station. Roadside stands. A motel.

'Think anybody saw us?' Leon asked.

'Must have.'

'Sure heard us,' Parkhurst said. 'We made a noise like God's indigestion when we hit.'

Vecchi stepped out onto the field. He swayed wildly, arms outstretched. 'I'm falling!'

Stone laughed. 'You'll get used to it. We've been in space too long. Come on.' He leaped down. 'Let's start walking.'

'Toward the town.' Parkhurst fell in beside him. 'Maybe they'll give us free eats . . . Hell—champagne!' His chest swelled under his tattered uniform. 'Returning heroes. Keys to the town. A parade. Military band. Floats with dames.'

'Dames,' Leon grunted. 'You're obsessed.'

'Sure.' Parkhurst strode across the field, the others trailing after him. 'Hurry up!'

'Look,' Stone said to Leon. 'Somebody over there. Watching us.'

'Kids,' Barton said. 'A bunch of kids.' He laughed excitedly. 'Let's go say hello.'

They headed toward the kids, wading through the moist grass on the rich earth.

'Must be spring,' Leon said. 'The air smells like spring.' He took a deep breath. 'And the grass.'

Stone computed. 'It's April ninth.'

They hurried. The kids stood watching them, silent and unmoving.

'Hey!' Parkhurst shouted. 'We're back!'

'What town is this?' Barton shouted.

The kids stared at them, eyes wide.

'What's wrong?' Leon muttered.

'Our beards. We look pretty bad.' Stone cupped his hands. 'Don't be scared! We're back from Mars. The rocket flight. Two years ago—remember? A year ago last October.'

The kids stared, white-faced. Suddenly they turned and fled. They ran frantically toward the town.

The six men watched them go.

'What the hell,' Parkhurst muttered, dazed. 'What's the matter?'

'Our beards,' Stone repeated uneasily.

'Something's wrong,' Barton said, shakily. He began to tremble. 'There's something terribly wrong.'

'Can it!' Leon snapped. 'It's our beards.' He ripped a piece of his shirt savagely away. 'We're dirty. Filthy tramps. Come on.' He started after the children, toward the town. 'Let's go. They probably got a special car on the way here. We'll meet them.'

Stone and Barton glanced at each other. They followed Leon slowly. The others fell in behind.

Silent, uneasy, the six bearded men made their way across the field toward the town.

A youth on a bicycle fled at their approach. Some railroad workers, repairing the train track, threw down their shovels and ran, yelling.

Numbly, the six men watched them go.

'What is it?' Parkhurst muttered.

They crossed the track. The town lay on the other side. They entered a huge grove of eucalyptus trees.

'Burlingame,' Leon said, reading a sign. They looked down a street. Hotels and cafes. Parked cars. Gas stations. Dime stores. A small suburban town, shoppers on the sidewalks. Cars moving slowly.

They emerged from the trees. Across the street a filling station attendant looked up—

And froze.

After a moment, he dropped the hose he held and ran down the main street, shouting shrill warnings.

Cars stopped. Drivers leaped out and ran. Men and women poured out of stores, scattering wildly. They surged away, retreating in frantic haste.

In a moment the street was deserted.

'Good God.' Stone advanced, bewildered. 'What—' He crossed onto the street. No one was in sight.

The six men walked down the main street, dazed and silent. Nothing stirred. Everyone had fled. A siren wailed, rising and falling. Down a side street a car backed quickly away.

In an upstairs window Barton saw a pale, frightened face. Then the shade was jerked down.

'I don't understand,' Vecchi muttered.

'Have they gone nuts?' Merriweather asked.

Stone said nothing. His mind was blank. Numb. He felt tired.

He sat down on the curb and rested, getting his breath. The others stood around him.

'My ankle,' Leon said. He leaned against a stop sign, lips twisting with pain. 'Hurts like hell.'

'Captain,' Barton said. 'What's the matter with them?'

'I don't know,' Stone said. He felt in his ragged pocket for a cigarette. Across the street was a deserted cafe. The people had run out of it. Food was still on the counter. A hamburger was scorching on the skillet, coffee was boiling in a glass pot on the burner.

On the sidewalk lay groceries spilling out from bags dropped by terrorized shoppers. The motor of a deserted parked car purred to itself.

'Well?' Leon said. 'What'll we do?'

'I don't know.'

'We can't just—'

'I don't know!' Stone got to his feet. He walked over and entered the cafe. They watched him sit down at the counter.

'What's he doing?' Vecchi asked.

'I don't know.' Parkhurst followed Stone into the cafe. 'What are you doing?'

'I'm waiting to be served.'

Parkhurst plucked awkwardly at Stone's shoulder. 'Come on, Captain. There's nobody here. They all left.'

Stone said nothing. He sat at the counter, his face vacant. Waiting passively to be served.

Parkhurst went back out. 'What the hell has happened?' he asked Barton. 'What's wrong with them all?'

A spotted dog came nosing around. It passed them, stiff and alert, sniffing suspiciously. It trotted off down a side street.

'Faces,' Barton said.

'Faces?'

'They're watching us. Up there.' Barton gestured toward a building. 'Hiding. *Why?* Why are they hiding from us?'

Suddenly Merriweather stiffened. 'Something's coming.'

They turned eagerly.

Down the street two black sedans turned the corner, headed toward them.

'Thank God,' Leon muttered. He leaned against the wall of a building. 'Here they are.'

The two sedans pulled to a stop at the curb. The doors opened. Men spilled out, surrounded them silently. Well-dressed. Ties and hats and long gray coats.

'I'm Scanlan,' one said. 'FBI.' An older man with iron-gray hair. His voice was clipped and frigid. He studied the five of them intently. 'Where's the other?'

'Captain Stone? In there.' Barton pointed to the cafe.

'Get him out here.'

Barton went into the cafe. 'Captain, they're outside. Come on.'

Stone came along with him, back to the curb. 'Who are they, Barton?' he asked haltingly.

'Six,' Scanlan said, nodding. He waved to his men. 'Okay. This is all.'

The FBI men moved in, crowding them back toward the brick front of the cafe.

'Wait!' Barton cried thickly. His head spun. 'What—what's happening?'

'What is it?' Parkhurst demanded deprecatorily. Tears rolled down his face, streaking his cheeks. 'Will you tell us, for God's sake—'

The FBI men had weapons. They got them out. Vecchi backed away, his hands up. 'Please!' he wailed. 'What have we done? What's happening?'

Sudden hope flickered in Leon's breast. 'They don't know who we are. They think we're Commies.' He addressed Scanlan. 'We're the Earth–Mars Expedition. My name is Leon. Remember? A year ago last October. We're *back*. We're back from Mars.' His voice trailed off. The weapons were coming up. Nozzles—hoses and tanks.

'We're back!' Merriweather croaked. 'We're the Earth–Mars Expedition, come back!'

Scanlan's face was expressionless. 'That sounds fine,' he said coldly. 'Only, the ship crashed and blew up when it reached Mars. None of the crew survived. We know because we sent up a robot scavenger team and brought back the corpses—six of them.'

The FBI men fired. Blazing napalm sprayed toward the six bearded figures. They retreated, and then the flames touched them. The FBI men saw the figures ignite, and then the sight was cut off. They could no longer see the six figures thrashing about, but they could hear them. It was not something they enjoyed hearing, but they remained, waiting and watching.

Scanlan kicked at the charred fragments with his foot. 'Not easy to be sure,' he said. 'Possibly only five here . . . but I didn't see any of them get away. They didn't have time.' At the pressure of his foot, a section of ash broke away; it fell into particles that still steamed and bubbled.

His companion Wilks stared down. New at this, he could not quite believe what he had seen the napalm do. 'I—' he said. 'Maybe I'll go back to the car,' he muttered, starting off away from Scanlan.

'It's not over positively,' Scanlan said, and then he saw the younger man's face. 'Yes,' he said, 'you go sit down.'

People were beginning to filter out onto the sidewalks. Peeping anxiously from doorways and windows.

'They got 'em!' a boy shouted excitedly. 'They got the outer space spies!'

Cameramen snapped pictures. Curious people appeared on all sides, faces pale, eyes popping. Gaping down in wonder at the indiscriminate mass of charred ash.

His hands shaking, Wilks crept back into the car and shut the door after him. The radio buzzed, and he turned it off, not wanting to hear anything from it or say anything to it. At the doorway of the cafe, the gray-coated Bureau men remained, conferring with Scanlan. Presently a number of them started off at a trot, around the side of the cafe and up the alley. Wilks watched them go. What a nightmare, he thought.

Coming over, Scanlan leaned down and put his head into the car. 'Feel better?'

'Some.' Presently he asked, 'What's this—the twenty-second time?'

Scanlan said, 'Twenty-first. Every couple of months . . . the same names, same men. I won't tell you that you'll get used to it. But at least it won't surprise you.'

'I don't see any difference between them and us,' Wilks said, speaking distinctly. 'It was like burning up six human beings.'

'No,' Scanlan said. He opened the car door and got into the back seat, behind Wilks. 'They only looked like six human beings. That's the whole point. They want to. They intend to. You know that Barton, Stone, and Leon—'

'I know,' he said. 'Somebody or something that lives somewhere out there saw their ship go down, saw them die, and investigated. Before we got there. And got enough to go on, enough to give them what they needed. But—' He gestured. 'Isn't there anything else we can do with them?'

Scanlan said, 'We don't know enough about them. Only this—sending in of imitations, again and again. Trying to sneak them past us.' His face became rigid, despairing. 'Are they crazy? Maybe they're so different no contact's possible. Do they think we're all named Leon and Merriweather and Parkhurst and Stone? That's the part that personally gets me down . . . Or maybe that's our chance, the fact that they don't understand we're individuals. Figure how much worse if sometime they made up a—whatever it is . . . a spore . . . a seed. But not like one of those poor miserable six who died on Mars—something we wouldn't know was an imitation . . .'

'They have to have a model,' Wilks said.

One of the Bureau men waved, and Scanlan scrambled out of the car. He came back in a moment to Wilks. 'They say there're only five,' he said. 'One got away; they think they saw him. He's crippled and not moving fast. The rest of us are going after him—you stay here, keep your eyes open.' He strode off up the alley with the other Bureau men.

Wilks lit a cigarette and sat with his head resting on his arm. Mimicry . . . everybody terrified. But–

Had anybody really tried to make contact?

Two policemen appeared, herding people back out of the way. A third black Dodge, loaded with Bureau men, moved along at the curb, stopped, and the men got out.

One of the Bureau men, whom he did not recognize, approached the car. 'Don't you have your radio on?'

'No,' Wilks said. He snapped it back on.

'If you see one, do you know how to kill it?'

'Yes,' he said.

The Bureau man went on to join his group.

If it was up to me, Wilks asked himself, what would I do? Try to find out what they want? Anything that looks so human, behaves in such a human way, must *feel* human . . . and if they– whatever they are–feel human, might they not become human, in time?

At the edge of the crowd of people, an individual shape detached itself and moved toward him. Uncertainly, the shape halted, shook its head, staggered and caught itself, and then assumed a stance like that of the people near it. Wilks recognized it because he had been trained to, over a period of months. It had gotten different clothes, a pair of slacks, a shirt, but it had buttoned the shirt wrong, and one of its feet was bare. Evidently it did not understand the shoes. Or, he thought, maybe it was too dazed and injured.

As it approached him, Wilks raised his pistol and took aim at its stomach. They had been taught to fire there; he had fired, on the practice range, at chart after chart. Right in the midsection . . . bisect it, like a bug.

On its face the expression of suffering and bewilderment deepened as it saw him prepare to fire. It halted, facing him, making no move to escape. Now Wilks realized that it had been severely burned; probably it would not survive in any case.

'I have to,' he said.

It stared at him, and then it opened its mouth and started to say something.

He fired.

Before it could speak, it had died. Wilks got out as it pitched over and lay beside the car.

I did wrong, he thought to himself as he stood looking down at it. I shot it because I was afraid. But I had to. Even if it was wrong. It came here to infiltrate us, imitating us so we won't recognize it. That's what we're told—we have to believe that they are plotting against us, are inhuman, and will never be more than that.

Thank God, he thought. It's over.

And then he remembered it wasn't . . .

It was a warm summer day, late in July.

The ship landed with a roar, dug across a plowed field, tore through a fence, a shed, and came finally to rest in a gully.

Silence.

Parkhurst got shakily to his feet. He caught hold of the safety rail. His shoulder hurt. He shook his head, dazed.

'We're down,' he said. His voice rose with awe and excitement. 'We're down!'

'Help me up,' Captain Stone gasped. Barton gave him a hand.

Leon sat wiping a trickle of blood from his neck. The interior of the ship was a shambles. Most of the equipment was smashed and strewn about.

Vecchi made his way unsteadily to the hatch. With trembling fingers, he began to unscrew the heavy bolts.

'Well,' Barton said, 'we're back.'

'I can hardly believe it,' Merriweather murmured. The hatch came loose and they swung it quickly aside. 'It doesn't seem possible. Good old Earth.'

'Hey, listen,' Leon gasped, as he clambered down to the ground. 'Somebody get the camera.'

'That's ridiculous,' Barton said, laughing.

'Get it!' Stone yelled.

'Yes, get it,' Merriweather said. 'Like we planned, if we ever got back. A historic record, for the schoolbooks.'

Vecchi rummaged around among the debris. 'It's sort of banged up,' he said. He held up the dented camera.

'Maybe it'll work anyhow,' Parkhurst said, panting with exertion as he followed Leon outside. 'How're we going to take all six of us? Somebody has to snap the shutter.'

'I'll set it for time,' Stone said, taking the camera and adjusting the knobs. 'Everybody line up.' He pushed a button, and joined the others.

The six bearded, tattered men stood by their smashed ship, as the camera ticked. They gazed across the green countryside, awed and suddenly silent. They glanced at each other, eyes bright.

'We're back!' Stone shouted. 'We're back!'

WAR GAME

In his office at the Terran Import Bureau of Standards, the tall man gathered up the morning's memos from their wire basket, and, seating himself at his desk, arranged them for reading. He put on his iris lenses, lit a cigarette.

'Good morning,' the first memo said in its tinny, chattery voice, as Wiseman ran his thumb along the line of pasted tape. Staring off through the open window at the parking lot, he listened to it idly. 'Say, look, what's wrong with you people down there? We sent that lot of'–a pause as the speaker, the sales manager of a chain of New York department stores, found his records–'those Ganymedean toys. You realize we have to get them approved in time for the autumn buying plan, so we can get them stocked for Christmas.' Grumbling, the sales manager concluded, 'War games are going to be an important item again this year. We intend to buy big.'

Wiseman ran his thumb down to the speaker's name and title.

'Joe Hauck,' the memo-voice chattered. 'Appeley's Children's.'

To himself, Wiseman said, 'Ah.' He put down the memo, got a blank and prepared to replay. And then he said, half-aloud, 'Yes, what about that lot of Ganymedean toys?'

It seemed like a long time that the testing labs had been on them. At least two weeks.

Of course, any Ganymedean products got special attention these days; the Moons had, during the last year, gotten beyond their usual state of economic greed and had begun–according to intelligence circles–mulling overt military action against competitive interest, of which the Inner Three planets could be called the foremost element. But so far nothing had shown up. Exports remained of adequate quality, with no special jokers, no toxic paint to be licked off, no capsules of bacteria.

And yet . . .

Any group of people as inventive as the Ganymedeans could be expected to show creativity in whatever field they entered. Subversion would be tackled like any other venture—with imagination and a flair for wit.

Wiseman got to his feet and left his office, in the direction of the separate building in which the testing labs operated.

Surrounded by half-disassembled consumers' products, Pinario looked up to see his boss, Leon Wiseman, shutting the final door of the lab.

'I'm glad you came down,' Pinario said, although actually he was stalling; he knew that he was at least five days behind in his work, and this session was going to mean trouble. 'Better put on a prophylaxis suit—don't want to take risks.' He spoke pleasantly, but Wiseman's expression remained dour.

'I'm here about those inner-citadel-storming shock troops at six dollars a set,' Wiseman said, strolling among the stacks of many-sized unopened products waiting to be tested and released.

'Oh, that set of Ganymedean toy soldiers,' Pinario said with relief. His conscience was clear on that item; every tester in the labs knew the special instructions handed down by the Cheyenne Government on the Dangers of Contamination from Culture Particles Hostile to Innocent Urban Populations, a typically muddy ukase from officialdom. He could always—legitimately—fall back and cite the number of that directive. 'I've got them off by themselves,' he said, walking over to accompany Wiseman, 'due to the special danger involved.'

'Let's have a look,' Wiseman said. 'Do you believe there's anything in this caution, or is it more paranoia about "alien milieux"?'

Pinario said, 'It's justified, especially where children's artifacts are concerned.'

A few hand-signals, and a slab of wall exposed a side room.

Propped up in the center was a sight that caused Wiseman to halt. A plastic life-size dummy of a child, perhaps five years in appearance, wearing ordinary clothes, sat surrounded by toys. At this moment, the dummy was saying, 'I'm tired of that. Do something else.' It paused a short time, and then repeated, 'I'm tired of that. Do something else.'

The toys on the floor, triggered to respond to oral instructions, gave up their various occupations, and started afresh.

'It saves on labor costs,' Pinario explained. 'This is a crop of junk that's got an entire repertoire to go through, before the buyer has his money's worth. If we stuck around to keep them active, we'd be in here all the time.'

Directly before the dummy was the group of Ganymedean soldiers, plus the citadel which they had been built to storm. They had been sneaking up on it in an elaborate pattern, but, at the dummy's utterance, they had halted. Now they were regrouping.

'You're getting this all on tape?' Wiseman asked.

'Oh, yes,' Pinario said.

The model soldiers stood approximately six inches high, made from the almost indestructible thermoplastic compounds that the Ganymedean manufacturers were famous for. Their uniforms were synthetic, a hodgepodge of various military costumes from the Moons and nearby planets. The citadel itself, a block of ominous dark metal-like stuff, resembled a legendary fort; peepholes dotted its upper surfaces, a drawbridge had been drawn up out of sight, and from the top turret a gaudy flag waved.

With a whistling pop, the citadel fired a projectile at its attackers. The projectile exploded in a cloud of harmless smoke and noise, among a cluster of soldiers.

'It fights back,' Wiseman observed.

'But ultimately it loses,' Pinario said. 'It has to. Psychologically speaking, it symbolizes the external reality. The dozen soldiers, of course, represent to the child his own efforts to cope. By participating in the storming of the citadel, the child undergoes a sense of adequacy in dealing with the harsh world. Eventually he prevails, but only after a painstaking period of effort and patience.' He added, 'Anyhow, that's what the instruction booklet says.' He handed Wiseman the booklet.

Glancing over the booklet, Wiseman asked, 'And their pattern of assault varies each time?'

'We've had it running for eight days now. The same pattern hasn't cropped up twice. Well, you've got quite a few units involved.'

The soldiers were sneaking around, gradually nearing the citadel. On the walls, a number of monitoring devices appeared and began tracking the soldiers. Utilizing other toys being tested, the soldiers concealed themselves.

'They can incorporate accidental configurations of terrain,' Pinario explained. 'They're object-tropic; when they see, for example, a dollhouse here for testing, they climb into it like mice. They'll be all through it.' To prove his point, he picked up a large toy spaceship manufactured by a Uranian company; shaking it, he spilled two soldiers from it.

'How many times do they take the citadel,' Wiseman asked, 'on a percentage basis?'

'So far, they've been successful one out of nine tries. There's an adjustment in the back of the citadel. You can set it for a higher yield of successful tries.'

He threaded a path through the advancing soldiers; Wiseman accompanied him, and they bent down to inspect the citadel.

'This is actually the power supply,' Pinario said. 'Cunning. Also, the instructions to the soldiers emanate from it. High-frequency transmission, from a shot-box.'

Opening the back of the citadel, he showed his boss the container of shot. Each shot was an instruction iota. For an assault pattern, the shot were tossed up, vibrated, allowed to settle in a new sequence. Randomness was thereby achieved. But since there was a finite number of shot, there had to be a finite number of patterns.

'We're trying them all,' Pinario said.

'And there's no way to speed it up?'

'It'll just have to take time. It may run through a thousand patterns and then—'

'The next one,' Wiseman finished, 'may have them make a ninety-degree turn and start firing at the nearest human being.'

Pinario said somberly, 'Or worse. There're a good deal of ergs in that power pack. It's made to put out for five years. But if it all went into something simultaneously—'

'Keep testing,' Wiseman said.

They looked at each other and then at the citadel. The soldiers had by now almost reached it. Suddenly one wall of the citadel flapped down, a gun-muzzle appeared, and the soldiers had been flattened.

'I never saw that before,' Pinario murmured.

For a moment nothing stirred. And then the lab's child-dummy, seated among its toys, said, 'I'm tired of that. Do something else.'

With a tremor of uneasiness, the two men watched the soldiers pick themselves up and regroup.

Two days later, Wiseman's superior, a heavy-set, short, angry man with popping eyes, appeared in his office. 'Listen,' Fowler said, 'you get those damn toys out of testing. I'll give you until tomorrow.' He started back out, but Wiseman stopped him.

'This is too serious,' he said. 'Come down to the lab and I'll show you.'

Arguing all the way, Fowler accompanied him to the lab. 'You have no concept of the capital some of these firms have invested in this stuff!' he was saying as they entered. 'For every product you've got represented here, there's a ship or a warehouse full on Luna, waiting for official clearance so it can come in!'

Pinario was nowhere in sight. So Wiseman used his key, bypassing the hand-signals that opened up the testing room.

There, surrounded by toys, sat the dummy that the lab men had built. Around it the numerous toys went through their cycles. The racket made Fowler wince.

'This is the item in particular,' Wiseman said, bending down by the citadel. A soldier was in the process of squirming on his belly toward it. 'As you can see, there are a dozen soldiers. Given that many, and the energy available to them, plus the complex instruction data—'

Fowler interrupted, 'I see only eleven.'

'One's probably hiding,' Wiseman said.

From behind them, a voice said, 'No, he's right.' Pinario, a rigid expression on his face, appeared. 'I've been having a search made. One is gone.'

The three men were silent.

'Maybe the citadel destroyed him,' Wiseman finally suggested.

Pinario said, 'There's a law of matter dealing with that. If it "destroyed" him—*what did it do with the remains?*'

'Possibly converted him into energy,' Fowler said, examining the citadel and the remaining soldiers.

'We did something ingenious,' Pinario said, 'when we realized that a soldier was gone. We weighed the remaining eleven plus the citadel. Their combined weight is exactly equal to that of the original set—the original dozen soldiers and the citadel. So he's in there somewhere.' He pointed at the citadel, which at the moment was pinpointing the soldiers advancing toward it.

Studying the citadel, Wiseman had a deep intuitive feeling. It had changed. It was, in some manner, different.

'Run your tapes,' Wiseman said.

'What?' asked Pinario, and then he flushed. 'Of course.' Going to the child-dummy, he shut it off, opened it, and removed the drum of video recording tape. Shakily, he carried it to the projector.

They sat watching the recording sequences flash by: one assault after another, until the three of them were bleary-eyed. The soldiers advanced, retreated, were fired on, picked themselves up, advanced again . . .

'Stop the transport,' Wiseman said suddenly.

The last sequence was re-run.

A soldier moved steadily toward the base of the citadel. A missile, fired at him, exploded and for a time obscured him. Meanwhile, the other eleven soldiers scurried in a wild attempt to mount the walls. The soldier emerged from the cloud of dust and continued. He reached the wall. A section slid back.

The soldier, blending with the dingy wall of the citadel, used the end of his rifle as a screwdriver to remove his head, then one arm, then both legs. The disassembled pieces were passed into the aperture of the citadel. When only the arm and rifle remained, that, too, crawled into the citadel, worming blindly, and vanished. The aperture slid out of existence.

After a long time, Fowler said in a hoarse voice, 'The presumption by the parent would be that the child had lost or destroyed one of the soldiers. Gradually the set would dwindle—with the child getting the blame.'

Pinario said, 'What do you recommend?'

'Keep it in action,' Fowler said, with a nod from Wiseman. 'Let it work out its cycle. But don't leave it alone.'

'I'll have somebody in the room with it from now on,' Pinario agreed.

'Better yet, stay with it yourself,' Fowler said.

To himself, Wiseman thought: *Maybe we all better stay with it. At least two of us, Pinario and myself.*

I wonder what it did with the pieces, he thought.

What did it make?

By the end of the week, the citadel had absorbed four more of the soldiers.

Watching it through a monitor, Wiseman could see in it no visible change. Naturally. The growth would be strictly internal, down out of sight.

On and on the eternal assaults, the soldiers wriggling up, the citadel firing in defense. Meanwhile, he had before him a new series of Ganymedean products. More recent children's toys to be inspected.

'Now what?' he asked himself.

The first was an apparently simple item: a cowboy costume from the ancient American West. At least, so it was described. But he paid only cursory attention to the brochure: the hell with what the Ganymedeans had to say about it.

Opening the box, he laid out the costume. The fabric had a gray, amorphous quality. *What a miserably bad job*, he thought. It only vaguely resembled a cowboy suit; the lines seemed unformed, hesitant. And the material stretched out of shape as he handled it. He found that he had pulled an entire section of it into a pocket that hung down.

'I don't get it,' he said to Pinario. 'This won't sell.'

'Put it on,' Pinario said. 'You'll see.'

With effort, Wiseman managed to squeeze himself into the suit. 'Is it safe?' he asked.

'Yes,' Pinario said. 'I had it on earlier. This is a more benign idea. But it could be effective. To start it into action, you fantasize.'

'Along what lines?'

'Any lines.'

The suit made Wiseman think of cowboys, and so he imagined to himself that he was back at the ranch, trudging along the gravel road by the field in which black-faced sheep munched hay with that odd, rapid grinding motion of their lower jaws. He had stopped at the fence—barbed wire and occasional upright posts—and watched the sheep. Then, without warning, the sheep lined up and headed off, in the direction of a shaded hillside beyond his range of vision.

He saw trees, cypress growing against the skyline. A chicken hawk, far up, flapped its wings in a pumping action . . . *as if*, he thought, *it's filling itself with more air, to rise higher*. The hawk glided energetically off, then sailed at a leisurely pace. Wiseman looked for a sign of its prey. Nothing but the dry mid-summer fields munched flat by the sheep. Frequent grasshoppers. And, on the road itself, a toad. The toad had burrowed into the loose dirt; only its top part was visible.

As he bent down, trying to get up enough courage to touch the warty top of the toad's head, a man's voice said nearby him, 'How do you like it?'

'Fine,' Wiseman said. He took a deep breath of the dry grass smell; he filled his lungs. 'Hey, how do you tell a female toad from a male toad? By the spots, or what?'

'Why?' asked the man, standing behind him slightly out of sight.

'I've got a toad here.'

'Just for the record,' the man said, 'can I ask you a couple of questions?'

'Sure,' Wiseman said.

'How old are you?'

That was easy. 'Ten years and four months,' he said, with pride.

'Where exactly are you, at this moment?'

'Out in the country, Mr Gaylord's ranch, where my dad takes me and my mother every weekend when we can.'

'Turn around and look at me,' the man said. 'And tell me if you know me.'

With reluctance, he turned from the half-buried toad to look. He saw an adult with a thin face and a long, somewhat irregular nose. 'You're the man who delivers the butane gas,' he said. 'For the butane company.' He glanced around, and sure enough, there was the truck, parked by the butane gate. 'My dad says butane is expensive, but there's no other–'

The man broke in, 'Just for the sake of curiosity, what's the name of the butane company?'

'It's right on the truck,' Wiseman said, reading the large painted letters. 'Pinario Butane Distributors, Petaluma, California. You're Mr Pinario.'

'Would you be willing to swear that you're ten years old, standing in a field near Petaluma, California?' Mr Pinario asked.

'Sure.' He could see, beyond the field, a range of wooded hills. Now he wanted to investigate them; he was tired of standing around gabbing. 'I'll see you,' he said, starting off. 'I have to go get some hiking done.'

He started running, away from Pinario, down the gravel road. Grasshoppers leaped away, ahead of him. Gasping, he ran faster and faster.

'Leon!' Mr Pinario called after him. 'You might as well give up! Stop running!'

'I've got business in those hills,' Wiseman panted, still jogging along. Suddenly something struck him full force; he sprawled on his hands, tried to get back up. In the dry midday air, something shimmered; he felt fear and pulled away from it. A shape formed, a flat wall . . .

'You won't get to those hills,' Mr Pinario said, from behind him. 'Better stay in roughly one place. Otherwise you collide with things.'

Wiseman's hands were damp with blood; he had cut himself falling. In bewilderment, he stared down at the blood . . .

Pinario helped him out of the cowboy suit, saying, 'It's as unwholesome a toy as you could want. A short period with it on, and the child would be unable to face contemporary reality. Look at you.'

Standing with difficulty, Wiseman inspected the suit; Pinario had forcibly taken it from him.

'Not bad,' he said in a trembling voice. 'It obviously stimulates the withdrawal tendencies already present. I know I've always had a latent retreat fantasy toward my childhood. That particular period, when we lived in the country.'

'Notice how you incorporated real elements into it,' Pinario said, 'to keep the fantasy going as long as possible. If you'd had time, you would have figured a way of incorporating the lab wall into it, possibly as the side of a barn.'

Wiseman admitted, 'I—already had started to see the old dairy building, where the farmers brought their market milk.'

'In time,' Pinario said, 'it would have been next to impossible to get you out of it.'

To himself, Wiseman thought, *If it could do that to an adult, just imagine the effect on a child.*

'That other thing you have there,' Pinario said, 'that game, it's a screwball notion. You feel like looking at it now? It can wait.'

'I'm okay,' Wiseman said. He picked up the third item and began to open it.

'A lot like the old game of Monopoly,' Pinario said. 'It's called Syndrome.'

The game consisted of a board, plus play money, dice, pieces to represent the players. And stock certificates.

'You acquire stock,' Pinario said, 'same as in all this kind, obviously.' He didn't even bother to look at the instructions. 'Let's get Fowler down here and play a hand; it takes at least three.'

Shortly, they had the Division Director with them. The three men seated themselves at a table, the game of Syndrome in the center.

'Each player starts out equal with the others,' Pinario explained, 'same as all this type, and during the play, their statuses change according to the worth of the stock they acquire in various economic syndromes.'

The syndromes were represented by small, bright plastic objects, much like the archaic hotels and houses of Monopoly.

They threw the dice, moved their counters along the board, bid for and acquired property, paid fines, collected fines, went to the 'decontamination chamber' for a period. Meanwhile, behind them, the seven model soldiers crept up on the citadel again and again.

'I'm tired of that,' the child-dummy said. 'Do something else.'

The soldiers regrouped. Once more they started out, getting nearer and nearer the citadel.

Restless and irritable, Wiseman said, 'I wonder how long that damn thing has to go on before we find out what it's for.'

'No telling.' Pinario eyed a purple-and-gold share of stock that Fowler had acquired. 'I can use that,' he said. 'That's a heavy uranium mine stock on Pluto. What do you want for it?'

'Valuable property,' Fowler murmured, consulting his other stocks. 'I might make a trade, though.'

How can I concentrate on a game, Wiseman asked himself, *when that thing is getting closer and nearer to—God knows what? To whatever it was built to reach. Its critical mass*, he thought.

'Just a second,' he said in a slow, careful voice. He put down his hand of stocks. 'Could that citadel be a pile?'

'Pile of what?' Fowler asked, concerned with his hand.

Wiseman said loudly, 'Forget this game.'

'An interesting idea,' Pinario said, also putting down his hand. 'It's constructing itself into an atomic bomb, piece by piece. Adding until–' He broke off. 'No, we thought of that. There're no heavy elements present in it. It's simply a five-year battery, plus a number of small machines controlled by instructions broadcast from the battery itself. You can't make an atomic pile out of that.'

'In my opinion,' Wiseman said, 'we'd be safer getting it out of here.' His experience with the cowboy suit had given him a great deal more respect for the Ganymedean artificers. And if the suit was the benign one . . .

Fowler, looking past his shoulder, said, 'There are only six soldiers now.'

Both Wiseman and Pinario got up instantly. Fowler was right. Only half of the set of soldiers remained. One more had reached the citadel and been incorporated.

'Let's get a bomb expert from the Military Services in here,' Wiseman said, 'and let him check it. This is out of our department.' He turned to his boss, Fowler. 'Don't you agree?'

Fowler said, 'Let's finish this game first.'

'Why?'

'Because we want to be certain about it,' Fowler said. But his rapt interest showed that he had gotten emotionally involved and wanted to play to the end of the game. 'What will you give me for this share of Pluto stock? I'm open to offers.'

He and Pinario negotiated a trade. The game continued for another hour. At last, all three of them could see that Fowler was gaining control of the various stocks. He had five mining syndromes, plus two plastics firms, an algae monopoly, and all seven of the retail trading syndromes. Due to his control of the stock, he had, as a byproduct, gotten most of the money.

'I'm out,' Pinario said. All he had left were minor shares which controlled nothing. 'Anybody want to buy these?'

With his last remaining money, Wiseman bid for the shares. He got them and resumed playing, this time against Fowler alone.

'It's clear that this game is a replica of typical interculture economic ventures,' Wiseman said. 'The retail trading syndromes are obviously Ganymedean holdings.'

A flicker of excitement stirred in him; he had gotten a couple of good throws with the dice and was in a position to add a share to his meager holdings. 'Children playing this would acquire a healthy attitude toward economic realities. It would prepare them for the adult world.'

But a few minutes later, he landed on an enormous tract of Fowler holdings, and the fine wiped out his resources. He had to give up two shares of stock; the end was in sight.

Pinario, watching the soldiers advance toward the citadel, said, 'You know, Leon, I'm inclined to agree with you. This thing may be one terminal of a bomb. A receiving station of some kind. When it's completely wired up, it might bring in a surge of power transmitted from Ganymede.'

'Is such a thing possible?' Fowler asked, stacking his play money into different denominations.

'Who knows what they can do?' Pinario said, wandering around with his hands in his pockets. 'Are you almost finished playing?'

'Just about,' Wiseman said.

'The reason I say that,' Pinario said, 'is that now there're only five soldiers. It's speeding up. It took a week for the first one, and only an hour for the seventh. I wouldn't be surprised if the rest go within the next two hours, all five of them.'

'We're finished,' Fowler said. He had acquired the last share of stock and the last dollar.

Wiseman arose from the table, leaving Fowler. 'I'll call Military Services to check the citadel. About this game, though, it's nothing but a steal from our Terran game Monopoly.'

'Possibly they don't realize that we have the game already,' Fowler said, 'under another name.'

A stamp of admissibility was placed on the game of Syndrome and the importer was informed. In his office, Wiseman called Military Services and told them what he wanted.

'A bomb expert will be right over,' the unhurried voice at the other end of the line said. 'Probably you should leave the object alone until he arrives.'

Feeling somewhat useless, Wiseman thanked the clerk and hung up. They had failed to dope out the soldiers-and-citadel war game, now it was out of their hands.

The bomb expert was a young man, with close-cropped hair, who smiled friendlily at them as he set down his equipment. He wore ordinary coveralls, with no protective devices.

'My first advice,' he said, after he had looked the citadel over, 'is to disconnect the leads from the battery. Or, if you want, we can let the cycle finish out, and then disconnect the leads before any reaction takes place. In other words, allow the last mobile elements to enter the citadel. Then, as soon as they're inside, we disconnect the leads and open her up and see what's been taking place.'

'Is it safe?' Wiseman asked.

'I think so,' the bomb expert said. 'I don't detect any sign of radioactivity in it.' He seated himself on the floor, by the rear of the citadel, with a pair of cutting pliers in his hand.

Now only three soldiers remained.

'It shouldn't be long,' the young man said cheerfully.

Fifteen minutes later, one of the three soldiers crept up to the base of the citadel, removed his head, arm, legs, body, and disappeared piecemeal into the opening provided for him.

'That leaves two,' Fowler said.

Ten minutes later, one of the two remaining soldiers followed the one ahead of him.

The four men looked at each other. 'This is almost it,' Pinario said huskily.

The last remaining soldier wove his way toward the citadel. Guns within the citadel fired at him, but he continued to make progress.

'Statistically speaking,' Wiseman said aloud, to break some of the tension, 'it should take longer each time, because there are fewer men for it to concentrate on. It should have started out fast, then got more infrequent until finally this last soldier should put in at least a month trying to–'

'Pipe down,' the young bomb expert said in a quiet, reasonable voice. 'If you don't mind.'

The last of the twelve soldiers reached the base of the citadel. Like those before him, he began to disassemble himself.

'Get those pliers ready,' Pinario grated.

The parts of the soldier traveled into the citadel. The opening began to close. From within, a humming became audible, a rising pitch of activity.

'Now, for God's sake!' Fowler cried.

The young bomb expert reached down his pliers and cut into the positive lead of the battery. A spark flashed from the pliers and the young bomb expert jumped reflexively; the pliers flew from his hands and skidded across the floor. 'Jeez!' he said. 'I must have been grounded.' Groggily, he groped about for the pliers.

'You were touching the frame of the thing,' Pinario said excitedly. He grabbed the pliers himself and crouched down, fumbling for the lead. 'Maybe if I wrap a handkerchief around it,' he muttered, withdrawing the pliers and fishing in his pocket for a handkerchief. 'Anybody got anything I can wrap around this? I don't want to get knocked flat. No telling how many–'

'Give it to me,' Wiseman demanded, snatching the pliers from him. He shoved Pinario aside and closed the jaws of the pliers about the lead.

Fowler said calmly, 'Too late.'

Wiseman hardly heard his superior's voice; he heard the constant tone within his head, and he put up his hands to his ears, futilely trying to shut it out. Now it seemed to pass directly from the citadel through his skull, transmitted by the bone. *We stalled around too long*, he thought. *Now it has us. It won out because there are too many of us; we got to squabbling . . .*

Within his mind, a voice said, 'Congratulations. By your fortitude, you have been successful.'

A vast feeling pervaded him then, a sense of accomplishment.

'The odds against you were tremendous,' the voice inside his mind continued. 'Anyone else would have failed.'

He knew then that everything was all right. They had been wrong.

'What you have done here,' the voice declared, 'you can continue to do all your life. You can always triumph over adversaries. By patience and persistence, you can win out. The universe isn't such an overwhelming place, after all . . .'

No, he realized with irony, it wasn't.

'They are just ordinary persons,' the voice soothed. 'So even though you're the only one, an individual against many, you have nothing to fear. Give it time—and don't worry.'

'I won't,' he said aloud.

The humming receded. The voice was gone.

After a long pause, Fowler said, 'It's over.'

'I don't get it,' Pinario said.

'That was what it was supposed to do,' Wiseman said. 'It's a therapeutic toy. Helps give the child confidence. The disassembling of the soldiers'—he grinned— 'ends the separation between him and the world. He becomes one with it. And, in doing so, conquers it.'

'Then it's harmless,' Fowler said.

'All this work for nothing,' Pinario groused. To the bomb expert, he said, 'I'm sorry we got you up here for nothing.'

The citadel had now opened its gates wide. Twelve soldiers, once more intact, issued forth. The cycle was complete; the assault could begin again.

Suddenly Wiseman said, 'I'm not going to release it.'

'What?' Pinario said. 'Why not?'

'I don't trust it,' Wiseman said. 'It's too complicated for what it actually does.'

'Explain,' Fowler demanded.

'There's nothing to explain,' Wiseman said. 'Here's this immensely intricate gadget, and all it does is take itself apart and then re-assemble itself. There *must* be more, even if we can't–'

'It's therapeutic,' Pinario put in.

Fowler said, 'I'll leave it up to you, Leon. If you have doubts, then don't release it. We can't be too careful.'

'Maybe I'm wrong,' Wiseman said, 'but I keep thinking to myself: *What did they actually build this for?* I feel we still don't know.'

'And the American Cowboy Suit,' Pinario added. 'You don't want to release that either.'

'Only the game,' Wiseman said. 'Syndrome, or whatever it's called.' Bending down, he watched the soldiers as they hustled toward the citadel. Bursts of smoke, again . . . activity, feigned attacks, careful withdrawals . . .

'What are you thinking?' Pinario asked, scrutinizing him.

'Maybe it's a diversion,' Wiseman said. 'To keep our minds involved. So we won't notice something else.' That was his intuition, but he couldn't pin it down. 'A red herring,' he said. 'While something else takes place. That's why it's so complicated. We were *supposed* to suspect it. That's why they built it.'

Baffled, he put his foot down in front of a soldier. The soldier took refuge behind his shoe, hiding from the monitors of the citadel.

'There must be something right before our eyes,' Fowler said, 'that we're not noticing.'

'Yes.' Wiseman wondered if they would ever find it. 'Anyhow,' he said, 'we're keeping it here, where we can observe it.'

Seating himself nearby, he prepared to watch the soldiers. He made himself comfortable for a long, long wait.

At six o'clock that evening, Joe Hauck, the sales manager for Appeley's Children's Store, parked his car before his house, got out, and strode up the stairs.

Under his arm he carried a large flat package, a 'sample' that he had appropriated.

'Hey!' his two kids, Bobby and Lora, squealed as he let himself in. 'You got something for us, Dad?' They crowded around him, blocking his path. In the kitchen, his wife looked up from the table and put down her magazine.

'A new game I picked for you,' Hauck said. He unwrapped the package, feeling genial. There was no reason why he shouldn't help himself to one of the new games; he had been on the phone for weeks, getting the stuff through Import Standards—and after all was said and done, only one of the three items had been cleared.

As the kids went off with the game, his wife said in a low voice, 'More corruption in high places.' She had always disapproved of his bringing home items from the store's stock.

'We've got thousands of them,' Hauck said. 'A warehouse full. Nobody'll notice one missing.'

At the dinner table, during the meal, the kids scrupulously studied every word of the instructions that accompanied the game. They were aware of nothing else.

'Don't read at the table,' Mrs Hauck said reprovingly.

Leaning back in his chair, Joe Hauck continued his account of the day. 'And after all that time, what did they release? One lousy item. We'll be lucky if we can push enough to make a profit. It was that Shock Troop gimmick that would really have paid off. And that's tied up indefinitely.'

He lit a cigarette and relaxed, feeling the peacefulness of his home, the presence of his wife and children.

His daughter said, 'Dad, do you want to play? It says the more who play, the better.'

'Sure,' Joe Hauck said.

While his wife cleared the table, he and his children spread out the board, counters, dice and paper money and shares of stock. Almost at once he was deep in the game, totally involved; his childhood memories of game-playing swam back, and he acquired shares of stock with cunning and originality, until, toward the con-clusion of the game, he had cornered most of the syndromes.

He settled back with a sigh of contentment. 'That's that,' he declared to his children. 'Afraid I had a head start. After all, I'm not new to this type of game.' Getting hold of the valuable holdings on the board filled him with a powerful sense of satisfaction. 'Sorry to have to win, kids.'

His daughter said, 'You didn't win.'

'You lost,' his son said.

'*What?*' Joe Hauck exclaimed.

'The person who winds up with the most stock *loses*,' Lora said.

She showed him the instructions. 'See? The idea is to get rid of your stocks. Dad, you're out of the game.'

'The heck with that,' Hauck said, disappointed. 'That's no kind of game.' His satisfaction vanished. 'That's no fun.'

'Now we two have to play out the game,' Bobby said, 'to see who finally wins.'

As he got up from the board, Joe Hauck grumbled, 'I don't get it. What would anybody see in a game where the winner winds up with nothing at all?'

Behind him, his two children continued to play. As stock and money changed hands, the children became more and more ani-mated. When the game entered its final stages, the children were in a state of ecstatic concentration.

'They don't know Monopoly,' Hauck said to himself, 'so this screwball game doesn't seem strange to them.'

Anyhow, the important thing was that the kids enjoyed playing Syndrome; evidently it would sell, and that was what mattered. Already the two youngsters were learning the naturalness of sur-rendering their holdings. They gave up their stocks and money avidly, with a kind of trembling abandon.

Glancing up, her eyes bright, Lora said, 'It's the best educational toy you ever brought home, Dad!'

IF THERE WERE NO
BENNY CEMOLI

Scampering across the unplowed field, the three boys shouted as they saw the ship: it had landed, all right, just where they expected, and they were the first to reach it.

'Hey, that's the biggest I ever saw!' Panting, the first boy halted. 'That's not from Mars; that's from farther. It's from all the way out, I know it is.' He became silent and afraid as he saw the size of it. And then looking up into the sky he realized that an armada had arrived, exactly as everyone had expected. 'We better go tell,' he said to his companions.

Back on the ridge, John LeConte stood by his steam-powered chauffeur-driven limousine, impatiently waiting for the boiler to warm. *Kids got there first*, he said to himself with anger. *Whereas I'm supposed to*. And the children were ragged; they were merely farm boys.

'Is the phone working today?' LeConte asked his secretary.

Glancing at his clipboard, Mr Fall said, 'Yes, sir. Shall I put through a message to Oklahoma City?' He was the skinniest employee ever assigned to LeConte's office. The man evidently took nothing for himself, was positively uninterested in food. And he was efficient.

LeConte murmured, 'The immigration people ought to hear about this outrage.'

He sighed. It had all gone wrong. The armada from Proxima Centauri had after ten years arrived and none of the early-warning devices had detected it in advance of its landing. Now Oklahoma City would have to deal with the outsiders here on home ground—a psychological disadvantage which LeConte felt keenly.

Look at the equipment they've got, he thought as he watched the commercial ships of the flotilla begin to lower their cargos. *Why, hell, they make us look like provincials.* He wished that his official car did not need twenty minutes to warm up; he wished—

Actually, he wished that CURB did not exist.

Centaurus Urban Renewal Bureau, a do-gooding body unfortunately vested with enormous inter-system authority. It had been informed of the Misadventure back in 2170 and had started into space like a phototropic organism, sensitive to the mere physical light created by the hydrogen-bomb explosions. But LeConte knew better than that. Actually the governing organizations in the Centaurian system knew many details of the tragedy because they had been in radio contact with other planets of the Sol system. Little of the native forms on Earth had survived. He himself was from Mars; he had headed a relief mission seven years ago, had decided to stay because there were so many opportunities here on Earth, conditions being what they were . . .

This is all very difficult, he said to himself as he stood waiting for his steam-powered car to warm. *We got here first, but* CURB *does outrank us: we must face that awkward fact. In my opinion, we've done a good job of rebuilding. Of course, it isn't like it was before . . . but ten years is not long. Give us another twenty and we'll have the trains running again. And our recent road-building bonds sold quite successfully, in fact were oversubscribed.*

'Call for you, sir, from Oklahoma City,' Mr Fall said, holding out the receiver of the portable field-phone.

'Ultimate Representative in the Field John LeConte, here,' LeConte said into it loudly. 'Go ahead; I say go ahead.'

'This is Party Headquarters,' the dry official voice at the other end came faintly, mixed with static, in his ear. 'We've received reports from dozens of alert citizens in Western Oklahoma Texas of an immense—'

'It's here,' LeConte said. 'I can see it. I'm just about ready to go out and confer with its ranking members, and I'll file a full report at the usual time. So it wasn't necessary for you to check up on me.' He felt irritable.

'Is the armada heavily armed?'

'Naw,' LeConte said. 'It appears to be comprised of bureaucrats and trade officials and commercial carriers. In other words, vultures.'

The Party desk-man said, 'Well, go and make certain they understand that their presence here is resented by the native population as well as the Relief of War-torn Areas Administrating Council. Tell them that the legislature will be calling to pass a special bill expressing indignation at this intrusion into domestic matters by an inter-system body.'

'I know, I know,' LeConte said. 'It's all been decided; I know.'

His chauffeur called to him, 'Sir, your car is ready now.'

The Party desk-man concluded, 'Make certain they understand that you can't negotiate with them; you have no power to admit them to Earth. Only the Council can do that and of course it's adamantly against that.'

LeConte hung up the phone and hurried to his car.

Despite the opposition of the local authorities, Peter Hood of CURB decided to locate his headquarters in the ruins of the old Terran capital, New York City. This would lend prestige to the CURBmen as they gradually widened the circle of the organization's influence. At last, of course, the circle would embrace the planet. But that would take decades.

As he walked through the ruins of what had once been a major train yard, Peter Hood thought to himself that when the task was done he himself would have long been retired. Not much remained of the pre-tragedy culture here. The local authorities—the political nonentities who had flocked in from Mars and Venus, as the neighboring planets were called—had done little. And yet he admired their efforts.

To the members of his staff walking directly behind him he said, 'You know, they have done the hard part for us. We ought to be grateful. It is not easy to come into a totally destroyed area, as they've done.'

His man Fletcher observed, 'They got back a good return.'

Hood said, 'Motive is not important. They have achieved results.' He was thinking of the official who had met them in his steam car; it had been solemn and formal, carrying complicated trappings. When these locals had first arrived on the scene years ago *they* had not been greeted, except perhaps by radiation-seared, blackened survivors who had stumbled out of cellars and gaped sightlessly. He shivered.

Coming up to him, a CURBman of minor rank saluted and said, 'I think we've managed to locate an undamaged structure in which your staff could be housed for the time being. It's underground.' He looked embarrassed. 'Not what we had hoped for. We'd have to displace the locals to get anything attractive.'

'I don't object,' Hood said. 'A basement will do.'

'The structure,' the minor CURBman said, 'was once a great homeostatic newspaper, the *New York Times*. It printed itself directly below us. At least, according to the maps. We haven't located the newspaper yet; it was customary for the homeopapes to be buried a mile or so down. As yet we don't know how much of this one survived.'

'But it would be valuable,' Hood agreed.

'Yes,' the CURBman said. 'Its outlets are scattered all over the planet; it must have had a thousand different editions which it put out daily. How many outlets function—' He broke off. 'It's hard to believe that the local politicos made no efforts to repair any of the ten or eleven world-wide homeopapes, but that seems to be the case.'

'Odd,' Hood said. Surely it would have eased their task. The post-tragedy job of reuniting people into a common culture depended on newspapers, ionization in the atmosphere making radio and TV reception difficult if not impossible. 'This makes me instantly suspicious,' he said, turning to his staff. 'Are they perhaps not trying to rebuild after all? Is their work merely a pretense?'

It was his own wife Joan who spoke up. 'They may simply have lacked the ability to place the homeopapes on an operational basis.'

Give them the benefit of the doubt, Hood thought. *You're right*.

'So the last edition of the *Times*,' Fletcher said, 'was put on the lines the day the Misadventure occurred. And the entire network of newspaper communication and news-creation has been idle since. I can't respect these politicos; it shows they're ignorant of the basics of a culture. By reviving the homeopapes we can do more to re-establish the pre-tragedy culture than they've done in ten thousand pitiful projects.' His tone was scornful.

Hood said, 'You may misunderstand, but let it go. Let's hope that the cephalon of the pape is undamaged. We couldn't possibly replace it.' Ahead he saw the yawning entrance which the CURB-men crews had cleared. This was to be his first move, here on the ruined planet, restoring this immense self-contained entity to its former authority. Once it had resumed its activity he would be freed for other tasks; the homeopape would take some of the burden from him.

A workman, still clearing debris away, muttered, 'Jeez, I never saw so many layers of junk. You'd think they deliberately bottled it up down here.' In his hands, the suction furnace which he operated glowed and pounded as it absorbed material, converting it to energy, leaving an increasingly enlarged opening.

'I'd like a report as soon as possible as to its condition,' Hood said to the team of engineers who stood waiting to descend into the opening. 'How long it will take to revive it, how much—' He broke off.

Two men in black uniforms had arrived. Police, from the Security ship. One, he saw, was Otto Dietrich, the ranking investigator accompanying the armada from Centaurus, and he felt tense automatically; it was a reflex for all of them—he saw the engineers and the workmen cease momentarily and then, more slowly, resume their work.

'Yes,' he said to Dietrich. 'Glad to see you. Let's go off to this side room and talk there.' He knew beyond a doubt what the investigator wanted; he had been expecting him.

Dietrich said, 'I won't take up too much of your time, Hood. I know you're quite busy. What is this, here?' He glanced about curiously, his scrubbed, round, alert face eager.

In a small side room, converted to a temporary office, Hood faced the two policemen. 'I am opposed to prosecution,' he said quietly. 'It's been too long. Let them go.'

Dietrich, tugging thoughtfully at his ear, said, 'But war crimes are war crimes, even a decade later. Anyhow, what argument can there be? We're required by law to prosecute. *Somebody* started the war. They may well hold positions of responsibility now, but that hardly matters.'

'How many police troops have you landed?' Hood asked.

'Two hundred.'

'Then you're ready to go to work.'

'We're ready to make inquiries. Sequester pertinent documents and initiate litigation in the local courts. We're prepared to enforce cooperation, if that's what you mean. Various experienced personnel have been distributed to key points.' Dietrich eyed him. 'All this is necessary; I don't see the problem. Did you intend to protect the guilty parties—make use of their so-called abilities on your staff?'

'No,' Hood said evenly.

Dietrich said, 'Nearly eighty million people died in the Misfortune. Can you forget that? Or is it that since they were merely local people, not known to us personally—'

'It's not that,' Hood said. He knew it was hopeless; he could not communicate with the police mentality. 'I've already stated my objections. I feel it serves no purpose at this late date to have trials and hangings. Don't request use of my staff in this; I'll refuse on the grounds that I can spare no one, not even a janitor. Do I make myself clear?'

'You idealists,' Dietrich sighed. 'This is strictly a noble task confronting us ... to rebuild, correct? What you don't or won't see is that these people will start it all over again, one day, unless we take steps now. We owe it to future generations. To be harsh now is the most humane method, in the long run. Tell me, Hood. What is this site? What are you resurrecting here with such vigor?'

'The *New York Times*,' Hood said.

'It has, I assume, a morgue? We can consult its backlog of information? That would prove valuable in building up our cases.'

Hood said, 'I can't deny you access to material we uncover.'

Smiling, Dietrich said, 'A day by day account of the political events leading up to the war would prove quite interesting. Who, for instance, held supreme power in the United States at the time of the Misfortune? No one we've talked to so far seems to remember.' His smile increased.

Early the next morning the report from the corps of engineers reached Hood in his temporary office. The power supply of the newspaper had been totally destroyed. But the cephalon, the governing brain-structure which guided and oriented the homeostatic system, appeared to be intact. If a ship were brought close by, perhaps its power supply could be integrated into the newspaper's lines. Thereupon much more would be known.

'In other words,' Fletcher said to Hood, as they sat with Joan eating breakfast, 'it may come on and it may not. Very pragmatic. You hook it up and if it works you've done your job. What if it doesn't? Do the engineers intend to give up at that point?'

Examining his cup, Hood said, 'This tastes like authentic coffee.' He pondered. 'Tell them to bring a ship in and start the homeopape up. And if it begins to print, bring me the edition at once.' He sipped his coffee.

An hour later a ship of the line had landed in the vicinity and its power source had been tapped for insertion into the homeopape. The conduits were placed, the circuits cautiously closed.

Seated in his office, Peter Hood heard far underground a low rumble, a halting, uncertain stirring. They had been successful. The newspaper was returning to life.

The edition, when it was laid on his desk by a bustling CURB-man, surprised him by its accuracy. Even in its dormant state, the newspaper had somehow managed not to fall behind events. Its receptors had kept going.

CURB LANDS, TRIP DECADE LONG,
PLANS CENTRAL ADMINISTRATION

Ten years after the Misfortune of a nuclear holocaust, the inter-system rehabilitation agency, CURB, has made its historic appearance on Earth's surface, landing from a veritable armada of craft—a sight which witnesses described as 'overpowering both in scope and in significance.' CURBman Peter Hood, named top co-ordinator by Centaurian authorities, immediately set up headquarters in the ruins of New York City and conferred with aides, declaring that he had come 'not to punish the guilty but to re-establish the planet-wide culture by every means available, and to restore—

It was uncanny, Hood thought as he read the lead article. The varied news-gathering services of the homeopape had reached into his own life, had digested and then inserted into the lead article even the discussion between himself and Otto Dietrich. The newspaper was—had been—doing its job. Nothing of news-interest escaped it, even a discreet conversation carried on with no outsiders as witnesses. He would have to be careful.

Sure enough, another item, ominous in tone, dealt with the arrival of the black jacks, the police.

SECURITY AGENCY VOWS 'WAR CRIMINALS' TARGET

Captain Otto Dietrich, supreme police investigator arriving with the CURB armada from Proxima Centauri, said today that those responsible for the Misfortune of a decade ago 'would have to pay for their crimes' before the bar of Centaurian justice.

Two hundred black-uniformed police, it was learned by the *Times*, have already begun exploratory activities designed to—

The newspaper was warning Earth about Dietrich, and Hood could not help feeling grim relish. The *Times* had not been set up to serve merely the occupying hierarchy. It served everyone, including those Dietrich intended to try. Each step of the police activity would no doubt be reported in full detail. Dietrich, who liked to work in anonymity, would not enjoy this. But the authority to maintain the newspaper belonged to Hood.

And he did not intend to shut it off.

One item on the first page of the paper attracted his further notice; he read it, frowning and a little uneasy.

CEMOLI BACKERS RIOT IN UPSTATE NEW YORK

Supporters of Benny Cemoli, gathered in the familiar tent cities associated with the colorful political figure, clashed with local citizens armed with hammers, shovels, and boards, both sides claiming victory in the two-hour melee which left twenty injured and a dozen hospitalized in hastily-erected first aid stations. Cemoli, garbed as always in his toga-style red robes, visited the injured, evidently in good spirits, joking and telling his supporters that 'it won't be long now,' an evident reference to the organization's boast that it would march on New York City in the near future to establish what Cemoli deems 'social justice and true equality for the first time in world history.' It should be recalled that prior to his imprisonment at San Quentin—

Flipping a switch on his intercom system, Hood said, 'Fletcher, check into activities up in the north of the county. Find out about some sort of a political mob gathering there.'

Fletcher's voice came back. 'I have a copy of the *Times*, too, sir. I see the item about this Cemoli agitator. There's a ship on the way up there right now; should have a report within ten minutes.'

Fletcher paused. 'Do you think—it'll be necessary to bring in any of Dietrich's people?'

'Let's hope not,' Hood said shortly.

Half an hour later the CURB ship, through Fletcher, made its report. Puzzled, Hood asked that it be repeated. But there was no mistake. The CURB field team had investigated thoroughly. They had found no sign whatsoever of any tent city or any group gathering. And citizens in the area whom they had interrogated had never heard of anyone named 'Cemoli.' And there was no sign of any scuffle having taken place, no first aid stations, no injured persons. Only the peaceful, semi-rural countryside.

Baffled, Hood read the item in the *Times* once more. There it was, in black and white, on the front page, along with the news about the landing of the CURB armada. What did it mean?

He did not like it at all.

Had it been a mistake to revive the great, old, damaged homeostatic newspaper?

From a sound sleep that night Hood was awakened by a clanging from far beneath the ground, an urgent racket that grew louder and louder as he sat up in bed, blinking and confused. Machinery roared. He heard the heavy rumbling movement as automatic circuits fitted into place, responding to instructions emanating from within the closed system itself.

'Sir,' Fletcher was saying from the darkness. A light came on as Fletcher located the temporary overhead fixture. 'I thought I should come in and wake you. Sorry, Mr Hood.'

'I'm awake,' Hood muttered, rising from the bed and putting on his robe and slippers. 'What's it doing?'

Fletcher said, 'It's printing an extra.'

Sitting up, smoothing her tousled blonde hair back, Joan said, 'Good Lord. What about?' Wide-eyed, she looked from her husband to Fletcher.

'We'll have to bring in the local authorities,' Hood said. 'Confer with them.' He had an intuition as to the nature of the extra roaring through the presses at this moment. 'Get that LeConte, the politico who met us on our arrival. Wake him up and fly him here immediately. We need him.'

It took almost an hour to obtain the presence of the haughty, ceremonious local potentate and his staff member. The two of them in their elaborate uniforms at last put in an appearance at Hood's office, both of them indignant. They faced Hood silently, waiting to hear what he wanted.

In his bathrobe and slippers Hood sat at his desk, a copy of the *Times'* extra before him; he was reading it once more as LeConte and his man entered.

NEW YORK POLICE REPORT CEMOLI LEGIONS

ON MOVE TOWARD CITY,

BARRICADES ERECTED, NATIONAL GUARD ALERTED

He turned the paper, showing the headlines to the two Earthmen. 'Who is this man?' he said.

After a moment LeConte said, 'I—don't know.'

Hood said, 'Come on, Mr LeConte.'

'Let me read the article,' LeConte said nervously. He scanned it in haste; his hands trembled as he held the newspaper. 'Interesting,' he said at last. 'But I can't tell you a thing. It's news to me. You must understand that our communications have been sparse, since the Misfortune, and it's entirely possible that a political movement could spring up without our—'

'Please,' Hood said. 'Don't make yourself absurd.'

Flushing, LeConte stammered, 'I'm doing the best I can, summoned out of my bed in the middle of the night.'

There was a stir, and through the office doorway came the rapidly-moving figure of Otto Dietrich, looking grim. 'Hood,' he said without preamble, 'there's a *Times* kiosk near my headquarters. It just posted this.' He held up a copy of the extra. 'The damn thing is running this off and distributing it throughout the world, isn't it? However, we have crack teams up in that area and they report absolutely nothing, no road blocks, no militia-style troops on the move, no activity of any sort.'

'I know,' Hood said. He felt weary. And still, from beneath them, the deep rumble continued, the newspaper printing its extra, informing the world of the march by Benny Cemoli's supporters on New York City–a fantasy march, evidently, a product manufactured entirely within the cephalon of the newspaper itself.

'Shut it off,' Dietrich said.

Hood shook his head. 'No. I want to know more.'

'That's no reason,' Dietrich said. 'Obviously, it's defective. Very seriously damaged, not working properly. You'll have to search elsewhere for your world-wide propaganda network.' He tossed the newspaper down on Hood's desk.

To LeConte, Hood said, 'Was Benny Cemoli active before the war?'

There was silence. Both LeConte and his assistant Mr Fall were pale and tense; they faced him tight-lipped, glancing at each other.

'I am not much for police matters,' Hood said to Dietrich, 'but I think you could reasonably step in here.'

Dietrich, understanding, said, 'I agree. You two men are under arrest. Unless you feel inclined to talk a little more freely about this agitator in the red toga.' He nodded to two of his police, who stood by the office doorway; they stepped obediently forward.

As the two policemen came up to him, LeConte said, 'Come to think of it, there was such a person. But–he was very obscure.'

'Before the war?' Hood asked.

'Yes.' LeConte nodded slowly. 'He was a joke. As I recall, and it's difficult . . . a fat, ignorant clown from some backwoods area. He had a little radio station or something over which he broadcast. He peddled some sort of anti-radiation box which you installed in your house, and it made you safe from bomb-test fallout.'

Now his staff member Mr Fall said, 'I remember. He even ran for the UN senate. But he was defeated, naturally.'

'And that was the last of him?' Hood asked.

'Oh yes,' LeConte said. 'He died of Asian flu soon after. He's been dead for fifteen years.'

*

In a helicopter, Hood flew slowly above the terrain depicted in the *Times* articles, seeing for himself that there was no sign of political activity. He did not feel really assured until he had seen with his own eyes that the newspaper had lost contact with actual events. The reality of the situation did not coincide with the *Times* articles in any way; that was obvious. And yet—the homeostatic system continued on.

Joan, seated beside him, said, 'I have the third article here, if you want to read it.' She had been looking the latest edition over.

'No,' Hood said.

'It says they're in the outskirts of the city,' she said. 'They broke through the police barricades and the governor has appealed for UN assistance.'

Thoughtfully, Fletcher said, 'Here's an idea. One of us, preferably you, Hood, should write a letter to the *Times*.'

Hood glanced at him.

'I think I can tell you exactly how it should be worded,' Fletcher said. 'Make it a simple inquiry. You've followed the accounts in the paper about Cemoli's movement. Tell the editor—' Fletcher paused. 'That you feel sympathetic *and you'd like to join the movement*. Ask the paper how.'

To himself, Hood thought, *In other words ask the newspaper to put me in touch with Cemoli*. He had to admire Fletcher's idea. It was brilliant, in a crazy sort of way. It was as if Fletcher had been able to match the derangement of the newspaper by a deliberate shift from common sense on his own part. He would participate in the newspaper's delusion. Assuming there was a Cemoli and a march on New York, he was asking a reasonable question.

Joan said, 'I don't want to sound stupid, but how does one go about mailing a letter to a homeopape?'

'I've looked into that,' Fletcher said. 'At each kiosk set up by the paper there's a letter-slot, next to the coin-slot where you pay for your paper. It was the law when the homeopapes were set up originally, decades ago. All we need is your husband's signature.' Reaching into his jacket, he brought out an envelope. 'The letter's written.'

Hood took the letter, examined it. *So we desire to be part of the mythical fat clown's throng*, he said to himself. 'Won't there be a headline reading CURB CHIEF JOINS MARCH ON EARTH CAPITAL?' he asked Fletcher, feeling a trace of wry amusement. 'Wouldn't a good, enterprising homeopape make front page use of a letter such as this?'

Obviously Fletcher had not thought of that; he looked chagrined. 'I suppose we had better get someone else to sign it,' he admitted. 'Some minor person attached to your staff.' He added, 'I could sign it myself.'

Handing him the letter back, Hood said, 'Do so. It'll be interesting to see what response, if any, there is.' *Letters to the editor*, he thought. *Letters to a vast, complex, electronic organism buried deep in the ground, responsible to no one, guided solely by its own ruling circuits. How would it react to this external ratification of its delusion? Would the newspaper be snapped back to reality?*

It was, he thought, *as if the newspaper, during these years of this enforced silence, had been dreaming, and now, reawakened, it had allowed portions of its former dreams to materialize in its pages along with its accurate, perceptive accounts of the actual situation. A blend of figments and sheer, stark reporting. Which ultimately would triumph? Soon, evidently, the unfolding story of Benny Cemoli would have the toga-wearing spellbinder in New York; it appeared that the march would succeed. And what then? How could this be squared with the arrival of CURB, with all its enormous inter-system authority and power? Surely the homeopape, before long, would have to face the incongruity.*

One of the two accounts would have to cease . . . but Hood had an uneasy intuition that a homeopape which had dreamed for a decade would not readily give up its fantasies. *Perhaps*, he thought, *the news of us, of CURB and its task of rebuilding Earth, will fade from the pages of the* Times, *will be given a steadily decreasing coverage each day, farther back in the paper. And at last only the exploits of Benny Cemoli will remain.*

It was not a pleasant anticipation. It disturbed him deeply. *As if*, he thought, *we are only real so long as the* Times *writes about us; as if we were dependent for our existence on it.*

*

Twenty-four hours later, in its regular edition, the *Times* printed Fletcher's letter. In print it struck Hood as flimsy and contrived—surely the homeopape could not be taken in by it, and yet here it was. It had managed to pass each of the steps in the pape's processing.

Dear Editor:
    Your coverage of the heroic march on the decadent plutocratic stronghold of New York City has fired my enthusiasm. How does an ordinary citizen become a part of this history in the making? Please inform me at once, as I am eager to join Cemoli and endure the rigors and triumphs with the others.

Cordially,

RUDOLF FLETCHER

Beneath the letter, the homeopape had given an answer; Hood read it rapidly.

Cemoli's stalwarts maintain a recruiting office in downtown New York; address, 460 Bleekman St, New York 32. You might apply there, if the police haven't cracked down on these quasi-legal activities, in view of the current crisis.

Touching a button on his desk, Hood opened the direct line to police headquarters. When he had the chief investigator, he said, 'Dietrich, I'd like a team of your men; we have a trip to make and there may be difficulties.'

After a pause Dietrich said dryly, 'So it's not all noble reclamation after all. Well, we've already dispatched a man to keep an eye on the Bleekman Street address. I admire your letter scheme. It may have done the trick.' He chuckled.

Shortly, Hood and four black-uniformed Centaurian policemen flew by 'copter above the ruins of New York City, searching for the remains of what had once been Bleekman Street. By the use of a map they managed after half an hour to locate themselves.

'There,' the police captain in charge of the team said, pointing. 'That would be it, that building used as a grocery store.' The 'copter began to lower.

It was a grocery store, all right. Hood saw no signs of political activity, no persons loitering, no flags or banners. And yet—something ominous seemed to lie behind the commonplace scene below, the bins of vegetables parked out on the sidewalk, the shabby women in long cloth coats who stood picking over the winter potatoes, the elderly proprietor with his white cloth apron sweeping with his broom. It was too natural, too easy. It was *too* ordinary.

'Shall we land?' the police captain asked him.

'Yes,' Hood said. 'And be ready.'

The proprietor, seeing them land in the street before his grocery store, laid his broom carefully to one side and walked toward them. He was, Hood saw, a Greek. He had a heavy mustache and slightly wavy gray hair, and he gazed at them with innate caution, knowing at once that they did not intend him any good. Yet he had decided to greet them with civility; he was not afraid of them.

'Gentlemen,' the Greek grocery store owner said, bowing slightly. 'What can I do for you?' His eyes roved speculatively over the black Centaurian police uniforms, but he showed no expression, no reaction.

Hood said, 'We've come to arrest a political agitator. You have nothing to be alarmed about.' He started toward the grocery store; the team of police followed, their side arms drawn.

'Political agitation here?' the Greek said. 'Come on. It is impossible.' He hurried after them, panting, alarmed now. 'What have I done? Nothing at all; you can look around. Go ahead.' He held open the door of the store, ushering them inside. 'See right away for yourself.'

'That's what we intend to do,' Hood said. He moved with agility, wasting no time on conspicuous portions of the store; he strode directly on through.

*

The back room lay ahead, the warehouse with its cartons of cans, cardboard boxes stacked up on every side. A young boy was busy making a stock inventory; he glanced up, startled, as they entered. *Nothing here*, Hood thought. *The owner's son at work, that's all.* Lifting the lid of a carton Hood peered inside. Cans of peaches. And beside that a crate of lettuce. He tore off a leaf, feeling futile and– disappointed.

The police captain said to him in a low voice, 'Nothing, sir.'

'I see that,' Hood said, irritably.

A door to the right led to a closet. Opening it, he saw brooms and a mop, a galvanized pail, boxes of detergents. And–

There were drops of paint on the floor.

The closet, some time recently, had been repainted. When he bent down and scratched with his nail he found the paint still tacky.

'Look at this,' he said, beckoning the police captain over.

The Greek, nervously, said, 'What's the matter, gentlemen? You find something dirty and report to the board of health, is that it? Customers have complained–tell me the truth, please. Yes, it is fresh paint. We keep everything spick and span. Isn't that in the public interest?'

Running his hands across the wall of the broom closet, the police captain said quietly, 'Mr Hood, there was a doorway here. Sealed up now, very recently.' He looked expectantly toward Hood, awaiting instructions.

Hood said, 'Let's go in.'

Turning to his subordinates, the police captain gave a series of orders. From the ship, equipment was dragged, through the store, to the closet; a controlled whine arose as the police began the task of cutting into the wood and plaster.

Pale, the Greek said, 'This is outrageous. I will sue.'

'Right,' Hood agreed. 'Take us to court.' Already a portion of the wall had given way. It fell inward with a crash, and bits of rubble spilled down onto the floor. A white cloud of dust rose, then settled.

It was not a large room which Hood saw in the glare of the police flashlights. Dusty, without windows, smelling stale and ancient . . . the room had not been inhabited for a long, long time, he realized, and he warily entered. It was empty. Just an abandoned storeroom of some kind, its wooden walls scaling and dingy. Perhaps before the Misfortune the grocery store had possessed a larger inventory. More stocks had been available then, but now this room was not needed. Hood moved about, flashing his beam of light up to the ceiling and then down to the floor. Dead flies, entombed here . . . and, he saw, a few live ones which crept haltingly in the dust.

'Remember,' the police captain said, 'it was boarded up just now, within the last three days. Or at least the painting was just now done, to be absolutely accurate about it.'

'These flies,' Hood said. 'They're not even dead yet.' So it had not even been three days. Probably the boarding-up had been done yesterday.

What had this room been used for? He turned to the Greek, who had come after them, still tense and pale, his dark eyes flickering rapidly with concern. *This is a smart man*, Hood realized. *We will get little out of him.*

At the far end of the storeroom the police flashlights picked out a cabinet, empty shelves of bare, rough wood. Hood walked toward it.

'Okay,' the Greek said thickly, swallowing. 'I admit it. We have kept bootleg gin stored here. We became scared. You Centaurians—' He looked around at them with fear. 'You're not like our local bosses; we know them, they understand us. You! You can't be reached. But we have to make a living.' He spread his hands, appealing to them.

From behind the cabinet the edge of something protruded. Barely visible, it might never have been noticed. A paper which had fallen there, almost out of sight; it had slipped down farther and farther. Now Hood took hold of it and carefully drew it out. Back up the way it had come.

The Greek shuddered.

It was, Hood saw, a picture. A heavy, middle-aged man with loose jowls stained black by the grained beginnings of a beard, frowning, his lips set in defiance. A big man, wearing some kind of uniform. Once this picture had hung on the wall and people had come here and looked at it, paid respect to it. He knew who it was. This was Benny Cemoli, at the height of his political career, the leader glaring bitterly at the followers who had gathered here. So this was the man.

No wonder the *Times* showed such alarm.

To the Greek grocery store owner, Hood said, holding up the picture, 'Tell me. Is this familiar to you?'

'No, no,' the Greek said. He wiped perspiration from his face with a large red handkerchief. 'Certainly not.' But obviously, it was.

Hood said, 'You're a follower of Cemoli, aren't you?'

There was silence.

'Take him along,' Hood said to the police captain. 'And let's start back.' He walked from the room, carrying the picture with him.

As he spread the picture out on his desk, Hood thought, *It isn't merely a fantasy of the* Times. *We know the truth now. The man is real and twenty-four hours ago this portrait of him hung on a wall, in plain sight. It would still be there this moment, if* CURB *had not put in its appearance. We frightened them. The Earth people have a lot to hide from us, and they know it. They are taking steps, rapidly and effectively, and we will be lucky if we can—*

Interrupting his thoughts, Joan said, 'Then the Bleekman Street address really was a meeting place for them. The pape was correct.'

'Yes,' Hood said.

'Where is he now?'

I wish I knew, Hood thought.

'Has Dietrich seen the picture yet?'

'Not yet,' Hood said.

Joan said, 'He was responsible for the war and Dietrich is going to find it out.'

'No one man,' Hood said, 'could be solely responsible.'

'But he figured largely,' Joan said. 'That's why they've gone to so much effort to eradicate all traces of his existence.'

Hood nodded.

'Without the *Times*,' she said, 'would we ever have guessed that such a political figure as Benny Cemoli existed? We owe a lot to the pape. They overlooked it or weren't able to get to it. Probably they were working in such haste; they couldn't think of everything, even in ten years. It must be hard to obliterate *every* surviving detail of a planet-wide political movement, especially when its leader managed to seize absolute power in the final phase.'

'Impossible to obliterate,' Hood said. *A closed-off storeroom in the back of a Greek grocery store . . . that was enough to tell us what we needed to know. Now Dietrich's men can do the rest. If Cemoli is alive they will eventually find him, and if he's dead—they'll be hard to convince, knowing Dietrich. They'll never stop looking now.*

'One good thing about this,' Joan said, 'is that now a lot of innocent people will be off the hook. Dietrich won't go around prosecuting them. He'll be busy tracking down Cemoli.'

True, Hood thought. And that was important. The Centaurian police would be thoroughly occupied for a long time to come, and that was just as well for everyone, including CURB and its ambitious program of reconstruction.

If there had never been a Benny Cemoli, he thought suddenly, *it would almost have been necessary to invent him.* An odd thought . . . he wondered how it happened to come to him. Again he examined the picture, trying to infer as much as possible about the man from this flat likeness. How had Cemoli sounded? Had he gained power through the spoken word, like so many demagogues before him? And his writing . . . Maybe some of it would turn up. Or even tape recordings of speeches he had made, the actual *sound* of the man. And perhaps video tapes as well. Eventually it would all come to light; it was only a question of time. *And then we will be able to experience for ourselves how it was to live under the shadow of such a man,* he realized.

The line from Dietrich's office buzzed. He picked up the phone.

'We have the Greek here,' Dietrich said. 'Under drug-guidance he's made a number of admissions; you may be interested.'

'Yes,' Hood said.

Dietrich said, 'He tells us he's been a follower for seventeen years, a real old-timer in the Movement. They met twice a week in the back of his grocery store, in the early days when the Movement was small and relatively powerless. That picture you have—I haven't seen it, of course, but Stavros, our Greek gentleman, told me about it—that portrait is actually obsolete in the sense that several more recent ones have been in vogue among the faithful for some time now. Stavros hung onto it for sentimental reasons. It reminded him of the old days. Later on when the Movement grew in strength, Cemoli stopped showing up at the grocery store, and the Greek lost out in any personal contact with him. He continued to be a loyal dues-paying member, but it became abstract for him.'

'What about the war?' Hood asked.

'Shortly before the war Cemoli seized power in a coup here in North America, through a march on New York City, during a severe economic depression. Millions were unemployed and he drew a good deal of support from them. He tried to solve the economic problems through an aggressive foreign policy—attacked several Latin American republics which were in the sphere of influence of the Chinese. That seems to be it, but Stavros is a bit hazy about the big picture . . . we'll have to fill in more from other enthusiasts as we go along. From some of the younger ones. After all, this one is over seventy years old.'

Hood said, 'You're not going to prosecute him, I hope.'

'Oh, no. He's simply a source of information. When he's told us all he has on his mind we'll let him go back to his onions and canned apple sauce. He's harmless.'

'Did Cemoli survive the war?'

'Yes,' Dietrich said. 'But that was ten years ago. Stavros doesn't know if the man is still alive now. Personally I think he is, and we'll go on that assumption until it's proved false. We have to.'

Hood thanked him and hung up.

As he turned from the phone he heard, beneath him, the low, dull rumbling. The homeopape had once more started into life.

'It's not a regular edition,' Joan said, quickly consulting her wristwatch. 'So it must be another extra. This is exciting, having it happen like this; I can't wait to read the front page.'

What has Benny Cemoli done now? Hood wondered. *According to the* Times, *in its misphased chronicling of the man's epic ... what stage, actually taking place years ago, has now been reached. Something climactic, deserving of an extra. It will be interesting, no doubt of that. The* Times *knows what is fit to print.*

He, too, could hardly wait.

In downtown Oklahoma City, John LeConte put a coin into the slot of the kiosk which the *Times* had long ago established there. The copy of the *Times'* latest extra slid out, and he picked it up and read the headline briefly, spending only a moment on it to verify the essentials. Then he crossed the sidewalk and stepped once more into the rear seat of his chauffeur-driven steam car.

Mr Fall said circumspectly, 'Sir, here is the primary material, if you wish to make a word-by-word comparison.' The secretary held out the folder, and LeConte accepted it.

The car started up. Without being told, the chauffeur drove in the direction of Party headquarters. LeConte leaned back, lit a cigar and made himself comfortable.

On his lap, the newspaper blazed up its enormous headlines.

CEMOLI ENTERS COALITION UN GOVERNMENT,
TEMPORARY CESSATION OF HOSTILITIES

To his secretary, LeConte said, 'My phone, please.'

'Yes sir.' Mr Fall handed him the portable field-phone. 'But we're almost there. And it's always possible, if you don't mind my pointing it out, that they may have tapped us somewhere along the line.'

'They're busy in New York,' LeConte said. 'Among the ruins.' *In an area that hasn't mattered as long as I can remember*, he said to himself. However, possibly Mr Fall's advice was good; he decided to skip the phone call. 'What do you think of this last item?' he asked his secretary, holding up the newspaper.

'Very success-deserving,' Mr Fall said, nodding.

Opening his briefcase, LeConte brought out a tattered, coverless textbook. It had been manufactured only an hour ago, and it was the next artifact to be planted for the invaders from Proxima Centaurus to discover. This was his own contribution, and he was personally quite proud of it. The book outlined in massive detail Cemoli's program of social change; the revolution depicted in language comprehensible to school children.

'May I ask,' Mr Fall said, 'if the Party hierarchy intends for them to discover a corpse?'

'Eventually,' LeConte said. 'But that will be several months from now.' Taking a pencil from his coat pocket he wrote in the tattered textbook, crudely, as if a pupil had done it:

DOWN WITH CEMOLI

Or was that going too far? No, he decided. There would be resistance. Certainly of the spontaneous, school boy variety. He added:

WHERE ARE THE ORANGES?

Peering over his shoulder, Mr Fall said, 'What does that mean?'

'Cemoli promises oranges to the youth,' LeConte explained. 'Another empty boast which the revolution never fulfills. That was Stavros's idea . . . he being a grocer. A nice touch.' *Giving it*, he thought, *just that much more semblance of verisimilitude. It's the little touches that have done it.*

'Yesterday,' Mr Fall said, 'when I was at Party headquarters, I heard an audio tape that had been made. Cemoli addressing the UN. It was uncanny; if you didn't know—'

'Who did they get to do it?' LeConte asked, wondering why he hadn't been in on it.

'Some nightclub entertainer here in Oklahoma City. Rather obscure, of course. I believe he specializes in all sorts of characterizations. The fellow gave it a bombastic, threatening quality . . . I must admit I enjoyed it.'

And meanwhile, LeConte thought, *there are no war-crimes trials. We who were leaders during the war, on Earth and on Mars, we who held responsible posts—we are safe, at least for a while. And perhaps it will be forever. If our strategy continues to work. And if our tunnel to the cephalon of the homeopape, which took us five years to complete, isn't discovered. Or doesn't collapse.*

The steam car parked in the reserved space before Party headquarters; the chauffeur came around to open the door and LeConte got leisurely out, stepping forth into the light of day, with no feeling of anxiety. He tossed his cigar into the gutter and then sauntered across the sidewalk, into the familiar building.

NOVELTY ACT

Lights burned late in the great communal apartment building Abraham Lincoln, because this was All Souls' night: the residents, all six hundred of them, were required by their charter to attend, down in the subsurface community hall. They filed in briskly, men, women and children; at the door Bruce Corley, operating their rather expensive new identification reader, checked each of them in turn to be sure that no one from outside, from another communal apartment building, got in. The residents submitted good-naturedly, and it all went very fast.

'Hey Bruce, how much'd it set us back?' asked old Joe Purd, oldest resident in the building; he had moved in with his wife and two children the day the building, in May of 1980, had been built. His wife was dead now and the children had grown up, married and moved on, but Joe remained.

'Plenty,' Bruce Corley said, 'but it's error-proof; I mean, it isn't just subjective.' Up to now, in his permanent job as sergeant of arms, he had admitted people merely by his ability to recognize them. But that way he had at last let in a pair of goons from Red Robin Hill Manor and they had disrupted the entire meeting with their questions and comments. It would not happen again.

Passing out copies of the agenda, Mrs Wells smiled fixedly and chanted, 'Item 3 A, Appropriation for Roof Repairs, has been moved to 4 A. Please make a note of that.' The residents accepted their agendas and then divided into two streams flowing to opposite sides of the hall; the liberal faction of the building seated themselves on the right and the conservatives on the left, each conspicuously ignoring the existence of the other. A few uncommitted persons—newer residents or odd-balls—took seats in the rear, self-conscious and silent as the room buzzed with many small conferences. The tone, the mood of the room, was tolerant, but the residents knew that tonight there was going to be a clash. Presumably, both sides were prepared. Here and there documents, petitions, newspaper clippings rustled as they were read and exchanged, handed back and forth.

On the platform, seated at the table with the four governing building trustees, chairman Donald Klugman felt sick at his stomach. A peaceful man, he shrank from these violent squabbles. Even seated in the audience he found it too much for him, and here tonight he would have to take active part; time and tide had rotated the chair around to him, as it did to each resident in turn, and of course it would be the night the school issue reached its climax.

The room had almost filled and now Patrick Doyle, the current building sky pilot, looking none too happy in his long white robe, raised his hands for silence. 'The opening prayer,' he called huskily, cleared his throat and brought forth a small card. 'Everyone please shut their eyes and bow their heads.' He glanced at Klugman and the trustees, and Klugman nodded for him to continue. 'Heavenly Father,' Doyle said, 'we the residents of the communal apartment building Abraham Lincoln beseech You to bless our assembly tonight. Um, we ask that in Your mercy You enable us to raise the funds for the roof repairs which seem imperative. We ask that our sick be healed and our unemployed find jobs and that in processing applicants wishing to live amongst us we show wisdom in whom we admit and whom we turn away. We further ask that no outsiders get in and disrupt our law-abiding, orderly lives and we ask in particular that lastly, if it be Thy will, Nicole Thibodeaux be free of her sinus headaches which have caused her not to appear before us on TV lately, and that those headaches not have anything to do with that time two years ago, which we all recall, when that stagehand allowed that weight to fall and strike her on the head, sending her to the hospital for several days. Anyhow, amen.'

The audience agreed, 'Amen.'

Rising from his chair, Klugman said, 'Now, before the business of the meeting, we'll have a few minutes of our own talent displayed for our enjoyment. First, the three Fettersmoller girls from apartment number 205. They will do a soft-shoe dance to the tune of "I'll Build a Stairway to the Stars."' He reseated himself, and onto the stage came the three little blonde-haired children, familiar to the audience from many talent shows in the past.

As the Fettersmoller girls in their striped pants and glittery silver jackets shuffled smilingly through their dance, the door to the outside hall opened and a late-comer, Edgar Stone, appeared.

He was late, this evening, because he had been grading test papers of his next-door neighbor, Mr Ian Duncan, and as he stood in the doorway his mind was still on the test and the poor showing which Duncan—whom he barely knew—had made. It seemed to him that without even having finished the test he could see that Duncan had failed.

On the stage the Fettersmoller girls sang in their scratchy voices, and Stone wondered why he had come. Perhaps for no more reason than to avoid the fine, it being mandatory for the residents to be here, tonight. These amateur talent shows, put on so often, meant nothing to him; he recalled the old days when the TV set had carried entertainment, good shows put on by professionals. Now of course all the professionals who were any good were under contract to the White House, and the TV had become educational, not entertaining. Mr Stone thought of great old late-late movies with comics such as Jack Lemmon and Shirley MacLaine, and then he looked once more at the Fettersmoller girls and groaned.

Corley, hearing him, glanced at him severely.

At least he had missed the prayer. He presented his identification to Corley's new machine and it allowed him to pass down the aisle toward a vacant seat. Was Nicole watching this, tonight? Was a White House talent scout present somewhere in the audience? He saw no unfamiliar faces. The Fettersmoller girls were wasting their time. Seating himself, he closed his eyes and listened, unable to endure watching. They'll never make it, he thought. They'll have to face it, and so will their ambitious parents; they're untalented, like the rest of us ... Abraham Lincoln Apartments has added little to the cultural store of the nation, despite its sweaty, strenuous determination, and you are not going to be able to change that.

The hopelessness of the Fettersmoller girls' position made him remember once more the test papers which Ian Duncan, trembling and waxen-faced, had pressed into his hands early that morning. If Duncan failed he would be even worse-off than the Fettersmoller girls because he would not even be living at Abraham Lincoln; he would drop out of sight—their sight, anyhow—and would revert to a despised and ancient status: he would find himself once more living in a dorm, working on a manual gang as they had all done back in their teens.

Of course he would also be refunded the money which he had paid for his apartment, a large sum which represented the man's sole major investment in life. From one standpoint, Stone envied him. What would I do, he asked himself as he sat, eyes closed, if I had my equity back right now, in a lump sum? Perhaps, he thought, I'd emigrate. Buy one of those cheap, illegal jalopies they peddle at those lots which—

Clapping hands roused him. The girls had finished, and he, too, joined in the applause. On the platform, Klugman waved for silence. 'Okay, folks, I know you enjoyed that, but there's lots *more* in store, tonight. And then there's the business part of the meeting; we mustn't forget that.' He grinned at them.

Yes, Stone thought. The business. And he felt tense, because he was one of the radicals at Abraham Lincoln who wanted to abolish the building's grammar school and send their children to a public grammar school where they would be exposed to children from other buildings entirely.

It was the kind of idea which met much opposition. And yet, in the last weeks, it had gained support. What a broadening experience it would be; their children would discover that people in other apartment buildings were no different from themselves. Barriers between people of all apartments would be torn down and a new understanding would come about.

At least, that was how it struck Stone, but the conservatives did not see it that way. Too soon, they said, for such mixing. There would be outbreaks of fights as the children clashed over which building was superior. In time it would happen . . . but not now, not so soon.

Risking the severe fine, Ian Duncan missed the assembly and remained in his apartment that evening, studying official Government texts on the religio-political history of the United States—*relpols*, as they were called. He was weak in this, he knew; he could barely comprehend the economic factors, let alone all the religious and political ideologies that had come and gone during the twentieth century, directly contributing to the present situation. For instance, the rise of the Democratic-Republican Party. Once it had been two parties, engaging in wasteful quarrels, in struggles for power, just the way buildings fought now. The two parties had merged, about 1985. Now there was just the one party, which had ruled a stable and peaceful society, and everyone belonged to it. Everyone paid dues and attended meetings and voted, each four years, for a new President—for the man they thought Nicole would like best.

It was nice to know that they, the people, had the power to decide who would become Nicole's husband, each four years; in a sense it gave to the electorate supreme power, even above Nicole herself. For instance, this last man, Taufic Negal. Relations between him and the First Lady were quite cool, indicating that she did not like this most recent choice very much. But of course being a lady she would never let on.

When did the position of First Lady first begin to assume stature greater than that of President? the *relpol* text inquired. In other words, when did our society become matriarchal, Ian

Duncan said to himself. Around about 1990; I know the answer to that. There were glimmerings before that; the change came gradually. Each year the President became more obscure, the First Lady became better known, more liked, by the public. It was the public which brought it about. Was it a need for mother, wife, mistress, or perhaps all three? Anyhow they got what they wanted; they got Nicole and she is certainly all three and more besides.

In the corner of his living room the television set said *taaaaang*, indicating that it was about to come on. With a sigh, Ian Duncan closed the official US Government text book and turned his attention to the screen. A special, dealing with activities at the White House, he speculated. One more tour, perhaps, or a thorough scrutiny (in massively-detailed depth) of a new hobby or pursuit of Nicole's. Has she taken up collecting bone-china cups? If so, we will have to view each and every Royal Albert blue.

Sure enough, the round, wattled features of Maxwell Jamison, the White House news secretary, appeared on the screen. Raising his hand, Jamison made his familiar gesture of greeting. 'Evening, people of this land of ours,' he said solemnly. 'Have you ever wondered what it would be like to descend to the bottom of the Pacific Ocean? Nicole has, and to answer that question she has assembled in the Tulip Room of the White House three of the world's foremost oceanographers. Tonight she will ask them for their stories, and you will hear them, too, as they were taped live, just a short while ago through the facilities of the Unified Triadic Networks' Public Affairs Bureau.'

And now to the White House, Ian Duncan said to himself. At least vicariously. We who can't find our way there, who have no talents which might interest the First Lady even for one evening: we get to see in anyhow, through the carefully-regulated window of our television set.

Tonight he did not really want to watch, but it seemed expedient to do so; there might be a surprise quiz on the program, at the end. And a good grade on a surprise quiz might well offset the bad grade he had surely made on the recent political test, now being corrected by his neighbor Mr Stone.

On the screen bloomed now lovely, tranquil features, the pale skin and dark, intelligent eyes, the wise and yet pert face of the woman who had come to monopolize their attention, on whom an entire nation, almost an entire planet, dwelt obsessively. At the sight of her, Ian Duncan felt engulfed by fear. He had failed her; his rotten test results were somehow known to her and although she would say nothing, the disappointment was there.

'Good evening,' Nicole said in her soft, slightly-husky voice.

'It's this way,' Ian Duncan found himself mumbling. 'I don't have a head for abstractions; I mean, all this religio-political philosophy—it makes no sense to me. Couldn't I just concentrate on concrete reality? I ought to be baking bricks or turning out shoes.' I ought to be on Mars, he thought, on the frontier. I'm flunking out here; at thirty-five I'm washed up, *and she knows it*. Let me go, Nicole, he thought in desperation. Don't give me any more tests, because I don't have a chance of passing them. Even this program about the ocean's bottom; by the time it's over I'll have forgotten all the data. I'm no use to the Democratic-Republican Party.

He thought about his brother, then. Al could help me. Al worked for Loony Luke, at one of his jalopy jungles, peddling the little tin and plastic ships that even defeated people could afford, ships that could, if luck was with them, successfully make a one-way trip to Mars. Al, he said to himself, you could get me a jalopy—wholesale.

On the TV screen, Nicole was saying, 'And really, it is a world of much enchantment, with luminous entities far surpassing in variety and in sheer delightful wonder anything found on other planets. Scientists compute that there are more forms of life in the ocean—'

Her face faded, and a sequence showing odd, grotesque fish segued into its place. This is part of the deliberate propaganda line, Ian Duncan realized. An effort to take our minds off of Mars and the idea of getting away from the Party . . . and from her. On the screen a bulbous-eyed fish gaped at him, and his attention, despite himself, was captured. Chrissakes, he thought, it is a weird world down there. Nicole, he thought, you've got me trapped. If only Al and I had succeeded; we might be performing right now for you, and we'd be happy. While you interviewed world-famous ocean-ographers Al and I would be discreetly playing in the background, perhaps one of the Bach 'Two Part Inventions.'

Going to the closet of his apartment, Ian Duncan bent down and carefully lifted a cloth-wrapped object into the light. We had so much youthful faith in this, he recalled. Tenderly, he unwrapped the jug; then, taking a deep breath, he blew a couple of hollow notes on it. The Duncan Brothers and Their Two-man Jug Band, he and Al had been, playing their own arrangements for two jugs of Bach and Mozart and Stravinsky. But the White House talent scout—the skunk. He had never even given them a fair audition. It had been done, he told them. Jesse Pigg, the fabulous jug-artist from Alabama, had gotten to the White House first, entertaining and delighting the dozen and one members of the Thibodeaux family gathered there with his version of 'Derby Ram' and 'John Henry' and the like.

'But,' Ian Duncan had protested, 'this is *classical* jug. We play late Beethoven sonatas.'

'We'll call you,' the talent scout had said briskly. 'If Nicky shows an interest at any time in the future.'

Nicky! He had blanched. Imagine being that intimate with the First Family. He and Al, mumbling pointlessly, had retired from the stage with their jugs, making way for the next act, a group of dogs dressed up in Elizabethan costumes portraying characters from *Hamlet*. The dogs had not made it, either, but that was little consolation.

'I am told,' Nicole was saying, 'that there is so little light in the ocean depths that, well, observe this strange fellow.' A fish, sport-ing a glowing lantern before him, swam across the TV screen.

Startling him, there came a knock on the apartment door. With anxiety Duncan answered it; he found his neighbor Mr Stone standing there, looking nervous.

'You weren't at All Souls?' Mr Stone said. 'Won't they check and find out?' He held in his hands Ian Duncan's corrected test.

Duncan said, 'Tell me how I did.' He prepared himself.

Entering the apartment, Stone shut the door after him. He glanced at the TV set, saw Nicole seated with the oceanographers, listened for a moment to her, then abruptly said in a hoarse voice, 'You did fine.' He held out the test.

Duncan said, 'I passed?' He could not believe it. He accepted the papers, examined them with incredulity. And then he understood what had happened. Stone had conspired to see that he passed; he had falsified the score, probably out of humanitarian motives. Duncan raised his head and they looked at each other, neither speaking. This is terrible, Duncan thought. What'll I do now? His reaction amazed him, but there it was.

I wanted to fail, he realized. Why? So I can get out of here, so I would have an excuse to give up all this, my apartment and my job, and go. Emigrate with nothing more than the shirt on my back, in a jalopy that falls to pieces the moment it comes to rest in the Martian wilderness.

'Thanks,' he said glumly.

In a rapid voice, Stone said, 'You can do the same for me sometime.'

'Oh yeah, be happy to,' Duncan said.

Scuttling back out of the apartment, Stone left him alone with the TV set, his jug and the falsely-corrected test papers, and his thoughts.

Al, you've got to help me, he said to himself. You've got to get me out of this; I can't even fail on my own.

In the little structure at the back of Jalopy Jungle No. 3, Al Duncan sat with his feet on the desk, smoking a cigarette and watching passers-by, the sidewalk and people and stores of downtown Reno, Nevada. Beyond the gleam of the new jalopies parked with flapping banners and streamers cascading from them he saw a shape waiting, hiding beneath the sign that spelled out LOONY LUKE.

And he was not the only person to see the shape; along the sidewalk came a man and woman with a small boy trotting ahead of them, and the boy, with an exclamation, hopped up and down, gesturing excitedly. 'Hey, Dad, look! You know what it is? Look, it's the papoola.'

'By golly,' the man said with a grin, 'so it is. Look, Marion, there's one of those Martian creatures, hiding there under that sign. What do you say we go over and chat with it?' He started in that direction, along with the boy. The woman, however, continued along the sidewalk.

'Come on, Mom!' the boy urged.

In his office, Al lightly touched the controls of the mechanism within his shirt. The papoola emerged from beneath the LOONY LUKE sign, and Al caused it to waddle on its six stubby legs toward the sidewalk, its round, silly hat slipping over one antenna, its eyes crossing and uncrossing as it made out the sight of the woman. The tropism being established, the papoola trudged after her, to the delight of the boy and his father.

'Look, Dad, it's following Mom! Hey Mom, turn around and see!'

The woman glanced back, saw the platter-like organism with its orange bug-shaped body, and she laughed. Everybody loves the papoola, Al thought to himself. See the funny Martian papoola. Speak, papoola; say hello to the nice lady who's laughing at you.

The thoughts of the papoola, directed at the woman, reached Al. It was greeting her, telling her how nice it was to meet her, soothing and coaxing her until she came back up the sidewalk toward it, joining her boy and husband so that now all three of them stood together, receiving the mental impulses emanating from the Martian creature which had come here to Earth with no hostile plans, no capacity to cause trouble. The papoola loved them, too, just as they loved it; it told them so right now—it conveyed to them the gentleness, the warm hospitality which it was accustomed to on its own planet.

What a wonderful place Mars must be, the man and woman

were no doubt thinking, as the papoola poured out its recollections, its attitude. Gosh, it's not cold and schizoid, like Earth society; nobody spies on anybody else, grades their innumerable political tests, reports on them to building Security committees week in, week out. Think of it, the papoola was telling them as they stood rooted to the sidewalk, unable to pass on. You're your own boss, there, free to work your land, believe your own beliefs, become *yourself*. Look at you, afraid even to stand here listening. Afraid to—

In a nervous voice the man said to his wife, 'We better go.'

'Oh no,' the boy said pleadingly. 'I mean, gee, how often do you get to talk to a papoola? It must belong to that jalopy jungle, there.' The boy pointed, and Al found himself under the man's keen, observing scrutiny.

The man said, 'Of course. They landed here to sell jalopies. It's working on us right now, softening us up.' The enchantment visibly faded from his face. 'There's the man sitting in there operating it.'

But, the papoola thought, what I tell you is still true. Even if it is a sales pitch. You could go there, to Mars, yourself. You and your family can see with your own eyes—if you have the courage to break free. Can you do it? Are you a real man? Buy a Loony Luke jalopy . . . buy it while you still have the chance, because you know that someday, maybe not so long from now, the law is going to crack down. And there will be no more jalopy jungles. No more crack in the wall of the authoritarian society through which a few—a few lucky people—can escape.

Fiddling with the controls at his midsection, Al turned up the gain. The force of the papoola's psyche increased, drawing the man in, taking control of him. You must buy a jalopy, the papoola urged. Easy payment plan, service warranty, many models to choose from. The man took a step toward the lot. Hurry, the papoola told him. Any second now the authorities may close down the lot and your opportunity will be gone forever.

'This is how they work it,' the man said with difficulty. 'The animal snares people. Hypnosis. We have to leave.' But he did not leave; it was too late: he was going to buy a jalopy, and Al, in the office with his control box, was reeling the man in.

Leisurely, Al rose to his feet. Time to go out and close the deal. He shut off the papoola, opened the office door and stepped outside onto the lot—and saw a once-familiar figure threading its way among the jalopies, toward him. It was his brother Ian and he had not seen him in years. Good grief, Al thought. What's he want? And at a time like this—

'Al,' his brother called, gesturing. 'Can I talk with you a second? You're not too busy, are you?' Perspiring and pale, he came closer, looking about in a frightened way. He had deteriorated since Al had last seen him.

'Listen,' Al said, with anger. But already it was too late; the couple and their boy had broken away and were moving rapidly on down the sidewalk.

'I don't mean to bother you,' Ian mumbled.

'You're not bothering me,' Al said as he gloomily watched the three people depart. 'What's the trouble, Ian? You don't look very well; are you sick? Come on in the office.' He led his brother inside and shut the door.

Ian said, 'I came across my jug. Remember when we were trying to make it to the White House? Al, we have to try once more. Honest to God, I can't go on like this; I can't stand to be a failure at what we agreed was the most important thing in our lives.' Panting, he mopped at his forehead with his handkerchief, his hands trembling.

'I don't even have my jug any more,' Al said presently.

'You must. Well, we could each record our parts separately on my jug and then synthesize them on one tape, and present that to the White House. This trapped feeling; I don't know if I can go on living with it. I have to get back to playing. If we started practicing right now on the "Goldberg Variations" in two months we—'

Al broke in, 'You still live at that place? That Abraham Lincoln?'

Ian nodded.

'And you still have that position down in Palo Alto, you're still a gear inspector?' He could not understand why his brother was so upset. 'Hell, if worst comes to worst you can emigrate. Jug-playing is out of the question; I haven't played for years, since I last saw you in fact. Just a minute.' He dialed the knobs of the mechanism which controlled the papoola; near the sidewalk the creature responded and began to return slowly to its spot beneath the sign.

Seeing it, Ian said, 'I thought they were all dead.'

'They are,' Al said.

'But that one out there moves and—'

'It's a fake,' Al said. 'A puppet. I control it.' He showed his brother the control box. 'It brings in people off the sidewalk. Actually, Luke is supposed to have a real one on which these are modeled. Nobody knows for sure and the law can't touch Luke because technically he's now a citizen of Mars; they can't make him cough up the real one, if he does have it.' Al seated himself and lit a cigarette. 'Fail your *relpol* test,' he said to Ian, 'lose your apartment and get back your original deposit; bring me the money and I'll see that you get a damn fine jalopy that'll carry you to Mars. Okay?'

'I tried to fail my test,' Ian said, 'but they won't let me. They doctored the results. They don't want me to get away.'

'Who's "they"?'

'The man in the next apartment. Ed Stone, his name is. He did it deliberately; I saw the look on his face. Maybe he thought he was doing me a favor . . . I don't know.' He looked around him. 'This is a nice little office you have here. You sleep in it, don't you? And when it moves, you move with it.'

'Yeah,' Al said, 'we're always ready to take off.' The police had almost gotten him a number of times, even though the lot could obtain orbital velocity in six minutes. The papoola had detected their approach, but not sufficiently far in advance for a comfortable escape; generally it was hurried and disorganized, with part of his inventory of jalopies being left behind.

'You're just one jump ahead of them,' Ian mused. 'And yet it doesn't bother you. I guess it's all in your attitude.'

'If they get me,' Al said, 'Luke will bail me out.' The shadowy, powerful figure of his boss was always there, backing him up, so what did he have to worry about? The jalopy tycoon knew a million tricks. The Thibodeaux clan limited their attacks on him to deep-think articles in popular magazines and on TV, harping on Luke's vulgarity and the shoddiness of his vehicles; they were a little afraid of him, no doubt.

'I envy you,' Ian said. 'Your poise. Your calmness.'

'Doesn't your apartment building have a sky pilot? Go talk to him.'

Ian said bitterly, 'That's no good. Right now it's Patrick Doyle and he's as bad off as I am. And Don Klugman, our chairman, is even worse off; he's a bundle of nerves. In fact our whole building is shot through with anxiety. Maybe it has to do with Nicole's sinus headaches.'

Glancing at his brother, Al saw that he was actually serious. The White House and all it stood for meant that much to him; it still dominated his life, as it had when they were boys. 'For your sake,' Al said quietly, 'I'll get my jug out and practice. We'll make one more try.'

Speechless, Ian gaped at him in gratitude.

Seated together in the business office of the Abraham Lincoln, Don Klugman and Patrick Doyle studied the application which Mr Ian Duncan of no. 304 had filed with them. Ian desired to appear in the twice-weekly talent show, and at a time when a White House talent scout was present. The request, Klugman saw, was routine, except that Ian proposed to do his act in conjunction with another individual *who did not live at Abraham Lincoln.*

Doyle said, 'It's his brother. He told me once; the two of them used to have this act, years ago. Baroque music on two jugs. A novelty.'

'What apartment house does his brother live in?' Klugman asked. Approval of the application would depend on how relations stood between the Abraham Lincoln and the other building.

'None. He sells jalopies for that Loony Luke—you know. Those cheap little ships that get you just barely to Mars. He lives on one of the lots, I understand. The lots move around; it's a nomadic existence. I'm sure you've heard.'

'Yes,' Klugman agreed, 'and it's totally out of the question. We can't have that act on our stage, not with a man like that involved in it. There's no reason why Ian Duncan can't play his jug; it's a basic political right and I wouldn't be surprised if it's a satisfactory act. But it's against our tradition to have an outsider participate; our stage is for our own people exclusively, always has been and always will. So there's no need even to discuss this.' He eyed the sky pilot critically.

'True,' Doyle said, 'but it is a blood relative of one of our people, right? It's legal for one of us to invite a relative to watch the talent shows . . . so why not let him participate? This means a lot to Ian; I think you know he's been failing, lately. He's not a very intelligent person. Actually, he should be doing a manual job, I suppose. But if he has artistic ability, for instance this jug concept—'

Examining his documents, Klugman saw that a White House scout would be attending a show at the Abraham Lincoln in two weeks. The best acts at the building would of course be scheduled that night . . . the Duncan Brothers and Their Baroque Jug Band would have to compete successfully in order to obtain that privilege, and there were a number of acts which—Klugman thought—were probably superior. After all, *jugs* . . . and not even electronic jugs, at that.

'All right,' he said aloud to Doyle. 'I agree.'

'You're showing your humane side,' the sky pilot said, with a grin of sentimentality which disgusted Klugman. 'And I think we'll all enjoy the Bach and Vivaldi as played by the Duncan Brothers on their inimitable jugs.'

Klugman, wincing, nodded.

On the big night, as they started into the auditorium on floor one of Abraham Lincoln Apartments, Ian Duncan saw, trailing along behind his brother, the flat, scuttling shape of the Martian crea-ture, the papoola. He stopped short. 'You're bringing that along?'

Al said, 'You don't understand. Don't we have to win?'

After a pause, Ian said, 'Not that way.' He understood, all right; the papoola would take on the audience as it had taken on side-walk traffic. It would exert its extra-sensory influence on them, coaxing out a favorable decision. So much for the ethics of a jalopy salesman, Ian realized. To his brother, this seemed perfectly nor-mal; if they couldn't win by their jug-playing they would win through the papoola.

'Aw,' Al said, gesturing, 'don't be your own worst enemy. All we're engaged in here is a little subliminal sales technique, such as they've been using for a century—it's an ancient, reputable method of swinging public opinion your way. I mean, let's face it; we haven't played the jug professionally in years.' He touched the controls at his waist and the papoola hurried forward to catch up with them. Again Al touched the controls—

And in Ian's mind a persuasive thought came, *Why not?* Every-one else does it.

With difficulty he said, 'Get that thing off me, Al.'

Al shrugged. And the thought, which had invaded Ian's mind from without, gradually withdrew. And yet, a residue remained. He was no longer sure of his position.

'It's nothing compared to what Nicole's machinery can accom-plish,' Al pointed out, seeing the expression on his face. 'One papoola here and there, and that planet-wide instrument that Nicole has made out of TV—there you have the real danger, Ian. The papoola is crude; you know you're being worked on. Not so when you listen to Nicole. The pressure is so subtle and so complete—'

'I don't know about that,' Ian said, 'I just know that unless we're successful, unless we get to play at the White House, life as far as I'm concerned isn't worth living. And nobody put that idea in my head. It's just the way I feel; it's my own idea, dammit.' He held the door open, and Al passed on into the auditorium, carrying his jug by the handle. Ian followed, and a moment later the two of them were on the stage, facing the partially-filled hall.

'Have you ever seen her?' Al asked.

'I see her all the time.'

'I mean in reality. In person. So to speak, in the flesh.'

'Of course not,' Ian said. That was the whole point of their being successful, of getting to the White House. They would see her really, not just the TV image; it would no longer be a fantasy—it would be true.

'I saw her once,' Al said. 'I had just put the lot down, Jalopy Jungle No. 3, on a main business avenue in Shreveport, La. It was early in the morning, about eight o'clock. I saw official cars coming; naturally I thought it was the police—I started to take off. But it wasn't. It was a motorcade, with Nicole in it, going to dedicate a new apartment building, the largest yet.'

'Yes,' Ian said. 'The Paul Bunyan.' The football team from Abraham Lincoln played annually against its team, and always lost. The Paul Bunyan had over ten thousand residents, and all of them came from administrative-class backgrounds; it was an exclusive apartment building of active Party members, with uniquely high monthly payments.

'You should have seen her,' Al said thoughtfully as he sat facing the audience, his jug on his lap. He tapped the papoola with his foot; it had taken up a position beneath his chair, out of sight. 'Yes,' he murmured, 'you really should. It's not the same as on TV, Ian. Not at all.'

Ian nodded. He had begun to feel apprehensive, now; in a few minutes they would be introduced. Their test had come.

Seeing him gripping his jug tautly, Al said, 'Shall I use the papoola or not? It's up to you.' He raised a quizzical brow.

Ian said, 'Use it.'

'Okay,' Al said, reaching his hand inside his coat. Leisurely, he stroked the controls. And, from beneath his chair, the papoola rolled forth, its antennae twitching drolly, its eyes crossing and uncrossing.

At once the audience became alert; people leaned forward to see, some of them chuckling with delight.

'Look,' a man said excitedly. It was old Joe Purd, as eager as a child. 'It's the papoola!'

A woman rose to her feet to see more clearly, and Ian thought to himself, *Everyone loves the papoola*. We'll win, whether we can play the jug or not. And then what? Will meeting Nicole make us even more unhappy than we are? Is that what we'll get out of this: hopeless, massive discontent? An ache, a longing which can never be satisfied in this world?

It was too late to back out, now. The doors of the auditorium had shut and Don Klugman was rising from his chair, rapping for order. 'Okay, folks,' he said into his lapel microphone. 'We're going to have a little display of some talent, right now, for everyone's enjoyment. As you see on your programs, first in order is a fine group, the Duncan Brothers and Their Classical Jugs with a medley of Bach and Handel tunes that ought to set your feet tapping.' He beamed archly at Ian and Al, as if saying, How does that suit you as an intro?

Al paid no attention; he manipulated his controls and gazed thoughtfully at the audience, then at last picked up his jug, glanced at Ian and then tapped his foot. The Little Fugue in G Minor opened their medley, and Al began to blow on the jug, sending forth the lively theme.

Bum, bum, bum. Bum-bum bum-bum bum bum de bum. DE bum, DE bum, de de-de bum . . . His cheeks puffed out red and swollen as he blew.

The papoola wandered across the stage, then lowered itself, by a series of gangly, foolish motions, into the first row of the audience. It had begun to go to work.

The news posted on the communal bulletin board outside the cafeteria of the Abraham Lincoln that the Duncan Brothers had been chosen by the talent scout to perform at the White House astounded Edgar Stone. He read the announcement again and again, wondering how the little nervous, cringing man had managed to do it.

There's been cheating, Stone said to himself. Just as I passed him on his political tests ... he's got somebody else to falsify a few results for him along the talent line. He himself had heard the jugs; he had been present at that program, and the Duncan Brothers, Classical Jugs, were simply not that good. They were *good*, admittedly ... but intuitively he knew that more was involved.

Deep inside him he felt anger, a resentment that he had falsified Duncan's test score. I put him on the road to success, Stone realized; I saved him. And now he's on his way to the White House.

No wonder Duncan did so poorly on his political test, Stone said to himself. He was busy practicing on his jug; he has no time for the commonplace realities which the rest of us have to cope with. It must be great to be an artist, Stone thought with bitterness. You're exempt from all the rules, you can do as you like.

He sure made a fool out of me, Stone realized.

Striding down the second floor hall, Stone arrived at the office of the building sky pilot; he rang the bell and the door opened, showing him the sight of the sky pilot deep in work at his desk, his face wrinkled with fatigue. 'Um, father,' Stone said, 'I'd like to confess. Can you spare a few minutes? It's very urgently on my mind, my sins I mean.'

Rubbing his forehead, Patrick Doyle nodded. 'Jeez,' he murmured. 'It either rains or it pours; I've had ten residents in today so far, using the confessionator. Go ahead.' He pointed to the alcove which opened onto his office. 'Sit down and plug yourself in. I'll be listening while I fill out these 4-10 forms from Boise.'

Filled with wrathful indignation, his hands trembling, Edgar Stone attached the electrodes of the confessionator to the correct spots of his scalp, and then, picking up the microphone, began to confess. The tape-drums of the machine turned as he spoke. 'Moved by a false pity,' he said, 'I infracted a rule of the building. But mainly I am concerned not with the act itself but with the motives behind it; the act merely is the outgrowth of a false attitude toward my fellow residents. This person, my neighbor Mr Duncan, did poorly in his recent *relpol* test and I foresaw him being evicted from Abraham Lincoln. I identified with him because subconsciously I regard myself as a failure, both as a resident of this building and as a man, so I falsified his score to indicate that he had passed. Obviously, a new *relpol* test will have to be given to Mr Duncan and the one which I scored will have to be voided.' He eyed the sky pilot, but there was no reaction.

That will take care of Ian Duncan and his Classical Jug, Stone said to himself.

By now the confessionator had analyzed his confession; it popped a card out, and Doyle rose to his feet wearily to receive it. After a careful study he glanced up. 'Mr Stone,' he said, 'the view expressed here is that your confession is no confession. What do you really have on your mind? Go back and begin all over; you haven't probed down deeply enough and brought up the genuine material. And I suggest you start out by confessing that you misconfessed consciously and deliberately.'

'No such thing,' Stone said, but his voice—even to him—sounded feeble. 'Perhaps I could discuss this with you informally. I did falsify Ian Duncan's test score. Now, maybe my motives for doing it—'

Doyle interrupted, 'Aren't you jealous of Duncan now? What with his success with the jug, White House-ward?'

There was silence.

'This could be,' Stone admitted at last. 'But it doesn't change the fact that by all rights Ian Duncan shouldn't be living here; he should be evicted, my motives notwithstanding. Look it up in the Communal Apartment-building Code. I know there's a section covering a situation like this.'

'But you can't get out of here,' the sky pilot said, 'without confessing; you have to satisfy the machine. You're attempting to force eviction of a neighbor to fulfill your own emotional needs. Confess that, and then perhaps we can discuss the code ruling as it pertains to Duncan.'

Stone groaned and once more attached the electrodes to his

scalp. 'All right,' he grated. 'I hate Ian Duncan because he's artistically gifted and I'm not. I'm willing to be examined by a twelve-resident jury of my neighbors to see what the penalty for my sin is—but I insist that Duncan be given another *relpol* test! I won't give up on this; he has no right to be living here among us. It's morally and legally *wrong*.'

'At least you're being honest, now,' Doyle said.

'Actually,' Stone said, 'I enjoy jug band playing; I liked their music, the other night. But I have to act in what I believe to be the communal interest.'

The confessionator, it seemed to him, snorted in derision as it popped a second card. But perhaps it was only his imagination.

'You're just getting yourself deeper,' Doyle said, reading the card. 'Look at this.' He passed the card to Stone. 'Your mind is a riot of confused, ambivalent motives. When was the last time you confessed?'

Flushing, Stone mumbled, 'I think last August. Pepe Jones was the sky pilot, then.'

'A lot of work will have to be done with you,' Doyle said, lighting a cigarette and leaning back in his chair.

The opening number on their White House performance, they had decided after much discussion and argument, would be the Bach Chaconne in D. Al had always liked it, despite the difficulties involved, the double-stopping and all. Even thinking about the Chaconne made Ian nervous. He wished, now that it had been decided, that he had held out for the simpler Fifth Unaccompanied Cello Suite. But too late now. Al had sent the information on to the White House A & R—artists and repertory—secretary, Harold Slezak.

Al said, 'Don't worry; you've got the number two jug in this. Do you mind being second jug to me?'

'No,' Ian said. It was a relief, actually; Al had the far more difficult part.

Outside the perimeter of Jalopy Jungle No. 3 the papoola moved, criss-crossing the sidewalk in its gliding, quiet pursuit of a

NOVELTY ACT

sales prospect. It was only ten in the morning and no one worth collaring had come along, as yet. Today the lot had set down in the hilly section of Oakland, California, among the winding tree-lined streets of the better residential section. Across from the lot, Ian could see the Joe Louis, a peculiarly-shaped but striking apartment building of a thousand units, mostly occupied by well-to-do Negroes. The building, in the morning sun, looked especially neat and cared for. A guard, with badge and gun, patrolled the entrance, stopping anyone who did not live there from entering.

'Slezak has to okay the program,' Al reminded him. 'Maybe Nicole won't want to hear the Chaconne; she's got very specialized tastes and they're changing all the time.'

In his mind Ian saw Nicole, propped up in her enormous bed, in her pink, frilly robe, her breakfast on a tray beside her as she scanned the program schedules presented to her for her approval. *Already she's heard about us*, he thought. *She knows of our existence.* In that case, we really do exist. Like a child that has to have its mother watching what it does; we're brought into being, validated consensually, by Nicole's gaze.

And when she takes her eye off us, he thought, then what? What happens to us afterward? Do we disintegrate, sink back into oblivion?

Back, he thought, into random, unformed atoms. Where we came from . . . the world of nonbeing. The world we've been in all our lives, up until now.

'And,' Al said, 'she may ask us for an encore. She may even request a particular favorite. I've researched it, and it seems she sometimes asks to hear Schumann's "The Happy Farmer." Got that in mind? We'd better work up "The Happy Farmer," just in case.' He blew a few toots on his jug, thoughtfully.

'I can't do it,' Ian said abruptly. 'I can't go on. It means too much to me. Something will go wrong; we won't please her and they'll boot us out. And we'll never be able to forget it.'

'Look,' Al began. 'We have the papoola. And that gives us–' He broke off. A tall, stoop-shouldered elderly man in an expensive natural-fiber blue pin-stripe suit was coming up the sidewalk. 'My God, it's Luke himself,' Al said. He looked frightened. 'I've only seen him twice before in my life. Something must be wrong.'

'Better reel in the papoola,' Ian said. The papoola had begun to move toward Loony Luke.

With a bewildered expression on his face Al said, 'I can't.' He fiddled desperately with the controls at his waist. 'It won't respond.'

The papoola reached Luke, and Luke bent down, picked it up and continued on toward the lot, the papoola under his arm.

'He's taken precedence over me,' Al said. He looked at his brother numbly.

The door of the little structure opened and Loony Luke entered. 'We received a report that you've been using this on your own time, for purposes of your own,' he said to Al, his voice low and gravelly. 'You were told not to do that; the papoolas belong to the lots, not to the operators.'

Al said, 'Aw, come on, Luke.'

'You ought to be fired,' Luke said, 'but you're a good salesman so I'll keep you on. Meanwhile, you'll have to make your quota without help.' Tightening his grip on the papoola, he started back out. 'My time is valuable; I have to go.' He saw Al's jug. 'That's not a musical instrument; it's a thing to put whiskey in.'

Al said, 'Listen, Luke, this is publicity. Performing for Nicole means that the network of jalopy jungles will gain prestige; got it?'

'I don't want prestige,' Luke said, pausing at the door. 'There's no catering to Nicole Thibodeaux by me; let her run her society the way she wants and I'll run the jungles the way I want. She leaves me alone and I leave her alone and that's fine with me. Don't mess it up. Tell Slezak you can't appear and forget about it; no grown man in his right senses would be hooting into an empty bottle anyhow.'

'That's where you're wrong,' Al said. 'Art can be found in the most mundane daily walks of life, like in these jugs for instance.'

Luke, picking his teeth with a silver toothpick, said, 'Now you don't have a papoola to soften the First Family up for you. Better think about that . . . do you really expect to make it without the papoola?'

After a pause Al said to Ian, 'He's right. The papoola did it for us. But—hell, let's go on anyhow.'

'You've got guts,' Luke said. 'But no sense. Still, I have to admire you. I can see why you've been a top notch salesman for the organization; you don't give up. Take the papoola the night you perform at the White House and then return it to me the next morning.' He tossed the round, bug-like creature to Al; grabbing it, Al hugged it against his chest like a big pillow. 'Maybe it would be good publicity for the jungles,' Luke said. 'But I know this. Nicole doesn't like us. Too many people have slipped out of her hands by means of us; we're a leak in mama's structure and mama knows it.' He grinned, showing gold teeth.

Al said, 'Thanks, Luke.'

'But I'll operate the papoola,' Luke said. 'By remote. I'm a little more skilled than you; after all, I *built* them.'

'Sure,' Al said. 'I'll have my hands full playing anyhow.'

'Yes,' Luke said, 'you'll need both hands for that bottle.'

Something in Luke's tone made Ian Duncan uneasy. What's he up to? he wondered. But in any case he and his brother had no choice; they had to have the papoola working for them. And no doubt Luke could do a good job of operating it; he had already proved his superiority over Al, just now, and as Luke said, Al would be busy blowing away on his jug. But still—

'Loony Luke,' Ian said, 'have you ever met Nicole?' It was a sudden thought on his part, an unexpected intuition.

'Sure,' Luke said steadily. 'Years ago. I had some hand puppets; my Dad and I traveled around putting on puppet shows. We finally played the White House.'

'What happened there?' Ian asked.

Luke, after a pause, said, 'She didn't care for us. Said something about our puppets being indecent.'

And you hate her, Ian realized. You never forgave her. 'Were they?' he asked Luke.

'No,' Luke answered. 'True, one act was a strip show; we had follies girl puppets. But nobody ever objected before. My Dad took it hard but it didn't bother me.' His face was impassive.

Al said, 'Was Nicole the First Lady that far back?'

'Oh yes,' Luke said. 'She's been in office for seventy-three years; didn't you know that?'

'It isn't possible,' both Al and Ian said, almost together.

'Sure it is,' Luke said. 'She's a really old woman, now. A grandmother. But she still looks good, I guess. You'll know when you see her.'

Stunned, Ian said, 'On TV—'

'Oh yeah,' Luke agreed. 'On TV she looks around twenty. But look in the history books yourself; figure it out. The facts are all there.'

The facts, Ian realized, mean nothing when you can see with your own eyes that she's as young-looking as ever. And we see that every day.

Luke, you're lying, he thought. We know it; we all know it. My brother saw her; Al would have said, if she was really like that. You hate her; that's your motive. Shaken, he turned his back to Luke, not wanting to have anything to do with the man, now. Seventy-three years in office—that would make Nicole almost ninety, now. He shuddered at the idea; he blocked it out of his thoughts. Or at least he tried to.

'Good luck, boys,' Luke said, chewing on his toothpick.

In his sleep Ian Duncan had a terrible dream. A hideous old woman with greenish, wrinkled claws scrabbled at him, whining for him to do something—he did not know what it was because her voice, her words, blurred into indistinction, swallowed by her broken-toothed mouth, lost in the twisting thread of saliva which found its way to her chin. He struggled to free himself . . .

'Chrissake,' Al's voice came to him. 'Wake up; we have to get the lot moving; we're supposed to be at the White House in three hours.'

NOVELTY ACT

Nicole, Ian realized as he sat up groggily. It was her I was dreaming about; ancient and withered, but still her. 'Okay,' he muttered as he rose unsteadily from the cot. 'Listen, Al,' he said, 'suppose she is old, like Loony Luke says? What then? What'll we do?'

'We'll perform,' Al said. 'Play our jugs.'

'But I couldn't live through it,' Ian said. 'My ability to adjust is just too brittle. This is turning into a nightmare; Luke controls the papoola and Nicole is old—what's the point of our going on? Can't we go back to just seeing her on the TV and maybe once in our lifetime at a great distance like you did in Shreveport? That's good enough for me, now. I want that, the image; okay?'

'No,' Al said doggedly. 'We have to see this through. Remember, you can always emigrate to Mars.'

The lot had already risen, was already moving toward the East Coast and Washington, DC.

When they landed, Slezak, a rotund, genial little individual, greeted them warmly; he shook hands with them as they walked toward the service entrance of the White House. 'Your program is ambitious,' he bubbled, 'but if you can fulfill it, fine with me, with us here, the First Family I mean, and in particular the First Lady herself who is actively enthusiastic about all forms of original artistry. According to your biographical data you two made a thorough study of primitive disc recordings from the early nineteen hundreds, as early as 1920, of jug bands surviving from the US Civil War, so you're authentic juggists except of course you're classical, not folk.'

'Yes sir,' Al said.

'Could you, however, slip in one folk number?' Slezak asked as they passed the guards at the service entrance and entered the White House, the long, carpeted corridor with its artificial candles set at intervals. 'For instance, we suggest "Rockabye My Sarah Jane." Do you have that in your repertoire? If not—'

'We have it,' Al said shortly. 'We'll add it toward the end.'

'Fine,' Slezak said, prodding them amiably ahead of him. 'Now may I ask what this creature you carry is?' He eyed the papoola with something less than enthusiasm. 'Is it alive?'

'It's our totem animal,' Al said.

'You mean a superstitious charm? A mascot?'

'Exactly,' Al said. 'With it we assuage anxiety.' He patted the papoola's head. 'And it's part of our act; it dances while we play. You know, like a monkey.'

'Well I'll be darned,' Slezak said, his enthusiasm returning. 'I see, now. Nicole will be delighted; she loves soft, furry things.' He held a door open ahead of them.

And there she sat.

How could Luke have been so wrong? Ian thought. She was even lovelier than on TV, and much more distinct; that was the main difference, the fabulous authenticity of her appearance, its reality to the senses. The senses knew the difference. Here she sat, in faded blue-cotton trousers, moccasins on her feet, a carelessly-buttoned white shirt through which he could see—or imagined he could see—her tanned, smooth skin . . . how informal she was, Ian thought. Lacking in pretense or show. Her hair cut short, exposing her beautifully-formed neck and ears. And, he thought, so darn young. She did not look even twenty. And the vitality. The TV could not catch that, the delicate glow of color and line all about her.

'Nicky,' Slezak said, 'these are the classical juggists.'

She glanced up, sideways; she had been reading a newspaper. Now she smiled. 'Good morning,' she said. 'Did you have breakfast? We could serve you some Canadian bacon and butterhorns and coffee if you want.' Her voice, oddly, did not seem to come from her; it materialized from the upper part of the room, almost at the ceiling. Looking that way, Ian saw a series of speakers and he realized that a glass barrier separated Nicole from them, a security measure to protect her. He felt disappointed and yet he understood why it was necessary. If anything happened to her—

'We ate, Mrs Thibodeaux,' Al said. 'Thanks.' He, too, was glancing up at the speakers.

We ate Mrs Thibodeaux, Ian thought crazily. Isn't it actually the other way around? Doesn't she, sitting here in her blue-cotton pants and shirt, doesn't she devour *us*?

Now the President, Taufic Negal, a slender, dapper, dark man, entered behind Nicole, and she lifted her face up to him and said, 'Look, Taffy, they have one of those papoolas with them—won't that be fun?'

'Yes,' the President said, smiling, standing beside his wife.

'Could I see it?' Nicole asked Al. 'Let it come here.' She made a signal, and the glass wall began to lift.

Al dropped the papoola and it scuttled toward Nicole, beneath the raised security barrier; it hopped up, and all at once Nicole held it in her strong hands, gazing down at it intently.

'Heck,' she said, 'it's not alive; it's just a toy.'

'None survived,' Al said. 'As far as we know. But this is an authentic model, based on remains found on Mars.' He stepped toward her—

The glass barrier settled in place. Al was cut off from the papoola and he stood gaping foolishly, seemingly very upset. Then, as if by instinct, he touched the controls at his waist. Nothing happened for a time and then, at last, the papoola stirred. It slid from Nicole's hands and hopped back to the floor. Nicole exclaimed in amazement, her eyes bright.

'Do you want it, dear?' her husband asked. 'We can undoubtedly get you one, even several.'

'What does it do?' Nicole asked Al.

Slezak bubbled, 'It dances, ma'am, when they play; it has rhythm in its bones—correct, Mr Duncan? Maybe you could play something now, a shorter piece, to show Mrs Thibodeaux.' He rubbed his hands together.

Al and Ian looked at each other.

'S-sure,' Al said. 'Uh, we could play that little Schubert thing, that arrangement of "The Trout." Okay, Ian, get set.' He unbuttoned the protective case from his jug, lifted it out and held it awkwardly. Ian did the same. 'This is Al Duncan, here, at the first jug,' Al said. 'And besides me is my brother Ian at the second jug, bringing you a concert of classical favorites, beginning with a little Schubert.' And then, at a signal from Al, they both began to play.

Bump bump-bump BUMP-BUMP buuump bump, ba-bump-bump bup-bup-bup-bup-bupppp.

Nicole giggled.

We've failed, Ian thought. God, the worst has come about: we're ludicrous. He ceased playing; Al continued on, his cheeks red and swelling with the effort of playing. He seemed unaware that Nicole was holding her hand up to cover her laughter, her amusement at them and their efforts. Al played on, by himself, to the end of the piece, and then he, too, lowered his jug.

'The papoola,' Nicole said, as evenly as possible. 'It didn't dance. Not one little step—why not?' And again she laughed, unable to stop herself.

Al said woodenly, 'I—don't have control of it; it's on remote, right now.' To the papoola he said, 'You better dance.'

'Oh really, this is wonderful,' Nicole said. 'Look,' she said to her husband, 'he has to *beg* it to dance. Dance, whatever your name is, papoola-thing from Mars, or rather imitation papoola-thing from Mars.' She prodded the papoola with the toe of her moccasin, trying to nudge it into life. 'Come on, little synthetic ancient cute creature, all made out of wires. Please.'

The papoola leaped at her. It bit her.

Nicole screamed. A sharp *pop* sounded from behind her, and the papoola vanished into particles that swirled. A White House security guard stepped into sight, his rifle in his hands, peering intently at her and at the floating particles; his face was calm but his hands and the rifle quivered. Al began to curse to himself, chanting the words over and over again, the same three or four, unceasingly.

'Luke,' he said then, to his brother. 'He did it. Revenge. It's the end of us.' He looked gray, worn-out. Reflexively he began wrapping his jug up once more, going through the motions step by step.

'You're under arrest,' a second White House guard said, appearing behind them and training his gun on the two of them.

'Sure,' Al said listlessly, his head nodding, wobbling vacuously. 'We had nothing to do with it so arrest us.'

Getting to her feet with the assistance of her husband, Nicole walked toward Al and Ian. 'Did it bite me because I laughed?' she said in a quiet voice.

Slezak stood mopping his forehead. He said nothing; he merely stared at them sightlessly.

'I'm sorry,' Nicole said. 'I made it angry, didn't I? It's a shame; we would have enjoyed your act.'

'Luke did it,' Al said.

'"Luke."' Nicole studied him. 'Loony Luke, you mean. He owns those dreadful jalopy jungles that come and go only a step from illegality. Yes, I know who you mean; I remember him.' To her husband she said, 'I guess we'd better have him arrested, too.'

'Anything you say,' her husband said, writing on a pad of paper.

Nicole said, 'This whole jug business . . . it was just a cover-up for an action hostile to us, wasn't it? A crime against the state. We'll have to rethink the entire philosophy of inviting performers here . . . perhaps it's been a mistake. It gives too much access to anyone who has hostile intentions toward us. I'm sorry.' She looked sad and pale, now; she folded her arms and stood rocking back and forth, lost in thought.

'Believe me, Nicole,' Al began.

Introspectively, she said, 'I'm not Nicole; don't call me that. Nicole Thibodeaux died years ago. I'm Kate Rupert, the fourth one to take her place. I'm just an actress who looks enough like the original Nicole to be able to keep this job, and I wish sometimes, when something like this happens, that I didn't have it. I have no real authority. There's a council somewhere that governs . . . I've never even seen them.' To her husband she said, 'They know about this, don't they?'

'Yes,' he said, 'they've already been informed.'

'You see,' she said to Al, 'he, even the President, has more actual power than I.' She smiled wanly.

Al said, 'How many attempts have there been on your life?'

'Six or seven,' she said. 'All for psychological reasons. Unresolved Oedipal complexes or something like that. I don't really care.' She turned to her husband, then. 'I really think these two men here—' She pointed at Al and Ian. 'They don't seem to know what's going on; maybe they are innocent.' To her husband and Slezak and the security guards she said, 'Do they have to be destroyed? I don't see why you couldn't just eradicate a part of their memory-cells and let them go. Why wouldn't that do?'

Her husband shrugged. 'If you want it that way.'

'Yes,' she said. 'I'd prefer that. It would make my job easier. Take them to the medical center at Bethesda and then let's go on; let's give an audience to the next performers.'

A security guard nudged Ian in the back with his gun. 'Down the corridor, please.'

'Okay,' Ian murmured, gripping his jug. But what happened? he wondered. I don't quite understand. This woman isn't Nicole and even worse there is no Nicole anywhere; there's just the TV image, the illusion, and behind it, behind her, another group entirely rules. A council of some kind. But who are they and how did they get power? Will we ever know? We came so far; we almost seem to know what's really going on. The actuality behind the illusion . . . can't they tell us the rest? What difference would it make now? How—

'Goodbye,' Al was saying to him.

'What?' he said, horrified. 'Why do you say that? They're going to let us go, aren't they?'

Al said, 'We won't remember each other. Take my word for it; we won't be allowed to keep any ties like that. So—' He held out his hand. 'So goodbye, Ian. We made it to the White House. You won't remember that either, but it's true; we did do it.' He grinned crookedly.

'Move along,' the security guard said to them.

Holding their jugs, the two of them moved down the corridor, toward the door and the waiting black medical van beyond.

It was night, and Ian Duncan found himself at a deserted street corner, cold and shivering, blinking in the glaring white light of an urban monorail loading platform. What am I doing here? he asked himself, bewildered. He looked at his wristwatch; it was eight o'clock. I'm supposed to be at the All Souls' Meeting, aren't I? he thought dazedly.

I can't miss another one, he realized. Two in a row—it's a terrible fine; it's economic ruin. He began to walk.

The familiar building, Abraham Lincoln with all its network of towers and windows, lay extended ahead; it was not far and he hurried, breathing deeply, trying to keep up a good steady pace. It must be over, he thought. The lights in the great central subsurface auditorium were not lit. Damn it, he breathed in despair.

'All Souls is over?' he said to the doorman as he entered the lobby, his identification held out.

'You're a little confused, Mr Duncan,' the doorman said, putting away his gun. 'All Souls was last night; this is Friday.'

Something's gone wrong, Ian realized. But he said nothing; he merely nodded and hurried on toward the elevator.

As he emerged from the elevator on his own floor, a door opened and a furtive figure beckoned to him. 'Hey, Duncan.'

It was Corley. Warily, because an encounter like this could be disastrous, Ian approached him. 'What is it?'

'A rumor,' Corley said in a rapid, fear-filled voice. 'About your last *relpol* test—some irregularity. They're going to rouse you at five or six A.M. tomorrow morning and spring a surprise quiz on you.' He glanced up and down the hall. 'Study the late 1980s and the religio-collectivist movements in particular. Got it?'

'Sure,' Ian said, with gratitude. 'And thanks a lot. Maybe I can do the same—' He broke off, because Corley had hurried back into his own apartment and shut the door; Ian was alone.

Certainly very nice of him, he thought as he walked on. Probably saved my hide, kept me from being forcibly ejected right out of here forever.

When he reached his apartment he made himself comfortable, with all his reference books on the political history of the United States spread out around him. I'll study all night, he decided. Because I have to pass that quiz; I have no choice.

To keep himself awake, he turned on the TV. Presently the warm, familiar being, the presence of the First Lady, flowed into motion and began to fill the room.

'. . . and at our musical tonight,' she was saying, 'we will have a saxophone quartet which will play themes from Wagner's operas, in particular my favorite, *Die Meistersinger*. I believe we will truly all find this a deeply rewarding and certainly an enriching experience to cherish. And, after that, my husband the President and I have arranged to bring you once again an old favorite of yours, the world renowned cellist, Henri LeClercq, in a program of Jerome Kern and Cole Porter.' She smiled, and at his pile of reference books, Ian Duncan smiled back.

I wonder how it would be to play at the White House, he said to himself. To perform before the First Lady. Too bad I never learned to play any kind of musical instrument. I can't act, write poems, dance or sing—nothing. So what hope is there for me? Now, if I had come from a musical family, if I had had a father or brothers to teach me how . . .

Glumly, he scratched a few notes on the rise of the French Christian Fascist Party of 1975. And then, drawn as always to the TV set, he put his pen down and turned to face the set. Nicole was now exhibiting a piece of Delft tile which she had picked up, she explained, in a little shop in Vermont. What lovely clear colors it had . . . he watched, fascinated, as her strong, slim fingers caressed the shiny surface of the baked enamel tile.

'See the tile,' Nicole was murmuring in her husky voice. 'Don't you wish you had a tile like that? Isn't it lovely?'

'Yes,' Ian Duncan said.

'How many of you would like someday to see such a tile?' Nicole asked. 'Raise your hands.'

Ian raised his hand hopefully.

'Oh, a whole lot of you,' Nicole said, smiling her intimate, radiant smile. 'Well, perhaps later we will have another tour of the White House. Would you like that?'

Hopping up and down in his chair, Ian said, 'Yes, I'd like that.'

On the TV screen she was smiling directly at him, it seemed. And so he smiled back. And then, reluctantly, feeling a great weight descend over him, he at last turned back to his reference books. Back to the harsh realities of his daily, endless life.

Against the window of his apartment something bumped and a voice called at him thinly, 'Ian Duncan, I don't have much time.'

Whirling, he saw outside in the night darkness a shape drifting, an egg-like construction that hovered. Within it a man waved at him energetically, still calling. The egg gave off a dull *putt-putt* noise, its jets idling as the man kicked open the hatch of the vehicle and then lifted himself out.

Are they after me already on this quiz? Ian Duncan asked himself. He stood up, feeling helpless. So soon . . . I'm not ready, yet.

Angrily, the man in the vehicle spun the jets until their steady white exhaust firing met the surface of the building; the room shuddered and bits of plaster broke away. The window itself collapsed as the heat of the jets crossed it. Through the gap exposed the man yelled once more, trying to attract Ian Duncan's faculties.

'Hey, Duncan! Hurry up! I have your brother already; he's on his way in another ship!' The man, elderly, wearing an expensive natural-fiber blue pin-stripe suit, lowered himself with dexterity from the hovering egg-shaped vehicle and dropped feet-first into the room. 'We have to get going if we're to make it. You don't remember me? Neither did Al. Boy, I take off my hat to them.'

Ian Duncan stared at him, wondering who he was and who Al was and what was happening.

'Mama's psychologists did a good, good job of working you over,' the elderly man panted. 'That Bethesda—it must be quite a place. I hope they never get me there.' He came toward Ian, caught hold of him by the shoulder. 'The police are shutting down all my jalopy jungles; I have to beat it to Mars and I'm taking you along with me. Try to pull yourself together; I'm Loony Luke—you don't remember me now but you will after we're all on Mars and you see your brother again. *Come on.*' Luke propelled him toward the gap in the wall of the room, where once had been a window, and toward the vehicle—it was called a jalopy, Ian realized—drifting beyond.

'Okay,' Ian said, wondering what he should take with him. What would he need on Mars? Toothbrush, pajamas, a heavy coat? He looked frantically around his apartment, one last look at it. Far off police sirens sounded.

Luke scrambled back into the jalopy, and Ian followed, taking hold of the elderly man's extended hand. The floor of the jalopy crawled with bright orange bug-like creatures whose antennae waved at him. Papoolas, he remembered, or something like that.

You'll be all right now, the papoolas were thinking. Don't worry; Loony Luke got you away in time, just barely in time. Now just relax.

'Yes,' Ian said. He lay back against the side of the jalopy and relaxed; for the first time in many years he felt at peace.

The ship shot upward into the night emptiness and the new planet which lay beyond.

WATERSPIDER

I

That morning, as he carefully shaved his head until it glistened, Aaron Tozzo pondered a vision too unfortunate to be endured. He saw in his mind fifteen convicts from Nachbaren Slager, each man only one inch high, in a ship the size of a child's balloon. The ship, traveling at almost the speed of light, continued on forever, with the men aboard neither knowing nor caring what became of them.

The worst part of the vision was just that in all probability it was true.

He dried his head, rubbed oil into his skin, then touched the button within his throat. When contact with the Bureau switchboard had been established, Tozzo said, 'I admit we can do nothing to get those fifteen men back, but at least we can refuse to send any more.'

His comment, recorded by the switchboard, was passed on to his co-workers. They all agreed; he listened to their voices chiming in as he put on his smock, slippers and overcoat. Obviously, the flight had been an error; even the public knew that now. But—

'But we're going on,' Edwin Fermeti, Tozzo's superior, said above the clamor. 'We've already got the volunteers.'

'Also from Nachbaren Slager?' Tozzo asked. Naturally the prisoners there would volunteer; their lifespan at the camp was no more than five or six years. And if this flight to Proxima were successful, the men aboard would obtain their freedom. They would not have to return to any of the five inhabited planets within the Sol System.

'What does it matter where they originate?' Fermeti said smoothly.

Tozzo said, 'Our effort should be directed toward improving the US Department of Penology, instead of trying to reach other stars.' He had a sudden urge to resign his position with the Emigration Bureau and go into politics as a reform candidate.

Later, as he sat at the breakfast table, his wife patted him sympathetically on the arm. 'Aaron, you haven't been able to solve it yet, have you?'

'No,' he admitted shortly. 'And now I don't even care.' He did not tell her about the other ship loads of convicts which had fruitlessly been expended; it was forbidden to discuss that with anyone not employed by a department of the Government.

'Could they be re-entering on their own?'

'No. Because mass was lost here, in the Sol System. To re-enter they have to obtain equal mass back, to replace it. That's the whole point.' Exasperated, he sipped his tea and ignored her. Women, he thought. Attractive but not bright. 'They need mass back,' he repeated. 'Which would be fine if they were making a round trip, I suppose. But this is an attempt to colonize; it's not a guided tour that returns to its point of origin.'

'How long does it take them to reach Proxima?' Leonore asked. 'All reduced like that, to an inch high.'

'About four years.'

Her eyes grew large. 'That's marvelous.'

Grumbling at her, Tozzo pushed his chair back from the table and rose. I wish they'd take her, he said to himself, since she imagines it's so marvelous. But Leonore would be too smart to volunteer.

Leonore said softly, 'Then I was right. The Bureau *has* sent people. You as much as admitted it just now.'

Flushing, Tozzo said, 'Don't tell anybody; none of your female friends especially. Or it's my job.' He glared at her.

On that hostile note, he set off for the Bureau.

*

As Tozzo unlocked his office door, Edwin Fermeti hailed him. 'You think Donald Nils is somewhere on a planet circling Proxima at this very moment?' Nils was a notorious murderer who had volunteered for one of the Bureau's flights. 'I wonder—maybe he's carrying around a lump of sugar five times his size.'

'Not really very funny,' Tozzo said.

Fermeti shrugged. 'Just hoping to relieve the pessimism. I think we're all getting discouraged.' He followed Tozzo into his office. 'Maybe we should volunteer ourselves for the next flight.' It sounded almost as if he meant it, and Tozzo glanced quickly at him. 'Joke,' Fermeti said.

'One more flight,' Tozzo said, 'and if it fails, I resign.'

'I'll tell you something,' Fermeti said. 'We have a new tack.' Now Tozzo's co-worker Craig Gilly had come sauntering up. To the two men, Fermeti said, 'We're going to try using pre-cogs in obtaining our formula for re-entry.' His eyes flickered as he saw their reaction.

Astonished, Gilly said, 'But all the pre-cogs are dead. Destroyed by Presidential order twenty years ago.'

Tozzo, impressed, said, 'He's going to dip back into the past to obtain a pre-cog. Isn't that right, Fermeti?'

'We will, yes,' his superior said, nodding. 'Back to the golden age of pre-cognition. The twentieth century.'

For a moment Tozzo was puzzled. And then he remembered.

During the first half of the twentieth century so many pre-cogs—people with the ability to read the future—had come into existence that an organized guild had been formed with branches in Los Angeles, New York, San Francisco and Pennsylvania. This group of pre-cogs, all knowing one another, had put out a number of periodicals which had flourished for several decades. Boldly and openly, the members of the pre-cog guild had proclaimed in their writings their knowledge of the future. And yet—as a whole, their society had paid little attention to them.

Tozzo said slowly, 'Let me get this straight. You mean you're going to make use of the Department of Archaeology's time-dredges to scoop up a famous pre-cog of the past?'

Nodding, Fermeti said, 'And bring him here to help us, yes.'

'But how can he help us? He would have no knowledge of our future, only of his own.'

Fermeti said, 'The Library of Congress has already given us access to its virtually complete collection of pre-cog journals of the twentieth century.' He smiled crookedly at Tozzo and Gilly, obviously enjoying the situation. 'It's my hope—and my expectation—that among this great body of writings we will find an article *specifically dealing with our re-entry problem*. The chances, statistically speaking, are quite good . . . they wrote about innumerable topics of future civilization, as you know.'

After a pause, Gilly said, 'Very clever. I think your idea may solve our problem. Speed-of-light travel to other star systems may yet become a possibility.'

Sourly, Tozzo said, 'Hopefully, before we run out of convicts.' But he, too, liked his superior's idea. And, in addition, he looked forward to seeing face to face one of the famous twentieth-century pre-cogs. Theirs had been one brief, glorious period—sadly, long since ended.

Or not so brief, if one dated it as starting with Jonathan Swift, rather than with H. G. Wells. Swift had written of the two moons of Mars and their unusual orbital characteristics years before telescopes had proved their existence. And so today there was a tendency in the textbooks to include him.

II

It took the computers at the Library of Congress only a short while to scan the brittle, yellowed volumes, article by article, and to select the sole contribution dealing with deprivation of mass and restoration as the modus operandi of interstellar space travel. Einstein's formula that as an object increased its velocity its mass increased proportionally had been so fully accepted, so completely unquestioned, that no one in the twentieth century had paid any attention to the particular article, which had been put in print in August of 1955 in a pre-cog journal called *If*.

In Fermeti's office, Tozzo sat beside his superior as the two of them pored over the photographic reproduction of the journal. The article was titled 'Night Flight,' and it ran only a few thousand words. Both men read it avidly, neither speaking until they had finished.

'Well?' Fermeti said, when they had come to the end.

Tozzo said, 'No doubt of it. That's our Project, all right. A lot is garbled; for instance he calls the Emigration Bureau "Outward, Incorporated," and believes it to be a private commercial firm.' He referred to the text. 'It's really uncanny, though. You're obviously this character, Edmond Fletcher; the names are similar but still a little off, as is everything else. And I'm Alison Torelli.' He shook his head admiringly. 'Those pre-cogs . . . having a mental image of the future that was always askew and yet in the main–'

'In the main correct,' Fermeti finished. 'Yes, I agree. This "Night Flight" article definitely deals with us and the Bureau's Project . . . herein called *Waterspider*, because it has to be done in one great leap. Good lord, that would have been a perfect name, had we thought of it. Maybe we can still call it that.'

Tozzo said slowly, 'But the pre-cog who wrote "Night Flight" . . . in no place does he actually give the formula for mass-restoration or even for mass-deprivation. He just simply says that "we have it."' Taking the reproduction of the journal, he read aloud from the article:

'Difficulty in restoring mass to the ship and its passengers at the termination of the flight had proved a stumbling block for Torelli and his team of researchers and yet they had at last proved successful. After the fateful implosion of the *Sea Scout*, the initial ship to–

'And that's all,' Tozzo said. 'So what good does it do us? Yes, this pre-cog experienced our present situation a hundred years ago– *but he left out the technical details.*'

There was silence.

At last Fermeti said thoughtfully, 'That doesn't mean he didn't *know* the technical data. We know today that the others in his guild were very often trained scientists.' He examined the biographical report. 'Yes, while not actually using his pre-cog ability he worked as a chicken-fat analyst for the University of California.'

'Do you still intend to use the time-dredge to bring him up to the present?'

Fermeti nodded. 'I only wish the dredge worked both ways. If it could be used with the future, not the past, we could avoid having to jeopardize the safety of this pre-cog–' He glanced down at the article. 'This Poul Anderson.'

Chilled, Tozzo said, 'What hazard is there?'

'We may not be able to return him to his own time. Or–' Fermeti paused. 'We might lose part of him along the way, wind up with only half of him. The dredge has bisected many objects before.'

'And this man isn't a convict at Nachbaren Slager,' Tozzo said. 'So you don't have that rationale to fall back on.'

Fermeti said suddenly, 'We'll do it properly. We'll reduce the jeopardy by sending a team of men back to that time, back to 1954. They can apprehend this Poul Anderson and see that *all of him* gets into the time-dredge, not merely the top half or the left side.'

So it had been decided. The Department of Archaeology's time-dredge would go back to the world of 1954 and pick up the pre-cog Poul Anderson; there was nothing further to discuss.

Research conducted by the US Department of Archaeology showed that in September of 1954 Poul Anderson had been living in Berkeley, California, on Grove Street. In that month he had attended a top-level meeting of pre-cogs from all over the United States at the Sir Francis Drake Hotel in San Francisco. It was probable that there, in that meeting, basic policy for the next year had been worked out, with Anderson, and other experts, participating.

'It's really very simple,' Fermeti explained to Tozzo and Gilly. 'A pair of men will go back. They will be provided with forged identification showing them to be part of the nation-wide pre-cog organization . . . squares of cellophane-enclosed paper which are pinned to the coat lapel. Naturally, they will be wearing twentieth century garments. They will locate Poul Anderson, single him out and draw him off to one side.'

'And tell him what?' Tozzo said skeptically.

'That they represent an unlicensed amateur pre-cog organization in Battlecreek, Michigan, and that they have constructed an amusing vehicle built to resemble a time-travel dredge of the future. They will ask Mr Anderson, who was actually quite famous in his time, to pose by their humbug dredge, and then they will ask for a shot of him within. Our research shows that according to his contemporaries, Anderson was mild and easy-going and also that at these yearly top-strategy assemblies he often became convivial enough to enter into the mood of optimism generated by his fellow pre-cogs.'

Tozzo said, 'You mean he sniffed what they called "airplane dope"? He was a "glue-sniffer"?'

With a faint smile, Fermeti said, 'Hardly. That was a mania among adolescents and did not become widespread in fact until a decade later. No, I am speaking about imbibing alcohol.'

'I see,' Tozzo said, nodding.

Fermeti continued, 'In the area of difficulties, we must cope with the fact that at this top-secret session, Anderson brought along his wife Karen, dressed as a Maid of Venus in gleaming breast-cups, short skirt and helmet, and that he also brought their new-born daughter Astrid. Anderson himself did not wear any disguise for purposes of concealing his identity. He had no anxieties, being a quite stable person, as were most twentieth century pre-cogs.

'However, during the discussion periods between formal sessions, the pre-cogs, minus their wives, circulating about, playing poker and arguing, some of them it is said stoning one another—'

'Stoning?'

'Or, as it was put, becoming stoned. In any case, they gathered in small groups in the antechambers of the hotel, and it is at such an occasion that we expect to nab him. In the general hubbub his disappearance would not be noted. We would expect to return him to that exact time, or at least no more than a few hours later or earlier . . . preferably not earlier because *two* Poul Andersons at the meeting might prove awkward.'

Tozzo, impressed, said, 'Sounds foolproof.'

'I'm glad you like it,' Fermeti said tartly, 'because you will be one of the team sent.'

Pleased, Tozzo said, 'Then I had better get started learning the details of life in the mid twentieth century.' He picked up another issue of *If*. This one, May of 1971, had interested him as soon as he had seen it. Of course, this issue would not be known yet to the people of 1954 . . . but eventually they would see it. And once having seen it they would never forget it . . .

Ray Bradbury's first textbook to be serialized, he realized as he examined the journal. *The Fisher of Men*, it was called, and in it the great Los Angeles pre-cog had anticipated the ghastly Gutmanist political revolution which was to sweep the inner planets. Bradbury had warned against Gutman, but the warning had gone—of course—unheeded. Now Gutman was dead and the fanatical supporters had dwindled to the status of random terrorists. But had the world listened to Bradbury—

'Why the frown?' Fermeti asked him. 'Don't you want to go?'

'Yes,' Tozzo said thoughtfully. 'But it's a terrible responsibility. These are no ordinary men.'

'That is certainly the truth,' Fermeti said, nodding.

III

Twenty-four hours later, Aaron Tozzo stood surveying himself in his mid twentieth century clothing and wondering if Anderson would be deceived, if he actually could be duped into entering the dredge.

The costume certainly was perfection itself. Tozzo had even been equipped with the customary waist-length beard and handlebar mustache so popular circa 1950 in the United States. And he wore a wig.

Wigs, as everyone knew, had at that time swept the United States as the fashion note par excellence; men and women had both worn huge powdered perukes of bright colors, reds and greens and blues and of course dignified grays. It was one of the most amusing occurrences of the twentieth century.

Tozzo's wig, a bright red, pleased him. Authentic, it had come from the Los Angeles Museum of Cultural History, and the curator had vouched for it being a man's, not a woman's. So the fewest possible chances of detection were being taken. Little risk existed that they would be detected as members of another, future culture entirely.

And yet, Tozzo was still uneasy.

However, the plan had been arranged; now it was time to go. With Gilly, the other member selected, Tozzo entered the time-dredge and seated himself at the controls. The Department of Archaeology had provided a full instruction manual, which lay open before him. As soon as Gilly had locked the hatch, Tozzo took the bull by the horns (a twentieth-century expression) and started up the dredge.

Dials registered. They were spinning backward into time, back to 1954 and the San Francisco Pre-Cog Congress.

Beside him, Gilly practiced mid twentieth-century phrases from a reference volume. 'Diz muz be da blace . . .' Gilly cleared his throat. 'Kilroy was here,' he murmured. 'Wha' hoppen? Like man, let's cut out; this ball's a drag.' He shook his head. 'I can't grasp the exact sense of these phrases,' he apologized to Tozzo. 'Twenty-three skidoo.'

Now a red light glowed; the dredge was about to conclude its journey. A moment later its turbines halted.

They had come to rest on the sidewalk outside the Sir Francis Drake Hotel in downtown San Francisco.

On all sides, people in quaint archaic costumes dragged along on foot. And, Tozzo saw, there were no monorails; all the visible traffic was surface-bound. What a congestion, he thought, as he watched the automobiles and buses moving inch by inch along the packed streets. An official in blue waved traffic ahead as best he could, but the entire enterprise, Tozzo could see, was an abysmal failure.

'Time for phase two,' Gilly said. But he, too, was gaping at the stalled surface vehicles. 'Good grief,' he said, 'look at the incredibly short skirts of the women; why, the knees are virtually exposed. Why don't the women die of whisk virus?'

'I don't know,' Tozzo said, 'but I do know we've got to get into the Sir Francis Drake Hotel.'

Carefully, they opened the port of the time-dredge and stepped out. And then Tozzo realized something. There had been an error. Already.

The men of this decade were clean-shaven.

'Gilly,' he said rapidly, 'we've got to shed our beards and mustaches.' In an instant he had pulled Gilly's off, leaving his bare face exposed. But the wig; that was correct. All the men visible wore head-dress of some type; Tozzo saw few if any bald men. The women, too, had luxurious wigs . . . or were they wigs? Could they perhaps be *natural* hair?

In any case, both he and Gilly now would pass. Into the Sir Francis Drake, he said to himself, leading Gilly along.

They darted lithely across the sidewalk—it was amazing how slowly the people of this time-period walked—and into the inexpressibly old-fashioned lobby of the hotel. Like a museum, Tozzo thought as he glanced about him. I wish we could linger . . . but they could not.

'How's our identification?' Gilly said nervously. 'Is it passing inspection?' The business with the facehair had upset him.

On each of their lapels they carried the expertly made false identification. It worked. Presently they found themselves ascending by a lift, or rather elevator, to the correct floor.

The elevator let them off in a crowded foyer. Men, all clean-shaven, with wigs or natural hair, stood in small clusters everywhere, laughing and talking. And a number of attractive women, some of them in garments called leotards, which were skin-tight, loitered about smilingly. Even though the styles of the times required their breasts to be covered, they were a sight to see.

Sotto voce, Gilly said, 'I am stunned. In this room are some of the–'

'I know,' Tozzo murmured. Their Project could wait, at least a little while. Here was an unbelievably golden opportunity to see these pre-cogs, actually to talk to them and listen to them . . .

Here came a tall, handsome man in a dark suit that sparkled with tiny specks of some unnatural material, some variety of synthetic. The man wore glasses and his hair, everything about him, had a tanned, dark look. The name on his identification . . . Tozzo peered.

The tall, good-looking man was A. E. van Vogt.

'Say,' another individual, perhaps a pre-cog enthusiast, was saying to van Vogt, stopping him. 'I read both versions of your *World of Null A* and I still didn't quite get that about it being *him*; you know, at the end. Could you explain that part to me? And also when they started into the tree and then just–'

Van Vogt halted. A soft smile appeared on his face and he said. 'Well, I'll tell you a secret. I start out with a plot and then the plot sort of folds up. So then I have to have another plot to finish the rest of the story.'

Going over to listen, Tozzo felt something magnetic about van Vogt. He was so tall, so spiritual. Yes, Tozzo said to himself; that was the word, a healing spirituality. There was a quality of innate goodness which emanated from him.

All at once van Vogt said, 'There goes a man with my pants.' And without a further word to the enthusiast, stalked off and disappeared into the crowd.

Tozzo's head swam. To actually have seen and heard A. E. van Vogt–

'Look,' Gilly was saying, plucking at his sleeve. 'That enormous, genial-looking man seated over there; that's Howard Browne, who edited the pre-cog journal *Amazing* at this time-period.'

'I have to catch a plane,' Howard Browne was saying to anyone who would listen to him. He glanced about him in a worried anxiety, despite his almost physical geniality.

'I wonder,' Gilly said, 'if Doctor Asimov is here.'

We can ask, Tozzo decided. He made his way over to one of the young women wearing a blonde wig and green leotards. 'WHERE IS DOCTOR ASIMOV?' he asked clearly in the argot of the times.

'Who's to know?' the girl said.

'Is he here, miss?'

'Naw,' the girl said.

Gilly again plucked at Tozzo's sleeve. 'We must find Poul Anderson, remember? Enjoyable as it is to talk to this girl—'

'I'm inquiring about Asimov,' Tozzo said brusquely. After all, Isaac Asimov had been the founder of the entire twenty-first century positronic robot industry. How could he not be here?

A burly outdoorish man strode by them, and Tozzo saw that this was Jack Vance. Vance, he decided, looked more like a big game hunter than anything else . . . we must beware of him, Tozzo decided. If we got into any altercation Vance could take care of us easily.

He noticed now that Gilly was talking to the blonde-wigged girl in the green leotards. 'MURRAY LEINSTER?' Gilly was asking. 'The man whose paper on parallel time is still at the very forefront of theoretical studies; isn't he—'

'I dunno,' the girl said, in a bored tone of voice.

A group had gathered about a figure opposite them; the central person whom everybody was listening to was saying, '. . . all right, if like Howard Browne you prefer air travel, fine. But I say it's risky. I don't fly. In fact even riding in a car is dangerous. I generally lie down in the back.' The man wore a short-cropped wig and a bow tie; he had a round, pleasant face but his eyes were intense.

It was Ray Bradbury, and Tozzo started toward him at once.

'Stop!' Gilly whispered angrily. 'Remember what we came for.'

And, past Bradbury, seated at the bar, Tozzo saw an older, care-weathered man in a brown suit wearing small glasses and sipping a drink. He recognized the man from drawings in early Gernsback publications; it was the fabulously unique pre-cog from the New Mexico region, Jack Williamson.

'I thought *Legion of Time* was the finest novel-length science-fiction work I ever read,' an individual, evidently another pre-cog enthusiast, was saying to Jack Williamson, and Williamson was nodding in pleasure.

'That was originally going to be a short story,' Williamson said. 'But it grew. Yes, I like that one, too.'

Meanwhile Gilly had wandered on, into an adjoining room. He found, at a table, two women and a man in deep conversation. One of the women, dark-haired and handsome, with bare shoulders, was—according to her identification plate—Evelyn Paige. The taller woman he discovered was the renowned Margaret St Clair, and Gilly at once said:

'Mrs St Clair, your article entitled "The Scarlet Hexapod" in the September 1959 *If* was one of the finest—' And then he broke off.

Because Margaret St Clair had not written that yet. Knew in fact nothing about it. Flushing with nervousness, Gilly backed away.

'Sorry,' he murmured. 'Excuse me; I became confused.'

Raising an eyebrow, Margaret St Clair said, 'In the September 1959 issue, you say? What are you, a man from the future?'

'Droll,' Evelyn Paige said, 'but let's continue.' She gave Gilly a hard stare from her black eyes. 'Now Bob, as I understand what you're saying—' She addressed the man opposite her, and Gilly saw now to his delight that the dire-looking cadaverous individual was none other than Robert Bloch.

Gilly said, 'Mr Bloch, your article in *Galaxy*: "Sabbatical," was—'

'You've got the wrong person, my friend,' Robert Bloch said. 'I never wrote any piece entitled "Sabbatical."'

Good Lord, Gilly realized. I did it again; "Sabbatical" is another work which has not been written yet. I had better get away from here. He moved back toward Tozzo . . . and found him standing rigidly.

Tozzo said, 'I've found Anderson.'

At once, Gilly turned, also rigid.

Both of them had carefully studied the pictures provided by the Library of Congress. There stood the famous pre-cog, tall and slender and straight, even a trifle thin, with curly hair—or wig—and glasses, a warm glint of friendliness in his eyes. He held a whiskey glass in one hand, and he was discoursing with several other pre-cogs. Obviously he was enjoying himself.

'Um, uh, let's see,' Anderson was saying, as Tozzo and Gilly came quietly up to join the group. 'Pardon?' Anderson cupped his ear to catch what one of the other pre-cogs was saying. 'Oh, uh, yup, that's right.' Anderson nodded. 'Yup, Tony, uh, I agree with you one hundred per cent.'

The other pre-cog, Tozzo realized, was the superb Tony Boucher, whose pre-cognition of the religious revival of the next century had been almost supernatural. The word-by-word description of the Miracle in the Cave involving the robot . . . Tozzo gazed at Boucher with awe, and then he turned back to Anderson.

'Poul,' another pre-cog said. 'I'll tell you how the Italians intended to get the British to leave if they did invade in 1943. The British would stay at hotels, the best, naturally. The Italians would overcharge them.'

'Oh, yes, yes,' Anderson said, nodding and smiling, his eyes twinkling. 'And then the British, being gentlemen, would say nothing—'

'But they'd leave the next day,' the other pre-cog finished, and all in the group laughed, except for Gilly and Tozzo.

'Mr Anderson,' Tozzo said tensely, 'we're from an amateur pre-cog organization at Battlecreek, Michigan and we would like to photograph you beside our model of a time-dredge.'

'Pardon?' Anderson said, cupping his ear.

Tozzo repeated what he had said, trying to be audible above the background racket. At last Anderson seemed to understand.

'Oh, um, well, where is it?' Anderson asked obligingly.

'Downstairs on the sidewalk,' Gilly said. 'It was too heavy to bring up.'

'Well, uh, if it won't take too awfully long,' Anderson said, 'which I doubt it will.' He excused himself from the group and followed after them as they started toward the elevator.

'It's steam-engine building time,' a heavy-set man called to them as they passed. 'Time to build steam engines, Poul.'

'We're going downstairs,' Tozzo said nervously.

'Walk downstairs on your heads,' the pre-cog said. He waved goodbye good-naturedly, as the elevator came and the three of them entered it.

'Kris is jolly today,' Anderson said.

'And how,' Gilly said, using one of his phrases.

'Is Bob Heinlein here?' Anderson asked Tozzo as they descended. 'I understand he and Mildred Clingerman went off somewhere to talk about cats and nobody has seen them come back.'

'That's the way the ball bounces,' Gilly said, trying out another twentieth century phrase.

Anderson cupped his ear, smiled hesitantly, but said nothing.

At last, they emerged on the sidewalk. At the sight of their time-dredge, Anderson blinked in astonishment.

'I'll be gosh darned,' he said, approaching it. 'That's certainly imposing. Sure, I'd, uh, be happy to pose beside it.' He drew his lean, angular body erect, smiling that warm, almost tender smile that Tozzo had noticed before. 'Uh, how's this?' Anderson inquired, a little timidly.

With an authentic twentieth-century camera taken from the Smithsonian, Gilly snapped a picture. 'Now inside,' he requested, and glanced at Tozzo.

'Why, uh, certainly,' Poul Anderson said, and stepped up the stairs and into the dredge. 'Gosh, Karen would, uh, like this,' he said as he disappeared inside. 'I wish to heck she'd come along.'

Tozzo followed swiftly. Gilly slammed the hatch shut, and, at the control board, Tozzo, with the instruction manual in hand, punched buttons.

The turbines hummed, but Anderson did not seem to hear them; he was engrossed in staring at the controls, his eyes wide.

'Gosh,' he said.

The time-dredge passed back to the present, with Anderson still lost in his scrutiny of the controls.

IV

Fermeti met them. 'Mr Anderson,' he said, 'this is an incredible honor.' He held out his hand, but now Anderson was peering through the open hatch past him, at the city beyond; he did not notice the offered hand.

'Say,' Anderson said, his face twitching. 'Um, what's, uh, this?'

He was staring at the monorail system primarily, Tozzo decided. And this was odd, because at least in Seattle there had been monorails back in Anderson's time . . . or had there been? Had that come later? In any case, Anderson now wore a massively perplexed expression.

'Individual cars,' Tozzo said, standing close beside him. 'Your monorails had only group cars. Later on, after your time, it was made possible for each citizen's house to have a monorail outlet; the individual brought his car out of its garage and onto the rail-terminal, from which point he joined the collective structure. Do you see?'

But Anderson remained perplexed; his expression in fact had deepened.

'Um,' he said, 'what do you mean "my time"? Am I dead?' He looked morose now. 'I thought it would be more along the lines of Valhalla, with Vikings and such. Not futuristic.'

'You're not dead, Mr Anderson,' Fermeti said. 'What you're facing is the culture-syndrome of the mid twenty-first century. I must tell you, sir, that you've been napped. But you will be returned; I give you both my personal and official word.'

Anderson's jaw dropped, but he said nothing; he continued to stare.

Donald Nils, notorious murderer, sat at the single table in the reference room of the Emigration Bureau's interstellar speed-of-light ship and computed that he was, in Earth figures, an inch high. Bitterly, he cursed. 'It's cruel and unusual punishment,' he grated aloud. 'It's against the Constitution.' And then he remembered that he had volunteered, in order to get out of Nachbaren Slager. That goddam hole, he said to himself. Anyhow, I'm out of there.

And, he said to himself, even if I'm only an inch high I've still made myself captain of this lousy ship, and if it ever gets to Proxima I'll be captain of the entire lousy Proxima System. I didn't study with Gutman himself for nothing. And if that don't beat Nachbaren Slager, I don't know what does . . .

His second-in-command, Pete Bailly, stuck his head into the reference room. 'Hey, Nils, I have been looking over the micro-repro of this particular old pre-cog journal *Astounding* like you told me, this Venus Equilateral article about matter transmission, and I mean even though I was the top vid repairman in New York City that don't mean I can build one of *these* things.' He glared at Nils. 'That's asking a lot.'

Nils said tightly, 'We've got to get back to Earth.'

'You're out of luck,' Bailly told him. 'Better settle for Prox.'

Furiously, Nils swept the micro-reproductions from the table, onto the floor of the ship. 'That damn Bureau of Emigration! They tricked us!'

Bailly shrugged. 'Anyhow we got plenty to eat and a good reference library and 3-D movies every night.'

'By the time we get to Prox,' Nils snarled, 'we'll have seen every movie—' He calculated. 'Two thousand times.'

'Well, then don't watch. Or we can run them backwards. How's your research coming?'

'I got going the micro of an article in *Space Science Fiction*,' Nils said thoughtfully, 'called "The Variable Man." It tells about faster-than-light transmission. You disappear and then reappear. Some guy named Cole is going to perfect it, according to the old-time pre-cog who wrote it.' He brooded about that. 'If we could build a faster-than-light ship we could return to Earth. We could take over.'

'That's crazy talk,' Bailly said.

Nils regarded him. 'I'm in command.'

'Then,' Bailly said, 'we got a nut in command. There's no returning to Terra; we better build our lives on Proxima's planets and forget forever about our home. Thank God we got women aboard. My God, even if we did get back . . . what could one-inch high people accomplish? We'd be jeered at.'

'Nobody jeers at me,' Nils said quietly.

But he knew Bailly was right. They'd be lucky if they could research the micros of the old pre-cog journals in the ship's reference room and develop for themselves a way of landing safely on Proxima's planets . . . even *that* was asking a lot.

We'll succeed, Nils said to himself. As long as everyone obeys me, does exactly as I tell them, with no dumb questions.

Bending, he activated the spool of the December 1962 *If*. There was an article in it that particularly interested him . . . and he had four years ahead of him in which to read, understand, and finally apply it.

Fermeti said, 'Surely your pre-cog ability helped prepare you for this, Mr Anderson.' His voice faltered with nervous strain, despite his efforts to control it.

'How about taking me back now?' Anderson said. He sounded almost calm.

Fermeti, after shooting a swift glance at Tozzo and Gilly, said to Anderson, 'We have a technical problem, you see. That's why we brought you here to our own time-continuum. You see—'

'I think you had better, um, take me back,' Anderson broke in. 'Karen'll get worried.' He craned his neck, peering in all directions. 'I knew it would be somewhat on this order,' he murmured. His face twitched. 'Not too different from what I expected ... what's that tall thing over there? Looks like what the old blimps used to catch onto.'

'That,' Tozzo said, 'is a prayer tower.'

'Our problem,' Fermeti said patiently, 'is dealt with in your article "Night Flight" in the August 1955 *If*. We've been able to deprive an interstellar vehicle of its mass, but so far restoration of mass has—'

'Uh, oh, yes,' Anderson said, in a preoccupied way. 'I'm working on that yarn right now. Should have that off to Scott in another couple of weeks.' He explained, 'My agent.'

Fermeti considered a moment and then said, 'Can you give us the formula for mass-restoration, Mr Anderson?'

'Um,' Poul Anderson said slowly. 'Yes, I guess that would be the correct term. Mass-restoration ... I could go along with that.' He nodded. 'I haven't worked out any formula; I didn't want to make the yarn too technical. I guess I could make one up, if that's what they wanted.' He was silent, then, apparently having withdrawn into a world of his own; the three men waited, but Anderson said nothing more.

'Your pre-cog ability,' Fermeti said.

'Pardon?' Anderson said, cupping his ear. 'Pre-cog?' He smiled shyly. 'Oh, uh, I wouldn't go so far as to say that. I know John believes in all that, but I can't say as I consider a few experiments at Duke University as proof.'

Fermeti stared at Anderson a long time. 'Take the first article in the January 1953 *Galaxy*,' he said quietly. '"The Defenders" ... about the people living beneath the surface and the robots up above, pretending to fight the war but actually not, actually faking the reports so interestingly that the people—'

'I read that,' Poul Anderson agreed. 'Very good, I thought, except for the ending. I didn't care too much for the ending.'

Fermeti said, 'You understand, don't you, that those exact conditions came to pass in 1996, during World War Three? That by means of the article we were able to penetrate the deception carried on by our surface robots? That virtually every word of that article was exactly prophetic—'

'Phil Dick wrote that,' Anderson said. '"The Defenders."'

'Do you know him?' Tozzo inquired.

'Met him yesterday at the Convention,' Anderson said. 'For the first time. Very nervous fellow, was almost afraid to come in.'

Fermeti said, 'Am I to understand that *none of you are aware that you are pre-cogs?*' His voice shook, completely out of control now.

'Well,' Anderson said slowly, 'some sf writers believe in it. I think Alf van Vogt does.' He smiled at Fermeti.

'But don't you understand?' Fermeti demanded. 'You described *us* in an article—you accurately described our Bureau and its inter-stellar Project!'

After a pause, Anderson murmured, 'Gosh, I'll be darned. No, I didn't know that. Um, thanks a lot for telling me.'

Turning to Tozzo, Fermeti said, 'Obviously we'll have to recast our entire concept of the mid twentieth century.' He looked weary.

Tozzo said, 'For our purposes their ignorance doesn't matter. Because the pre-cognitive ability was there anyhow, whether they recognized it or not.' That, to him, was perfectly clear.

Anderson, meanwhile, had wandered off a little and stood now inspecting the display window of a nearby gift store. 'Interesting bric-a-brac in there. I ought to pick up something for Karen while I'm here. Would it be all right—' He turned questioningly to Fermeti. 'Could I step in there for a moment and look around?'

'Yes, yes,' Fermeti said irritably.

Poul Anderson disappeared inside the gift shop, leaving the three of them to argue the meaning of their discovery.

'What we've got to do,' Fermeti said, 'is sit him down in the situation familiar to him: *before a typewriter*. We must persuade him to compose an article on deprivation of mass and its subsequent restoration. Whether he himself takes the article to be factual or not has no bearing; it still will be. The Smithsonian must have a workable twentieth-century typewriter and 8½ by 11 white sheets of paper. Do you agree?'

Tozzo, meditating, said, 'I'll tell you what I think. It was a cardinal error to permit him to go into that gift shop.'

'Why is that?' Fermeti said.

'I see his point,' Gilly said excitedly. 'We'll never see Anderson again; he's skipped out on us through the pretext of gift-shopping for his wife.'

Ashen-faced, Fermeti turned and raced into the gift shop. Tozzo and Gilly followed.

The store was empty. Anderson had eluded them; he was gone.

As he loped silently out the back door of the gift shop, Poul Anderson thought to himself, I don't believe they'll get me. At least not right away.

I've got too much to do while I'm here, he realized. What an opportunity! When I'm an old man I can tell Astrid's children about this.

Thinking of his daughter Astrid reminded him of one very simple fact, however. Eventually he had to go back to 1954. Because of Karen and the baby. No matter what he found here—for him it was temporary.

But meanwhile . . . first I'll go to the library, *any* library, he decided. And get a good look at history books that'll tell me what took place in the intervening years between 1954 and now.

I'd like to know, he said to himself, about the Cold War, how the US and Russia came out. And—space explorations. I'll bet they put a man on Luna by 1975. Certainly, they're exploring space now; heck, they even have a time-dredge so they must have *that*.

Ahead Poul Anderson saw a doorway. It was open and without hesitation he plunged into it. Another shop of some kind, but this one larger than the gift shop.

'Yes sir,' a voice said, and a bald-headed man—they all seemed to be bald-headed here—approached him. The man glanced at Anderson's hair, his clothes . . . however the clerk was polite; he made no comment. 'May I help you?' he asked.

'Um,' Anderson said, stalling. What did this place sell, anyhow?

He glanced around. Gleaming electronic objects of some sort. But what did they do?

The clerk said, 'Haven't you been nuzzled lately, sir?'

'What's that?' Anderson said. *Nuzzled?*

'The new spring nuzzlers have arrived, you know,' the clerk said, moving toward the gleaming spherical machine nearest him. 'Yes,' he said to Poul, 'you do strike me as very, very faintly introve— no offense meant, sir, I mean, it's legal to be introved.' The clerk chuckled. 'For instance, your rather odd clothing . . . made it yourself, I take it? I must say, sir, to make your own clothing is highly introve. Did you weave it?' The clerk grimaced as if tasting something bad.

'No,' Poul said, 'as a matter of fact it's my best suit.'

'Heh, heh,' the clerk said. 'I share the joke, sir; quite witty. But what about your head? You haven't shaved your head in *weeks*.'

'Nope,' Anderson admitted. 'Well, maybe I do need a nuzzler.' Evidently everyone in this century had one; like a TV set in his own time, it was a necessity, in order for one to be part of the culture.

'How many in your family?' the clerk said. Bringing out a measuring tape, he measured the length of Poul's sleeve.

'Three,' Poul answered, baffled.

'How old is the youngest?'

'Just born,' Poul said.

The clerk's face lost all its color. 'Get out of here,' he said quietly. 'Before I call for the polpol.'

'Um, what's that? Pardon?' Poul said, cupping his ear and trying to hear, not certain he had understood.

'You're a criminal,' the clerk mumbled. 'You ought to be in Nachbaren Slager.'

'Well, thanks anyhow,' Poul said, and backed out of the store, onto the sidewalk; his last glimpse was of the clerk still staring at him.

'Are you a foreigner?' a voice asked, a woman's voice. At the curb she had halted her vehicle. It looked to Poul like a bed; in fact, he realized, it was a bed. The woman regarded him with astute calm, her eyes dark and intense. Although her glistening shaved head somewhat upset him, he could see that she was attractive.

'I'm from another culture,' Poul said, finding himself unable to keep his eyes from her figure. Did all the women dress like this here in this society? Bare shoulders, he could understand. But not—

And the bed. The combination of the two was too much for him. What kind of business was she in, anyhow? And in public. What a society this was . . . morals had changed since his own time.

'I'm looking for the library,' Poul said, not coming too close to the vehicle which was a bed with motor and wheels, a tiller for steering.

The woman said, 'The library is one bight from here.'

'Um,' Poul said, 'what's a "bight"?'

'Obviously, you're wanging me,' the woman said. All visible parts of her flushed a dark red. 'It's not funny. Any more than your disgustingly hairy head is. Really, both your wanging and your head are not amusing, at least not to me.' And yet she did not go on; she remained where she was, regarding him somberly. 'Perhaps you need help,' she decided. 'Perhaps I should pity you. You know of course that the polpol could pick you up any time they want.'

Poul said, 'Could I, um, buy you a cup of coffee somewhere and we could talk? I'm really anxious to find the library.'

'I'll go with you,' the woman agreed. 'Although I have no idea what "coffee" is. If you touch me I'll nilp at once.'

'Don't do that,' Poul said, 'it's unnecessary; all I want to do is look up some historical material.' And then it occurred to him that he could make good use of any technical data he could get his hands on.

What one volume might he smuggle back to 1954 which would be of great value? He racked his brains. An almanac. A dictionary . . . a school text on science which surveyed all the fields for laymen; yes, that would do it. A seventh grade text or a high school text. He could rip the covers off, throw them away, put the pages inside his coat.

Poul said, 'Where's a school? The closest school.' He felt the urgency of it, now. He had no doubt that they were after him, close behind.

'What is a "school"?' the woman asked.

'Where your children go,' Poul said.

The woman said quietly, 'You poor sick man.'

V

For a time Tozzo and Fermeti and Gilly stood in silence. And then Tozzo said in a carefully controlled voice, 'You know what's going to happen to him, of course. Polpol will pick him up and mono-express him to Nachbaren Slager. Because of his appearance. He may even be there already.'

Fermeti sprinted at once for the nearest vidphone. 'I'm going to contact the authorities at Nachbaren Slager. I'll talk to Potter; we can trust him, I think.'

Presently Major Potter's heavy, dark features formed on the vidscreen. 'Oh, hello, Fermeti. You want more convicts, do you?' He chuckled. 'You use them up even faster than we do.'

Behind Potter, Fermeti caught a glimpse of the open recreation area of the giant internment camp. Criminals, both political and nonpol, could be seen roaming about, stretching their legs, some of them playing dull, pointless games which, he knew, went on and on, sometimes for months, each time they were out of their work-cells.

'What we want,' Fermeti said, 'is to prevent an individual being brought to you at all.' He described Poul Anderson. 'If he's monoed there, call me at once. And don't harm him. You understand? We want him back safe.'

'Sure,' Potter said easily. 'Just a minute; I'll have a scan put on our new admissions.' He touched a button to his right and a 315-R computer came on; Fermeti heard its low hum. Potter touched buttons and then said, 'This'll pick him out if he's monoed here. Our admissions-circuit is prepared to reject him.'

'No sign yet?' Fermeti asked tensely.

'Nope,' Potter said, and purposefully yawned.

Fermeti broke the connection.

'Now what?' Tozzo said. 'We could possibly trace him by means of a Ganymedean sniffer-sponge.' They were a repellent life form, though; if one managed to find its quarry it fastened at once to its blood system leech-wise. 'Or do it mechanically,' he added. 'With a detec beam. We have a print of Anderson's EEG pattern, don't we? But that would really bring in the polpol.' The detec beam by law belonged only to the polpol; after all, it was the artifact which had, at last, tracked down Gutman himself.

Fermeti said bluntly, 'I'm for broadcasting a planet-wide Type II alert. That'll activate the citizenry, the average informer. They'll know there's an automatic reward for any Type II found.'

'But he could be manhandled that way,' Gilly pointed out. 'By a mob. Let's think this through.'

After a pause Tozzo said, 'How about trying it from a purely cerebral standpoint? If you had been transported from the mid twentieth century to our continuum, what would you want to do? *Where would you go?*'

Quietly, Fermeti said, 'To the nearest spaceport, of course. To buy a ticket to Mars or the outplanets—routine in our age but utterly out of the question at mid twentieth century.'

They looked at one another.

'But Anderson doesn't know where the spaceport is,' Gilly said. 'It'll take him valuable time to orient himself. We can go there directly by express subsurface mono.'

A moment later the three Bureau of Emigration men were on their way.

'A fascinating situation,' Gilly said, as they rode along, jiggling up and down, facing one another in the monorail first-class compartment. 'We totally misjudged the mid twentieth-century mind;

it should be a lesson to us. Once we've regained possession of Anderson we should make further inquiries. For instance, the Poltergeist Effect. What was their interpretation of it? And table-tapping—did they recognize it for what it was? Or did they merely consign it to the realm of the so-called "occult" and let it go at that?'

'Anderson may hold the clue to these questions and many others,' Fermeti said. 'But our central problem remains the same. We must induce him to complete the mass-restoration formula in precise mathematical terms, rather than vague, poetic allusions.'

Thoughtfully, Tozzo said, 'He's a brilliant man, that Anderson. Look at the ease by which he eluded us.'

'Yes,' Fermeti agreed. 'We mustn't underestimate him. We did that, and it's rebounded.' His face was grim.

Hurrying up the almost-deserted sidestreet, Poul Anderson wondered why the woman had regarded him as sick. And the mention of children had set off the clerk in the store, too. Was birth illegal now? Or was it regarded as sex had been once, as something too private to speak of in public?

In any case, he realized, if I plan to stay here I've got to shave my head. And, if possible, acquire different clothing.

There must be barbershops. And, he thought, the coins in my pockets; they're probably worth a lot to collectors.

He glanced about, hopefully. But all he saw were tall, luminous plastic and metal buildings which made up the city, structures in which incomprehensible transactions took place. They were as alien to him as—

Alien, he thought, and the word lodged chokingly in his mind. Because—something had oozed from a doorway ahead of him. And now his way was blocked—deliberately, it seemed—by a slime mold, dark yellow in color, as large as a human being, palpitating visibly on the sidewalk. After a pause the slime mold undulated toward him at a regular, slow rate. A human evolutionary development? Poul Anderson wondered, recoiling from it. Good Lord . . . and then he realized what he was seeing.

This era had space travel. He was seeing a creature from another planet.

'Um,' Poul said, to the enormous mass of slime mold, 'can I bother you a second to ask a question?'

The slime mold ceased to undulate forward. And in Poul's brain a thought formed which was not his own. 'I catch your query. In answer: I arrived yesterday from Callisto. But I also catch a number of unusual and highly interesting thoughts in addition . . . you are a time traveler from the past.' The tone of the creature's emanations was one of considerate, polite amusement—and interest.

'Yes,' Poul said. 'From 1954.'

'And you wish to find a barbershop, a library and a school. All at once, in the precious time remaining before they capture you.' The slime mold seemed solicitous. 'What can I do to help you? I could absorb you, but it would be a permanent symbiosis, and you would not like that. You are thinking of your wife and child. Allow me to inform you as to the problem regarding your unfortunate mention of children. Terrans of this period are experiencing a mandatory moratorium on childbirth, because of the almost infinite sporting of the previous decades. There was a war, you see. Between Gutman's fanatical followers and the more liberal legions of General McKinley. The latter won.'

Poul said, 'Where should I go? I'm confused.' His head throbbed and he felt tired. Too much had happened. Just a short while ago he had been standing with Tony Boucher in the Sir Francis Drake Hotel, drinking and chatting . . . and now this. Facing this great slime mold from Callisto. It was difficult—to say the least—to make such an adjustment.

The slime mold was transmitting to him. 'I am accepted here while you, their ancestor, are regarded as odd. Ironic. To me, you look quite like them, except for your curly brown hair and of course your silly clothing.' The creature from Callisto pondered. 'My friend, the polpol are the political police, and they search for deviants, followers of the defeated Gutman, who are terrorists now, and hated.

Many of these followers are drawn from the potentially criminal classes. That is, the non-conformists, the so-called introves. Individuals who set their own subjective value-system up in place of the objective system in vogue. It is a matter of life and death to the Terrans, since Gutman almost won.'

'I'm going to hide,' Poul decided.

'But where? You can't really. Not unless you wish to go underground and join the Gutmanites, the criminal class of bomb-throwers . . . and you won't want to do that. Let us stroll together, and if anyone challenges you, I will say you're my servant. You have manual extensors and I have not. And I have, by a quirk, decided to dress you oddly and to have you retain your head-hair. The responsibility then becomes mine. It is actually not unusual for higher out-world organisms to employ Terran help.'

'Thanks,' Poul said tautly, as the slime mold resumed its slow forward motion along the sidewalk. 'But there are things I want to do—'

'I am on my way to the zoo,' the slime mold continued.

An unkind thought came to Poul.

'Please,' the slime mold said. 'Your anachronistic twentieth-century humor is not appreciated. I am not an inhabitant of the zoo; it is for life forms of low mental order such as Martian glebs and trawns. Since the initiation of interplanetary travel, zoos have become the center of—'

Poul said, 'Could you lead me to the space terminal?' He tried to make his request sound casual.

'You take a dreadful risk,' the slime mold said, 'in going to any public place. The polpol watch constantly.'

'I still want to go.' If he could board an interplanetary ship, if he could leave Earth, see other worlds—

But they would erase his memory; all at once he realized that, in a rush of horror. *I've got to make notes*, he told himself. At once!

'Do, um, you have a pencil?' he asked the slime mold. 'Oh, wait; I have one. Pardon me.' Obviously the slime mold didn't.

On a piece of paper from his coat pocket—it was convention material of some sort—he wrote hurriedly, in brief, disjointed phrases, what had happened to him, what he had seen in the twenty-first century. Then he quickly stuck the paper back in his pocket.

'A wise move,' the slime mold said. 'And now to the spaceport, if you will accompany me at my slow pace. And, as we go, I will give you details of Terra's history from your period on.' The slime mold moved down the sidewalk. Poul accompanied it eagerly; after all, what choice did he have? 'The Soviet Union. That was tragic. Their war with Red China in 1983 which finally involved Israel and France . . . regrettable, but it did solve the problem of what to do with France—a most difficult nation to deal with in the latter half of the twentieth century.'

On his piece of paper Poul jotted that down, too.

'After France had been defeated—' The slime mold went on, as Poul scratched against time.

Fermeti said, 'We must glin, if we're to catch Anderson before he boards a ship.' And by 'glin' he did not mean glinning a little; he meant a full search with the cooperation of the polpol. He hated to bring them in, and yet their help now seemed vital. Too much time had passed and Anderson had not yet been found.

The spaceport lay ahead, a great disk miles in diameter, with no vertical obstructions. In the center was the Burned Spot, seared by years of tail-exhausts from landing and departing ships. Fermeti liked the spaceport, because here the denseness of the close-packed buildings of the city abruptly ceased. Here was *openness*, such as he recalled from childhood . . . if one dared to think openly of childhood.

The terminal building was set hundreds of feet beneath the rexeroid layer built to protect the waiting people in case of an accident above. Fermeti reached the entrance of the descent ramp, then halted impatiently to wait for Tozzo and Gilly to catch up with him.

'I'll nilp,' Tozzo said, but without enthusiasm. And he broke the band on his wrist with a single decisive motion.

The polpol ship hovered overhead at once.

'We're from the Emigration Bureau,' Fermeti explained to the polpol lieutenant. He outlined their Project, described–reluctantly–their bringing Poul Anderson from his time-period to their own.

'Hair on head,' the polpol lieutenant nodded. 'Quaint duds. Okay, Mr Fermeti; we'll glin until we find him.' He nodded, and his small ship shot off.

'They're efficient,' Tozzo admitted.

'But not likeable,' Fermeti said, finishing Tozzo's thought.

'They make me uncomfortable,' Tozzo agreed. 'But I suppose they're supposed to.'

The three of them stepped onto the descent ramp–and dropped at breathtaking speed to level one below. Fermeti shut his eyes, wincing at the loss of weight. It was almost as bad as takeoff itself. Why did everything have to be so rapid, these days? It certainly was not like the previous decade, when things had gone leisurely.

They stepped from the ramp, shook themselves, and were approached instantly by the building's polpol chief.

'We have a report on your man,' the gray-uniformed officer told them.

'He hasn't taken off?' Fermeti said. 'Thank God.' He looked around.

'Over there,' the officer said, pointing.

At a magazine rack, Poul Anderson was looking intently at the display.

It took only a moment for the three Emigration Bureau officials to surround him.

'Oh, uh, hello,' Anderson said. 'While I was waiting for my ship I thought I'd take a look and see what's still in print.'

Fermeti said, 'Anderson, we require your unique abilities. I'm sorry, but we're taking you back to the Bureau.'

All at once Anderson was gone. Soundlessly, he had ducked away; they saw his tall, angular form become smaller as he raced for the gate to the field proper.

Reluctantly, Fermeti reached within his coat and brought out a sleep-gun. 'There's no other choice,' he murmured, and squeezed.

The racing figure tumbled, rolled. Fermeti put the sleep-gun away and in a toneless voice said, 'He'll recover. A skinned knee, nothing worse.' He glanced at Gilly and Tozzo. 'Recover at the Bureau, I mean.'

Together, the three of them advanced toward the prone figure on the floor of the spaceport waiting room.

'You may return to your own time-continuum,' Fermeti said quietly, 'when you've given us the mass-restoration formula.' He nodded, and a Bureau workman approached, carrying the ancient Royal typewriter.

Seated in the chair across from Fermeti in the Bureau's inner business office, Poul Anderson said, 'I don't use a portable.'

'You must cooperate,' Fermeti informed him. 'We have the scientific know-how to restore you to Karen; remember Karen and remember your newly-born daughter at the Congress in San Francisco's Sir Francis Drake Hotel. Without full cooperation from you, Anderson, there will be no cooperation from the Bureau. Surely, with your pre-cog ability you can see that.'

After a pause Anderson said, 'Um, I can't work unless I have a pot of fresh coffee brewing around me at all times, somewhere.'

Curtly, Fermeti signaled. 'We'll obtain coffee beans for you,' he declared. 'But the brewing is up to you. We'll also supply a pot from the Smithsonian collection and there our responsibility ends.'

Taking hold of the carriage of the typewriter, Anderson began to inspect it. 'Red and black ribbon,' he said. 'I always use black. But I guess I can make do.' He seemed a trifle sullen. Inserting a sheet of paper, he began to type. At the top of the page appeared the words:

NIGHT FLIGHT
—Poul Anderson

'You say *If* bought it?' he asked Fermeti.

'Yes,' Fermeti replied tensely.

Anderson typed:

Difficulties at Outward, Incorporated had begun to nettle Edmond Fletcher. For one thing, an entire ship had disappeared, and although the individuals aboard were not personally known to him he felt a twinge of responsibility. Now, as he lathered himself with hormone-impregnated soap

'He starts at the beginning,' Fermeti said bitingly. 'Well, if there's no alternative we'll simply have to bear with him.' Musingly, he murmured, 'I wonder how long it takes . . . I wonder how fast he writes. As a pre-cog he can see what's coming next; it should help him to do it in a hurry.' Or was that just wishful thinking?

'Have the coffee beans arrived yet?' Anderson asked, glancing up.

'Any time now,' Fermeti said.

'I hope some of the beans are Colombian,' Anderson said.

Long before the beans arrived the article was done.

Rising stiffly, uncoiling his lengthy limbs, Poul Anderson said, 'I think you have what you want, there. The mass-restoration formula is on typescript page 20.'

Eagerly, Fermeti turned the pages. Yes, there it was; peering over his shoulder, Tozzo saw the paragraph:

If the ship followed a trajectory which would carry it into the star Proxima, it would, he realized, regain its mass through a process of leeching solar energy from the great star-furnace itself. Yes, it was Proxima itself which held the key to Torelli's problem, and now, after all this time, it had been solved. The simple formula revolved in his brain.

And, Tozzo saw, there lay the formula. As the article said, the mass would be regained from solar energy converted into matter, the ultimate source of power in the universe. The answer had stared them in the face all this time!

Their long struggle was over.

'And now,' Poul Anderson said, 'I'm free to go back to my own time?'

Fermeti said simply, 'Yes.'

'Wait,' Tozzo said to his superior. 'There's evidently something you don't understand.' It was a section which he had read in the instruction manual attached to the time-dredge. He drew Fermeti to one side, where Anderson could not hear. 'He can't be sent back to his own time with the knowledge he has now.'

'What knowledge?' Fermeti inquired.

'That—well, I'm not certain. Something to do with our society, here. What I'm trying to tell you is this: the first rule of time travel, according to the manual, is don't change the past. In this situation just bringing Anderson here has changed the past merely by exposing him to our society.'

Pondering, Fermeti said, 'You may be correct. While he was in that gift shop he may have picked up some object which, taken back to his own time, might revolutionize their technology.'

'Or at the magazine rack at the spaceport,' Tozzo said. 'Or on his trip between those two points. And—*even the knowledge that he and his colleagues are pre-cogs.*'

'You're right,' Fermeti said. 'The memory of this trip must be wiped from his brain.' He turned and walked slowly back to Poul Anderson. 'Look here,' he addressed him. 'I'm sorry to tell you this, but everything that's happened to you must be wiped from your brain.'

After a pause, Anderson said, 'That's a shame. Sorry to hear that.' He looked downcast. 'But I'm not surprised,' he murmured. He seemed philosophical about the whole affair. 'It's generally handled this way.'

Tozzo asked, 'Where can this alteration of the memory cells of his brain be accomplished?'

'At the Department of Penology,' Fermeti said. 'Through the

same channels we obtained the convicts.' Pointing his sleep-gun at Poul Anderson he said, 'Come along with us. I regret this . . . but it has to be done.'

VI

At the Department of Penology, painless electroshock removed from Poul Anderson's brain the precise cells in which his most recent memories were stored. Then, in a semi-conscious state, he was carried back into the time-dredge. A moment later he was on his trip back to the year 1954, to his own society and time. To the Sir Francis Drake Hotel in downtown San Francisco, California and his waiting wife and child.

When the time-dredge returned empty, Tozzo, Gilly and Fermeti breathed a sigh of relief and broke open a bottle of hundred-year-old Scotch which Fermeti had been saving. The mission had been successfully accomplished; now they could turn their attention back to the Project.

'Where's the manuscript that he wrote?' Fermeti said, putting down his glass to look all around his office.

There was no manuscript to be found. And, Tozzo noticed, the antique Royal typewriter which they had brought from the Smithsonian—it was gone, too. But why?

Suddenly chill fear traveled up him. He understood.

'Good Lord,' he said thickly. He put down his glass. 'Somebody get a copy of the journal with his article in it. At once.'

Fermeti said, 'What is it, Aaron? Explain.'

'When we removed his memory of what had happened we made it impossible for him to write the article for the journal,' Tozzo said. 'He must have based "Night Flight" on his experience with us, here.' Snatching up the August 1955 copy of *If* he turned to the table-of-contents page.

No article by Poul Anderson was listed. Instead, on page 78, he saw Philip K. Dick's "The Mold of Yancy" listed instead.

They had changed the past after all. And now the formula for their Project was gone—gone entirely.

'We shouldn't have tampered,' Tozzo said in a hoarse voice. 'We should never have brought him out of the past.' He drank a little more of the century-old Scotch, his hands shaking.

'Brought who?' Gilly said, with a puzzled look.

'Don't you remember?' Tozzo stared at him, incredulous.

'What's this discussion about?' Fermeti said impatiently. 'And what are you two doing in my office? You both should be busy at work.' He saw the bottle of Scotch and blanched. 'How'd that get open?'

His hands trembling, Tozzo turned the pages of the journal over and over again. Already, the memory was growing diffuse in his mind; he struggled in vain to hold onto it. They had brought someone from the past, a pre-cog, wasn't it? But who? A name, still in his mind but dimming with each passing moment . . . Anderson or Anderton, something like that. And in connection with the Bureau's interstellar mass-deprivation Project.

Or was it?

Puzzled, Tozzo shook his head and said in bewilderment, 'I have some peculiar words in my mind. "Night Flight." Do either of you happen to know what it refers to?'

"Night Flight," Fermeti echoed. 'No, it means nothing to me. I wonder, though—it certainly would be an effective name for our Project.'

'Yes,' Gilly agreed. 'That must be what it refers to.'

'But our Project is called *Waterspider*, isn't it?' Tozzo said. At least he thought it was. He blinked, trying to focus his faculties.

'The truth of the matter,' Fermeti said, 'is that we've never titled it.' Brusquely, he added, 'But I agree with you; that's an even better name for it. *Waterspider*. Yes, I like that.'

The door of the office opened and there stood a uniformed, bonded messenger. 'From the Smithsonian,' he informed them. 'You requested this.' He produced a parcel, which he laid on Fermeti's desk.

'I don't remember ordering anything from the Smithsonian,' Fermeti said. Opening it cautiously he found a can of roasted, ground coffee beans, still vacuum packed, over a century old.

The three men looked at one another blankly.

'Strange,' Torelli murmured. 'There must be some mistake.'

'Well,' Fletcher said, 'in any case, back to Project *Waterspider*.'

Nodding, Torelli and Gilman turned in the direction of their own office on the first floor of Outward, Incorporated, the commercial firm at which they had worked and the Project on which they had labored, with so many heartaches and setbacks, for so long.

At the Science Fiction Convention at the Sir Francis Drake Hotel, Poul Anderson looked around him in bewilderment. Where had he been? Why had he gone out of the building? And it was an hour later; Tony Boucher and Jim Gunn had left for dinner by now, and he saw no sign of his wife Karen and the baby, either.

The last he remembered was two fans from Battlecreek who wanted him to look at a display outside on the sidewalk. Perhaps he had gone to see that. In any case, he had no memory of the interval.

Anderson groped about in his coat pocket for his pipe, hoping to calm his oddly jittery nerves—and found, not his pipe, but instead a folded piece of paper.

'Got anything for our auction, Poul?' a member of the Convention committee asked, halting beside him. 'The auction is just about to start—we have to hurry.'

Still looking at the paper from his pocket, Poul murmured, 'Um, you mean something here with me?'

'Like a typescript of some published story, the original manuscript or earlier versions or notes. You know.' He paused, waiting.

'I seem to have some notes in my pocket,' Poul said, still glancing over them. They were in his handwriting but he didn't remember having made them. A time-travel story, from the look of them. Must have been from those Bourbons and water, he decided, and not enough to eat. 'Here,' he said uncertainly, 'it isn't much but I guess you can auction these.' He took one final glance at them.

'Notes for a story about a political figure called Gutman and a kidnapping in time. Intelligent slime mold, too, I notice.' On impulse, he handed them over.

'Thanks,' the man said, and hurried on toward the other room, where the auction was being held.

'I bid ten dollars,' Howard Browne called, smiling broadly. 'Then I have to catch a bus to the airport.' The door closed after him.

Karen, with Astrid, appeared beside Poul. 'Want to go into the auction?' she asked her husband. 'Buy an original Finlay?'

'Um, sure,' Poul Anderson said, and with his wife and child walked slowly after Howard Browne.

WHAT THE DEAD MEN SAY

I

The body of Louis Sarapis, in a transparent plastic shatterproof case, had lain on display for one week, exciting a continual response from the public. Distended lines filed past with the customary sniffling, pinched faces, distraught elderly ladies in black cloth coats.

In a corner of the large auditorium in which the casket reposed, Johnny Barefoot impatiently waited for his chance at Sarapis's body. But he did not intend merely to view it; his job, detailed in Sarapis's will, lay in another direction entirely. As Sarapis's public relations manager, his job was—simply—to bring Louis Sarapis back to life.

'Keerum,' Barefoot murmured to himself, examining his wrist-watch and discovering that two more hours had to pass before the auditorium doors could be finally closed. He felt hungry. And the chill, issuing from the quick-pack envelope surrounding the casket, had increased his discomfort minute by minute.

His wife Sarah Belle approached him, then, with a thermos of hot coffee. 'Here, Johnny.' She reached up and brushed the black, shiny Chiricahua hair back from his forehead. 'You don't look so good.'

'No,' he agreed. 'This is too much for me. I didn't care for him much when he was alive—I certainly don't like him any better this way.' He jerked his head at the casket and the double line of mourners.

Sarah Belle said softly, 'Nil nisi bonum.'

He glowered at her, not sure of what she had said. Some foreign language, no doubt. Sarah Belle had a college degree.

'To quote Thumper Rabbit,' Sarah Belle said, smiling gently, '"If you can't say nothing good, don't say nothing at all."' She added, 'From *Bambi*, an old film classic. If you attended the lectures at the Museum of Modern Art with me every Monday night—'

'Listen,' Johnny Barefoot said desperately, 'I don't want to bring the old crook back to life, Sarah Belle; how'd I get myself into this? I thought sure when the embolism dropped him like a cement block it meant I could kiss the whole business goodbye forever.' But it hadn't quite worked out that way.

'Unplug him,' Sarah Belle said.

'W-what?'

She laughed. 'Are you afraid to? Unplug the quick-pack power source and he'll warm up. And no resurrection, right?' Her blue-gray eyes danced with amusement. 'Scared of him, I guess. Poor Johnny.' She patted him on the arm. 'I should divorce you, but I won't; you need a mama to take care of you.'

'It's wrong,' he said. 'Louis is completely helpless, lying there in the casket. It would be—unmanly to unplug him.'

Sarah Belle said quietly, 'But someday, sooner or later, you'll have to confront him, Johnny. And when he's in half-life you'll have the advantage. So it will be a good time; you might come out of it intact.' Turning, she trotted off, hands thrust deep in her coat pockets because of the chill.

Gloomily, Johnny lit a cigarette and leaned against the wall behind him. His wife was right, of course. A half-lifer was no match, in direct physical tête-à-tête, for a living person. And yet—he still shrank from it, because ever since childhood he had been in awe of Louis, who had dominated 3-4 shipping, the Earth to Mars commercial routes, as if he were a model rocket-ship enthusiast pushing miniatures over a papier-mâché board in his basement. And now, at his death, at seventy years of age, the old man through Wilhelmina Securities controlled a hundred related—and non-related—industries on both planets. His net worth could not be calculated, even for tax purposes; it was not wise, in fact, to try, even for Government tax experts.

It's my kids, Johnny thought; *I'm thinking about them, in school back in Oklahoma.* To tangle with old Louis would be okay if he wasn't a family man . . . nothing meant more to him than the two little girls and of course Sarah Belle, too. *I got to think of them, not myself,* he told himself now as he waited for the opportunity to remove the body from the casket in accordance with the old man's detailed instructions. *Let's see. He's probably got about a year in total half-life time, and he'll want it divided up strategically, like at the end of each fiscal year. He'll probably proportion it out over two decades, a month here and there, then towards the end as he runs out, maybe just a week. And then—days.*

And finally old Louis would be down to a couple of hours; the signal would be weak, the dim spark of electrical activity hovering in the frozen brain cells . . . it would flicker, the words from the amplifying equipment would fade, grow indistinct. And then— silence, at last the grave. But that might be twenty-five years from now; it would be the year 2100 before the old man's cephalic processes ceased entirely.

Johnny Barefoot, smoking his cigarette rapidly, thought back to the day he had slouched anxiously about the personnel office of Archimedean Enterprises, mumbling to the girl at the desk that he wanted a job; he had some brilliant ideas that were for sale, ideas that would help untangle the knot of strikes, the spaceport violence growing out of jurisdictional overlapping by rival unions— ideas that would, in essence, free Sarapis of having to rely on union labor at all. It was a dirty scheme, and he had known it then, but he had been right; it was worth money. The girl had sent him on to Mr Pershing, the Personnel Manager, and Pershing had sent him to Louis Sarapis.

'You mean,' Sarapis had said, 'I launch from the *ocean*? From the Atlantic, out past the three-mile limit?'

'A union is a national organization,' Johnny had said. 'Neither outfit has a jurisdiction on the high seas. But a business organization is international.'

'I'd need men out there; I'd need the same number, even more. Where'll I get them?'

'Go to Burma or India or the Malay States,' Johnny had said. 'Get young unskilled laborers and bring them over. Train them yourself on an indentured servant basis. In other words, charge the cost of their passage against their earnings.' It was peonage, he knew. And it appealed to Louis Sarapis. A little empire on the high seas, worked by men who had no legal rights. Ideal.

Sarapis had done just that and hired Johnny for his public relations department; that was the best place for a man who had brilliant ideas of a non-technical nature. In other words, an uneducated man: a *noncol*. A useless misfit, an outsider. A loner lacking college degrees.

'Hey Johnny,' Sarapis had said once. 'How come since you're so bright you never went to school? Everyone knows that's fatal, nowadays. Self-destructive impulse, maybe?' He had grinned, showing his stainless-steel teeth.

Moodily, he had replied, 'You've got it, Louis. I want to die. I hate myself.' At that point he had recalled his peonage idea. But that had come after he had dropped out of school, so it couldn't have been that. 'Maybe I should see an analyst,' he had said.

'Fakes,' Louis had told him. 'All of them—I know because I've had six on my staff, working for me exclusively at one time or another. What's wrong with you is you're an envious type; if you can't have it big you don't want it, you don't want the climb, the long struggle.'

But I've got it big, Johnny Barefoot realized, had realized even then. *This is big, working for you. Everyone wants to work for Louis Sarapis; he gives all sorts of people jobs.*

The double lines of mourners that filed past the casket . . . he wondered if all these people could be employees of Sarapis or relatives of employees. Either that or people who had benefited from the public dole that Sarapis had pushed through Congress and into law during the depression three years ago. Sarapis, in his old age the great daddy for the poor, the hungry, the out of work. Soup kitchens, with lines there, too. Just as now.

Perhaps the same people had been in those lines who were here today.

Startling Johnny, an auditorium guard nudged him. 'Say, aren't you Mr Barefoot, the PR man for old Louis?'

'Yes,' Johnny said. He put out his cigarette and then began to unscrew the lid of the thermos of coffee which Sarah Belle had brought him. 'Have some,' he said. 'Or maybe you're used to the cold in these civic halls.' The City of Chicago had lent this spot for Louis to lie in state; it was gratitude for what he had done here in this area. The factories he had opened, the men he had put on the payroll.

'I'm not used,' the guard said, accepting a cup of coffee. 'You know, Mr Barefoot, I've always admired you because you're a non-col, and look how you rose to a top job and lots of salary, not to mention fame. It's an inspiration to us other noncols.'

Grunting, Johnny sipped his own coffee.

'Of course,' the guard said, 'I guess it's really Sarapis we ought to thank; he gave you the job. My brother-in-law worked for him; that was back five years ago when nobody in the world was hiring except Sarapis. You hear what an old skinflint he was—wouldn't permit the unions to come in, and all. But he gave so many old folks pensions . . . my father was living on a Sarapis pension-plan until the day he died. And all those bills he got through Congress; they wouldn't have passed any of the welfare for the needy bills without pressure from Sarapis.'

Johnny grunted.

'No wonder there're so many people here today,' the guard said. 'I can see why. Who's going to help the little fellow, the noncols like you and me, now that he's gone?'

Johnny had no answer, for himself or for the guard.

*

As owner of the Beloved Brethren Mortuary, Herbert Schoenheit von Vogelsang found himself required by law to consult with the late Mr Sarapis's legal counsel, the well-known Mr Claude St Cyr. In this connection it was essential for him to know precisely how the half-life periods were to be proportioned out; it was his job to execute the technical arrangements.

The matter should have been routine, and yet a snag developed almost at once. He was unable to get in touch with Mr St Cyr, trustee for the estate.

Drat, Schoenheit von Vogelsang thought to himself as he hung up the unresponsive phone. *Something must be wrong; this is unheard of in connection with a man so important.*

He had phoned from the bin—the storage vaults in which the half-lifers were kept in perpetual quick-pack. At this moment, a worried-looking clerical sort of individual waited at the desk with a claim check stub in his hand. Obviously he had shown up to collect a relative. Resurrection Day—the holiday on which the half-lifers were publicly honored—was just around the corner; the rush would soon be beginning.

'Yes sir,' Herb said to him, with an affable smile. 'I'll take your stub personally.'

'It's an elderly lady,' the customer said. 'About eighty, very small and wizened. I didn't want just to talk to her; I wanted to take her out for a while.' He explained, 'My grandmother.'

'Only a moment,' Herb said, and went back into the bin to search out number 3054039-B.

When he located the correct party he scrutinized the lading report attached; it gave but fifteen days of half-life remaining. Automatically, he pressed a portable amplifier into the hull of the glass casket, tuned it, listened at the proper frequency for indication of cephalic activity.

Faintly from the speaker came, '. . . and then Tillie sprained her ankle and we never thought it'd heal; she was so foolish about it, wanting to start walking immediately . . .'

Satisfied, he unplugged the amplifier and located a union

man to perform the actual task of carting 3054039-B to the loading platform, where the customer could place her in his 'copter or car.

'You checked her out?' the customer asked as he paid the money due.

'Personally,' Herb answered. 'Functioning perfectly.' He smiled at the customer. 'Happy Resurrection Day, Mr Ford.'

'Thank you,' the customer said, starting off for the loading platform.

When I pass, Herb said to himself, *I think I'll will my heirs to revive me one day a century. That way I can observe the fate of all mankind.* But that meant a rather high maintenance cost to the heirs, and no doubt sooner or later they would kick over the traces, have the body taken out of quick-pack and—God forbid—buried.

'Burial is barbaric,' Herb murmured aloud. 'Remnant of the primitive origins of our culture.'

'Yes sir,' his secretary Miss Beasman agreed, at her typewriter.

In the bin, several customers communed with their half-lifer relations, in rapt quiet, distributed at intervals along the aisles which separated the caskets. It was a tranquil sight, these faithfuls, coming as they did so regularly, to pay homage. They brought messages, news of what took place in the outside world; they cheered the gloomy half-lifers in these intervals of cerebral activity. And—they paid Herb Schoenheit von Vogelsang; it was a profitable business, operating a mortuary.

'My dad seems a little frail,' a young man said, catching Herb's attention. 'I wonder if you could take a moment to check him over. I'd really appreciate it.'

'Certainly,' Herb said, accompanying the customer down the aisle to his deceased relative. The lading report showed only a few days remaining; that explained the vitiated quality of cerebration. But still—he turned up the gain, and the voice from the half-lifer became a trifle stronger. *He's almost at an end*, Herb thought. It was obvious that the son did not want to see the lading, did not actually care to know that contact with his dad was diminishing, finally. So

Herb said nothing; he merely walked off, leaving the son to commune. Why tell him? Why break the bad news?

A truck had now appeared at the loading platform, and two men hopped down from it, wearing familiar pale blue uniforms. Atlas Interplan Van and Storage, Herb realized. Delivering another half-lifer, or here to pick up one which had expired. He strolled toward them. 'Yes, gentlemen,' he said.

The driver of the truck leaned out and said, 'We're here to deliver Mr Louis Sarapis. Got room all ready?'

'Absolutely,' Herb said at once. 'But I can't get hold of Mr St Cyr to make arrangements for the schedule. When's he to be brought back?'

Another man, dark-haired, with shiny-button black eyes, emerged from the truck. 'I'm John Barefoot. According to the terms of the will I'm in charge of Mr Sarapis. He's to be brought back to life immediately; that's the instructions I'm charged with.'

'I see,' Herb said, nodding. 'Well, that's fine. Bring him in and we'll plug him right in.'

'It's cold, here,' Barefoot said. 'Worse than the auditorium.'

'Well of course,' Herb answered.

The crew from the van began wheeling the casket. Herb caught a glimpse of the dead man, the massive, gray face resembling something cast from a break-mold. *Impressive old pirate*, he thought. *Good thing for us all he's dead finally, in spite of his charity work. Because who wants charity? Especially his.* Of course, Herb did not say that to Barefoot; he contented himself with guiding the crew to the pre-arranged spot.

'I'll have him talking in fifteen minutes,' he promised Barefoot, who looked tense. 'Don't worry; we've had almost no failures at this stage; the initial residual charge is generally quite vital.'

'I suppose it's later,' Barefoot said, 'as it dims ... then you have the technical problems.'

'Why does he want to be brought back so soon?' Herb asked.

Barefoot scowled and did not answer.

'Sorry,' Herb said, and continued tinkering with the wires

which had to be seated perfectly to the cathode terminals of the casket. 'At low temperatures,' he murmured, 'the flow of current is virtually unimpeded. There's no measurable resistance at minus 150. So–' He fitted the anode cap in place. 'The signal should bounce out clear and strong.' In conclusion, he clicked the amplifier on.

A hum. Nothing more.

'Well?' Barefoot said.

'I'll recheck,' Herb said, wondering what had gone afoul.

'Listen,' Barefoot said quietly, 'if you slip up here and let the spark flicker out–' It was not necessary for him to finish; Herb knew.

'Is it the Democratic-Republican National Convention that he wants to participate in?' Herb asked. The Convention would be held later in the month, in Cleveland. In the past, Sarapis had been quite active in the behind-the-scenes activities at both the Democratic-Republican and the Liberal Party nominating conventions. It was said, in fact, that he had personally chosen the last Democratic-Republican Presidential candidate, Alfonse Gam. Tidy, handsome Gam had lost, but not by very much.

'Are you still getting nothing?' Barefoot asked.

'Um, it seems–' Herb said.

'Nothing. Obviously.' Now Barefoot looked grim. 'If you can't rouse him in another ten minutes I'll get hold of Claude St Cyr and we'll take Louis out of your mortuary and lodge charges of negligence against you.'

'I'm doing what I can,' Herb said, perspiring as he fiddled with the leads to the casket. 'We didn't perform the quick-pack installation, remember; there may have been a slip-up at that point.'

Now static supervened over the steady hum.

'Is that him coming in?' Barefoot demanded.

'No,' Herb admitted, thoroughly upset by now. It was, in fact, a bad sign.

'Keep trying,' Barefoot said. But it was unnecessary to tell Herbert Schoenheit von Vogelsang that; he was struggling desper-

WHAT THE DEAD MEN SAY

ately, with all he had, with all his years of professional competence in this field. And still he achieved nothing; Louis Sarapis remained silent.

I'm not going to be successful, Herb realized in fear. *I don't understand why, either. WHAT'S WRONG? A big client like this, and it has to get fouled up.* He toiled on, not looking at Barefoot, not daring to.

At the radio telescope at Kennedy Slough, on the dark side of Luna, Chief Technician Owen Angress discovered that he had picked up a signal emanating from a region one light-week beyond the solar system in the direction of Proxima. Ordinarily such a region of space would have held little of interest for the UN Commission on Deep-Space Communications, but this, Owen Angress realized, was unique.

What reached him, thoroughly amplified by the great antennae of the radio telescope, was, faintly but clearly, a human voice.

'... probably let it slide by,' the voice was declaring. 'If I know them, and I believe I do. That Johnny; he'd revert without my keeping my eye on him, but at least he's not a crook like St Cyr. I did right to fire St Cyr. Assuming I can make it stick...' The voice faded momentarily.

What's out there? Angress wondered, dazedly. 'At one fifty-second of a light-year,' he murmured, making a quick mark on the deep-space map which he had been recharting. 'Nothing. That's just empty dust-clouds.' He could not understand what the signal implied; was it being bounced back to Luna from some nearby transmitter? Was this, in other words, merely an echo?

Or was he reading his computation incorrectly?

Surely this couldn't be correct. Some individual ruminating at a transmitter out beyond the solar system ... a man not in a hurry, thinking aloud in a kind of half-slumbering attitude, as if free-associating ... it made no sense.

I'd better report this to Wycoff at the Soviet Academy of Sciences, he said to himself. Wycoff was his current supervisor; next month it would be Jamison of MIT. *Maybe it's a long-haul ship that—*

The voice filtered in clearly once again. '. . . that Gam is a fool; did wrong to select him. Know better now but too late. Hello?' The thoughts became sharp, the words more distinct. 'Am I coming back?—for God's sake, it's about time. Hey! Johnny! Is that you?'

Angress picked up the telephone and dialed the code for the line to the Soviet Union.

'Speak up, Johnny!' the voice from the speaker demanded plaintively. 'Come on, son; I've got so damn much on my mind. So much to do. Convention's started yet, has it? Got no sense of time stuck in here, can't see or hear; wait'll you get here and you'll find out . . .' Again the voice faded.

This is exactly what Wycoff likes to call a 'phenomenon,' Angress realized.

And I can understand why.

II

On the evening television news, Claude St Cyr heard the announcer babbling about a discovery made by the radio telescope on Luna, but he paid little attention: he was busy mixing martinis for his guests.

'Yes,' he said to Gertrude Harvey, 'ironic as it is, I drew up the will myself, including the clause that automatically dismissed me, canceled my services out of existence the moment he died. And I'll tell you why Louis did that; he had paranoid suspicions of me, so he figured that with such a clause he'd insure himself against being–' He paused as he measured out the iota of dry wine which accompanied the gin. 'Being prematurely dispatched.' He grinned, and Gertrude, arranged decoratively on the couch beside her husband, smiled back.

'A lot of good it did him,' Phil Harvey said.

'Hell,' St Cyr protested. 'I had nothing to do with his death; it was an embolus, a great fat clot stuck like a cork in a bottleneck.' He laughed at the image. 'Nature's own remedy.'

Gertrude said, 'Listen. The TV; it's saying something strange.' She rose, walked over to it and bent down, her ear close to the speaker.

'It's probably that oaf Kent Margrave,' St Cyr said. 'Making another political speech.' Margrave had been their President now for four years; a Liberal, he had managed to defeat Alfonse Gam, who had been Louis Sarapis's hand-picked choice for the office. Actually Margrave, for all his faults, was quite a politician; he had managed to convince large blocs of voters that having a puppet of Sarapis's for their President was not such a good idea.

'No,' Gertrude said, carefully arranging her skirt over her bare knees. 'This is—the space agency, I think. Science.'

'Science!' St Cyr laughed. 'Well, then let's listen; I admire science. Turn it up.' *I suppose they've found another planet in the Orionus System,* he said to himself. *Something more for us to make the goal of our collective existence.*

'A voice,' the TV announcer was saying, 'emanating from outer space, tonight has scientists both in the United States and the Soviet Union completely baffled.'

'Oh no,' St Cyr choked. 'A voice from outer space—please, no more.' Doubled up with laughter, he moved off, away from the TV set; he could not bear to listen any more. 'That's what we need,' he said to Phil. 'A voice that turns out to be—you know Who it is.'

'Who?' Phil asked.

'God, of course. The radio telescope at Kennedy Slough has picked up the voice of God and now we're going to receive another set of divine commandments or at least a few scrolls.' Removing his glasses he wiped his eyes with his Irish linen handkerchief.

Dourly, Phil Harvey said, 'Personally I agree with my wife; I find it fascinating.'

'Listen, my friend,' St Cyr said, 'you know it'll turn out to be a transistor radio that some Jap student lost on a trip between Earth and Callisto. And the radio just drifted on out of the solar system entirely and now the telescope has picked it up and it's a huge mystery to all the scientists.' He became more sober. 'Shut it off, Gert; we've got serious things to consider.'

Obediently but reluctantly she did so. 'Is it true, Claude,' she asked, rising to her feet, 'that the mortuary wasn't able to revive old Louis? That he's not in half-life as he's supposed to be by now?'

'Nobody tells me anything from the organization, now,' St Cyr answered. 'But I did hear a rumor to that effect.' He knew, in fact, that it was so; he had many friends within Wilhelmina, but he did not like to talk about these surviving links. 'Yes, I suppose that's so,' he said.

Gertrude shivered. 'Imagine not coming back. How dreadful.'

'But that was the old natural condition,' her husband pointed out as he drank his martini. 'Nobody had half-life before the turn of the century.'

'But we're used to it,' she said stubbornly.

To Phil Harvey, St Cyr said, 'Let's continue our discussion.'

Shrugging, Harvey said, 'All right. If you really feel there's something to discuss.' He eyed St Cyr critically. 'I could put you on my legal staff, yes. If that's what you're sure you want. But I can't give you the kind of business that Louis could. It wouldn't be fair to the legal men I have in there now.'

'Oh, I recognize that,' St Cyr said. After all, Harvey's drayage firm was small in comparison with the Sarapis outfits; Harvey was in fact a minor figure in the 3-4 shipping business.

But that was precisely what St Cyr wanted. Because he believed that within a year with the experience and contacts he had gained working for Louis Sarapis he could depose Harvey and take over Elektra Enterprises.

Harvey's first wife had been named Elektra. St Cyr had known her, and after she and Harvey had split up St Cyr had continued to see her, now in a more personal—and more spirited—way. It had always seemed to him that Elektra Harvey had obtained a rather bad deal; Harvey had employed legal talent of sufficient caliber to outwit Elektra's attorney . . . who had been, as a matter of fact, St Cyr's junior law partner, Harold Faine. Ever since her defeat in the courts, St Cyr had blamed himself; why hadn't he taken the case personally? But he had been so tied up with Sarapis business . . . it had simply not been possible.

WHAT THE DEAD MEN SAY

Now, with Sarapis gone and his job with Atlas, Wilhelmina and Archimedean over, he could take some time to rectify the imbalance; he could come to the aid of the woman (he admitted it) whom he loved.

But that was a long step from this situation; first he had to get into Harvey's legal staff—at any cost. Evidently, he was succeeding.

'Shall we shake on it, then?' he asked Harvey, holding out his hand.

'Okay,' Harvey said, not very much stirred by the event. He held out his hand, however, and they shook. 'By the way,' he said, then, 'I have some knowledge—fragmentary but evidently accurate—as to why Sarapis cut you off in his will. And it isn't what you said at all.'

'Oh?' St Cyr said, trying to sound casual.

'My understanding is that he suspected someone, possibly you, of desiring to prevent him from returning to half-life. That you were going to select a particular mortuary which certain contacts of yours operate . . . and they'd somehow fail to revive the old man.' He eyed St Cyr. 'And oddly, that seems to be exactly what has happened.'

There was silence.

Gertrude said, at last, 'Why would Claude not want Louis Sarapis to be resurrected?'

'I have no idea,' Harvey said. He stroked his chin thoughtfully. 'I don't even fully understand half-life itself. Isn't it true that the half-lifer often finds himself in possession of a sort of insight, of a new frame of reference, a perspective, that he lacked while alive?'

'I've heard psychologists say that,' Gertrude agreed. 'It's what the old theologists called *conversion*.'

'Maybe Claude was afraid of some insight that Louis might show up with,' Harvey said. 'But that's just conjecture.'

'Conjecture,' Claude St Cyr agreed, 'in its entirety, including that as to any such plan as you describe; in actual fact I know absolutely no one in the mortuary business.' His voice was steady, too; he made it come out that way. But this all was very sticky, he said to himself. Quite awkward.

The maid appeared, then, to tell them that dinner was ready. Both Phil and Gertrude rose, and Claude joined them as they entered the dining room together.

'Tell me,' Phil Harvey said to Claude. 'Who is Sarapis's heir?'

St Cyr said, 'A granddaughter who lives on Callisto; her name is Kathy Egmont and she's an odd one . . . she's about twenty years old and already she's been in jail five times, mostly for narcotics addiction. Lately, I understand, she's managed to cure herself of the drug habit and now she's a religious convert of some kind. I've never met her but I've handled volumes of correspondence passing between her and old Louis.'

'And she gets the entire estate, when it's out of probate? With all the political power inherent in it?'

'Haw,' St Cyr said. 'Political power can't be willed, can't be passed on. All Kathy gets is the economic syndrome. It functions, as you know, through the parent holding company licensed under the laws of the state of Delaware, Wilhelmina Securities, and that's hers, if she cares to make use of it—if she can understand what it is she's inheriting.'

Phil Harvey said, 'You don't sound very optimistic.'

'All the correspondence from her indicates—to me at least—that she's a sick, criminal type, very eccentric and unstable. The very last sort I'd like to see inherit Louis's holdings.'

On that note, they seated themselves at the dinner table.

In the night, Johnny Barefoot heard the phone, drew himself to a sitting position and fumbled until his hands touched the receiver. Beside him in the bed Sarah Belle stirred as he said gratingly, 'Hello. Who the hell is it?'

A fragile female voice said, 'I'm sorry, Mr Barefoot . . . I didn't mean to wake you up. But I was told by my attorney to call you as soon as I arrived on Earth.' She added, 'This is Kathy Egmont, although actually my real name is Mrs Kathy Sharp. Do you know who I am?'

'Yes,' Johnny said, rubbing his eyes and yawning. He shivered from the cold of the room; beside him, Sarah Belle drew the covers back up over her shoulders and turned the other way. 'Want me to come and pick you up? Do you have a place to stay?'

'I have no friends here on Terra,' Kathy said. 'But the spaceport people told me that the Beverely is a good hotel, so I'm going there. I started from Callisto as soon as I heard that my grandfather had died.'

'You made good time,' he said. He hadn't expected her for another twenty-four hours.

'Is there any chance—' The girl sounded timid. 'Could I possibly stay with you, Mr Barefoot? It scares me, the idea of a big hotel where no one knows me.'

'I'm sorry,' he said at once. 'I'm married.' And then he realized that such a retort was not only inappropriate . . . it was actually abusive. 'What I mean is,' he explained, 'I have no spare room. You stay at the Beverely tonight and tomorrow we'll find you a more acceptable apartment.'

'All right,' Kathy said. She sounded resigned but still anxious. 'Tell me, Mr Barefoot, what luck have you had with my grandfather's resurrection? Is he in half-life, now?'

'No,' Johnny said. 'It's failed, so far. They're working on it.'

When he had left the mortuary, five technicians had been busy at work, trying to discover what was wrong.

Kathy said, 'I thought it might work out that way.'

'Why?'

'Well, my grandfather—he was so different from everyone else. I realize you know that, perhaps even better than I . . . after all, you were with him daily. But—I just couldn't imagine him inert, the way the half-lifers are. Passive and helpless, you know. Can you imagine him like that, after all he's done?'

Johnny said, 'Let's talk tomorrow; I'll come by the hotel about nine. Okay?'

'Yes, that's fine. I'm glad to have met you, Mr Barefoot. I hope you'll stay on with Archimedean, working for me. Goodbye.' The phone clicked; she had rung off.

My new boss, Johnny said to himself. *Wow.*

'Who was that?' Sarah Belle murmured. 'At this hour?'

'The owner of Archimedean,' Johnny said. 'My employer.'

'Louis Sarapis?' His wife sat up at once. 'Oh . . . you mean his granddaughter; she's here already. What's she sound like?'

'I can't tell,' he said meditatively. 'Frightened, mostly. It's a finite, small world she comes from, compared with Terra, here.' He did not tell his wife the things he knew about Kathy, her drug addiction, her terms in jail.

'Can she take over now?' Sarah Belle asked. 'Doesn't she have to wait until Louis's half-life is over?'

'Legally, he's dead. His will has come into force.' *And,* he thought acidly, *he's not in half-life anyhow; he's silent and dead in his plastic casket, in his quick-pack, which evidently wasn't quite quick enough.*

'How do you think you'll get along with her?'

'I don't know,' he said candidly. 'I'm not even sure I'm going to try.' He did not like the idea of working for a woman, especially one younger than himself. And one who was—at least according to hearsay—virtually psychopathic. But on the phone she had certainly not sounded psychopathic. He mulled that over in his mind, wide-awake now.

'She's probably very pretty,' Sarah Belle said. 'You'll probably fall in love with her and desert me.'

'Oh no,' he said. 'Nothing as startling as that. I'll probably try to work for her, drag out a few miserable months, and then give up and look elsewhere.' *And meanwhile,* he thought, *WHAT ABOUT LOUIS? Are we, or are we not, going to be able to revive him?* That was the really big unknown.

If the old man could be revived, he could direct his granddaughter; even though legally and physically dead, he could continue to manage his complex economic and political sphere, to some extent. But right now this was simply not working out, and the old man had planned on being revived at once, certainly before the Democratic-Republican Convention. Louis certainly knew—or

WHAT THE DEAD MEN SAY

rather had known—what sort of person he was willing his holdings to. Without help she surely could not function. *And*, Johnny thought, *there's little I can do for her. Claude St Cyr could have, but by the terms of the will he's out of the picture entirely. So what is left? We must keep trying to revive old Louis, even if we have to visit every mortuary in the United States, Cuba and Russia.*

'You're thinking confused thoughts,' Sarah Belle said. 'I can tell by your expression.' She turned on the small lamp by the bed, and was now reaching for her robe. 'Don't try to solve serious matters in the middle of the night.'

This must be how half-life feels, he thought groggily. He shook his head, trying to clear it, to wake up fully.

The next morning he parked his car in the underground garage of the Beverely and ascended by elevator to the lobby and the front desk where he was greeted by the smiling day clerk. It was not much of a hotel, Johnny decided. Clean, however; a respectable family hotel which probably rented many of its units by the month, some no doubt to elderly retired people. Evidently Kathy was accustomed to living modestly.

In answer to his query, the clerk pointed to the adjoining coffee shop. 'You'll find her in there, eating breakfast. She said you might be calling, Mr Barefoot.'

In the coffee shop he found a good number of people having breakfast; he stopped short, wondering which was Kathy. The dark-haired girl with the stilted, frozen features, over in the far corner out of the way? He walked toward her. Her hair, he decided, was dyed. Without makeup she looked unnaturally pale; her skin had a stark quality, as if she had known a good deal of suffering, and not the sort that taught or informed one, made one into a 'better' person. It had been pure pain, with no redemptive aspects, he decided as he studied her.

'Kathy?' he asked.

The girl turned her head. Her eyes, empty; her expression totally flattened. In a little voice she said, 'Yes. Are you John Barefoot?' As he came up to the booth and seated himself opposite her she watched as if she imagined he would spring at her, hurl himself on her and—God forbid—sexually assault her. *It's as if she's nothing more than a lone, small animal*, he thought. *Backed into a corner to face the entire world.*

The color, or rather lack of it, could stem from the drug addiction, he decided. But that did not explain the flatness of her tone, and her utter lack of facial expression. And yet—she was pretty. She had delicate, regular features . . . animated, they would have been interesting. And perhaps they had been, once. Years ago.

'I have only five dollars left,' Kathy said. 'After I paid for my one-way ticket and my hotel and my breakfast. Could you—' She hesitated. 'I'm not sure exactly what to do. Could you tell me . . . do I own anything yet? Anything that was my grandfather's? That I could borrow against?'

Johnny said, 'I'll write you a personal check for one hundred dollars and you can pay me back sometime.' He got out his checkbook.

'Really?' She looked stunned, and now, faintly, she smiled. 'How trusting of you. Or are you trying to impress me? You were my grandfather's public relations man, weren't you? How were you dealt with in the will? I can't remember; it's all happened so fast, it's been so blurred.'

'Well,' he said, 'I wasn't fired, as was Claude St Cyr.'

'Then you're staying on.' That seemed to relieve her mind. 'I wonder . . . would it be correct to say you're now working for *me?*'

'You could say that,' Johnny said. 'Assuming you feel you need a PR man. Maybe you don't. Louis wasn't sure, half the time.'

'Tell me what efforts have been made to resurrect him.'

He explained to her, briefly, what he had done.

'And this is not generally known?' she asked.

'Definitely not. I know it, a mortuary owner with the unnatural name of Herb Schoenheit von Vogelsang knows it, and possibly news has trickled to a few high people in the drayage business, such as Phil Harvey. Even Claude St Cyr may know it, by now. Of course, as time goes on and Louis has nothing to say, no political pronouncements for the press—'

'We'll have to make them up,' Kathy said. 'And pretend they're from him. That will be your job, Mr Funnyfoot.' She smiled once more. 'Press-releases by my grandfather, until he's finally revived or we give up. Do you think we'll have to give up?' After a pause she said softly, 'I'd like to see him. If I may. If you think it's all right.'

'I'll take you there, to the Blessed Brethren Mortuary. I have to go there within the hour anyhow.'

Nodding, Kathy resumed eating her breakfast.

As Johnny Barefoot stood beside the girl, who gazed intently at the transparent casket, he thought bizarrely, *Maybe she'll rap on the glass and say, 'Grandfather, you wake up.' And,* he thought, *maybe that will accomplish it. Certainly nothing else has.*

Wringing his hands, Herb Schoenheit von Vogelsang burbled miserably, 'I just don't understand it, Mr Barefoot. We worked all night, in relays, and we just aren't getting a single spark. And yet we ran an electrocephalograph and the 'gram shows faint but unmistakable cerebral activity. So the after-life is there, but we can't seem to contact it. We've got probes at every part of the skull, now, as you can see.' He pointed to the maze of hair-wires connecting the dead man's head to the amplifying equipment surrounding the casket. 'I don't know what else we can do, sir.'

'Is there measurable brain metabolism?' Johnny asked.

'Yes, sir. We called in outside experts and they detected it; it's a normal amount, too, just what you'd expect, immediately after death.'

Kathy said calmly, 'I know it's hopeless. He's too big a man for this. This is for aged relatives. For grandmothers, to be trotted out once a year on Resurrection Day.' She turned away from the casket. 'Let's go,' she said to Johnny.

Together, he and the girl walked along the sidewalk from the mortuary, neither speaking. It was a mild spring day, and the trees here and there at the curb had small pink flowers. Cherry trees, Johnny decided.

'Death,' Kathy murmured, at last. 'And rebirth. A technological miracle. Maybe when Louis saw what it was like on the other side he changed his mind about coming back . . . maybe he just doesn't *want* to return.'

'Well,' Johnny said, 'the electrical spark is there; he's inside there, thinking something.' He let Kathy take his arm as they crossed the street. 'Someone told me,' he said quietly, 'that you're interested in religion.'

'Yes, I am,' Kathy said quietly. 'You see, when I was a narcotics addict I took an overdose—never mind of what—and as a result my heart action ceased. I was officially, medically, dead for several minutes; they brought me back by open-chest heart massage and electroshock . . . you know. During that time I had an experience, probably much like what those who go into half-life have experienced.'

'Was it better than here?'

'No,' she said. 'But it was different. It was—dreamlike. I don't mean vague or unreal. I mean the logic, the weightlessness; you see, that's the main difference. You're free of gravity. It's hard to realize how important that is, but just think how many of the characteristics of the dream derive from that one fact.'

Johnny said, 'And it changed you.'

'I managed to overcome the oral addictive aspects of my personality, if that's what you mean. I learned to control my appetites. My greed.' At a newspaper stand Kathy halted to read the headlines. 'Look,' she said.

VOICE FROM OUTER SPACE BAFFLES SCIENTISTS

'Interesting,' Johnny said.

Kathy, picking up the newspaper, read the article which accompanied the headline. 'How strange,' she said. 'They've picked up a sentient, living entity . . . here, you can read it, too.' She passed the newspaper to him. 'I did that, when I died . . . I drifted out, free of the solar system, first planetary gravity then the sun's.

I wonder who it is.' Taking the newspaper back she reread the article.

'Ten cents, sir or madam,' the robot vender said, suddenly.

Johnny tossed it the dime.

'Do you think it's my grandfather?' Kathy asked.

'Hardly,' Johnny said.

'I think it is,' Kathy said, staring past him, deep in thought. 'I know it is; look, it began one week after his death, and it's one light-week out. The time fits, and here's the transcript of what it's saying.' She pointed to the column. 'All about you, Johnny, and about me and about Claude St Cyr, that lawyer he fired, and the Convention; it's all there, but garbled. That's the way your thoughts run, when you're dead; all compressed, instead of in sequence.' She smiled up at Johnny. 'So we've got a terrible problem. We can hear him, by use of the radio telescope at Kennedy Slough. But he can't hear us.'

'You don't actually—'

'Oh, I do,' she said matter-of-factly. 'I knew he wouldn't settle for half-life; this is a whole, entire life he's leading now, out in space, there, beyond the last planet of our system. And there isn't going to be any way we can interfere with him; whatever it is he's doing—' She began to walk on, once more; Johnny followed. 'Whatever it is, it's going to be at least as much as he did when he was alive here on Terra. You can be sure of that. Are you afraid?'

'Hell,' Johnny protested, 'I'm not even convinced, let alone afraid.' And yet—perhaps she was right. She seemed so certain about it. He could not help being a little impressed, a little convinced.

'You should be afraid,' Kathy said. 'He may be very strong, out there. He may be able to do a lot. Affect a lot . . . affect us, what we do and say and believe. Even without the radio telescope—he may be reaching us, even now. Subliminally.'

'I don't believe it,' Johnny said. But he did, in spite of himself. She was right; it was just what Louis Sarapis would do.

Kathy said, 'We'll know more when the Convention begins,

because that's what he cares about. He failed to get Gam elected last time, and that was one of the few times in his life that he was beaten.'

'Gam!' Johnny echoed, amazed. 'That has-been? Is he even still in existence? Why, he completely disappeared, four years ago—'

'My grandfather won't give up with him,' Kathy said meditatively. 'And he is alive; he's a turkey farmer or some such thing, on Io. Perhaps it's ducks. Anyhow, he's there. Waiting.'

'Waiting for what?'

Kathy said, 'For my grandfather to contact him again. As he did before, four years ago, at the Convention then.'

'No one would vote for Gam again!' Repelled, he gazed at her.

Smiling, Kathy said nothing. But she squeezed his arm, hugging him. As if, he thought, she were afraid again, as she had been in the night, when he had talked to her. Perhaps even more so.

III

The handsome, dapper, middle-aged man wearing vest and narrow, old-fashioned necktie, rose to his feet as Claude St Cyr entered the outer office of St Cyr and Faine, on his way to court. 'Mr St Cyr—'

Glancing at him, St Cyr murmured, 'I'm in a rush; you'll have to make an appointment with my secretary.' And then he recognized the man. He was talking to Alfonse Gam.

'I have a telegram,' Gam said. 'From Louis Sarapis.' He reached into his coat pocket.

'Sorry,' St Cyr said stiffly. 'I'm associated with Mr Phil Harvey now; my business relationship with Mr Sarapis was terminated several weeks ago.' But he paused, curious. He had met Gam before; at the time of the national campaign, four years ago, he had seen a good deal of the man—in fact, he had represented Gam in several libel suits, one with Gam as the plaintiff, the other as defendant. He did not like the man.

Gam said, 'This wire arrived the day before yesterday.'

'But Sarapis has been–' Claude St Cyr broke off. 'Let me see it.' He held out his hand, and Gam passed him the wire.

It was a statement from Louis Sarapis to Gam, assuring Gam of Louis's utter and absolute support in the forthcoming struggle at the Convention. And Gam was correct; the wire was dated only three days before. It did not make sense.

'I can't explain it, Mr St Cyr,' Gam said dryly. 'But it sounds like Louis. He wants me to run again. As you can see. It never occurred to me; as far as I'm concerned I'm out of politics and in the guinea-fowl business. I thought you might know something about this, who sent it and why.' He added, 'Assuming that old Louis didn't.'

St Cyr said, 'How could Louis have sent it?'

'I mean, written it before his death and had someone send it just the other day. Yourself, perhaps.' Gam shrugged. 'Evidently it wasn't you. Perhaps Mr Barefoot, then.' He reached out for his wire.

'Do you actually intend to run again?' St Cyr asked.

'If Louis wants me to.'

'And lose again? Drag the party to defeat again, just because of one stubborn, vindictive old man–' St Cyr broke off. 'Go back to raising guinea fowl. Forget politics. You're a loser, Gam. Everyone in the party knows it. Everyone in America, in fact.'

'How can I contact Mr Barefoot?'

St Cyr said, 'I have no idea.' He started on.

'I'll need legal help,' Gam said.

'For what? Who's suing you now? You don't need legal help, Mr Gam; you need medical help, a psychiatrist to explain why you want to run again. Listen–' He leaned toward Gam. 'If Louis alive couldn't get you into office, Louis dead certainly can't.' He went on, then, leaving Gam standing there.

'Wait,' Gam said.

Reluctantly, Claude St Cyr turned around.

'This time I'm going to win,' Gam said. He sounded as if he meant it; his voice, instead of its usual reedy flutter, was firm.

Uneasy, St Cyr said, 'Well, good luck. To both you and Louis.'

'Then he *is* alive.' Gam's eyes flickered.

'I didn't say that; I was being ironic.'

Gam said thoughtfully, 'But he is alive; I'm sure of it. I'd like to find him. I went to some of the mortuaries, but none of them had him, or if they did they wouldn't admit it. I'll keep looking; I want to confer with him.' He added, 'That's why I came here from Io.'

At that point, St Cyr managed to break away and depart. *What a nonentity*, he said to himself. *A cypher, nothing but a puppet of Louis's.* He shuddered. *God protect us from such a fate: that man as our President.*

Imagine us all *becoming like Gam!*

It was not a pleasant thought; it did not inspire him for the day ahead. And he had a good deal of work on his shoulders.

This was the day that he, as attorney for Phil Harvey, would make Mrs Kathy Sharp—the former Kathy Egmont—an offer for Wilhelmina Securities. An exchange of stock would be involved; voting stock, redistributed in such a fashion that Harvey gained control of Wilhelmina. The worth of the corporation being almost impossible to calculate, Harvey was offering not money but real estate in exchange; he had enormous tracts of land on Ganymede, deeded to him by the Soviet Government a decade ago in exchange for technical assistance he had rendered it and its colonies.

The chance of Kathy accepting was nil.

And yet, the offer had to be made. The next step—he shrank from even thinking about it—involved a fracas to the death in the area of direct economic competition, between Harvey's drayage firm and hers. And hers, he knew, was now in a state of decay; there had been union trouble since the old man's death. The thing that Louis hated the most had started to take place: union organizers had begun to move in on Archimedean.

He himself sympathized with the unions; it was about time they came onto the scene. Only the old man's dirty tactics and his boundless energy, not to speak of his ruthless, eternal imagination, had kept them out. Kathy had none of these. And Johnny Barefoot—

What can you ask of a noncol? St Cyr asked himself caustically. *Brilliant strategy-purse out of the sow's ear of mediocrity?*

And Barefoot had his hands full building up Kathy's image before the public; he had barely begun to succeed in that when the union squabbles broke out. An ex-narcotics addict and religious nut, a woman who had a criminal record . . . Johnny had his work cut out for him.

Where he had been productive lay in the area of the woman's physical appearance. She looked sweet, even gentle and pure; almost saintly. And Johnny had seized on this. Instead of quoting her in the press he had photographed her, a thousand wholesome poses: with dogs, children, at county fairs, at hospitals, involved in charity drives—the whole business.

But unfortunately Kathy had spoiled the image he had created, spoiled it in a rather unusual way.

Kathy maintained—simply—that she was in communication with her grandfather. That it was he who lay a light-week out in space, picked up by Kennedy Slough. She heard him, as the rest of the world did . . . and by some miracle he heard her, too.

St Cyr, riding the self-service elevator up to the 'copter port on the roof, laughed aloud. Her religious crankery couldn't be kept from the gossip columnists . . . Kathy had said too much in public places, in restaurants and small, famous bars. And even with Johnny beside her. Even he couldn't keep her quiet.

Also, there had been that incident at that party in which she had taken off her clothes, declaring the hour of purification to be momentarily arriving; she had daubed herself in certain spots with crimson nail polish, as well, a sort of ritual ceremony . . . of course she had been drinking.

And this is the woman, St Cyr thought, *who operates Archimedean.*

The woman we must oust, for our good and *the public's.* It was, to him, practically a mandate in the name of the people. Virtually a public service to be performed, and the only one who did not see it that way was Johnny.

St Cyr thought, *Johnny LIKES her. There's the motive.*

I wonder, he mused, *what Sarah Belle thinks of that.*

Feeling cheerful, St Cyr entered his 'copter, closed the hatch and inserted his key in the ignition. And then he thought once again of Alfonse Gam. And his good humor vanished at once, again he felt glum.

There are two people, he realized, *who are acting on the assumption that old Louis Sarapis is alive; Kathy Egmont Sharp and Alfonse Gam.*

Two most unsavory people, too. And, in spite of himself, he was being forced to associate with both of them. It seemed to be his fate.

He thought, *I'm no better off than I was with old Louis. In some respects, I'm even worse off.*

The 'copter rose into the sky, on its way to Phil Harvey's building in downtown Denver.

Being late, he snapped on the little transmitter, picked up the microphone and put in a call to Harvey. 'Phil,' he said, 'can you hear me? This is St Cyr and I'm on my way west.' He listened, then.

—Listened, and heard from the speaker a far-off weird babble, a murmur as if many words were being blended into a confusion. He recognized it; he had come onto it several times now, on the TV news programs.

'. . . spite of personal attacks, much superior to Chambers, who couldn't win an election for house of ill repute janitor. You keep up faith in yourself, Alfonse. People know a good man, value him; you wait. Faith moves mountains. I ought to know, look what I've accomplished in my life . . .'

It was, St Cyr realized, the entity a light-week out, now emitting an even more powerful signal; like sunspots, it beclouded normal transmission channels. He cursed, scowled, then snapped off the receiver.

Fouling up communications, he said to himself. *Must be against the law; I ought to consult the FCC.*

Shaken, he piloted his 'copter on, across open farm land.

My God, he thought, *it did sound like old Louis!*

Could Kathy Egmont Sharp possibly be right?

*

At the Michigan plant of Archimedean, Johnny Barefoot appeared for his appointment with Kathy and found her in a state of gloom.

'Don't you see what's happening?' she demanded, facing him across the office which had once been Louis's. 'I'm not managing things right at all; everybody knows that. Don't you know that?' Wild-eyed, she stared at him.

'I don't know that,' Johnny said. But inside he did know it; she was correct. 'Take it easy and sit down,' he said. 'Harvey and St Cyr will be here any minute now, and you want to be in command of yourself when you meet with them.' It was a meeting which he had hoped to avoid. But, he had realized, sooner or later it would take place, and so he had let Kathy agree to it.

Kathy said, 'I—have something terrible to tell you.'

'What is it? It can't be so terrible.' He set himself, waiting in dread to hear.

'I'm back on drugs, Johnny. All this responsibility and pressure; it's too much for me. I'm sorry.' She gazed down at the floor sadly.

'What is the drug?'

'I'd rather not say. It's one of the amphetamines. I've read the literature; I know it can cause a psychosis, in the amounts I'm taking. But I don't care.' Panting, she turned away, her back to him. He saw, now, how thin she had gotten. And her face was gaunt, hollow-eyed; he now understood why. The overdosage of amphetamines wasted the body away, turned matter into energy. Her metabolism was altered so that she became, as the addiction returned, a pseudo-hyperthyroid, with all the somatic processes speeded up.

Johnny said, 'I'm sorry to hear it.' He had been afraid of this. And yet when it had come he had not understood; he had had to wait until she told him. 'I think,' he said, 'you should be under a doctor's care.' He wondered where she got the drug. But probably for her, with her years of experience, it was not difficult.

'It makes a person very unstable emotionally,' Kathy said. 'Given to sudden rages and also crying jags. I want you to know that, so you won't blame me. So you'll understand that it's the drug.' She tried to smile; he saw her making the effort.

Going over to her he put his hand on her shoulder. 'Listen,' he said, 'when Harvey and St Cyr get here, I think you better accept their offer.'

'Oh,' she said, nodding. 'Well.'

'And then,' he said, 'I want you to go voluntarily into a hospital.'

'The cookie factory,' Kathy said bitterly.

'You'd be better off,' he said, 'without the responsibility you have, here at Archimedean. What you need is deep, protracted rest. You're in a state of mental and physical fatigue, but as long as you're taking that amphetamine—'

'Then it doesn't catch up with me,' Kathy finished. 'Johnny, I can't sell out to Harvey and St Cyr.'

'Why not?'

'Louis wouldn't want me to. He—' She was silent a moment. 'He says no.'

Johnny said, 'Your health, maybe your life—'

'My sanity, you mean, Johnny.'

'You have too much personally at stake,' he said. 'The hell with Louis. The hell with Archimedean; you want to find yourself in a mortuary, too, in half-life? It's not worth it; it's just property, and you're a living creature.'

She smiled. And then, on the desk, a light came on and a buzzer sounded. The receptionist outside said, 'Mrs Sharp, Mr Harvey and Mr St Cyr are here, now. Shall I send them in?'

'Yes,' she answered.

The door opened, and Claude St Cyr and Phil Harvey came swiftly in. 'Hey, Johnny,' St Cyr said. He seemed to be in a confident mood; beside him, Harvey looked confident, too.

Kathy said, 'I'll let Johnny do most of the talking.'

He glanced at her. *Did that mean she had agreed to sell?* He said, 'What kind of deal is this? What do you have to offer in exchange for a controlling interest in Wilhelmina Securities of Delaware? I can't imagine what it could be.'

'Ganymede,' St Cyr said. 'An entire moon.' He added, 'Virtually.'

'Oh yes,' Johnny said. 'The USSR land deed. Has it been tested in the international courts?'

'Yes,' St Cyr said, 'and found totally valid. Its worth is beyond estimate. And each year it will increase, perhaps double, in value. My client will put that up. It's a good offer, Johnny; you and I know each other, and you know when I say it that it's true.'

Probably it was, Johnny decided. It was in many respects a generous offer; Harvey was not trying to bilk Kathy.

'Speaking for Mrs Sharp,' Johnny began. But Kathy cut him off.

'No,' she said in a quick, brisk voice. 'I can't sell. He says not to.'

Johnny said, 'You've already given me authority to negotiate, Kathy.'

'Well,' she said in a hard voice, 'I'm taking it back.'

'If I'm to work with you and for you at all,' Johnny said, 'you must go on my advice. We've already talked it over and agreed—'

The phone in the office rang.

'Listen to him yourself,' Kathy said. She picked up the phone and held it out to Johnny. 'He'll tell you.'

Johnny accepted the phone and put it to his ear. 'Who is this?' he demanded. And then he heard the drumming. The far-off uncanny drumming noise, as if something were scratching at a long metal wire.

'. . . imperative to retain control. Your advice absurd. She can pull herself together; she's got the stuff. Panic reaction; you're scared because she's ill. A good doctor can fix her up. Get a doctor for her; get medical help. Get an attorney and be sure she stays out of the hands of the law. Make sure her supply of drugs is cut. Insist on . . .' Johnny yanked the receiver away from his ear, refusing to hear more. Trembling, he hung the phone back up.

'You heard him,' Kathy said. 'Didn't you? *That was Louis.*'

'Yes,' Johnny said.

'He's grown,' Kathy said. 'Now we can hear him direct; it's not just the radio telescope at Kennedy Slough. I heard him last night, clearly, for the first time, as I lay down to go to sleep.'

To St Cyr and Harvey, Johnny said, 'We'll have to think your proposition over, evidently. We'll have to get an appraisal of the worth of the unimproved real estate you're offering and no doubt you want an audit of Wilhelmina. That will take time.' He heard his voice shake; he had not gotten over the shock of picking up the telephone and hearing the living voice of Louis Sarapis.

After making an appointment with St Cyr and Harvey to meet with them once more later in the day, Johnny took Kathy out to a late breakfast; she had admitted, reluctantly, that she had eaten nothing since the night before.

'I'm just not hungry,' she explained, as she sat picking listlessly at her plate of bacon and eggs, toast with jam.

'Even if that was Louis Sarapis,' Johnny said, 'you don't—'

'It was. Don't say "even"; you know it's him. He's gaining power all the time, out there. Perhaps from the sun.'

'So it's Louis,' he said doggedly. 'Nonetheless, you have to act in your own interest, not in his.'

'His interests and mine are the same,' Kathy said. 'They involve maintaining Archimedean.'

'Can he give you the help you need? Can he supply what's missing? He doesn't take your drug addiction seriously; that's obvious. All he did was preach at me.' He felt anger. 'That's damn little help, for you or for me, in this situation.'

'Johnny,' she said, 'I feel him near me all the time; I don't need the TV or the phone—I *sense* him. It's my mystical bent, I think. My religious intuition; it's helping me maintain contact with him.' She sipped a little orange juice.

Bluntly, Johnny said, 'It's your amphetamine psychosis, you mean.'

'I won't go into the hospital, Johnny. I won't sign myself in; I'm sick but not that sick. I can get over this bout on my own, because I'm not alone. I have my grandfather. And—' She smiled at him. 'I have you. In spite of Sarah Belle.'

'You won't have me, Kathy,' he said quietly, 'unless you sell to Harvey. Unless you accept the Ganymede real estate.'

'You'd quit?'

'Yes,' he said.

After a pause, Kathy said, 'My grandfather says go ahead and quit.' Her eyes were dark, enlarged, and utterly cold.

'I don't believe he'd say that.'

'Then talk to him.'

'How?'

Kathy pointed to the TV set in the corner of the restaurant. 'Turn it on and listen.'

Rising to his feet, Johnny said, 'I don't have to; I've already given my decision. I'll be at my hotel, if you should change your mind.' He walked away from the table, leaving her sitting there. Would she call after him? He listened as he walked. She did not call.

A moment later he was out of the restaurant, standing on the sidewalk. She had called his bluff, and so it ceased to be a bluff; it became the real thing. He actually had quit.

Stunned, he walked aimlessly on. And yet—he had been right. He knew that. It was just that . . . damn her, he thought. Why didn't she give in? Because of Louis, he realized. Without the old man she would have gone ahead and done it, traded her controlling, voting stock for the Ganymede property. Damn Louis Sarapis, not her, he thought furiously.

What now? he asked himself. Go back to New York? Look for a new job? For instance approach Alfonse Gam? There was money in that, if he could land it. Or should he stay here in Michigan, hoping that Kathy would change her mind?

She can't keep on, he decided. *No matter what Sarapis tells her. Or rather, what she believes he's telling her. Whichever it is.*

Hailing a cab, he gave the driver the address of his hotel room. A few moments later he was entering the lobby of the Antler Hotel, back where he had started early in the morning. Back to the forbidding empty room, this time merely to sit and wait. To hope that Kathy would change her mind and call him. This time he had no appointment to go to; the appointment was over.

When he reached his hotel room he heard his phone ringing.

*

For a moment Johnny stood at the door, key in hand, listening to the phone on the other side of the door, the shrill noise reaching him as he stood in the hall. *Is it Kathy?* he wondered. *Or is it* him*?*

He put the key in the lock, turned it and entered the room; sweeping the receiver off its hook he said, 'Hello.'

Drumming and far-off, the voice, in the middle of its monotonous monologue, its recitation to itself, was murmuring, '. . . no good at all, Barefoot, to leave her. Betrayal of your job; thought you understood your responsibilities. Same to her as it was to me, and you never would have walked off in a fit of pique and left me. I deliberately left the disposition of my body to you so you'd stay on. You can't . . .' At that point Johnny hung up, chilled.

The phone rang again, at once.

This time he did not take it off the hook. *The hell with you,* he said to himself. He walked to the window and stood looking down at the street below, thinking to himself of the conversation he had held with old Louis years ago, the one that had made such an impression in his mind. The conversation in which it had come out that he had failed to go to college because he wanted to die. Looking down at the street below, he thought, *Maybe I ought to jump. At least there'd be no more phones . . . no more of* it.

The worse part, he thought, *is its senility. Its thoughts are not clear, not distinct; they're dreamlike; irrational. The old man is not genuinely alive. He is not even in half-life. This is a dwindling away of consciousness toward a nocturnal state. And we are forced to listen to it as it unwinds, as it develops step by step, to final, total death.*

But even in this degenerative state, it had desires. It *wanted,* and strongly. It wanted him to do something; it wanted Kathy to do something; the remnants of Louis Sarapis were vital and active, and clever enough to find ways of pursuing him, of getting what was wanted. It was a travesty of Louis's wishes during his lifetime, and yet it could not be ignored; it could not be escaped.

The phone continued to ring.

Maybe it isn't Louis, he thought then. *Maybe it's Kathy.* Going to it he lifted the receiver. And put it back down at once. The drum-

ming once more, the fragments of Louis Sarapis's personality . . .
he shuddered. *And is it just here, is it selective?*

He had a terrible feeling that it was *not* selective.

Going to the TV set at the far end of the room he snapped the
switch. The screen grew into lighted animation, and yet, he saw, it
was strangely blurred. The dim outlines of–it seemed to be a face.

And everyone, he realized, *is seeing this.* He turned to another
channel. Again the dully-formed features, the old man half-
materialized here on the television screen. And from the set's
speaker the murmur of indistinct words. '. . . told you time and
again your primary responsibility is to . . .' Johnny shut the set off;
the ill-formed face and words sank out of existence, and all that
remained, once more, was the ringing phone.

He picked up the phone and said, 'Louis, can you hear me?'

'. . . when election time comes they'll see. A man with the spirit
to campaign a second time, take the financial responsibility, after all
it's only for the wealthy men, now, the cost of running . . .' The voice
droned on. No, the old man could not hear him. It was not a conversation; it was a monologue. It was not authentic communication.

And yet the old man knew what was occurring on Earth; he
seemed to understand, to somehow see, that Johnny had quit his
job.

Hanging up the phone he seated himself and lit a cigarette.

I can't go back to Kathy, he realized, *unless I'm willing to change my
mind and advise her not to sell. And that's impossible; I can't do that. So
that's out. What is there left for me?*

How long can Sarapis hound me? Is there any place I can go?

Going to the window once more he stood looking down at the
street below.

At a newsstand, Claude St Cyr tossed down coins, picked up the
newspaper.

'Thank you, sir or madam,' the robot vender said.

The lead article . . . St Cyr blinked and wondered if he had lost
his mind. He could not grasp what he was reading–or rather

unable to read. It made no sense; the homeostatic news-printing system, the fully automated micro-relay newspaper, had evidently broken down. All he found was a procession of words, randomly strung together. It was worse than *Finnegans Wake*.

Or was it random? One paragraph caught his eye.

At the hotel window now ready to leap. If you expect to conduct any more business with her you better get over there. She's dependent on him, needs a man since her husband, that Paul Sharp, abandoned her. The Antler Hotel, room 604. I think you have time. Johnny is too hot-headed; shouldn't have tried to bluff her. With my blood you can't be bluffed and she's got my blood, I

St Cyr said rapidly to Harvey, who stood beside him, 'Johnny Barefoot's in a room at the Antler Hotel about to jump, and this is old Sarapis telling us, warning us. We better get over there.'

Glancing at him, Harvey said, 'Barefoot's on our side; we can't afford to have him take his life. But why would Sarapis—'

'Let's just get over there,' St Cyr said, starting toward his parked 'copter. Harvey followed on the run.

IV

All at once the telephone stopped ringing. Johnny turned from the window—and saw Kathy Sharp standing by it, the receiver in her hand. 'He called me,' she said. 'And he told me, Johnny, where you were and what you were going to do.'

'Nuts,' he said, 'I'm not going to do anything.' He moved back from the window.

'He thought you were,' Kathy said.

'Yes, and that proves he can be wrong.' His cigarette, he saw, had burned down to the filter; he dropped it into the ashtray on the dresser and stubbed it out.

'My grandfather was always fond of you,' Kathy said. 'He wouldn't like anything to happen to you.'

Shrugging, Johnny said, 'As far as I'm concerned I have nothing to do with Louis Sarapis any more.'

Kathy had put the receiver to her ear; she paid no attention to Johnny—she was listening to her grandfather, he saw, and so he ceased talking. It was futile.

'He says,' Kathy said, 'that Claude St Cyr and Phil Harvey are on their way up here. He told them to come, too.'

'Nice of him,' he said shortly.

Kathy said, 'I'm fond of you, too, Johnny. I can see what my grandfather found about you to like and admire. You genuinely take my welfare seriously, don't you? Maybe I could go into the hospital voluntarily, for a short period anyhow, a week or a few days.'

'Would that be enough?' he asked.

'It might.' She held the phone out to him. 'He wants to talk to you. I think you'd better listen; he'll find a way to reach you, in any case. And you know that.'

Reluctantly, Johnny accepted the phone.

'. . . trouble is you're out of a job and that depresses you. If you're not working you feel you don't amount to anything; that's the kind of person you are. I like that. The same way myself. Listen, I've got a job for you. At the Convention. Doing publicity to make sure Alfonse Gam is nominated; you'd do a swell job. Call Gam. Call Alfonse Gam. Johnny, call Gam. Call—'

Johnny hung up the phone.

'I've got a job,' he told Kathy. 'Representing Gam. At least Louis says so.'

'Would you do that?' Kathy asked. 'Be his PR man at the nominating convention?'

He shrugged. Why not? Gam had the money; he could and would pay well. And certainly he was no worse than the President, Kent Margrave. And—*I must get a job*, Johnny realized. *I have to live. I've got a wife and two children; this is no joke.*

'Do you think Gam has a chance this time?' Kathy asked.

'No, not really. But miracles in politics do happen; look at Richard Nixon's incredible comeback in 1968.'

'What is the best route for Gam to follow?'

He eyed her. 'I'll talk that over with him. Not with you.'

'You're still angry,' Kathy said quietly. 'Because I won't sell. Listen, Johnny. Suppose I turned Archimedean over to you.'

After a moment he said, 'What does Louis say to that?'

'I haven't asked him.'

'You know he'd say no. I'm too inexperienced. I know the operation, of course; I've been with it from the start. But—'

'Don't sell yourself short,' Kathy said softly.

'Please,' Johnny said. 'Don't lecture me. Let's try to stay friends; cool, distant friends.' *And if there's one thing I can't stand*, he said to himself, *it's being lectured by a woman. And for my own good.*

The door of the room burst open. Claude St Cyr and Phil Harvey leaped inside, then saw Kathy, saw him with her, and sagged. 'So he got you to come here, too,' St Cyr said to her, panting for breath.

'Yes,' she said. 'He was very concerned about Johnny.' She patted him on the arm. 'See how many friends you have? Both warm and cool?'

'Yes,' he said. But for some reason felt deeply, miserably sad.

That afternoon Claude St Cyr found time to drop by the house of Elektra Harvey, his present employer's ex-wife.

'Listen, doll,' St Cyr said, 'I'm trying to do good for you in this present deal. If I'm successful—' He put his arms around her and gave her a bear hug. 'You'll recover a little of what you lost. Not all, but enough to make you a trifle happier about life in general.' He kissed her and, as usual, she responded; she squirmed effectively, drew him down to her, pressed close in a manner almost uncannily satisfying. It was very pleasant, and in addition it lasted a long time. And that was *not* usual.

Stirring, moving away from him finally, Elektra said, 'By the way, can you tell me what ails the phone and the TV? I can't call—there always seems to be someone on the line. And the picture on the TV screen; it's all fuzzy and distorted, and it's always the same, just a sort of *face*.'

'Don't worry about it,' Claude said. 'We're working on that right now; we've got a crew of men out scouting.' His men were going from mortuary to mortuary; eventually they'd find Louis's body. And then this nonsense would come to an end . . . to everyone's relief.

Going to the sideboard to fix drinks, Elektra Harvey said, 'Does Phil know about us?' She measured out bitters into the whiskey glasses, three drops to each.

'No,' St Cyr said, 'and it's none of his business anyhow.'

'But Phil has a strong prejudice about ex-wives. He wouldn't like it. He'd get ideas about you being disloyal; since he dislikes me, you're supposed to, too. That's what Phil calls "integrity".'

'I'm glad to know that,' St Cyr said, 'but there's damn little I can do about it. Anyhow, he isn't going to find out.'

'I can't help being worried, though,' Elektra said, bringing him his drink. 'I was tuning the TV, you see, and—I know this sounds crazy, but it actually seemed to me—' She broke off. 'Well, I actually thought I heard the TV announcer mention us. But he was sort of mumbling, or the reception was bad. But anyhow I did hear that, your name and mine.' She looked soberly up at him, while absent-mindedly rearranging the strap of her dress.

Chilled, he said, 'Dear, it's ridiculous.' Going over to the TV set he clicked it on.

Good Lord, he thought. *Is Louis Sarapis everywhere? Does he see everything we do from that locus of his out there in deep space?*

It was not exactly a comforting thought, especially since he was trying to involve Louis's granddaughter in a business deal which the old man disapproved of.

He's getting back at me, St Cyr realized as he reflexively tuned the television set with numbed fingers.

*

Alfonse Gam said, 'As a matter of fact, Mr Barefoot, I intended to call you. I have a wire from Mr Sarapis advising me to employ you. I do think, however, we'll have to come up with something entirely new. Margrave has a considerable advantage over us.'

'True,' Johnny admitted. 'But let's be realistic; we're going to get help this time. Help from Louis Sarapis.'

'Louis helped last time,' Gam pointed out, 'and it wasn't sufficient.'

'But his help now will be of a different order.' *After all*, Johnny thought, *the old man controls all the communication media, the newspapers, radio and TV, even the telephones, God forbid*. With such power Louis could do almost anything he chose.

He hardly needs me, he thought caustically. But he did not say that to Alfonse Gam; apparently Gam did not understand about Louis and what Louis could do. And after all, a job was a job.

'Have you turned on a TV set lately?' Gam asked. 'Or tried to use the phone, or even bought a newspaper? There's nothing but a sort of decaying gibberish coming out. If that's Louis, he's not going to be much help at the Convention. He's—disjointed. Just rambles.'

'I know,' Johnny said guardedly.

'I'm afraid whatever scheme Louis had for his half-life period has gone wrong,' Gam said. He looked morose; he did not look like a man who expected to win an election. 'Your admiration for Louis is certainly greater than mine, at this stage,' Gam said. 'Frankly, Mr Barefoot, I had a long talk with Mr St Cyr, and his concepts were totally discouraging. I'm determined to press on, but frankly—' He gestured. 'Claude St Cyr told me to my face I'm a loser.'

'You're going to believe St Cyr? He's on the other side, now, with Phil Harvey.' Johnny was astonished to find the man so naive, so pliable.

'I told him I was going to win,' Gam murmured. 'But honest to God, this drivel from every TV set and phone—it's awful. It discourages me; I want to get as far away from it as possible.'

Presently Johnny said, 'I understand.'

'Louis didn't use to be like that,' Gam said plaintively. 'He just drones on, now. Even if he can swing the nomination to me . . . do I want it? I'm tired, Mr Barefoot. Very tired.' He was silent, then.

'If you're asking me to give you pep,' Johnny said, 'you've got the wrong man.' The voice from the phone and the TV affected him much the same way. Much too much for him to say anything encouraging to Gam.

'You're in PR,' Gam said. 'Can't you generate enthusiasm where there is none? Convince me, Barefoot, and then I'll convince the world.' From his pocket he brought a folded-up telegram. 'This is what came from Louis, the other day. Evidently he can interfere with the telegraph lines as well as the other media.' He passed it over and Johnny read it.

'Louis was more coherent then,' Johnny said. 'When he wrote this.'

'That's what I mean! He's deteriorating rapidly. When the Convention begins—and it's only one more day, now—what'll he be like? I sense something dreadful, here. And I don't care to get mixed up in it.' He added, 'And yet I want to run. So Barefoot—you deal with Louis for me; you can be the go-between.' He added, 'The psychopomp.'

'What's that mean?'

'The go-between between God and man,' Gam said.

Johnny said, 'If you use words like that you won't get the nomination; I can promise you that.'

Smiling wryly, Gam said, 'How about a drink?' He started from his living room, toward the kitchen. 'Scotch? Bourbon?'

'Bourbon,' Johnny said.

'What do you think of the girl, Louis's granddaughter?'

'I like her,' he said. And that was true; he certainly did.

'Even though she's a psychotic, a drug addict, been in jail and on top of that a religious nut?'

'Yes,' Johnny said tightly.

'I think you're crazy,' Gam said, returning with the drinks. 'But I agree with you. She's a good person. I've known her for some time, as a matter of fact. Frankly, I don't know why she took the bent that she has. I'm not a psychologist . . . probably though it has something to do with Louis. She has a peculiar sort of devotion to him, a kind of loyalty that's both infantile and fanatic. And, to me, touchingly sweet.'

Sipping his drink, Johnny said, 'This is terrible bourbon.'

'Old Sir Muskrat,' Gam said, grimacing. 'I agree.'

'You better serve a better drink,' Johnny said, 'or you really are through in politics.'

'That's why I need you,' Gam said. 'You see?'

'I see,' Johnny said, carrying his drink into the kitchen to pour it back in the bottle—and to take a look at the Scotch instead.

'How are you going about getting me elected?' Alfonse Gam asked.

Johnny said, 'I—think our best approach, our only approach, is to make use of the sentimentality people feel about Louis's death. I saw the lines of mourners; it was impressive, Alfonse. Day after day they came. When he was alive, many persons feared him, feared his power. But now they can breathe easier; he's gone, and the frightening aspects of—'

Gam interrupted. 'But Johnny, he's not gone; that's the whole point. You know that gibbering *thing* on the phones and on TV—that's him!'

'But they don't know it,' Johnny said. 'The public is baffled—just as the first person to pick it up was baffled. That technician at Kennedy Slough.' Emphatically, he said, 'Why should they connect an electrical emanation one light-week away from Earth with Louis Sarapis?'

After a moment Gam said, 'I think you're making an error, Johnny. But Louis said to hire you, and I'm going to. And you have a free hand; I'll depend on your expertise.'

'Thanks,' Johnny said. 'You can depend on me.' But inside, he was not so sure. *Maybe the public is smarter than I realize*, he thought. *Maybe I'm making a mistake.* But what other approach was there?

None that he could dream up; either they made use of Gam's tie with Louis or they had absolutely nothing by which to recommend him.

A slender thread on which to base the campaign for nomination—and only a day before the Convention convened. He did not like it.

The telephone in Gam's living room rang.

'That's probably him,' Gam said. 'You want to talk to him? To be truthful, I'm afraid to take it off the hook.'

'Let it ring,' Johnny said. He agreed with Gam; it was just too damn unpleasant.

'But we can't evade him,' Gam pointed out. 'If he wants to get in touch with us; if it isn't the phone it's the newspaper. And yesterday I tried to use my electric typewriter . . . instead of the letter I intended to compose I got the same mishmash—I got a text from *him*.'

Neither of them moved to take the phone, however. They let it ring on.

'Do you want an advance?' Gam asked. 'Some cash?'

'I'd appreciate it,' Johnny said. 'Since today I quit my job with Archimedean.'

Reaching into his coat for his wallet, Gam said, 'I'll give you a check.' He eyed Johnny. 'You like her but you can't work with her; is that it?'

'That's it,' Johnny said. He did not elaborate, and Gam did not press him any further. Gam was, if nothing else, gentlemanly. And Johnny appreciated it.

As the check changed hands the phone stopped ringing.

Was there a link between the two? Johnny wondered. Or was it just chance? No way to tell. Louis seemed to know everything . . . anyhow, this was what Louis had wanted; he had told both of them that.

'I guess we did the right thing,' Gam said tartly. 'Listen, Johnny. I hope you can get back on good terms with Kathy Egmont Sharp. For her sake; she needs help. Lots of it.'

Johnny grunted.

'Now that you're not working for her, make one more try,' Gam said. 'Okay?'

'I'll think about it,' Johnny said.

'She's a very sick girl, and she's got a lot of responsibility now. You know that, too. Whatever caused the rift between you—try to come to some kind of understanding *before it's too late*. That's the only proper way.'

Johnny said nothing. But he knew, inside him, that Gam was right.

And yet—how did he do it? He didn't know how. *How do you approach a psychotic person?* he wondered. *How do you repair such a deep rift?* It was hard enough in regular situations . . . and this had so many overtones.

If nothing else, this had Louis mixed in it. And Kathy's feelings about Louis. Those would have to change. The blind adoration—that would have to cease.

'What does your wife think of her?' Gam asked.

Startled, he said, 'Sarah Belle? She's never met Kathy.' He added, 'Why do you ask?'

Gam eyed him and said nothing.

'Damn odd question,' Johnny said.

'Damn odd girl, that Kathy,' Gam said. 'Odder than you think, my friend. There's a lot you don't know.' He did not elaborate.

To Claude St Cyr, Phil Harvey said, 'There's something I want to know. Something we must have the answer to, or we'll never get control of the voting stock of Wilhelmina. *Where's the body?*'

'We're looking,' St Cyr said patiently. 'We're trying all of the mortuaries, one by one. But money's involved; undoubtedly someone's paying them to keep quiet, and if we want them to talk—'

'That girl,' Harvey said, 'is going on instructions from beyond the grave. Despite the fact that Louis is devolving . . . she still pays attention to him. It's—unnatural.' He shook his head, repelled.

'I agree,' St Cyr said. 'In fact, you expressed it perfectly. This morning when I was shaving–I picked him up on the TV.' He shuddered visibly. 'I mean, it's coming at us from every side, now.'

'Today,' Harvey said, 'is the first day of the Convention.' He looked out of the window, at the cars and people. 'Louis's attention will be tied up there, trying to swing the vote onto Alfonse Gam. That's where Johnny is, working for Gam–that was Louis's idea. Now perhaps we can operate with more success. Do you see? Maybe he's forgotten about Kathy; my God, he can't watch everything at once.'

St Cyr said quietly, 'But Kathy is not at Archimedean now.'

'Where is she, then? In Delaware? At Wilhelmina Securities? It ought to be easy to find her.'

'She's sick,' St Cyr said. 'In a hospital, Phil. She was admitted during the late evening, last night. For her drug addiction, I presume.'

There was silence.

'You know a lot,' Harvey said finally. 'Where'd you learn this, anyhow?'

'From listening to the phone and the TV. But I don't know where the hospital is. It could even be off Earth, on Luna or on Mars, even back where she came from. I got the impression she's extremely ill. Johnny's abandoning her set her back greatly.' He gazed at his employer somberly. 'That's all I know, Phil.'

'Do you think Johnny Barefoot knows where she is?'

'I doubt it.'

Pondering, Harvey said, 'I'll bet she tries to call him. I'll bet he either knows or will know, soon. If we only could manage to put a snoop-circuit on his phone . . . get his calls routed through here.'

'But the phones,' St Cyr said wearily. 'All it is now–just the gibberish. The interference from Louis.' He wondered what became of Archimedean Enterprises if Kathy was declared unable to manage her affairs, if she was forcibly committed. Very complicated, depending on whether Earth law or–

Harvey was saying, 'We can't find her and we can't find the body. And meanwhile the Convention's on, and they'll nominate that wretched Gam, that creature of Louis's. And next we know, he'll be President.' He eyed St Cyr with antagonism. 'So far you haven't done me much good, Claude.'

'We'll try all the hospitals. But there's tens of thousands of them. And if it isn't in this area it could be anywhere.' He felt helpless. *Around and around we go*, he thought, *and we get nowhere.*

Well, we can keep monitoring the TV, he decided. *That's some help.*

'I'm going to the Convention,' Harvey announced. 'I'll see you later. If you should come up with something—which I doubt—you can get in touch with me there.' He strode to the door, and a moment later St Cyr found himself alone.

Doggone it, St Cyr said to himself. *What'll I do now? Maybe I ought to go to the Convention, too.* But there was one more mortuary he wanted to check; his men had been there, but he also wanted to give it a try personally. It was just the sort that Louis would have liked, run by an unctuous individual named, revoltingly, Herbert Schoenheit von Vogelsang, which meant, in German, Herbert Beauty of the Bird's Song—a fitting name for a man who ran the Beloved Brethren Mortuary in downtown Los Angeles, with branches in Chicago and New York and Cleveland.

When he reached the mortuary, Claude St Cyr demanded to see Schoenheit von Vogelsang personally. The place was doing a rush business; Resurrection Day was just around the corner and the petite bourgeoisie, who flocked in great numbers to just such ceremonies, were lined up waiting to retrieve their half-lifer relatives.

'Yes sir,' Schoenheit von Vogelsang said, when at last he appeared at the counter in the mortuary's business office. 'You asked to speak to me.'

St Cyr laid his business card down on the counter; the card still described him as legal consultant for Archimedean Enterprises. 'I am Claude St Cyr,' he declared. 'You may have heard of me.'

Glancing at the card, Schoenheit von Vogelsang blanched and mumbled, 'I give you my word, Mr St Cyr, we're trying, we're really trying. We've spent out of our own funds over a thousand dollars in trying to make contact with him; we've had high-gain equipment flown in from Japan where it was developed and made. And still no results.' Tremulously, he backed away from the counter. 'You can come and see for yourself. Frankly, I believe someone's doing it on purpose; a complete failure like this can't occur naturally, if you see what I mean.'

St Cyr said, 'Let me see him.'

'Certainly.' The mortuary owner, pale and agitated, led the way through the building into the chill bin, until, at last, St Cyr saw ahead the casket which had lain in state, the casket of Louis Sarapis. 'Are you planning any sort of litigation?' the mortuary owner asked fearfully. 'I assure you, we—'

'I'm here,' St Cyr stated, 'merely to take the body. Have your men load it onto a truck for me.'

'Yes, Mr St Cyr,' Herb Schoenheit von Vogelsang said in meek obedience; he waved two mortuary employees over and began giving them instructions. 'Do you have a truck with you, Mr St Cyr?' he asked.

'You may provide it,' St Cyr said, in a forbidding voice.

Shortly, the body in its casket was loaded onto a mortuary truck, and the driver turned to St Cyr for instructions.

St Cyr gave him Phil Harvey's address.

'And the litigation,' Herb Schoenheit von Vogelsang was murmuring, as St Cyr boarded the truck to sit beside the driver. 'You don't infer malpractice on our part, do you, Mr St Cyr? Because if you do—'

'The affair is closed as far as we're concerned,' St Cyr said to him laconically, and signaled the driver to drive off.

As soon as they left the mortuary, St Cyr began to laugh.

'What strikes you so funny?' the mortuary driver asked.

'Nothing,' St Cyr said, still chuckling.

When the body in its casket, still deep in its original quick-pack, had been left off at Harvey's home and the driver had departed, St Cyr picked up the telephone and dialed. But he found himself unable to get through to the Convention Hall. All he heard, for his trouble, was the weird distant drumming, the monotonous litany of Louis Sarapis—he hung up, disgusted but at the same time grimly determined.

We've had enough of that, St Cyr said to himself. *I won't wait for Harvey's approval; I don't need it.*

Searching the living room he found, in a desk drawer, a heat gun. Pointing it at the casket of Louis Sarapis he pressed the trigger.

The envelope of quick-pack steamed up, the casket itself fizzed as the plastic melted. Within, the body blackened, shriveled, charred away at last into a baked, coal-like clinker, small and nondescript.

Satisfied, St Cyr returned the heat gun to the desk drawer.

Once more he picked up the phone and dialed.

In his ear the monotonous voice intoned, '. . . no one but Gam can do it; Gam's the man what am—good slogan for you, Johnny. Gam's the man what am; remember that. I'll do the talking. Give me the mike and I'll tell them; Gam's the man what am. Gam's—'

Claude St Cyr slammed down the phone, turned to the blackened deposit that had been Louis Sarapis; he gaped mutely at what he could not comprehend. The voice, when St Cyr turned on the television set, emanated from that, too, just as it had been doing; nothing had changed.

The voice of Louis Sarapis was not originating in the body. Because the body was gone. There simply was no connection between them.

Seating himself in a chair, Claude St Cyr got out his cigarettes and shakily lit up, trying to understand what this meant. It seemed almost as if he had it, almost had the explanation.

But not quite.

V

By monorail—he had left his 'copter at the Beloved Brethren Mortuary—Claude St Cyr numbly made his way to the Convention Hall. The place, of course, was packed; the noise was terrible. But he managed to obtain the services of a robot page; over the public address system, Phil Harvey's presence was requested in one of the side rooms used as meeting places by delegations wishing to caucus in secret.

Harvey appeared, disheveled from shoving through the dense pack of spectators and delegates. 'What is it, Claude?' he asked, and then he saw his attorney's face. 'You better tell me,' he said quietly.

St Cyr blurted, 'The voice we hear. It isn't Louis! It's someone else trying to sound like Louis!'

'How do you know?'

He told him.

Nodding, Harvey said, 'And it definitely was Louis's body you destroyed; there was no deceit there at the mortuary—you're positive of that.'

'I'm not positive,' St Cyr said. 'But I think it was; I believe it now and I believed it at the time.' It was too late to find out now, in any case, not enough remained of the body for such an analysis to be successfully made.

'But who could it be, then?' Harvey said. 'My God, it's coming to us from beyond the solar system—could it be nonterrestrials of some kind? Some sort of echo or mockery, a non-living reaction unfamiliar to us? An inert process without intent?'

St Cyr laughed. 'You're babbling, Phil. Cut it out.'

Nodding, Harvey said, 'Whatever you say, Claude. If you think it's someone here—'

'I don't know,' St Cyr said candidly. 'But I'd guess it's someone right on this planet, someone who knew Louis well enough to have introjected his characteristics sufficiently thoroughly to imitate them.' He was silent, then. That was as far as he could carry his logical processes . . . beyond that he saw nothing. It was a blank, and a frightening one at that.

There is, he thought, *an element of the deranged in it. What we took to be decay—it's more a form of madness than degeneration. Or is madness itself degeneration?* He did not know; he wasn't trained in the field of psychiatry, except regarding its legal aspects. And the legal aspects had no application, here.

'Has anyone nominated Gam yet?' he asked Harvey.

'Not yet. It's expected to come sometime today, though. There's a delegate from Montana who'll do it, the rumor is.'

'Johnny Barefoot is here?'

'Yes.' Harvey nodded. 'Busy as can be, lining up delegates. In and out of the different delegations, very much in evidence. No sign of Gam, of course. He won't come in until the end of the nominating speech and then of course all hell will break loose. Cheering and parading and waving banners . . . the Gam supporters are all prepared.'

'Any indication of—' St Cyr hesitated. 'What we've assumed to be Louis? His presence?' *Or its presence,* he thought. *Whatever it is.*

'None as yet,' Harvey said.

'I think we'll hear from it,' St Cyr said. 'Before the day is over.'

Harvey nodded; he thought so, too.

'Are you afraid of it?' St Cyr asked.

'Sure,' Harvey said. 'A thousand times more so than ever, now that we don't even know who or what it is.'

'You're right to take that attitude,' St Cyr said. He felt the same way.

'Perhaps we should tell Johnny,' Harvey said.

St Cyr said, 'Let him find out on his own.'

'All right, Claude,' Harvey said. 'Anything you say. After all, it was you who finally found Louis's body; I have complete faith in you.'

In a way, St Cyr thought, *I wish I hadn't found it. I wish I didn't know what I know now; we were better off believing it was old Louis talking to us from every phone, newspaper and TV set.*

That was bad—but this is far worse. Although, he thought, *it seems to me that the answer is there, somewhere, just waiting.*

I must try, he told himself. *Try to get it. TRY!*

Off by himself in a side room, Johnny Barefoot tensely watched the events of the Convention on closed-circuit TV. The distortion, the invading presence from one light-week away, had cleared for a time, and he could see and hear the delegate from Montana delivering the nominating speech for Alfonse Gam.

He felt tired. The whole process of the Convention, its speeches and parades, its tautness, grated on his nerves, ran contrary to his disposition. *So damn much show,* he thought. Display for what? If Gam wanted to gain the nomination he could get it, and all the rest of this was purposeless.

His own thoughts were on Kathy Egmont Sharp.

He had not seen her since her departure for UC Hospital in San Francisco. At this point he had no idea of her condition, whether she had responded to therapy or not.

The deep intuition could not be evaded that she had not.

How sick really was Kathy? Probably very sick, with or without drugs; he felt that strongly. Perhaps she would never be discharged from UC Hospital; he could imagine that.

On the other hand—if she wanted out, he decided, *she would find a way to get out.* That he intuited, too, even more strongly.

So it was up to her. She had committed herself, gone into the hospital voluntarily. And she would come out—if she ever did—the same way. No one could compel Kathy . . . she was simply not that sort of person. And that, he realized, could well be a symptom of the illness-process.

The door to the room opened. He glanced up from the TV screen.

And saw Claude St Cyr standing in the entrance. St Cyr held a heat gun in his hand, pointed at Johnny. He said, 'Where's Kathy?'

'I don't know,' Johnny said. He got slowly, warily, to his feet.

'You do. I'll kill you if you don't tell me.'

'Why?' he said, wondering what had brought St Cyr to this point, this extreme behavior.

St Cyr said, 'Is it on Earth?' Still holding the gun pointed at Johnny he came toward him.

'Yes,' Johnny said, with reluctance.

'Give me the name of the city.'

'What are you going to do?' Johnny said. 'This isn't like you, Claude; you used to always work within the law.'

St Cyr said, 'I think the voice is Kathy. I know it's not Louis, now; we have that to go on but beyond that it's just a guess. *Kathy is the only one I know deranged enough, deteriorated enough.* Give me the name of the hospital.'

'The only way you could know it isn't Louis,' Johnny said, 'would be to destroy the body.'

'That's right,' St Cyr said, nodding.

Then you have, Johnny realized. *You found the correct mortuary; you got to Herb Schoenheit von Vogelsang.* So that was that.

The door to the room burst open again; a group of cheering delegates, Gam supporters, marched in, blowing horns and hurling streamers, carrying huge hand-painted placards. St Cyr turned toward them, waving his gun at them—and Johnny Barefoot sprinted past the delegates, to the door and out into the corridor.

He ran down the corridor and a moment later emerged at the great central hall in which Gam's demonstration was in full swing. From the loudspeakers mounted at the ceiling a voice boomed over and over.

'Vote for Gam, the man what am. Gam, Gam, vote for Gam, vote for Gam, the one fine man; vote for Gam who really am. Gam, Gam, Gam, he really am—'

Kathy, he thought. *It can't be you; it just can't.* He ran on, out of the hall, squeezing past the dancing, delirious delegates, past the glazed-eyed men and women in their funny hats, their banners wiggling . . . he reached the street, the parked 'copters and cars, throngs of people clustered about, trying to push inside.

If it is you, he thought, *then you're too sick ever to come back. Even if you want to, will yourself to. Had you been waiting for Louis to die, is that it? Do you hate us? Or are you afraid of us? What explains what it is you're doing . . . what's the reason for it?*

He hailed a 'copter marked TAXI. 'To San Francisco,' he instructed the driver.

Maybe you're not conscious that you're doing it, he thought. *Maybe it's an autonomous process, rising out of your unconscious mind. Your mind split into two portions, one on the surface which we see, the other one—*

The one we hear.

Should we feel sorry for you? he wondered. *Or should we hate you, fear you? HOW MUCH HARM CAN YOU DO? I guess that's the real issue. I love you,* he thought. *In some fashion, at least. I care about you, and that's a form of love, not such as I feel toward my wife or my children, but it is a concern. Damn it,* he thought, *this is dreadful. Maybe St Cyr is wrong; maybe it isn't you.*

The 'copter swept upward into the sky, cleared the buildings and turned west, its blade spinning at peak velocity.

On the ground, standing in front of the Convention Hall, St Cyr and Phil Harvey watched the 'copter go.

'Well, so it worked,' St Cyr said. 'I got him started moving. I'd guess he's on his way either to Los Angeles or to San Francisco.'

A second 'copter slid up before them, hailed by Phil Harvey; the two men entered it and Harvey said, 'You see the taxi that just took off? Stay behind it, just within sight. But don't let it catch a glimpse of you if you can help it.'

'Heck,' the driver said, 'if I can see it, it can see me.' But he clicked on his meter and began to ascend. Grumpily, he said to Harvey and St Cyr, 'I don't like this kind of stuff; it can be dangerous.'

'Turn on your radio,' St Cyr told him. 'If you want to hear something that's dangerous.'

'Aw hell,' the driver said, disgusted. 'The radio don't work; some kind of interference, like sun spots or maybe some amateur operator—I lost a lot of fares because the dispatcher can't get hold of me. I think the police ought to do something about it, don't you?'

St Cyr said nothing. Beside him, Harvey peered at the 'copter ahead.

*

When he reached UC Hospital at San Francisco, and had landed at the field on the main building's roof, Johnny saw the second ship circling, not passing on, and he knew that he was right; he had been followed all the way. But he did not care. It didn't matter.

Descending by means of the stairs, he came out on the third floor and approached a nurse. 'Mrs Sharp,' he said. 'Where is she?'

'You'll have to ask at the desk,' the nurse said. 'And visiting hours aren't until—'

He rushed on until he found the desk.

'Mrs Sharp's room is 309,' the bespectacled, elderly nurse at the desk said. 'But you must have Doctor Gross's permission to visit her. And I believe Doctor Gross is having lunch right now and probably won't be back until two o'clock, if you'd care to wait.' She pointed to a waiting room.

'Thanks,' he said. 'I'll wait.' He passed through the waiting room and out the door at the far end, down the corridor, watching the numbers on the doors until he saw room number 309. Opening the door he entered the room, shut the door after him and looked around for her.

There was the bed, but it was empty.

'Kathy,' he said.

At the window, in her robe, she turned, her face sly, bound up by hatred; her lips moved and, staring at him, she said with loathing, 'I want Gam because he am.' Spitting at him, she crept toward him, her hands raised, her fingers writhing. 'Gam's a man, a *real* man,' she whispered, and he saw, in her eyes, the dissolved remnants of her personality expire even as he stood there. 'Gam, gam, gam,' she whispered, and slapped him.

He retreated. 'It's you,' he said. 'Claude St Cyr was right. Okay. I'll go.' He fumbled for the door behind him, trying to get it open. Panic passed through him, like a wind, then; he wanted nothing but to get away. 'Kathy,' he said, 'let go.' Her nails had dug into him, into his shoulder, and she hung onto him, peering sideways into his face, smiling at him.

'You're dead,' she said. 'Go away. I smell you, the dead inside you.'

'I'll go,' he said, and managed to find the handle of the door. She let go of him, then; he saw her right hand flash up, the nails directed at his face, possibly his eyes—he ducked, and her blow missed him. 'I want to get away,' he said, covering his face with his arms.

Kathy whispered, 'I am Gam, I am. I'm the only one who am. Am alive. Gam, alive.' She laughed. 'Yes, I will,' she said, mimicking his voice perfectly. 'Claude St Cyr was right; okay, I'll go. I'll go. I'll go.' She was now between him and the door. 'The window,' she said. 'Do it now, what you wanted to do when I stopped you.' She hurried toward him, and he retreated, backward, step by step, until he felt the wall behind him.

'It's all in your mind,' he said, 'this hate. Everyone is fond of you; I am, Gam is, St Cyr and Harvey are. What's the point of this?'

'The point,' Kathy said, 'is that I show you what you're really like. Don't you know yet? You're even worse than me. I'm just being honest.'

'Why did you pretend to be Louis?' he said.

'I am Louis,' Kathy said. 'When he died he didn't go into half-life because I ate him; he became me. I was waiting for that. Alfonse and I had it all worked out, the transmitter out there with the recorded tape ready—we frightened you, didn't we? You're all scared, too scared to stand in his way. He'll be nominated; he's been nominated already, I feel it, I know it.'

'Not yet,' Johnny said.

'But it won't be long,' Kathy said. 'And I'll be his wife.' She smiled at him. 'And you'll be dead, you and the others.' Coming at him she chanted, 'I am Gam, I am Louis and when you're dead I'll be you, Johnny Barefoot, and all the rest; I'll eat you all.' She opened her mouth wide and he saw the sharp, jagged, pale-as-death teeth.

'And rule over the dead,' Johnny said, and hit her with all his strength, on the side of her face, near the jaw. She spun backward, fell, and then at once was up and rushing at him. Before she could catch him he sprinted away, to one side, caught then a glimpse of her distorted, shredded features, ruined by the force of his blow—and then the door to the room opened, and St Cyr and Phil Harvey, with two nurses, stood there. Kathy stopped. He stopped, too.

'Come on, Barefoot,' St Cyr said, jerking his head.

Johnny crossed the room and joined them.

Tying the sash of her robe, Kathy said matter-of-factly, 'So it was planned; he was to kill me, Johnny was to. And the rest of you would all stand and watch and enjoy it.'

'They have an immense transmitter out there,' Johnny said. 'They placed it a long time ago, possibly years back. All this time they've been waiting for Louis to die; maybe they even killed him, finally. The idea's to get Gam nominated and elected, while keeping everyone terrorized with that transmission. She's sick, much sicker than we realized, even sicker than *you* realized. Most of all it was under the surface where it didn't show.'

St Cyr shrugged. 'Well, she'll have to be certified.' He was calm but unusually slow-spoken. 'The will named me as trustee; I can represent the estate against her, file the commitment papers and then come forth at the sanity hearing.'

'I'll demand a jury trial,' Kathy said. 'I can convince a jury of my sanity; it's actually quite easy and I've been through it before.'

'Possibly,' St Cyr said. 'But anyhow the transmitter will be gone; by that time the authorities will be out there.'

'It'll take months to reach it,' Kathy said. 'Even by the fastest ship. And by then the election will be over; Alfonse will be President.'

St Cyr glanced at Johnny Barefoot. 'Maybe so,' he murmured.

'That's why we put it out so far,' Kathy said. 'It was Alfonse's money and my ability; I inherited Louis's ability—you see. I can do anything. Nothing is impossible for me if I want it; all I have to do is want it *enough*.'

'You wanted me to jump,' Johnny said. 'And I didn't.'

'You would have,' Kathy said, 'in another minute. If they hadn't come in.' She seemed quite poised, now. 'You will, eventually; I'll keep after you. And there's no place you can hide; you know I'll follow you and find you. All three of you.' Her gaze swept from one of them to the next, taking them all in.

Harvey said, 'I've got a little power and wealth, too. I think we can defeat Gam, even if he's nominated.'

'You have power,' Kathy said, 'but not imagination. What you have isn't enough. Not against me.' She spoke quietly, with complete confidence.

'Let's go,' Johnny said, and started down the hall, away from room 309 and Kathy Egmont Sharp.

Up and down San Francisco's hilly streets Johnny walked, hands in his pockets, ignoring the buildings and people, seeing nothing, merely walking on and on. Afternoon faded, became evening; the lights of the city came on and he ignored that, too. He walked block after block until his feet ached, burned, until he became aware that he was very hungry—that it was now ten o'clock at night and he had not eaten anything since morning. He stopped, then, and looked around him.

Where were Claude St Cyr and Phil Harvey? He could not remember having parted from them; he did not even remember leaving the hospital. But Kathy; he remembered that. He could not forget it even if he wanted to. And he did not want to. It was too important ever to be forgotten, by any of them who had witnessed it, understood it.

At a newsstand he saw the massive, thick-black headlines.

GAM WINS NOMINATION, PROMISES BATTLING CAMPAIGN
FOR NOVEMBER ELECTION

So she did get that, Johnny thought. *They did, the two of them; they got what they're after exactly. And now—all they have to do is defeat Kent Margrave. And that thing out there, a light-week away; it's still yammering. And will be for months.*

They'll win, he realized.

At a drugstore he found a phone booth; entering it he put money into the slot and dialed Sarah Belle, his own home phone number.

The phone clicked in his ear. And then the familiar monotonous voice chanted, 'Gam in November, Gam in November; win with Gam, President Alfonse Gam, our man—I am for Gam. *I am for Gam. For GAM!*' He rang off, then, and left the phone booth. It was hopeless.

At the counter of the drugstore he ordered a sandwich and coffee; he sat eating mechanically, filling the requirements of his body without pleasure or desire, eating by reflex until the food was gone and it was time to pay the bill. *What can I do?* he asked himself. *What can anyone do? All the means of communication are gone; the media have been taken over. They have the radio, TV, newspapers, phone, wire services . . . everything that depends on microwave transmission or open-gap electric circuitry. They've captured it all, left nothing for us, the opposition, by which to fight back.*

Defeat, he thought. *That's the dreary reality that lies ahead for us. And then, when they enter office, it'll be our—death.*

'That'll be a dollar ten,' the counter girl said.

He paid for his meal and left the drugstore.

When a 'copter marked TAXI came spiraling by, he hailed it.

'Take me home,' he said.

'Okay,' the driver said amiably. 'Where is home, buddy?'

He gave him the address in Chicago and then settled back for the long ride. He was giving up; he was quitting, going back to Sarah Belle, to his wife and children. The fight—for him—apparently was over.

When she saw him standing in the doorway, Sarah Belle said, 'Good God, Johnny—you look terrible.' She kissed him, led him inside, into the warm, familiar living room. 'I thought you'd be out celebrating.'

'*Celebrating?*' he said hoarsely.

'Your man won the nomination.' She went to put the coffee pot on for him.

'Oh yeah,' he said, nodding. 'That's right. I was his PR man; I forgot.'

'Better lie down,' Sarah Belle said. 'Johnny, I've never seen you look so beaten; I can't understand it. What happened to you?'

He sat down on the couch and lit a cigarette.

'What can I do for you?' she asked, with anxiety.

'Nothing,' he said.

'Is that Louis Sarapis on all the TV and phones? It sounds like him. I was talking with the Nelsons and they said it's Louis's exact voice.'

'No,' he said. 'It's not Louis. Louis is dead.'

'But his period of half-life—'

'No,' he said. 'He's dead. Forget about it.'

'You know who the Nelsons are, don't you? They're the new people who moved into the apartment that—'

'I don't want to talk,' he said. 'Or be talked at.'

Sarah Belle was silent, for a minute. And then she said, 'One thing they said—you won't like to hear it, I guess. The Nelsons are plain, quite commonplace people . . . they said even if Alfonse Gam got the nomination they wouldn't vote for him. They just don't like him.'

He grunted.

'Does that made you feel bad?' Sarah Belle asked. 'I think they're reacting to the pressure, Louis's pressure on the TV and phones; they just don't care for it. I think you've been excessive in your campaign, Johnny.' She glanced at him hesitantly. 'That's the truth; I have to say it.'

Rising to his feet, he said, 'I'm going to visit Phil Harvey. I'll be back later on.'

She watched him go out the door, her eyes darkened with concern.

When he was admitted to Phil Harvey's house he found Phil and Gertrude Harvey and Claude St Cyr sitting together in the living room, each with a glass in hand, but no one speaking. Harvey glanced up briefly, saw him, and then looked away.

'Are we going to give up?' he asked Harvey.

Harvey said, 'I'm in touch with Kent Margrave. We're going to try to knock out the transmitter. But it's a million to one shot, at that distance. And with even the fastest missile it'll take a month.'

'But that's at least something,' Johnny said. It would at least be before the election; it would give them several weeks in which to campaign. 'Does Margrave understand the situation?'

'Yes,' Claude St Cyr said. 'We told him virtually everything.'

'But that's not enough,' Phil Harvey said. 'There's one more thing we must do. You want to be in on it? Draw for the shortest match?' He pointed to the coffee table; on it Johnny saw three matches, one of them broken in half. Now Phil Harvey added a fourth match, a whole one.

St Cyr said, 'Her first. Her right away, as soon as possible. And then later on if necessary, Alfonse Gam.'

Weary, cold fright filled Johnny Barefoot.

'Take a match,' Harvey said, picking up the four matches, arranging and rearranging them in his hand and then holding out the four even tops to the people in the room. 'Go ahead, Johnny. You got here last so I'll have you go first.'

'Not me,' he said.

'Then we'll draw without you,' Gertrude Harvey said, and picked a match. Phil held the remaining ones out to St Cyr and he drew one also. Two remained in Phil Harvey's hand.

'I was in love with her,' Johnny said. 'I still am.'

Nodding, Phil Harvey said, 'Yes, I know.'

His heart leaden, Johnny said, 'Okay. I'll draw.' Reaching, he selected one of the two matches.

It was the broken one.

'I got it,' he said. 'It's me.'

'Can you do it?' Claude St Cyr asked him.

He was silent for a time. And then he shrugged and said, 'Sure. I can do it. Why not?' *Why not indeed?* he asked himself. *A woman that I was falling in love with; certainly I can murder her. Because it has to be done. There is no other way out for us.*

'It may not be as difficult as we think,' St Cyr said. 'We've consulted some of Phil's technicians and we picked up some interesting advice. Most of their transmissions are coming from nearby, not a light-week away by any means. I'll tell you how we know. Their transmissions have kept up with changing events. For example, your suicide-attempt at the Antler Hotel. *There was no time-lapse there or anywhere else.*'

'And they're not supernatural, Johnny,' Gertrude Harvey said.

'So the first thing to do,' St Cyr continued, 'is to find their base here on Earth or at least here in the solar system. It could be Gam's guinea-fowl ranch on Io. Try there, if you find she's left the hospital.'

'Okay,' Johnny said, nodding slightly.

'How about a drink?' Phil Harvey said to him.

Johnny nodded.

The four of them, seated in a circle, drank, slowly and in silence.

'Do you have a gun?' St Cyr asked.

'Yes.' Rising to his feet he set his glass down.

'Good luck,' Gertrude said, after him.

Johnny opened the front door and stepped outside alone, out into the dark, cold evening.

NOTES

All notes in italics are by Philip K. Dick. The year when the note was written appears in parentheses following the note. Most of these notes were written as story notes for the collections *The Best of Philip K. Dick* (published 1977) and *The Golden Man* (published 1980). A few were written at the request of editors publishing or reprinting a PKD story in a book or magazine.

When there is a date following the name of a story, it is the date the manuscript of that story was first received by Dick's agent, per the records of the Scott Meredith Literary Agency. Absence of a date means no record is available. The name of a magazine followed by a month and year indicates the first published appearance of a story. An alternate name following a story indicates Dick's original name for the story, as shown in the agency records.

These four volumes include all of Philip K. Dick's short fiction, with the exception of short novels later published as or included in novels, childhood writings, and unpublished writings for which manuscripts have not been found. The stories are arranged as closely as possible in chronological order of composition; research for this chronology was done by Gregg Rickman and Paul Williams.

THE CRAWLERS ('FOUNDLING HOME')
Oct. 29, 1953. *Imagination*, July 1954.

SALES PITCH
Nov. 19, 1953. *Future*, June 1954.
When this story first appeared, the fans detested it. I read it over, perplexed by their hostility, and could see why: it is a superdowner story, and relentlessly so. Could I rewrite it I would have it end differently, I would have the man and the robot, i.e. the fasrad, form a partnership at the end and become friends. The logic of paranoia of this story should be deconstructed into its opposite; Y, the

human-against-robot theme, should have been resolved into null-Y, human-and-robot-against-the-universe. I really deplore the ending. So when you read the story, try to imagine it as it ought to have been written. The fasrad says, 'Sir, I am here to help you. The hell with my sales pitch. Let's be together forever.' Yes, but then I would have been criticized for a false upbeat ending, I guess. Still, this ending is not good. The fans were right. (1978)

SHELL GAME
Dec. 22, 1953. *Galaxy*, Sept. 1954.

UPON THE DULL EARTH
Dec. 30, 1953. *Beyond Fantasy Fiction*, Nov. 1954.

FOSTER, YOU'RE DEAD
Dec. 31, 1953. *Star Science Fiction Stories No. 3*, edited by Frederik Pohl, New York, 1955.

One day I saw a newspaper headline reporting that the President suggested that if Americans had to buy their bomb shelters, rather than being provided with them by the government, they'd take better care of them, an idea which made me furious. Logically, each of us should own a submarine, a jet fighter, and so forth. Here I just wanted to show how cruel the authorities can be when it comes to human life, how they can think in terms of dollars, not people. (1976)

PAY FOR THE PRINTER ('PRINTER'S PAY')
Jan. 28, 1954. *Satellite Science Fiction*, Oct. 1956.

WAR VETERAN
Feb. 17, 1954. *If*, Mar. 1955.

THE CHROMIUM FENCE
Apr. 9, 1954. *Imagination*, July 1955.

MISADJUSTMENT
May 14, 1954. *Science Fiction Quarterly*, Feb. 1957.

A WORLD OF TALENT ('TWO STEPS RIGHT')
June 4, 1954. *Galaxy*, Oct. 1954.

PSI-MAN HEAL MY CHILD! ('OUTSIDE CONSULTANT')
June 8, 1954. *Imaginative Tales*, Nov. 1955. [Also published in a story collection as 'Psi-Man.']

AUTOFAC

Oct. 11, 1954. *Galaxy*, Nov. 1955.

Tom Disch said of this story that it was one of the earliest ecology warnings in sf. What I had in mind in writing it, however, was the thought that if factories became fully automated, they might begin to show the instinct for survival which organic living entities have . . . and perhaps develop similar solutions. (1976)

SERVICE CALL

Oct. 11, 1954. *Science Fiction Stories*, July 1955.

When this story appeared many fans objected to it because of the negative attitude I expressed in it. But I was already beginning to suppose in my head the growing domination of machines over man, especially the machines we voluntarily surround ourselves with, which should, by logic, be the most harmless. I never assumed that some huge clanking monster would stride down Fifth Avenue, devouring New York; I always feared that my own TV set or iron or toaster would, in the privacy of my apartment, when no one else was around to help me, announce to me that they had taken over, and here was a list of rules I was to obey. I never like the idea of doing what a machine says. I hate having to salute something built in a factory. (Do you suppose all those White House tapes came out of the back of the President's head? And programmed him as to what he was to say and do?) (1976)

CAPTIVE MARKET

Oct. 18, 1954. *If*, Apr. 1955.

THE MOLD OF YANCY

Oct. 18, 1954. *If*, Aug. 1955.

Obviously, Yancy is based on President Eisenhower. During his reign we all were worrying about the man-in-the-gray-flannel-suit problem; we feared that the entire country was turning into one person and a whole lot of clones. (Although in those days the word 'clone' was unknown to us.) I liked this story enough to use it as the basis for my novel The Penultimate Truth; *in particular the part where everything the government tells you is a lie. I still like that part; I mean, I still believe it's so. Watergate, of course, bore the basic idea of this story out.* (1978)

THE MINORITY REPORT

Dec. 22, 1954. *Fantastic Universe*, Jan. 1956.

RECALL MECHANISM
If, July 1959.

THE UNRECONSTRUCTED M
June 2, 1955. *Science Fiction Stories*, Jan. 1957.

If the main theme throughout my writing is, 'Can we consider the universe real, and if so, in what way?' my secondary theme would be, 'Are we all humans?' Here a machine does not imitate a human being, but instead fakes evidence of a human being, a given human being. Fakery is a topic which absolutely fascinates me; I am convinced that anything can be faked, or anyhow evidence pointing to any given thing. Spurious clues can lead us to believe anything they want us to believe. There is really no theoretical upper limit to this. Once you have mentally opened the door to the reception of the notion of fake, you are ready to think yourself into another kind of reality entirely. It's a trip from which you never return. And, I think, a healthy trip . . . unless you take it too seriously. (1978)

EXPLORERS WE
May 6, 1958. *Fantasy & Science Fiction*, Jan. 1959.

WAR GAME ('DIVERSION')
Oct. 31, 1958. *Galaxy*, Dec. 1959.

IF THERE WERE NO BENNY CEMOLI ('HAD THERE NEVER BEEN A BENNY CEMOLI')
Feb. 27, 1963. *Galaxy*, Dec. 1963.

I have always believed that at least half the famous people in history never existed. You invent what you need to invent. Perhaps even Karl Marx was invented, the product of some hack writer. In which case– (1976)

NOVELTY ACT ('AT SECOND JUG')
Mar. 23, 1963. *Fantastic*, Feb. 1964. [Included in PKD's novel *The Simulacra*.]

WATERSPIDER
Apr. 10, 1963. *If*, Jan. 1964.

WHAT THE DEAD MEN SAY ('MAN WITH A BROKEN MATCH')
Apr. 15, 1963. *Worlds of Tomorrow*, June 1964.